Willi

HOOLIGANS

SHARKY'S MACHINE

William Diehl Omnibus

HOOLIGANS

SHARKY'S MACHINE

WILLIAM DIEHL

time**warner**
paperbacks

A *Time Warner* Paperback

This omnibus edition first published in Great Britain by
Time Warner Paperbacks in 2003
William Diehl Omnibus Copyright © William Diehl 2003

Previously published separately:
Hooligans first published in Great Britain in 1984 by Michael Joseph Ltd
Published by Sphere Books Ltd in 1985
Reprinted 1985 (twice), 1987, 1988, 1990
Reprinted by Warner Books in 1992
Reprinted 1994, 1995, 1996, 1997, 2000
Copyright © 1984 by Hooligans Inc.

Sharky's Machine first published in Great Britain in 1978 by
Hutchinson & Co (Publishers) Ltd
Published by Sphere Books in 1979
Reprinted 1979, 1982 (twice), 1983, 1985, 1986, 1987, 1988, 1990
Reprinted by Warner Books in 1994
Reprinted 1995, 1996, 1997
Copyright © William Diehl 1978

A CIP catalogue record for this book is
available from the British Library.

ISBN 0 7515 3521 4

Printed and bound in Great Britain by
Mackays of Chatham plc, Chatham, Kent

Time Warner Paperbacks
An imprint of
Time Warner Books UK
Brettenham House
Lancaster Place
London WC2E 7EN

www.TimeWarnerBooks.co.uk

HOOLIGANS

This book is dedicated to Virginia, who is the love of my life;
To Michael Parver, for his support and friendship through
the tough times, and for Stick;
And to my father, the most gentle and loving man I have
ever known, who died before it was completed.

SPECIAL OPERATIONS BRANCH

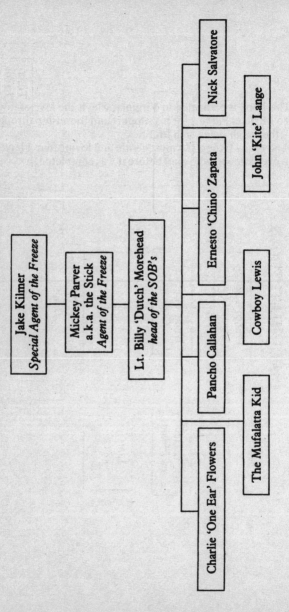

CINCINNATI TRIAD

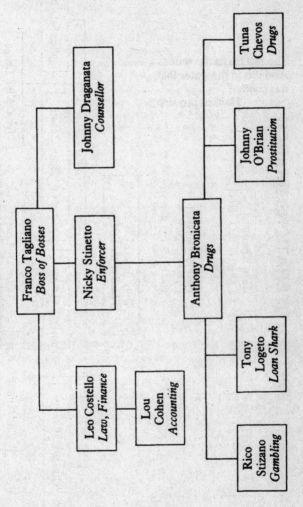

Franco Tagliano — *Boss of Bosses*

Johnny Draganata — *Counsellor*

Nicky Stinetto — *Enforcer*

Leo Costello — *Law, Finance*

Lou Cohen — *Accounting*

Anthony Bronicata — *Drugs*

Johnny O'Brian — *Prostitution*

Tuna Chevos — *Drugs*

Rico Stizano — *Gambling*

Tony Logeto — *Loan Shark*

The fish trusts the water,
And it is in the water that
it is cooked.
    – Haitian proverb

PREFACE

DUNETOWN

Dunetown is a city forged by Revolutionaries, hammered and shaped by rascals and southern rebels, and mannered by genteel ladies.

Dunetown is grace and unhurried charm, azalea-lined boulevards and open river promenades, parks and narrow lanes; a city of squares; of ironwork and balustrades, shutters and dormers, porticos and steeples and dollops of gingerbread icing; of bricks, ballast, and oyster shells underfoot; a waterfront place of massive walls and crude paving, of giant shutters on muscular hinges and winding stairwells and wrought-iron spans; a claustrophobic vista where freighters glide by on the river, a mere reach away, and seagulls yell at robins.

It is a city whose heartbeat changes from block to block as subtly as its architecture; a city of seventeenth-century schoolhouses, churches, taverns; of ceilings fans and Tiffany windows, two-storey atriums, blue barrel dormers, Georgian staircases and Palladian windows and grand, elegant antebellum mansions that hide from view among moss-draped oaks and serpentine vines.

Dunetown is a stroll through the eighteenth century, its history limned on cemetery tablets:

HERE LIES JENIFER GOLDSMITH
LOVING WYF OF JEREMY
WHO DIED OF THE PLAGUE THAT KILED SO MENY
IN THESE PARTS IN THE YEAR OF OUR LORD, 1744

or

JAMES OLIVER
A FAST TONGUE AND HOT TEMPER
DEAD AT 22 YRS. OF HIS AGE
IN A DUEL WITH LT. CHARLES MORAY
WHO SHOT QUICKER AND WITH KEENER EYE

These are its ancestors. The survivors become the city's power brokers, the rulers of the kingdom, dictating an archaic social structure that is unchanging, and defined by its metaphor, the Dune Club, restricted to the elite, whose money is oldest, whose roots are deepest, and who, for more than a century, have sequestered it from time.

Thus the years have passed Dunetown, leaving behind a treasure: an eighteenth-century serfdom whose history trembles with ghost stories, with wars and brawls and buried loot on shaggy Atlantic beaches; whose people have the heritage and independence of islanders, their bloodlines traced to Irish colliers, Spanish privateers, to Haiti and Jamaica, and Cherokee reservations.

Its bays, marches, and rivers still weave a city comprised of islands: Alee, Skidaway, Thunderhead, Buccaneer, Oceanby, Sea Oat, and the wistful, Gatsby-like Isle of Sighs, a haunt of the rich, its antique houses serene against the backwaters of the sea, where one might easily envision a solitary and forlorn Jay Gatz, staring across the water at the solemn light on Daisy's pier.

The past is everywhere,
If you listen,
For that is not the wind you hear,
It is the whispering ghost of yesteryear.

Reality, to Dunetown, is history to the rest of the world.

INTRODUCTION
A Walk Through Dunetown
J. THOMPSON, 1972

PROLOGUE

Sunday: Dawn *The small trawler was heading north an hour before dawn on the eighth day out of Cumaná, Venezuela, when the captain of the four-man crew first spotted the red trouble light blinking on the mast of the sailboat. He made it a mile or so away when he saw it the first time. The trawler was ten miles at sea and thirty-five miles northeast of Fernandina, Florida, at the time. The captain watched the light for half an hour as his rusty scow drew closer.*

In the grey light just before the sun broke, they were close enough to see the sailboat, a rich man's toy, dead in the water. It was a forty-footer, with a man on deck. The man had removed his shirt and was waving it overhead.

The captain, a deeply tanned man in his early forties wearing four days' growth of beard, stroked his jaw with a greasy hand. Two of the crew members watched the sailboat draw closer with mild interest. The mate, a black man with a scar from the corner of his mouth to his ear, squinted through the dim light and then urged the captain to pass up the stricken boat.

'Fuck em, man. We ain't got time to mess with no honky sailors,' he said quietly.

But the captain had been a seaman too long to pass up any vessel in distress. Besides, the shirtless man was obviously rich; a soft, Sunday sailor, becalmed far beyond his limit and probably scared to death.

'No guns,' the captain said softly in Spanish. 'Just stand easy and see what they want. If gas is their problem, we can help the gringos out.'

He turned on a powerful light and swept its beam along the sailboat from bow to stern. He steered the trawler close beside the sailboat and tossed the man a line.

'Habla español?' the captain asked.

'No,' the sailor answered, putting his shirt back on.

'What ees your problem?' the captain asked in broken English.

'Not enough wind.' The sailor, who was wearing white jeans and designer sneakers, pointed at the limp sail. 'And no gas. Can you sell me some gas?'

'I geev you enough gas to make Saint Simons Island,' the captain said, pointing towards the horizon. 'Fifteen, maybe twenty miles northwest.'

'Thank you, thank you very much. Muchas gracias, señor.' The man bowed and waved a thank-you.

The captain ordered one of his men to take a gas can aboard the sailboat. The man went below and emerged a few minutes later with a ten-gallon can in hand. He and one of the other crewmen scrambled aboard the sailboat.

The captain and the mate watched from aboard the trawler.

'Messin' with trouble,' the black mate mumbled.

'No problem,' said the captain.

The two crewmen had not quite reached the stern tanks of the sailboat when the hatch to the cabin suddenly slid back and another man jumped on deck from below. He was holding a submachine gun. The mate uttered an oath and reached for the pistol in his belt but he was too late. The man with the machine gun raked the deck and bridge of the trawler.

Bddddddddddddd . . .

Bddddddddddddd . . .

The windshield of the captain's cabin exploded, showering glass across the deck. The first burst blew away the captain's chest. He flew backwards through the door and landed on his back on the bridge. His foot twitched violently for a few seconds before he died.

The second burst ripped into the mate as he clawed under his coat for the .38. It lifted him high in the air, twisted him around, and tossed him halfway across the deck. He fell like an empty sack, face down, most of his head blown away.

The remaining two crew members, the ones who had boarded the sailboat, turned wild-eyed towards the gunner. The shirtless man stabbed one of them in the chest with a bowie knife. He fell across the stern, babbling incoherently. The man with the submachine gun fired a burst into the chest of the last crewman, who dropped the gas can and flipped backward over the railing into the sea.

The shirtless man pulled his knife free, cleaned the blade on the dead man's pants, and tossed his victim overboard.

The shooter sent another burst into the light and it exploded into darkness.

It was all over in thirty seconds.

They worked very quickly, searching the boat. It took less than half an hour to find their prize. They transferred the three small, heavy bags to the sailboat, threw the captain and his mate into the sea, doused the trawler with gasoline, and set it afire.

The shirtless man cranked up the engine of the sailboat and guided it away from the trawler; then, setting the wheel, he joined the shooter and they checked out the prize.

'What d'ya think?' the shirtless man said, leaning over and staring into one of the bags.

'Beautiful,' the shooter said. He moved behind his partner, took a .357 Magnum from his belt, and stepped closer.

'Sorry,' he said. He held the gun an inch or so from the back of the shirtless man's head and squeezed the trigger. The gun roared and the bullet smacked into the back of the man's head, knocking him forward against the railing.

The shooter reached out for the body but it fell sideways, was caught for an instant in the line of the foresail, and then rolled over it and plunged face forward into the sea.

'Shit!' cried the shooter and made a frantic last grab, but it was gone. The body bobbed to the surface like a cork on a fishing line, then went under.

The shooter ran back to the tiller, shoved the throttle on full, and turned the boat sharply around. He searched for ten minutes, hoping to get a glimpse of his victim, but he finally gave up.

He was a mile or so away when the gasoline on the trawler exploded, spewing up a broiling ball of fire that for a moment or two rivalled the rising sun.

He watched the trailing smoke grow smaller and smaller until he could see it no longer.

1

ACE, DEUCE, TRAY

Going back to Dunetown was worse than going to Vietnam. I didn't know what was in store for me in Nam; I knew what was waiting in Dunetown.

As the plane veered into its final approach, memories began to ambush me, memories that pulled me back to a place I had tried to forget for a lot of years, and to a time that was, in my mind, the last green summer of my life. After that, everything seemed to be tinted by the colours of autumn, colours of passage. Dying colours.

The colours of Nam.

Brown, muddy rivers. Dark green body bags. Black cinders where trees and villages had once stood. Grey faces with white eyes, waiting to be zipped up and shipped back to the World and laid away in the auburn earth.

Those were the hues that had painted my life since that summer. 1963, that was the year.

A long time ago.

For over twenty years I had tried to erase the scars of that year. Now, suddenly, it was thrust back at me like a dagger, and the names and faces of another time besieged me. Chief. Titan. Wally Butts and Vince Dooley. Teddy.

Doe.

Time had dulled the blade, sanded down the brittle edges, but it had only sharpened that one persistent pain. Doe Findley was the last fantasy I had left. I had flushed most of my other dreams, but that one I hung on to, protecting it, nurturing it, seeking shelter in it, and I wasn't ready yet to surrender it to reality.

It was raining, a steady downpour, as the small jet swept in low over the marshes. I squinted through the oval window, tear-streaked with raindrops, looking for something to orient me in time and place. I suppose I was expecting that same one-room shed that passed for a depot, with its coffee machine and half a dozen chairs they jokingly called a waiting room. Time plays crazy head tricks on you. In your head, time is a freeze frame. People don't grow older; the paint on houses doesn't chip or fade; trees don't get taller. The grass doesn't even grow. ·

What I really expected to see through that window was the past. What I saw was a low, glass and chrome terminal, exploding strobe lights limning the runways, other jets jockeying for position. There was more action on the runway than in Las Vegas on a Saturday night. Twenty years is a lot of reality to swallow in one dose, but that's what I got.

As I scampered down the stairs from the plane and across the ramp through the rain, I remembered something my father used to say:

'Anything that comes easily isn't worth having.'

Well, actually it was my mother who said it. My father died in action in the Pacific three months before I was born. I was never very much for geography, but by the time I was in kindergarten, I knew everything there was to know about the island called Iwo Jima. I knew its geographic coordinates, its shape; I knew it was less than five miles long and less than three miles wide and had five villages at 0915 on February 19, 1945, when Captain J. L. Kilmer ceased to be my father and became my mother's legend. I also knew it was an ugly, worthless piece of lava in the middle of nowhere that nobody ever should have died for. Later I was to learn about that kind of dying firsthand.

Anyway, his LST was blown out from under him on the first wave going in. He never even got his feet wet.

But I know about my old man, about what he believed, and about the place where he died. My mother made sure about that. The lessons she taught me while I was growing up always started the same way: 'Your father used to say . . .'

Then she'd hit me with the payoff line.

I was probably sixteen or seventeen before I figured out that in order for my father to have passed on to my mother all the bromides fed to me during my formative years and attributed to him, he would have had to talk constantly, twenty-four hours a day, for the entire two years they were married. My father image was created by the mother. But it worked. By the time I got on to her, I figured my dad at twenty-two was wiser than Homer, Socrates, Newton and Ben Franklin all rolled up in one. Funny thing is, I guess I still do.

2

'Your father used to say, "Anything that comes too easily isn't worth having."'

I should have listened to that reprise as I ran through the rain, but I had other things on my mind. It went in one ear, out the other, and never slowed down along the way.

When I entered the Dunetown terminal, I was slapped back to reality in a hurry. It was a city block long, with a moving sidewalk, a twenty-four-hour snack shop, a fancy European-type restaurant, and two bars.

In the time it took me to walk the length of the terminal and pick up my bags, I saw a first-class dip from Albuquerque named Digit Dan Delaney, two hookers from San Diego whose names eluded me, and a scam artist from Detroit named Spanish Eddie Fuereco, spinning the coin with a mark in a seersucker suit and a Hawaiian shirt.

They were all working. That told me a lot.

The lady at the airline counter had an envelope for me with car keys, registration, confirmed reservations at the Ponce Hotel, and a map of the town showing me how to get there. There was also a message that had been phoned in twenty minutes earlier:

'Urgent. Meet me at emergency entrance, city hospital, soon as possible.'

It had been phoned in by a Lieutenant Morehead of the local police. And that reminded me of why I was there, which certainly wasn't to weep over my lost youth. A man named Franco Tagliani was the reason I was there, a mobster who headed an outfit called the Cincinnati Triad. For five years I had dogged Tagliani; for five years I had listened to his voice on wiretaps, watched him through binoculars, snapped pictures of him through a telephoto lens. For five years I had tried to bring Tagliani and his bunch down. I had tried everything due process would allow.

Zip.

In those five years I never got close enough to him to tip my hat good morning. It was embarrassing, five years and nothing to show for it but a goose egg.

Then he had disappeared. And with him, his whole bunch. Poof, just like that. The magic trick of the year. And now, nine months later, he had popped back up. And in Dunetown, the last place on earth I cared to be. Thanks a bunch, Franco.

3

This time we were going to play hard cheese. This time the score was going to be a little different.

I finessed the hotel and drove straight to the city hospital. The lieutenant was waiting at the entrance, an enormous man who towered over me.

'I'm Morehead,' he said as my hand disappeared into his. 'Call me Dutch.'

'Jake Kilmer,' I said.

Five minutes later I came face-to-face with Franco Tagliani for the first time. He was in a drawer in the basement freezer with a hole in his back, a nick in the shoulder, one more in his forehead, and an insurance shot in the right eye.

The tag on his toe said his name was Frank Turner but I knew better.

In the drawer beside him and just as dead was his number one boy, Nicky Stinetto. He had been shot three times, two of them good-bye hits. His tag said he was Nat Sherman, another lie.

Both bodies were badly burned, both had multiple body hits.

Two different guns. You don't need to be a coroner to tell the difference between the hole a .22 makes, and one made by a .357.

'Couple of pros?' I suggested.

'That or Wyatt Earp,' Morehead said. He went on, sounding like an official police report. 'The homicides occurred at approximately seven fifteen p.m. at the residence of the deceased, Turner . . . or Tagliani, whichever way you want it. The shooting was followed by an explosion. We're working on the bomb angle now. Tagliani's old lady got caught in the blowup. She's up in ICU, hangin' on by her pinky.'

I looked at my watch. It was a little after nine.

'You've put together a pretty good sheet on this thing, considering it happened less than two hours ago,' I said.

'We got a play-by-play on tape,' he said and winked. Billy Morehead, head of the Special Operations Branch, local police, had Kraut written all over his battered face. He stared down at me through pale blue, hooded eyes that lurked behind gold-rimmed glasses. Morehead was the size of a prize bull with hands like cantaloupes, sandy hair going grey, a soft but growling voice, and a penchant for swearing in German, all of which had earned him the nickname Dutch. He was cordial, but cautious, and although I had only known him for thirty minutes, I was beginning to like his style.

I said, 'Well, so much for them. Let's hope his widow makes it. Maybe she saw something.'

'She'll never stool if she did. They're all alike.'

There was nothing more to do there until the autopsy, so we went up to the intensive care unit on the second floor. Mrs Tagliani looked like she was on her way to the moon; lines sticking out of both arms, a mask over her face, and behind the bed, three different monitors recording her life signs, what was left of them. The coronary reader seemed awfully lazy, *bip, bip, bipping* slowly as its green lines moved across the centre of the monitor screen, streaking up with each *bip*.

Nobody from the family was in sight. I asked Dutch about that. He shrugged and smoothed the corners of his Bavarian moustache with the thumbs and forefingers of each hand.

'Probably hiding under the bed' was his only comment.

The intern, a callow young man with a teenager's complexion, told us the widow had suffered first-degree burns over seventy per cent of her body, had glass imbedded in her chest and stomach, and had been buried under debris which had caused severe head injuries.

'What're her chances?'

'A Kansas City shoe clerk might take the odds,' he said, and went away.

'I got a man on the front door, another one in a green robe on this floor,' Dutch said. 'Nobody can get near her. Whyn't ya come with me? I gotta debrief my people.'

Mrs Tagliani made the decision for me. While we were standing there the heart monitor went sour. It stopped bipping and the green lines settled into a continuous streak.

The machine went *deeeeeeeee*.

'*Schmerz!*' Dutch muttered. I had heard the expression before. Roughly translated, it meant a sorry state of affairs. I couldn't have put it better.

A moment later the intern and two nurses rushed in, followed by the trauma unit with their rolling table filled with instruments.

We stayed around for ten minutes or so until they gave it up.

'*Eins, zwei, drei,*' Dutch growled. 'One more and we'd have us a home run. Looks like you made a long trip for naught, Mr Kilmer.'

'Yeah,' I said.

'I gotta call homicide, tell 'em Tagliani's missus went across. I'll be a minute. You're stayin' at the Ponce, right?'

'Right.'

'Nice digs,' Dutch said.

He went into the ICU office, made two phone calls in the time it took me to straighten my tie, and came back.

'I hear you know the town,' he said as we headed for the parking lot.

'I do if it hasn't changed in twenty years,' I answered.

He laughed, but it was a sardonic, humourless laugh. 'You're in for a surprise,' he said. 'Follow me over to the hotel. You can plant your car and run out to the Warehouse with me.'

'The Warehouse?'

'That's what we call our layout.'

I told him that was damn white of him and we headed out into the hot, rainy night.

2

SIGHTSEEING

It was only a few blocks back to the hotel but I saw enough through the windshield wipers and rain to tell me what twenty years had done to Dunetown. These were not the wrinkles of time; this was a beautiful woman turned whore. Tagliani's death had started the worms nibbling at my stomach. One look at downtown Dunetown turned the worms to writhing, hissing snakes, striking at my insides.

Twenty years ago Ocean Avenue was a dark, romantic, two-lane blacktop, an archway of magnolias dripping with Spanish moss, that meandered from Dunetown to the sea, six miles away. Now it was Ocean Boulevard, a six-lane highway that slashed between an infinity of garish streetlights like a scar. Neither tree nor bush broke up the eerie green glow, but a string of hotel billboards did, their flashing neon fingers beckoning tourists to the back.

Front Street was worse. I was so shocked by what had happened here that I stopped the car, got out, and stood in the rain, staring at a street gone mad. It was so far from the Front Street in my freeze frame, I couldn't relate to it.

The Front Street I remembered was like the backdrop of a Norman Rockwell painting. There were two old movie houses that showed double features. There was Bucky's drugstore, which had a marble-top soda fountain where you could still get a milk-shake made out of real ice cream and sit in an old-fashioned wire-back chair to enjoy it. And there was the town landmark, Blaine's Department Store, which filled an entire block. The people of Dunetown once got everything from their diapers to their funeral clothes at Blaine's.

Gone. No more Bucky's, no more Blaine's, and the two theatres were twenty-four-hour porno houses. A neon blight had settled over the heart of the town like a garish cloud. Hookers peddled their bodies from under marquees to keep out of the rain, hawkers lured out-of-towners and footloose horseplayers into all-nudie revues, and 'bottomless' and 'topless' signs glittered everywhere. The blaring and oppressive beat of disco music was the street's theme song.

I had been there before, along Hollywood's strip and in the Boston combat zone. The scenario was always the same. You couldn't buy a drink in any bar on the street without staring at a naked bosom or getting propositioned by a waitress – or waiter, depending on your inclination.

My God, I thought, what's happened here? How could Chief and Titan have let this happen to a town they had once treated like a new bride?

The neon blight held the next six blocks in its fist.

And then, as if some medieval architect had built an invisible wall right through the middle of the city, the neon vanished and Dunetown turned suddenly elegant. It was as if time had tiptoed past this part of town with its finger to its lips. Old trees embraced mansions and two-hundred-year-old townhouses. The section had been restored to Revolutionary grandeur with spartan and painstaking accuracy. Gas lamps flickered on the corners, the streets were mostly window-lit, and there were flower-laced squares every three or four blocks, fountained oases that added a sense of symmetry and beauty to the place.

My reaction was simple.

The town was shizo to the core.

3

DOOMSTOWN

Dutch was waiting for me under the awning in front of the Ponce, the political watering hole of Dunetown, a grand, old, creaky hotel, dripping with potted plants, and one of the few things in Dunetown that hadn't changed. His hands were stuffed in the pockets of a bagged-out, nondescript suit, and a Camel was tucked in the corner of his mouth. If he had a care in the world, it didn't show. I parked behind a large black limo, gave the keys to the garageman, checked in, gave a bellhop five bucks to drop my bag in my room, and tossed my briefcase into Dutch's backseat.

As I crawled into the front seat, I was still shell-shocked from the sights and sounds of Dunetown.

'Okay, let's roll,' he said, pulling into the dark, palm-lined street.

He didn't have anything to volunteer; his attitude was still cooperative but cautious. And while I was interested in getting the lowdown on Tagliani-Turner, for the moment I was more interested in what had happened to the local landscape.

After a block or two of silence I asked, 'What in hell happened to Dunetown?'

He stared over at me with a funny look on his face, then, as if answering his own question, said, 'Oh, yeah, I keep forgetting you lived here once.'

'Not here,' I said. 'Not in *this* town. Anyway, I didn't live here. I was, uh . . . I guess you could say I was a summer guest.'

'When was that again?'

I was trying to be casual, trying to keep away from personal history. I didn't know him well enough to show him any scars.

'Twenty years ago, just for a couple of months. It's hardly worth mentioning,' I answered in an offhand way.

'You were just a kid then.'

'Yeah, a senior in college.' While I didn't want to get too personal, I didn't want to play games, either.

'Teddy Findley was my best friend,' I added after a second or two.

'Oh,' he said. 'Then you know what's been going on.'

'No, I got out of touch with the family,' I said.

'You know the Findley kid is dead?'

'You mean Teddy?'

'Yeah.'

'Yes,' I said. 'It's after that I kind of lost track of things.'

'Well, what happened was the racetrack, that's what. The town got bent. Twenty years ago there was probably, what, seventy-five, a hundred thousand people?'

'Sounds about right.'

'Probably three hundred thousand now, about half of 'em from the shady side of the tracks. What you got here, you got a major racetrack, and a beauty. Looks like Saratoga. A classy track, okay? That's a gimmee.'

'Where is it?'

'Back behind us, on Thunderhead Island, about halfway to the beach. It's dark now, anyway.'

'Okay, so you got a classy track. Then what?'

'I think maybe what the money in town expected was kind of another Ascot. Everybody standing around sipping tea, wavin' their pinkies in the air. What they got is horseplayers, which come in every shape, size, and variety known to mankind, and about half of them smoke tea, they don't drink it.'

'So that's what Front Street's all about?'

'It appeals to some of that element. It isn't Front Street's gonna make your gonads shrink. It's what happened to the rest of the town. They turned it into a little Miami.'

'They? Who's they?'

'The wimps that took over. Look, Chief Findley's an old man. Most of the rest of the old power structure's dead. They turned it over to their heirs. Keepers of the kingdom, right? Wrong. Wimps, the lot of 'em, with maybe an exception or two.'

'I probably know some of them,' I said.

'Probably. But it wasn't just them, it was anybody had a square foot of ground they could sell. Condos all over the place. High-rise apartments. Three big hotels on the beach, another one going up. Real estate outta sight. Two marinas as big as Del Mar. You feel bad now, wait'll you see Doomstown in the daylight.'

That was the first time I heard it called Doomstown, but it was far from the last.

'I'm still surprised Chief Findley and the old power structure let it happen,' I said.

'Couldn't do anything about it,' Dutch growled. 'They died or were too old to cope.'

An edge had crept into his tone, a touch of anger mixed with contempt. He seemed to sense it himself and drove quietly while he calmed down.

I tried to fill in the dead space. 'My father used to say you can inherit blood but you can't inherit backbone.'

For the first few blocks we drove through the Dunetown I wanted to remember, the large section of the midtown area that had been restored to its Revolutionary elegance.

I remembered driving through the section with Chief and Teddy one Sunday afternoon a long time ago. It had fallen on hard times; block after block of broken-down row houses that were either boarded-over or had been converted into cheap rooming houses. We were in Chief's black Rolls convertible and he was sitting on the edge of his seat, shoulders square, his white hair thrashing in the wind.

'We're going to restore this whole damn part of town,' he had said grandly, in his soft, Irish-southern accent, while waving his arm at the drab ruins. 'Not a damn museum like Williamsburg. I mean a livin', breathin' place where people will be proud to live. Feel like they're part of her history. Share bed and board with her ghosts. This is the heart of the city, by God! And if the heart stops, the city dies. You boys just remember that.' He paused to appraise the street, then added, half under his breath, 'Someday it'll be your responsibility.' And Teddy looked over at me and winked. In those days I was one of the boys.

It seemed he had kept that bargain, although God knows what miserable trade he had made, allowing the business section to go to hell. That part of it didn't make sense. This part did. The parks and squares opened the town up, letting it breathe and flourish naturally, giving it a personality of its own. Here and there, expensive-looking ships and galleries nudged up against the town-houses. You could tell that zoning here was communal, that the rules were probably shaped by common consent.

'This is better,' I said. 'But Front Street, Jesus!'

'They had to give the two-dollar betters someplace to play,' Dutch said matter-of-factly.

We took a left and a right and were back to reality again. We were on the edge of Back O'Town, a kind of buffer between Dunetown and the black section. You could feel poverty in the air. The fancy shops gave way to army-navy stores and cut-rate furniture outlets. It was the worn-out part of town. A lot of used car lots and flophouse hotels.

We drove in silence for a minute or two, then I asked, 'How long you been here, Dutch?'

'Came down from Pittsburgh almost four years ago, right after they passed the referendum for the track.'

'They built it when?'

'It opened for business year before last and the town went straight to hell. From white Palm Beach suits to horse blanket jackets and plaid pants overnight. You gotta bust an eardrum to hear a southern accent anymore.' His own was a kind of guttural Pennsylvania Dutch.

'You mean like yours?' I joked.

He chuckled. 'Yeah, like mine.'

'Town on the make,' I said, half aloud.

'You got that right.'

'How long you been a cop?'

'Forever,' he said, without even thinking.

He turned down a dark residential street, driving fast but without circus lights or siren.

'Hell of a note,' I said. 'Chief and his bunch pampered Dunetown. It was like a love affair.'

'Well, pal, that's a long time ago. It's a one-night stand now.' He paused and added, 'You know the Findleys that well, huh?'

I thought about that for a minute before answering.

'Well, twenty years dims the edges,' I said.

'Ain't that the truth.' Dutch lit a cigarette and added, 'Sounds like you thought a lot of the old man.'

I nodded. 'You could say that.'

'The way it comes to me, his kid was a war hero, got himself wasted over in Nam. After that the old guy just folded up. Least that's the way I hear it.'

'Too bad,' I said. I was surprised at how indifferent my words sounded.

'I guess.'

11

'I gather you've got reservations about Findley,' I said.

He shrugged. 'It's the machine. I don't trust anybody's been in politics longer than it takes me to eat lunch. And I'm a fast eater.'

Old feelings welled up inside me, noodling at my gut again, a passing thing I couldn't quite get in touch with. Or didn't want to.

'It was like a fiefdom, y'know,' he went on. 'A couple of heavyweights calling all the shots. Now it's a scramble to see who can get richest.'

It was an accurate appraisal and I said so.

'It's what power's all about,' I told him.

'So I got a dollar, you got two. That makes you twice as good as me?'

'No,' I said, 'twice as dangerous.'

He thought about that for a few seconds.

'I guess it all depends on who you are,' Dutch said. Then he dropped the bomb. 'Findley's daughter tried to take up the slack. After his son was zeroed, I mean.'

Bang, there it was.

'How's that?' I asked, making it sound as casual as a yawn.

'Married herself a hotshot all-American. He grabbed the ball from Findley and took off with it. Harry Raines is his name. Talk about ironic.'

'How so?'

'Findley's own son-in-law's head of the racetrack commission.'

That one caught me a little off guard.

'How did that happen?' I asked.

'Wasn't for Raines, there wouldn't be a racetrack. We'd all be dustin' our kiesters someplace else.'

'Raines . . .' I echoed.

'Harry Raines, the son-in-law,' he said.

'Yeah, I know. I was just thinking about the name. Harry Raines,' I said.

'Know him?'

'Vaguely.'

Harry Raines. I remembered the name but I couldn't put a face with it. Faces come hard after twenty years.

'Raines put it all together. This whole racetrack thing.'

'Why?'

'You'll have to ask him that,' said Dutch.

'This Raines a stand-up guy?'

12

'I couldn't say different. What I hear, old Harry's gonna be governor one of these days.'

'You mean because of the racetrack?'

'I guess that's part of it.'

'What's the rest of it?' I asked.

'It's a long story,' he said. 'Worth a dinner.'

'Fair enough,' I said. 'What do you think?'

'About what?'

'About whether Harry Raines is going to be governor or not?'

'I think the sun rises in the east and sets in the west,' he said. And that was the end of that.

4

LEADBETTER'S LEGACY

The rain had turned into a driving storm by the time we got to Dutch Morehead's war room, which was in a small, rundown shopping centre in the suburbs, a mile or two from the centre of town. Lightning etched in purple monochromes a shabby, flat, one-storey building that had once been a supermarket. Its plate-glass windows were boarded over and the entire building was painted flat black.

'Looks like Gestapo headquarters,' I said.

'Psychological,' Dutch grunted.

A less than imposing sign beside the entrance announced that it was the SPECIAL OPERATIONS BRANCH. Below it, even less imposing letters whispered DUNETOWN POLICE DEPARTMENT. I had to squint to read that line.

'Nice of you to mention the police department,' I said.

'I thought so,' Dutch said.

'What exactly does Special Operations Branch mean?' I asked.

'I'm not real sure myself,' he said. 'I think they just wanted to call us the SOB's.'

A moment later Dutch roared like a lion demanding lunch.

'That sorry, flat-assed, pea-brained sappenpaw!' he said, curling his lip.

'Who?' I said, thinking maybe I had offended him.

13

'That six-toed, web-footed, sappenpaw, *klommenshois* Callahan,' he raved on. 'The mackerel-snapping, redheaded putz stole my damn parking place *again*! If I told him once, I told him – arrgh . . .' His voice trailed off as he whispered further insults under his breath.

A half dozen cars in various stages of disrepair were angle-parked along the front of the building. Dented fenders, cracked windshields, globs of orange primer where paint jobs had been started and never finished, hood ornaments and hubcaps gone; it looked like the starting line of a demolition derby.

'Your boys got something against automobiles?' I asked.

He growled something under his breath and wheeled into a spot marked only 'The Kid'.

'I'll take Mufalatta's place,' he said defensively. 'He's never around anyway.'

We were fifty yards from the front door, a long way in the raging storm. He cut the engine and leaned back, offering me a Camel.

'No thanks, I quit,' I said.

'I don't wanna hear about it,' he said, lighting up. He cracked the window and let the smoke stream out into the downpour.

'I can understand about your feelings towards old man Findley,' he said. 'The old boy had a lotta class, I'll give him that. He dealt one last hand before he retired.'

'How's that?'

'His last hurrah. He brought in Ike Leadbetter to head up the force here. Findley was smart enough to know the burg needed some keen people to keep an eye on things when the track was built – the local cops were about as sophisticated as a warthog in a top hat. Leadbetter had been through the mill already. He'd done a turn up in Atlantic City before he came here, so he was savvy. Was Leadbetter brought me in.'

'And Leadbetter is good?'

'Was.'

'Where'd he go?'

'No place. He's dead. Leadbetter knew what was gonna happen, I mean law-wise. He had learned a lot in Atlantic City. And he was honest.'

'What happened to him?' I asked.

'Three years ago, ran his car into the river, if you can believe that.'

'You don't?'

'I stopped believin' in accidents an hour after I got here.'

I was beginning to wonder how Tagliani fit into the picture. Killing a police chief was not exactly his way of doing things.

Anger crept back into Dutch's tone. 'The way it was, the case went to the homicide boys. You lump that whole bunch together, what you end up with is a bigger lump. Not a one of 'em can count to eleven without takin' off his shoes.' Pause. 'It went down as an accident, period, end, of course.'

'Who took Leadbetter's place?'

'Herb Walters.'

'What's the score with him?'

'Old-timer. Up through the ranks. Scared for his job. He don't swim upstream, if that's what you mean. Herb likes calm waters.'

'Is he honest?'

'That's an excellent question. I just don't know. I guess old Herb's okay; he just hasn't had an original thought since the first time he went to the john by himself.' He stopped, then after a moment added: 'Actually he's just a kiss-ass to the people on the green side of town.'

I laughed. 'I gather you don't like him.'

'That's very smart gathering.'

'Why would anybody want to blitz Leadbetter?'

'Why would a lotta people *not* want to? A smart, tough, no-nonsense cop, honest as the Old Testament, in a town going to hell. When Leadbetter was running the show, you couldn't find a pimpmobile anywhere on Front Street. Now every other vehicle you see's either a pink Caddy or a purple Rolls-Royce.'

'How does your outfit fit into all this?'

'It's borderline. We try to monitor the out-of-towners, but local stuff is handled by vice. Don't even ask me about them.'

I slid down in my seat and shook my head.

'Wonderful,' I said. 'Maybe I'll just take some sick leave and sleep this one out.'

'Stick around and watch the fireworks,' he said.

'You think that's going to happen, eh?'

'Well, what I don't think is that Turner and his pistol and his wife had a suicide pact,' he said.

I laughed. 'His name's Tagliani,' I said.

'Whatever.'

15

'I agree,' I said. 'It's my experience that when a *mafioso capo di tutti capi* gets wasted, it doesn't just quietly blow over.'

'*Verdammt!*'

'If you're right and Leadbetter was assassinated, that could have been the kickoff, right there.'

Dutch threw away his butt and checked the weather. It was still like a monsoon outside. He sighed.

'Look,' he said, 'here's the long and short of it, okay? The way it went was that big daddy Findley plugged in Leadbetter, tells him keep the town clean. But Leadbetter inherits a department so old and leaky, if it was a bucket you couldn't carry rocks in it. He can't just vacuum out the whole outfit. That's where I come into the picture. Ike brings me in, gives me a decent budget, says, "Go out, get yourself a dozen or so of the toughest no-shit lads you can find. Boys who know something about the LCN and can't be bent." So I went lookin'. What I got is one mean bunch of hooligans. They're savvy and tough enough to take heat. And they're about as friendly as a nest of copperheads.'

I said 'Uh-huh' pensively. There was a message in all that for me.

'I just want you to understand the way the land rolls, see,' he went on. 'What it was, Leadbetter didn't trust anybody on the old force. Our job was to keep our eyes open, build up our snitches, hassle the out-of-town conmen, grifters, dips, hustlers. Put a little heat under the undesirables so they'd move on. Try to keep a line on who's who and what's what. The tough thing is to do it without walkin' on toes. We hassle a hooker, vice gets pissed. We break down an out-of-town dice game, bunco goes crazy. So we pretty much been spinning our wheels up till now. I mean, we do okay, but . . .' He paused, looking for the next sentence, and finally said, 'Maybe I'm just tired of doin' rounds with the front office.'

I let it all sink in. What I thought I was hearing was that the local police were either stupid or on the take. It was Morehead's job to cover all the bases.

'Leadbetter and Findley played it real smart,' Dutch continued. 'They gave us very loose power, so to speak, and fixed it so we report to a select committee of the city commission.'

'You're not part of the department, then?'

'Yeah. We deal with them when we have to. But Walters can't fire any of us, so we pretty much play it our way. He don't like it, but it's a tough-*sheiss* situation for him. Otherwise, we'd probably all be sorting files in Short Arm, Kansas, by now.'

'He fights you?'

'Not in the open. But he wants control. He's a back fighter. Hell, I'm talkin' too much,' he growled suddenly, and fell silent. I could tell from his flat monotone that he was having trouble trusting me. He was being just friendly enough not to be unfriendly.

The storm rolled over and the rain turned to a fine mist.

He locked the car and we headed for the front door, squeezing up against the building to keep out of the rain that swirled under its eaves.

'Once ya get t'know the gang, you can come, go as ya please,' Dutch said as we hurried towards the door. 'For now, they ain't gonna give you a dime for the toilet unless I'm with you.'

I stopped and he almost ran into me. He loomed over me, his hands jammed in his pockets and an unlit butt in his mouth.

'You got a hard-on for Feds?' I asked.

'Let's just say we've had a few bad rounds with 'em,' he said, studying me through eyes the colour of sapphires. Rainwater dribbled from the brim of his battered, brown felt hat.

'Well, who hasn't?' I said.

'You *are* the Fed,' he said.

'Look, I'm on *your* side. I'm not the Feebies or the Leper Colony. You've dealt with the Freeze before. You and Mazzola are practically old pals by now.'

'Like I said, it's one-on-one in there. These guys don't even trust each other sometimes.'

'How about you?' I asked. 'Am I on probation with you, too? Where do you stand?'

'Out here in the rain getting soaked,' he said. 'Can we maybe continue this inside? There's a lot more of me getting wet than there is of you.'

And he turned and stomped off towards the door.

5

THE WAREHOUSE

Dutch Morehead herded me towards the door with his sheer bulk. I'd been this route before, getting the red eye from the local police. Local cops don't like to deal with Feds because they get treated like kids and because they get the runaround from the Feebies and the shaft from the Lepers. My outfit, the Federal Racket Squad, was different. Part of the job was working on the local level, pointing them in the right direction on interstate cases. Sometimes it took a while for that to sink in.

I decided to save a little time, so I put on my tough guy act.

'I just like to know where I stand without reading a road map,' I snapped as we hurried along through the rain. 'If I'm on some kind of probation with this bunch of yours, then screw it. I'll go it alone.'

He stopped me and smiled condescendingly.

'Cut the bullshit,' he said.

'No bullshit,' I said. 'The hell with this one-on-one, sink-or-swim crap. I didn't come here to audition for you and yours.'

'What the hell got under your saddle all of a sudden?'

'You know what the Freeze is all about?' I demanded, and went on before he could answer. 'We're the only federal agency around who works with the street cops. The FBI, the IRS, Justice Department, they're all in it for themselves.'

'And you're not?' he demanded. 'You came here to bust this Tagliani's balls, right or wrong?'

'I came here to find out what he's doing here – '

'Was,' he interrupted.

'Was,' I agreed. 'But if he was here, then the rest of his bunch is close by. I know this outfit, Dutch. I know this gang better than anyone alive. Sure, I want to bring the whole bunch down. What do you want to do, send flowers?'

He lit his Camel and took a long pull, staring hard at me all the while.

'Look here,' he said. 'Before, when I was talking about what our assignment is, I left one thing out. We were supposed to keep organised crime out of Doomstown. All of a sudden, your boss tells me we got Mafia up to our eyeballs. How do you think that makes me feel? All of us, the whole bunch. Like monkeys, that's how.'

'Cisco didn't invite them down here, y'know. He just recognised a face and turned them up for you, that's all. If it was the Feebies, you can bet your sweet by-and-by they'd be all over town and you couldn't find out what day it is from any of them.'

'You're right there.'

'So we throw in together and bring them down?'

'If somebody doesn't beat us to it.'

'Okay. So tell your boys to forget this college Charlie shit,' I said, still acting irritated. 'This isn't pledge week at the old frat house and I'm not here to impress anybody. If these guys are as tough as you make them sound, it'll help if you give me a vote of confidence off the top.'

Not bad, Kilmer, not bad at all. Hard case but not hard nose. They can live with that.

Dutch started laughing.

'Sensitive, ain't you,' he said, and led me into the building. We walked through the front door into what looked like the entrance to a prison block: a small boxlike room, a door with a bell on one side, and a mirror in the wall beside it. One-way glass. Dutch shoved a thumb against the bell. A second later the door buzzed open. Inside, a black, uniformed cop sat in a darkened cubicle, watching the entrance. An Uzi machine gun was leaning on the wall beside him. I nodded and got a blank stare back.

'Looks like you're expecting an invasion,' I said.

'Security. Nobody gets in here without one of us saying so. That includes everybody from the chief of police and the mayor to the President of the United States.

'Nice weapon,' I said, with a nod towards the Uzi.

'We liberated it. My bunch is pretty good at dog robbing,' Dutch said, then added, almost as an afterthought, 'Among other things.'

Inside, the front of the place had been divided into half a dozen office cubicles. Behind them, in the centre of the building, was a fairly sophisticated computer system and a telephone switchboard. Behind that was what appeared to be a large meeting room, walled with chalk- and corkboards. A six-foot television screen was mounted in the wall at the front of the room and twenty or so old-fashioned movable chairs were scattered about, the kind with writing platforms attached, like they had in school when I was a kid – and still do, for all I know.

The big room in the back was affectionately known as the Kindergarten.

Two rooms filled the back end of the old supermarket. One was a holding cell that looked big enough to accommodate the entire D-Day invasion force, and the other was behind a door marked simply VIDEO OPERATIONS. I counted three uniformed cops on duty, including the man on the door and a black woman who was operating the switchboard.

A pretty classy setup: Morehead's war room.

'Are the uniform people part of your gang or on loan-out?'

'Probation. If they can hack the everyday stuff, they maybe can work their way into the gang. Also we find out pretty quick whether they can keep their mouths shut.'

I decided to take one last shot at my immediate problem. 'Before the rest of your guys show up,' I said, 'can we settle this Fed problem?'

'It's settled. We don't have a problem,' he said, trying to brush it off.

'Right,' I said with more than a little acid. I decided to let him blow off a little steam.

'Okay,' he snapped, 'let's put it this way. At first we tried workin' with the IRS, but cooperating with the Leper Colony is no different than loanin' your watch to Jesse James. They're either young turks just out of college, in it so they can learn how to beat the system and get rich, or they're misfits none of the other agencies'll touch. Either way, it's every man for himself. Like workin' in a patch of skunk cabbage.'

'No argument,' I said.

'A bunch of *Pfutzilukers*!' he bellowed.

'Absolutely,' I agreed. 'Whatever that means.'

'If I broke half the laws they do, I'd be doing time.'

'Life plus twenty, at least.' Now it was his turn and I let him rage on.

He leaned over me, jabbing his chest with his thumb. 'I wouldn't let one of 'em in here, not if he showed up with a court order and the entire Marine Corps to back 'em up!' he roared. 'And the Feebies aren't much better! All they wanna do is make nickels in Washington. If it looks good on the daily report and they can get a press conference out of it, that's all they care about. Ask them for a little help, you get senile waitin' for the phone to ring.'

'I've had the same experience,' I said with sympathy.

'Dipshits and robots!' he said. Now his arms were in the act. He was waving them around like a symphony conductor. 'Bastards steal our information, make deals that sour our cases, violate civil rights, and we get the enema. They always ride off with the chick in the end.'

I nodded agreement. He was running out of steam.

'All my boys get is to kiss the horse at the fadeout, know what I mean?'

'Sure.' Pause. 'How about you?'

'How about me what?'

'You feel all you get out of them is to kiss the horse?'

He stopped and stared me up and down and then he figured it all out and started to laugh.

'Aw, hell, pal,' he said, 'I been around so long I'm glad for all the kissin' I can get, even if it's a horse's ass.'

'Okay, Dutch,' I said quietly. 'I'm not looking for any fadeout kisses. If these people are looting your town, I'll help you put them away. All the Freeze wants out of it is information. Connections. How they operate. How did they infiltrate the town? Who did they have to buy? How are they connected with the other mobs? No conflict, okay?'

'We'll just play it by ear,' he said, still coy. It was like kicking a brick wall.

'Shit, if that's the play, that's the play,' I said with a shrug.

'You'll do fine. You got a hair up your ass just like the rest of us.'

'I just do the best I can,' I said, throwing in a little humility.

'According to your boss, that's pretty damn good,' he said.

'Far as I'm concerned, if we get enough to make a case against somebody, it can go state or federal,' I said. 'My style is give it to whoever has the strongest case – and the best prosecutor. I get a little crazy when somebody walks on me.'

'That's fair enough,' he said. 'Who doesn't?'

'What kind of DA do you have?'

'A woman. Her name's Galavanti and she's meaner than a three-day hangover.'

'On us or them?'

He smiled. 'On *every*body. You put a case on her with holes in it, you'll hear language would turn a lifer purple.'

'Good. Maybe we can help each other.'

'Thing of it is, I never heard of your bunch until a couple of months ago. This guy Mazzola shows up one day outta the blue, buys me lunch, gives me the same buck and wing you're givin' me.'

Mazzola was Cisco Mazzola, my boss in the Freeze. He had told me Dutch Morehead was a man who said his piece and I was beginning to believe him.

'Which you sneezed off,' I said.

'Not exactly. For starters, he put something in the pot.'

'Like what?'

'Like the Stick.'

'The Stick? What's the Stick?'

He looked at me kind of funny, one of those 'what year were you born' looks.

'Not what, who. You know . . . the Stick. Parver. So far he fits right in.'

I didn't have the foggiest idea what he was talking about and before I could pursue it any further, he picked up a bright red bullhorn, turned up the volume, and summoned his men to the back room.

I took the opportunity to step into an empty office and call the hotel. They patched me through to Cisco, who was in the restaurant, eating. He had flown in from Washington to brief me on the local situation. Since it had changed radically in the last couple of hours, I didn't know what to expect.

Cisco and I were friends in a remote kind of way. He was one of several shadows that wove in and out of my life, altering its course without ever touching me directly, our main connection provided by the telephone company. In the seven or so years I had known him, I had never seen the inside of his house, never met his family, and knew little about his personal taste other than that he had a penchant for vitamins and health food. He also had an obsession about saving his hair, most of which was gone.

It took him a minute to get to the phone.

'Sorry to take you away from dinner,' I said. 'I would have called sooner but I've been busy. There's been a takeout. Tagliani, Stinetto, and Tagliani's wife.'

'Yes, I've heard,' he said in his flat, no-nonsense voice. 'Any details yet?'

'At his place, about three hours ago. Pistols and a fire bomb. The woman was killed by the bomb. Whoever scratched the other two knew what he, or they, were doing. It looks like a couple of Petes to me.'

'I want you to stay with this,' he said.

'Good. How many have you made so far?'

'The whole mob's here except for Tuna Chevos and his gunslinger – '

'Nance,' I hissed, cutting him off. Anger roiled inside me at the mention of Turk Nance. We went back a ways, Nance and I, and it wasn't a friendly trip. 'They're here too,' I said. 'I'll give you odds.'

'Maybe so, but this isn't a vendetta. Nance is just a tinhorn shooter. Forget him.'

'Right.'

'Forget him, Jake.'

'I heard you!'

'What are you so edgy about?'

'Oh, nothing at all. I've been hounddogging this mob for what, four, five years?'

'Closer to five,' he sighed.

'I'm just a little burned that the iceman beat me to it.'

'Understandable. Just remember why you're here. I want information. Where are you now?'

'Morehead's war room.'

'A good man,' Cisco said. 'A little short on procedure, maybe.'

That was the understatement of the year.

I said, 'So far he's treating me like I just broke his leg.'

'Cautious,' said Cisco. 'Give him a little time.'

'What happens if things pick up speed and I need some backup?' I asked.

'Mickey Parver will help you,' he said.

'He the one they call Stick?'

'Right.'

'I felt a little like an idiot. How come I never heard of this guy before now?'

'Because you never read the weekly report, that's why,' he snapped. 'He files a report every – '

I cut him off, trying to change the subject.

23

'Oh, yeah, I do seem to remember – '

'Don't bullshit me,' said Cisco. 'You haven't read the weekly poop sheet since the pope was a plumber.'

'How long's he been in the squad?' I asked, trying to avoid that issue.

'He's been in the squad for a year or so,' Cisco said, with annoyance. 'You'll like him. He's young and not too jaded yet. Please don't spoil him by getting lost out in left field someplace. He's a lot like you, a lone wolf. You two can be good for each other.'

'I don't have time to baby-sit some – '

'Who said anything about baby-sitting? Did I say that?'

'It sounded like – '

'It sounded like just what I said. Don't stray off the dime, Jake. I want information, period. You're a lawyer and you always stick to due process. I'd like a little of that to rub off on Stick.'

'I got a feeling he's not going to get a lot of help in that respect from Morehead's bunch.'

'That's what I mean,' Cisco said. 'Give the lad a little balance, okay?'

'What if I need some *professional* backup?' I asked.

'He wouldn't be in the Freeze if he wasn't first class, and you know it,' Cisco growled. 'You get in trouble, he's as good a man to have at the back door as you could ask. All I'm saying is, if we do happen to turn up a RICO case, I want it to be airtight. No illegal wiretaps, no hacking their computers. Nothing that won't hold up in court.'

'Yeah, okay,' I said.

Cisco couldn't resist throwing in a little jab.

'Maybe he can get you to file a report now and again, once a week or so, y'know.'

'Mm-hmm.'

'Dutch has a computer setup. You can tie directly into our terminal in Washington.'

'Right,' I said, and before I could move on to something else, he added sarcastically, 'Maybe he can help you a little in that area.'

'Sure thing.'

'Stick sent the Tagliani photos up to me in his weekly report; that's how we made them.'

I was beginning to hate this kid they called Stick, already. He sounded like a miserable little eager beaver.

'How long you in town for?' I asked.

'I'm in town to say hello,' Cisco answered. 'I head back to Washington tomorrow.'

'Aw, and just when the fun's starting.'

'Somebody has to put food on the table. We're in the middle of the annual battle of the budget – which reminds me, you're two months behind in your expense reports and you haven't filed a field report for – '

'Tell me more about this Stick fellow,' I said, trying to avoid another issue.

Mazzola paused. 'I want those expense reports,' he said. 'Clear?'

'Right. You got 'em.'

'Now, about Parver. Before he came with us, he was a DC plainclothes, then a narc, then he worked on the DC mob squad. Before all that he did time in Nam. Army intelligence or something. He's tough enough.'

'Not too jaded, huh?'

Cisco chuckled like he'd just heard a dirty joke. 'I loaned him to Dutch. I don't think anybody else in the outfit knows he's one of us. Dutch'll fix it so the two of you can pair up. You'll like him.'

'Says who?'

'All the ladies do.'

'Great.'

'Sorry about Tagliani,' Mazzola said. 'I know how long you been working on his case.'

'Well, saves the Fed a lot of money, I suppose,' I said. 'But it would have been nice to put the bastard in Leavenworth with his brother.'

'One more thing,' Cisco said before hanging up. 'You're not here to solve any murder cases. You're here to find out if there were any outside Mob strings on Tagliani and who holds them. That's number one. We could have a classic case working here, Jake.'

'Morehead said something funny,' I told him. 'He said, "I've got the whole thing on tape."'

'What whole thing? You mean the Tagliani hit?'

'I guess so. He was evasive when I asked him.'

'Well, ask him again. You can fill me in at breakfast.'

'Sure.'

'I'll meet you in the hotel restaurant. Eight o'clock suit you?'

'Nine might be better.'

'See you at eight,' he said, ending the conversation.

6

INSTANT REPLAY

When I got back to the Kindergarten, Dutch Morehead's SOB's were beginning to gather in the room. One or two had drifted in. Dutch had a handful of photographs which he was about to pin on a corkboard. A quick glance confirmed that the Tagliani gang was in Dunetown and was there in force. Only two pictures were missing: Tuna Chevos and his gunman, Turk Nance. And as I told Cisco, I knew they had to be in Dunetown somewhere.

'That's Tagliani's outfit all right,' I told Dutch. 'All but two of them. Otherwise known as the Cincinnati Triad. Mind if I ask you what put you on to him in the first place?'

'Ever hear of Charlie Flowers?' Dutch asked.

'Charlie "One Ear" Flowers?' I asked, surprised.

'Could there be more than one?' he said with a smile.

'Everybody in the business has heard of Charlie One Ear,' I said.

'What've you heard?' he asked.

Charlie One Ear was a legend in the business. It was said that he had the best string of snitches in the country, had a computer for a brain, was part Indian, and was one of the best trackers alive. If rumour was correct, Flowers could find a footprint in a jar of honey, and I told Dutch that.

'Ever meet him?'

'No,' I said, 'I've never met a living legend.'

'What have you heard lately?'

He asked the way people who already know the answers ask questions.

I hesitated for a moment, then said, 'Word is, he got on the sauce and had to retire.'

'You been listening to a bunch of *sheiss kopfes*,' he said. 'That gent in the tweeds, second row there, that's Charlie One Ear. He's never had a drink in his life.'

I looked at him. He was short and squat, a barrel of a man, impeccably dressed in a tweed suit, tan suede vest, and a perfectly matched tie. His moustache was trimmed to perfection, his nails immaculately manicured. He had no right ear, just a little bunch of balled-up flesh where it should have been. I had heard the story too. When Flowers was a young patrolman in St Louis, a mugger bit his ear off.

He was chatting with a middling, wiry tiger of a man who was dressed on the opposite end of the sartorial scale; Hell's Angels' leather and denim. His face looked like it had been sculpted with a waffle iron.

'Flowers remembers every face, rap sheet, stiff, he's ever seen or met,' said Dutch. 'Photographic memory, total recall – whatever you call it – he's got it. Anyway, he didn't make Tagliani, but he made a couple of Tagliani's out-of-town pals. A lot of heavy-weights from out of state spent time with Tagliani at the track, none of them exactly movie star material. Tagliani was also a very private kind, but he flashed lots of money. Big money. So Charlie One Ear got nosy, shot some pictures one day out at the track. Stick sends the photos up to DC to Mazzola and tells him Turner, which is how we knew him then, is keeping fast company and spending money like he owns the Bank of England. Cisco takes one look and bingo, we got a Tagliani instead of a Turner on our hands. That was last week.'

'Great timing,' I said.

'Ain't it though,' Dutch said woefully.

'Who's that he's talking to?' I asked.

'You mean the dude in black tie and tails?' Dutch said with a snicker. 'That's Chino Zapata. He mangles the king's English and thinks *Miranda* is a South American banana republic, but he can follow a speck of dust into a Texas tornado and never lose sight of it. And in a pinch, he's got a punch like Dempsey.'

'Where'd you find him?'

'LAPD. The story is they recruited him to get him off the street, although nobody in the LAPD will admit it. When I found him, he was undercover with the Hell's Angels.'

'How'd you get him down here?'

'I told him he could bring his bike and wear whatever he pleased.'

'Oh.'

By this time the room had gathered three more men – about half of Dutch Morehead's squad – a strange-looking gang whose dress varied from Flowers' tweeds and brogans to Zapata's black leather jacket and hobnail boots. They stood, or sat, smoking, drinking coffee, making nickel talk and eyeballing me. It was my first view of the hard-case bunch I would get to know a lot better, and fast.

Morehead sidled around so his back was to the room and started quietly giving me a rundown on the rest of his gang.

'Sitting right behind Zapata is Nick Salvatore, a real rough-neck. His old man was *soldato* for a small-time *mafioso* in south Philly, blew himself up trying to wire a bomb to some poli-tician's car. You'll probably get the whole story from him if you stick around long enough, but the long and short of it is he hates the outfit with a passion. Calls our job the Dago roundup. He's more streetwise than Zapata. I guess you might call Salvatore our resident LCN expert. He doesn't know that many of the people, but he knows the way they think.'

Salvatore was dressed haphazardly at best: a T-shirt with GRATEFUL DEAD printed over a skull and crossbones, a purple Windbreaker, and jeans. A single gold earring peeked out from under his long black hair. It was hard to tell whether he was growing a beard or had lost his razor.

'The earring is his mother's wedding band,' Dutch whis-pered. 'He's touchy about that. He also carries a sawed-off pool cue with a leaded handle in his shoulder holster.'

On my card it was a split decision whether Zapata or Salva-tore was the worst dresser, although Dutch gave the nod to Salvatore.

'Zapata doesn't know any better,' he said. 'Salvatore doesn't give a damn. If you blindfold him and ask him what he's wearing, he couldn't even guess.'

Dutch continued the thumbnail sketch of his gang:

'Across from him is Cowboy Lewis.' The man he referred to was as tall as Dutch, thirty pounds trimmer, and wore a black patch over his left eye. He was dressed in white jeans and a tan Windbreaker zipped halfway down, had very little hair on his chest. A black baseball cap with a gold dolphin on the crown covered a tangled mop of dishwater-blond hair. There wasn't a spare ounce of fat on the guy.

'Pound for pound, the hardest man in the bunch. He doesn't have much to say, but when he does, it's worth listening to,' Dutch said. 'He thinks in a very logical way. A to b to c to d, like that. If there's a bust on the make, Lewis is the man you want in front. He's kind of like our fullback, y'know. You say to Cowboy, We need to lose that door, Cowboy, and the door's gone, just like that, no questions asked. I suppose if I told him to lose an elephant, he'd waste the elephant. He's not afraid of anything that I can think of.'

'Are any of them?' I asked.

Dutch chuckled. 'Not really,' he said. 'Lewis is kind of . . .' He paused a moment, looking for the proper words, and then said, 'He's just very single-minded. Actually, he started out to be a hockey player but he never made the big time. His fuse was too short, even for hockey. Y'see, if Cowboy was going for a goal, and the cage was way down at the other end of the rink, he'd go straight for it. Anybody got in his way, he'd just flatten them.'

'Doesn't sound like the perfect team man,' I said.

'Nobody's perfect,' said Dutch.

The last man in the room was also lean and hard-eyed, in his mid- to late thirties, and over six feet tall. He looked like he had little time for nonsense or small talk.

'The tall guy in the three-piece suit and the flower in his lapel, that's Pancho Callahan,' Dutch continued. 'He's a former veterinarian, graduated from UCLA, and can tell you more about horse racing than the staff of Calumet Farms. He spends most of his time at the track. He doesn't say too much unless you get him on horses; then he'll talk your ear off.' Callahan seemed restless. It was obvious he would rather have been elsewhere, which was probably true of all of them.

Altogether, about as strange a bunch of lawmen as I've ever seen gathered in one room. And there were a few more to go: the Mufalatta Kid and Kite Lange, more of whom later, and, of course, Stick, who was still an enigma to me. Eight in all, nine if you counted Dutch.

'Tell me a little about the Stick,' I said. 'What kind of guy is he?'

Dutch stared off at a corner of the room for a moment, tugging at his moustache.

29

'Very likable,' he said finally. 'You could call him amiable. Bizarre sense of humour. But not to be messed with. I'll tell you a little story about Stick. He has this old felt hat, I mean this hat looks like an ape's been playing with it. One day he leaves the hat in the car while he goes to get a haircut. He comes back, somebody lifted the hat. Don't ask me why anybody would *want* the hat, but there you are. About a week later Stick is cruising up Bay Street one afternoon and there this guy is, strolling up the boulevard wearing his hat.

'Stick pulls up, starts following the guy on foot. The guy goes into a record store. At that point Stick remembers he left his piece in his glove compartment. So what does he do? He hops in a hardware store, buys a number-five Stillson wrench, and when the little putz comes out of the record store, Stick falls in behind him, shoves him in the first alley they come to, and whaps the bejesus out of the guy. The guy never saw him and never knew what hit him, but he sure knew Stick got his hat back.'

He paused for another moment and then added: 'Resourceful, that's what Stick is, resourceful.'

I filed that information away, then said to Dutch, 'Look, I don't want to seem pushy this early in the game, but I know this Tagliani mob. There's something I'd like to run by your people. Maybe it'll help a little.'

He gave the request a second's worth of thought and nodded. 'Okay,' he said. 'But let me ease you into the picture first.'

'Anything you say.'

I went over and grabbed a desk near the side of the room.

Dutch, as rumpled as an unmade bed, stood in front of the room.

'All right, listen up,' he told his gashouse gang. 'You all know by now what happened tonight. We lost the ace in the deck and we had a man sitting two hundred yards away.'

He did an eyeball roll call and then bellowed loud enough to wake the dead in Milwaukee:

'*Sheiss*, we're missin' half the squad here. Didn't they hear this is a command performance?'

'They're still out on the range,' a voice mumbled from the back of the room.

'Hmmm,' Dutch muttered. 'Okay, you all know about Tagliani and Stinetto getting chilled. Those are the two we knew as Turner and Sherman. Well, first, I got a little good news, if you

30

want to call it that. Then we'll talk about who was where and how we screwed up tonight. Anyway, we had the house bugged and as happens, one of the rooms on the wire was the den, which is where the hit was made. So we got the whole thing on tape, thanks to Lange, who did his telephone repairman act.'

Dutch punched a button on a small cassette player and a moment later the room's hollow tone hissed through the speaker.

For maybe two minutes that's all there was, room tone.

Then a doorbell, far off, in another part of the house.

Seconds later someone entered the room.

Sounds of someone sitting down, a paper rustling, a lighter being struck, more paper noises. Then a voice, getting closer to the room:

'Hey, Nicky, *bon dia*, how ya do at the track?'

It was Tagliani's voice; I'd heard it on tape enough times to know.

'I dropped a bundle.' Stinetto's voice.

'How the fuck you lose? It was a fix. I gave it to yuh just this morning. Din't I tell yuh, it's on for Midnight Star, third race. Huh?'

'Ya tol' me. Too bad the other seven heats wasn't fixed.'

Laughter. 'I don' believe yuh. I give you a sure thing, you turn right aro – '

At that point there was a sound of glass crashing, a lot of jumbled noise, swearing and yelling . . .

Tagliani: 'God – no, no . . .'

Stinetto: 'Motherfu – '

Several shots, from two different guns.

A man's scream.

'Nicky . . .'

Brrrddt. A muffled rapid-fire gun, probably a submachine gun. It fired so fast it sounded like a dentist's drill.

Two screams; terrible, terrified, haunting screams.

Two more shots.

Bang . . . bang. Something heavy, a .357 maybe.

Somebody gagged.

Something heavy hit the floor, crunching glass as it fell.

Two more shots, spaced.

Bang . . . bang!

Footsteps running and the sound of something else hitting the floor.

The something else was sizzling.
A woman's voice,
screaming,
getting closer,
entering the room.
Baroomf!

The explosion blew out the mike. Dutch punched the off button.

'That's it,' he said.

Charlie One Ear said, 'Utterly charming. Too bad about the woman.'

'Too bad about all of them,' Dutch snapped caustically. 'They were worth more to us alive than dead.'

Dutch ran the tape back and played it again. We all leaned forward, hoping to hear something significant, but there wasn't much. I listened to the shots, counting them.

'That one, sounds like a dentist's drill, I make that some kind of submachine gun,' Zapata said.

Dutch played it again.

It was a chilling tape. Just when you think you've seen it all and heard it all, you run across something like this, listening to three people die. Mobsters or not, it raised the hair on my arms.

'Definitely two guns,' Charlie One Ear said.

'That's pretty good, Charlie. Stinetto's gun was still in his belt when we found him,' Dutch said. 'Loaded and clean. The old man was light.'

'Pretty good shooting,' Chino ventured.

'Had to be two of 'em,' said Salvatore.

'Or an ambidextrous marksman,' Charlie One Ear said.

'Fuckin' nervy one,' Zapata added.

'Any other ideas?' Dutch asked.

I kept mine to myself.

'Okay, now pay attention. We got a man here can maybe shed a little glimmer on the night's proceedings, so everybody just relax a minute. This here's Jake Kilmer. Kilmer's with the Freeze and he's an expert on this outfit.'

A moan of discontent rippled through the room.

'You wanna listen to him, or stay dumb?' Dutch snapped without a hint of humour in his tone.

The room got quiet.

And colder than an ice cube sandwich.

7

EXIT SCREAMING

The house was a two-storey brick and stone structure nestled against high dunes overlooking the bay. The backyard was terraced, rising from the swimming pool to a flat that looked like a child's dream. There was a gazebo and an eight-horse carousel and a monkey bar set and a railroad with each car just large enough to accommodate one child.

Two men smoked quietly in the gazebo.

From high above, on top of the dunes that separated the house from the bay, the sound of the child laughing could be heard, followed by his grandfather's rough laughter. Their joyous chorus was joined by the sound of a calliope playing East Side, West Side, All Around the Town. *The child was on the carousel, his grandfather standing beside him with an arm around the boy. The horses, eyes gleaming, nostrils flaring, mouths open, jogged up and down in an endless, circular race. Below them, in the pool, an inner tube floated forgotten.*

The figure, dressed entirely in black, crouched as it moved silently and swiftly through the sea grass on top of the dune to a point above the house. Only the swimming pool was visible. The figure was carrying a weapon that had the general conformity of a rifle but was larger.

The figure slid to the ground and eased quietly to the edge of the dune, looking down at the old man and the child. He waited.

A woman appeared at the sliding glass door at the back of the house.

'Ricardo, bedtime,' she yelled.

The child protested but the woman persisted.

'Once more around,' the old man yelled back, and the woman agreed and waited.

The figure on the dune also waited.

His last ride finished, the little boy ran gleefully down the terrace and then turned back to the older man.

'Come kiss me good night, Grandpa,' he called back.

The grandfather smiled and waved his hand.

'Uno momento,' *he called back, and then motioned to the men in the gazebo to shut down the carousel.*

The child skipped to his grandmother and they entered the house together.

The figure on the dune fitted what looked like a pineapple onto the end of the weapon and adjusted a knob on the rear of the barrel. There was the faint sound of metal clinking against metal.

The old man looked around, not sure where the sound had come from.

One of the men in the gazebo stood up, stepped out onto the terrace, and looked up.

'Something?' *the other one said.*

The first one shrugged and walked back into the gazebo.

There was a muffled explosion –

Pumf!

A sigh in the night air over their heads.

Then the terraced backyard of the house was suddenly bathed in a sickening orange-red glow.

The two men in the gazebo were blown to the ground. The grandfather arced like a diver doing a backflip as he was blown off the terrace. He landed in the pool. The merry horses were blown to bits.

The night calm was shattered by the explosion, by a crescendo of broken glass, by the screams.

8

THE CINCINNATI TRIAD

Morehead had pinned six photographs on a corkboard in the front of the big room, each one identified with a felt-tip pen. Since we had already made Tagliani and Frank Turner as one and the same, ditto Stinetto and Nat Sherman, Dutch crossed them out.

Until a couple of hours ago Tagliani had been *capo di tutti capi*, 'boss of all bosses' of the Cincinnati Tagliani family, known as the Cincinnati Triad.

For fifty years the Taglianis had ruled the mob world in

south-west Ohio, operating out of Cincinnati. The founder of the clan, Giani, its first *capo di tutti capi*, died when he was eighty-three and never saw the inside of a courtroom, much less did time for his crimes. The empire was passed to his son, Joe 'Skeet' Tagliani. While the old man had a certain Old World charm, Skeet Tagliani was nothing less than a butcher. Under his regime the Taglianis had formed an alliance with two other gang leaders. One was Tuna Chevos, who married Skeet Tagliani's sister and was also one of the Midwest's most powerful dope czars. Across the Ohio River, in Covington, an old-time *mafioso* named Johnny Draganata controlled things. When a black Irish hood named Bannion tried to take over, Skeet threw in with Draganata. The war lasted less than three months. It was a bloodbath and to my knowledge there isn't a Bannion hoodlum left to talk about it.

Thus the Cincinnati Triad was formed: Skeet Tagliani, Tuna Chevos, and Johnny Draganata.

I had put Skeet away for a ten spot, but it had taken three years of my life to do it and I had spent the better part of the next two trying to prove that his brother, Franco, had taken over as *capo* in Skeet's place. It was a nasty job and costly. Several of our agents and witnesses had died trying to gather evidence against the Taglianis.

Then Franco had vanished, poof, just like that, no trace – and another year had gone down the drain while I chased every hokum lead, every sour tip, up and down every dead-end alley in the country. The Cincinnati Triad had simply disappeared.

A clever move, Tagliani selling out and hauling stakes like that. Clever and frustrating. Now, almost a year later, he had turned up in Dunetown – stretched out in the morgue with a name tag on his toe that said he was Frank Turner. The name change was easy to understand.

What he was doing on ice was not.

The other five faces in Dutch's photos were familiar although their names, too, were new. They were the princes of Tagliani's hoodlum empire, the *capi* who helped rule the kingdom: Rico Stizano, who was now calling himself Robert Simons; Tony Logeto, who had become Thomas Lanier; Anthony Bronicata, now known as Alfred Burns; and Johnny Draganata, the old fox, whose nom de plume was James Dempsey. The subject in the last picture was less familiar to me, although I knew who he was: Johnny 'Jigs' O'Brian, a nickel-dime hoodlum who had been doing odd jobs for the Mob in Pheonix until he married Tagliani's youngest daughter, Dana. At the time the Triad had done its disappearing act, O'Brian was doing on-the-job training running prostitution.

Cute, but not all that original. The new names helped explain initials on suitcases, gold cuff links, silk shirts, sterling silverware, that kind of thing. The Tagliani bunch was big on monograms.

Then there were the two missing faces, Tuna Chevos and his chief executioner and sycophant, Turk Nance. In the whole mob, Chevos and his henchman Nance were the most deadly. The setup here seemed too perfect for them to be too far away. Besides, Chevos was a dope runner and the coastline of Georgia from South Carolina to Florida was the Marseilles of America. Dope flowed through there as easily as ice water flowed through Chevos' veins.

'Recognise these people?' Dutch asked, pointing to the rogues' gallery.

I nodded. 'All of 'em. Cutthroats to the man.'

'Okay,' he said, 'let's get on with it.'

I decided to play it humble and sat down on the corner of the desk.

'I don't want to sound like I know it all,' I said, 'but I've been hounddogging these bastards for years. I know a lot about this mob because I've been trying to break up their party ever since I got out of short pants.'

Not a grin. A tough audience. Salvatore was cleaning his fingernails with a knife that made a machete look like a safety pin. Charlie One Ear was doing a crossword puzzle. I kept trying.

'Just what is the Freeze?' Charlie One Ear asked without looking up from his puzzle.

They were going to make it tough.

'Well, I'll tell you what it's not. It's not the Feebies or the Leper Colony,' I said. 'We have two jobs. We work with locals on anything where there's a hint of an interstate violation. And we go after the LCN. We're not in a league with the Leper Colony. We don't kiss ass in Washington by victimising some little taxpayer who can't protect himself, and we don't hold press conferences every five minutes like the Feebies.'

'What's the LCN?' Zapata asked.

'La Cosa Nostra, you fuckin' moron,' Salvatore taunted.

Zapata looked back over his shoulder at Salvatore. 'Big deal. So I never heard it called LCN before. My old man didn't suck ass for some broken-down old *mafioso*.'

'That's right,' Salvatore said. 'Your old man swept floors in a Tijuana whorehouse.'

'You shoulda been brung up in a whorehouse,' Zapata shot back. 'Maybe you wouldn't wear an earring, like a fuckin' fag.'

'Hey, you're talking about my mother's wedding ring!' roared Salvatore.

'All right, all right,' Charlie One Ear said, holding up his hand.

'You keep outta this,' said Salvatore. 'At least I got an ear to put it in; some dip didn't eat it for dinner.'

I wondered why Dutch didn't step in and stop things before they got out of hand. Then Zapata started snickering and Salvatore broke out in a laugh and Charlie One Ear smiled, and I got a sudden sense of what was happening. You see it in combat, this kind of barbed-wire humour. It's a great equaliser. It says: I trust you; we're buddies; you can say anything about me you want; nobody else has the privilege. It bonds that unspoken sense of love and trust among men under pressure, a macho camaraderie in which the insult becomes the ultimate flattery.

I was beginning to understand what Dutch meant. This was a tight little society and they were letting me know it in their own way.

They all got into it except Pancho Callahan, who never cracked a smile. He stared at me over a pyramid of fingers through cold grey eyes, the way you stare at a waiter in a restaurant when he forgets your order. I got the message. 'Screw the buddy-buddy humour, hotshot,' he was saying. 'Show us what you got.'

'You guys can rehearse your act later,' Dutch said, throwing a wet towel in the works. 'If we listen, maybe we can learn something. Did all of you forget that part of our deal was to keep organised crime out of this town? Look what we ended up with.'

They all eyeballed me.

'Not him,' Dutch growled, 'the *pfutzlüker* Taglianis.'

Dutch never swore in English, only German. I doubt that any of his gang knew what the hell he meant most of the time. Nobody ever asked, either.

'Go on,' he said to me. 'Keep trying.'

'Look, this gang up here on the wall is no penny-ante outfit and they didn't come here for the waters. They came here to buy

37

this town. I been after these bastards since the day I joined the Freeze.'

'So what d'you want outta all this?' Cowboy Lewis asked.

'I'll tell you what I want,' I said. 'The RICO anti-crime laws refer to any monies earned from illegal sources as igg,' I said, 'which stands for *ill-gotten gains*.'

That drew a laugh from Charlie One Ear. 'Ah,' he said, 'the wonders of the government never cease.'

'What's RICO stand for?' Lewis asked, seriously.

'Racketeer Influenced and Corrupt Organisations – gangland fronts,' I said.

'Igg simply means the kiwash they make from dope, gambling, prostitution, extortion, pornography . . . all the LCN's favourite tricks. The LCN has to wash that money, and it isn't easy. So they invest in legitimate business – even banks – to clean it up. RICO gives us the power to bust them if we can prove that any business depends for its support on igg. If we can prove that, we can confiscate their money, their businesses, their equipment, their yachts and Rolls-Royces and all the rest of their toys. And we can also make cases against the racketeers and *everybody* connected with them. That goes for legitimate businessmen, politicians, or anybody else that gets in bed with them.'

Zapata piped up: 'Do we get credit for this course?'

'Yeah,' Salvatore chimed in. 'When's the final?'

More laughter.

'Give him a chance,' Dutch snapped.

'Okay,' I said. 'Let's forget the bureaucratic bullshit. Here's what you're dealing with. In the Freeze we spend most of our time working with the locals, tying known LCN racketeers to igg, and the igg to legitimate sources that have been corrupted. That's what I'm after – I want to know how they got their hooks into Dunetown and who they had to buy to do it. I'm not interested in making individual cases for prostitution or gambling or even homicide. Anything I get that can help you in those areas is yours.'

'We've heard that song before, old man,' Charlie One Ear said caustically.

'Enough of this true-and-false crap,' Dutch said. 'Let's get to the meat and potatoes.'

I gave them a brief history of the Triad, very brief so they wouldn't fall asleep.

'Franco Tagliani was very cautious,' I said. 'Before we nailed Skeet, Franco had made quite a name for himself. He was a big shot in Cincy. He contributed to the arts, ballet, symphony, local sports teams, everything including the humane society. He loved animals. Everybody's lovable old Uncle Franco, right? When we dumped Skeet, we figured Franco would have to come out of the closet, so we started a matrix on him. What we call a link analysis. We charted every scrap of information that came our way that related to the Triad, even the most insignificant stuff. Bits of bullshit from snitches, restaurants they frequented, social gatherings, weddings, pals, acquaintances, habits, police records, vacation trips. Hell, we even had Interpol checking on them when they left the country. It all went on the matrix, and we kept refining it, and finally we ended up with this.'

'There it is,' I said. 'The Cincinnati Triad. Anybody thinks they came here for their health should go back to school.'

No grumbling this time. I had their attention.

I started down the list while I was still ahead, beginning with Franco, once the *consigliere*, the legal brains, for Skeet, and until a few hours ago, godfather to the Triad.

'Tagliani was a classic *mafioso*,' I said. 'His religion was family, friends, and fuck everybody else; Tagliani's three daughters are married to family *capi*. The Triad's respected in La Cosa Nostra. Nobody messes with them. At least nobody has until now.

'Stinetto was Franco's executioner, the official enforcer for the outfit, and Tagliani's bodyguard. One of the few people Tagliani trusted. All the other *capi* were under Stinetto's direct command. Stinetto was an old-timer. He made his bones in the fifties, about the time Buggsby Siegel bought his. So what I'm saying, they were both tough old pros. Taking them out together like that was ingenious and gutsy.'

Dutch jumped in at this point. 'Whoever pulled this off poisoned two guard dogs and got past three armed guards. Nobody laid an eye on him or them.'

There was another face that was not on the board: Leo Costello, Mr Clean, the *consigliere* of the outfit, summa cum lauda graduate of Chicago Law School, mid- to late thirties, married to Tagliani's daughter, Maria.

'Costello was a major in Nam,' I said. 'Adjutant general's

39

office. He never saw combat, spent most of his time preparing court-martial cases. The man won't touch a gun, doesn't even hunt. He prefers the country club set to his own family.'

'Mazzola put us on to him,' said Charlie One Ear. 'Him and his friend.'

'Lou Cohen?' I asked.

'The same,' said Flowers. 'Neither one of them changed their names.'

'That sounds like him,' I said. 'Costello avoids as much contact as possible with the rest of the mob. He doesn't have any shooters around him. And Cohen is a quiet, reclusive accountant. The money brains and the bagman for the outfit. The Lepers've been trying to burn Cohen for at least ten years. Zip. But Costello may have to show his colours now.'

'How come?' asked Zapata.

'Because he's the most likely one of the bunch to take over as *capo di tutti capi* now that Franco's bought the farm. That's unless there's something we don't know,' I added.

'Such as?' asked Dutch.

'Such as somebody else in the family pushing the old man across and taking over.'

'Oh,' said Dutch, '*that* such as.'

I went on, running down the list of felons who were now in residence in Doomstown:

Johnny Draganata, the tough, no-quarter Moustache Pete from the old school, and professor and priest to all the Tagliani soldiers, the final authority on tradition and protocol; Rico Stizano, also known as the Barber, because that's what he had once been in Chicago, until he married Tagliani's sister. Now his speciality was gambling. A big family man. They all were.

Tony Logeto, Tagliani's son-in-law, was a cannon and a muscle man, married to Tagliani's oldest daughter, Sheila, and a specialist in loan sharking, extortion, and anything that required more muscle than brains. Logeto saw himself as a big ladies' man. A lot of ladies apparently did too.

'Anthony Bronicata is another old-timer,' I told them. 'He's a one-time *soldato* with a lot of notches on his gun. In dope circles he's known as the Peg, short for Il Peggiore, which means the Worst, and that – in the trade – means don't mess with him. He's king pusher, pipeline to the street, and we've never been able to put a finger on him for anything – possession, conspiracy, distribution, nothing. Bronicata's front is always a restaurant. The only good thing I can say about him is he makes pretty fair fettuccine. You want him? If we can nail his ass, he's yours.'

I had very little recollection of O'Brian. In my mind I remembered him as a short little Irishman with a blustery red face and bad teeth. Dutch's photo showed that he had a pug nose and a go-to-hell smile, and his picture was the only pleasant one in the bunch, but I didn't let that fool me for a minute. As the newest member of the clan, he still had to prove himself, and that made him more unpredictable than any of the rest.

Dutch observed, 'All these guns around, and it didn't help Tagliani for a minute.'

'Never does if they want you bad enough,' I said.

I pulled two new photographs out of my briefcase and held them up.

'These two look familiar to anybody?' I asked.

There were no takers.

I held up the clearer of the two photos, that of a round-faced man in his sixties with a pleasant smile, his snake eyes hidden behind sunglasses.

'This is Tuna Chevos,' I said. 'We'll turn him up.'

'How would you know that?' Charlie One Ear asked.

My stomach started to churn just thinking about Chevos and Nance, his personal assassin.

'I have this little buzzer inside me goes off whenever I'm within fifty miles of the son of a bitch.'

'Something personal?' Charlie One Ear asked, raising his eyebrows.

I stared at him dead-eyed for a full minute before he looked away. Then I held up the other picture, a somewhat fuzzy photograph of a lean, hard, ferret-faced man in his mid-thirties, his eyes also obscured by sunglasses.

'You see Chevos, this one is close behind. He's the Greek's numero uno, your friendly little neighbourhood assassin. His name is Turk Nance and he's the deadliest one of the lot, a psychopath with a temper as thin as a shadow. They're both cobras. Chevos married into the family but they're outsiders. They play by their own rules.'

'Maybe they did the old bastard in,' Zapata suggested.

'Maybe, but I don't think so.'

'Why not?' Dutch asked.

'I don't say I'm ruling them out,' I replied. 'I said I don't think they did it. It's still family. Salvatore, you know what I mean?'

'He's right,' Salvatore said. 'I mean, what you say, this Chevos was the old man's brother-in-law. Unless there was real bad blood . . .' He let the sentence dangle.

'So where do these two bombos fit in?' Cowboy Lewis asked.

'Chevos brings the stuff in, Bronicata gets it to the wholesalers,' I said. 'Nance is Chevos' personal *soldato*. If Chevos says go flush your head in the toilet, Nance's head is as good as in the bowl. There's one other thing – don't let Chevos fool you because he's got Nance for backup. The story goes that Chevos killed his own brother to make his bones for Skeet. I don't know if his brother needed killing, but if he was in the same league as Chevos, it was no big loss.

'Nance started in the streets, got a postgrad course in Vietnam, probably killed at least half of the Bannion gang himself. He favours a nine-millimetre Luger with a twelve-inch barrel and hollow points soaked in arsenic. A real sweetheart. He's also a muscle freak. Sooner or later, when he can plant Chevos someplace safe for an hour or two, he'll show up at the best fitness centre in town. Everybody in the family is scared shitless of both of them.

'Turk Nance. Remember that name. If you have trouble with him, shoot first.'

'You keep tellin' us what you don't want,' Callahan said in a dead monotone. 'What the hell do you want?'

I thought about that, about why I was here and what had happened to Dunetown and was going to happen to it. I thought about a lot of things in the next few seconds.

'I want the whole damn bunch off the street. I don't care if you do it or I do it or we do it together. They're the cockroaches of our society.'

I looked at Charlie One Ear. 'You ask me is it personal? I got five years invested in this bunch. In the whole rat pack only Costello and Cohen are clean. The rest of them have rap sheets that'll stretch from here to Malibu and back.'

I started pacing. I had lost my temper for a moment, not because of Charlie One Ear or because Dutch Morehead's hooligans didn't trust me. I was used to that. It was because of Cincinnati. I stopped and looked at each of them in turn.

'Yeah, fuckin'-A it's personal,' I said. 'One of my partners on the Tagliani job was Harry Nome, Wholesome Harry we called him. Best inside man I ever met. He was undercover in Chevos' dope operation. Nance tumbled him. They took him for a ride and Nance stuck his gun up Harry's nose, ripped it off with the gunsight – I mean he *ripped it off*. Then he tossed Harry out of a car doing about fifty. Harry came out of it a paraplegic.

'We had another man, on loan from the Drug Enforcement Agency. He tried to burrow into the operation at the New Orleans end. We never saw him or heard from him again. Nothing. He just disappeared. That's been three years now.

'I had an informant, a hooker named Tammi. She was eighteen years old, recruited by Stizano, who hooked her on horse when she was fifteen. They had her working interstate and she wanted out, so she agreed to talk to the attorney general about how hookers are moved around on the national circuit, who runs it, that sort of thing. Very strong stuff. Nance got her away from us. He cut off her nose and both ears, stuffed them down her throat, and strangled her with them. Costello – Mr Clean? He was Nance's mouthpiece. The bastard wasn't even indicted.'

I paused for a minute, letting it all sink in.

'Naw,' I said, 'it isn't personal. It's never personal, right? I mean, why should I be pissed? I was lucky. When they took a shot at me, the bullet went in my side, here, just below the ribs, popped out my back, and went on its merry way. The bullet hurt, but not like the arsenic it was soaked in.'

I sat down.

Not bad, I thought. Not bad at all. Save up the rough stuff until the end.

Nobody said anything else for a minute or two.

I didn't know it at the time, but there was another name I should have added to the list that night:

Longnose Graves,

I would get to know him well in the next few days. I would get to know a lot of people well in the next few days, very damn few of them for long.

9

SCREWING UP ROYALLY

Dutch stood in front of the room, a Teutonic frown etched into his heavy features.

'Thanks,' he said.

'Anytime.'

'I don't want to upset anybody,' he said, turning to his troops, 'but these . . . *ash lochers* have been under our surveillance two weeks. A whole family of them, and we didn't even know it!'

The group looked stricken, none more than Charlie One Ear.

'I can't believe it,' he said, shaking his head in disbelief. 'Not so much as a hint from any of my canaries about this. I should think somebody, *somebody*, would have heard some goddamn thing!'

The rest of them stared at the floor and moved imaginary objects around with their feet. All except Lewis, who stared at a corner of the room through squinted eyes, and Callahan, who spoke up again.

'Why you getting steamed up, Dutch?' he said. 'We didn't know who they were until last week. Up till then we were just following them because Charlie One Ear had a hunch.'

'I'm including myself,' Dutch said. 'We been making a lot of racket for these past nine months. Busting pimps and pros, dropping dealers with a nickel bag in their shorts. We got a little too big for our hats.'

'We didn't *know* until – ' Salvatore started.

'He's right,' Charlie One Ear said. 'We were much too casual about this mob. I was one of the worst.'

'You, Chino, you were on Tagliani tonight, right?' Dutch asked.

'Who?'

'Franco Tagliani,' Dutch said, leaning an inch from the Mexican's face. 'He's the one got killed tonight while you were parked in his front yard. Remember?'

'I keep forgetting the new names,' Zapata said.

44

'Well, stop forgetting them. I don't want to hear any more about Frank Turner or Nat Sherman or any of the other monikers there people are using. From now on, we use their *real-life* names, okay?'

The group nodded in unison.

'So what happened?'

'On Sundays, uh . . . Tagliani and . . . uh . . . Nicky Stinetto go to . . . Bronicata's joint for dinner, so I went there and waited. Shit, you stand out like a blind man at a tit show, out there on Thunderhead Island. There's only one other house on Tur . . . Tagliani's street. Twice I been hassled by the fuckin' downtown blue and whites, fer Christ sakes.'

'So it's your call to jump ahead of your mark that way?' Dutch asked.

'It was just a routine surveillance, Dutch. Shit, I was hungry, nothing to eat for seven hours. I went ahead, grabbed some groceries so I'd be ready when he split. Who had any thought he was gonna get hit?'

'I'm sorry you didn't get a printed invitation!' Dutch said. 'How about Stinetto, who had him?'

Charlie One Ear sank a little lower in his chair.

'I'm afraid I have to plead guilty,' he said. 'It was a double-up, Dutch. We knew they were going to dinner together, so I told – '

'So you told Chino to go to the restaurant and you'd cover the house,' he said, finishing the sentence.

'Right.'

Callahan said, 'It's routine with him, Chief. Tagliani goes to Bronicata's every Sunday for dinner. He usually meets one or two of his *capi* there. Draganata, Stizano, Logeto. Like that. Bronicata usually sits with them.'

'Big deal, so who does the dishes? What I want to know is who was at dinner?'

'Logeto and, uh, the red-haired guy . . .' Chino said.

'O'Brian,' I coached.

'Yeah. And, of course, Bronicata.'

'I suppose you was eyeballing Bronicata, too, right, since you was there anyway,' Dutch growled at Chino.

'I had Bronicata,' Callahan said quietly. 'They all split together. I put Bronicata home before I came back here.'

'Who had O'Brian?'

Lewis raised his hand. 'Same thing,' he said. 'He went straight home too.'

'What happened there in the restaurant?' Dutch said.

Chino said, 'I was inside, watching the whole team. So Bronicata gets this phone call, comes back looking like he just swallowed a jar of jalapeña peppers. There's some chi chi – '

'Chi chi? What the hell's chi chi?' Dutch asked.

'They was whispering.'

'Oh.'

'Then the Irishman and Logeto both split like the place was on fire. Coupla minutes later the waiter brings the bill, tells me the joint's closing for the night. "What the hell's goin' on?" I say. He tells me the chef had a heart attack. I guess the call was to tell them the old man got aced.'

Dutch, who was twirling one side of his moustache and staring at the ceiling, said, 'It don't make a lot of sense, y'know. Tagliani follows the same procedure every Sunday. There he is, in the car with only Stinetto and the chauffeur, who couldn't shoot the shit with the Pope. An easy mark, yet the shooter chooses to waste two guard dogs and blow up Turner and Sherman in the house.'

'It's Tagliani and Stinetto,' Charlie One Ear said sedately.

All that bought him was a dirty look.

'Salvatore,' Dutch went on, 'who was your mark?'

'Stizano,' he said. 'He's home also. I left his place when you called us in.'

'Cowboy?'

'The playboy – what's his name?'

'Logeto?' I suggested.

'Yeah, him. He's home too.'

'Everyody's home tonight,' Zapata said with a chuckle.

'Is any of this stuff from the past few weeks, from when you started watching these guys, is any of this on paper?' I asked.

Dutch said, 'We don't make reports. You put it on paper and somebody can read it.'

'Like who?' I asked.

'Somebody, anybody,' he said vaguely.

'You know what burns me?' said Chino. 'What fuckin' burns me is that these assholes have got themselves watertight alibis and they don't even know it.'

'Wouldn't it be fun not to tell them,' Charlie One Ear said wistfully.

46

Dutch said, 'Okay, Charlie, put your good ear to the ground, see if you can turn up something. The rest of you, back out on the range; see if we can stop this daisy chain before it goes any further. If you run across the Mufalatta Kid, Kite Lange, or the Stick, tell them to get in touch. Any questions?'

There weren't any.

As the gang started to disperse, Cowboy Lewis got up and walked straight towards me. He moved two desks out of his way to get to me.

'It's Jake, right?' he said.

'Yeah.'

He stuck out his hand.

'My name's Chester Lewis. They call me Cowboy.'

'Right.'

'You want this asshole Nance, right?'

'Yeah, I want him, Cowboy.'

'Then he's yours.'

'Thanks,' I said, pumping his hand.

'You got a right,' he said, whirled on his heel, and headed straight out the door. As he left, a new face appeared in the doorway.

I knew who it was without asking.

10

STICK

The new guy was ignored by the rest of the bunch, who were too busy talking about the tapes to notice him. He came straight towards me.

He was what some women would call a primal beauty. Indian features, high cheekbones, long, narrow face, hard jaw, brown eyes, thick, shining black hair that tumbled over his forehead and ears. Six feet tall and lean, he was my height and ten pounds trimmer. His seersucker suit looked like he balled it up and put it under his pillow at night; his tie had a permanent knot in it and was hanging two inches below an open collar. The points of his shirt collar curled up towards the ceiling, and I doubt that his loafers had ever seen a shoeshine rag. Obviously, dressing wasn't a real big thing with him.

He looked bagged out, and not just from a bad night. The circles under his eyes were permanent and his dimples were turning into crevices. He had the deep, growling voice that comes from too many drinks or too many cigarettes or too many late nights or all three. He was wearing a battered old brown felt hat, and a cigarette dangled from the corner of his mouth.

Twenty-nine going on forty. One look, you knew he drove the women crazy.

Not jaded yet?

'I'm Parver,' he said. 'Everybody calls me Stick.'

We moved away from the rest of the bunch, back towards the coffeepot.

'You a poolshooter?' I asked, to get the conversation off the ground.

'Not really, why?'

'The moniker.'

'It's short for Redstick. Everybody thinks I look like a damn Indian,' he said with disgust. 'Truth is, I'm Jewish and I'm from Boston.'

'I'm Jake Kilmer,' I said. 'That's all I ever was.'

We shook hands.

'This about the Tagliani chill?' he asked. He said it casually as though murder in Dunetown were as common as sand fleas on the beach.

I nodded.

'It looks like two gunners,' I said. 'They killed a couple of guard dogs, got by a couple of armed guards, and killed all three of them.'

'Three?' Stick said. 'When Cowboy raised me, he said Tagliani and Stinetto got it.'

'After wasting Tagliani and Stinetto, they dropped off a bomb to finish the job. Tagliani's wife walked in. She died in the hospital.'

'Too bad,' he said. 'Though I can't say as I'm too upset over the two goons.' So much for sympathy. 'How do you figure there were two shooters?'

'The house was wired. Dutch has the whole scene on tape, what there was of it. It was all over in about thirty seconds.'

'Not so great for you. In town for an hour and your mark gets snuffed out from under you.'

48

'That's the breaks.'

'Guns and bombs,' he mused. 'Sounds the Lincoln County war.'

I said I hoped not.

'The boys giving you a hard time?' he asked.

'How'd you guess it.'

'I got some jazz when I first came on. Kind of like an initiation. But they think Dutch hired me, so they weren't as suspicious as they will be towards you. You're a Fed, man. That makes you a badass. Don't let it get you down; they'll come around.'

'So as far as they're concerned, you're just another one of the boys, that it?'

'You got it.'

'What's your angle in all this?' I asked.

'Dutch's had me playing the field, kind of getting my feet wet. One day this guy, the next somebody else. But the last week, since Mazzola made the Tagliani gang, I've been hawking Costello and that little fink, Cohen.'

'And . . . ?'

'Hell, you know the outfit better than any of us,' he said. Then, smiling, Stick added, 'Don't you ever do reports? I didn't know shit about Tagliani until Cisco filled me in. I mean, there's some chicken-shit stuff in the box about them, but nothing with any meat on it.'

'Yeah, I know. I'm bad about reports. I'm like Dutch. Anybody can read them.'

'In answer to your question, Costello keeps away from the rest of the players.'

'How about Cohen?'

'The same. A mousy bookkeeper.'

'Don't undersell him. He's got more tricks than a gypsy magician.'

'I'll keep that in mind. Have you seen Cisco yet?'

'Talked to him on the phone. I'm meeting him for breakfast. Maybe you ought to join us.'

'I think I'll pass. If any of these guys spot me they could get antsy. Right now they trust me. I'd like to keep it that way.'

'Whatever,' I said as Dutch joined us.

'That was a nice job,' he said to me. 'I liked the little heart tug at the end.' And then to Stick: 'What have you been up to?'

'Hounddogging Costello. He and Cohen spent the day on his yacht, talking business.'

'Great. That's two more we can alibi.' Then back at me: 'You talk to Cisco yet?'

'Just before the meeting. He suggested maybe Stick and I should team up. Is that a problem?'

'I guess not. It's a pretty loose operation. I'll move you around a little bit, just so's the rest of the boys don't wonder why I've put the two newcomers together. So what can I tell you, you don't know already?'

'Anybody on the local scene I ought to know about?' I asked, not really expecting an answer.

'Just Longnose Graves,' Dutch said.

'Longnose Graves?' I said, chuckling at the moniker.

Dutch stared at me through his hooded eyes. 'He ain't a laughing matter,' the big man said.

'Oh? Who is he?'

Dutch scratched the edge of his jaw with a thumb. 'The local bandit,' he said. 'Not *a* local bandit, *the* local bandit.' He tossed a sideways glance at the Stick. 'This business tonight, I hope it doesn't blow up like the Cherry McGee thing.'

'Cherry McGee?' I said. 'Would that be the McGee from up in Pittsburgh?'

'The McGee I'm talking about is planted in the local cemetery,' said Dutch. 'Compliments of Nose.'

The Stick drew himself a cup of coffee and poured me one. It was strong enough to swim the English Channel.

'So what's the story on Graves? What's he called? Longnose?'

'Not to his face,' Dutch said. Then he ran down the pedigree: 'Graves once had a beak, made Durante look like he had a nose job. He had an inch or so shaved off it in a fight, but the name sticks. He's black, a dandy, but not pimp-dandy, know what I mean? Sports jackets, shirt and tie, likes sports cars – that's more his style. Long before I got here, Graves controlled whatever underworld Dunetown had in the old days. Ladies, sharking, the book. He doesn't deal in hard drugs; in fact, he probably kept them out of Doomstown.'

'That's a switch,' I said.

'Moral fibre,' said the Stick.

'Sure,' Dutch snickered, and went on. 'About two years ago this outsider, Cherry McGee, moved into town with a bunch of roughnecks and decided to take some of the action. First he tried easing Nose out. When that didn't work, he tried buying Nose out. Still no dice. So then McGee decides to burn down one of Graves' clubs, to show Nose he was serious. A mistake.'

Stick chimed in with a character observation.

'Graves has great comeback talent,' he volunteered. 'Going against him was no different than McGee jumping off the Bay Bridge and thinking he could fly.'

Dutch continued, 'McGee did something uncharacteristic. He dropped a frame on Graves. Extortion. And it washed. Graves did a deuce off a nickel in Little Q.'

'Little Q?'

'Felony Disneyworld,' said the Stick. 'A very hard-time joint in this state – or any other for that matter.'

'When Nose comes out, he comes out like a Brahman bull comin' out of the chute,' said Dutch.

'Did he keep the business while he was gone?' I asked.

'It was nip and tuck. The trip cost everybody. In the end it was a trade-off – three of Graves' boys went down in the street; a couple of McGee's shooters ended up in the swamp.'

'Is it still going on?'

'Not since McGee and his top gun got their brains handed to them, wham, bam, just like that,' said Dutch.

'Hey, Chief, it's the phone for you,' Chino yelled from across the room. 'It's Kite Lange, babblin' like Niagara Falls.'

'Excuse me,' Dutch said, and dashed for the phone.

'Who's this Mufalatta Kid?' I asked the Stick.

'Black cop, out from New Orleans. He's very good. Moves easy on the range. A real cool operator, but make him mad, you got a ton of bad nigger on a hundred-and-fifty-pound frame.'

Dutch's *'Schmerz!'* could be heard for miles. The room got as quiet as a prayer meeting. Then he said it again, this time louder and, to everyone's shock, in English. 'Holy shit!'

He slammed down the phone.

'Somebody just blew up Johnny Draganata in the family swimming pool while Lange was sittin' shiva half a block from his house,' the Dutchman bellowed.

The war room sounded suddenly like a hen house.

'Now listen t'me,' Dutch boomed. 'I want Tagliani's bunch covered like a strawberry sundae, and now. I'm goin' up to

Draganata's. Chino, you come with me. The rest of you know your marks. Let's roll before the whole town gets snuffed.'

He rushed back to us.

'You two wanna join us?'

'We wouldn't miss it for the world,' I said.

'Let's roll,' the Dutchman roared, and moved faster than any big man I ever saw.

11

DEATH HOUSE ON FLORAL STREET

It was like Saturday afternoon at the county fair and the Stick was Joey Chitwood. He slapped the blue light on the top of his black Firebird and took off, driving with one hand while he lit cigarettes, tuned the police radio, and hit the siren with the other, cigarette bobbing in the corner of his mouth as he talked. Pedestrians and traffic ran for cover before the screaming Pontiac. I hunkered down in my seat and stiff-armed the console.

'You nervous?' he asked.

'Not a bit,' I lied.

He hit Azalea Boulevard sideways and straightened out doing seventy. I could feel the seat moving out from under me.

I liked the Stick's cavalier attitude, but his driving was downright hazardous. I knew he had to be a good cop or he wouldn't be in the Freeze. The Federal Racket Squad, which everybody called the Freeze, was three years old, understaffed, underpublicised, underlobbied, and under the gun. The FBI wanted to make it part of their dodge, but so far we had maintained our integrity because our job was mainly gathering information, not strict law enforcement. At least, that's what it was supposed to be. Sometimes it didn't work out just that way. Cisco Mazzola, who had formed the outfit, was an ex-street cop and he hired only street cops. As far as I could tell, the Stick fit in perfectly.

He seemed to know the town. His course took us down a few alleys and past an impressive row of old homes, restored to Revolutionary grandeur, their lights blurring into a single streak as we vaulted down the street.

'How long you been here?'

'Couple months,' he said around the cigarette dangling from his lips.

'So you were here for the Graves-McGee showdown?'

'Just after it happened.'

'I knew a Philly shooter who operated out of Pittsburgh named McGee,' I said, still making small talk. 'But he called himself Ipswitch.'

'I wouldn't know about that,' Stick said. 'Actually, it was all over when I got here. All I know is what I heard on the gaspipe.'

More turns. More screaming tires. More fleeing pedestrians.

'What's this Graves like?' I asked.

'Like Dutch said, for years he had the town sewed up. I get the idea the local law left him alone as long as he didn't get too far out of line.'

'Wasting McGee wasn't getting out of line?' I asked.

'Y'know, I don't think anybody blamed him for the McGee thing. In fact, I get the feeling the locals were glad he did McGee in.'

'Could he be behind this Tagliani chill?'

'I suppose he could. Mufalatta's keeping an eye on him. If anybody will know, the Kid will.'

We drove away from the downtown section and across the Bridge to Thunderhead Island, which lay between the city and the beach. The rain had stopped and the moon seemed to be racing in and out of the clouds. As we crossed the bridge, the old-town charm of Dunetown vanished, swallowed up by redwood apartment complexes and condos that looked like grey boxes in the fleeting moonlight. There was something sterile and antiseptic about Thunderhead. Twenty years ago it was a wild, undeveloped island, a refuge for wildlife and birds. Now it appeared almost overpopulated.

Stick took Ocean Boulevard like it was Indianapolis. The souped-up engine growled angrily beneath us and the needle of the speedometer inched past one twenty. The landscape became a blur. Five minutes of that and he downshifted and swerved off the four-lane and headed off through a subdivision, its houses set back from the road behind carefully planted trees and shrubs. In the dark it could have been any planned community.

'Cisco says you lived here once,' Stick said past the cigarette clenched between his teeth.

'I just spent a summer here,' I answered, trying to adjust my eyes to the fleeing landscape.

'When was that?'

'I hate to tell you. Kennedy was still the president.'

'That long ago, huh?' he said, somewhat surprised.

'I was still a college boy in those days,' I said. I was beginning to feel like an antique.

He made a hairpin turn with one hand.

'Surprised you, huh, how much it changed?'

I laughed, only it didn't come out like a laugh; it sounded like I was gagging.

'Oh, yeah, you could say that. You could say I was surprised, and I haven't even seen the place in the daylight.'

'I couldn't tell you about all that. No frame of reference, y'know.'

'This used to be a wildlife refuge,' I said. 'That give you an idea?'

He flipped the cigarette out the window and whistled through his teeth.

'I doubt if you'll see a sparrow out here now. Rents are too high.'

He swerved into Highland Drive without even making a pass at the brakes and lit another cigarette at the same time. I started thinking about taking a cab when I saw half a dozen blue and whites blocking the street ahead, their red and blue lights flashing. We pulled up behind one of them, leaving a mile or so of hot rubber in the process. Ground never felt better underfoot.

I could smell salt air when we got out of the car.

'Lock up,' the Stick said. 'Some fuckhead stole my hat once.'

'So I heard,' I said as we headed towards the house, which sat a hundred yards or so back from the road against high dunes. An electric fence was the closest thing to a welcome mat.

I began to get the feeling that this whole bunch of hooligans, Stick included, were like Cowboy Lewis. They definitely believed the shortest distance between two points was a straight line. I also began to wonder where due process fit into all this, if it fit in at all.

We reached the fence, showed some bronze to the man on the gate, and started up the long drive on foot. Dutch was there already. I could see his enormous hulk silhouetted against the floodlights. The body lay, uncovered, at the pool's edge. A

54

breeze blew in off the bay, rattling the sea oats along the dunes above.

The old man was unrecognisable. Whatever had blown up, had blown up right in his face. One of his arms had been blown off and either he had been knocked into the pool or was in it when the bomb went off. The water was the colour of cherry soda.

There were blood and bits of flesh splattered on the wall of the brick house.

All the windows in the back were blown out.

A woman was hysterical somewhere inside.

'What kind of maniac we got here?' Dutch said, as quietly as I'd heard him say anything since I arrived in Dunetown.

'Right under my fuckin' nose,' Kite Lange said. And quite a nose it was. It looked like it had been reworked with a flat iron, and he talked through it like a man with a bad cold or a big coke habit. To make it worse, he was neither. His nose simply had been broken so many times that his mother probably cried every time she saw him. He had knuckles the size of Bermuda onions.

Ex-fighter, had to be.

He was wearing ragged jeans, a faded and nicked denim battle jacket, no shirt under it, and a pair of cowboy boots that must have set him back five hundred bucks. The headband he wore had to be for show – he didn't have enough dishwater-blond hair left to bother with. He also had a gold tooth, right in the front of his bridgework. I was to find out later that he was a former Golden Gloves middleweight champion, a West Coast surfer, and, for ten years, a bounty hunter for a San Francisco bail bondsman before he went legit and joined the police.

Salvatore appeared through the bright lights, nosing around.

'I thought you were gonna check out Stizano,' Dutch said. 'What the hell are you doin' here?'

'A look-see, okay? Where's Stizano gonna go anyway? He's an old fart and it's past ten o'clock.'

'You don't think the whole bunch ain't hangin' on by their back teeth at this point? Somebody just wasted their king.'

'They're on the phones,' Salvatore said confidently. 'They're jawin' back and forth, tryin' to figure out what the hell to do next. What they ain't gonna do at this point is bunch up. Jesus, will you look at this!'

I was beginning to get a handle on Dutch's hooligans, on the common strain that bonded them into a unit. What they lacked in finesse, they made up for with what could mercifully be called individuality. There's an old theory that the cops closest to the money are the ones most likely to get bent. Dutch went looking for mavericks, men too proud to sell out and too tough to scare off. Whatever their other merits, they seemed to have one thing in common – they were honest because it probably didn't occur to them to be anything else.

'First Tagliani's wife gets whacked,' Lange said. 'And the old man's grandson almost got it here.'

'This here don't read like a Mafia hit t'me,' Salvatore said. 'Killing family members ain't their style.'

'Maybe it was a mistake,' the Stick volunteered.

'Yeah,' Dutch said, 'like Pearl Harbour.'

'More like a warning,' I said.

'Warning?' Lange and Dutch asked at the same time. A lot of eyebrows made question marks.

'Yeah,' I said, 'a warning that he or she or it – whoever he, she, or it is – means to waste the whole clan.'

'Tell me some more good news,' said Dutch.

'So why warn them?' Lange said.

'It's the way it's done,' said Salvatore. 'All that Sicilian bullshit.'

'Now we got four stiffs, and we're still as confused as we ever were,' Dutch said. 'Hey, Doc, you got any idea what caused this?'

The ME, who was as thin as a phalanx and looked two hundred years old, was leaning over what was left of the old man. His sleeves were rolled up and he wore rubber gloves stained red with blood. He shook his head.

'Not yet. A hand grenade, maybe.'

'Hand grenade?' the Stick said.

'Yeah,' the ME said. 'From up there. He was blown down here from the terrace. See the bloodstains?'

'There were two,' Lange said.

'Two what?' the ME asked.

'Explosions. I was sittin' right down there. The first one was a little muffled, like maybe the thing went off underwater. The second one sounded like Hiroshima.'

'Woke ya up, huh,' Dutch said.

56

The ME still would not agree. He shook his head. 'Let's wait until I get up there and take a look. The pattern of stains on the wall there and the condition of the body indicate a single explosion.'

'I heard two bangs,' Lange insisted.

'How far apart?' I asked.

'Hell, not much. It was like . . . bang, bang! Like that.'

I had a terrifying thought but I decided to keep it to myself for the moment. The whole scene was terrifying enough.

The woman screaming uncontrollably inside the house didn't help.

'Homicide'll clean this up,' Dutch said. 'I'm just interested in the autopsy. Maybe there's something with the weapons'll give us a lead.'

The homicide man was a beefy lieutenant in his early forties, dressed in tan slacks, a tattersall vest, a dark brown jacket, and an atrocious flowered tie. His name was Lundy. He came over shaking his head.

'Hey, Dutch, what d'ya think? We got a fuckin' mess on our hands here, wouldn't ya say?'

'Forget that Lindbergh shit, Lundy. This isn't a "we", it's a "you". Homicide ain't my business.'

Lundy said with a scowl, 'I need all the help I can get.'

Dutch smiled vaguely and nodded. 'I would say that, Lundy.'

'Can ya believe it, Dutch,' Lundy said, 'that little kid almost bought it!'

It occurred to me that nobody had expressed any concern for Grandpa Draganata, whose face was all over the side of the house. I mentioned my feelings quietly to the Stick.

'What'd you expect, a twenty-one-gun salute?'

'Four stiffs in less than three hours,' Dutch mused again. 'This keeps up, I'll be out of work before morning.'

'Yeah, and I'll have a nervous breakdown,' Lundy said.

I looked over the entire scene. The pool was directly adjacent to the rear of the house; then there was a terrace with a carousel, a miniature railroad, a gazebo, and three picnic tables. Beyond that, the land rose sharply to the dunes above, maybe a hundred yards behind and above the house.

'I'm gonna take the Stick and have a look-see up on the terrace,' I told Dutch. To the Stick I said, 'Get a light.'

A young patrolman came down the hill and said, 'There's a

couple of Draganata's goons up there, acting like they own the place.'

'We'll talk to them,' the Stick said. 'Let me bum your torch a minute.'

'Three gets you five they ain't sayin' a fuckin' word about what happened. It's that goddamn wop salad code of theirs,' Dutch growled. Lundy went back to the scene.

'Want to come along?' I asked Dutch.

He looked up the hill and laughed.

'In a pig's ass. Call collect when you get there.'

The Stick and I went up to the terrace and looked around. One of Draganata's bodyguards approached me. He was no more than six four or five and didn't weigh a pound over two hundred and fifty, with a face that would scare the picture of Dorian Gray.

A finger the size of a telephone pole tried to punch a hole in my chest.

'Private property,' he said.

I stared him as straight in the eye as I could, considering the eye was four inches above me.

'You jab me once more with that finger, I'll break it off and make you eat it,' I said in my tough guy voice.

The goon looked at me and smiled.

'Sure thing.'

'I'm a federal officer and you're obstructing the scene of a crime. That's a misdemeanour. You jab me again, asshole, that's assaulting a federal officer, which is a felony. Can you stand still for a felony toss, sonny?'

He shuffled from one foot to the other for a moment or two, trying to work that out in whatever he used for a brain. While he was sorting through my threat, the other gorilla came over.

'Don't take no shit, Larry,' he said. He was just as big and just as ugly.

'You two already fucked up royally once tonight,' I said. 'How's it feel, knowing you screwed up and your boss got his head handed to him?'

Larry's face turned purple. He made a funny sound in his throat and took a step towards me. But before he could raise his hand a fist came from my left and caught him on the corner of the jaw. The top part of his face didn't budge; the bottom part went west. His jaw cracked like a gunshot. He was so ugly, it was hard to tell whether the look on his face was one of pain or surprise. A second later his eyes did a slow roll and he dropped to his knees.

He made a noise that sounded like 'Arfroble'.

The Stick was standing beside me, shaking out his knuckles.

The other tough went for the Stick and I pulled my .38 from under my arm and stuck the barrel as far up his left nostril as the gunsight would permit.

'Don't you hear good?' I said.

He stared at the gun and then at me and then back at the gun. The Stick kicked him in the nuts as hard as I've ever seen anybody kicked anywhere. He hit the ground beside his partner; his teeth cracked shut, trapping the cry of pain. It screeched in the back of his throat. Tears flooded his eyes. He fell forward on his hands and threw up. The other one was shaking his head, his jaw wobbling uselessly back and forth.

'Gladolabor,' he said.

I thought about what Cisco had told me, about how Stick was young and not too jaded, and about how I might give him a few pointers on due process. Now was hardly the time. He was doing just fine. I put my artillery away and smiled.

'Y'know,' he said, 'we got a pretty good act here.'

'Yeah. Maybe we should tighten it up a little, take it on the road,' I agreed.

Stick and I checked over the terrace, ignoring the two stricken mastodons.

'Obstructing the scene of a crime,' he mused. 'Where did you come up with that?'

'It sounded good,' I said. 'Did it sound good to you?'

'I was convinced,' he said. 'Cisco says you're a lawyer; I figured you should know.'

He stepped into the gazebo and threw on the lights. The calliope music started, but the merry-go-round was destroyed, tilted on one side like a bloody beret. It was eerie, the mutilated horses frozen in up-and-down positions, heads blown away, feet missing, while the calliope played its happy melody.

'Cisco likes to tell people I'm a lawyer, to impress them,' I said. 'I never practised law.'

'How come?' he asked.

A bloody horse's head, with flared nostrils and fiery, bloody eyes, lay at my feet. I lifted it slightly with the toe of one shoe and peered under it, as though I expected to find an important bit of evidence under there.

'I had the stupid notion it was still an honourable profession,' I said.

He laughed this crazy laugh, his eyes dancing between the lids, his mouth turned down at the corners instead of up. It could have been mistaken for a snarl.

'I knew better than that the first time I was briefed by a prosecutor. He as much as told me to perjure myself.'

'And what'd you tell him?'

'I told him to get fucked. It didn't happen the way he wanted it to happen and that was that. He ended up plea bargaining the case away rather than taking a shot with the true facts.'

'Just after I took the bar I was interviewed by this big law firm in San Francisco,' I said. 'This was one of the most prestigious law firms in the city. The old partner who did the interviewing spent an hour explaining to me how fee splitting works. Nothing is ever said between two opposing lawyers; they just exchange D and B's on the clients and decide how much they can milk them for. When the well's dry, they reach a settlement. When I left, I was so disgusted I almost threw up. I wandered around the hill for a while, then went down and joined the police force.'

'But you felt good about it,' he said, flashing that crazy smile again.

'No, I felt like shit if you want to know the truth,' I admitted to him. 'Four years in law school and I end up driving a blue and white.'

The Stick listened to the music for several seconds and finally flicked the switch off. I looked above us, up to the top of the dunes.

'Up there,' I said.

We huffed and puffed through the sand to the top of the sharp embankment and found ourselves staring at the ocean far below. It twinkled in the moonlight.

'What're we looking for?' the Stick asked.

'You were in the army,' I said. 'What makes a discharge when it's fired and another one when it hits?'

'Mortar?'

'Too close.'

He snapped his fingers. 'Grenade launcher.'

'It fits,' I said.

We checked the trajectory from the hill to the pool. The terrace could only be seen from the very edge of the dune. It didn't take us long to find a scorched place in the grass on the back of the dune with a smear of gun grease behind it.

'Right here,' I said. 'Whoever killed the old man lobbed his shot from here, right onto the terrace. He couldn't even see him; he lined up his shot with some point on the pool and it blew up right in the old man's lap.'

I flashed the light around the dune, looking for footprints.

'There,' the Stick said, pointing to several depressions in the side of the dune leading towards the ocean.

We looked closer.

'Looks like Bigfoot,' the Stick said. The depressions were fairly shallow and about the size of a small watermelon. There was no definition to them.

I pointed the light to the hard sand at the bottom of the dune. The tide was almost full. Ridges of foam lay near the foot of the dune.

'Great,' I said. 'The tide's in. There goes any tracks on the beach.'

'Knew what he was doin',' the Stick said. 'A blind shot like that and the timing was perfect.'

'This took a little planning. He had to know the setup. He knew when high tide was. And with those two goons down there, he only had one shot. Confident son of a bitch. We better not make too many tracks; forensics may turn something up.'

'One Ear,' the Stick said.

'Right. Let's get him over here.'

We went back down and told Lundy what we had found and he sent two men and a photographer up the hill.

'Those two gorillas up there may need some medical assistance, too,' the Stick said. 'They give you any shit, book 'em for assaulting an officer.'

Lundy's eyebrows arched in surprise. 'Yeah, thanks,' he said with a touch of awe.

'I'm goin' inside,' said the Stick. 'See if I can raise Charlie One Ear.'

I joined Dutch, who was leaning on the corner of the house gnawing on a toothpick. He was obviously impressed.

'You guys weren't gone long to be so busy,' he said with a grin.

I looked at my watch. It was past ten and my stomach was telling me it hadn't been fed since noon.

'I've gotta fill Mazzola in and get something to eat,' I said. 'Then I'm calling it a night.'

'I could use some food too,' the Stick said, rejoining us. 'Charlie's on his way and not too happy about it. I told Lundy to keep people off the hill.'

The Stick produced a small, tan calling card.

'You ever need me,' he said, handing me a card, 'my home number's on the back. There's a machine on it. If it rings four times before it answers, I'm there, just takin' a shit or a shower or something. Leave a number, I'll usually get back to you in a coupla minutes. If it answers after one ring, I'm out.'

'Meet us at the Feed Mill,' Dutch said to the Stick. 'Jake can drive down with me.'

I was grateful for that.

As we walked back to the cars I said, 'We can throw in with you on this. I think we can assume the weapon was a grenade launcher and that's an illegal weapon and that makes it federal.'

'Gee whiz,' Dutch growled. 'Ain't due process grand.'

12

STONEWALL TITAN

We drove across town to a bluff overlooking the Dunetown River. The rain had stopped and the river steamed in the warm southern wind that had brought it. Ancient brick buildings, shrouded in fog and dating back to God knows when, lined the bluff, like sentinels guarding the waterfront from Front Street and the Strip, and history swirled around us in the fog as we edged down a narrow cobblestone alley from Bay Street to the river's edge.

I felt the cold breath of ghosts on my neck. Unseen signs, hidden in the mist, creaked before the wind. The dim shape of a freighter drifted eerily down the river, not twenty yards from us, its foghorn bleating a path to the sea.

This was the Dunetown I remembered.

Doomstown seemed a Saturn ride away.

The Feed Mill was a long, narrow place on River Street facing the waterfront. The menu was written out on a green chalkboard at one end and between it and the front door there were maybe twenty tables and booths. We sat near the front. Dutch took out his glasses and squinted at the bill of fare.

'The chicken fried steak is great; so's the mulligan stew. All the vegetables are good,' he said as he studied the menu.

He ordered the steak, three vegetables, a side dish of mashed potatoes and gravy, another side of stew, and two orders of tapioca pudding. I got heartburn listening to him.

The Stick and I ordered a normal meal and coffee.

'I think I'm ruling out Nose,' Dutch said, diving into his banquet.

'How's that?' I asked.

'It's just not his style. When Nose came out of Little Q after doing that stretch, he went straight after Cherry McGee, blew him away in broad daylight as McGee was comin' out of a bank on Bay Street. People were all over the place but he didn't take out anybody but McGee and one of his strongarms. We got a woman kayoed here.'

'Could have been a mistake,' the Stick argued.

'Why's Graves still on the street?' I asked.

'No proof. I had twenty people who were standin' right there when it went down, couldn't identify him in the stand-up.'

'Twenty-two,' the Stick corrected.

'He was wearing a stocking cap, and the car he did the trick from was boosted from a downtown parkin' lot half an hour earlier. We couldn't prove doodly-shit. He walked. And he was laughing as he went out the door.'

'Nevertheless, I kind of like Nose,' the Stick said.

'Why?' I asked.

'Because he's not afraid of anybody. One spook against the lot.'

'I give him credit for still being alive,' Dutch said between mouthfuls.

'So where does that leave us?' I said.

'No-fuckin'-where,' said Stick.

'Tell you the truth,' Dutch added, 'I think about it, we got about a hundred good suspects we could hassle on this score so far.'

'I thought homicide was out of your league,' I said.

'Wel-l-l, you can't stop a man from thinking. Besides, we'll be in wheelchairs before Lundy and his bunch come up with anything. He needs a road map to find his ass when it itches.'

'I got explicit orders,' I said. 'Cisco says he'll hang me higher than the Washington Monument if I stick my nose in a homicide investigation.'

'Well, nobody can stop us from thinking.'

'You can blow a circuit trying to separate all the suspects,' I said. 'You've got the whole Tagliani outfit, what's left of them. Stizano, Logeto, Bronicata, Chevos – '

'If he's here,' Dutch interrupted.

'Yeah, if he's here. Then there's Leo Costello. He's not only Tagliani's son-in-law, he's *consigliere* for the whole outfit.'

'You may as well throw in Cohen,' Stick said.

'He's afraid of his own shadow,' I said, and then after thinking it over, I tossed in: 'On the other hand, if he burned the books, they'd all end up doing the clock. They've all got a motive. That's assuming it's in the family.'

'Even if it isn't, there's got to be lots of nervous Taglianis out there tonight.'

'With Tagliani, Stinetto, and Draganata out of the way, that just about takes out all the old line. Except for the Barber,' I said.

'They gotta figure it's Nose,' said the Stick. 'Some hothead Tagliani torpedo will take a pop at one of Graves' boys and we'll have a three-way war on our hands.'

'That's if they don't start shootin' each other,' said Dutch.

'Hell,' the Stick said. 'It's probably a coupla Philly shooters on their way home already.'

'Or a coupla China soldiers with nothing to do right now,' Dutch said.

'Shit, it could be anybody,' the Stick sighed.

'Which is why I'm finishing my meal and going home,' I said. 'We can sit here all night speculating on who shot who. Let's hit it fresh in the morning.'

We paid the bill; the Stick said good night and left. Dutch and I drove the ten minutes back to the hotel in silence.

The black limo was still parked under the marquee of the Ponce when we got back. As I got out of the car I noticed the tag: ST-1. I told Dutch I would check my messages and meet him in the bar for a nightcap.

There was a phone call from Cisco and a hotel envelope, sealed, with my name printed meticulously across the front.

I called Cisco, gave him the latest body count, and told him I'd give him the details over breakfast.

As I started towards the bar I finally saw him, the first of several spectres from the past. I was tired and getting irritable and I wasn't ready to face up yet, but there he was in his three-piece dark blue suit and a grey fedora, leaning on a gold-handled ebony cane, his snowy hair clipped neatly above the ears, his sapphire eyes twinkling fiercely under thick white brows.

Stonewall Titan, sheriff and kingmaker of Oglethorpe County, Mr Stoney to everything that walked on two feet in the town, was standing under the marquee wiggling a short, thick finger under the nose of a tall and uncomfortable-looking guy in a tweed jacket and grey flannels. Titan had made or destroyed more than one political dream with a wave of that finger. The man in tweeds went back into the bar.

Finished, Titan turned and, leaning on the cane, limped towards his car, where a tall and ugly bird in a tan and black county policeman's uniform held the door for him. As he was about to enter the car, he saw me and hesitated for an instant. His bright blue eyes glittered in brief recognition, then his hard jaw tightened and he climbed into the limousine and was gone.

Then I saw her.

I moved behind a fern, watching her through its slender leaves, like a high school swain eyeing his first crush. I don't know what made me think I could have avoided seeing her. It had to happen sooner or later. Later would have been better.

Doe Findley still looked nineteen, still had the long blonde silky hair, the caramel tan, eyes as grey as ever. A flash of memories tumbled through my mind: Doe on water skis, her silken hair twisting in the wind; roaring across the beach in a dune buggy; playfully wrestling on the boat dock with Teddy and pushing him into the bay in his best sports coat and pants, then chasing me across the wide lawn down to the edge of the bay.

Doe watching the sun set off the point at Windsong, an image as soft and fragile as a Degas painting.

Time had erased a lot of images from my mind, but those were as clear as a painting on the wall, even after twenty years.

It came and went quickly.

She was talking to a chic blonde woman; then she laughed and turned and joined a tall guy in Ultrasuede who was holding open the door of a dark blue Mercedes sedan.

So that was Harry Raines. My dislike for him was intense and immediate, a feeling I didn't like but could not control. I looked for flaws, blemishes on the face of this golden boy who had it all. His blond hair was thinning out the way a surfer's hair thins out, and he had traded his tan for an office pallor, but he was a handsome man nonetheless, with the bearing and presence that most powerful men exude. Harry Raines wore success the way a beautiful woman wears diamonds. If he had flaws, they were not apparent. I watched as he helped her into the car, trying to ignore the feelings that hit me in waves, like the aftershock of an earthquake. A handsome, good-looking pair. I tried to shove my feelings down in the dark places where they had hidden for all those years but it didn't work. As the Mercedes drove off into the dark I was aware that my hand was shaking.

Easy, Kilmer, I told myself; that was then, this is now. The lady probably doesn't even remember your name.

I tried shrugging it off and joined Dutch. Some things never change. The Ponce Bar was one of them. It was a dark, oaken room with a brick floor, a zinc-topped bar, and Tiffany lamps over the stalls and tables. The mirror behind the bar itself ran half the length of the room and was etched glass. They had built the hotel around it, rather than change a brick of the place. Politicians had been made and trashed in this room, business deals closed with a handshake, schemes planned and hatched. It was the heartland of the makers and breakers of Dunetown. For two hundred years the room had crackled with electricity generated by the power brokers, arm wrestling for position.

Only Findley and Titan seemed immune to the games. Together they called the business and political shots of the entire county, unchallenged by the other robber barons of Dunetown. It was in this room that Chief had given Teddy and me one of our first lessons in business.

'Right over in that corner,' he had told us, 'that's where Vic Larkin and I locked horns for the last time. We owned half the beach property on Oceanby together; our fathers had been partners. But we never got along. Larkin wanted to develop the beach front, turn it into a damn tinhorn tourist trap. He just didn't have any class. I favoured leaving it alone.

'One night it came to a head. We had one helluvan argument

sitting right over there. "Damn it, Victor," I says to him, "we're never gonna get along and you know it. I'll cut you high card. Winner buys the loser out for a dollar."

'Vic turned pale but he had guts, I'll give him that. I told the bartender to bring us a deck of cards and we cut. He pulled a six, I pulled a nine. That nine bought me a million dollars' worth of real estate for one buck.'

'You call that good business?' Teddy had asked.

'I call it gambling,' Chief had said. 'And that's what business is all about, boys. It's a gambler's game.'

From the look of the crowd, there weren't too many gamblers left among the Dunetown elite. What was missing was the electricity. There was no longer a hum in the air, just a lot of chatter.

The blonde woman who had been outside with Doe had returned to the room and was talking to a small group of people. She was wearing a wraparound mauve silk dress and an off-yellow wide-brimmed hat and her eyes moved around the room as she spoke, taking in everything.

'The blonde you're eyeballin' is Babs Thomas,' Dutch said. 'Don't say hello unless you want everybody in town to know it five minutes later.'

'Local gossip?' I asked.

'You could call her that. She does a snitch column in the *Ledger* called "Whispers". Very apropos. You wanna know the inside on Doomstown's aristocracy, ask her. She knows what bed every pair of shoes in town is under.'

I jotted that down in my memory for future reference and then said, 'I just saw Stonewall Titan out front.'

'Yeah?' Dutch said.

'I figured Titan was probably dead by now,' I said.

'Mr Stoney will tell God when he's ready to go, and offhand I'd say God's gonna have to wait awhile. How well do you know him?'

'Too long ago to matter,' I said, which was far from the truth. I don't think Dutch believed it either, although he was kind enough to let it pass.

'I saw him, too, coming out of the bar,' said Dutch. 'We had words. He gave me some *sheiss*.'

'What does Titan expect you to do?' I asked.

'End it.'

'Just like that?'

'Yeah, just like that. "Get it done before Harry gets wind of it,"' he says.

'Gets wind of it!' I replied. 'How the hell does he hope to keep Raines in the dark? And why?'

'He's hoping we'll nail this thing down fast so the Committee can shove it under the carpet.'

'What Committee?' I asked.

Dutch hesitated, staring into his drink. He rattled ice in his glass for a few moments, then shrugged. 'Local power structure,' he said, brushing it off.

'You just took a left turn,' I said.

'Y'see, Raines doesn't think beyond the racetrack,' Dutch said, still ignoring my question. 'The paper and the TV stations tend to play down any violence that happens. Now we got Mafia here, it could be Raines' worst nightmare come true. I could get my walking papers over this.'

'So you said.'

The waitress brought our drinks. I decided not to press him on who or what the Committee was for the moment.

'Fill me in on Titan,' I said.

He jiggled the ice in his highball.

'Only trouble with Stoney Titan, he's been sheriff for too damn long. Forty years plus; that's one hell of a long time.'

'You think he's on the take?'

'Not the way you mean,' Dutch said. 'Nothin' goes down in this town he don't know about. Not a card game, not a floating crap game, not numbers. Not a horse parlour. He knows every hooker by her first *and* last name, every bootlegger, dope runner, car booster. A man can't be around that long, know that much, he isn't bent just a little, know what I mean? On the other hand, he's a tough little bantam, not a man to take sides against.'

I remembered Titan differently. I remembered him on soft summer afternoons with his coat across his knees, drinking bourbon with Chief and talking on the porch at Windsong. I remember he always put his gun in the boot before coming up to the house and took off his coat because he wore his badge pinned on the inside pocket and I guess that was his way of saying it was a friendly call. And I remembered him as thinner and not as grey, a wiry little man with a fast step and twinkling eyes. Hell, I thought, he's pushing hard on eighty. Funny how people never age in your memory.

'I wonder if he was on Tagliani's payroll?' I thought aloud.

'He isn't bent in that direction. No way,' Dutch said. 'Stoney doesn't need money or power. And he's too old to get sucked into that kind of game. Titan coulda been a state senator, probably governor. God knows he's got the power. But he's like a man who can't swim – he never goes in over his head.'

'Then maybe he had Tagliani killed,' I suggested.

'Not his style. Squeeze Tagliani out, maybe. But this high-style execution isn't gonna be good for Dunetown. And I don't see a hope in hell of cleaning this up right away, do you?'

I admitted that there was very little to go on at that point. I also told him I didn't think the town could keep the gang slayings a secret for too long.

'A day or two,' I said, 'maybe.'

'When Cherry McGee and Nose Graves were going at it, the press kept it buried,' he said. 'As far as most folks know, the hoods that went down during that mêlée were robbers and thieves, part of the body count that can be chalked up to your normal, everyday crime statistics.'

'Can't you sneak some of this information to them?' I said. 'Having the press on your side can help sometimes.'

He leaned over the table towards me and said, 'You don't understand, Jake m'boy. They know it already. It's their option to underplay it. It's the way things have always been done here.'

'As I recall, a sheriff is a very big man in this state,' I said.

'Nothing like Stoney. Big doesn't even cover it. The way I hear it, he's delivered the swing vote for two governors, half a dozen senators, and this county helped give the state to Kennedy in 1960.'

'A lot of people owe him then,' I said.

'Yeah.'

'He could probably put Raines in the statehouse.'

'He could give him one helluva shove.'

'And the town blowing up around them could sink Raines, right?'

'Yeah, I suppose you could say that. But Raines is a heavy hitter. He might could slug his way out of a scandal if it didn't touch him directly.'

I leaned across the table and said very quietly, 'You know as

69

well as I do they can't ignore this. It's going to blow up bigger than Mount St Helens.'

'Stoney's point is well made,' said Dutch. 'The sooner we stop it, the better.'

'For Raines?'

'For everybody.'

'Do you like Titan?' I asked bluntly.

'He's a relic,' Dutch said. 'And I love relics.'

13

THE COMMITTEE

Dutch looked as if he was getting ready to pack it in for the night, but there was still a question left hanging in the air. He had avoided it. I didn't want him to. I decided to back into it with a shocker.

'You think there's any chance Harry Raines is behind this?' I asked. It worked. He looked up as if I had thrown cold water in his face.

'I'm just trying to get a fix on all the players,' I said.

'Why would Harry want to create this kind of problem for himself? I told you, it's his worst nightmare come true.'

'Maybe he thinks he can keep it quiet like the Cherry McGee affair. Get rid of these hoodlums and pass it off as some kind of kook slaying.'

'You're reaching, son,' he said. 'Harry Raines has more to lose in this than anybody.'

'Maybe that's what he wants everybody to think.'

'You're serious, aren't you?'

'You can look at it two ways. He's got the most to lose when this gets out, but he also has the most to gain by getting rid of the Triad.'

'You know, if I didn't know better, I might think that's the way you want it to play out.'

'Just asking. Like I said, I'm trying to cover all the bases.'

'You're out of the ballpark on that one,' he said, scowling at me over his drink. He looked around the room and jiggled his ice some more.

It was time to force the issue. Dutch Morehead knew more than he wanted me to know, I was sure of it.

'Look, Dutch,' I said, 'I don't mind standing muster for your SOB's. I understand all that. I'll make my peace with them in my own way. But I think it's time we started trusting each other. Right now I have the feeling I'm not playing with all the cards and you hold the missing ones.'

He continued to play with his drink. Finally he said, 'All right, what's stuck in your craw?'

'What about this Committee you mentioned? What's that all about? I mean, look around, Dutch. This is the crème de la crème of Dunetown in here. Society, politics, money. This is their watering hole. They act like nothing's happened. Three mainline mobsters and a woman have been butchered and there isn't a frown in the place.'

'They don't know about it yet,' he said. 'And the local press is gonna keep it under wraps as long as they're told to.'

'By whom?'

He sighed as only a big man can sigh. It shook the table.

'I got a few questions first,' he said.

'My old man used to say, "You can't listen when you're talking."'

'Is that a fact,' he said. 'Well, my old man used to say, "You can't get water out of a low well without priming it."'

I started chuckling. 'You're older than I am, Dutch, I suppose you can keep this up a lot longer. What do you want to know?'

'You been playing coy ever since you got here, acting like this is your first trip to town,' he said. 'See, I ain't buying that because I don't think you're on the level and it ain't a one-way street, y'know, it's give and take.'

I had been underestimating the big man. He was either a lot more perceptive than I had given him credit for or he knew more about me than I thought he did.

'Give me a for instance.'

'For instance, I got this gut feeling you know all about Chief and Titan and the Findleys.'

I wasn't sure I could trust Dutch Morehead, I wasn't sure I could trust anybody. But I had to start someplace. I decided to prime the pump a little.

'No bullshit,' he said.

'No bullshit,' I answered. 'I lived with Chief Findley and his family for one summer. That was 1963. Teddy Findley was my best friend. We played football together. We were in Nam together. I was with him when he died.'

'Uh-huh.'

That's all he said. He was waiting for more.

'I never knew my own father,' I went on. 'He died at Iwo Jima before I was born. I guess Chief was like a father figure to me. What he said was gospel. You could . . . you could feel the power of the man when he walked in the room. It made the room hum. I've got mixed feelings about all that now.'

'I've heard that about him. There isn't much left anymore.'

'No, now Raines is doing the humming.'

'So what's that to you?'

'Bottom line, if Raines is the man now, then he has to take the rap for what's happened here. Sooner or later it's going to fall on him.'

'So?'

'So how come he's got his head stuck so far in the sand?'

'Harry Raines is a local boy,' he said. 'Surprised everybody because he was kind of a hell-raising kid who grew up to be a shrewd businessman and a tough politician. His old man was a barely respectable judge, had a passion for all the things judges ain't supposed to lust after – women, racehorses, gambling. Hell, the old man died in his box at Hialeah with a fistful of winning tickets in his hand.'

'So that's where the interest in horse racing started,' I said.

'From what I hear, by the time Harry was old enough to pee by himself, he'd been to every racetrack in the country. He handicapped his way through Georgia, played football, was one of Vince Dooley's first all-Americans, got a law degree at Harvard, came back, went to work as a lawyer for Chief, married Doe Findley, and inherited the political power of the city, then ran for the Senate and was elected, thanks in no little way to Stoney Titan. There it is in about two paragraphs, the story of Harry Raines.'

'Nice merger,' I said, with more acid than I had planned.

Dutch's eyebrows rose. Then he pursed his lips and said, 'I suppose you could say that.'

'So Chief picked him out, right?'

'I don't know, that's before my time. We ain't exactly drinking buddies, Raines and me. I don't know the particulars.'

'How'd he get to be racing commissioner?'

'Gave up his seat in the state senate and stumped one end of this state to the other, selling the idea. His big edge was that it would raise tax money for the school system. He also turned over the operation of Findley Enterprises to his best friend, Sam Donleavy. That way nobody could accuse him of any conflict of interest. Hell, he won't even let his wife race her Thoroughbreds. The man's clean, Jake.'

'Yeah, I know, he's going to be governor one of these days soon.'

'Probably, if this mess doesn't blow him out of the water.'

'Anybody jealous of his success? The fact that he married a rich girl and got richer?'

'I suppose so.'

'Anybody who might be out to destroy him?'

He stared hard at me.

'Lissen here, a lot of people in this town got rich in the boom and they thank Harry for that. If you think he's unpopular around here, think again. He's the favourite son of Dunetown.'

'And the most powerful,' I added.

'I would say that.'

'Because of Chief's clout,' I went on.

'In the beginning maybe. Not anymore. He's got his own power base; he doesn't need a worn-out old man.'

'He uses Titan.'

I realized that was a mistake the minute I said it. I was letting my own feelings intrude on the conversation. Dutch shook his head and stared down into his drink.

'You're gonna waste a lot of time if you try to stretch that one out,' he said. 'Raines doesn't *use* Titan any more than Titan uses him. As far as the town goes, the people that run Doomstown don't have to drive down Front Street anymore. They can afford to shop in Atlanta.'

'So they drew the battle line at Front Street,' I said. 'Gave that to the hoodlums.'

'More or less.'

I stared him hard in the eye.

'What's the Committee?' I asked bluntly.

He paused again. I had the feeling he wanted more out of me

before going on but I waited him out. Finally he talked:

'Before he stepped out of local affairs, Harry formed an ex-officio committee. The five most powerful men in town. They have no legislative power per se. They don't have a name, an office, don't even meet any one place in particular. They're just old friends who feel it's their responsibility to look out for the town, just like your friend Chief used to do, and Titan still does. It's the way things're done down here.'

'What do they do?'

'As I get it, the idea was that they screen everybody who comes near this town with a dollar to invest.'

I said, 'To make sure people like Tagliani don't get a foothold, is that it?'

'Part of it. And to contain the roughhouse element, so nobody gets out of line.'

'That what you've been doing, containing the roughhouse element?'

'Part of it.'

'That gives them ten points for awareness and none for performance.'

'Thanks. I appreciate that.'

'I don't mean you. It wasn't your job to spot Tagliani.'

'They're local boys, Jake. They don't know from the Mafia. Babes in the woods. That was what Leadbetter was supposed to do, keep an eye on the new shakers that moved in.'

'That makes a strong case against the Tagliani clan for Leadbetter's murder,' I said. 'Maybe he tumbled them and they hit him before he could say anything.'

'I've been thinking the same thing. When Leadbetter took the wash, it kinda fell in my lap. What can I tell you, Tagliani got by all of us.'

'Hell, I can't knock that,' I said. 'I lost them for a year. But how could five men operating ex-officio have any effect on the town?'

''Cause they're the most powerful men in the city, son,' he said. 'This is still a small town to them. Since the day they laid the first cobblestone, a handful of men have run Dunetown. Them, their wives and families – hell, they own or control most of the property on the islands. They *are* the political power. They set the social standards. They screen people who want to do business here. And they directly or indirectly control most of the

74

big banks. They are Roman emperors, Jake. Thumbs up, you're in; thumbs down, you're out. Now, that may not be to your likin' or mine, but that's the way it is. Nobody bucks that kind of power.'

'So they'd know who owns the hotels, the marinas, condos, apartments, what have you?'

'I suppose so, unless they're all owned by blind corporations. The hotels are owned by a local combine.'

'You're sure about that?'

'Straight from the horse's mouth.'

'And which horse would that be?'

'Sam Donleavy. He's Harry's right-hand man, the second most powerful man in Dunetown. If there's a head of the Committee, he'd be it.'

'How about Raines?'

'He doesn't sit. Donleavy's his voice. Raines is funny about conflict of interest. Right now he devotes all his time to the track. If he can prove it's worthwhile, he'll waltz into the governor's mansion.'

'Who else is on this Committee?'

He wiggled his head like an old bear. 'Shit, pal, you don't stop, do you? You prime the pump with a cup of water and get a gallon outta me. You could turn out to be a real son of a bitch.'

'I have been accused of that.'

His flaccid face flowed back into a smile.

'I'll just bet so,' he said.

'It's what I do,' I said, smiling back.

'Don't we all. Okay, first, there's Donleavy. That's him sitting right over there in the tweed jacket.'

He nodded towards the man whom I had seen talking to Stoney Titan as I came in. He was a big guy with a bull neck and shoulders that threatened to split his green blazer down the middle. He appeared to be in his thirties, wore his hair in a crew cut, and had a nose that had been flattened more than once. An ex-ballplayer, I guessed looking at him. He was entertaining the ladies at the table, there was a lot of giggling, but the lines around his mouth were tight and the laughter didn't spread to his eyes. He looked like a man with a lot of trouble trying to have a good time and I mentioned it to Dutch.

'I imagine Stoney's driven a spike up his tail,' said Dutch.

'Sam'll fall before Harry, and if he falls out of grace, he doesn't have the Findley millions to lean on.'

'Which means they'll put the heat on you.'

'Us, partner.'

'Yeah, us.'

'Our feet are already in the fire, make no mistake.'

'Who else is on this Committee?'

'Charles Seaborn. He's president of the Seacoast National Bank chain, largest in these parts. He's old money. His father was chairman of the board when he died last year. Then there's Arthur Logan, who'll be president of the town's most prestigious and successful law firm in another year or two, soon's his old man dies or quits. Next, Roger Sutter, he's Sutter Communications. That's the newspaper and the television station. Between them, they own most of the ground with grass on it in the county. That's power.'

'That covers all the bases but one,' I said. 'You said there were five members on the Committee.'

'Before I answer that,' he said, 'I got one more question to ask you.'

'Shoot.'

'It's personal, Jake. You can tell me to suck eggs if you want to.'

I guess I knew what the question was going to be before he asked it.

'Were you in love with Doe Findley twenty years ago?' he asked.

I was ready for him. I smiled a big fifty-dollar smile. 'Hell, I'm just like you, Dutch. I always end up kissing the horse at the finish. Who's number five?'

'Who else?' he said. 'Stonewall Titan.'

14

DOE

I finished my drink and said good night. My room on the third floor had a dormer window with a chintz loveseat and coffee table in front of it, a vintage TV set, a double bed, and ceilings so high you could fly a kite in it. Everything – the drapes, walls, carpeting, sills, and baseboards – was a combination of green and white. The room looked like it had been designed by a rampant garden club. I got out a bottle of amaretto and poured myself a couple of fingers.

Burned out, my bones aching with jet lag, I couldn't erase the images of the night from my mind. Tagliani and Stinetto in the icebox. Mrs Tagliani's monitor going *deeeeeeee* right in front of my eyes. The haunting tape of two killers delivering their coup de grace and the bloody back wall of Draganata's house. I had seen worse, but never in any civilised place I could remember.

Then I looked at the note I had picked up at the desk. The handwriting was so precise it could have been calligraphed. I recognised it immediately and the old electricity streaked from my stomach to my throat.

'I know you are here,' it said. 'I'll be in the boathouse at Windsong, tomorrow night, nine p.m. Please. D.'

She must have written it before she went into the restaurant, before I had seen her downstairs.

I suppose you always remember the good things in life as being better than they really were. To me, Dunetown was a slow-motion movie shot through a hazy lens. Everything was soft, the reflections glittered like stars, and there were no hard edges on anything. It was the end of adolescence and being exposed to the sweet life for what was an instant in my time. It was living high, dancing at the country club, open cars and laughter and cool nights on the beach.

Fat City is what it was.

And it was Doe Findley.

Doe Findley had risen out of my past like a spectre. For twenty years she had been the hope in my nightmares, a gauzy sylph brightening the dark corners of bad dreams like the nightlight at the end of a long, dark hall.

I thought about that boathouse and about Doe, dancing tightly against me to the music from the radio as we fumbled with buttons and snaps and zippers. I couldn't remember the song now, but it had stayed with me for a long time before Nam erased it.

The thought of her spread through me like a shot of good brandy. She was the memory of that lost summer, the last green

77

summer I could remember. It had all vanished that fall on a Saturday afternoon in Sanford Stadium.

It's funny, Teddy and I used to joke about those days later in Nam. Anything for a laugh over there. I remember Teddy once saying to me, 'Y'know something, Jake, we should have been born a little earlier or a little later. Our timing was terrible. Think about it – we played during three of the worst seasons the Bulldogs ever had. You remember what our record was for those three years?' Did I remember? Hell, yes, I remembered. 'Ten, sixteen, and four,' I answered with disgust. 'Yeah,' he said, 'and the season after we graduated, Dooley came in and they had a seven, three, and one. Now we're here. See what I mean? A dollar short and a day late, that's us.'

Looking back on it, he was right. Maybe we were just jinxed from the start. That Saturday that changed my life, I was going wide to the right with Teddy in front of me and I made one of those hard stopping turns I had become known for. The foot hit wrong. I could hear the ankle go before the pain knocked my back teeth loose. It sounded like a branch cracking. All I remember after that is the backfield coach staring down at my face, saying 'Shit! So much for this halfback.'

I got the letter from Chief Findley while I was still in the hospital. 'Too bad, son,' it said. 'Keep the car. Doe sends her regards.' The pink slip for the MG was attached. That was it. That's how I found out what an ex-running halfback with a bum ankle is worth in Dunetown. Findley had been my sponsor. They couldn't pay us for playing football at the university, but there was always some rich alumnus willing to provide a sports coat now and then, a car, a summer on the house. Sometimes even a daughter.

She didn't even send a card.

Eighteen years. I hadn't seen or heard from her since, not even when Teddy was killed. I can understand that; I can understand not being able to deal with that kind of pain. Hell, I can understand it all. When you love someone you forgive everything.

I had kicked most of the other monkeys off my back, all but Doe. I couldn't purge her from my fantasies, what was left of them. Vietnam was bad for the soul. It was bad enough, what you saw and did, but the worst thing was what you thought. You get over the rest of it but you never forget what it does to the soul.

78

Teddy Findley was the best friend I ever had, from the day I arrived at Georgia until the day in Saigon that he bled to death in my arms. Teddy was a golden boy. Teddy hadn't hit a false note. He was Chief's hope for immortality. The plan was perfect: football for four years at Georgia, show what the kid could do, then law school somewhere in the north to erase the jock image. Then back to take over the reins and keep the Findley hand in the Dunetown pot.

Vietnam screwed it all up. Instead of Harvard Law School, Teddy ended up in Nam with me, a couple of shavetail lieutenants doing the best we could to keep sane and alive.

Then all of a sudden Teddy was dead and the moment it sank in that he was dead, what I thought was:

Christ, Teddy, how can you do this to me, how can you leave me to tell Doe and Chief about this.

I still remember thinking that. I have pretty much erased everything else from my mind, but I still remember that when Teddy died, I didn't think about Teddy, I worried about me. That's what I mean about Nam and your soul.

Eventually, of course, I wrote the letter. I told them what I knew Chief wanted to hear.

I created the lie and I wrote the letter and I never got an answer, not even an acknowledgment that he had received it.

So I started forgetting in earnest. Football heroes exist only on bright fall afternoons, and pretty girls stay young only in picture frames.

Except there was Doe, who hadn't changed a bit. She still had that young, amazed look she'd had in the early sixties. Still had the long, golden hair. Silk. Slim, firm body. Breasts that some women would pay a fortune to try and imitate. Skin like cream. And suddenly she was no longer out of reach. She wasn't a sylph or a fantasy; she was as painfully real as a shin splint and just a phone call away.

And now, twenty years after the fact, she expected me to come trotting to the boathouse like it never happened.

Meet her in the boathouse? Who am I kidding, of course I'd meet her in the boathouse. I'd walk from Pittsburgh to meet her in the boathouse.

Shit.

I got in bed with a copy of Donleavy's *Meet My Maker, The Mad Molecule* and read myself to sleep. At two a.m. the phone woke me up. I put the book on the table and turned off the light.

The phone rang twelve times before it finally quit.

Fuck it, it had to be bad news.

15

BAD DREAMS

I had the dream again that night. The first time in four or five years. It had been so long I had forgotten it. It had started a year after I got back from Nam. I understand that's normal. It's called delayed nocturnal shock or something like that. At first it was just this one persistent dream. I could never remember all of it, just bits and pieces. After a while it was such a familiar nightmare that I knew I was dreaming and it didn't bother me as much.

Then it changed.

The way it started, I am in a hang glider soaring over a city. It could be Saigon, but I don't recognise it. Suddenly people on the ground are shooting at me. I can't see them, but the bullets are tearing through the wings of the glider. Next the bullets are hitting me. They bounce off as if my skin is bulletproof. I don't feel the bullets. I don't feel anything. I don't hear anything either. This is a silent dream. The next thing I remember, I see Teddy. He is on top of a ridge and he's running. I don't know what he's running from. Maybe he's running towards something. He starts waving at me. I try to soar down to pick him up, but the glider won't move up or down. Teddy starts screaming at me, this soundless scream. I feel desperate to get to him. Finally I get out of the seat of the glider and I hang over the side and let go and I fall. There's no ground, just me, falling through an empty space.

Then I wake up.

After a while it began to get more complicated, after I got used to it and it didn't bother me anymore.

There were other hang gliders trying to collide with me. The other gliders were black and the pilots were all masked. It was like an obstacle course in the sky. Before I got comfortable with that version, the people in the other gliders started taking off their masks. One was my mother. Another was a fifth-grade schoolteacher whom I had not seen or thought about for fifteen years. Another was my father, only a face in a photograph to me. Then the parish priest in the New Jersey town where I was born. I couldn't remember his name; all I could remember about him was that he had 'silent collections' – that meant folding money, no silver. It used to make me angry. And there was also a captain named Grant, a martinet Teddy and I had served under in Nam when we were still second lieutenants.

They were all yelling at me, but of course I couldn't hear anything. It was a silent horror movie that never ended.

A couple of years later, when I was working the street in San Francisco, I became friendly with another patrolman who had served in Nam. His name was Winfield. He was a black guy and he was taking college courses in psychology because he thought it would help him make detective.

One night over too many beers we started talking about dreams, so I told him mine and he gave me a nickel's worth of psychology 101:

'Your values are all fucked up, Jake. One thing is, you think you're different. Shit, join the club. I figure it like this: It was one way here, the other way over there, okay? You get a lot of guilt over such shit. Gets so you're afraid to trust anybody because you don't want them to find out. It happened to us all, man. What you do, see, you decide what makes sense to you. Settle for that and fuck everything else.'

After that we talked a lot. The dreams got fewer and farther between. Finally they stopped.

That night in Doomstown I had the dream again, only this time it wasn't Teddy running on the ridge.

It was Franco Tagliani.

16
PLAYING BY THE BOOK

The Palm Room of the Ponce Hotel was a big, cheery room, as bright as a hothouse and decked out in as many hanging plants, ferns, and potted flowers. It was decorated in soft hues of green, yellow, and pink, with windows down one side that faced the hotel courtyard. Once, in summertimes past, the cream of Dunetown society had sunned itself and gossiped around the pool. It had since been converted into a giant fish pond spiked with lily pads, and while there were still a few old deck chairs scattered about the area, the place had a forlorn, faded, unused look about it. The restaurant, however, was breezy, cheerful, and buzzing with early morning conversation.

I showed up the next morning at a few minutes after eight with my head pounding and the taste of old overshoes and amaretto in my mouth. I put on my sunglasses and groped my way through the restaurant.

Francisco Mazzola, the peerless leader of the Freeze, was seated near a window overlooking the courtyard. He had a half a dozen vitamin pills of varying sizes and colours lined up in front of his plate and was gulping them down with orange juice. He pumped my hand, threw an arm around my back, and slid the morning paper in front of me as I sat down.

'I ordered your breakfast,' he said. 'Fresh orange juice, a dozen dollar pancakes, one egg over easy, no meat. Your system needs a break, I'm sure. She's bringing your coffee now and I got some great vitamins here for you.'

'If I eat all that, I'll die,' I said.

'Got to keep up the old strength.'

'There are enough vitamins here for the whole room.'

He ignored the complaint. 'Vitamins do great things for the brain,' he said.

Mazzola did vitamins like a speed freak does amphetamines. He was also fighting a losing battle with his hair. He spent an hour every morning, weaving what few strands were left over a pate as bald as a kitchen table. To compensate he had grown a beard which made his dark mediterranean looks and intense brown eyes more intimidating than usual. He slid a handful of vitamins across the table to me.

'These are yours,' he said. 'This stuff's from China. Incredible, has all kinds of – '

'Cisco, I'm not into vitamins, okay? I'm into coffee and a little booze, an occasional lay, rare steaks, wine, mashed potatoes and gravy . . .'

He looked like he was going to throw up.

82

'I'm not into vitamins and weird herbs.'

'In two days you'll notice an improvement.'

'If I got a good night's sleep I'd notice an improvement. I was up half the night thanks to the sudden departure of half the Tagliani clan.'

'We'll get to that,' he said, digging in to his breakfast, a plate of health food that looked like it had been dredged from the bottom of a swamp.

'Besides,' I said, 'I read where overdosing on vitamins makes your hair fall out.'

He looked up, aghast.

'Where did you read that?'

'In the paper. One of those health columns. Rots out the roots of the hair.'

I tried to keep the gag going but I started to laugh. He leaned back in his chair and narrowed his eyes.

'No more jokes about the hair, okay? Do I joke about your knee?'

'It's my ankle.'

'See, you're touchy about that.'

'I'm not touchy about it. I happen to have shitty ankles. Great wheels, shitty ankles; otherwise I wouldn't be here, I'd be a retired millionaire football player living in Tahiti. On the other hand, you only have about four strands of hair left, although I'll say the beard helps.'

'Fuck you,' he said. 'Fill me in.'

I gave him a fairly thorough walk-through of the events of Sunday night.

'You're the expert on the Triad – what the hell's going on here?' he asked.

'I'll tell you what I don't think's going on,' I said. 'I don't think it's an outside mob and I don't think it's an inside job.'

'That's interesting,' he said. 'That just about rules out everybody. Who do you think did it, the tooth fairy?'

'It's logical. The last thing the Triad wanted to do was create attention. They uprooted their families and sneaked in here. If it had been a family feud, it makes more sense that it would have been done before they left Cincinnati. Besides, this thing just doesn't read like a Mafia hit. Salvatore agrees with me.'

'Salvatore's an expert, huh?' he said, looking over his breakfast plate and raising his eyebrows.

'He knows their style. Hell, he ought to, his father was an LCN cannon in south Philly.'

'I know that.' He went back to his breakfast, waving a fork at my plate. 'Talk and eat, it'll get cold.'

'The only exception to that is that maybe it could be Chevos and Nance.'

He looked up, surprised.

'I didn't know they were here.'

'They're here somewhere.'

'Oh, you're guessing again.'

'It's logical.'

'You and your logic,' he said. 'You can make any argument sound good. One minute you tell me you don't think it's internal and the next you tell me it is.'

'Chevos and Nance are different.'

'That's 'cause you want them to be,' he said, pointing a finger at me. 'This is department business, pal. I didn't bring you in here to carry out a personal vendetta.'

'I'm just running the possibilities past you. Chevos is devious enough to try it and Nance is psychotic enough to do the work. So, if the shot fits . . .' I let the rest of the sentence dangle.

'It's "if the shoe fits",' he said.

'Not in this case.'

'All right, tell me more.'

'We have reason to believe whoever's in on this did time in Nam.'

'How do you figure that?'

'Weapons, mo, style.'

'Uh-huh.'

'Nance was in Nam, right in the thick of it.'

'Uh-huh. And so were you, Stick, and half of Dutch Morehead's bunch. Hell, I was even in Nam. That doesn't make Nance an assassin. Some people might even consider him a hero.'

'The war's over,' I said.

'I think maybe you're grabbing for flies,' he said.

'Maybe,' I said with a shrug.

'Anything else.'

'Well, uh . . .'

He leaned over the table and dropped his voice to a whisper.

'Before you go any further,' he said, 'let me remind you that you're not here to solve homicides. Just between us, I don't care if Yankee Doodle Dandy's doing it, unless it's relevant. I want the package on Tagliani.'

He didn't wait for me to say anything.

'This used to be a nice, quiet, historical tourist trap,' he said. 'It's turning into Rotten City, USA. I want to know how deep Tagliani had his hooks in. What did he own? Who did he buy? How did he pull it off? Hell, I don't have to give you the lecture, you know what the Freeze is all about.'

'If you're interested in what I think,' I said, 'I think the homicides have to be relevant.'

He pointed at me with his fork.

'Don't get lost on me, Jake. And don't lead Stick astray.'

'Lead Stick astray! You got to be joking. And what's all this shit about him not being jaded?'

'What do you think of him?' he asked with a smile.

'He's as off the wall as the rest of Dutch Morehead's hooligans,' I said.

'He's just like you were,' he said. 'Eager, tough, a lone wolf. You two can help each other. Working with Dutch and his boys'll give you both a sense of team play.'

'I know all about team play, remember?'

'You been playing your own game for a while,' Cisco said. 'Now you got plenty of help. I want to nail the Cincinnati Triad. I think we got a giant washing machine here, Jake, and I want to see the inside of it. I want to know how it works. That's what this trip is all about, okay?' He paused for a moment and added, 'And I'd like to find out while a few of them are still breathing. Seen the morning paper?'

Cisco could change the subject in mid-sentence. When he had said all he had to say on a subject, he just dropped it and moved on.

He laid the paper beside my plate. It was turned to page twelve where the Tagliani killing was reported quietly, under a one-column headline:

THREE DIE IN
HOUSE ROBBERY

I read the story, which was vague, inaccurate, and short. The police weren't saying anything except that they expected an arrest 'shortly'.

'They're expecting an arrest, I see,' I commented.

'Keep reading,' Cisco said. 'It gets worse.'

Tagliani was identified as Frank Turner, a Cincinnati businessman with interests in racehorses. Stinetto – Nat Sherman in the story – was listed as 'a business associate of Mr Turner's'. Robbery was the suspected motive. Not a mention of the Molotov cocktail the killer had dropped on his way out. According to the story, the police believed that Turner and Sherman surprised the robbers and were killed in so doing. There was a very fuzzy picture of Tagliani and his wife getting into a car, obviously shot from somewhere in New Jersey and blown up until the grain was as big as the moon.

'Not a mention of Draganata.'

'That's on page eighteen,' Cisco said without looking up from his breakfast.

The Draganata story, identifying him as John Dempsey, a retired businessman, was even more ludicrous. It was three paragraphs long and said he died in his swimming pool. The police did not expect foul play.

'Well,' I said, 'the police got the Draganata kill right. He certainly did die in his swimming pool.'

'Point is, that's the kind of reporting you can expect here. Nobody's gonna dig for anything; they'll print what they're told to print.'

'Dutch told me this would happen and I as much as laughed in his face.'

'Yeah, well, he's got the last laugh. Just keep this in mind, pal, everybody supported the track. The press supported it and the businessmen's association and the chamber of commerce *and* the local politicians. Even the board of education endorsed it. Don't you get it? They don't want anything to make their town look sour. So they'll play it down, make it look like exactly what they want it to look like, and hope somebody will solve the case so they can cover it up. Let the killer cop a plea and keep his mouth shut.'

'That's bullshit,' I said.

'It's the way the world turns,' he said. 'That's why I don't want you spinning your wheels on the homicide angle. Just find out how the Tagliani clan got their foot in the door and how far in it is now, okay? Forget local politics. Things here haven't changed in two hundred years, and a little massacre isn't gonna make a bit of difference.'

86

'These islands have been raped,' I said bitterly.

'Maybe so,' he went on, 'but look around you. These are the people who pull the strings in Dunetown. When you talk about the rape of paradise, these are the people who are doing the raping. They're the ones making the big bucks. Tagliani didn't ruin the place. He just got in on the kill.' Then he did another fast change-up. 'Anything else for now?'

'Did you hear the tape of the Tagliani chill?' I said.

He nodded.

'Did you catch that, about a fix at the track?'

He gave me one of those 'what do you think I am, stupid' looks. 'So?' he said.

'So, if Tagliani knew about it, maybe the track's dirty too.'

Cisco's dark brown eyes bored into me. 'It's an illegal tape,' he said. 'Anyway, it's probably just some owner building up odds on one of his ponies. On the other hand . . .' He paused for a few moments and stared off into space.

'On the other hand what?' I asked.

'On the other hand, this commissioner, Harry Raines? He might be worth looking into. He's got more muscle than anyone else in the town.'

Bingo, there it was. I felt a twinge of indication.

'He controls gambling in the whole state,' Cisco went on. 'The racetrack commission is also the state gaming commission. It's the way the law was written.'

'Interesting,' I said.

'Yeah. If they want anything, Harry Raines is the man they need to deal with – or bypass.'

'Maybe they bought him,' I suggested.

'From what I hear, not likely, although always a possibility,' said Cisco. 'I'll give you some logic. Whether they bought him or not, the last thing anybody wants right now is a gang war. If Raines is in their pocket, it puts him on the dime and destroys his effectiveness. If they haven't bought him, this mêlée still hurts everybody, the Triad included. The bottom line is that Raines needs this kind of trouble like he needs a foot growing out of his forehead. He and his partner, Sam Donleavy, are both up the proverbial creek right now.'

'Donleavy was in here last night,' I said. 'I saw Titan talking to him, and the old man didn't look he was giving away any merit badges.'

87

'They're all edgy,' he said, sliding the bill across the table to me. 'Here, put this on your tab. I've got to catch a plane.'

He stood up and threw his napkin on the table. 'It's time somebody put a turd in the Dunetown punch bowl,' he said. 'Glad you're here – I can't think of a better person to do it. Finish your breakfast and get to work. See you in about a week.'

And with that he left.

I didn't have to leave the restaurant to get to work. Babs Thomas walked in as Cisco walked out. I decided it was time to find out whose shoes were under whose bed in Doomstown.

17

CHEAP TALK, RICH PEOPLE

The Thomas woman was tallish, honey blonde, coiffured and manicured, dressed in printed silk, with a single strand of black pearls draped around a neck that looked like it had been made for them. Her sunglasses were rimmed in twenty-four-carat gold. An elegant lady, as chic as a pink poodle in a diamond collar.

I scratched out a note on my menu: 'A gangster from Toronto would love to buy you breakfast,' and sent it to her table by waiter. She read it, said something to the waiter, who pointed across the room at me, lowered her glasses an inch or two, and peered over them. I gave her my fifty-dollar, Toronto gangster smile. The waiter returned.

'Ms Thomas said she'd be delighted if you'd join her,' he said. I gave him a fin, dug through my wallet and found a card that identified me as a reporter for a fictional West Coast newspaper, and went to her table.

She looked me up and down. I was wearing unpressed corduroy jeans, a blue Oxford shirt, open at the collar, and an old, scarred Windbreaker. Definitely not the latest mobster look.

'If you're a gangster from Toronto, I'm Lady Di,' she said, in a crisp voice laced with magnolias, 'and I've got a good ten years on her.'

Closer to fifteen, I thought, but a very well-disguised fifteen.

'You don't look a day over twenty-six,' I lied.

'Oh, I think we're going to get along,' she said, pointing to a chair. 'Sit.'

I sat and slid the card across the table to her. It identified me as Wilbur Rasmussen from the Las Andreas *Gazette* in San Francisco. She looked at it, snorted, looked at the back, and slid it back across the table.

'Phooey, a visiting fireman,' she said. 'And here I thought I was going to be wooed by some dashing *mafioso*.'

'Do I look like a dashing *mafioso*?'

'You look like an English professor with a hangover.'

'You're half right.'

'Try a screwdriver. At least the orange juice makes you feel like you're doing something decent for your body.'

'I couldn't stand the vodka.'

'It'll get your heart beating again. What can I do for you? I'll bet you're here about that mess last night.' She leaned over the table and said quietly, 'Everybody in town's talking about it,' flagging down a waiter as she spoke and ordering me a screwdriver.

'No kidding?' I said, trying to act surprised.

'It was ghastly. I had calls before the maid even opened my drapes this morning. I hardly knew this Turner man, but he seemed like a charming old gentleman.'

'Charming?' I said. Uncle Franco was probably smiling in his grave.

'Well, you know. He contributed to the ballet and the symphony. He was on the board of the children's hospital. And he was quite modest about it all.'

'No pictures, no publicity, that sort of thing?'

'Mm-hmm. Why?'

'Just wondering. I always suspect modesty. It's unnatural.'

'You're a cynic.'

'Very possibly.'

'I always suspect cynics,' she said.

'Why's that?' I asked.

'There's security in cynicism,' she said. 'Usually it covers up a lot of loneliness.'

'You the town philosopher?' I asked, although I had to agree with her thesis.

'Nope,' she said rather sadly. 'I'm the town cynic, so I know one when I see one.'

'So what's the pipeline saying about all this?' I asked, changing the subject.

She lowered the glasses again, peering over them at me. 'That he's a gangster from Toronto,' she said with a smirk.

'Couldn't be, I never heard of him,' I said.

'Just what is your angle?'

'I do travel pieces.'

'Really.'

'Yeah.'

'And lie a lot?'

'That too.'

'To gossip columnists?' she said.

'I don't discriminate.'

'Thanks.'

'Maybe I ought to try and get a job on the *Ledger*,' I said, changing the subject.

'Why, for God's sakes?'

'I don't know much about women's clothes but I can tell a silk designer dress when I see one. They must pay well over there.'

She threw back her head and laughed hard. 'Now that is a joke,' she said. 'Did you ever know any newspaper that paid well?'

The waiter brought my screwdriver. I took a swallow or two and it definitely got the blood flowing again.

'Actually my husband died young, the poor dear, and left me wonderfully provided for,' Babs said.

'You don't sound real upset over losing him.'

'He was a delight, but he drank himself to death.'

'What did he do?' I asked, sipping at the screwdriver.

'Owned the hotel,' she said casually, but with a glint in her eyes.

'What hotel?'

'This hotel.'

'You own the Ponce?' I said.

'Every creaky inch of it. Actually I hired a very good man from California to run it before Logan died. I love owning it but I dread the thought of having to run it.'

'You live here?'

She nodded and pointed towards the ceiling. 'Six flights up. The penthouse, darling. Owning the joint does have its perks. I have a beach place out on the Isle of Sighs but I don't go out there much anymore. It's a bit too solitary.'

'I'm on the third floor,' I said. 'I don't have any perks.'

'Is there something wrong with your accommodation?' she asked. 'If there's a problem, I have a lot of pull with the management.'

'The room's fine, thank you.' I ordered coffee to chase the taste of vodka out of my mouth.

'What's your room number? I'll have them send up a basket of fruit.'

'Three sixteen. I love fresh pineapple.'

'I'll remember that. You were telling me what you're doing here.'

'I was?'

'Mm-hmm.'

'Actually I'm interested in doing a piece on the social order in Dunetown. Movers and shakers, that kind of thing.'

'For the Los Aghast *Gazette* or whatever it was?'

I would have bet my underwear that she remembered the name of the paper and everything else I had said since joining her.

'Yeah, kind of a background piece.'

She said 'Mm-hmm' again and didn't mean a syllable of it. She lit a pink Sherman cigarette, leaned back in her chair, and blew smoke towards the ceiling. 'Well, it was founded in 1733 by – '

'Not that far back.'

'Just what do you want, Wilbur whatever-your-name-is, and I don't believe that for a minute, either.'

'Who would make up a name like Wilbur Rasmussen?' I said. She dipped her dark glasses at me again but made no comment.

'I hear it's an old town run by old money,' I said.

'You're looking at some of it, darling.'

'Accurate?'

'Fairly accurate.'

'They making any money off the track?'

'Honey, *every*body's making money off the track. If you own a bicycle concession in this town you can get rich.' She sighed. 'I suppose we are going to have to talk about this, aren't we?'

'Sooner or later.'

The waiter brought my coffee and as I was diluting it with cream and sugar she made an imperceptible little move with a finger towards the hostess, a pretty, trim young black woman, no more than nineteen or twenty, who, a second or two later, appeared at the table.

''Scuse me,' she said. 'You have a phone call, Ms Babs.'

'My public is after me,' she said with mock irritation. 'Excuse me for a moment, would you, darling?'

I watched her in the row of mirrors at the entrance to the restaurant. She picked up the phone at the hostess desk and punched out a number. That would be the desk she was calling, checking me out. She said a few words, waited, then hung up and came back to the table, still smiling, but a little colder than when I first sat down.

I smiled back.

'Jake Kilmer,' she said.

'Nice trick with the hostess. I could see you calling the desk in the mirrors.'

'That obvious, huh? Hmm. I wonder how many other people have caught me at it.'

'Lots. The others were just too nice to mention it.'

'Why do I know your name?'

'It's fairly common.'

'Hmm. And you're a cop,' she said.

'Kind of.'

'How can you be kind of a cop?'

'Well, you know, I do statistical profiles, demographs, that kind of thing.'

'You're much too cute to be that dull.'

'Thanks. You're pretty nifty too.'

'You're also an outrageous flirt.'

'I am?' I said. 'Nobody's ever complained about that before.'

'Who's complaining?' she said, dipping her head again and staring at me with eyes as grey as a rainy day. I passed.

'So tell me who makes Dunetown click,' I said.

'Persistent too,' she said, then shrugged. 'Why not, but it'll cost you a drink at the end of the day.'

'Done.'

She knew it all. Every pedigree, every scalawag, every bad leaf on every family tree in town. She talked about great-grandfathers and great-great-grandfathers who came over in the early 1800s and made a fortune in privateering, cotton, land, and shipping; who rose to become robber barons and worse, what Babs called 'varmints,' a word that seemed harmless somehow, the way she used it, but which I took to mean tough men who destroyed each other in power brawls. She talked about a one-time Irish highwayman named Larkin who escaped the noose by becoming an indentured slave to a Virginia tobacco man and then ran off, arriving in Dunetown where, fifteen years later, he became its first banker; about Tim Clarke, the stevedore from Dublin who stowed away to Dunetown and ended up owning the shipyard; and an Irish collier named Findley who once killed a man in a duel over a runaway pig, and who went on to make a fortune in cotton and converted his millions to land before the bottom dropped out, and was the man who talked Sherman out of burning Dunetown because he owned most of the town and didn't want to see it torched like Atlanta. Doe's great-grand-father.

Hooligans, the bunch of them, the Findleys, Larkins, Clarkes, and the second generation, with names like Colonel and Chief, the ones who said yes, no and maybe to every decision that affected the city for two centuries. And finally the third generation, the Bubbas and Chips and Juniors, so intimidated by their fathers that they were reduced to panderers, more interested in golf than empires.

Once she started it was like turning on a tape recorder with no stop button. A twenty-minute dialogue at the end of which I knew about every inbred mongoloid child, every lady of colour who had married across the line, all the bastard and aborted children, the adulterers and adulteresses, the covered-up suicides, the drunks, gays, and feuding families, the banker's daughter who was a prostitute in LA, and the two Junior Leaguers who ran off together and left two confused husbands and five children behind.

Routine for any small money town.

Three names stood out: Findley, Clarke, and Larkin.

The Findleys and the Larkins had been cautious partners through the years.

The Clarkes were their adversaries – in politics, business, even in love affairs.

'Jimmy Clarke would have died to marry Doe Findley,' Babs said, 'but Chief wouldn't hear of it. He picked an outsider for her. Not old money but respectable. His father was a lawyer and later a judge.'

'Harry Raines?' I said. Funny, I couldn't remember Jimmy Clarke, although the name rang a bell.

'You do get around,' Babs said.

'What about Raines?'

'What about him?'

'The way I get it, he married rich and got richer.'

'My, my,' she said, 'aren't we being a little catty?'

'No. I've been doing a lot of listening, that's all.'

'Did they tell you Harry's going to be governor one of these days soon?'

'I keep hearing that. Has he been nominated yet?'

'Cute,' she said.

'Well?'

'As well as, darling.'

'Why?'

'Because he's Dunetown's golden boy. He's handsome, he's rich, he's young. He's a lawyer, married to a beautiful woman, and an ex-football star. His politics are moderate. His family's acceptable. And he's the state racing commissioner. Isn't that enough?'

'Sounds like he was born for the job.'

'Besides, Dunetown's long overdue for a governor, particularly with the city growing so, and Harry's just perfect.'

'Couldn't that be a hot spot?'

'Governor?' she said.

'Racing commissioner.'

'Anything but, dear boy. Harry's brought a lot of money to the state. And a lot of tax money for the schools.'

'I never trust a politician who was born with his mouth full of silver,' I said.

'Ah, but he wasn't.'

'So he married the money, that it?'

'Do you know Harry?' she asked. Her tone was turning cautious. I had the feeling I had stretched my luck a little thin.

'Nope,' I said. 'Just trying to get the feel of things. Obviously he's a man with a lot of drive. A lot of ambition.'

'Is there something wrong with that?' she asked.

'Not necessarily. Depends on how much ambition and how big a drive. What you're willing to trade for success.'

'He didn't have to trade anything for it, darling. He got all the prizes. The town's richest and most desirable young woman, her father's political clout. But he didn't sit on his little A-frame and drink it up the way a lot of them have. He made a name for himself.'

'What's he like personally?'

She leaned back in her chair and eyed me suspiciously. I was beginning to sound a little too much like a man with an axe to grind and Babs Thomas was nobody's fool.

'Just what the hell is your game, Kilmer?' she said.

'Told you, I'm trying to get a line on the town.'

'No, you're trying to get a line on Harry Raines.'

'Well, he's part of the big picture,' I said, trying to sound as casual as I could.

She leaned forward and said flippantly, 'You don't have to like a man to vote for him. Personally I find him a bit cold, but he gets things done. The rest of the state is in a depression and Dunetown is in the middle of a boom. You can't have everything. If he was any better he'd probably be in the movies.'

I laughed at her rationale. I'm sure most of the voters in the state would look at Harry Raines in the same way. Babs Thomas had a bit of Everywoman in her, although I'm sure she would have killed anyone who accused her of same.

'Anyway,' she said, tossing her head, 'the sheriff's on his side. That's reason enough to get elected.'

'That would be this Titan fellow?'

'No, darling, not "this Titan fellow". *Mister* Stoney. God owes *him* favours.'

'And he and Raines are buddies?'

I was coaxing information now.

'When Chief's son, Teddy, was killed in Vietnam,' she said, 'Chief almost died with him. Doe married Harry less than a year later. Chief faded out of the picture right after that.'

'As soon as he was sure the keys to the kingdom were in the right pocket,' I said. It was not a question. 'And now Sam Donleavy's running the store for Raines, isn't that it?'

'Yes. They're inseparable friends.'

Listening to her was like a déjà vu.

'Is Donleavy one of the landed aristocracy?'

'No, he's just plain people. He's from New *Joisey*,' she said playfully. 'Nouveau riche. You'd like him.'

I grimaced at her. 'Thanks a lot.'

'Just joking. Actually Sam's quite a charmer. His wife left him about a year ago. Ran off with her karate instructor. Sam took it quite hard at first, but he's over it now. In fact, right now I'd say he's the town's most eligible bachelor – and enjoying every minute of it.'

'Is this Raines clean?' I asked.

'Clean? You mean does he bathe?' She wasn't joking; it was obvious she didn't understand me.

'No, you know – does he cheat on his wife, that sort of thing?'

'Harry, cheat? He wouldn't dare.' She stared over my shoulder as she spoke and her eyes grew wide. 'Speak of the devil,' she said. 'There's Doe Findley now.'

18

LITTLE TONY LUKATIS

It's hard to be casual when every muscle in your body has turned to ice. I tried playing for time.

'Who?' I asked, in a voice that seemed to me to be at least an octave above normal

'Doe Findley,' Babs said impatiently, pointing over my shoulder. 'Turn around!'

I turned in slow motion, still playing the charade, still acting like the whole thing was a bore. Doe was coming out of a small meeting room with a dozen other well-dressed women. She was wearing tan silk slacks and a dark green silk blouse and her golden hair was pulled back in a tight ponytail and tied with a red ribbon.

'That's the horsey set,' Babs said. 'Thoroughbred breeders.'

But I wasn't paying any attention. I was remembering the first time I ever saw Doe. Her hair was tied back just like that, except she was only fifteen at the time. Teddy brought her into the dorm, where we shared a room. She was wearing tight white jeans and a red pullover and she didn't look any more like a fifteen-year-old than I look like Muhammad Ali. I had seen her pictures, of course; Teddy was big on family pictures. But she didn't look like that in pictures. No way. All I clearly remember was that she had an absolutely sensational rear end. I couldn't take my eyes off it. I was embarrassed, but my eyes kept straying. It was like a magnet. I tried, I tried really hard, but it didn't do any good. I kept sneaking peaks. Then Teddy suddenly buried an elbow in my side.

'She's fifteen,' he hissed under his breath.

'What's the matter with you?' I whispered back.

'Clicking eyeballs, Junior,' he said. 'Lay a finger on that behind before she's eighteen and I'll disengage your fucking clutch.' Then he broke down and started laughing.

That was the fall of 1960, a couple of weeks after Teddy Findley and I met, became roommates, and began a friendship that would last far beyond college. He started calling me Junior the day we met. I don't know why, and he never explained it. I finally figured it was because he was taller than me. Two, three inches. Nobody else, not even Doe, shared that privilege.

Anyway, I waited until she was eighteen. Two and a half years; that's a lot of waiting. And during that two and a half years she kept getting better and better, blossoming from little sister to big sister to woman, while I watched it happen. Teddy didn't help. He became a verbal calendar, taunting me every week of the way.

'How about it, Junior,' he'd say, 'only four months to go.' It never occurred to me until later that I was being sized up all that time: that waiting until she was eighteen had as much to do with me as it did with her.

'Jake! Jake Kilmer. Is that really you?'

She was standing a foot away. I could feel the fire starting in the small of my back and coursing up to my neck, like the fuse on a stick of dynamite.

Time seemed to have evaded her. No lines, no wrinkles. Just pale grey eyes staring straight at me and the warmth of her hand as she squeezed mine.

I stood up and said something totally inadequate like, 'Hi, Doe.'

Then she put her arms around me and I was smothered by the warmth of her body pressing against mine, by the hard muscles in her back and the softness of the rest of her. I was consumed with wanting her.

Then she stepped back and looked up at my face, cocking her head to one sied.

'Hardly a grey hair,' she said. 'And every line in the right place.'

'Is that your way of saying I'm growing old gracefully?' I tried to joke.

'Oh, no,' she said softly, 'not that. You look beautiful.' She stared hard at me for another second or two, and just as quickly turned her attention to Babs.

'I see you've cornered him already,' she said playfully, and then back at me: 'Call me . . . please. I have a private line. It's listed under D. F. Raines. Chief would love to see you.'

I didn't buy that. To Chief I would just be bad news, a vague face from the past, a painful reminder that his son was dead. What she was really asking was, Are you coming to Windsong tonight?

'Sure,' I said.

'Promise?'

'Promise.'

She didn't just leave, she turned and fled.

I sat back down and looked across the table at Babs, whose mouth was dangling open. She reached up slowly and pushed it closed with a finger.

'You sly son of a bitch,' she said.

'What're you talking about?'

'You know Doe Findley *that* well?' she said.

'What do you mean, *that* well?'

'I mean *that* well.'

'We knew each other in college. Twenty years ago.'

'Uh-uh, honey. That wasn't a "gee it's nice to see you again after all these years" look. That was a "where the hell have you been for the last twenty years" look.'

'It was probably a shock seeing me again. I knew her brother.'

'I don't care who you knew. These old eyes are not that bad yet. Twenty years, huh?'

'What are you raving about?' I said to her.

'So where did she fall in love with you? She didn't go to Georgia, she went to . . . oh, let's see, one of those snotty colleges up north.'

Now she was doing the coaxing.

'Vassar,' I said. 'Real hard to remember.'

'So you have kept track?'

'Through Teddy.'

'Oh, right. And you just sat there, letting me jabber on about the Findleys and Harry Raines . . .'

'Trash it,' I said.

'Trash it?'

'Trash it. There's nothing there.'

She wasn't about to back off. She leaned back in her chair and appraised me through narrowed eyes.

'Jake Kilmer. That name ought to mean something to me,' she said.

She sat there struggling with her memories, trying to sort me out of the hundreds of names and faces from her past. Then recognition slowly brightened her eyes.

'Of course,' she said. 'You played football for the Dogs.'

'You have some memory,' I said, wondering how often that interlude was going to keep haunting me. I doubt that it had been mentioned once in the last ten years, and now it seemed to pop up every time I said hello, or maybe it was just popping up in my mind.

'You and Teddy played on the same team, didn't you?'

'For a while.'

'She's not a real happy woman, Kilmer.'

'How would you know that?'

'I know *every*thing, darling. It's what I do, remember I'm the town snoop.'

'I thought you said Raines had a wonderful family.'

'I didn't say he had a happy one. Raines is married to politics and Doe doesn't play second fiddle well at all.'

'People seem to think she married well.'

'Tom Findley couldn't have picked a better man for the job.'

'Christ, you are bitchy.'

'I like Doe,' she said, ignoring the slur. 'She's very honest. Not too bright, though, do you think?'

'I don't remember. When I was in college I thought everybody was brilliant but me.'

'She had an affair, you know.'

I leaned over towards her. 'I haven't heard a word about her since Teddy died, okay? I am not hooked into the Dunetown hot line.'

'You're really not going to ask who she had the affair with?'

'Nope.'

'It was Tony Lukatis.'

'No kidding. Little old Tony, huh?'

'You're much too blasé to really be blasé, I know it. I know all

99

the tricks. Listen, we have name entertainers coming out to the beach hotels now. I get some big-time gossip. They all try to act blasé, too, but it doesn't work – and they've been at it forever. Tony Lukatis was the guy. The golf pro at the country club. His father was the manager.'

My memory jumped back to that summer like the ball bouncing over the lyrics of some old song at an old-time movie matinee.

'Nick?'

'Ah, you do remember.'

'I remember Nick. I don't remember Tony.'

But then suddenly I did remember him, a little kid with incredibly curly hair who spent most of his time on the putting green when he wasn't caddying. He must have been fifteen or sixteen that summer.

'Aha, I see recognition in those green eyes.'

'Yeah, he's younger than she is.'

'The best kind, darling.'

'He had a sister.'

'Deidre . . . DeeDee?' Babs pressed on.

'Skinny little kid, used to hang around the club?' I asked.

'Skinny little kid? I can tell you haven't seen *her* in a while.'

'What's she doing these days?' I asked, trying to seem interested.

'She's Charlie Seaborn's secretary – Seacoast National Bank.'

'Did Raines know about the affair?' I tried not to sound too interested.

'Not so you could tell.'

'What happened?'

'Poor little Tony. Rumour has it he decided to get rich quick and got mixed up in some pot smuggling. He went to prison for five years. I've lost track of him since. It almost killed DeeDee.'

The conversation was cutting close to the bone. I decided it was time to ease on out.

'You've been a lot of help,' I said. 'I've got to get moving but I owe you a drink.'

'You better believe you do, dearie,' she said. 'You know how to get in touch. And if you don't, I will.'

I headed out of the restaurant, feeling like I had barely averted disaster.

No such luck.

19

HIDE AND SEEK

Stick was hiding behind the morning paper in the lobby of the hotel when I left the restaurant. He flashed the crazy smile of his when I spotted him.

'Not bad, not bad at all,' he said. 'Doe Findley and Babs Thomas for breakfast. And I was afraid you'd get lonely.'

'Strictly business,' I said.

'Hey,' he said, spreading his arms out at his sides, 'I never doubted it for a minute.'

'I'm sure you have my social calender filled for the day,' I said. 'What's up?'

'A little war conference with the troops.'

'You mean they're speaking to me?'

'They're thinking about it,' he said, leading me out the door. His Black Maria was hunched down in the loading zone, like it was looking for trouble.

'Why don't I take my car?' I suggested. 'In case we have to split up.'

'No worry,' he said, opening the door for me. 'I'm your tour guide for the day. It was a raffle. I lost.'

'Keep it under ninety, will you?' I asked as I got in.

'It stutters under ninety,' he answered.

'Fine, let's listen to it stutter for a while.'

He took me to a bright, airy place in a row house overlooking the river. It didn't look like a restaurant; it was more like having coffee in someone's living room. The place was about five minutes away, hardly time for the Maria to get up to speed, for which I was momentarily thankful. I was sure I wouldn't be that lucky for the entire day. Zapata, Salvatore, and Flowers were seated at a table in the back.

'Hey, Mildred,' Salvatore yelled across the room as we entered, 'two more javas.'

They all stared at me as I approached their table.

'What's the matter, is my fly open?' I asked as I sat down.

101

'Sorry,' Charlie One Ear said. 'We haven't seen you in the daytime.'

'What you see, gentlemen, is a ruin,' I said. 'Give me a couple of days to get some sun. I look much better with a decent night's sleep and a little colour.'

'It's the fluorescent lights in the Warehouse,' Charlie One Ear joked. 'They give everyone a ghastly pallor.'

'Well,' I said, smiling at everybody, 'thanks for not judging me on first appearances.

'Yeah, you're welcome,' said Salvatore.

'Y'see what it is, Kilmer, we decided to throw in with you,' Zapata said. 'On a temporary basis, see what happens.'

'Gee whiz, I don't know what to say,' I replied sarcastically.

'"Thank you" will be fine,' said Charlie One Ear.

'Thanks again.'

'Our pleasure,' Charlie One Ear replied. 'Now, just what specifically is it we're looking for?'

'What I need,' I said, 'is connections.'

'Like such as?' Chino Zapata asked.

'Like maybe a hooker who's been bending her heels in Louisville, suddenly shows up here. Chances are, she's on the circuit. The mob moves them around like that.'

'How about pimps?' Charlie One Ear queried.

'Sure, the same thing. Maybe I can tie a pimp to some outfit in Cincy or Chicago. Next step is, who's he working for? How did he get here? Pimps don't move from town to town. What I mean is, they don't freelance. They move when the heat's on. They usually work for the man. He tells them where to go.'

'So what's different about Dunetown?' Salvatore said. 'That's pretty common, isn't it?'

'What's different is that the Tagliani family is here,' Stick threw in.

'Right,' I said. 'If I can make a connection between here and someplace else, that's the start of an interstate case. If I can tie it to Tagliani's mob, that's part two. If I can prove it, then I can take it to the Justice Department. That's three, and then it's their problem. Anything else I lay off on you guys. I'm not here to make collars, okay?'

'All that is by way of telling us you're looking for out-of-town talent, correct?' Charlie One Ear said.

'Right. I'd also like to know the names of companies owned by the Triad. Where they bank. Who they do business with. What kind of straight businesses they're into.'

'That's a little outta our line,' Zapata said.

'The key man is the accountant, Cohen,' I said. 'He's the bagman. Unless he's changed his mo, he makes three or four pickups a day, never at the same spots. He carries a little black satchel, like one of those old-fashioned doctor's bags, and it's probably full of cash. That's the skim, the money they need to wash.'

'The Igg,' offered Charlie One Ear.

'Correct.'

'This is street money, right?' Stick said, playing along with me. 'Gambling, prostitution, dope, that kind of thing.'

I nodded.

'So why don't we just grab the bag away from the little shit and take a look?' Zapata suggested.

'For one thing, he's probably got four or five cannons escorting him,' I said.

'Yes,' Charlie One Ear said snidely. 'It's also against the law. It's called robbery. One to five for first offence, which might not be applicable in your case.'

Zapata looked at him and laughed.

'They don't usually put their swag in the bank,' Salvatore offered.

'I agree,' I said. 'But Cohen's a crafty son of a bitch. He may have something worked out at the bank.'

'They're in cahoots?' Zapata asked.

'Not necessarily,' I said. 'He may be depositing in several different accounts or putting it in a safe deposit box. The bank doesn't have to be involved.'

I was trying to be honest about it, but I couldn't help wondering whether Charles Seaborn, president of that bank, and a member of the Committee, knew Cohen personally. And if so, whether Sam Donleavy knew that Seaborn knew Cohen. And whether Raines knew that Donleavy knew that Seaborn knew Cohen. It was time I faced up to the facts. I *wanted* Raines and Donleavy to be up to their necks in it, because if things had gone differently and Teddy were still alive, I would have been in Donleavy's boots. I didn't want to feel that way, but coming back to Dunetown had stirred old emotions that I thought were long dead, and the lies, the hurt, the resentments, were as visceral as fresh wounds. I could taste the blood. So there it was. What can a man do?

'We should maybe talk to Cowboy,' said Salvatore, breaking up my train of thought. 'He shagged the little weed for a couple days.'

'Good,' I said. 'If we can put together enough evidence to show cause, we might find a judge who'll let us look into their bank accounts or let us have some wiretaps.'

'Kite Lange can handle that,' said Zapata.

'He means *legal* wiretaps, el retardo,' said Salvatore.

'In the meantime, I can throw a few crumbs your way,' I offered.

'How's that?' said Zapata, slurping his coffee.

I decided to try Charlie One Ear out, to see if he was as good as everybody said he was.

'I spotted Spanish Eddie Fuereco on the way in,' I said.

'At the airport, no doubt,' Charlie One Ear piped up immediately.

Zapata stared over at him, obviously impressed.

'Right,' I said.

'How'd you know that, Charlie?' asked Zapata, who appeared to be genuinely in awe of the one-eared detective.

'And in the bar,' Charlie One Ear added.

'Right again,' I said.

'Geez,' Zapata said.

'The old coin trick,' Charlie One Ear said. 'Was he spinning heads and tails?'

'You got it,' I said.

'What's the coin trick?' Zapata asked.

'He marks the top of a quarter, say on the heads side but along the ridges so you can't see it unless you're looking for it,' said Charlie One Ear. 'He lets the mark spin the coin. Spanish Eddie never touches it. The mark doesn't suspect anything, y'see, because he's controlling the spin and Eddie's calling whether it'll fall heads or tails. He can tell by the mark on the coin. He's also a sleight-of-hand artist. If the mark wants to switch coins, he always has another one ready.'

'Geez,' Zapata said again, his wonder still growing.

'He's very good,' Charlie One Ear said. 'On a real good night he can score enough to buy a new car.'

'So how come you knew he was at the airport?'

'If the mark starts getting pushy,' Charlie One Ear said, 'Fuereco switches to a regular coin, plays on the mark's money for a few rounds, then has to catch a plane. That's why he does airports. Gives him an excuse to end the game.'

'I'll be damned,' Zapata said. He looked over at me. 'Charlie knows every scumbag in the business,' he said with great pride.

'Only the cream of the crop,' Charlie One Ear threw in. 'And Spanish Eddie Fuereco only by reputation. I'd love to go a few rounds with him, before I put the arm on him.'

'He'll beatcha,' Zapata said. 'He can read the coin.'

'I'm not too bad at sleight of hand myself,' Charlie One Ear said proudly. 'I'll mark two coins and switch them back and forth so he keeps reading them wrong. What a coup, beating Fuereco at his own game!'

'He's all yours,' I said.

'I love con games,' Zapata said. 'Did you ever wonder who dreams them up?'

Charlie One Ear stared at Zapata for a moment or two, then said, 'No, I never really thought about it before.'

'I also saw Digit Dan out there,' I said.

'Ah, now there's a man with talent,' said Charlie One Ear. 'Fastest hands I've ever seen. Nobody works the shoulder bump like Dan.'

'The shoulder bump?' Zapata said, his sense of wonderment continuing to grow as Charlie One Ear showed off.

'He works crowds, bumps the shoulder of the mark. Usually the mark will touch his wallet to make sure he hasn't been boosted. That does two things for Digit. One, it tells him where the mark's wallet is. Two, the next time he bumps him, the mark is too embarrassed to check his belongings. Bingo! The wallet's gone and so is Dan.'

'You don't miss a trick, there Charlie,' Zapata said, shaking his head.

'The thing about Digit Dan that's remarkable,' said Charlie One Ear, 'is that he always hits somebody who's well heeled. He has that talent. He can look at a mark and tell how much money he's got in his kick.'

'Amazing,' Zapata said, shaking his head.

'He'll be working track tomorrow,' Charlie One Ear said. 'We'll nail him. Now, about your problem. Perhaps we can give you something there.'

That didn't surprise me.

'A pimp named Mortimer Flitch, alias Mort Tanner,' he continued. 'A wimpy sort and not too flashy. Handles high-class clientele, usually four or five girls at most. He calls Saint Louis home. He also has a thing for ladies of means.'

'Rich broads, you mean,' Zapata said.

'Yes, Chino, rich broads.'

'A gigolo, eh?' said Stick.

'I hate to give him that distinction,' said Charlie One Ear.

'Where'd you see him at?' Zapata asked.

'Out on the Strip, a week or two ago. This Turner thing came up and I never followed through.'

'It's Tagliani,' said Salvatore.

'What's he look like?' Zapata asked.

'Tallish, a little under six feet. Slender. I'd say one forty, one forty-two. Wears three-piece suits. Lightweight for the climate. Goes in for coloured shirts and has atrocious taste in ties. Flowers, lots of bad colours, that kind of thing. Brown hair and not a lot of it. Combs it over his forehead to stretch it out. Brown eyes. Always wears black boots.'

'Quirks?' Zapata asked.

'Bites his fingernails.'

Zapata turned to me. 'You want this guy?'

I wasn't sure what I'd do with him, but I said, 'Sure, it's a start.'

'Thirty minutes,' Zapata said. 'Wait here. Come on, Salvatore, I need company,' and they were gone.

'Zapata's amazing,' Charlie One Ear said, watching them rush out the door. 'Nose like a bloodhound.'

'Looks more like a waffle iron,' I said with a laugh.

'True,' said Charlie One Ear. 'But that doesn't impede his instinct for finding people. He's unerring.'

I got the impression maybe Zapata had been hit one or two times too many on the soft part of his head. Later I learned that he was as streetwise as any cop I've ever known. He may have been short on Shakespeare, but he was long on smarts.

'He was a middleweight contender, you know,' Charlie One Ear continued. 'Got full of patriotism, volunteered for the army, and spent a year in Vietnam. Then he came back and joined the Hell's Angels. I've never quite understood why.'

'You seem to have a nice team going,' I said. 'You spot them, Zapata finds them, and Salvatore sticks to them.'

'Like flypaper,' said Charlie One Ear.

Stick excused himself to go call the coroner and see if there were any autopsy reports yet. When he left, I leaned over the table towards Charlie One Ear.

'I've got to ask you something,' I said. 'It's a personal thing.'

'Yes?'

'I heard your father was an English lord and your mother was a Ute Indian. Whenever your name comes up, somebody says that.'

'Only partly correct. It was my grandparents and she was a Cree. I inherited my memory from my father and my instincts from my mother. Thank God it wasn't the other way around. I'm quite flattered you've heard of me.'

'Charlie Flowers, the man who smashed the Wong Yang Fu opium ring in San Francisco almost single-handed! You're a legend in your time,' I said with a smile.

'I really enjoy this, y'know,' he said, grinning back. 'I have an enormous ego.'

'Is it true you once busted so many moonshiners in Georgia that they threw together and hired a couple of Philly shooters to do you in?'

'Actually it was four, including Dancing Rodney Shutz out of Chicago, who was reputed to have killed over sixty people, a lot of whom didn't deserve the honour.'

'And you got 'em all?'

'Yes. Without a scratch, I might add. They made a mistake. They all took me on at once – I suppose they thought there was safety in numbers.' He paused for a minute and then flashed a twenty-dollar smile. 'Dancing Rodney was so aghast I don't think he realized to this day that he's dead.' And we both broke out laughing.

'So what're you doing here?' I asked.

His smile stayed but got a little brittle. 'Well, I don't share Dutch Morehead's consternation with condos. My wife and I enjoy outs quite a lot. Beautiful view. We're near the water. The climate's wonderful . . .' He paused. He could have let it drop there, but he went on. 'Besides, I couldn't get a job anywhere else.'

'What!'

He took out one of those long, thin Dutch cigars, lit it, and blew smoke rings at the ceiling. 'I was working internal affairs for the state police out in Arizona a couple of years back. There had been a lot of killing going on and they suspected it was dope-related. The main suspect was a big-time dealer named Mizero. They sent me in, undercover, to check it out. It was Mizero's game all right, but he had an inside man, a narc named Burke, who was very highly situated. What they were doing, Mizero would make a big sale. Maybe a hundred pounds of grass. Then Burke would step in, bust the buyer, confiscate his money and goods, tell him get lost and he wouldn't press charges. If the buyer got antsy, Mizero would push him over.

'I got too close to the bone and blew my cover. So Burke decided he had to get rid of Mizero. The trouble was, it went the other way. Mizero dropped Burke. The locals made a deal with the state to keep Burke out of it. It was an election year and this was a big case. Nobody wanted to deal with a bad-cop scandal.

'I was a key witness for the prosecution. They knew they couldn't muzzle Mizero, so they wanted me to testify that Burke was working undercover with me. I said no, I won't do that. Some things I'll do, but I won't perjure myself for anyone, particularly a bad cop. Next thing you know, they ship me out of state so the defence can't call me, and put out the word I'm a drinker, a big trouble-maker. And, get this, they put it out that I committed perjury! For over a year everybody in the business thought I was a drunken liar. And I don't even drink.'

'How about the Fed's?' I said.

'They didn't want me back. I was always too independent to suit the bureaucrats. Anyway, Dutch heard about it. I was living in Trenton working a security job and he showed up one day, didn't ask any questions, just offered me a job. After I took it, I said, "I don't drink and I've never told a lie under oath in my life," and he says, "I know it," and it's never come up since.'

Then he leaned across the table towards me. 'That's my excuse, what's yours?'

'I know the rest of the Cincinnati Triad is here. I just want to dig a hole under all of them. I don't care where they fall, but I want them to drop.'

'Is it because you couldn't nail them up there?'

'That's part of it.'

'And the rest of it's personal?' he said.

I nodded. 'Absolutely.'

He gave me another big smile. 'Splendid,' he said. 'I truly

admire a man who's strongly motivated.' He offered me his hand. 'I think Zapata and I will have a go at finding this Nance chap.'

'I'd like that a lot,' I said.

A minute or two later Stick came back to the table. 'Zapata just called,' he said. 'They've already spotted Tanner. He's at the Breakers Hotel eating breakfast.'

'See what I mean about Chino?' Charlie One Ear said with a grin, and we were on our way.

20

MEMORANDUM

Okay, Cisco, you're always complaining that I don't file reports. So I have a thing about that. I can't type and it takes me forever to peck out one lousy report. Also there are never enough lines on the forms and I can't get the stuff in between the lines that are there. If you want to know the truth, it's a royal pain in the ass. But if I were going to write a memorandum, it would probably go something like this:

I've been in Dunetown less than twenty-four hours. So far I've witnessed one death, seen three other victims, fresh on the slab, been treated like I got smallpox by Dutch Morehead and his bunch of hooligans, and seen just enough of Dunetown to understand why they call it Doomstown. It's an understatement.

Due process? Forget it. It went out the window about the time Dunetown got its first paved road. As far as the hooligans are concerned, due process is the notice you get when you forget to pay your phone bill. Most of them think *Miranda* is the president of a banana republic in South America.

Stick understands the territory but he's kind of in the squeeze. He has to go along with the hooligans so they won't tumble that he's a Fed. On the other hand, he's smart enough to know that any evidence these guys might gather along the way would get stomped flat at the door to the courthouse.

What we're talking about, Cisco, is education. Stick is a smooth operator. The rest of Dutch Morehead's people would rather kick ass then eat dinner. Today I tried to discuss the RICO statutes with them and Chino Zapata thought I was talking about a mobster he knows in Buffalo.

The only exception is Charlie 'One Ear' Flowers, who knows the game but doesn't buy the rules. He's like the rest of these guys – they've been fucked over so much by the system that they walk with their legs crossed. I'm not making any value judgments, mind you. Maybe some of them deserved their lumps.

Take Salvatore, for instance. He was up on charges in New York City when Dutch found him. The way I get it, Salvatore was on stakeout in one of those mom and pop stores in the Bronx. It had been robbed so often, the people who owned it took out the cash and put it on the counter everytime somebody walked into the store. The old man had been shot twice. Classic case. It's the end of the year and Salvatore is behind two-way glass and this freak comes into the store and starts waving a Saturday night special around. Salvatore steps out from his hiding place, says, 'Merry Christmas, motherfucker,' and blows the guy into the middle of the street with an 870 riot gun loaded with rifle slugs. The police commissioner took issue with the way Salvatore did business. Now he's down here.

One thing about them, they don't complain. Between you and me, I'm glad they're here.

You can add this to everything else: Every time I go around a corner I get another rude shock. Like going out to the beach today. I wasn't ready for that. The traffic should have been a clue. It got heavy about a quarter mile from where the boulevard terminates at Dune Road, which runs parallel to the ocean. See, the way I remember Dune Road, it was this kind of desolate macadam strip that merged with the dunes. It went out to the north end of the island and petered out at the sea; one of those old streets that go nowhere in particular.

Now it's four lanes wide with metered parking lots all over the place. There are three hotels that remind me a lot of Las Vegas, and shops and fast-food joints one on top of the other, and seawalls to protect the hotel guests from the common people. Two more going up and beyond them condos polluting the rest of the view. And the noise! It was a hurricane of sound. Stereos, honking horns, and hundreds of voices, all jabbering at once.

La Côte de Nightmare is what it is now.

See what I mean about rude shocks? The Strip, that's one rude shock.

Anyway, I'm on my way out there with Stick and Charlie One Ear. Going anywhere with Stick is taking your life in your hands. He doesn't drive a car, he flies it. He can do anything in that Pontiac but a slow roll and I wouldn't challenge him on that. I ought to be getting combat pay.

Without boring you with details, Savatore and Zapata made this St Louis pimp named Mortimer Flitch and we went out to have a chat with him.

He was hanging out on the Strip and before I go any farther with that, let me tell you about the Strip. The first thing I noticed when we got there, the hotels are almost identical triplets. Take the Breakers, for instance. The lobby is the size of the Dallas stadium. It would take about five minutes to turn it into a casino. I could almost hear the cards ruffling and the roulette balls rattling and the gears crinking in the slot machines. When Raines pushed through the pari-mutuel law, he promised there would never be any casino gambling in Dunetown. Well, you can forget that, Cisco. They're ready. It's just a matter of time. I'll give them a year, two at the most. What we're looking at is Atlantic City, Junior. About fifteen minutes told me all I wanted to know about the Strip.

When we get there, the pimp, Mortimer, is sitting in a booth in the coffee shop looking like he just swallowed a 747. Salvatore is sitting across from him, kind of leaning over the table, grinning like he's running for mayor. One thing I left out: Salvatore carries a sawed-off pool cue in his shoulder holster. It's about eighteen inches long and it's always catching on things, which doesn't seem to bother him a bit. Zapata is standing by the door. That's their idea of backup.

When we arrived, Zapata split. He's on the prowl for Nance and Chevos. That makes me feel real fine, because if Chevos and Nance are within a hundred miles of here, Zapata will find them. I'll make book on it.

We join Salvatore and Mortimer at the table and then I see why this Mortimer Flitch has got that screwy look on his face. Salvatore has his pool cue between Mortimer's legs and every once in a while he gives the cue a little jerk and rings Mortimer's bells.

'Tell him what you told me there, Mort,' Salvatore says, and bong! he rings the bells and Mortimer starts singing like the fat lady in the opera.

111

'I got in a little trouble in Louisville about two months ago – '

Bong! 'Tell 'em what for,' says Salvatore.

'Beating up this chippie. She had it coming – '

Bong! 'Forget the apologies,' says Salvatore.

'Anyway, the DA was all over me and –

Bong! 'Tell 'em why,' says Salvatore.

'It, uh, it – '

Bong!

'It was my fifth offence. Anyway, I give a call to a friend of mine, does a little street business in Cincy, and he says forget it out there, things are real hot, I should try calling Johnny O'Brian down here. So I did and he sends me the ticket.'

Mortimer stopped to catch his breath and Salvatore gave him another little shot.

'Tell 'em about the hotel and all,' he says.

'Look, O'Brian did me all right. I could get blitzed over this.'

Bong! 'Tell 'em about the fuckin' hotel, weed.'

'He gets me a suite here in the Breakers, give me two G's, and says I got a couple of weeks to line up some ladies. It's a sixty-forty split. He gets the forty.'

Salvatore looked over at me and smiled.

'What else you want to know?'

'Did you bring any ladies with you?' I asked.

'Uh – '

Bong!

'Yeah, yeah. Two.'

'That's the Mann Act,' I said.

'Look, could we maybe meet somewhere else if we're going to keep this up?' Mortimer pleaded. 'I could take a boxcar ride just talking to you guys.'

'How many pimps does O'Brian have working down here?' I asked.

Mortimer looks at Salvatore wild-eyed and says, 'Swear to God, I don't know. I got the hotel, that's all I know.'

'This is your territory exclusively?' Charlie One Ear asked, and Mortimer nodded vigorously.

'Okay,' I said. 'Finish your breakfast. We wanted information; we're not going to tell anybody about our chat. Don't screw up and leave town.'

He shakes his head, Salvatore pockets the cue, and we split.

'Can we use this?' Charlie One Ear asks on the way out.

'No,' I said, 'but it's nice to know.'

'Coercion, huh?'

'Yeah.'

Now I know why Salvatore carries a pool cue. He calls it his sweet nutcracker.

See what I mean about due process, Cisco?

21

DRIVE-IN

Stick drove intelligently on the way back. Neither one of us had much to say. About halfway to town he wheeled into a drive-in and got us each a hamburger and a beer. He pulled around behind the place and parked under some palm trees in the parking lot and we opened the doors to let the breeze blow through.

'You okay?' he asked.

'Sure, why?'

'I figure maybe you got the blues.'

'How come?'

'You got that look in your eye.'

'I'm doing fine.'

'I know the blues when I see them.' He looked at me with that crazy sideways smile. 'I just thought I'd let you know I'm a good listener and I got an awful memory.'

'It's nothing you haven't heard before,' I said.

'I'm only thirty-one,' he replied. 'You'd be surprised what I haven't heard yet.'

'I'll keep that in mind.'

There was a lot of activity in the parking lot; a lot of young girls wearing just about as little as the law allowed and young men with acne and cutoff jeans making awkward passes at them. The beer was ice cold and it tickled the tongue and made the mouth feel clean and fresh, and the hamburgers were real meat and cooked just right. So I hunkered down in the seat, bracing my knees on the dashboard, and took a long pull on my bottle. It had been a long time since I had spent lunch watching pretty young girls at play.

'Just look at that, would you,' Stick said wistfully.

'I'm looking,' I said, just as wistfully.

After a while two girls in a TR-3 pulled in and parked near us. One of them got out and threw something into the trash can. She was wearing thin white shorts that barely covered her bottom and a man's white shirt tied just under her breasts, which were firm and perilously close to popping out. She stood by the door of the TR-3 for a minute, flirting with Stick, and then she leaned over and whispered something to her friend. When she did the shorts tightened around every curve and into every crevice and you could see the lines of her skimpy bikinis through the cotton cloth and see the half-circles of her cheeks.

'Holy shit,' Stick muttered, 'that's damn near criminal.'

'She's not a day over fifteen, Stick.'

'I don't remember fifteen-year-olds being stacked like that when I was a kid,' he said somewhat mournfully. 'Do you remember them looking like that?'

I remembered Doe at fifteen, coming up to Athens with Chief for homecoming, flirting with me every time Teddy or Chief looked the other way. She definitely looked like that.

'Seems to me they were all flat-chested and giggled a lot,' Stick went on.

'They're giggling,' I pointed out.

'That's a different kind of giggling.'

'They're just beginning to figure it out,' I said.

'Figure what out?'

'How to drive a man up the wall.'

'She's got the angle, all right,' he said, drumming the fingers of one hand on his steering wheel and staring back at the little cutie, who lowered her sunglasses and stared back.

'Oh my,' Stick moaned. 'You just don't know where to draw the line.'

'About two years older than that,' I said.

'What a shame.'

He took a long pull on his beer, smacked his lips, and sighed.

'I missed all that,' he said. 'They were little girls when I went to Nam and they were grown up and spoken for when I got back. What a fuckin' ripoff.'

The girl in the TR-3 leaned her head way back and shook her long black hair across her face, and then she leaned forward and flipped it back and smoothed it out with her hands. The shirt came perilously close to falling completely open.

114

'She's doing that on purpose,' Stick said, watching every move. He looked back over at me. 'Fifteen, huh?'

'At the most.'

'Shit. What a fuckin' ripoff.'

The driver of the TR-3 cranked up and pulled around in a tight little arc so they drove past us.

'Love your hat,' the girl in the white cotton shorts purred as they went by. Stick whipped the hat off and scaled it like a Frisbee in the wake of the TR-3. It hit the parking lot and skipped to a stop as the sports car vanished around the building. Stick retrieved his hat and got back behind the wheel.

'All bluff,' he muttered, and then added, 'I may have to take the night off.'

'I wouldn't mind taking the rest of my life off,' I said. 'I been on this case too long. Almost six years. I'm sick and tired of the Taglianis. They're enough to give anybody the blues.'

'Relax. The way things are going there won't be any of them left to be sick and tired of,' he said almost jauntily, staring at another young girl in a bikini bathing suit who was sitting on the back of a convertible, her face turned up towards the sun. Her long, slender legs were stretched out in front of her and her breasts bubbled over the skimpy top. The driver, a skinny kid in surfing trunks and a cutoff T-shirt, stared dumbly at her in the rearview mirror.

'Look at that kid in the front seat,' Stick said. 'He doesn't know what the hell to do about all that.'

'It'll come to him,' I said.

'They're all over the place,' Stick cried lasciviously. 'You know what this is? It's a plague of young flesh. Do you get the feeling this is a plague of young flesh?'

'Yeah,' I said. 'God's throwing the big final at us. He's testing our mettle.'

'Mettle, shmettle,' Stick said. 'If that little sweetie on the back of the convertible takes a deep breath, her top'll fly off and kill that kid up front.' After a moment he added, 'What a way to go.'

He finished his beer and put the empty bottle on the floor between his legs. 'That's all it is then? You're tired of the Tagliani case?'

I wondered whether he was fishing and what he was fishing for. Then I thought, Who cares, so he's fishing. Suddenly I had this crazy thought that while Stick was younger than me and newer at the game, he was protecting me. It was a feeling I had known in the past and it scared me because it made me think about Teddy.

'I've been chasing Taglianis longer than anything else I've done in my whole life,' I said. 'Longer than college, longer than law school, longer than the army. I know everything there is to know about the fucking Taglianis.'

'That's why you're here enjoying the land of sunshine and little honeys,' Stick replied. 'Think about it – you could be back in Cincinnati. Now that's something to get blues over.'

'I hope you're not gonna be one of those jerks who always looks on the bright side,' I said caustically.

In a crazy kind of way, I felt a strange sense of kinship with the Taglianis, as if I were the black sheep of the family. My life had been linked to theirs for nearly six years. I knew more about the Tagliani clan than I did about Findleys or any of the hooligans. I knew what their wives and their girlfriends were like, what they liked to eat, how they dressed, what they watched on television, where they went on vacation, what they fought about, how often they made love. I even knew when their children were born.

'You want to hear something really nuts?' I said. 'I almost sent one of the Tagliani kids a birthday card once.'

'I knew a detective in DC, used to send flowers to the funeral when he wasted somebody. He always signed the cards "From a friend".'

'That's sick,' I said.

'You know what we oughta do, buddy? When this fiasco is all over we ought to take a month's leave, go down to the Keys. I got a couple of buddies live down there, sit around all day smoking dope and eating shrimp. That's the fuckin' life. Or maybe get the hell out of the country, hit the islands, Aruba, one of those. Sit around soaking up rays, getting laid, forget all this shit.'

'Wouldn't that be nice?' I said.

'We'll do it,' he said, slapping the steering wheel with the palm of his hand, and then he said suddenly, 'Hey, you married?'

'No, are you?'

'Hell no. What woman in her right mind would spend more than a weekend at the Holiday Fuckin' Inn.'

'That's where you're staying, the Holiday Inn?'

'Yeah. It's kind of like home, y'know. They're all exactly alike, no matter where you are. If you get one of the inside rooms overlooking the pool, the view doesn't even change.'

116

'I had this little basement apartment when I was in Cincy,' I said. 'I took it by the month because I didn't think I'd be there that long. There weren't even any pictures on the wall. Finally I went out and bought some used books and a couple of cheap prints to try and doll the place up but it didn't work. It always seemed like I was visiting somebody else when I came home.'

'Yeah, I know,' he said. 'It's been like that since Nam. We're disconnected.'

That was the perfect word for it. Disconnected. For years I had worked with other partners but always at arm's length, like two people bumping each other in a crowd. I didn't know whether they were married, divorced; whether they had kids or hobbies. All I knew was whether they were good or bad cops and that we all suffered from the same anger, frustration, boredom, and loneliness.

'Don't you ever wonder why in hell you picked this lousy job?' I asked him.

'That's your trouble right there, Jake, you think too much. You get in trouble when you think too much.'

'No shit?'

'No shit. Thinking can get you killed. You didn't make it through Nam thinking about it. Nobody did. The thinkers are still over there, doing their thinking on Boot Hill.'

There was a lot of truth in what he said. I was thinking too much. There was this thing about Cisco telling me to forget murder unless it was relevant. That bothered me. Hell, I was a cop and murder is murder, and part of the job, like it or not, is to keep people alive, like them or not, and keeping them alive meant finding the killer, no matter what Cisco said. It was all part of the territory. And there was the lie about Teddy which I hadn't thought about for years, because I had stuffed it down deep, along with the rest of my memories. I had walked away from the past, or thought I had. I had even stopped dreaming, though dreams are an occupational hazard for anyone who has seen combat. Now the dreams had started again. You can't escape dreams. They sneak up on you in the quiet of the night, shadow and smoke, reminding you of what had been. You don't dream about the war, you dream about things that are far worse. You dream about what *might* have been

'Hell, it's very complicated, Stick,' I said, finally. 'I don't

117

think I've got it sorted out enough to talk about. Sometimes I feel like I'm juggling with more balls than I can handle.'

'Then throw a couple away.'

'I don't know which ones to throw.'

'That's what life's all about,' he said. 'A process of elimination.'

'I thought I had it all worked out before I got here,' I said. 'It was very simple. Very uncomplicated.'

'That's the trap,' he replied. 'Didn't Nam teach you anything, Jake? Life is full of incoming mail. You get comfortable, you get dead.'

'That's what it's all about, Alfie?'

'Sure. It's also the answer to your question. We're cops because we have to keep ducking the incoming. That's what keeps us alive.'

Finally I said, 'Yeah, that's what we'll do, go down to the islands, lay out, and forget it all.'

'That's all that's bugging you, a little cabin fever then?'

'Right.'

He flashed that crazy smile again.

'I don't believe that for a fuckin' minute,' he said as he cranked up the Black Maria.

22

HEY, MISTER BAGMAN

Cowboy Lewis was waiting in the Warehouse when we got back. The big, raw-boned man was sitting at a desk, laboriously hunting and pecking out a report on a form supplied by the department. He didn't worry about the little lines or how many there were. He typed over them, under them, through them, and past them. Getting it down, that was his objective. There were a lot of words x'd out and in one or two places he had forgotten to hit the spacer, but I had to give him A for effort. At least he was doing it. His face lit up like the aurora borealis when he saw me.

'Hey, I was writing you a memo,' he said, ripping it out of the Selectomatic in mid-word. 'I'll just tell you.'

I looked at the partially completed report and told him that would be just fine. The thought occurred to me that I could sign it myself and send it to Cisco. That would probably end his bitching about my reports, or lack thereof, forever.

'Salvatore says you're interested in that little weed, uh . . .' He paused, stymied temporarily because he had forgotten the name.

'Cohen?' I helped.

'Yeah. Little four-eyed wimp, got his head on a swivel?' he said, twisting his head furiously back and forth to illustrate what he meant.

'That's him,' I replied. 'Unless times have changed, he's the bagman for the outfit.'

'Yeah,' he said, which was his way of agreeing. 'Carries one of those old-timey doctor's bags, black. Hangs on to that sucker like he's got the family jewels in there.'

'That's about what it is,' said Stick, 'The family jewels.'

'I shadowed him three days – Tuesday, Wednesday, Friday, last week – and got him cold.' Lewis took out a small black notebook. 'He stays real busy in the morning. Moves around a lot. Goes to the bank every day at two o'clock, just as it closes.'

'Every day?' I asked.

'All three days he went to the bank there on the river.' He nodded.

'This activity in the morning – does he always go to the same places?' Stick asked.

Lewis shook his head. 'He's all over town. But he always seems to wind up on the Strip around noon. Leastwise he did these three days.'

'Where does he bank?' I queried.

'Seacoast National, down there by the river like I said. Although sometimes he makes deposits at the branches.'

The good news worm nibbled at my stomach. That was Charles Seaborn's homeplate.

'Cash deposits?' I asked.

'Never got that close,' Lewis said with a shrug. 'Didn't wanna tip my hand, y'see. He travels first class. Big black Caddy limo with a white driver looks like he could carry the heap in his arms. Then there's another pug in the front seat and a souped-up Dodge Charger with a high-speed rear end following them. Usually two, three mutts in it.'

'Like a little parade?' Stick suggested.

'Yeah,' he said with a smile, 'a little parade. Any one of 'em could win an ugly contest, hands down. The Charger is usually in pretty tight. Half a block behind at best.'

'And he moves around a lot, you say?' I threw in.

'Uh-huh. But he always ends up there at the bank by the river, just before it closes.'

He offered me his notebook, which had notations scrawled everywhere. Slantwise, up the sides of the pages, upside down. It was far worse than his typed report.

'What does all this mean?' I asked.

He looked a little hurt. 'That's addresses and stuff,' he said. 'See here, 102 Fraser, that's an address where he stopped. Here's Bay Br. That's the Bay branch of the bank. Uh, I don't know what this one is for sure, but I can figure it out.'

'Any of these addresses mean anything to you?'

'Well, some of 'em do. See here where I wrote down "Port"? That's the Porthole Restaurant on the way out to the Strip. He hit there two days, Tuesday and Friday. "Bron", that's Bronicata's joint. That was Wednesday.'

'He sure eats a lot,' I said.

'Naw. Never stays that long. Five minutes, sometimes ten. I ambled in behind him once at the Porthole. He has a cup of coffee at the corner of the bar, goes to the can, and leaves. Two guys from the Charger sat a few stools away, another grabs a table near the door. The other two stand by the car. He sure ain't lonely.'

It was an excellent tail job, but it was impossible for me to decipher his notes.

'This is a great job,' I told him, 'but I need a big favour. Can you list the places he stopped with the dates and times for me? Nothing fancy, just write them down in a straight line on a sheet of paper.'

'Can't read my writing, huh?' he said, looking hurt again.

I tried to ease the pain. 'It's strictly my problem,' I said. 'I have a very linear mind.'

His 'Oh' told me that he didn't quite get my meaning but wasn't interested in pursuing it any further.

'Does Dutch have you shadowing Cohen anymore?' I asked.

'Tomorrow,' he said. 'I'm pulling a double. Logeto tonight, Cohen in the morning. Then I'm off a day.'

'Maybe he ought to watch the car instead of Cohen,' Stick

suggested. 'Some of his operators probably have a key to the boot. He parks in a lot or on a side street somewhere, goes into a place, and while he's gone, the henchman makes a drop in the boot.'

'Excellent idea,' I said. 'Also you might switch cars with one of the other guys. These people are very nervous. They keep their eyes open; that's their job.'

'That and cutting down anybody that gets near the family jewels,' Stick said.

'Got it,' Cowboy said. 'I'll get right on this list.' He returned to his desk.

I pulled Stick out of earshot. 'When he gets finished,' I said, 'we need to pull a Link matrix on this stuff, just to see where these pickups overlap. The same with the rest of the gang. This Cohen is very particular. I'm sure he's smart enough to avoid any obvious patterns, but in the long run he's going to end up setting patterns whether he likes it or not.'

'What's the significance of the restaurants?' Stick asked.

'I'd have to guess.'

'So guess.'

'Bronicata probably owns the Porthole, as well as his own place. Maybe some other eateries around town as well. That's probably dope money. The hotels is probably skim. I'm sure they have double-entry books to keep the Lepers off their ass.'

Stick said, 'We might have Salvatore pay Mortimer another visit and find out who he pays and when. That could give us a lead on the pros take.'

He had learned his lessons well, the Stick. He was revealing himself as a first-class detective with a handle on how the mob operates and I told him so.

'Thanks, teacher,' he said with that crooked smile of his. 'Anything else?'

'Yeah. It wouldn't hurt to know who owns the businesses they frequent. We've got to start putting together some kind of profile on the whole Triad operation here.'

'Charlie One Ear's the man for that. He knows all the tricks and you can't beat that computer he uses for a brain. I can help with the legwork.'

'Good enough,' I said.

'How about dinner tonight?' Stick asked. 'Maybe hit a few hot spots afterwards.'

'I'm tied up tonight,' I said. 'Can we shoot for tomorrow night?'

Stick smiled. 'I'll check my dance card,' he said.

Charlie One Ear appeared from the back of the building with an expression that spelled trouble.

'You need to have a chat with Dutch, old man,' he said to me.

'Trouble?'

'I think his feelings are hurt.'

'Oh, splendid,' I replied.

'I'll fill Charlie in,' Stick said as I headed back towards the big man's office. Dutch operated out of a room the size of a walk-in closet. A desk, two chairs, one of which he occupied, and a window. The desk could have qualified for disaster aid. It was so littered with paper that he kept the phone, which he was using when I knocked, on the windowsill.

'Talk to ya later,' he barked into the phone, and slammed it down. I decided to close the door.

'You don't have t'do that,' he growled. 'We ain't got any secrets here.' He pointed to the other chair. 'Take a load off.'

I sat down. He cleared his throat and moved junk around on his desktop for a minute or so, then took off his glasses and leaned back in his chair, staring at the ceiling.

'I don't wanna sound unappreciative,' he started, 'but I got a way of doing things, okay? It may not be SOP, and it may not be to the Fed's liking, but that's the way it is. Now, it seems to me that all of a sudden you're kind of running this operation, got my people running errands all over town, doing little numbers on wayward pimps, like that, and I like to get things off my chest, so I'm speaking my piece right up front.'

'Is that all that's bothering you?' I asked. I sensed that there was something else behind his annoyance but I wasn't sure exactly what.

'So far.'

'Okay,' I said. 'Since it's your ballgame, maybe you better tell me the rules.'

He opened a drawer and took out a sheet of paper.

'This here's my schedule sheet. I spend a lot of time working this out, make sure all the bases are covered, people have some time off when they need it. You go short-stoppin' me and it's going to get to be a big mess.'

I don't like to be put on the defensive, nor do I like apologies

122

and excuses. 'That's fair enough,' I said. 'Can we work out a compromise?'

'Such as what?'

'Such as you and me sitting down and drawing up a list of priorities.'

'I got a list of priorities.'

'It would help if you explained them to me.'

'When it comes up, I will.'

'See here, Dutch, I didn't come here to screw up your operation. You've got a good bunch of people here. A little rough around the edges, but that may be good in the long pull. All I'm trying to do is give them a little direction.'

'There's channels,' he said brusquely.

'What channels? You? You're the channel, Dutch. I'm sorry if I stepped on your toes – '

'It ain't that,' he said, cutting me off.

'Then what is it? Look here, if you want to keep boosting dips and hassling street pushers and hookers, that's your business. I didn't come here to kick ass, I came here to do a job which is to dump the Tagliani outfit. I thought we saw eye to eye on that.'

'Don't screw up my schedule!' he bellowed, slamming his fist on the desk.

I jumped to my feet.

'Fuck your schedule,' I said quietly. 'Maybe I better get some help in here from the field and go it alone. And don't raise your voice to me. This isn't high school.'

It was a bluff but I decided to call his hand before the pot got too big to cover. Sometimes the best way to defuse a situation is to light the fuse. He didn't like it one bit. It caught him off guard. His eyes glittered dangerously and beads of sweat popped out in his moustache. I started for the door.

'You shoulda told me about you and Doe Raines,' he said, before I could get to it.

So that was it. Titan had let the tiger loose.

'Why? It's personal business. Titan knows that.'

'Titan didn't tell me.'

'Nobody else knows about it,' I said. 'That was twenty years ago, damn it.'

He leaned back and raised his eyebrows. 'Babs Thomas' is all he said.

I felt like a fool. The last thing I needed to show Dutch at this point was misjudgment. We stared at each other for what seemed like an hour. Finally his shoulders loosened and he wiped his mouth with the back of his hand.

'*Sheiss*,' he growled, half under his breath, then waved at the chair. 'Sit down. Let's start over.'

I sat down. There was no point in pushing it any further. We both had made out points.

'Suppose you tell me how you want to run the show,' I said.

The storm was over. 'It ain't that,' he said quietly. 'I just got hot under the collar, see. I didn't like hearing things about a man I'm workin' sock and shoe with from the local gossip.'

'She's guessing,' I said.

'Is she guessing right? Did you have an affair with Doe Raines.'

'Shit, Dutch, I had a college romance with Doe Findley. That was over and done with a long time ago. Besides, what's that got to do with the price of eggs?'

'Right now a scandal could really upset the apple cart.'

I felt like getting righteously indignant except that he was cutting close to the bone. I wasn't sure how to deal with the situation without straight-out lying to the man.

'There's not going to be any scandal,' I said finally.

'Is that a fact?' he asked seriously.

'That's a fact.'

He nodded slowly. 'Okay,' he said. 'I'm sorry I brought it up but I'm just as glad we got it out of the way. Anyway, I got run through the ringer this morning. Titan and Donleavy both shoved it up and broke it off.'

'Does Donleavy know about Doe and me?'

'I doubt it. It didn't come up?'

'So what's their beef?'

'No more'n you could expect,' he moaned. 'My job was to keep people like Tagliani outta here. Now they want the whole mess cleaned up. Titan's idea is to just run them out of town.'

'That stuff went out with Buffalo Bill.'

'Tell them that. So far, Raines hasn't figured it all out. The name of the game is sweep it under the rug.'

'It's gone too far for that.'

'You know it and I know it.'

'But they don't, is that it?'

'Livin' in the past,' he mused. 'Donleavy doesn't know

anything about the rackets. He's seen too many James Cagney movies.'

'Unless I'm mistaken,' I said, 'Donleavy had a hand in all this. He was supposed to screen these people.'

'I think it goes something like this: the buck stops here,' he said, pointing to himself. 'It doesn't go any higher.'

'How did you get yourself in this fix?' I asked. 'You're not the kind of man that kisses the ass of people like Donleavy.'

I was thinking of what Charlie One Ear had told me, about the way Dutch hired him and Salvatore. I was sure Dutch had used the same kind of judgment in hiring all the hooligans.

'The rules changed on me,' he said sadly. 'Leadbetter was supposed to be the in-between man. When he went down, it fell to me. Up until now, I didn't have any bitch.'

'Up to now it didn't matter,' I said.

He looked over at me for a long time. I was putting the squeeze on him and he knew it. What he wanted was for me to let him off the hook, but I couldn't do that. I needed Dutch right where he was, standing between me and the damned Committee. And that meant he had to stand up to them, like it or not.

'You don't give a man much, do you, son?'

'I'm not telling you how to run your business, Dutch. I could ask you to trust me but you don't know me that well. What I will tell you is that this thing is going to blow and soon. The powder keg's in the fire.'

'So what's the answer?' he said, holding his hands out like a man going down for the third time.

'Try to beat the explosion,' I said. 'I need to find the key that will put the Triad against the wall.'

'What key?'

'I need to build a RICO case against these bastards.'

'That could take years!' he cried.

'Except we have one edge,' I said. 'I already know the players and how they operate. It's not like we were starting with scratch. What I need is the local buy-out.'

'Who do you suspect,' he asked.

'Hell, there's so many termites in this woodpile it's hard to say. Just give me free reign with you SOB's for a few days. We can work together. But if something pops, I don't want to have to run you down and explain it. Trust me that far. I may work your boys to death, but it'll be worth it in the long pull.'

'I'll give you this – you already made believers outta Charlie One Ear, Salvatore, and Cowboy Lewis. Zapata's still on the fence but he's about to come around. That leaves only Kite Lange, the Mufalatta Kid, and Pancho Callahan to convince. I don't know how you did it, but you sure moved fast.'

'I'm just a charming fellow,' I said with a smile, trying to ease the pressure.

'You don't have any ideas?' he asked, pressing the question.

'It could be Raines. Maybe that's the reason he's so coy. He's keeping arm's length from the action. And Donleavy could be his front.'

'That don't even make good sense, Jake. They got more to lose than anybody, particularly Harry.'

'Harry Raines didn't get where he is by running on empty,' I said. 'He's ambitious and he's got more than his share of pride. The mob might be making him a bigger offer than just governor of the state. Their clout in Washington is scary.'

He shook his head. 'You got one helluva devious mind,' he said.

I didn't say any more. I couldn't tell him that I wanted Raines to be in it. Or Donleavy. Or that my reasons were purely selfish because I was in love with Raines' wife. Hell, I'm only human.

23

DUE PROCESS

Charlie One Ear was killing time near the water fountain when I left Dutch's office. His expression asked the question. I made a circle with thumb and forefinger and winked.

'Just your basic lack of communication,' I said.

'Good,' he said. 'He's a fine man, Dutch. There's not a man in the squad who wouldn't kill for him.'

'He deserves it,' I said. 'He's got a mean job and right now the local hotshots have got him shoved against the wall.'

'I just wanted to make sure you understood,' said Charlie One Ear. 'You're a nice chap and all that, but we're throwing in with you because it appears to be the only chance he's got.'

It was obvious that Charlie One Ear was the spokesman for the SOB's, or perhaps chairman would be closer to it.

'I appreciate your honesty, Charlie. Just so there's no misunderstanding either way, I intend to take advantage of that loyalty every chance I get.'

He smiled and put out his hand. 'Thus far you seem to know what you're doing. Someday I hope to add a new chapter to the legend that seems to be growing around me. Busting the Triad with Jake Kilmer.'

'Let's hope you can write it,' I said. 'We got the clock against us.'

'I have already come to that conclusion,' he said as we walked towards the door. 'There seems to be a covert attempt in Dunetown to ignore the Tagliani kill-out.'

'You noticed that, huh?'

'Yes. Obviously they're hoping for a break before they have to fess up,' he continued. 'I'm certain the powers that be are aware that the homicide division couldn't find their collective asses if they were all farting "Dixie" in harmony.'

'Did Stick talk to you about the information we need?'

'Yes,' he said. 'I'll start on it this afternoon. I just wanted to make sure everything was A-one with Dutch.'

'He just wants me to stop fucking up his schedule,' I said, laughing.

'He's been days behind on the bloody schedule since the first week we started,' Charlie One Ear said with a grin.

'I think he just needed to blow off a little steam,' I answered.

'By the way, just so you'll know. Cowboy may seem a bit dense at times, but he's really quite bright. He's on about a ten-second flash-to-bang delay.'

'Okay,' I said. 'Has he always been like that?'

Charlie One Ear shook his head. 'He got the back of his head blown off in Vietnam. There's a steel plate in there. That's why he wears that ridiculous baseball cap. It covers up the bald spot.'

I didn't know how to respond to that. What do you say? Gee, that's tough? Everybody knows it's tough.

'Actually I mentioned that because Cowboy was a sheriff in Waco, Texas, before he went off to war. When he came back nobody would hire him. Dutch found him working on the docks in New Orleans.'

'Thanks, Charlie, I'm glad to know that.'

'I'm sure he'll have that list up for you by tomorrow, even if he has to work on it all night.'

'Tell him I said thanks,' I said.

'Tell him yourself,' said Charlie Ear. 'I'm off for the hall of records.'

Cowboy Lewis was right where I left him, labouring over his errant notebook.

'Cowboy, don't kill yourself on that, okay?'

'Tomorrow,' he said, shoving the baseball cap back on his head. 'I got to tail that Logeto tonight but I'll have it by tomorrow.'

'Thanks.'

'By the way, Zapata said to tell you he went out to find that creep that shot you.'

'His name's Turk Nance,' I said.

'Turk Nance, right.' He smiled. 'Zapata'll find him, you can put that in the bank.'

'I'll thank him when I see him,' I said.

'I think I'm going to have to take writing lessons,' he said as I was leaving. 'I can't read my own fuckin' writing.'

As I headed for the door a new figure loomed in my path. It was the cop with the waffle-iron features.

'We didn't have a chance to get acquainted last night,' he said. 'I'm Kite Lange.'

'Jake Kilmer.'

'I'm a good wire man,' he said. 'You need anything wired, you call me, okay? I can bug a fly in motion right in front of your face, you wouldn't see me do it.'

'Terrific.'

'I'm not bragging,' he said, and his battered features broke into a smile. 'It's a God-given talent.'

'And I'm sure you don't abuse it,' I said.

'Not unless somebody asks me to,' said Kite, then he added, 'I hear you were in Nam.'

'Yeah,' I said.

'When was that?'

''67, '68. I got held up coming home by the Tet.'

'What outfit?'

'Military intelligence. How about you?'

'Medevac chopper pilot,' he said.

'How many missions did you fly?' I asked.

128

'You'd throw up if I told you.'

I hesitated for a moment before asking him the next question, but I figured, what the hell. I was getting to be one of the boys.

'Mind if I ask you a personal question?' I said.

'Shoot.'

'How did you fuck up and get in this squad?'

Lange's smashed face bunched up and he howled.

'Hey, that's getting right to the point,' he said. 'Well, I was flying helicopter traffic control for the Denver PD. Three guys heisted a bank and I was tailing them at about five hundred feet. A blue and white was closing in on them but he lost his car and went off the road. So I dropped right down on top of the getaway car. You know, a couple of feet. I was hanging right in there, radioing back his position, trying to force him off the road, when we came to a railroad bridge. At the last minute I had to pull up to get over it.'

'Yeah?'

'I didn't see the freight train that was crossing the bridge at the time. Flew right into an open boxcar. It happened to be the mayor's favourite chopper. Had his name on the side and everything. You should of seen it, the chopper, I mean.' He stopped a moment and chuckled. 'It looked like the Jolly Green Giant had it for lunch.'

'So you got the old heave-ho for breaking the mayor's toy, huh?'

'That and the city had to buy a new boxcar for the train. They didn't even give me a going-away party.'

I said, 'You're lucky you lived through it.'

'What d'ya think happened to my face?' Kite said, still grinning.

'What were you doing when Dutch found you?' I asked, expecting him to tell me he was selling used cars or something.

'A traffic gig in Roanoke, Virginia, with a lady reporter,' he said. 'It was kind of demeaning after doing police work, but it had its moments. She used to give me head on the way back from the afternoon rush every day.'

It was my turn to laugh. 'You must be some kind of pilot,' I said.

'After Nam, it's all pie à la mode.'

Then I got an idea. I still don't believe what I did next, Old Mr Due Process, ex-lawyer, always-do-it-right Kilmer. Maybe the hooligans were beginning to rub off on me.

'I got an idea,' I said.

'Shoot.'

'You know the Seacoast Bank's main branch down near the river?'

'I can find it.'

'I'd like to know who the president's doing business with. Who he talks to during the day, that kind of thing. His name's Charles Seaborn.'

'How about the phone?' Lange asked. 'You want it bugged, too? I got a two-for-one special on.'

'No, they wouldn't be that dumb.'

Lange spread another smile over his boxcarred face.

'Done.'

24

LIGHTNING PEOPLE

All the way back to the hotel I was thinking she had probably called and left a message cancelling out. It kept building up in my mind until I broke out in a sweat, the way you do when you want something so bad you're sure you won't get it. I started getting pissed and by the time I got to the hotel I had this dialogue between us worked out in my head. I would get it all off my chest, once and for all.

Then I got to the room and there were no phone calls or messages. It was almost a letdown.

I was still in a sweat so I peeled off my shirt and pants and sat down in front of the air conditioner in my shorts. I sat there until I got chilled. That took about fifteen minutes, which meant I had four more hours to go.

I kept waiting for the phone to ring, expecting her to call the whole thing off. The suspense was awful. I took the phone off the hook but it started screeching like bad brakes do and I hung it up. I sat on the bed and took it off the hook and waited until it screeched; then I'd depress the little bar and wait a minute and let it up again. I killed another fifteen minutes that way until my finger got tired.

About six o'clock I ordered a steak, potatoes, salad, and coffee. I had forgotten how bad room service food is until I took the first bite. I wasn't hungry anyway. The coffee was in one of those ugly purple Thermos pitchers that always look dirty and it was lukewarm but I drank it because it was something to do.

I was killing time. Hell, who am I kidding, I was watching it crawl by on its hands and knees, checking the clock every five minutes. In desperation I started to read Cisco's report on Dunetown. It might just as well have been written by the chamber of commerce for all it told me. I dropped it in the wastebasket and stared at the television set for another thirty minutes.

At about seven I decided to take a bath, soak my tired muscles, and kill another half hour. I turned on the spigots and the radio. The water was so hot it took ten minutes of juggling and dipping before I settled in. A bath is great therapy, particularly when it's just about too hot to bear. It opens up the head, clears away the cobwebs, helps you sort the real stuff from the bullshit. Kind of like meditation.

About ten minutes after I got into the tub the muses began to whisper to me. They were saying things I didn't want to hear. The muses don't always cooperate.

Wake up, Kilmer, the voices said, you made Dutch a promise. No scandal, you told him, and he took you at your word, no questions asked.

Wake up, Kilmer, you can't erase twenty years with a kiss and a smile and a roll in the hay. 1963 is history. You had prospects then. What have you got now? Stick spelled it out, the Holiday Fucking Inn, that's what you've got. Now that would really give Doe a laugh – for about the first five minutes.

Wake up, Kilmer. You don't even know what's real and what's fantasy anymore.

I was getting pretty fed up with the muses, and the radio didn't help. It was set on one of those easy-listening stations and Eydie Gorme was singing 'Who's Sorry Now?'. Just what I needed, background music with a sob in every note.

I lifted my foot and turned on the hot water with my toes and waited until I had to grit my teeth to stand it. The water was reaching the boiling point when I turned it off. That killed another fifteen minutes.

I needed to get a little perspective on things, separate what was real and what I wanted to be real. I needed to be objective.

But that's not what I did. What I did was think about that

place at the base of her throat, the soft spot, the one where you can see the pulse beating. I used to stare at it and count the beats. I could tell when she started getting excited.

I thought about the way she closed her eyes and parted her lips about a quarter of an inch when I was about to kiss her. She had the softest lips. You could get buried in those lips. I never felt her teeth. I don't know how she did it. Her lips were as soft as a down quilt.

Three years, that's how long I had waited, watching her grow from a fifteen-year-old tease to an eighteen-year-old woman, playing the brother-sister act when they came up to Athens for football weekends. That was to appease Chief. When she was about sixteen, her good-bye kisses started getting softer. And longer.

Talk about strung out.

Get off it, Kilmer. Think about something else. Details, concentrate on details. And events. Reality is what we're after here.

I concentrated on her eighteenth birthday party. It came to me in flashes, like a movie when the film breaks and they lose a few frames.

She wouldn't let me see her all that day. The way she acted, you'd have thought it was her wedding day. About midmorning Chief, Teddy, and I went to the Findley office on Factors' Walk. It was part of the ritual when we came down for the weekend, going to the office on Saturday morning. We had to wear ties and sports jackets, setting an example so the workers wouldn't get the feeling that they could take it easy because it was the weekend. Chief was big on setting examples. The office was only open half a day, so the employees thought they were getting a break. 'Give us four hours' jump on the competition come Monday morning,' Chief said with a wink. He winked a lot for emphasis, a habit Teddy had picked up.

He'd always pull off some kind of deal, usually on the phone, just to show us how it was done. When he was wheeler-dealing, his left eye would close about halfway. Teddy called it the Evil Eye. When the Eye started to narrow, watch out, he was on to something, closing in for the kill. It's one of the things the rich inherited, that predatory sense. I guess that's why they're rich – they have a built-in instinct for the jugular.

I never got a true handle on the business. They were into

everything. Cotton, shipping, real estate, industry, farming, you name it. All it did was bedazzle the hell out of me. I don't think Teddy got into it either. He was more interested in hell-raising. And poon. That's what he called it, poon. 'Let's go down to the beach, Junior, check out the poon.'

I got another flash. On that particular morning the office was closed in honour of Doe's eighteenth birthday. When we got there, the janitor let us in and we went up to the third floor. I always loved that building. It was all brass and oak and everything was oiled and polished so it sparkled.

Chief stood in his office, which seems now like it was maybe half the top floor. He stood there and swept his hand around.

'I'm going to divide this room up into three rooms, boys,' he said. 'I'll take this corner. One of you can have the river view; the other one, the park.' Then he flipped a coin.

'Call it, Jake,' he cried. I don't remember what I called. He covered the coin with his hand and peeked under it, looked up very slowly, and smiled at me. 'You win, Jake. Take your choice, river or park?' I figured Teddy wanted the river and he had a right to it because it was obviously the choice view, so I picked the park.

And I remember Chief looking at me and that left eye narrowing down for just an instant, and then he said, 'That's very generous of you, Jake.'

The Evil Eye. Looking back on it, I think Chief saw that move as a sign of weakness. To him, it was winner take all.

The more I got into it, the faster and faster the flashes came. The way the place looked. Daisies all over Windsong, hundreds of them. And candles – my God, there must have been ten thousand candles. It was a fire hazard there were so many candles.

And people. Three hundred maybe, the top of the list. Black tie, a live orchestra, champagne, the works. Chief had seen to that. It's what you call taste, another thing the born rich inherit.

'I got to give you credit, Junior,' Teddy had said as I was straightening his black tie. 'Three years, man, you really stick in there.'

Was that it? Was it a test?

Before the guests arrived, Chief took the two of us out onto the porch and popped a bottle of champagne and we stood there watching the sun go down. We drank a toast to Doe and threw our glasses at the big oak tree at the corner of the house.

'One more year, boys,' Chief said. 'And you'll be off to law school. The time'll fly. You'll be back here in business before you know it.'

That was another part of the trap, Chief laying it all out for us that way, planning our lives. Only then it felt good. When you're on the inside it always feels good. When he put his hand on my shoulder, there was lightning in his fingers. That's the way Chief was. That's the way all three of them were. They were Lightning People. You could feel their aura crackling around them.

'It's a helluva night, lads,' he said. He didn't know the half of it.

It was dark and all the candles were lit and the guests were all assembled when she made her entrance. I still have trouble breathing when I think about that moment. My mouth gets dry and my hands shake thinking about her walking into the eerie candlelight, dressed in white, with a scarlet sash that tightened her waist and moulded every magnificent line of her body. Talk about lightning. Everybody applauded when she came in. She went straight to Chief and kissed him. Chief always came first. Then she came to us and that soft spot was twitching like crazy and it was all I could do to keep my hands off her. It was like that all night. I couldn't get close enough to her. I guess I never will.

The party ended about three in the morning and we were all a little drunk from champagne. Teddy had latched on to this kind of dippy girl and the four of us piled into the dune buggy and drove out to the beach. He threw me the keys. He was in the back, working up a little poon. When we got in the car it was all Doe and I could do to keep our hands off each other. Well, we didn't. She leaned over and put her hand down inside of my thigh and wrapped her fingers around my knee and squeezed it hard and the electricity started humming.

When we got out there we took some dunes and spun around a few times in the moonlight. Teddy popped a bottle of champagne, shook it up, and used his thumb to squeeze off a stream of it. We were all soaked with champagne and the dippy girl jumped out and ran down to the surf and jumped in, clothes and all, Teddy right behind her. We drove off and left them there, clawing at each other in the surf.

And I remember Doe saying, 'Stop soon, Jake. Please!' I never heard that tone in her voice before. Husky, with a lot of breath behind it. I topped a dune and slammed on the brakes and we tumbled out before the buggy was fully stopped. It rolled down to the bottom of the hill and stalled.

We were like animals freed from a cage. Touching, feeling, pulling. I found the soft spot in her throat and when I kissed it I could feel her heart beating in my mouth and she cried out and pulled her dress down and her breasts jumped free and I slid my lips down to her and opened my mouth as wide as I could and sucked her up into it, feeling her nipple grow hard under my tongue. Then her hands reached down and found me and she turned me sideways and began stroking me. Finally I unzipped the dress and slid it down over her feet and she hooked her thumbs in the sides of her panties and slid them off too. Then she helped me undress and we lay back for a minute and just stared at each other. Then there was more touching and pulling and stroking until finally I felt her open under my fingertips and she pulled me over on top of her and guided me into her, enveloping me, crushing me, devouring me with her soft muscles . . .

Nice going, Kilmer. That's putting it all in the proper perspective. Objective, right?

Sure.

25

SILVER DOLLAR WOMAN

Oh, Jesus, just keep it in me!
Take it, take it all, baby.
Oh, God, don't stop!
You're all alike, can't get enough, can you baby?
Never!
There . . .
More . . . oh, yes, MORE!
There . . .
What are you doing?
There . . .
Come on, you bastard, fuck me!
Hereitcomes, hereitcomes . . .

OH . . . ohoh, nownow, ohoh, nownow . . .
Here comes the fuckin freight train!
Now . . . yes, now . . .
ONE potato, TWO potato, THREE potato, FOUR . . .
Oh, you . . . fucking . . . m-m-machine . . .
GodDAMN!
Don't stop now, oh, sweet Jesus, don't stop now!
Gonna . . . fuck you . . . dead . . . l-a-a-a-d-e-e-e
Oh . . . God . . . NOW!
Yeah.
NOW!
YEAH!
NOW . . .

Later . . .
I'm going to be sore for a week, you damn crazy . . .
Hey, you're the one keeps cryin' for more.
Yes. More.
Not enough anything for you, is there?
Not that.
Not just cock, ANYthing.
After tonight we'll have it all.
No such thing as ALL, baby. And no such thing as enough.
Fuck me again.
Gotta save up some spunk, lady. It's gonna be a long night.
When it's over . . .
We'll celebrate. I'll fuck your head off . . .
Promise?
You got it.
Crazy doin' it tonight.
When'll he be here?
Fifteen minutes.
That's takin' it to the edge.
I love it. Gimme a kiss.
Sure. So long, babe.

He caressed her throat with his thumbs, running them, side by side, from her collarbone up along her carotid to her chin and back and then again, and this time he pressed harder and her face bunched up.

Too hard . . .

Too late. His thumbs suddenly seemed to spasm, digging deep into both sides of her adam's apple.

136

Her eyes bulged, her tongue shot out, quivering obscenely.

He pressed deeper. Something cracked. She gagged, fought, tried to scratch.

He stopped suddenly, straightened up, struck her sharply with two fingers in the temple, and her life blinked out.

He rolled her over in the bed, arranged her as if sleeping, killed the light, and went to the window.

Ten minutes. Two black limousines pulled up. Four men jumped out of the first limo, perused the street. Two of them entered the apartment house while the other two waited at the door.

Footsteps on the stairs, some muffled talk. He moved silently across the room and entered the closet.

One of the men inside opened the front door of the apartment house and nodded to the two outside and one of them ran to the second car and opened the rear door. A tall, chunky man, whose face indicated that he had once been thinner, got out and hustled into the apartment. He was nattily dressed in a dark blue blazer, tan gaberdine pants, a pale blue shirt, and a dark striped tie. He climbed the stairs, nodded to the man by the door of the apartment, who went back down. The chunky man took out his key and let himself in.

The four men gathered just inside the front door of the apartment and started pitching silver dollars against the wall in the carpeted hallway.

The chunky man stood inside the doorway, looking at the woman on the bed, sleeping on her side, the bed a mess. He started getting hard, thinking about it. What a wanton bitch she was. He smiled and walked to the end of the bed and began to shake it very easily.

The closet door opened without a sound. The chunky man never heard anything until the whirr of the rope as it whipped around his throat, then the sudden, awful vice around his neck. He reacted almost instantly.

Almost.

A leg wrapped around both his legs and he lost his balance and fell forward on the bed. He was thrashing, trying to break loose, but the vice tightened.

He began to jerk . . .

And jerk . . .

And jerk . . .

Downstairs in the hall, the boys pitching dollars could hear the bedsprings squeaking.

That Tony, he didn't waste no time.
Fuckin' bull. Go on, Ricky, pitch.
The silver dollar twinkled as it soared down the hall and hit the
carpet and bounced against the wall.
And the winner sang:

'Yuh kin t'row a silver dollar, across thu floor,
It'll roo-ool, cause it's ro-ound,
Woman never knows what a good man she's got,
Until she lets him down.'

26

BUSINESS AS USUAL

After I got out of the tub and dried off, I went in and laid down
naked on the bed to cool off. I stared at the ceiling fan for a long
time. Objectivity is a painful enterprise at best, and I had avoided
it for twenty years. Now, as it grew dark outside, shadows
stretched across the room like accusing fingers pointing at me. In
the loneliness of the dark, romance wore off and reality took
over. Other memories started coming back to me. The past began
to materialise again, unfettered by candlelight and daisies. One
face emerged from the harsh shadows and began to taunt me. It
was Stonewall Titan.

I remembered Titan the night of the party, a little man, a shade
under five five, who chose not to wear a tux, opting instead for his
usual dark, three-piece winter suit, and arriving just minutes
before Doe made her entrance.

More than once during the evening I caught him staring across
the room at me with those agate eyes glittering in the candlelight.
I didn't pay any attention to it at the time; it didn't seem
important. Mr Stoney never smiled much anyway; he was a quiet
man, constantly introspective or contemplative or both, not an
uncommon demeanour for short people. But now, reflecting on
it, it strikes me that it was a hard look, almost angry, as if I had
offended him in some way.

After Doe came over and officially welcomed Teddy and me to

her party, after she had taken my hand and almost squeezed my fingers off and then drifted off to greet the rest of the guests, I worked my way across the room and greeted the taut little man. He stared up at me and said, 'You really stick to it, don't you, boy? Been waiting a long time for tonight.'

'What do you mean?' I had asked with a smile.

'Just don't count your chickens,' he said, and moved away.

That was the end of it. A caustic remark which he never repeated again during the summer I spent with the Findleys. I had forgotten it. Looking back on the moment, it occurred to me that the little man probably thought me unworthy of the Findley dowry. And since that night seemed to be the end of my probation period, he apparently had been overruled. After that, I was treated more like family than ever before. But Stonewall Titan never warmed up to me, I presume because I had offended him by going the distance.

Was I really being tested during those years or was it just my paranoia, an excuse to back away from another emotional commitment, to remain disconnected, as Stick called it? None of this had occurred to me at the time. When you're nineteen or twenty years old and it's all going your way, you don't think about such things.

But now in the darkness of the room, my suspicions were stirred.

Was that it? Was it all part of the Findley test? Were Doe and Teddy part of that three-year probation during which they sized me up and checked me out for longevity, consistency, durability, loyalty, all the *important* things? Perhaps I had never passed the test at all. Perhaps they had seen in me some fatal flaw that I myself did not perceive, something more ominous than bad ankles, something that did not prevent Teddy from accepting me as his best friend, but precluded my becoming one of the Findley inheritors. Perhaps my blood had never been blue enough.

Wake up, Kilmer.

Lying there, I began to feel like a piece of flux caught between two magnets. One drew me towards Doe and Chief and the sweet life that might still be there. The other, towards the Taglianis of the world, which was, ironically, a much safer place to be. In a funny way, I trusted the Taglianis precisely because I knew I *couldn't* trust them and there was safety in that knowledge.

A lot of raw ends were showing. It scared me. It clouded my judgment. Dunetown was dangerous for me. It was opening me up. My Achilles' heel was showing.

The magnets were drawing me out of my safe places.

I lay there, immobilised, staring at the lazy ceiling fan until the room was totally dark. At five past nine the phone rang. It rang for a long time. At twenty past, it rang again. I didn't move. I lay there like a statue. I couldn't talk to her, not right then. At nine thirty it rang twelve times; I counted them. After that every five minutes. At five to ten I heard a scratching at the door. It sounded like a cockroach crawling across a kitchen cabinet. I raised up on one elbow and looked over. There was a slip of paper under the door.

I picked it up and sat on the edge of the bed for a few minutes before I turned on the light. It was a phone message from Dutch Morehead.

Tony Logeto had made the list.

27

THE SINGING ROPE

It didn't take me five minutes to get dressed. As I hurried through the lobby towards the garage, the Black Maria roared into the motor lobby and screeched to a stop. The front door swung open and I crawled in. Stick dropped it into first and left an inch of rubber in the drive.

'I hope to hell the place isn't far,' I moaned.

'Ten minutes,' he said, putting the red light on the top of the car and flicking on the siren. It was the longest ten minutes of my life. We boomed south along the river where late-returning shrimp boats were reduced to streaks of light.

The place was near Back O'Town, a row house that had been converted into pleasant apartments facing the river. Flat roof, fancy front door; a classy-looking place. There were a lot of police cars parked haphazardly in the narrow street in front.

Cowboy Lewis was standing by the door, looking very unhappy.

'I fucked up,' he said tightly. 'They got by me.'

'Who got by you, Cowboy?' I asked.

'Whoever did them in,' he said, looking at my feet.

'Them?' Stick said.

'There's two of 'em,' he said, jabbing a thumb over his shoulder towards the building. 'Second floor in the front.'

'Who else?' I asked as we headed for the door.

'Della Norman,' he said.

A new name!

'Should that mean something to me?' I asked.

'She was Longnose Graves' favourite lady,' said Stick.

'Yeah, but she was in bed with Logeto when he got hit,' Lewis added.

I whistled through my teeth.

The mess was in a second floor bedroom.

'The singing rope,' I said, looking at the man's neck.

Dutch's 'Huh?' told me he had never heard of the trick.

'That's what the Vietnamese call it, the singing rope. A knock off of the Thuggee knot.'

It was also known among the British as the Bombay Burke – Bombay because the Thuggee stranglers operated in India, Burke being British slang for strangulation, named after an Englishman who tried to kill Queen Victoria, failed, and had his neck stretched for this trouble.

It had been more than a dozen years since I had last seen that particular kind of bruise. It was blood red and about the size of a half dollar, in the soft place at the base of Logeto's skull on the back of his neck. The deep, gnarled, bloody ring around his throat filled in the picture.

'Anybody else here?' Stick asked Dutch.

'Salvatore,' Dutch answered. 'He's out checking the neighbourhood.'

'I haven't seen a mark like that since Nam,' I said.

'Beautiful. What in hell next?' said the weary lieutenant.

Cowboy Lewis filled the doorway, the handle of a Cobra .357 looming from the front of his pants, right over the fly.

'If that goes off accidentally, you're gonna have to change your name,' Dutch said. Lewis didn't say anything. 'Okay,' said Dutch, 'let's have the long and short of it.'

'It's SOP, Logeto coming over here. It's every Monday night, rain or shine, six o'clock or close to it. He usually stays an hour,

141

hour and a half. He had two limos and four shooters. He goes in, the four goons start pitching coins in the hall. Two hours later the marks still there. About eight thirty I started getting nervous. Finally I decided to take the door, have a look.'

'By yourself, with four gorillas between you and Logeto? That don't call for backup in your book?' Dutch demanded.

Cowboy shrugged. 'I had buckshot loads in the Magnum. I got in, start up the stairs, get some shit, show the cannon. "You wanna get picked up in a dustpan, fuck around" is all I told 'em. I put my ear against the door, give a call or two. Nothin'. So I kicked it in.'

He swung his arm casually around the room, indicating what he had found.

The bed looked like a ploughed field. Covers and sheets half on the floor, pillows on head and foot. The woman lay on her side naked, her hair sprawled across her face. Logeto was on his face, fully dressed, both fists clutching the sheets, his feet hanging off the bed but not quite touching the floor.

'So that's Della Norman,' I said. Even in death, you could tell she was a dish.

'Apeshit,' Stick said.

'He means Longnose ain't gonna handle this too well,' Dutch said, and shook his head ruefully. 'A new wrinkle,' he went on. 'What in hell was Tony Logeto doin', shacked up with the Nose's favourite lady?'

The arrival of Chess, the ME, broke his thought train. Chess was short and on the tubby side, wearing old pants and a pyjama top stuffed half in and half out of his pants. He was not too happy about being there.

'And who do we have here?' he asked.

'Tagliani's son-in-law and Longnose Graves' girlfriend.'

Chess looked up with a lascivious grin. 'Isn't that interesting,' he said. 'It's the best part of the job, y'know, the inside stuff. I wonder how Longnose is going to take this.'

'Badly,' Stick chimed in.

Chess put down his black satchel. 'Ladies first. Let's get some pictures before I mess things up.'

The photographer appeared, shot the room top and bottom, and was gone in ten minutes. The doc stepped in and started his work, jabbering continually as he did.

'We got a simple strangulation here, on the woman. From the

142

front I'd say. See the thumbprints here on her larynx. Death was quick. My guess's her carotid, jugular, the whole shooting match in her throat is crushed. Powerful set of hands at work here.'

He kept probing, talking while studying the corpse.

'You gotta slow down there, Dutch. The freezer downtown is full and we don't have but five people in pathology and I got a vacation comin' up in three months. It would be nice to be finished by then.'

'Ho, ho, ho,' Dutch said, his sense of humour wearing thin, as was all of ours.

I looked around the apartment while the ME continued his work. It occupied the front side of the building. The living room, bedroom, and kitchen all faced the street. The place was decorated in early nothing. Expensive furniture that didn't go together. Her closet had enough clothes in it to start a salon.

The bathroom and several closets were adjacent to an alley that ran along the side of the building. There was only one door into the apartment, the one we had all come in through.

I ambled into the bathroom. It was large, with a double sink, commode, step-in tub, and stall shower.

The window over the commode was open and the curtains shifted idly in the breeze. I took a look out.

Straight up to the roof, straight down to the street.

I went back to the scene of the crime.

A new face had appeared. His name was Braun, out of homicide, a short, slender, hawk-faced man with age spots on the backs of his hands and dark hair turning white.

Braun said in a nasal voice, 'I hear, Dutch, that you're planning to retire tomorra. There won't be anything left for you t'do.'

Dutch said, 'Don't make me laugh too hard, I'll wet my pants.'

'How many is this between last night and tonight?' Braun asked, continuing to needle the big man. 'Got enough for a football game yet?'

'Just do yer job, okay, Braun? Leave the comedy to Bob Hope.'

The homicide cop looked down at Della Norman.

'Lookit that spook's tits. Bet there was some good pussy went through the window when she blinked out.'

'You want maybe we should all step out in the hall for a minute or two while you get a little?' Dutch chided.

'Up yours,' Braun said.

All class.

Chess finished his work on the woman and turned to Logeto.

'What've we got here?' Chess said. 'Looks as though there's been a hangin'.'

'Jake here says this job looks like an old Vietnam trick called the singin' string or something.'

'D'they learn it on *The Lawrence Welk Show*?' Braun asked.

'It's called the singing rope,' I corrected. 'The way it works, you take a rope, tie a knot halfway down it, and tie a small stick in the end. The Arvies would come up behind their target, whip the rope around his throat, catch the stick, and twist. The knot pops the main nerve in the back of the neck and paralyses the mark. After that, all it takes is about sixty seconds or so to finish the job.'

'You like havin' the Feds do yer thinkin' fer yuh?' Braun asked.

Cowboy Lewis made a growling sound deep in his throat and balled up his fists. Dutch laid a gentle hand on the big man's shoulder.

'Anybody touch anything up here?' Chess asked.

The Cowboy shifted from one foot to the other.

'I used toilet paper when I phoned it in. No prints,' Cowboy said.

'Excellent, m'boy. I see you teach them right,' Chess said to Dutch.

'Yeah, all yuh gotta do now's teach 'em to talk,' Braun said.

'Cowboy, g'downstairs, see what you can shake outta those dago coin-tossers,' Dutch said, probably saving Braun a trip to intensive care. When Lewis was gone, Dutch said to Braun, 'What's your problem, putz?'

'You and your special headquarters and shit,' said Braun. 'So far looks t'me like all you've done is fuck up.'

'You make a lot of noise for somebody with thirteen unsolved murders in his lap,' Dutch said.

Braun said, 'We got enough bodies downtown for one night.'

'Braun, you cry too much. You can't see straight through all the tears,' Dutch said.

'Fuck you,' Braun said.

Tension crackled in the room. Chess broke up the witty repartee.

144

'Well,' he said, 'if you two Shirtley Temples are tired of goosin' each other, I'd like to get this pair down on a slab and start work.'

'It ain't my beat anymore,' Dutch said. 'I get 'em alive, putz here gets 'em dead.'

'What's your guess about the time, Doc?' I interjected, hoping to ease things a little.

'I'd guess – and I'm guessing remember, don't hold me to this – I'd guess they were both killed close together, the girl first. One to two hours ago, give or take.'

It was ten thirty-five.

The ME turned Logeto's body over and the dead mobster lay on his back, staring sightlessly at the ceiling with his tongue stretched out of his mouth. The corpse was nattily dressed. His tie wasn't even loose.

An idea or two began to brew in my head.

I ambled out into the hall, found the stairs to the roof, and climbed up them. The door to the roof was unlocked. I checked it out, looking down to the open bathroom window and giving the brick wall a close check. There were three grooves in the ledge above Della Norman's bathroom window.

As I came back down I saw the Stick talking to one of the four coin-tossers, a weasel-faced little hood who stood sideways, looking off down the street someplace as he spoke, as if the Stick were not there.

Stick finally nodded and left his stoolie, entering the building and joining me on the second floor.

'I got sidetracked,' he said. 'That little shit I was talking to, his brother's in the dock waiting to be sentenced for pushing. He's hoping I'll go to bat, get the bastard a reduced sentence. But he doesn't know shit about what happened and neither do the other three. What he says, Logeto came here at six twelve. They saw him go into the girl's apartment, which is usual for Wednesday night. They heard some bedsprings rattling a coupla minutes later, figure Logeto was so horny he jumped right to it. They made a couple of jokes, then pitched dollars until Cowboy Lewis showed up and busted in.'

'Go take a look inside.'

We went back in the apartment together. Della Norman's body was already wrapped up and on a stretcher. The ambulance lads worked a body bag over Logeto's feet and wheeled both

145

bodies out. Braun followed them into the hall and Dutch, Stick, and I were alone in the room.

'What's this bit about them getting burked?' Dutch asked. 'What's that all about?'

Stick said, 'I saw this once down country. The CRIPS used it. Silent and quick.'

'What's a CRIP?'

'Combined Recon and Intelligence Platoons. They were kind of the army's on-the-spot Green Berets. Only they didn't have the training. They recruited everybody. Guys in the brig, misfits, old French Legionnaires, mercenaries, people who didn't want to come back after their tour was up. Basically they were assassination squads. Send 'em out, kill a village leader or a tax collector, some rebel leader who's getting a little muscle. Like that.'

Morehead shook his head. 'Different kind of army,' he said.

'You were in the army?' said Stick.

'Korea. Foot soldier. Sixteen months,' the big German said. 'You remember Korea, boys? Nowadays most people think Korea's the name of an all-night grocery stand.'

'Poor old Della,' the Stick said. 'Why would anybody want to ice her.'

'What about her?' I asked.

He shrugged. 'Della and I got along. I had occasion to bust her once. A pot charge. It was just a fishing expedition, see if maybe we could turn up something on Nose. She figured it out and took it like a sport.'

'Wonder what Logeto was doing with her.'

'Maybe she was just a good piece of ass,' the Stick conjectured. 'Wasn't he supposed to be the Taglianis' resident cocksman?'

'That's a simple enough explanation,' Dutch said.

I was barely listening. I was too busy wondering how Logeto and Della Norman had been killed without being seen or heard by four goons not twenty feet away in the hall.

'I can thing of one reason Della was killed,' I said.

'We're holding our breath,' said Dutch.

I did some verbal logic, to hear what the ideas sounded like:

'Logeto came here every Monday night. Whoever killed him knew that, knew what time he usually came, and he or she also knew that there was a lot of heat on. Getting past Logeto's bodyguards wouldn't be easy. So what's the answer? Come in first and kill the girl. Killer knew Logeto would come in alone;

146

he's too macho to have his boys sweep the place first. So he or she killed the girl and then waited. When Logeto came in, the killer burked him. Logeto never made a sound.'

'Then he or she dusted off through the bathroom using a dropline,' Stick finished.

'Except they went up, not down,' I said. 'And got away across to the roof next door so they wouldn't be seen from the ground.'

'That's probably how he got in,' Stick said. 'Went down the line, killed them both, then went back up.'

'Beautiful planning,' I said.

Dutch chewed that over for a moment or two. 'Yeah, I don't have a problem with that. Got a lot of guts, acing out a mobster with four of his handymen down the hall.'

'Yeah. Or desperate,' I said.

'Desperate?'

'Yeah. Either somebody with more guts than Moses or somebody who can't afford *not* to get it done.'

Dutch said, 'In that case, if it's Nance doing this number for Chevos, that leaves only Costello, Bronicata, Stizamo, O'Brian and Cohen left.'

'Five to go,' said Stick.

Dutch was leaning against the wall of the apartment with his hands stuffed deep in his pockets.

'It's the full moon,' he said woefully. 'Pregnant women have babies, men go apeshit. What can I tell yuh.'

'That's good,' the Stick said. 'That's what we'll tell the papers, that it was the full moon.'

28

DISAWAY

I went back to the hotel and went to bed.

The phone rang several times during the night. How many times, I couldn't tell you. Finally I put it on the floor, threw a pillow over it, and died. The next thing I knew, someone was trying to knock down my door. I flicked on the lamp, struggled into a pair of pants, and found Pancho Callahan standing on the threshhold.

'Change in plans' was all he said.

'Huh?' was all I could muster.

'Tried to call,' he said.

'Appreciate it,' I mumbled, and started back to bed.

'Going out to the track,' he said in his abbreviated patois.

'What, now?'

'Yep.'

'What time is it?'

'Five.'

'In the morning!'

'Yep.'

'Tuesday morning?'

I stared bleakly at him. He looked like a page out of *GQ* magazine. Grey cotton trousers, a tattersall vest under a blue linen blazer, pale blue shirt, a wine tie with delicate grey horses galloping aimlessly down its length, and a checkered cap, cocked jauntily over one eye.

He didn't look any more like a cop than John Dillinger looked like the Prince of Wales.

'Not on your life,' I croaked.

He put his hand gently on the door.

'Gonna be a great day.'

I was too tired to argue.

'Smashing.'

At exactly 5:15 we were in a red sports car with more gadgets than a 747, heading out into a damp, musty morning. As we crossed the tall suspension bridge to the mainland, we picked up fog so thick I couldn't see the shoulder of the road. Callahan, a tall, muscular chap, with high cheekbones and a hard jaw that looked like it might have been drawn with a T-square, chose to ignore it. He drove like it was a sunny afternoon on the interstate. I was beginning to think the whole bunch was suicidal.

'Foggy' was the only word out of him during the twenty-minute trip. Not a mention of the previous night's events.

He eased back on the throttle when we reached the entrance to Palmetto Gardens, tossed a jaunty salute to the guard, who had to look twice to see him through the soup, and parked near the stables.

'Here, pin this on your jacket,' he said, handing me a green badge that identified me as a track official. I did as I was told and followed him to the rail, which popped out of the damp haze so suddenly I bumped into it. So far, all I could tell about the track was that it was in Georgia and about twenty minutes from town, if you drove like Mario Andretti.

'Wait here,' Callahan said, and disappeared for five minutes. I could hear, but not see, horses snorting, men coughing, laughter, and the clop of hoofs on the soft earth as I stood in fog so thick I couldn't see my own feet. When Callahan returned, he brought black coffee in plastic foam cups and warm, freshly made sinkers. I could have kissed him.

'What the hell are we doing out here?' I asked, around a mouthful of doughnut.

'Workin' three-year-olds,' he answered.

'That's it? That's what we're doing here in the middle of the night? Listening to them work the three-year-olds?'

'So far.'

'Is this something special? How often do they do this?'

'Every morning.'

'You're shitting me.'

He looked at me through the fog and shook his head.

'You're not shitting me. Great. I got dragged out of bed for, uh . . . to stand around in this . . . this *gravy* listening . . . just *listening* . . . to a bunch of nags doing calisthenics.'

Callahan turned to me and smiled for the first time. 'Flow with it, pal. You're here, enjoy it. Put a little poetry back in your soul.'

'What are you, some kind of guru, Callahan?'

'Horse sense. Besides, Dutch says you need to learn about the track.'

'I can't even see the track. And don't call me pal. I'm not a dog, my name's Jake.'

'Sure.'

He moved down the rail and I followed. Dim shapes began to take form in the fog. The outriders were leading their riderless charges through an opening in the fence and out onto the track.

'This is the morning workout,' Callahan said. 'Gets the kinks out of the ponies.' He pointed to a stately looking cinnamon-brown gelding, frisky and hopping about at the end of its tether. 'Keep your eye on that boy there,' he advised.

'What about him?' I asked.

149

'That's one fine horse.'

'Oh.'

'If you don't mind my asking,' he said, 'just how much do you know about racing?'

I had been to the horse races twice in my life, both times out in California with Cisco Mazzola, who loved three things in life: his family, vitamins, and betting the ponies, and I'm not real sure in what order. Both times I had lost a couple of hundred dollars I couldn't afford to lose making sucker bets. After that, Cisco stopped inviting me.

I said, 'I know the head from the tail and that's about the size of it.'

'That's okay,' Callahan said, although he seemed surprised at my ignorance. 'Keep your ear open, I will give you the course.'

Before the day was out, I was to learn a lot about Pancho Callahan and a lot more about racing, for he talked to me constantly and it was like listening to a poet describe a beautiful woman.

'First, I will tell you a little about Thoroughbreds,' he said. 'Thoroughbreds are different from all other animals. Thoroughbreds are handsome, hard, spooky, temperamental. They are independent and proud. And they are also conceited as hell because, see, they *know* how good they are. The jockey, if he is worth his weight, he takes his kid in tow and he talks to him and he disciplines him around the track. The trainer may tell the jock how he wants him to run the race, like maybe hold the pony in until the backstretch or let him loose at the five-eighths pole or the clubhouse turn, like that, but once that gate opens up, it is just the jock and the horse and that is what it's all about.'

In the fog, with the sun just beginning to break behind the large water oaks nearby, we could hear the horses but not see them until they were on top of us. The three-year-old gelding was frisky and playful and the outrider was having trouble with him. He was snorting and throwing his long neck across the saddlehorn of the outrider and trying to bite his hand as they galloped past in the fog, which was eerily magenta in the rising sun's first light.

It was one hell of a sight. Callahan was right, there was poetry here.

The three-year-old was to become a lot more important than

150

either Callahan or I realised then. His name was Disaway. And on this particular morning, he wanted to run.

'He is full of it,' Callahan said. 'A real Thoroughbred feeling frisky. Is that a sight?'

I allowed as how it was a sight.

'Thoroughbreds are trained to break fast out of the gate and open up and run quickly and flat away to the finish line, save up a little extra and put it on hard near the end, like a swimmer doing the two twenty,' Callahan said. 'This horse wants to go, so they have to calm him down a bit. Otherwise he will be too brash and spooky when the rider is up.'

So they were not running hard and instead were trotting in and out of the cotton wads of fog, working out the early morning kinks. When they brought him in, he made one more halfhearted effort to bite the outrider and then, hopping slightly sideways, he kicked his heels a couple of times and settled down. The trainer led him to the tie-up to be saddled.

Disaway was a fine-looking animal with very strong front legs and a sweat-shiny chest, hard as concrete. The muscles were quivering and ready. Callahan walked close and stroked first one foreleg, then the other, then strolled back to the rail.

No comment.

The owner was a short, heavy man in a polo shirt with a stop-watch clutched in a fat fist and binoculars dangling around his neck. His name was Thibideau. He stood with his back to the jockey, chewing his lip. When he spoke, his voice was harsh and sounded it was trapped deep in his throat.

'Okay,' he said, without turning around or looking at the rider, 'let's see what he can do. You open him up at the three-quarter post.'

The exercise rider looked a little surprised and then said, 'The three-quarter, yes, sir.'

They threw the saddle over the gelding's back, all the time talking to him and gentling him, and got ready to let him out.

'All these characters are interested now,' Callahan said. 'The track handicappers, the owners, the trainers, the railbirds – all standing by to see just how much horse he is today.'

The exercise rider led the gelding out onto the track, lined him up, and then, standing straight up in the stirrups and leaning far over the horse's mane, egged him on until he stretched out his long legs and took off down the track into the fog. Half a dozen stopwatches clicked in unison somewhere in the mist.

I could hear him coming long before he burst through the haze, snorting like an engine, his hoofs shaking the earth underfoot. Then, pow! he came out of it and thundered past us, his head up and his mane waving like the flag. The watches clicked again Callahan looked at the chronograph on his wrist.

Still no comment.

'Let's get some breakfast,' he said. 'The jockeys'll be showing up about now.'

I watched Disaway as they led him out to be hosed and squeegeed down and fed. His nostrils were flared open, his ears standing straight up and slightly forward, and there was a look of defiant madness in his eyes. I was beginning to understand why Pancho had a thing about Thoroughbreds.

'Well, what do you think?' I asked as we walked down the shedrows.

'About what?'

'What was all that about, feeling the horse's legs, the stopwatches, all the inside track stuff?'

'Well, he's not a bad kid,' Callahan said as we walked through the dissipating fog. 'He's strong, good bloodlines, has good legs, but he's a mudder. He just does okay on the fast track. If I were a betting man I'd put my money on him to show. He's about half a length short of a champion.'

'You got all that from feeling his forelegs?'

'I got all that from reading the racing form.'

As we walked past the shedrows and headed across a dirt road towards the jockeys' cafeteria, I saw a dark blue Mercedes, parked near the stables. It was empty. I looked around, trying not to be obvious, but the fog was still too heavy to see anybody farther away than twenty feet.

'Old Dracula's here,' Callahan said.

'Dracula?'

'Raines. The commissioner.'

'You don't like him?' I found myself hoping Callahan would say no.

'Runs a tight operation. Like him a lot better if he had blood in his veins. One cold piece of work. That's his wife right over there.'

It caught me by surprise. I turned quickly, getting a glimpse of

152

Doc through the fog, talking nose to nose with a horse in one of the stables. Then the mist swirled back around her and she vanished.

'Let's mosey to the commissary,' Callahan said. 'Grab some groceries. Listen to the jocks and trainers.'

I didn't know Callahan well, but he was acting like a man who's on to something.

The fog had lifted enough for me to see the contours of the cafeteria, a long, low clapboard building. The dining room was a very pleasant, bright room that smelled of fresh coffee and breakfast. It was about half-filled with track people: jocks, trainers, owners, handicappers, exercise riders, stewards. The talk was all horses. Mention Tagliani to this group, they'd want to know what race he was in and who was riding him.

I stayed close to Callahan, ordered a breakfast that would have satisfied a stevedore, and listened. Callahan was as tight with these people as a fat man's hand in a small glove. He talked to the track people from one side of his mouth and me from the other:

'The little guy with the hawk nose and no eyes, that's Johnny Gavilan. Very promising jock until he took a bad spill at Delray a couple years ago. Turned trainer . . .'

Or:

'The little box in the coat and cap is Willie the Clock, the track handicapper. He works for the track and sets the beginning odds for each race. Knows more about horses than God and he's just as honest . . .'

Or:

'The guy in the red sweater, no hair, that's Charlie Entwhistle. A great horse breeder. Started out as a trainer, then won this horse called Justabout in a poker game. At first it was a joke because old Justabout was just about the ugliest animal God ever created. He had no teeth. He'd stand around the paddock munching away on his gums and from the front he looked bowlegged. People would come down to the paddock, stick their tongues out at him, throw things at him, laugh at him. The Toothless Terror they called him, and he didn't look like he could beat a fat man around the track.

'Everybody was laughing at Charlie Entwhistle.

'But it turns out there's only one thing Justabout was any good for, and that was running. He not only loved to run, he couldn't stand for anything to be in front of him. Brother, could that kid

153

run. He was home in bed before the rest of the field got to the wire. He rewrote the record books, made Sunday school teachers out of a lot of horseplayers, and he made old Charlie Entwhistle rich.'

Callahan looked at me and smiled.

'And that's what horse racing's all about.'

We had finished breakfast, and he picked up his coffee. 'Now let's go to work,' he said, and we moved towards the other side of the room.

29

MAGIC HANDS

'Just listen,' Callahan said as we drew fresh cups of coffee, though I hadn't so much as cleared my throat for the last thirty minutes.

'Every day of the season, Willie the Clock judges the top three horses in each race and sets the opening odds. His choice is printed in the programme as a service to the betters. No guarantees, of course, but that doesn't matter. The players are always pissed at him. He's maybe the best handicapper in the business, but it's a thankless damn job.'

'Why?'

'Because favourites lose more than they win. They get a bad break out of the gate or get caught in a traffic jam in the backstretch and can't find a slot. Here comes a long shot paying thirty to one and the players yell 'boat race'. Everybody wants to lynch Willie.'

We sat down next to the square little man, who was about sixty, had a face the texture of weatherbeaten wood, wore the same coat, rain or shine, winter or summer, and had a black cap pulled down hard over his eyes. His binoculars were as big as he was. He didn't talk much and was very cautious about his clipboard, which is where all his information was scribbled.

He peered suspiciously from under the peak of his cap, recognised Callahan, gave him what I assume passed for a smile for Willie, and scowled at me.

'This's Jake, Willie,' said Callahan. 'He's on our side.' Willie grunted and returned to his breakfast.

'What's lookin' good?' Callahan asked.

The little man shrugged and ate a while longer. We sipped coffee while Callahan eyeballed the room. He nudged me once and nodded towards a wiry little guy, obviously a jockey, who came into the restaurant and sat by himself in a corner. The newcomer didn't look a day over fifteen and wouldn't have weighed a hundred pounds in a diving suit.

'Ginny's Girl looks good in the fifth,' Willie said finally, then closed up for another five minutes. Callahan didn't press but finally said, 'How about Disaway?'

Willie looked at him from the corner of his eye.

'Something special?' he asked.

Callahan shrugged. 'Just wondering, y'know, after he dozed off in the stretch Sunday.'

'He's lookin' fair.'

Another minute or so of silence, then:

'Not too crazy this morning; clocked out at 3:22. Not bad since they opened him up at the three-quarter and he's usually a stretch runner . . .'

He washed down a piece of dry toast with a gulp of black coffee, searched for something in the corner of his mouth with a forefinger, then added:

'Track gets a little harder later in the day, he may tiptoe around. Right now I'd say he's a toss-up to place behind Polka Dits, who was kinda wild at the workout.'

'Talk at ya,' Callahan said, and we moved on again.

'You get all that?' he asked when we were a respectable distance from Willie.

'I think so,' I said. 'If the track's hard, Disaway'll probably fold in the stretch again. If it stays soft, he could come in second.'

'Very good. You're learning.'

'The little guy you gave me the nudge on,' I said. 'What was that all about?'

'That's Scoot Impastato. Out of Louisiana. Started racing quarter horses when he was thirteen. Moved up to Thorough-breds when he was sixteen, if you believe his birth certificate. He's a seasoned jockey, great legs, magic hands, and he's all of twenty, soakin' wet.'

'Very impressive,' I said. 'So why the nudge?'

155

'He was riding Disaway on Sunday,' Callahan said, and headed towards the little guy.

The jockey, Scoot Impastato, was a man in a child's body, with a voice that sounded like it was still trying to decide whether it was going to change or not. Right now it was kind of low choirboy. But the boy had hands made of stainless steel.

'Hey, Mr Callahan,' he said as we sat down.

'How they runnin', Scoot?' Callahan asked.

'So-so,' the youngster answered. 'You know how it goes – some days it don't pay to answer the call.'

'Still upset about the race Sunday?' Callahan said. He was fishing. I don't know much about horse racing but I know fishing when I hear it.

The kid chuckled 'Which one?' he asked. 'I was up four times and I ran out of the money four times.' He seemed to be taking it in stride.

'Well, maybe it was some little thing, y'know, maybe you handled them a little different than usual and they got pissed. You know Thoroughbreds.'

He laughed aloud. 'I oughta,' he said. He poured half his cup of coffee into an empty water glass and filled the cup with cream until it looked like weak chocolate milk, the way New Orleanians like it.

He added some sugar and kept talking as he stirred it up. 'Once at Belmont I was up on Fancy Dan, fifty wins in two seasons, the horse couldn't lose. He went off a three-to-two favourite. The bell rings, the gate pops, he just stands there! I'm whackin' him with the bat, I'm bootin' hell outta him, I'm cussin' him, I'm sweet-talkin' him. He ain't goin' nowhere, he just stands there lookin' at the crowd and smellin' the grass. For all I know, he's still standin' there.'

'So what happened with Disaway?'

Definitely fishing.

'Crapped out,' he said with an aimless shrug. 'He came outta that three stall like Man O' War and led the pack all the way around the backstretch; then we come into the clubhouse and all of a sudden he starts fallin' asleep on me. Midnight Star comes by like we was stopped for gas, then half the field passes us. I guess he just decided to walk home. I was yellin' at him just to keep him awake.'

'How'd he look in the morning workout?'

156

'Fine. Not too spooky. Ran good. Two-tenths ahead of his usual speed.'

'Well,' Callahan said, 'at least he got out of the gate.'

'Sunday was like that. Seems every horse I rode wanted to be someplace else for the day. Well, it's Thoroughbreds for you, like you said.'

His breakfast came. Steak, three eggs, and grits, and he dug in. I wondered how he stayed so small. Callahan kept fishing.

'You up on Disaway today?'

'Nope. No more. Got me another ride. Chigger Bite.'

'How come?'

'Me and Smokey had it out. After the race he starts chewin' my ass for lettin' Disaway out early. Finally I says, "Hey, it wasn't me, it was Mr Thibideau," and he looks at me like he thinks maybe I'm lyin' or somethin'. Who needs that shit anyways? The owner says let him loose at the five-eighths, I let him loose at the five-eighths.' And he laughed again. 'Maybe he thought the seven-eighths pole was the wire.' He kept talking while he ate. 'It ain't like it was some big surprise. Hell, we been talkin' about it. Mr Thibideau wanted to try a change-up, letting him out at the five-eighths 'stead of the stretch, maybe cut a coupla tenths off his time. He just didn't have anything left for the stretch. Anyways, I never argue with the owners.'

'You didn't disagree with Thibideau, then?'

'Not out loud. Hell, he comes up just before post time, tells me boot him on the backstretch, and that's what I did. I just figure you want to try a change-up, why do it when you're the favourite? I'd rather wait until we're not on the board – nothin' to lose that way.'

'Well, he probably had his reasons.'

'Afterwards he comes up, says he's sorry, and gives me a double century, make up for the purse. "I made a mistake" is all he says.'

'He had the exercise boy break him out at the three-quarters again this morning,' Callahan said casually over his coffee cup.

'Disaway's a marginal. Put him in a field with a bunch of heavyweights he might pull in third if he's feeling just right, it's been raining, track's soft, like that. Give him a little mud, a slow field, he takes the money.'

'Thibideau ought to handicap him a little better.'

'Mr Thibideau, he keeps tryin', y'know, hopin' the horse'll

show a little more stamina. You wanna know what I think, the pony's a stretch runner. He don't have it to run wide open then last three furlongs. Also he was favouring his left front gam. Anyways, I got another ride.'

'When was he favouring the leg?'

'Just after the race. Probably got a pebble in his shoe. I told Smokey about it.'

'Well, good luck today,' Callahan said, and we moved outside.

The fog had burned off and left behind a beautiful day, with a cool breeze under a cloudless sky.

Callahan said, 'That was probably Greek to you.'

'I followed it pretty well. I just don't understand the drift of it all.'

As we walked around the corner of the cafeteria, I got my first good look at the track and whistled between my teeth.

'Impressive, huh?' Callahan said.

Impressive was an understatement.

It sprawled out in the morning sun, a white structure framed against a forest of trees. It was three tiers high with cupolas on each end and a glass clubhouse that stretched from one end of the top floor to the other. The designer had modelled the building after Saratoga and other venerable tracks. It looked like it had been there for fifty years. There were azalea gardens to give it colour and giant oak trees standing sentinel at its corners. Great care had obviously been taken to remove only those trees necessary. The parking lot even had free standing oaks and pines breaking up the blacktop. It was a stunning sight and, I had to admit, a tribute to Harry Raines' taste. The clubhouse windows sparkled in the morning sun, and in the infield the grass was the colour of emeralds.

'Wow!' I said.

'Some nice operation,' Callahan agreed.

The Mercedes was gone.

I decided to get back to the subject at hand.

'Why are you so interested in Disaway?' I asked.

'He was two horse in the third race Sunday.'

'Is that good luck or something?'

'Remember the tape Sunday night?'

'How could anybody forget it?'

'You forgot something,' Callahan said. 'Tagliani told Stinetto it was a fix for the four horse in the third heat.'

158

'I still don't get the point.'

'The four horse was Midnight Star. He went off as place favourite, eight to one, won, paid a bundle. The favourite was Disaway. Wasn't set up for Midnight Star to win, was set up for Disaway to lose. No sense any other way. Sunday, everything was A-one for him, up against a weak field, track was soft, he went off a five-to-two favourite. Strolled in eighth.'

'Eighth!'

'It can happen. We all have bad days.'

'So the trick was to slow Disaway down?' I said.

Callahan nodded. 'Midnight Star romped first, paid $46.80. You bet Midnight Star, you got $46.80 for every two bucks you put down. Figure it out, bet a thousand bucks, go home with $23,400 smackers – not a bad day's work. My way of thinking, Disaway wasn't just having a bad day Sunday.'

'Supposing Midnight Star had a bad day?'

Callahan smiled. 'That's horse racing,' he said.

'How did they do it? Make him lose, I mean?'

'Lots of ways. Legal ways.'

'You think the jockey was in on it.'

'Maybe, not likely. Scoot doesn't like Thibideau or the trainer. He's a straight-up kid; like to think it wasn't him.'

'How about the trainer?'

'Smokey? Maybe again, but he was pissed because he thought the boy booted the horse early. Didn't know Thibideau told him to.'

'So that makes it the owner?'

'Looks that way. Thing is, Tagliani knew about it. Tagliani got wasted couple of hours later. Maybe there's no connection, but got to think about the possibilities.'

'So what do we do about it, go to Raines?'

'Can't. Illegal wiretap. Dutch can't afford to have anybody know about it. No tape, all we got's guesswork.'

'So we forget it?'

'I don't forget it,' he said ominously. 'Happens once, it'll happen again.'

30

INVITATION

'I was tired of the track and anxious to get back to town. There were a lot of loose ends that needed tying up and I suddenly felt out of touch with things. It was pushing noon, so I told Callahan I needed to make a phone call or two and then I'd grab a cab back to town.

'Stick's on his way out,' Callahan said. 'Back gate, fifteen minutes.'

'How do you know that?' I asked, wondering whether Callahan was psychic in addition to his other talents.

'Arranged it last night,' he said, and added in his cryptic dialogue, 'Due at the clubhouse. See ya.'

'Thanks for the education,' I said.

Callahan stood for a moment appraising me and then nodded. 'Disaway runs Thursday afternoon. Ought to be here.'

'It's a date,' I said.

He started to leave, then turned back around and offered me his hand. 'You're okay,' he said. 'Like a guy who listens. Thought maybe you'd turn out to be a know-everything.'

'What I don't know would fill the course.'

'You know plenty,' he said, turning and heading across the infield towards the clubhouse.

I went looking for a phone to check the hotel for messages. By daylight, I had started having second thoughts about the night before. I knew some of the phone calls had been from Dutch. I wondered whether any of them had been Doe calling.

I was walking past the stables when I heard her voice.

'Jake?'

The voice came from one of the stalls. I peered inside but saw nothing, so I went in cautiously. I could hear a horse grumbling and stomping his foot and the pungent odour of hay and manure tickled my nose, but my eyes were slow adjusting to the dark stable after leaving the bright sunlight.

'Are you going blind in your old age?' she said from behind

160

me. I turned around and she was standing in the doorway, framed against the brash sunlight, like a ghost. My eyes gradually picked out details. She was all dolled up in jodhpurs, a Victorian blouse with a black bow tie, and a little black derby. Twenty years vanished, just like that. She looked eighteen again, standing there in that outfit, scratching her thigh with her riding crop. My knees started bending both ways. I felt as awkward as a schoolboy at his first dance.

'You could have called,' she chided, as if she were scolding a kid for stealing cookies.

'I got tied up,' I said.

She came over to me and ran the end of the riding crop very gently down the edge of my jaw and down my throat, stopping at the soft depression where the pulse hides.

'I can see your heart beating,' she said.

'I don't doubt it for a moment.'

'Can you forgive me?'

'For what?'

'Twenty years ago?'

'There's nothing to forgive,' I lied. 'Those things happen.'

She shook her head slowly and moved closer. 'No,' she said, 'there's a lot to forgive. A lot to forget, if you can forget that kind of thing.'

'What kind of thing?'

'You know what I'm talking about,' she said evasively.

'Look, Doe, I . . .'

She put the tip of the crop against my lips, cutting off the sentence.

'Please don't say anything. I'm afraid you're going to say something I don't want to hear.'

I didn't know how to answer that, so I just stood there like a fool, grinning awkwardly, wondering if we could be seen from outside the stall. If we could, it didn't seem to concern her. She stepped even closer, put the riding crop behind my neck, and, holding it with both hands, drew me closer. Her mouth opened a hair, her eyes narrowed.

'Oh, God, I'm so sorry,' she whispered. 'I never wanted to hurt you. I didn't know Chief had written that letter until Teddy told me. You just stopped writing and calling, like you'd died.'

'The phone works both ways,' I heard myself say, and I

161

thought, Shut up, you fool, play it out. Let her talk. You've been dreaming about this moment for twenty years; don't blow it now.

'Pride,' she said. 'We all have our faults. That's one of my worst. I wanted to write, then Teddy told me to leave you alone. He said you'd had enough. Please forgive me for being so foolish.'

I wondered if she really thought we could puff off twenty years so easily. Say we're sorry and forget it. Was she that sure of my vulnerability? The armour started slipping around me but she moved closer, six inches away, and shaking her head gently, she breathed, 'There will never be anyone like you for me. Never again. I've known it ever since I lost you, just as I knew you wouldn't come last night.'

'How did you know that?' I said, my voice sounding hoarse and uncertain.

'Because I don't deserve it,' she said, and her lips began to tremble. 'Because I wanted you to come so much and – '

'Hey, easy,' I said, putting a finger against that full, inviting mouth.

What's happening here? I thought. How about all the decisions I had silently made to myself the night before? Is this all it takes to break old Kilmer down?

Yeah, that's all it takes.

Then she closed her eyes, and her lips spread apart again, and she moved in and it was like the old days. I got lost in her mouth, felt her tentative tongue taking a chance, and responded with mine. And then she was in my arms and it was all I could do to keep from crushing her. I felt her knee rubbing the outside of mine, heard the riding crop fall into the sawdust, felt her hands sliding down the small of my back, pressing me closer to her.

I forgot all the things I was going to say to her. The accusations, the questions that would clear up the dark corners of my mind. Whatever anger lurked inside me vanished at that moment. I slid my hands down and felt the rise of her buttocks and pressed her to me.

'Oh, Jake,' she said huskily, 'I wish it was that summer again. I wish the last twenty years never happened.'

Don't we all, I thought; wouldn't that be nice. But I didn't say it.

'Forget all that,' I mumbled without taking my lips away. 'Nothing to forgive.'

162

'Oh, Jake, I want it to be like it used to be,' she said, with her lips still brushing mine. 'Come tonight. Please come tonight. Don't stay away again.'

And without thinking anymore about it, I said, 'Yes.' And I knew I meant yes. I knew I would go and the hell with Dutch and the Taglianis and the hell with safety and distance and vulnerability. I would go because I wanted to and because it was my payoff for twenty years. I said it again. And again.

'Yes . . . yes . . . yes.'

31

UP JUMPS THE DEVIL

When I left the stable, the first person I saw was Stick. He was leaning against the dreaded black Pontiac and was looking right at me when I came out. She was a couple of feet behind me, standing inside the stall but visible nevertheless. His expression never changed; he simply looked the other way as he took out a cigarette and lit it up.

'Later,' I said quietly, without turning, and walked straight to the car. Stick had traded in his slept-in seersucker for a pair of ratty chinos, dirty tennis shoes, and a black boatneck T-shirt, but the brown fedora was still perched on the back of his head.

'Sorry if I'm late,' I said, staring out the windshield.

'First things first,' he said, swinging around and heading back out the gate.

We drove a couple of minutes in silence and I finally said, 'That wasn't what it looked like.'

'I didn't see a thing.'

'Look, I knew her a long time ago. It's no big thing.'

'No big thing. Gotcha.'

'It's no big thing!'

'Jake, it's nothing to me,' he said. 'See no evil, hear no evil, that's me.'

'What do you mean, evil!'

'It's a saying. Hey, there's no need to be touchy, man.' He drove a moment or two more and added, 'I admire the hell out of the way you gather information.' And he started to laugh. I started to get burned, then he looked over at me and winked. He reminded me of Teddy. I was waiting for him to add the 'Junior' on the end of the sentence. I started laughing too.

'Shit,' I said.

'Is it that important?'

'I don't know,' I said with disgust. 'It's one of the balls I've been juggling.'

I was surprised at how easily it came out.

'Well, if you want an amateur's opinion, I sure wouldn't throw that one away.'

'Her husband's the fucking racing commissioner,' I said.

'I know who her fucking husband is,' he said with a chuckle. 'Anybody who's been in town for fifteen minutes knows who her husband is.'

More driving. More silence. Then he started to chuckle again. 'I got to tell you, Jake, I really do admire your style.'

'It hasn't got anything to do with the job,' I told him. 'This is old, personal business. Something that was never finished properly.'

'O-kay,' he said, drawing out the 'Oh' for about five minutes. 'Well, I'm glad you're doing it up right this time.'

'Don't be an asshole,' I grumbled.

'Why don't you talk about it?'

'I don't want to talk about it.'

'Okay.' A long pause. 'But I know you want to.'

'I don't want to talk about anything!'

'It's just like the blues. I can tell.'

'Damnit, Stick, drop it.'

'Done,' he said, and dropped it. I didn't. He was right – I had to get it off my chest.

'There was a time – in my . . . late-blooming youth – when I thought I was going to marry her. I took it for granted, one of my more spectacular mistakes.'

'Marry her, huh. Shit, you do have a problem.'

'It's no problem.'

'Hey, this is the Stick, my friend. You can bullshit me about not finishing things properly and all that crap, but don't tell me it's no problem.'

'It's no problem,' I said emphatically. It sounded more like I was trying to convince myself than him.

164

'Jake, getting into it is never the problem. Getting out of it, that's the problem.'

'I'm already out of it. What I'm trying to avoid is getting back in.'

'Oh, that's what you're trying to do?'

'Yes!'

'You got a unique approach,' he said, and after a few seconds he asked, 'Are you still in love with her?'

'Shit.'

'No shit.'

I sighed. 'Hell, I don't know. Maybe I'm in love with the idea of her. Maybe I never took the time to get out of love with her. I haven't worked it out.'

'When are you going to see her again?'

I had a moment of panic, as though I'd told him too much already. The old paranoia.

'What time tonight are you going to see her?' he repeated.

'Who says I'm going to see her tonight?'

He shot me another crazy smile.

'Nine o'clock,' I said.

'You need some backup?'

'Don't get funny.'

'I don't mean that, Jake,' he said seriously. 'I mean do you want me to cover you? Keep an eye on the place, make sure nobody's hounddogging you? What I'm trying to say is, I'm for you. Whatever it means to you, I hope it comes out right.'

I was moved by his concern. There was a lot of Teddy in Stick. But I was wary of him. I was wary of everybody. I had taken two steps, back to back. First opening up to Doe, and now Stick. I was moving farther away from my safe spots. It scared hell out of me.

'I shouldn't have come back to this fucking place,' I snapped finally.

'Aw, c'mon,' he said. 'Then you wouldn't have met me. I'm the magic man, my friend. I can wave my hand and make the impossible come true.'

'Where are we going?' I asked, deciding to change the subject.

'City docks.'

'What's out there?'

'We got a surprise for you.'

'Who's "we"?'

'Me and Zapata.'

'Well, try to keep it under ninety, will you?'

'The Bird here runs a little rough under ninety,' he said, grinning as he patted the steering wheel.

'Too bad about the Bird,' I said. 'I run a little rough over ninety. What happens at the city docks?'

'The shrimpers unload there,' he said, as if that explained everything. I decided to be surprised and said no more.

He turned right onto Front Street and drove slowly in the direction of the beach. In the first two blocks I saw six hookers, working in pairs. Two were chatting with a very friendly policeman whose hands moved from one rear end to the other throughout the conversation; another pair was negotiating something with a middle-aged couple in a Winnebago wearing Iowa plates; and two more almost jumped in front of the car trying to get our attention. After that I lost interest.

'I took a detour. This is the scenic route,' Stick said as I watched the strip joints, lingerie stores, and porno houses glide past the window. 'I thought you'd like to see it in the daytime.'

'So this is what America's all about,' I said. 'Fifty-year-old swingers in recreation vans are replacing Norman Rockwell, Stick. The Front Streets of America are replacing Bunker Hill. Whatever happened to Beaver Cleaver and the father who knew best and the days when a major crisis was whether Rickie was going to run out of gas in the Nelsons' Chevy?'

'Who's Beaver Cleaver?' he said, sarcastically.

When I'd seen enough, Stick turned off Front, went two blocks north, and turned east on Ocean Boulevard. There was very little traffic to disturb the palmettos, palm trees, and azaleas that lined the divided highway. It looked much better in the daylight, without benefit of Day-Glo streetlights.

The day had turned hot and humid and we drove with the windows down, back over the bridge to Thunderhead Island and past the entrance to the track. We were still an island away from the ocean, but I could feel the air getting cooler.

I was remembering Oglethorpe County twenty years ago, and riding the two-lane blacktop out to the beach on warm summer nights. The county spread out over six or seven islands and the people had a fierce kind of pride that all islanders seem to possess, an independence which, I suppose, comes from living in a place that is detached from the mainland. The islanders I knew

166

didn't give a damn what anybody else thought or did. They did it their own way.

'Y'know, years before booze was legal in the state, drinks were sold openly across the bar in this county,' I told him. 'They called it the free state of Oglethorpe.'

'Breaking the law in those days had a certain charm to it,' he said. 'That's probably where Titan's power started.'

I had never thought about it before, but Stick was probably right. That's where the patronage had begun. God knows where it had spread.

'What do you think of Titan?' I asked.

'The toughest seventy-five-year-old man I ever met,' he said emphatically.

Twenty years had transformed Thunderhead Island from a deserted, marshy wonderland to a nightmare of condos; stark, white, three-storey monoliths that lined the river to the north, while to the south, the marsh had been dredged out, cleaned up, and concreted into a sprawling marina. There was hardly a tree in sight, just steel and stone, and the masts of dozens of sailboats, endlessly bobbing up and down, up and down, like toothpicks.

I wondered who got rich – or richer – when they plundered this piece of paradise.

The Stick interrupted my angst.

'I had the computer pull the military files on everybody in the Triad who was in Nam,' he said. 'Costello was in Saigon for about six weeks on some legal thing. The rest of the time he was in Washington. Adjutant general's office. Big shot. A couple of their musclemen did time too. But Harvey Nance – that's his real name, Harvey – he's another case entirely. He was in Nam for two years. He was in CRIP, operating out of Dau Tieng. You know about CRIP?'

'Headhunters,' I said, with a nod.

'I know this is gonna sound strange,' Stick said, 'but I still have this funny feeling about guys from Nam. You know, the chemistry. After a while you get so used to a guy, he starts a sentence, you finish it. And when he's hurting, you know he's hurting. Like you are now.'

I knew what he was talking about. Once, just after I came back from Nam, I was in San Francisco and I went to the movies and when I came out there was this top kick sitting on the stairs. He had hashmarks up to his shoulder and I don't think I ever saw so many decorations and he was sitting there crying so hard he was sobbing. People were walking by, looking at him like maybe he was unglued. Well, maybe he was, he probably had the right. Anyway, I sat down beside him and put my arm around him and he looked up and all he said was 'Ah, Jesus,' and we sat that way for a long time and finally he got over it and said thanks and we left the theatre. He went that way and I went this, so I knew what Stick was talking about.

And he was right, I was hurting.

'You lose track of reality fast,' I said. 'When I first went into combat, the Hueys took us into U Minh Forest. It was a free-strike zone. The B-52's had done it in that afternoon, and there was this old man sitting against a wall and he was clutching his leg to his chest, like he was afraid somebody was going to steal it. He bled to death like that, just clutching that leg. This old man, probably, I don't know, maybe sixty, sixty-five, too old to do anything to anybody. I started thinking, Holy shit, there's some weird people over here. Whoever's running this war needs to get his head rewired.'

He was nodding along with me.

'It was the ultimate scam, Nam,' he agreed. 'Nam the scam, the big con. Shit, from the day we're born we get sold the big con about war and manhood. We get conned up for that all our lives. The big fuckin' war payoff. Be a hero – except there weren't any heroes in Nam. All it was was a giant fuck-up with a high body count.'

'That's what you wanted, Stick? To be a hero and have a parade.'

Stick laughed. 'Would have been nice if somebody had made the offer.'

'I never did figure out what it was all about,' I said. 'That was the worst part of it.'

'Guilt is what it's all about.'

I knew about that. First you're exhilarated because you're still alive and others around you are dead. You don't want to admit it, but that's the way it is. The guilt sets in later. That's the way it was with Teddy.

'Anyway,' I said, 'you get over the thing about camaraderie the first time one of them takes a shot at you. That's part of the scam.'

'I didn't mean to get off the subject,' Stick said. 'The thing is, the CRIPS were mean motherfuckers and Nance was one of them.'

'Why all this interest in Nance?' I asked.

'I'm about to show you.'

He peeled off Ocean Boulevard just before we reached the bridge to Oceanby Island and the beaches. The city docks were clean, well-kept, concrete wharves, stretching several hundred feet along the river. It was early for the shrimpers. There was one boat unloading. It was jet black, its nets draped from the outriggers like the wings of a bat. The strikers were shovelling shrimp from the hold onto a conveyor belt that carried it into a sheet-metal building that was little more than an elaborate icehouse.

Stick pulled in to a large parking lot flyspecked with battered fishing cars and stopped near a beat-up Ford that looked vaguely familiar. Zapata peered out of the front seat and grinned.

'Hey, amigo,' he said. 'How's everything at the track?'

'I got an education,' I answered.

'You're about to get another one,' he said.

'How's that?'

He reached out between the cars and handed me a pair of binoculars.

'Check the belt.'

I checked the belt running into the building. It appeared deserted.

'Nobody around,' I said.

'Just keep watching for a minute,' said Zapata.

Stick put lighter to cigarette and hunched down behind the wheel.

A man with a clipboard came out of the shrimp house. He was a short man with a white beard, rather benevolent looking, with a stomach that was used to too many beers. His bullet head was covered by a bright green fishing cap, and he was checking wooden crates piled against the back of the building. I watched him for a full minute before I realised it was Tuna Chevos. A new beard and dark glasses were my only excuses. I knew that face well.

'Son of a bitch,' I said. 'There he is, the missing link. I knew it! I knew that old bastard had to be around here. That means Nance can't be too far away. How did you tumble on to them?'

'Shit, this was easy,' Zapata said. 'You said Chevos ran barges on the Ohio River. Seemed logical he'd stick to the same trade, especially since shrimp boats move a lot of grass. So I got out the phone book, turned to shrimp companies. I got lucky. This is the third place I checked out.'

'What's the name of this joint?' I asked.

'Jalisco Shrimp Company,' Stick answered.

'Let's find out who owns it.'

'Check.'

Another man joined Chevos, a tall, lean, ferret of a man who walked on the balls of his feet, loose and rangy. His head moved constantly, as though he were stalking some unsuspecting prey. I could almost smell his feral odour three hundred yards away.

'There he is,' I said, no longer trying to conceal my hatred of Turk Nance. 'That's Nance.'

'Yeah, I figured,' Zapata said. He was grinning like the man in the moon.

'You did good, Chino,' I said.

'Thanks. Piece of cake, this one.'

'You really have a hard-on for Nance, don't you?' the Stick said.

'I owe the son of a bitch.'

'Well, maybe we can fix it so you'll be accommodated,' Zapata said almost gleefully.

'That would be nice,' I answered. 'At least we know they're all here.'

I watched them taking inventory of the shrimp boxes.

'They look like they're actually working for a living,' I said.

'These are the real bad ones, huh?' asked Zapata.

I kept watching Nance, his snake eyes gleaming malevolently. Nance had killed a dozen men I could think of.

'The real badasses,' I affirmed. 'The way it is, if anybody in the Tagliani outfit is capable of wasting the whole family, it's Chevos, with Nance probably doing the batting.

'Twenty-four hour surveillance on these two, okay?' I said to Zapata.

'I'll see to it personally,' he said, obviously proud of his score.

'It also might help to know where the two of them were last night. Particularly Nance. But don't let them on to you.'

'That may be a little tougher but I'll see what I can do. You want Nance, you got him.'

I gave the glasses back to Zapata. 'I'll tell you how I want

Nance. I want Nance doing the full clock in the worst joint there is. I want him screaming in solitary for the rest of his natural life.'

The Stick stared at me with surprise for several moments, then broke into his grin.

'We got the point,' he said.

32

ISLE OF SIGHS

It was eight thirty when I started out to the Isle of Sighs and it was dusk by the time I had put Front Street and Dunetown behind me. Crab fishermen were standing hard against the railing of the two-lane bridge that connects the main island to Skidaway. Below it, an elderly woman, as freckled as an Iowa corn picker, and wearing a battered white fishing hat with its brim folded down around her ears, fished from a flat-bottom skiff that drifted idly among the reeds in the backwater. The hyenas hadn't got this far yet.

Skidaway was the buffer, a pancake-shaped, marshy islet that separated the whore-city from the wistful Isle of Sighs. There were few cars, the road was populated mostly by weathered natives on bikes. The islanders seemed to have prevailed here, stubbornly refusing to surrender to time or progress. I passed what seemed to be an abandoned city square, its weeds crowding the wreck of a building at its centre, then half a mile farther on, a small settlement of restored tabby houses, surrounded by laughing children and barking dogs. Streets narrowed to lanes, oyster shells crackled beneath my tyres, and the oaks, bowed with age, turned the roadways into living arches, their beards of grey Spanish moss *shushing* across the top of my car.

I was racing the sun, hoping to get to Windsong before dark, but as I got closer to the old, narrow, wooden bridge that ties the Isle of Sighs to Skidaway, I unsuspectingly burst out of the trees for several hundred yards and the marsh spread out before me for miles, like an African plain. It was as if I had suddenly driven to the edge of the world.

I pulled over, got out of the car, and leaned against a fender.

The sun, a scorched orb hanging an inch or two above the sprawling sea grass, lured birds and ducks and buzzing creatures aloft for one last flight before nightfall I watched the sun sink to the ground like a forest fire. The world was red for a minute or so and then the sun dropped silently behind the sea oats and marsh grass.

Whoosh; just like that it was dark.

When I got back into the car, I had a momentary attack of guilt. My mind flashed on Dutch and the promise I had made to him. No scandal, I had told him. I thought about that for at least sixty seconds as I drove on through the oak archways and across the narrow bridge to the Isle of Sighs. Nothing here had changed. It was like driving into a time warp. Here and there, along the rutted lanes, hand-carved signs announced the names of houses hidden away among pine and palm. Once this had been the bastion of Dunetown, a fiefdom for the power brokers who took the gambles, claimed the spoils, divided them up, and ruled the town with indulgent authority. The homes were unique, each a masterpiece of casual grace.

Windsong was the fortress.

It stood at the edge of the woods and a mile from the main road, down a narrow dirt corridor, tortured by palmettos and dwarf palms, that was more path than lane; a stately, two-storey frame house, ghost-white in the moonlight, surrounded by sweeping porches, with a cap of cedar shingles and dark oblong shutters framing its windows. Before it, a manicured lawn spread a hundred yards down to the bay's edge. Beyond it, past the south point of Thunderhead Island, a mile or so away, was the Atlantic Ocean. The gazebo, where bands had once played on summer nights, stood near the water like a pawn on an empty chessboard.

Memories stirred.

A lamp burned feebly in a corner room on the second floor and another spilled light from the main room to a corner of the porch. Otherwise the place was dark.

I stopped near a dark blue Mercedes coupé that was parked haphazardly on the grass near the end of the driveway, got out, and stood for a minute or two, letting my eyes deal with the darkness. Moon shadows were everywhere. A south wind drifted idly across the bay and rattled the tree branches. Out beyond the house, a night bird sang a mournful love song and waited for an answer that never came. It was obvious why Chief had called it Windsong; no other name could possibly have fit.

I remembered Chief and Stonewall Titan, ending each day sipping whisky on that porch. I opened the boot and put my pistol under the spare tyre and pressed it shut as quietly as I could. This was no place for sudden noises.

The boathouse was a dark square, jutting out into the bay to the east of the house. I walked down towards it. The night bird started singing again and then, suddenly, flew off in a rustle of leaves. Then there was only the wind.

I knew what I was going to say; I had been rehearsing it in my head ever since I saw her.

Hang tough, Jake, don't let soft memories shake you. Get it said and get out.

I was ready.

She was standing in the boathouse, haloed by the moon, swinging on a twenty-five-foot Mako bow line clamped to a hook above her head. She didn't see me at first. Eyes closed, she was lost in the moonlight, stirring her own memories.

A small Sony tape deck was whispering on the dock beside her. And that summer came back, a riptide that erased whatever scenario I had planned. I recognised Phil Spector's breakaway guitar on the old Drifters version of 'On Broadway'. Twenty years ago I could whistle every note and break, right along with him. I didn't even think, I just started whistling softly between my teeth, amazed that I could still keep up with all the riffs and pauses.

She turned, startled, her fawnlike eyes fluttering as they tried to adjust to the darkness. The bay was slapping the pilings beneath us and the Mako bumped easily against the rubber tyres in the side of the dock.

Nothing else but the wind.

'Jake?' she said, a decibel above the night sounds.

'Yeah.'

She moved away from the line.

'You can still do it,' she said, and laughed.

'I'm a little rusty,' I said.

'No. Not rusty at all.'

There was an awkward pause, where you feel you should say something just to fill the silence. She did it for me.

'I'm so glad you came. I wanted it so bad it hurt.'

'You haven't changed at all,' I said huskily. 'Time has passed you by.'

'You always say the perfect thing, you always did.' Another pause, then, 'I didn't even hear you. I was lost for a minute.'

'I can't think of a better place to be lost.'

She eased towards me, a shimmering vision, still moving slightly with the music.

'Remember the night party? Dewey Simpson got drunk and tried to swim the channel marker in his tuxedo . . .'

I remembered it and said so.

'. . . and you kept egging him on . . .'

The moon silhouetted her, trim legs etched behind a white cotton skirt.

'. . . and we kept playing that song, over and over, while Teddy swam out to pull him in . . .'

The brief triangle of her bikini panties, the swell of one of her breasts, tinted by a moonbeam.

'And my 18th birthday, when we took the dune buggy out to South Beach and left Teddy and that girl in the ocean . . .'

Her blonde hair swirling in the wind, whipping the shadow of her face.

'We were at the very end, remember? Down at the point . . . the breakers were running so high.'

She whisked her fingertips down her neck.

'It was so hot that night. Remember how hot it was?'

I began to feel the same heat, rising round my neck. She was some piece of work, make no mistake.

'It was just like tonight . . . the moon was full . . .'

She was close enough to smell.

'. . . that was the first time I ever saw you naked . . .'

And now she was close enough to feel my heat.

'We were lying there in the dunes and you let the buggy roll down the hill . . .'

'Oh yes, I remember . . .'

'You were gorgeous . . .'

'You still are,' I heard myself say. My voice was as shaky as a spinster's dream.

'I feel the same way now, Jake. I feel like I'm on fire inside . . .'

She moved against me, her breasts exploring my chest as tentatively as a butterfly exploring a blossom.

174

But it was not 1963 and we were not on South Beach; it was now and here and she stepped back from me, her dress already unbuttoned, her breasts pushing out past the white bodice, and she lifted her shoulders so gracefully that she hardly moved, and the dress slipped away, hovering down to the dock at her feet, and she leaned forward, her hands sweeping swiftly down her thighs, and suddenly she was naked before me again.

If anything, time had improved her body.

She moved against me and I ran my hands slowly across the swell of her buttocks, pressing her hard against me. She began to rock back and forth, urging me to rise to her. I let the flat of my hand slip down along her thigh and then back up, and she urged herself against it. She was warm and moist and she clamped her legs together, trapping my hand, and began to rock harder. Her fingers moved nimbly to my belt, unfastening it, and then she slid her hand down and began to caress me and then we were moving together.

'Oh, God, Jake,' she moaned, 'where have you been?'

I lowered her slowly to the cushions in the boat and she stretched out before me, her hands over her head as I teased her, my hand barely touching her soft down until suddenly she thrust up against my hand. She began to tremble under my touch, took my hand and pressed it harder, and began to move my hand with hers, showing me where to touch, what to explore, orchestrating her pleasure. Her hands groped for something to hang on to, found the edge of the seat and clutched it. Every muscle in her body seemed to be responding. She was moving back and forth as my fingers sought all her secret places.

She started to whimper and the whimper became a growl, deep in her throat, and she stiffened suddenly, wrapped her arms around me, buried her head in my shoulder, and her cries were muffled against my flesh. She reached down, searching desperate fingers, and turning slightly, guided me into her. Then there was only the feel of her, her soft muscles engulfing me, urging me to come with her, and the rush of her mouth against mine.

There was nothing else.

No Ciscos, no Taglianis, no hooligans, no wounds or screams of grief. There were only our own cries of joy and relief, whisked to sea on the wind.

33

LATE CALL

The tape recorder had run its course and turned itself off and I had pulled my Windbreaker over us, although I didn't need it. Her warm body lay across mine like a blanket. We didn't say much, we just lay there holding each other. Half an hour crept by and then my beeper broke the spell, like a phone that's been left off the hook too long.

I shifted under her enough to reach up on the dock and rifle through my clothes until I found it and turned it off. My watch said eleven fifteen.

She twisted back against me and sighed. 'What was that?' she asked.

I was wondering who would be beeping me at this time of night.

'The beeper,' I whispered. 'I gotta call the office.'

She rose up an inch or so, a tousled head peering through tangled hair with one half-open eye.

'Wha' time is it?'

'Past eleven.'

'You have to call the office at this time of night?'

'I have terrible hours.'

'Ridiculous. Besides, it's too early to leave.'

'You've got a husband, remember?'

'I have a husband in Atlanta for the night,' she said. She looked up at me and smiled. There wasn't a hint of remorse on her face. She looked as innocent as a five-year-old.

'He may call.'

She snuggled up again.

'Uh-uh. Out of sight, out of mind. Besides, he trusts me.'

I didn't feel like dealing with that. I didn't feel like dealing with any of it. Guilt gnawed at my stomach like an ulcer and it had nothing to do with Harry Raines. I kept lying to myself that it had been inevitable. I shifted again and reached for my clothes. She sat up, leaning naked against the bulkhead, her tawny form outlined by the dying moon.

'More,' she whispered, and it was more of a demand than a plea.

A new fire ignited deep in my gut, but the old devils were creeping back: guilt, frustration, jealousy, distrust.

I threw the Windbreaker over her.

'Give me a break,' I said, squeezing out a smile.

'You never asked for a break before,' she said, putting a hand as soft as a chamois on my chest.

'I was in training then.'

'Please come back,' she said as I started to dress.

'I never know about later. I could be on my way to Alaska an hour from now.'

'No.'

I laughed. 'No? What do you mean, no?'

'I waited all these years for you to come back. You are not going to just up and leave, not again.'

She closed her eyes and put her head back against the side of the boat. 'I went crazy inside when I saw you at the restaurant yesterday and then at the track this morning,' she said. 'It all came rushing back at me. Like a tidal wave inside me.' She opened her eyes and looked at me. 'It happened, and it wasn't one of those things you question. Do you know what I mean?'

Instant replay: a rampant fantasy from the past. For months after Chief had written his good-bye letter, fantasies had infested my days. Uncontrollable, they were like panes of glass, separating me from reality. The fantasies were impossible dreams; that she would show up at my door in the middle of night to tell me she couldn't live another instant without me; that I would find her waiting in the corner of some restaurant. I looked for her everywhere I went, in supermarkets, in the windows of other cars as I drove down the highway. I bought a pair of cheap binoculars so I could scan Chief's box at Sanford Stadium on football weekends. Even a glimpse, I thought, would help. Finally I accepted the danger of fantasies. They sour into nightmares and vanish, leaving scars on the soul. Tonight could not change that, even though the fantasy was becoming real again.

I could feel the armour, like a steel skin, slipping around me.

'Don't go away again,' she said. 'Not for a while, at least. Give it a chance.'

I let some anger out, not much, just relieving the valve for a moment.

'That isn't exactly the way it played,' I said harshly.

'It was Chief. He never understood how we really felt about each other.'

'He understood all right.'

She looked away, fiddling with a strand of cotton ravelling from her dress.

'Hell, Jake, you know Chief. He always made whatever he said sound so . . . so, right. Nobody ever argued with Chief.'

'Maybe somebody should have.'

She stared at me for several seconds before saying, 'Why didn't you?'

I didn't know how to answer that properly.

What I said was 'Pride,' and let it go at that.

She nodded. 'Beats us all, doesn't it.'

'Well, it's a little hard, coming to grips with the feeling that you're a failure at twenty-one because you have bad ankles. It made me readjust some of my values.'

'Jake,' she said suddenly, changing the mood entirely. 'I want to hear about Teddy.'

'I wrote you all there is to know.'

'I want to hear it from you.'

'Why, for God's sakes?'

'So I'll know it's true and I can forget it, once and for all.'

'It's true, believe me. I won't replay it, Doe. It's not one of my favourite images.'

It had been so long I had almost forgotten the lie. It was heroic, a real Greek tragedy, that much I remembered.

'Time you laid Teddy to rest,' I said softly. 'Forget the war. That wasn't reality, it was madness. Remember him the way he was the day you pushed him into the bay. That's what he'd want.'

Then she started to cry, very softly so you would hardly notice it.

'He'd like it, that we're together here. He was all for us, Jake.'

'I know it.'

She went on, ignoring the tears. 'When I think back, I think of all of us together. Such bright promises, and all of them broken. Everything seemed to go bad and stay bad. They kept taking things away from me. First you, then Teddy, then . . . oh, just everything.'

'Then what? You started to say something, finish it.'

'Lots of thens. I have this horse, a beautiful stallion, Georgia-bred. He had real promise. Chief gave him to me when I turned thirty. He said Firefoot – it was a silly name but he had this white splash on one foot, jet black only he had this white streak, so I called him Firefoot – anyway, Chief said Firefoot and I would stay young together. I wanted to race him, oh, how I wanted that. But Harry got involved with this racetrack thing. I guess inheriting Dunetown from Chief wasn't enough. It wouldn't look right, he said, the racing commissioner's wife racing horses. So Firefoot's up for stud now. When I go out there, he runs across the meadow to me with his head up, so proud . . . he wanted to race; it's what Thoroughbreds are all about, Jake, they're born to run, to prove themselves. He really deserved the chance. He deserved that. An animal like that, it has rights.'

She stopped and bit off another strand ravelling from her dress, wiggled it off her fingers, then turned back to me.

'It's been that way ever since you left. Everything went bad.'

'I'll buy that,' I said bitterly.

'It just seems like nobody's what they appear to be,' she went on angrily. 'At first Harry reminded me of you. He was fun and he laughed a lot and he made me laugh. Then Chief decided to retire and Harry changed overnight. It was business, business, business!'

'That went with the territory.'

'I didn't know he was so ambitious. Suddenly Findley Enterprises wasn't enough. Next it was politics and then the track. It's always something new. He's like a man on a roller coaster; he can't seem to stop. I didn't want that. There's no reason for it. We've got more than we'll ever need.'

For a few moments I felt sorry for Raines, because I understood that drive. Harry Raines had to prove himself. He couldn't be satisfied with the role of Mr Doe Findley, and for that I respected him. I wondered if I would have done the same thing. But I didn't say anything, I just listened. I had very little respect for his political aspirations. In my book, politicians usually rank one step above bank robbers and child molesters. That was my prejudice and my problem to deal with, of course, but I had met damn few of them I either liked or trusted.

'I love Harry,' she said. 'I'm just not *in* love with him anymore. He's not Harry anymore, he's already Governor Raines.'

'Maybe he's got troubles,' I said, buttoning my shirt.

'Tiger by the tail, that's all he keeps saying.'

'More like a two-ton elephant on a piece of string.'

'Is it that bad? Is he in trouble?' she asked.

'I don't know. Is he honest?'

'Chief believed . . . believes in him.'

'Oh, so Chief picked him out,' I said. It was a cruel comment. I was sorry I said it before all the words were out of my mouth.

She stood up, her back as straight as a slat, smoothing her dress. '*I* picked him out,' she snapped.

'Sorry,' I said. 'Anyway, I'm not interested in what Chief thinks, Doe. What do you think?'

She pulled on the dress, but didn't button it, and gave me back my Windbreaker.

'I don't think he could be dishonest.'

'That's a nice vote of confidence.'

'I'm trying to be honest myself. Are you here because of something to do with the track?'

'Hell, I'm not sure of anything,' I answered. 'I'm new in town. Can I use the phone up at the house?'

She opened a metal box on the wall of the boathouse, reached in and took out a wall phone, handed me the receiver, and leaned back against the wall, staring at me.

I dialled the war room and Dutch answered.

'Where are you?' he bellowed.

'With friends,' I said. 'What's up?'

'You got a weird phone call about an hour ago. Kite fielded it. He says a guy wanted to talk to you real bad, but he hung up when Kite tried to press him. Thing is, Kite says the guy didn't exactly sound like Mary Poppins. The reason I'm calling, before Kite put it together he told this guy he might be able to reach you at the hotel. So you might want to keep your eyes open.'

'Thanks. Maybe we ought to have breakfast and do a little catch-up.'

'I'll pick you up at nine,' he said. I told him that was real civilised of him and hung up.

'More trouble?' Doe asked, anxiety in her voice.

'I don't think so.'

'Please, come back.'

I played it tough. 'Sure,' I said, and leaned over and kissed her. As I started to leave I felt her hand on my sleeve.

180

'Jake?'

'Yeah?'

'What did they do to us?'

'The hyenas got us,' I said. 'The bastards never let up.'

When I got back to the car, the light was still on in the upper bedroom. Then I remembered that that was Teddy's old room. I wondered if the light was left on permanently, like the eternal torch at Arlington.

I drove as fast I could back to reality.

34

WESTERN UNION

A grey Olds picked me up a couple of blocks before I got back to the hotel and followed at a respectable distance. The driver was pretty good. I did a couple of figure-eights, trying to throw him off, but he didn't panic and he didn't close the gap. He stayed a block or so behind me all the way to the hotel.

I parked in front and let the doorman take the car. The Olds pulled in half a block away and sat with the lights out. I checked the desk. Then I walked across the lobby and ducked behind a small forest of ferns and ficus trees near the elevators.

A medium-sized man got out of the Olds and drifted across Palm Drive, acting like he wasn't in a hurry. I got a better look at him in the light of the lobby. He was neither tall nor short, fat nor thin, old nor young. He was decked out in a nondescript grey business suit, no hat, and his chiselled features might have been handsome except for the deep acne scars that pitted his cheeks. Once he got inside, he picked up his pace, his deep-set eyes darting back and forth, perusing the lobby. He headed straight for the elevators and speared the up button with a forefinger.

I stepped in behind him, grabbed a handful of jacket and collar, slammed him face-forward against the wall, bent his left arm behind him, reached under his arm, and relieved him of a Smith & Wesson .38.

'Wha'dya think yer doin?' he whined.

I leaned close to his ear and put a rasp in my voice.

'You just took the words right out of my mouth,' I whispered. 'You've been following me for the last ten minutes. I don't think you're attracted by my beautiful eyes.'

'Lemme go,' he continued to whine.

I shoved his gun between his shoulder blades.

'You got a name?' I asked.

He paused and I shoved harder. He turned his face sideways, glared at me through yellow-flecked snake eyes, and snarled, 'Harry Nesbitt.'

'Just why are you so attracted to me, Harry?'

'I came to talk. Lemme loose.'

'You talk with your arm?'

'You got the gun, hotshot.'

'Yeah, and I'm kind of jumpy, homicide being the hottest game in town right now. Talk first.'

'Look, all I'm doin' is a Western Union. You wanna lissen or not?'

'I'm listening, Harry.'

'Johnny O'Brian wants a meet.'

'Is that a fact? And what's that to you?'

'I work for him.'

'What do you do, carry his gun?'

'Very funny,' he said, beginning to put an edge back into his voice. I let him go, slipped his gun into my belt, and backed away from the potted plants, out to the edge of the lobby.

'Do you mind,' he said, his eyes beginning to dance around the room again. 'O'Brian ain't anxious the whole fuckin' world should know we're talking.'

'Uh-huh,' I said.

He moved farther back among the plants.

'This joint is crawling with people,' he said, although all I could see was one sleepy bellhop and a desk clerk who was busy sorting bills.

'Just speak your piece and shag,' I said.

'O'Brian says he'll meet you anywhere you say, anytime. One on one. Nobody knows but him and you.'

'What about you? You planning an attack of amnesia?'

'Cute,' he chuckled. 'Anyway, I already got it.'

'And how do I contact O'Brian?'

'You don't. I do the go-between, okay? You tell me, I give it to the boss.'

'And why should I trust you? Because I like your taste in ties?'

'Lookee here,' said Nesbitt. 'He wants to make a deal with you, okay? He ain't got nothing to do with this hit parade goin' down.'

'Now how would I know that?'

'Look, it comes to O'Brian that you burned Skeet Tagliani and gave Uncle Franco and the rest of them a hotfoot there. It also comes to him that you're a stand-up guy when it comes to your word. He wants to do business. What's the matter, you got something against free enterprise?'

'Am I supposed to be flattered by all this?' I asked.

'You wanna talk or you wanna audition for vaudeville? O'Brian ain't lookin for trouble, okay? Am I drifting your way?'

'Getting scared, is he?'

'O'Brian don't scare,' Nesbitt said matter-of-factly.

'Pigs don't lie in the mud, either.'

'Look, my boss don't go to the party empty-handed, know what I mean? You wanna be the smartass, don't wanna listen, fuck off.'

I thought about it for a moment or two – not about meeting O'Brian, that was a gimme – but about where and when to meet him. It could be a setup, except there was no reason to set me up. Was he representing the family? Or was he freelancing? What was he willing to talk about that could interest me? I was still guessing that O'Brian was running scared, looking for an umbrella to hide under.

'Does he know who scratched Tagliani and the rest?' I asked.

Nesbitt shifted from one foot to the other and sighed. 'Whyn't yuh ask him? I told yuh, I'm just doing a Western Union. I don't know shit besides that and my orders are to forget it!'

'When?' I asked finally.

'Sooner the better.'

'How's tomorrow morning sound?'

'Worse than now, better than later,' he said with a shrug.

'It's too late to do anything now,' I said. 'It's got to be tomorrow, middle of the morning.' I make a lot of bad decisions at two in the morning.

'That's the best you can do, that's the best you can do. You wanna pick the spot?'

I didn't know or remember the town well enough. I decided to test the water a little.

'Does O'Brian have a place in mind?'

'Yeah, but he don't want you should get nervous, him pickin' it out, I mean.'

'Try me.'

'He has this little fishing camp out on Oceanby. On the bay side, sits out over the water. It's private; his old lady don't even go out there. Also it has good sight lines; there ain't a blade of grass within twenty yards of the place.'

I thought some more about it. It would have been smarter to leave then and follow Nesbitt to the meet, but I wanted to let somebody know where I was.

'Where is this place exactly?' I asked.

'You hang a right three blocks after you cross the bridge from Thunderhead to Oceanby. It's a mile or so down the road, on the bay, like I said. You can't miss it, the road ends there.'

I studied him for a long minute, tugged my ear, and then nodded. 'What's the name of the street?'

'Bayview.'

'I have a breakfast appointment,' I said. 'It'll be about ten thirty.'

· 'No problem, he's spending the night out there. Ten thirty.' He smiled and held out his hand, palm up. 'How about the piece?' he said.

I took out the revolver, pulled the retaining pin, dropped the cylinder into my palm, and handed him his gun.

'I'll give O'Brian the rest of it when I see him,' I said.

His acne scars turned purple and pebbles of sweat began to ridge his forehead. He looked at me quizzically. 'Why the badass act?' he said. 'You don't have to prove how tough you are. Like I told ya, we know all about Cincy.'

'I'm a cautious man,' I said. 'Too many people are dying in town right now.'

'Did I lay any heat on you, Kilmer? No. I just come and delivered the message like I was supposed to. Y'know, I get caught in the middle on this thing, I'll end up in the bay, parley-vooin' with the fuckin' shrimps.'

'That's your problem.'

'So I come back with half a gun? It gets everything off on the wrong foot, know what I mean?'

I tossed him the cylinder for his .38 and he caught it without taking his yellow eyes off mine.

'You owe me one,' I said.

'You talk to O'Brian, you'll be paid in spades,' he said, and was gone, darting across the lobby like a dragonfly and out the nearest exit.

35

BREAKFAST TALK

There was a message in my box when I went down to meet Dutch the next morning. It was a handwritten note from Babs Thomas:

'Cocktails in the penthouse tomorrow at 6. I expect you there. Love and kisses, B.T.'

She wasn't in the breakfast room but Dutch and Charlie One Ear were. I slid the note across the table to Dutch as I sat down. He read it and chuckled.

'You better be there,' he said. 'It's a felony in Doomstown to turn down a command performance from the duchess.'

'Just what I need,' I said, 'a fucking cocktail party.'

'Give you a chance to see how the other half lives,' Charlie One Ear said without looking up from his fruit cocktail.

'I don't like crowds,' I said.

He looked up and smiled. 'Perhaps it'll be just the two of you,' he suggested.

That earned him a dirty look from me and a bit of contemplation from Dutch.

'Well,' Dutch said, 'you could do worse.'

'Let's forget cocktail parties for the moment,' I said, ending the conjecture. 'Something's come up. It could be our first real break.'

'Oh?' Dutch retorted.

'Johnny O'Brian sent one of his gunmen to see me last night. He wants to have a powwow. Sounds like he could be running scared.'

'Are you going to meet him?' Dutch asked.

'Yeah. At ten thirty. Do you have anybody on O'Brian's tail?'

He nodded. 'Salvatore's doing the honours today.'

'Has he reported in?'

'Do any of these guys ever report in?' Dutch said. 'I can check the Warehouse and see, but I can tell you what the chances are.'

'We've got to raise him,' I said. 'My deal is that I go alone. If O'Brian tumbles onto Salvatore it could blow the whole deal.'

'I'll see what I can do,' Dutch said, heading for the phone.

'Is that real smart?' Charlie One Ear asked.

'You mean going alone?'

He nodded. The muscles in his face had tightened up. I knew what he was thinking.

'Don't worry,' I said. 'If this is some kind of a trap they wouldn't warn me first. They can't be that sure I won't have some kind of backup with me.'

'You know this bunch better than I do,' he answered, turning back to his breakfast. 'But I wouldn't stray too far from the range, just in case.'

'I appreciate your concern,' I said. 'The thing is, if O'Brian wants to make some kind of a deal, we can't afford to lose it. I've been down this road before, Charlie. I'll watch my step.'

He shrugged. 'You're a big boy now,' he said. 'I assume you know what you're doing.'

I ordered a light breakfast and doctored my coffee. Dutch was gone about five minutes. He seemed concerned when he got back.

'Okay,' he said. 'Zapata was in the Warehouse and he beeped Salvatore. Zapata's going to call me back if he raises him.'

'I thought Zapata was tailing Nance,' I said.

Dutch was scowling. He lit a cigarette and blew smoke towards the ceiling.

'He lost him,' Dutch said. 'Followed him out to the docks at dawn. Nance went out on a shrimp boat and left Zapata at the altar.'

I got a sudden chill, as if a cold breeze had blown across the back of my neck. Nance being on the loose was a wild card I hadn't counted on.

'An awful lot of people know about this gig,' I mused.

'Are you worried about Salvatore and Zapata?' Dutch asked stiffly.

'No. But I don't want anybody screwing this thing up.'

'Don't worry about it,' Dutch replied. 'We'll raise Salvatore and call him off, if you're sure that's the way you want to play it.'

'That was my deal,' I said as the waitress brought my breakfast.

'You want to tell us where you're going?' Charlie One Ear asked.

'Not really,' I said. 'You know how it is with these people, Charlie. They spook real easily.'

I decided we had talked enough about O'Brian and changed the subject again.

'Anything new on the Logeto killing?' I asked.

Dutch shook his head. 'We combed the neighbourhood. Nobody saw anybody on the roof or coming down the walls. So far it's a blank. But I do have something for you.' He took an envelope out of his pocket and handed it to me. 'Here's that list of drops Cohen made. Cowboy finally got it together for you.'

I opened it up and checked over the list. Most of the addresses didn't mean anything to me. The most significant note was that on two of the three days, Cohen had visited both a branch bank of the Seacoast National *and* made his usual two o'clock visit to the bank.

'Have you checked this over?' I asked Dutch.

He nodded. 'I can give you chapter and verse and the drops if you want.'

'I don't have time now,' I said. 'There's one thing that jumps out. I wonder why Cohen has been hitting the bank twice. On Wednesday and Friday he went to a branch *and* the main bank. Now why would he do that?'

'Maybe he doesn't like to carry a lot of cash around for too long,' Charlie One Ear suggested.

'Maybe,' I said, staring at the list. 'But I don't think so. Unless things have changed, he's used to moving large sums of money.'

'You got another idea?' asked Dutch.

'Yeah. Maybe he's skimming a little off the top for himself.'

'If he is, he's got more guts than I give him credit for,' said Dutch.

'Or he could be working with Costello,' I said.

'Wouldn't that be sweet, to catch them in the middle like that,' Charlie thought aloud. 'We could probably get a whole chorus of canaries out of it.'

'That's *if* he's playing games,' I said.

'Cowboy's on him again today,' Dutch said. 'Maybe he'll turn up something new.' Then his eyebrows went up. 'I'll be damned,' he said. 'Speak of the devil. See the two guys that just walked in? The one that looks like a football player and the jellyfish with him?'

The two men sat down at a corner table and immediately began

187

to jabber like two spinsters gossiping. One was Donleavy. The other one was as tall, but slender, and older, probably in his mid-forties, with wavy, greying hair that framed a weak, flaccid face. His manicured hands jittered nervously as he talked, fiddling with the bits of toast on his plate the way a spider fiddles with an ant. Both of them looked like they spent a lot of time in the sun.

'The one on the left is Donleavy,' said Dutch. 'The bird in the navy blue suit is the banker, Charles Seaborn. From the looks of things, they're having a lovers' spat.'

'I think I'll just stir the pot a little,' I said.

'What are you going to do?' Dutch asked nervously.

'Just introduce myself,' I said, patting his shoulder as I rose. 'I'm not going to bite anybody.'

I strolled across the restaurant towards the table where Donleavy and Seaborn were bickering over breakfast. Donleavy saw me from the corner of his eye. He kept talking, but it was obvious that he sensed I was heading their way and he didn't want to be disturbed. As I reached them, he looked up angrily, trouble clouding in his brown eyes.

'I'm Jake Kilmer,' I said before he had a chance to explode. 'I think it's about time we met.'

He wasn't sure what to do. The anger in his hard features was suddenly replaced by a wide grin, a car salesman's grin, the kind that makes you want to count your fingers after you've shaken hands.

'Yes, yes, yes,' he suddenly babbled, and jumped up. 'Of course.' He pumped my hand and introduced me to Seaborn, who looked like he'd just bitten his tongue. Seaborn offered me a hand that was as clammy as it was insincere.

It was obvious that neither of them was overjoyed at meeting me.

'I'd like to have a talk with you,' I said to Donleavy, 'whenever it's convenient.'

'Is it urgent?' he said. 'Aren't we going to see you tomorrow night?'

'Tomorrow night?'

'At Babs' cocktail party,' he said with a lame grin. 'You better not forget – she's touting you as the guest of honour. She's got a short temper and a long memory.'

'I'll be there,' I said. 'But I need a little time alone with you. It's nothing unpleasant. Information mostly.'

He dug a small notebook from an inside pocket and leafed through it. 'How about Friday around noon?' he asked. 'I'll take the phone off the hook and send out for sandwiches.'

'Sounds like a winner,' I said. 'I'll buy.'

'Not in my town you won't,' he said. His smile had grown more relaxed and genuine. 'It's number three warehouse, overlooking the Quadrangle. We have the whole top floor.'

'I'm afraid I won't be seeing you tomorrow evening,' Seaborn said. 'I have the bank examiners in town. You know how that can be.'

'By the way,' I said to Seaborn. 'I believe you have a customer I know from Cincinnati. His name's Cohen.'

'Cohen?' he echoed, raising his eyebrows much too high. He looked like he had just swallowed something much too big for his throat, which was bobbing up and down like a fishing cork.

'Yes. Lou Cohen?'

'Oh, yes, I believe I've seen him in the bank from time to time.'

'Give him my regards the next time you see him,' I said.

I could almost hear their sighs of relief when I left the table. And I knew enough about human nature to know that Charles Seaborn had more than a casual acquaintance with Cohen.

Perhaps Cowboy Lewis would confirm my suspicions. In the meantime, I couldn't help wondering why tiny beads of sweat had been twinkling from Seaborn's upper lip. I usually don't make people *that* nervous.

When I got back to the table, Dutch still looked nervous.

'What'd you say to them?' he asked. 'Seaborn looked like he swallowed a lemon.'

'I just asked Seaborn if he knew my old friend Lou Cohen,' I said with a smile.

'*Verdammt*,' Dutch said, shaking his head. 'You sure do play hard cheese.'

'Is there any other way to play?' I replied.

On the way out Dutch was paged. He spoke into the lobby phone for a few moments and hung up.

'That was Zapata,' he said. 'Salvatore's screaming bloody murder, but he's giving up O'Brian. He thinks you're nuts.'

'I've been accused of that before too,' I said.

'Just so you'll know,' Dutch added, 'Salvatore knows where O'Brian is. If you're not back in two hours, we're going in with the marines, although I don't know why we should bother.'

'We're just getting accustomed to that ugly pan of his,' Charlie One Ear commented.

It was nice to know they cared.

36

LURE

The fat old pelican sat on a corner post of the deck surrounding the fishing shack, looking bored. He surveyed the broad spanse of bay which emptied into the Atlantic Ocean a mile away to the east at Thunder Point. A warm breeze ruffled in from the sound and the old bird stared, half asleep, across the surface of the water, looking for the tell-tale signs of lunch. Then, spotting a school of mullet, he flapped his broad wings and soared off the post, climbing twenty feet or so above the water, wheeling over and diving straight in, hitting with a splat and bobbing back up with a fish flopping helplessly in his bucket of a beak.

The Irishman watched the pelican make his catch. He was making a fishing lure. He had set up a small vice on the edge of a table and was carefully twining and retwining nylon, hook, and feathers, weaving them into a shiny lure. He had stopped to watch the pelican, keeping the line taut so it would not ravel.

He was a big man with one of those florid Irish faces that would look fifteen years old until he was ninety. A few lines grooved its smooth surface, but not enough to mar his youthful, carefree expression.

There was very little traffic along the river. A few shrimp boats had gone out against the rising tide and a weekend sailor was trying, without much success, to get a lacklustre wind in the sails of his boat a couple of hundred yards away. Otherwise it was so quiet he could hear what little wind there was rattling the marsh grass.

This was the Irishman's love, his escape from a business he neither liked nor understood. He felt like a misfit, a Peter Principled gunman forced to act like a businessman. O'Brian liked to settle disputes his own way. Negotiating confused him. But here he was king; he was alone and free, master of himself and his tiny domain, for O'Brian had mastered the secrets of fishing. It was one of the few things he did well, and he loved the sport with consummate passion.

When the phone rang, he snapped 'Damn!' under his breath and weighted down the loose end of the lure with a metal clamp before he went into the main room of the cabin to answer it.

'It's me, boss, Harry,' the gravelly voice on the other end of the line said. 'He's through eating breakfast. You sure you don't want I should follow him out, make sure he isn't bringin' company?'

'I said alone.'

'He could bring company.'

'Naw, he won't do that.'

'You never know with these Feds.'

'He don't have nothin' on me,' the Irishman said.

'He's pretty quick, this guy.'

'Just camp out at Benny's down the road. I need ya, I holler.'

'Want I should ring once and hang up when he leaves?'

'Good idea.'

'Everything calm out there?'

'No problem. Coupla shrimp boats went by. Nobody's been down the road. There's some jerk out here trying to get his sailboat back to the city marina, which is kinda funny.'

'What's so funny about it?'

'There ain't no wind.'

'Well, don't take no chances.'

'Don't worry. You just hang out there at Benny's, have a coupla beers, come on in when you see him leave.'

'Gotcha.'

They hung up and the Irishman switched on the radio and walked out onto the deck for a stretch. The sailboat had drifted four hundred feet or so west of the shack, towards the city, and the sailor was trying vainly to crank up his outboard, a typically sloppy weekend sailor in a floppy white hat, its brim pulled down around his ears. The putz, he thought, probably out of gas. But he had learned one thing since discovering the sea – sailors helped each other.

He cupped his hands and yelled:

'See if you can get it over here, maybe I can help.'

The sailor waved back, took an oar from the cockpit of the sailboat, and began to paddle towards the Irishman.

FLASHBACK: NAM DIARY, THE FIRST SIX

The first day: *First off, I was a replacement. I sat around the Cam Ranh Bay repo-depot for about ten days and then they send me down to Third Brigade HQ and from there down here to Dau Tieng and here's where I pick up my squad. I'm only five weeks out of Advanced Infantry school, I don't know shit, and I am plenty scared.*

I'm not here five minutes, the lieutenant, who looks about sixteen, red hair and freckles, his name is Carmody, sits down, pops two beers, and he says, 'Now listen good to me. I been out here, it's going on eight months. I got my own way of doing things after all that time, so you do what I say, don't even argue, don't tell me you didn't learn it that way back in the World, you just do it and I'll get you home alive. You don't I give you two weeks, you'll be dead or missing something you don't want to lose.'

I don't say anything, I just listen. I try not to shake but I am real nervous.

'I got a few rules,' he says. 'In the beginning, no matter what happens, follow me. If Charlie starts busting caps, you just follow me. Don't talk, don't start yelling at anybody else. If I go down, you go down. Find a pebble or a mound of dirt or a paddy and get below it. Get under his horizon. If you get hit, don't say anything and don't move. You do, and you're dead. Just lay there, somebody'll get you. That's my last rule – we don't leave anybody behind. Dead or alive, everybody goes out together.'

I was so scared my stomach hurt.

'These VC are good, goddamn good,' he says. 'Don't let anybody tell you different because that's bullshit. All that shit they gave you back in AI, forget it. They got tunnels out there, they go on for miles. They got whole operating rooms under the ground, not just some little pooch hole you throw a grenade in and forget it. You do and they pop up fifty feet away and your ass is in a bucket. These fuckers can run into a village and vanish. We don't get heroic, okay, we call in some air, let the Black Ponies burn it out. We move on. That's our mission, search and destroy. What it is not is search and be destroyed.'

I remember thinking, This is for real. Jesus, in five minutes we could be doing it for real.

'Any questions.' he says.

I shake my head no.

'Welcome to the war,' he says.

The fifth day: *Today I killed a man for the first time. I have a hard time talking about this. What happened, we're moving on this village, which was actually about a dozen hooches in this rice field seven or eight kliks downriver. This village was at the bottom of some foothills. There were rice paddies on both sides and a wide road lined with pepper trees and bamboo kind of dead-ending at it.*

Before we start down, Doc Ziegler, our medic, hands me a couple of buttons. 'What are these for?' I ask. 'Dex,' he says. 'Make you see better, hear better, move faster. Just do it.' So I popped the speed. It took about twenty seconds to kick my ass. I've never had speed before. I felt like taking on the village all by myself. I mean, I was ready!

We go down towards it, two squads on each side in the rice paddies, because they make good cover, and we have the Three Squad backing us up in reserve. We go in on the left and the One Squad on the right. They take the first hit. The VC opens up with mortars and machine gun fire and starts just chewing them up. One guy, the whole top of his head went off. The noise was horrendous; I couldn't believe the racket.

The lieutenant runs straight towards the village with his head down just below the edge of the ditch and I'm right behind him. The radio man is having trouble calling up the reserve platoon because we're in this little valley and the reception is for shit, so the lieutenant sends back a runner and then he says, 'Fuckin' gooks are eating One Squad up, we got to take them,' and he goes out of the paddy and runs for this stretch of bamboo which is maybe twenty yards from the gooks and me still right behind him.

That tips Charlie and they start cutting away at us. They're shooting the bamboo down all around us, just cutting it off. Then I see this VC in his black pyjamas and he's got his head out just a little, checking it out, and I sight him in and, ping! he goes down, just throws his hands up in the air and goes over backwards. Then another one comes running over and he's shooting as he comes, only he's aiming about ten metres to my left and I drop him. Then I see the machine gun, which is in the dirt out in front of the first hooch, and there's two of them and they're just cutting One Squad to shit, so I run up through the bamboo and get in position and blitz them both, pow, pow, pow, pow, pow!

Next thing I know, the lieutenant and the rest of the squad are running past me and the One Squad breaks loose and then it's all over. Five minutes, maybe. I was thinking, Jesus, I did more in the last five minutes than I ever did in my whole life. I mean, it was such a high. And to still be in one piece!

There wasn't anybody left. Women, kids, old people, VC. The entire village was blitzed. Nobody seemed to pay any attention to that; it was just business as usual. Then they brought in a flamethrower and scorched the whole place. I didn't look at the civilians, I just looked the other way. I figure, this is the way it's done, but it doesn't change how I feel about it.

Otherwise we were all feeling pretty good because none of our guys was hurt.

'You okay?' the lieutenant says after he makes the body count, and I says, 'Yeah, I feel good.' And I did.

'You looked okay in there,' he says.

I wasn't a virgin anymore and I was still alive. Jesus, I felt good.

It took me a long time to get used to it, that I had killed those people and it was okay, that it was what they expected me to do. For a while I kept dreaming they would come at night and arrest me.

38th day: *Doc Ziegler doesn't even believe in all this. He's a medic, doesn't carry any weapons. He says he would have gone to Canada but his old man had a bad heart and Doc figured it would kill him if Doc jumped the border. So he said 'Fuck it!' when he got his notice. 'I can put up with anything for a year,' he says. Among other things, Doc supplies the speed. He doesn't do it himself, says he doesn't need it since he doesn't carry a weapon. But he smokes pot a lot. Morning, noon, and night. Hell, I don't think I've ever seen Doc unstoned. But when there's trouble he can move with the best of them. What the hell, if it makes it easier. He's been on the line a month longer than me and he acts like he was born here.*

Carmody is the best officer I ever knew. All he thinks about is what's out there. He never talks about home, his wife, nothing. Just business and his men. He was a green shavetail when he got to Nam ten months ago. He has a funny sense of humour, like no matter what you ask him, he's got a one-liner for you. I asked him once where he was from.

'My old man had the poorest farm in Oklahoma,' he says. 'Our hog

194

was so skinny, if you put a dime on its nose, its back feet would rise up off the ground.'

Then there's Jesse Hatch, who used to drive a truck all over the country, one of those big semis; and Donny Flagler, who's like me, just out of college. Both of them are black guys. And there's Jim Jordan, who was in law school; his old man was a senator and still couldn't get him deferred. Jordan is one pissed-off guy. He's a short-timer, has two months to go, a first-class pain in the ass. Hatch is the M-60 man; he can really handle that mother. Flagler is our radio. None of us are regulars, but after a month out here, I feel like one.

The 42nd day: *We get orders to take this knob for an LZ. Charlie is all over the place. He won't give it up. They have the high ground; they sit up there and lob mortars down on us all after-fuckin'-noon. Carmody gets on the radio and calls in the Hueys. He wants them to blitz the place so we can rush it, only it's raining and a little foggy, and they're giving him some stand-down shit and he starts yelling:*

'I want some air in here, now! Don't gimme any of that fog shit. Nobody's told us to go home because it's raining. Get me some goddamn air support fast!'

He slams the phone down.

'Listen, kid, if you can't get a chopper in when you fuckin' need one, forget it. That's the edge. You don't have the edge, you're in trouble. We can't beat these motherfuckers at this kind of game, for Christ sake, they been doing it for fifteen fuckin' years. When you need air, get nasty.'

That's the way he was, always teaching me something.

About ten minutes later these two Hueys come over and really waste that knob. Carmody doesn't wait for shit, we're off up the hill while the Hueys are still chewing it up. Six or eight 50-millimetre and 20-millimetre cannons working. Good God, there were VC's flying all over the place in bits and pieces. A boot with a foot in it hit me in the shoulder and splashed blood down my side. I was getting sick. Then the gooks broke and ran and we took the knob and sat up there picking them off as they went down the other side. We must've shot ten, twelve of them in the back. After a while I stopped counting. It didn't seem right. Maybe I've seen too many cowboy movies, but shooting all those people in the back seemed to be pushing it. But then, I've only been on the line two months. I'm still learning.

* * *

The 56th day: *Last night a bunch of sappers jumped this airstrip eight or nine kliks north of here and pillaged two cargo planes. They got ahold of some of our own Bouncing Bettys. What you got there is a daisy cutter, a 60-millimetre mortar round, and it's rigged so it jumps up about waist high when you trip it, and it goes off there, at groin level, cuts you in half.*

We're always real careful about mines, but the motherfuckers have these Bettys all over the fucking pace. A couple of places they rigged phony trip lines so you'd see the line and move out of the way and they'd have another trip line next to it and you'd nick that and it was all over.

I hear it go off. Nobody screams or anything, it just goes boomf! *and shakes some leaves off the trees where I am. I run back. It's maybe a hundred metres. Flagler's laying there and he's blown in half. Two parts of him. I can't believe it. I start shaking. I sit down and shake all over. Then Doc comes up and gives me a downer.*

Carmody is taking it the worst. He just keeps swearing over and over. Later in the day we catch up with a couple of VC. We don't know whether they rigged the Bouncing Bettys, but we tie the two of them to these two trees, side by side, and we set one of the mines between the trees and rig it and then we back off about a hundred feet and we keep shooting at the line and those two gooks are screaming bloody-fucking- murder. It was Jesse finally tripped it. We left them hanging in the trees.

Psychological warfare, that's what we call it.

38

DEAD MAN'S FLOAT

It took me twenty minutes to make the drive to Oceanby Island. Three blocks on the far side of the bridge I found Bayview, a deserted gravel lane, hardly two cars wide, that twisted through a living arch of oak trees heavy with Spanish moss. Here and there, ruts led to cabins hidden away among trees, palmettos, and underbrush. I passed a roadhouse called Benny's Barbecue, which looked closed except for a grey Olds parked at the side of the place that looked suspiciously like the car Harry Nesbitt was driving when he followed me the night before. After that there was nothing but foliage for almost a mile before I came to O'Brian's shack.

It wasn't much more than that, although it seemed a sturdy enough place. It was built on stilts about twenty yards off shore and was connected to land by a wooden bridge no more than three feet wide. The tide was in and the cabin, which looked about two rooms large with a deck surrounding it and a screened porch at one end, was perched barely three feet above the water. A small boat, tied to one end of the platform, rocked gently on the calm surface of the bay.

Nesbitt was right – there wasn't a blade of grass within twenty yards of the cabin.

The place was as still as a church at dawn.

A slate-grey Continental was parked under the trees near the water's edge. It had been there awhile; the bonnet was as cool as the rest of the car. I walked out to the edge of the clearing and held my hands out, prayer style, palms up.

'O'Brian? It's me, Kilmer.'

A mockingbird cried back at me and darted off through the palmettos. Somewhere out near the shack a fish jumped in the water. Then, not a sound.

I waited a moment or two.

'It's Jake Kilmer,' I yelled. 'I'm coming on out.'

Still nothing.

I tucked both sides of my jacket in the back of my belt to show him I wasn't wearing a gun and started walking out onto the platform, holding onto both railings so he could see my hands.

'O'Brian!'

A fish jumped underfoot and startled me. I could see why O'Brian had built his shack on this spot. He could drop a line out the window and fish without getting out of bed.

'O'Brian, it's Kilmer. You around?'

Still no answer.

I reached the cabin. The front door was locked, so I went around to the porch, held my face up against the screen cupped my eyes, and peered inside. The place was as empty as a dead man's dream.

'O'Brian?'

Still no sounds, except the tie line of the boat, grinding against the wooden railing.

Worms began to nibble at my stomach.

'Hey, O'Brian, are you in there?' I yelled. I startled an old pelican sitting on a corner of the deck and he lumbered away, squawking as he went. There was no answer.

I tried the screen door and it was open. The cabin was empty; nobody was under the bed or stuffed in the shower. But the radio was on with the volume turned all the way down, and the beginnings of a fishing lure dangled from a vice on the porch table.

The worms stopped nibbling and started gnawing at my insides.

I went back outside and started around the deck. The boat was empty.

I might have missed the two bullet holes except for the blood. It was splattered around two small nicks in the rear wall of the cabin; crimson, baked almost brown in the hot sunlight, yet still sticky to the touch.

The worms in my stomach grew to coiled snakes.

'Oh, shit!' I heard myself whisper.

I knelt down on the deck and peered cautiously under the cabin. The first thing I saw was a foot in a red sweat sock jammed in the juncture of two support posts. The foot belonged to Jigs O'Brian. The rest of him was floating face down, hands straight out at his sides, as if he were trying to embrace the bay.

Fish were nibbling at the thin red strands that laked from his head like the tentacles of a jellyfish.

I didn't need a medical degree to tell that he was DOA.

39

SKEELER'S JOINT

Dutch almost swallowed the phone when I got him on the line. He was on his way before I hung up. The coroner reacted in much the same way.

Dutch arrived fifteen minutes later with Salvatore at the wheel, followed by an ambulance with the coroner and his forensics team close behind.

The big German lumbered out to the cabin with his hands in his pants pockets, an unlit Camel dangling from the corner of his mouth, and stared ruefully down at me through his thick glasses. Salvatore was behind him, glowering like a man looking for a fight.

'I take the full rap for this one,' I said. 'If you hadn't called Salvatore off, O'Brian might be alive now.'

'I should have left Salvatore on his tail,' Dutch said. 'That was my mistake.'

'You just did what I asked,' I said. 'I told O'Brian I'd be alone. Where are your pals from homicide?'

'On the way,' he said with a roll of his eyes, adding, 'What did it this time, a flame thrower?'

'Small calibre, very likely a submachine gun,' I said.

'How do you figure that?'

'He's got a row of .22's from his forehead to his chin so perfect the line could've been drawn with a straightedge. My guess is, the first couple of shots knocked his head back. The gun was firing so fast it just drew a line right down his face, zip, like that.'

I drew an invisible line from my forehead to my chin with a forefinger.

'Some gun,' he said.

'Yeah,' I said. 'There's only one weapon I can think of that fits the bill.'

'Well, don't keep us in suspense,' said Dutch. Salvatore began to show signs of interest. He stopped staring into space long enough to give me the dead eye.

'The American 180. Fires thirty rounds a second. Sounds like a dentist's drill when it goes off.'

'Like on the tape of the Tagliani job,' Dutch said.

'Yeah, just like that. I figure whoever aced him came in by boat and whacked O'Brian when he came out of the cabin. Two of the slugs went through his head; they're in the back wall.'

'So what does all that mean to us?' Dutch said.

While the coroner was studying the bloodstained holes in the back wall of the cabin, his men were shooting pictures of O'Brian's body from everywhere but underwater.

'Chevos owns boats,' I said. 'It's his thing. And he lives at the Thunder Point Marina. Where would that be from here?'

Dutch pointed due east. Thunder Point was a mile away, a misty, low, white structure surrounded by miniature boats.

199

'You really want to pin this one on Nance, don't you?' Dutch asked.

'Maybe.'

'Look, I got nothing against headhunting; sometimes it can get great results. You got something to settle with that *sheiss kopf* it's okay with me.'

The coroner dug the two bullets out of the wall and went back across the bridge to shore.

'Maybe he's holed up on a boat,' I said.

'That's assuming he knows we're looking for him.'

'Well, hell, I make a lot of mistakes,' I said.

Dutch put a paw on my shoulder. 'Aw, don't we all,' he said, putting that discussion to bed. He strolled up and down the deck of O'Brian's shack, berating himself, like an orator grading his own speech.

Salvatore stood in one place, staring back into space and grinding fist into palm, like a bomb looking for someplace to go off.

'We should've brought 'em all in, the whole damn bunch,' Dutch said, 'Get it out in the open. I laid off because it's homicide's baby. Well, it's our baby too. The Red Sea'll turn kelly green before that bunch of *pfutzlükers* get their heads out far enough to see daylight. Ain't it just wonderful!' He stared off towards 'Thunder Point'. 'I'm gonna haul that bunch of *Ash lochers* in and get some answers. If nothing else, maybe we can throw these killers off their stride.'

His tirade brought only a grunt from Salvatore, who was glaring back into space.

Dutch sighed. 'Okay, let's see who we got left.'

He started counting them off on his fingers. 'There's the Bobbsey Twins, Costello and Cohen. Then there's Stizano and the pasta king, Bronicata, and your pals, Chevos and Nance. I miss anybody?'

There wasn't anybody else. Like Christie's Ten Little Indians, the field was running out.

'One thing,' I said. 'If you start hauling these people in, you better have a lot of help. They come complete with pistoleros. And you'll also be dealing with Leo Costello. He's quick and a helluva lot smarter than you'd like him to be. The son of a bitch sleeps with a habeas corpus under his pillow.'

'I'll keep that in mind,' Dutch said.

200

Salvatore finally broke his silence. He looked at me and said, 'What it is with me, see, I coulda followed that ugly fuckin' Mick into his bedroom and held his nuts while he balled his old lady and he still wouldn't know I was there. I got a talent for that kind of thing. Me and Zapata, we're the invisible men.'

'I told him I'd be alone,' I protested. 'We took a chance, what can I tell you? Next time I'll know better.'

He stared at me for a beat or two longer and suddenly said, 'Ah, shit, let's forget it.'

'What do you think O'Brian wanted,' Dutch asked.

'I don't know, but if anybody knows, Nesbitt does,' I said. 'Let's put him on the radio, find out his story.'

'Done,' said Dutch. 'I'll add him to the list.'

We walked back across the narrow pier to solid land where the coroner flagged us down.

'Stoney Titan's on his way out,' he said, and turned to me. 'He says he wanted a word or two with you.'

'Looks like the old man's finally throwing his oar in,' Dutch said.

I didn't feel up to my first round with Titan; I had something else on my mind. 'I've got some things to do,' I told Dutch. 'You know as much about this mess as I do; you talk to the old man.'

'He's not gonna like that even a little bit,' the big man growled.

'Tough shit,' I said, and drove off towards Benny's Barbecue. I was anxious to see if the grey Olds was still there. It wasn't, but as I turned into the place, Stonewall Titan's black limo passed me, going like he was late for the policemen's ball.

I pulled around to the back of Benny's, oyster shells crunching under my tyres, and found a tallish, deeply tanned man with dishwater-blond hair that had seen too much sun and surf loading soft-drink crates through the back door of the place. He was wearing black denim shorts and dirty sneakers, no shirt, and could have been thirty, fifty, or anything between.

'We don't open until five,' he said as I got out of the car.

'I'm looking for a pal of mine,' I said, following him inside. The place was dark and there was the leftover chill of last night's air conditioning lingering in the air, which smelled of stale beer and shrimp. He looked at me over his shoulder.

'I don't know anybody,' he said flatly. 'Half the time I can't remember my kids' names.'

'I saw his car here a little earlier,' I said.

'No kidding. Maybe he had a flat.'

'He wasn't around.'

'Probably ran outta gas. Maybe he had to walk up to the boulevard, pick up a can.'

'Could be. I kind of felt he was in here.'

'Hmm,' he said, stacking the soft drinks in the corner. 'You know how long I been here in this spot?'

'No, but I bet you're going to tell me.'

He drew two beers from the spigot behind the bar and slid one across the bar to me. It was colder than Christmas in the Yukon.

'Thirty-three years. Be thirty-four in September.'

I sipped the beer and stared at him.

'You know why I been here this long?' he went on.

'You mind your own business,' I said.

'Right on the button.'

'This guy's name is Nesbitt. Little squirt with roving eyeballs.'

'You ain't been listening to me,' he said.

'Sure I have,' I said, sipping my beer. 'If a fellow looks like that should come back by, tell him Kilmer says we need to have a talk. Real bad.'

'That you Kilmer?'

'Uh-huh.'

'A guy I knew once had a mark on him, thought he was safe in downtown Pittsburgh. Then a wheelbarrow full of cement fell off a six-storey building right on his head.'

The metaphore seemed a little vague to me, but I took a stab at retorting.

'Tell him I won't drop any cement on his head.'

The bartender chuckled and held out a hand. 'Ben Skeeler,' he said. 'The place used to be called Skeeler's but everybody kept sayin' "Let's go to Benny's" so I finally changed the sign.'

He shook hands like he meant it.

'Long as we're being so formal, maybe I could see some ID,' the cautious man said.

'That's fair enough,' I said, and showed him my buzzer.

He looked at it and nodded. 'I hope you're straight. The way I get it, you're straight, but this town can bend an evangelist faster than he can say amen.'

I waited for more.

'Tough, too. I heard you was tough.'

202

'I talk a good game,' I said finally.

'These days, you know, you never can be too sure.'

'Uh-huh.'

'County ambulance just went by actin' real serious,' he said. 'You wouldn't know anything about that, would you.'

'Man named O'Brian just got himself killed out on the bay,' I said.

His eyes got startled for a moment and then he looked down into his beer glass. 'That so' was all he said. He pulled on his ear, then took a folded-up paper napkin out of his pocket and handed it to me.

'Dab your lips,' he said. 'I gotta get back to work.'

He went outside and I unfolded the napkin. The message was written hurriedly in ballpoint that had torn through the napkin in a couple of places and left several inkblots at the end of words. It said, 'Uncle Jolly's Fillup, route 14 south about 18 miles. Tonight, nine p.m. Come alone.'

No signature. Skeeler came back with another crate of soft drinks.

'You know a place called Jolly's Fillup, route fourteen south of town?'

'Sounds like a filling station, don't it?' he said.

'Now that you mention it.'

'You'll know it when you get there,' he said, and went back outside. I finished my beer and followed him.

'Thanks for the beer. Maybe I'll come back and try the shrimp,' I said as I got into the car.

'You do that, hear?' he said. 'Be sure to introduce yourself again. I'm bad on names.' And he vanished back inside.

40

RELICS

I started back towards Dunetown but when I got to the boulevard I went east instead of going back towards town. I really didn't have anything to do after I left Skeeler's, but I had to put some distance between me and Dunetown. I needed a little time to myself, away from Stick, Dutch, and the hooligans. Away from Doe. Away from them all. I was tired of trying to make some sense out of a lot of disparate jigsaw pieces, pieces like Harry Raines, Chief, and Stoney Titan. Like Donleavy and his sweaty banking friend, Seaborn. Like Chevos and Nance, a bad luck horse named Disaway, and a black gangster I didn't even know whom everybody called Nose, but not to his face. I suddenly had the feeling that using people had become a way of life for me and I didn't like the feeling and I needed some room to deal with that. I needed to get back to my safe places again, at least for a little while.

When I got to the Strip I headed south, putting the tall hotels that plundered the beach behind me. I drove south with the ocean at my left, not sure where I was going. I just smelled the sea air and kept driving. Finally I passed a decrepit old sign peering out from behind the weeds that told me I had reached someplace called South Beach. It was desolate. Progress had yet to discover it.

I parked my car in a deserted public lot. Weeds grew up through the cracks in the macadam, and small dunes of sand had been collected by the wind along its curbs. I sat looking out at the Atlantic for a while. The sea here was calm, a mere ripple in the bright sunlight, and the beach was broad and clean. It revived memories long buried, the good times of youth that age often taints with melancholy.

My mind was far from Dunetown. It was at a place called Beach Haven, a village on the Jersey coast where I had spent several summers living on a houseboat with the family of my best friend in grammar school. I couldn't remember his name but I did remember that his father was Norwegian and spoke with a marvellous accent and wore very thick glasses and that the family was not in the least modest and that he had a sister of high school age who thought nothing at all of taking a shower in front of us. Sitting there in the hot sedan with sweat dribbling off my chin, I also recalled that I had spent a good part of that summer trying to hide a persistent erection.

After a while I got out and took off shoes, socks, jacket, and tie and put them in the boot. I slammed it shut, then opened it again, dropped my beeper in with them, and went down to the beach.

I rolled my pants legs to the knee and walked barefoot with the sand squeaking underfoot. I must have walked at least a mile when I came upon a small settlement of summer cottages, protected by walls of granite rock that were meant to hold back the ocean. It had been a futile gesture. The houses were deserted. Several had already broken apart and lay lopsided and forlorn, awash with the debris of tides.

One of them, a small two-bedroom house of cyprus and oak, was still perched tentatively over the rocks, its porch supported by two-by-fours poised on the granite boulders. A faded sign, hanging crookedly from the porch rail, told me the place was for sale, and under that someone had added, with paint, the words 'or rent'. There was a phone number.

I went up over the big grey rocks, climbed the porch railing, and looked through the place, a forlorn and lonely house. The floor creaked and sagged uncertainly under each step and the wind, sighing through its broken windows, sounded like the ghost of a child's summer laughter.

I stripped down to my undershorts, went down to the deserted beach, and ran into the water, swimming hard and fast against the tide until arms and legs told me to turn back. I had to breast-stroke the last few yards and when I got out I was breathing heavily and my lungs hurt, but I felt clean and my skin tingled from the saltwater. I went back up to the house and stretched out on the porch in the sun.

I was dozing when the woman came around the corner of the house. She startled us both and as I scrambled for my pants she laughed and said, 'Don't bother. Most of the gigolos hanging around the hotel pools wear far less than that.'

She was an islander, I could tell; a lovely woman, delicate in structure with sculptured features textured by wind and sun, tiny white squint-lines around her eyes, and amber hair coiffured by the wind. I couldn't guess how old she was; it didn't matter. She was carrying a seine net – two five-foot wooden poles with the net attached to each and topped by cork floats. The net was folded neatly around the poles.

'I was halfway expecting my friend. He sometimes waits up here for me,' she said, peering inside without making a show of it. Then she added, 'Are you flopping here?'

I laughed.

'No, but it's a thought.'

She looked around the place.

205

'This was a very dear house once,' she said. She said it openly and without disguising her sadness.

'Do you know the owners?' I asked.

'It once belonged to the Jackowitz family, but the bank has it now.'

Her sad commentary told me all I needed to know of its history.

'What a shame. There's still some life left to it.'

'Yes, but no heart,' she said.

'Banks are like that. They have a blind appetite and no soul. They're the robots of our society.'

'Well, I see my friend down on the beach. I'm glad you like the house.'

A skinny young man in cutoffs with long blond hair that flirted with his shoulders was coming up the beach carrying a bucket. She went down over the boulders to the sand.

'Hey?' I said.

She turned and raised her eyebrows.

'Is your name Jackowitz?'

'It used to be,' she said, and went on to join her friend.

I got dressed and walked back through the surf to the parking lot. I found a phone booth that still worked and called the number that was on the sign at the house. It turned out to be the Island Trust and Savings bank. I managed, by being annoyingly persistent, to get hold of a disagreeable little moron named Ratcher who, I was told, was 'in beach property'.

'I'm interested in a piece of land on South Beach,' I said. 'It might have belonged to a family called Jackowitz.'

I could hear papers rustling in the background.

'Oh, yes,' he said, probably after turning up the foreclosure liens. 'I know the place.' I could tell he knew as much about that cottage as I know about Saudi Arabian oil leases.

'Are you in real estate?' he asked curtly.

'No, I thought I might just rent it for the rest of the summer,' I told him.

'The place is condemned,' he said nastily. 'And this establishment prosecutes trespassers.' He hung up. I stood there for a minute or two then invested another quarter and got Ratcher back on the phone.

'Ratcher?'

'Yes!'

'You're a despicable little asshole,' I said, and hung up.

I drove back down towards the beach and, by trial and error, found a neglected road that led to the house and sat there, watching the woman whose name was once Jackowitz and her young man with the long hair, dragging their seine nets slowly along the water's edge, picking the shrimp and mullet out after each drag and putting them in the bucket. After a while it started to rain and they quit. I waved to them as they walked off down the beach. I'm not sure they saw me but it would be nice to think they did and that they knew the house still meant something to someone. Finally I drove back towards town in the rain, feeling beach-tired but recharged.

I thought about that place a lot in the days that followed, but I never went back. I didn't have to. Driving back to Dunetown, I realised I had left the safe places behind forever.

41

FIGHT NIGHT AT THE WAREHOUSE

I drove back to the Warehouse, and into bedlam.

A dozen men, including a couple of brass buttons, were jammed in the doorway. There was a lot of shoving, pushing, cursing, threatening. The Stick was standing outside, back from the crowd, watching the mêlée with a smile.

'Be goddamned,' he said as I rolled up. 'Dutch's put the arm on Costello and all his merry men!'

I jumped out of the car and we ran into the building.

A lot of racket from the back.

A cop stopped the Stick long enough to tell him they had Costello; his number one bodyguard and shooter, Drack Moreno, who looked and talked like a moron but had a genius IQ; two of his top button men, Silo Murphy, a.k.a. the Weasel, because he looked like one, and Arthur Pravano, whose moniker was Sweetheart, for reasons I'll never understand; and two other musclemen. In addition, they also had Chevos and Bronicata on tap with their various gunsels. Nance was missing, as was Stizano.

A small army of twelve, all of them but Costello raising almighty hell.

We headed for the war room, which is exactly what it had turned into from the sound of things.

The hooligans were well represented: Pancho Callahan, Salvatore, Chino Zapata, Charlie One Ear, Cowboy Lewis, and Dutch Morehead. Everyone but Kite and Mufalatta, who seemed to have vanished from the earth. With the Stick and me, it kind of rounded the teams off at eight to eight.

The yelling, cursing, and threats had continued down through the Warehouse and into the war room, which was as chaotic as the floor of the stock exchange at the closing bell.

Dutch had separated the big shots and shoved them into one of the cubicles. The gunsels were all in the war room. Dutch was standing in front of the room bellowing like a wounded whale.

'Everybody ease off, y'hear me, or some heads are gonna get loosened!' he roared.

The room settled down to a low rumble.

With Costello's bunch and the hooligans, the room was full of the meanest-looking gang of cutthroats I've ever seen gathered in one place.

I was standing in the doorway, eyeballing Costello and Chevos. In all the years I had been bonded to this gang, I had never seen either of them closer than fleetingly and from across the street or through binoculars. Now they were both fifteen feet away. I made no attempt to conceal my contempt for them.

Costello alone seemed calm. He was a tall man and better looking than I would have liked, his sharp features and hard-set jaw deeply tanned, his longish black hair bronzed by a lot of sun, his lean body decked out in a blue blazer, a pale blue shirt open at the collar, white slacks, and white loafers. He was one of those people whose age is superfluous. There were a lot of reasons to dislike him. Only his brown eyes were a clue to his anger. They glittered with suppressed rage. My rage was open, my hatred obvious, but I kept my mouth shut for the time being.

Chevos stood stoically in a corner of the cubicle, alone, staring at the wall, and Bronicata was jabbering like a monkey in heat.

The rest of the Tagliani mob was dressed casually for the

208

beach, looking like graduates of a Sing Sing cellblock disguised as the Harvard crew team.

The hooligans rounded out the scene. A novice would have had one hell of a time separating the good guys from the bad.

'Kick that door shut there, Pancho,' Dutch said, and Callahan closed the door.

Everybody chose up sides and lined up against opposite walls of the room, hooligans near the door, Costello's gunsels against the far wall.

Cowboy Lewis, wearing aged jeans, a faded Levi's jacket, a Derringer-type cowboy hat, and a brilliant red sunburn, was carrying a large grocery sack.

'We dumped 'em comin' offa Costello's rowboat,' Cowboy said, in a voice that sounded like he swabbed his throat with number four sandpaper. I was to learn that Costello's 'rowboat', as Lewis had genteely put it, was a sixty-foot yacht that slept ten.

Cowboy carried a brown paper bag to the front of the room and dumped its contents on Dutch's desk.

Eight pistols of every kind and calibre, slip knives, brass knucks, two rolls of quarters, and other assorted tools of the trade. 'The heavyweights were all light,' he said.

Dutch's eyebrows rose with the corners of his lips.

'Neat. Did you all hear the Russians are in Charleston or some such?' he asked nobody in particular. Nobody answered, but there was a lot of grumbling and grousing.

'Definitely concealed weapons,' said Lewis, who was nursing a split lip.

'Where'd ya get the fat lip?' Dutch asked.

'The little asshole with the mouse clipped me when I wasn't looking,' he said, jerking a thumb towards one of the goons, who was wearing a black eye the size of a pancake. 'I had to use reasonable force to subdue him.'

The little asshole with the mouse got very tense.

'Okay, let's start makin' a list'r two here,' said Dutch. 'First off, we got concealed weapons – '

'They's all registered,' said one of Costello's rat pack, cutting Dutch off.

'Shut up,' Sweetheart Pravano said quietly. 'L.C. says we don't say nuthin' to these monkeys, period.'

Salvatore's eyes narrowed to slits and his fists balled and unballed. Cowboy Lewis stared at a spot in the corner of the ceiling and looked bored. Callahan just chuckled, and Chino Zapata took the gold tooth out of the front of his bridgework, put it in the change pocket of his jeans, and shook out his hands. Charlie One Ear mumbled something that could have been 'shithouse mouse,' although I'm not sure.

The Stick and I ambled into a neutral corner on the opposite side of the room from Dutch and laid back, waiting for something to happen.

Callahan started it.

'Tag these and put 'em away,' Dutch told him. The dapper cop found paper and pencil and went up to the desk to complete his chore. He picked up a palm-sized .25 with a pearl handle, a cute little weapon, accurate for maybe three feet if the wind isn't blowing.

'Which one of you girls belongs to this?' Callahan said with a snicker, holding it between thumb and forefinger, like a dead fish.

Sweetheart Pravano, well over six feet tall and built like a Russian weightlifter, stepped up and slapped the carnation out of Callahan's lapel.

'Whyn't ya eat that daisy, ya fuckin' fag,' he said.

His comment was greeted with a right hook that hurt my jaw and sent Sweetheart soaring across the room, head over heels over a table.

All hell broke loose.

Dutch was so appalled, he just watched it openmouthed.

Cowboy swept the artillery back into the paper bag and threw it in a desk drawer.

I held my corner of the room.

The Stick waded right in.

Makeshift weapons appeared from under jackets, armpits, pants legs.

Salvatore drew his sawed-off pool cue from the leather sheath strapped to his leg and whapped Weasel Murphy across the back of the head as if he were swinging at a fastball. A tuft of Murphy's hair lifted straight up and Murphy slid across a table, sweeping file folders, baskets, and other stenographic paraphernalia before him to the floor.

Callahan took the meanest looking of Costello's mutts, squared off in a fighting stance, and as the goon closed in on him, kicked him in the jaw. The toe of his sneaker was loaded with ball bearings. It burst open like a squashed grapefruit, and steel marbles rattled all over the floor. Callahan's target destroyed a typing stand and landed in a corner, spitting out his front teeth.

The floor was covered with ball bearings. It looked like amateur night at the roller derby, everybody dilly-dancing on the things like three-year-olds at ballet school.

Charlie One Ear, who had seemed a little overweight to me and far too elegant to mix it up with this bunch, slid out of his tweed jacket, spun around on the ball of one foot, kicked a goon in the diaphragm with a perfectly aimed toe-shot, slashed him across the temple with the flat of his hand, and was back on both feet before the goon hit the floor. A lovely little *pas de solo*.

Zapata relied on nothing more than his fists, waltzing across the ball-bearinged floor and hitting any and all targets of opportunity.

The Stick picked Drack Moreno and they went at it, Moreno outweighing him by twenty pounds and outreaching him by three inches, a condition Stick quickly remedied by first kicking Moreno in the kneecap, then pulling a handkerchief loaded with silver dollars from his pocket and swinging it around and around like a bolo. It caught Moreno more than once. Moreno's face bunched up in pain. The Stick hit him in the throat. Moreno's tongue almost hit the far wall. His eyes crossed. He gasped for air. Zapata stepped in and flattened Moreno with a lovely one-two, a short jab to the face, followed by a gorgeous right uppercut to the jaw.

The Stick's silver dollars and Salvatore's pool cue finished off Weasel Murphy, who made the mistake of trying to get up off the floor.

Charlie One Ear gave another of his brief karate demonstrations and put another one away.

Salvatore held the last of Costello's strongarms by the collar of his shirt at arm's length and was socking him, almost casually, in the face, over and over again, with his pool cue.

Dutch ended the mêlée with two shots into the ceiling.

All motion was suspended.

'*Verdammt*, Salvatore, drop that guy!' he boomed.

Salvatore opened his hand and let him go, the tough dropping face first into a typewriter that lay on the floor.

Weasel Murphy groaned and slid down the wall.

The asshole with the mouse now had a pair of mice and no front teeth.

Drack Moreno's face looked like Omaha Beach on June seventh.

To my knowledge, not one of the hooligans had suffered so much as a bruise, except for cowboy Lewis' fat lip.

The entire gala had lasted maybe a full minute, no more.

Dutch stood in front of the room, gun in hand, dust drizzling down on his shoulders from two holes on the ceiling.

'What's the matter with everybody? You all comin' unwired? Book these punks here for resisting arrest.'

The door opened cautiously and three uniformed cops peered in nervously before entering the room. There were a lot of clinking handcuffs and groans as they cleared out the Tagliani goons.

Lewis and the others helped Callahan clean up his ball bearings.

'Brand-new sneakers,' he complained, surveying the split toe of his Nikes.

All clubs and other weapons had magically vanished back to their nesting places.

The Stick returned to my solitary corner. He was smiling. 'I feel much better,' he said.

'I thought maybe one of them stole your hat,' I said.

42

DOG WITH A BAD COLD

With things back under control, we left the war room and went back to the front of the Warehouse.

Costello remained in his corner, still tense, like a big cat waiting to spring. He looked back at me and stared for a few seconds, as though not quite sure who I was, and then recognition swept over his features. I could feel the hatred across the room. I smiled at him and stared back. My turn was coming.

Our group had narrowed down to the Stick, Dutch, and me. Most of the aggravated tension moved into the other room with us.

'Excuse me,' Costello said in a voice that was flat, harsh, and no less venomous than the bite of an asp. 'Do you mind reading us our rights and telling us what we're charged with?'

Dutch said, 'The rest of them I'm gonna charge with, let's see, how about assaulting an officer, resisting arrest, creating a riot, destroying city property – '

'All right, let's make it simple,' Costello interrupted. 'What the hell are we doing here?'

'Things were a little too quiet, we only had one murder so far today,' Dutch said. 'So I thought we'd have us all a little picnic.'

'Look,' Costello said to Dutch, 'I realise you're a well-respected police officer, Morehouse, but you're pushing – '

Now it was Dutch's turn to do the interrupting.

'Morehead,' Dutch said in a growl. 'Lieutenant Morehead.'

'All right, Morehead – '

'*Lieutenant.*'

Costello glared a moment or two more. '*Lieutenant* Morehead, what the hell do you want from us? Why are we here?'

Dutch said, 'Maybe you haven't noticed, but a lot of your relatives have dropped suddenly dead in the last couple of days.'

'Is that why that bunch of beach bums of yours has been harassing us for the past few weeks?'

'Oh, I would hardly call that harassment, Mr Costello,' Dutch said. 'I'll be glad to show you real harassment, if you'd like.'

Throughout the exchange, Chevos never took his eyes off me. They glittered like the eyes of a night predator. It had suddenly occurred to him who I was, a man whose assassination he had once ordered. I looked back and for a moment we were eye to eye. A lot went on in that face in a couple of seconds: hate, fear, annoyance, curiosity, anger, frustration. He finally looked away.

I finally cut into the conversation. 'So you're representing all these people, right Costello?'

'That's right. I'm glad somebody finally remembered I'm an attorney.'

'Then let's just you and us talk,' I said, and I stepped back into the war room. Dutch ushered Costello in and the Stick followed.

I slammed the door and said, 'Look, let's stop fucking around. You're just a mobster, Costello. We all know it so let's stop the bullshit. Uncle Franco is dead and that makes you primo candidate for *capo di capi* – that's if you don't join the rest of your worthless ancestors, which wouldn't hurt my feelings at all.'

He started to say something but I held my hand up and kept

talking. 'Now we figure two things, Costello; either some mob from up country has decided to muscle you out of Dunetown and take over, or somebody inside your clan has got a real bad beef going on.'

'Are you implying that I engineered these killings?' he said angrily.

'You haven't got the guts,' I said, letting my feelings hang out. 'I'm telling you what we know and what we're guessing.'

'It's our problem.'

'Wrong again, asshole,' I said. 'We just made it our problem.'

'Not likely,' he said, very slowly and deliberately. 'Whatever the problem is, it's our problem and we'll take care of it.'

'Yeah,' I said with a smile. 'Just like you have so far?'

His face turned red. Dutch said, 'Wrong, anyway. We're talking about homicide, lots of it. It's out of your hands, Costello. It's officially a police matter. As such, what we're suggesting is your cooperation.'

'I'll tell it one more time,' he said, holding up a forefinger. 'I don't know who is doing this, or why. And that's all any of us will have to say on the matter.'

'That's hardly what we call cooperation, counsellor,' Dutch said. Then he piped up, 'Right now, I got you down as an A-number-one client for a hit *and* an A-number-one suspect. You could be in a lot of trouble, Mr Costello. I could book you as a material witness for starters.'

'I'd be out before the desk sergeant cleared his throat,' Costello said.

'Where's Turk Nance?' I asked.

'I barely know Turk Nance. Why, is he missing?' Costello hissed, then turning to Dutch, added, 'I'm leaving now and I'm taking my people with me.'

'I'm booking that bunch of muggers of yours for disorderly conduct,' Dutch said. 'Seventy-five bucks apiece.'

'Don't be silly . . .'

'Disorderly conduct, period,' Dutch said. 'You want to argue, we'll see you all in court. Otherwise you can pay the night judge on your way out. It'll fix the holes in the ceiling.' He jabbed a thumb towards two bullet holes.

Costello turned back to me. 'You, I know about. Your name came down from Cincy. I hear you're on the list, buddy boy. Way up. My wife's uncle Skeet had a lot of friends.'

214

'I'm all torn up over your wife's uncle Skeet,' I said. 'I'll make you a promise, wimp. I'm going to send you up there with him. A Christmas present, so he doesn't get lonely.'

'You know, you could work yourself to death, Kilmer.'

'I doubt even you're stupid enough to knock over a Fed,' the Stick said to Costello.

'Sure he is,' I said. 'He's real stupid.'

'Maybe you ought to be on the list too,' Costello said to Stick

'Love it,' said the Stick, and started laughing.

'You've been a flea bite to my family for a long time, Kilmer,' Costello said.

'Sure, that's why you all ran out of Cincinnati,' I said with a leer. 'You couldn't stand the itch.'

'I suggest you back off,' he said coldly. 'We've done nothing illegal here. This is none of your business.'

'Everything you do's my business,' I snarled. 'I've made you my favourite charity.'

There was one of those tense moments when nobody says anything. I decided to fill in the blanks.

'There's an African proverb, goes like this,' I said. '"When the skunk saw the lion run from him, he thought he was king of the jungle. And then he met a dog with a bad cold." That's me, Costello, I'm your dog with a bad cold. I know all about your lily-white record and I don't care. I'm going to turn you up. Sooner or later this dog is going to bite. That's if you're still around.'

'Oh, I'll be around,' he said, and turned to leave. He hesitated at the door. 'This is a family affair,' he said. 'Resolving it is a matter of honour to us.'

'That explains the problem.' I said. 'If honour's concerned in this, you're dead already.'

Costello turned and left. I followed back out and went up to Chevos, standing so I was a few inches from his face. He looked like one of those Russian assassins that usually get elected to the Politburo.

I put on my toughest voice, almost a whisper with an edge like a carving knife.

'Where's Nance, old man?'

He stared at me, snake eyed, his jaws shivering. He didn't answer and he couldn't look me in the eye; he just kept staring over my shoulder.

'Where's Nance, *old man?*' I snarled again, with as much menace as I could put in it.

Blood filled his face at the insult but he still didn't answer.

'Give him a message from me,' I hissed angrily. 'You tell that gutless back-shooter he fucked up when he missed me in Cincinnati that night. Tell him the next time he tries, I'm gonna take his gun away from him, stick it up his ass, and blow his brains out. Do you think you can remember that, or are you too senile?'

He was so angry his eyes started to water. His Adam's apple was bobbing like a bubble in the surf as he swallowed his spit.

'I know all about you, you disgusting freak,' I went on, getting all the venom I could out of my system. 'You make junkies out of children. You kill women. You're scum, Chevos, and you're on my list too.'

It felt good. Damn did it feel good. I may not have had ball bearings in my sneakers or a sawed-off pool cue in my knickers, but I felt good.

I turned and went back into the war room, followed momentarily by Stick and Dutch.

'Well, that's throwing down the old gauntlet,' Stick said.

'That was some touchy stuff bein' said in there,' Dutch agreed.

'Blood feud,' I said. 'I put their patron saint in the place and sooner or later some punk asshole's gonna try to even the score and make a name for himself. I just decided to give it a nudge.'

'That's a comforting thought,' said the Stick. Then he turned to Dutch. 'What the hell did all that accomplish, anyway?' he asked.

'Blew off a little steam. I figured you boys needed some close-up contact, see these guys eyeball to eyeball. Us too. It's good to see the enemy up close. Also to get it out in the open air, so there's no question about where everybody stands.'

Stick's face curled up into that crazy-eyed smile and he shook his head. 'You made it clear all right.'

At that point Dutch stared past us in surprise.

'Well, I'll be damned,' he said. 'Look who finally blew in with the wind.'

I turned to check out the new arrival.

'You're about to meet the Mufalatta Kid, Jake,' Dutch said.

The Mufalatta Kid was not what I expected. I had pictured a man smaller and leaner, almost emaciated. I suppose because the

216

Stick had implied as much. The Mufalatta Kid was a shade under six feet tall and built like a swimmer. He walked loose, his hands dangling at his sides, fingers limp, shoulders sagging from side to side, only the balls of his feet touching. No jewellery. The Kid was dressed for yachting: a pale blue sailcloth shirt, jeans, and dirty, white, low-cut sneakers. All he needed was a rugby shirt and a pipe. But what surprised me most was that he didn't look a day over sixteen. Even his pencil-thin moustache didn't help. The Kid was well named – that's exactly what he looked like.

'Welcome home,' Dutch growled. 'I hope you had a nice trip.'

The Kid didn't say anything, but he didn't look too concerned about anything, either.

'Okay,' Dutch demanded, what's your story? We got World War Three going on here, and you drop off the face of the earth.'

'I've been shagging Mr Badass since Sunday morning, eleven A.M.' His voice was soft, dusty, confident. I assumed Mr Badass was Longnose Graves.

'You eyeballed him that entire time?' Dutch said.

'Until about thirty minutes ago. He's been in a highstakes poker game at the Breakers Hotel with two horseplayers from California, some asshole from Hot Springs, Texas, in a Stetson hat who insulted everybody at the table, a white pimp off Front Street, and a few fast losers. A Louisiana horse breeder came into the game late today and Nose stayed around to clean his tank also. Fucker dropped fifteen grand before he could wipe his nose.'

'Graves was the big winner, then?' I asked.

'That's it. Who the hell are you, anyway?'

Dutch did the honours. Mufalatta had a handshake that almost crippled me for life. He stuck up his nose at me upon learning I was a Fed. Another one to educate.

'Do you know what's been happening?' Dutch asked.

'No details. Just that all these bozos are from points north and somebody has a hard-on for them.' He paused and looked at me for the blink of an eye, then added, 'All of a sudden.'

Dutch said, 'Kilmer was on the plane when Tagliani got wasted. I picked him up myself at the airport.'

The Kid shrugged. 'No offence,' he said. 'My mother sold

me for six bucks to a Canal Street vegetable man when I was four years old. I ain't trusted anybody since.'

'How the hell did you keep him in sight for thirty-six hours?' Dutch asked.

'Nose don't know me from a brick shithouse, so I bribed the bellhop who's got the room, give him a Franklin and all the tips I took in, he let me take the job. I handled the room, mixed drinks, keep the place tidy. Kept the ladies in the other room happy. Let me tell you, the only time that nigger left the table was to go to the growler. He didn't do so much as a Ma Bell the whole time.'

'Was he by himself?' Dutch asked.

'Just him and his bodyguard. A Chinee called Song. Big Chinee,' the Kid said, giving it a little vibrato for emphasis. 'I mean, that fucker makes King Kong look like an organ grinder's monkey.'

'Graves probably wouldn't be doing the dirty work himself, anyway,' I offered.

'I'd want long odds, if I made that bet,' the Kid said, glaring at me.

'You think he would?' I asked.

'He did Cherry McGee in, personally. And in broad fuckin' daylight. We couldn't bend him for disturbing the peace. And he disturbed the hell out of McGee's fuckin' peace.'

'What do you know about McGee?' I asked.

'He's a dead fuckin' honky,' the Kid said.

I had a wild hunch and I threw it at the Kid. 'That Louisiana horse breeder that came in the game late, his name wasn't Thibideau, was it?'

He looked surprised. 'Thibideau? Yeah, I think that was the name. Short guy, dark hair, built like a crate?'

'Close enough. How much did he drop?'

'Fifteen and change. How you know he was in the game?'

'I'm psychic,' I said.

'No shit?' he said. 'Maybe you should read my palm. I been told I got a life line shorter than a lovebird's pecker.'

'I wouldn't know,' I said. 'I've never seen a lovebird's pecker.'

'See what I mean,' he said. Then he turned back to Dutch. 'What the hell's goin' on here? Who are all these people fuckin' up the place?'

218

'Kid, it's a long, *long* story,' Dutch said wearily. 'You're about three days behind. I'll buy you a sandwich; maybe Kilmer here can fill you in.'

He looked back at me. 'A fuckin' Fed, huh,' he said. 'We ain't got enough trouble.'

'You'll learn to love me,' I said, and begged off dinner with some vague excuse. I had to meet Harry Nesbitt at Uncle Jolly's and this time I decided to keep the meeting to myself.

I headed back to the hotel to take a quick shower.

There were four phone messages in my box. Three of them were from Doe Findley. The fourth was from DeeDee Lukatis.

43

UNCLE JOLLY'S

I put on my oldest jeans, a faded cotton shirt, clodhopper boots, a nasty old Windbreaker from my narc days, put my .357 under my arm, and slipped a bob-nosed .22 into my boot. It was about eight o'clock when I headed out Highway 35 south.

I was thinking about Doe, and I was also thinking about DeeDee Lukatis. She had obviously left the message at the desk. It was handwritten.

> Dear Jake:
> You probably don't remember me. The last time I saw you I was barely 15. I need to talk to you about a matter of some urgency. My phone number is below. If we miss each other I'll be at Casablanca after ten tonight.
>
> An old friend,
> DEEDEE LUKATIS

It was followed by a PS with her phone number. I had tried it but there was no answer. I might have ignored the message except for two things. DeeDee Lukatis was Tony Lukatis' sister, and Tony Lukatis had once been Doe's lover. That would have been enough to warrant a phone call. But Babs Thomas had also told me that DeeDee Lukatis was the personal secretary of my favourite Dunetown banker, Charles Seaborn. That made it very important. She might know a lot about Lou Cohen's relationship with Seaborn.

Then I started thinking about Doe. Her first two phone messages had been simple and to the point: 'Please call Mrs Rains about the stud fee.' Nice and subtle. The last message informed me that she was out for the evening but I could call her after ten in the morning. That was to let me know Harry was back in town. I felt a sudden urgency to see her, knowing I couldn't, and I felt some sense of guilt at not calling her earlier in the day.

Uncle Jolly's Fillup ended that reverie. The place wasn't hard to find. It would have been harder not to find.

It looked like a Friday night football game. A country cop was directing traffic, most of which was going down the same dirt road I went down. I followed the crowd about two miles through pine trees and palmetto bushes to the parking lot. Through the cracks and peeling paint I could just make out the sign: PARK HERE FOR UNCLE JOLLY'S FILLUP.

A hundred cars in the space, at least.

I parked among dusty Chevys and Dodges, Pontiacs with high-lift rear ends, and pickup trucks with shotguns in the rear window gunracks, and drifted with the crowd. As I passed one of those big-wheel pickups, the kind with wheels about six feet high, the door opened and the Mufalatta Kid stuck his caramel-coloured face out.

'You take a wrong turn someplace?' he asked.

'What're you doin' here?' I asked.

'Just checkin' out the territory.'

'Me too.'

'Glide easy, babes. Strangers make these people real nervous.'

'What's this all about, anyway?' I asked him.

'You mean you don't know why you came all the way out here?' he said incredulously. 'Shit, man, I guess you are psychic. This is the dog fights, babes.'

It jolted me.

Dog fighting was the last thing I expected. Bare-knuckle boxing, a porno show, a carnival, a lot of things had occurred to me when I saw the traffic jam, but dog fighting was the farthest thing from my mind.

'Dog fighting,' he repeated. 'Not your thing, huh?'

'Jesus, dog fighting. I didn't know they still did that kind of thing.'

220

'Well, you do now, man, 'cause that's what it's all about.'

'You going to bust this little picnic?'

'Me? All by myself? Shit. If I was that fucked up I wouldn't have *any* life line. These people take their sports real serious. You wanna die in a backwoods swamp in south fuckin' Georgia? If I was you, what I would do is, I would hightail my ass back up the road and be glad you're gone.'

'I don't want to start a thing,' I said lamely.

'So how the fuck did you wind up here?'

'I was invited,' I said.

'You are a piece of work, all right. Stick was tellin' me about you. "He's a real piece of work," he said. He left off that you're nuts.'

'Well, that's what happens when you're in a strange town,' I said. 'You'll do anything for laugh.'

We watched a lot of coming and going, a lot of lean men in felt hats, overalls, and galluses, a lot of weary women in Salvation Army duds dragging four and five-year-olds with them, a few friendly arguments over the merits of the dogs, two freckle-bellied high school kids wandering off into the brush to settle a dispute over a cheerleader who looked thirteen years old except for a bosom you could set Thanksgiving dinner on, a woman nursing a child old enough to tackle a two-dollar steak, and a few blacks, all of whom were men and all face-creased, gaunt looking, and smiling.

As it started getting dark, the visiting team rolled up, a group of edgy, sharp-faced badgers in polyester knits. Mug book faces. Twenty in all and travelling in a herd. The Romans had arrived; time for the festivities to begin.

'Track dudes,' Mufalatta said. 'Always a bunch don't get enough action at the races. Look at those threads, man. Now there's a fuckin' crime.'

Next the emperor arrived – in a silver and grey stretch Lincoln limo big enough to throw a Christmas party in. The chariot stopped for a chat with the guard at the road.

'That's Elroy Luther Graves in that car there,' the Mufalatta Kid said. Now I knew what the Kid was doing there.

'Elroy Luther?'

'That's his name, babes, Elroy Luther Graves,' he said.

'Nice to know,' I said, and decided to get a peek at the man everybody seemed to have a healthy respect for. As I started toward the limo, I ran into the back of Mufalatta's hand. He never looked at you when he spoke; he was always staring off somewhere at nothing in particular.

'Uh-uh,' he said.

'Uh-uh?' I said.

'Uh-uh. Not that way.'

'Fuck him,' I growled.

Mufalatta moved his hand. 'Okay,' he said, 'but you're on his turf, man. No place to start trouble.'

I thought about that for a minute. What Mufalatta was telling me was that it wasn't just Graves' turf, it was the Kid's too.

'I didn't know you had something going,' I said. 'Sorry.'

'Don't be. It's the way things happen. You'll get the hang of it.'

'Okay,' I said, 'so we do it your way.'

'That's cool,' he said. 'For now, the Kid's way is to hang loose, don't splash the water, don't wave your face around a lot, lay back, see what comes along.'

'Is there gonna be trouble here?'

'Anyplace Elroy Luther is, there could be trouble. It comes to him like flies to a two-holer.'

'Well, are you *expecting* trouble?'

'I just answered that,' the Kid said, and shut up.

'I'm going to mosey around,' I said.

I followed the silver chariot a hundred yards down the road until it ended at an old frame roadhouse, a big place with a cone-shaped roof, boarded-up windows, and a lot of noise inside.

And there were the dogs. Mean dogs. Not yipping dogs. These were angry, snarling, growling, scarred, teeth-snapping, gum-showing, slobbering dogs, biting at their cages with yellow teeth. I could feel the gooseflesh on my arms rising like biscuits in a stove.

In all, I estimated three hundred and fifty to four hundred people were packed inside, all of whom had paid ten dollars a head, man, woman, and child, to the giant at the door. He was bald and black-bearded, wore overalls and no shirt, had arms like a truck tyre and curly hair on his shoulders. For those who were not impressed by his size, there was a .38 police special hanging haphazardly from his rear pocket.

When the crowd outside the arena had thinned to half a dozen, a tall, pole-thin black man got out of the front seat of the Lincoln.

The window glided silently down as he reached in and drew back a wad of bills big enough to strangle Dumbo. I got a quick look at a handsome black face at the window. I had imagined Nose Graves to be ugly. If that was Nose Graves, and I was fairly sure it was, he was the lady-killer type. Older than I'd thought, probably forty-five or so, give or take a couple of years either way. His bushy hair was greying at the temples and he had a deep scar almost the width of one eyebrow, another over his ear that carried a grey streak with it. His nose was straight and larger than mine. He was wearing gold-rimmed sunglasses. My guess was, Nose Graves probably wore those glasses to bed.

The window went back up without a sound and the skinny man headed for the rear door of Uncle Jolly's. So that was the pitch, then. Longnose Graves was the banker. It was his house.

I sauntered up to the gate. My sawbuck vanished into the keeper's fist. He cut me about six ways with his black eyes before jerking his head for me to go in.

Noise, heat, odour, hit me like a bucket of hot water. Tiers had been built up and away from a pit in the middle of the room. Fruit jars of moonshine were being passed back and forth. Some of the families had brought picnics and were wolfing down dinner, waiting for the tournament to start. Smoke swirled around half a dozen green-shaded two-hundred-watt bulbs that hung from the ceiling over the plywood rink.

Most of the crowd could have been dirt farmers living on food stamps – until the betting started. That's when the US Grants and Ben Franklins appeared.

The place suddenly sounded like a tobacco auction. Graves' man stood in the ring and handled it with the bored finesse of a maitre d'. A wizened, mean-looking little creep, with a flimsy white beard, whom I took to be Uncle Jolly, stood behind him with a large roll of movie tickets over one wrist, handing out Chits as the bets were made, after scribbling what I assumed to be the size of the bet and the number of the dog on the back.

A lot of money was going down, big money. And this was only the first fight. Clyde Barrow could have knocked over this soirée and retired.

44

DOUBLE FEATURE

It had seen better days, the South Longbeach Cinema, a movie palace once long ago, when Garbo and Taylor were the stars and glamour and double features eased the pain of the Depression. Its flamingo-painted walls were chipped and faded now, and the art deco curves around its marque were terminally spattered by pigeons and sea birds.

It stood alone, consuming, with its adjacent parking lot, an entire block, facing a small park. Behind it, looming up like some extinct prehistoric creature, was the tattered skeleton of a roller coaster, stirring bleak memories of a time when the world was a little more innocent and South Longbeach was the playground of the city's middle class.

Now the theatre was an ethnic showplace, specialising in foreign films shown in their original language. It attracted enough trade to stay open, but not enough to be cared for properly. The park across the street was rundown too. Its nests of palm trees dry and dusty, the small lake polluted, most of its lights broken or burned out. At night nobody went near the place but drunks, hobos, and predators.

The ocean was hidden from the area by an abutment, the foot of one of the many towering dunes from which the city had taken its name. The road that wound around it to the beach was pockmarked by weather and strewn with broken bottles and beer cans.

A long black limousine was parked in the 'no stand' zone in front of the theatre. The double feature was Roma *and* La Strada. *Stizano and his bunch had come only for the last feature,* La Strada. *Stizano, an inveterate movie buff, had dropped his wife off, and come back to the movies with his number one button and two other gunsels. It was his way of relaxing.*

They were still dressed in black. First came the shooters, both of whom looked like beach bums in mourning, their necks bulging over tight collars. They studied the street, then one of them stepped back and opened the theatre doors and the number one button exited, a thin, sickly-looking man, the colour of wet cement. He shrugged and summoned his boss.

Stizano was portly, with white hair that flowed down over his ears, and looked more like the town poet than a mobster. He walked with an ebony cane, his fingers glittering with rings.

The chauffeur walked around the back of the car to open the door.

Suddenly they were marionettes, dancing to the tune of a silent drummer. Tufts flew from their clothes; popcorn boxes were tossed in the air.

The only sound was the thunk of bullets tearing into the five of them, then the shattering of glass as bullets ripped into the show windows of the theatre and an explosion of shards as the box office was obliterated, then the popping of the bulbs in the marque.

Poppoppoppop . . . poppopoppop . . .

Poppoppoppoppoppop . . .

Broken bulbs showered down on the street.

Five people lay in the outer lobby, on the sidewalk, in the gutter.

It had happened so fast there were no screams.

Nor the sound of gunfire.

Nor the flash from a weapon.

Nothing.

Nothing but five puppets dancing on the string of death.

Then, just like that, it was all over. Silence descended over the park.

There was only the wind, rattling the dried-out palms.

A bird crying.

Somewhere, far on the other side of the park, a car driving lazily past on the way to the beach.

And the sizzling wires dangling in front of the theatre.

45

DOGS

Harry Nesbitt was sitting up in the back of the arena, in a corner under a burned-out light. I stopped a couple of rows below him and checked out the crowd. Nobody was interested in us; they were concentrating on the two dogs getting ready for the first fight. One was a dirty grey pug, its lacerated face seamed with the red scars of other battles. The other, a white mutt, part bulldog, was fresh and unscathed and an obvious virgin to the pit.

Two men, obviously the owners of the dogs, were on opposite sides of the pit but not in it, and they seemed to be washing the dogs down with a white substance. One of the men reached over and nipped the bulldog's neck.

I moved up and sat down next to Nesbitt.

'I wasn't sure you'd show,' he said.

'I'm a real curious fellow,' I said. 'Besides, I like your pal Benny Skeeler.'

'Yeah, what a guy.'

'What are they doing?' I asked, nodding towards the arena.

'Checking out each other's dogs. That white stuff there, that's warm milk. They're checking for toxics in the dog.'

'Why's that one guy biting it on the neck?'

'Tastin' the skin. Some claim they can taste it if the dog's been juiced up.'

He pointed down at the small bulldog.

'Lookit there, see that little no-hair mutt down there, looks like a bulldog only uglier.'

'I really don't like dog fights, Nesbitt.'

'Call me Harry. Makes me feel secure, okay?'

'Sure, Harry.'

'Anyways, that ugly little bowser, that's called a hog dog. You know why? Because they use them kind of mutts to hunt wild boars. The dog grabs the boar by the ear, see, and he just hangs on for dear life, pulls that fuckin' hog's head right down to the ground and holds him there. Tough motherfuckers. I got a hundred down on that one.'

'You do this often?'

'Every week. Better than horse racing. The reason I picked the place, nobody'll ever go with me. So I know I ain't meeting unexpected company, see what I mean?'

The owners retrieved their animals and took them into the pit. For the first time the two animals were aware of each other, although they were tail to tail across the arena. Hackles rose like stalks of wheat down the back of the scarred old warrior. The bulldog hunkered down, sleeked out, his lips peeled back to show gum and tooth.

Neither of the dogs made a sound, no growling, no barking. It was eerie.

226

The betting was done. The crowd grew quiet, leaning forward on the benches.

The referee, a lean man with a warty face and a jaw full of chewing tobacco, whistled between his teeth and the place was silent.

'Gentlemen,' warty-face said, 'face yer dogs.'

I turned away, looking over at Nesbitt, who was wide-eyed, waiting for two dogs to tear each other to pieces.

'So let's get on with it,' I said.

I heard the referee cry, 'Pit!'

The crowd went crazy. The dogs still did not bark. I was to learn later that they are trained to fight without a sound. It conserves energy.

My companion was really into it. He was on his feet. 'Get 'im, ya little pissant!' he screamed.

'So let's get on with it,' I yelled to Nesbitt. 'This isn't one of my favourite things here, with the dogs.'

'You know what's goin' down, man. Do I look like I wanna end up a chopped liver sandwich?' he said, without taking his eyes off the pit. He was almost yelling so I could hear him above the crowd.

'Okay, speak your piece,' I said.

'Look, Kilmer, I din't have nothin' to do with Jigs' getting pushed across.'

'What are you telling me for?'

His speech came in a rush. He was talking so fast he almost stuttered.

'I'll tell you why, see. Because I was eyeballin' you in the restaurant up until you left. You had breakfast with a couple of guys, then you talked with a couple of other guys, then you went down and got your own car, okay? I drive on out the highway ahead of you, see, wait at the place, at Benny's. You pass it goin' in. I was there when you come by. It was exactly five to eleven.'

'So?'

'So I couldn't of killed him. Shit, I talked to him on the phone right after you finished breakfast.'

'Why?'

'Why what?'

'Why did you talk to him?'

'Look, I don't trust none of this, okay? I mean, O'Brian says he wants to bullshit with you. Lay off, he says, I promised him

227

I'd be alone. It's one on one, he says. So I keep an eye on you when you come down in the morning, I call to tell him where everything's at, he says go to Benny's and wait until you leave. I din't have *time* to nix him, fer Chrissakes.'

One of the dogs let out the damnedest sound I ever heard. It was a cry of agony that seemed to go on forever. My eyes were drawn to the pit.

The old fighter had the little hog dog by the thigh and was shaking his head while the newcomer was trying desperately to back away.

'He's got my boy fanged,' Nesbitt said.

'What's fanged?'

'Bit right through his thigh and impaled his own lip. He can't let go, that ugly one can't.'

The referee cautiously approached the fighting animals and took a stick and started prying the old warrior's jaws loose. I'd seen enough.

'Look, can we go outside and talk? This definitely is not my thing.'

'Weak stomach?'

'Yeah, right.'

'They take a little time out here, when the ref has to use the breaking stick like that.'

'So what'd O'Brian say when you called him?' I asked.

'Nothin'. Nobody was around. Some shrimpers, a guy trying to make city marina in a sailboat. That was it.'

'What time was that?'

'You left at ten-oh-five.'

'You'd be up shit creek if I turned the time around a little, wouldn't you?'

'Where you think I am right now? Up shit creek without the proverbial, no less, is where I'm at. Everybody's on my ass, okay? The locals, the Fed, the Tagliani family, what's left of them. I mean, I got everybody on my ass but the fuckin' marines . . .'

'Somebody threaten you?'

'I don't have to hear from the Pope, pal. I was O'Brian's chief button. My job was keepin' him alive. I fucked up. You think I'm gonna get a second chance? O'Brian was family, he was son-in-law to old man Franco.'

'Maybe that's what they wanted.'

228

'What the hell's that mean?'

'I'm talking about supposing somebody wanted Jigs out of the way, somebody big in the family. Supposing they put it to somebody to ice Jigs. And this somebody rigs the whole thing to provide himself with a perfect alibi – like me, for instance. Shit, Harry, what do you take me for – '

'Hey, you think I done O'Brian in? You think I done that thing? C'mon. And the family put my nose to it? Come *on*. Shit, you need help, dreamin' up a story like that. The whole fuckin' family's getting aced one on top of the other, you think it's one of *them* behind it?'

'Why not? This is quite a plum, Doomstown. Be a nice place to control.'

'Shit, you think this is an inside job, you're on the wrong trolley.'

'How about Chevos? Or Nance?'

'That's family!'

'Not really.'

'There ain't any bad blood there. Everybody was happy until the Tagliani knockover. Everybody had their thing.'

'It's happened before, y'know. Somebody gets greedy. Like that.'

'Not this time, pal. I mean, that Nance, he's a badass and all that, but I don't see him and Chevos doing that. Look, I'm tellin' you, except for that local nigger there wasn't any problems.'

'I still don't trust you, Harry,' I said. 'You could've dragged me all the way out to this pasture to try to get me to fix yourself up an alibi.'

He was sweating. The dogs were at it again but he had lost interest. He was mine for now. He wiped his forehead with the back of his hand and leaned closer to me, whispering over the bellowing crowd.

'What d'ya want to know? Uh, the guys, with you, one was the size of a semi, the other one was missing an ear . . . uh, you had a feast would choke a fuckin' hippopotamus. Then you went over and talked to two other birds . . .'

He rambled on, filling in details as they came to him, things nobody would have thought to tell him. He was a very observant man.

'Okay,' I said, cutting him off, 'so maybe for now I choose to believe you. You got something to trade? This is your party so I assume you want something, and since Christmas is long gone, I figure you got something to throw in the pot. Otherwise we wouldn't be out here in this shithouse.'

'Look, I know I'm probably on the shit list. I can't take a chance on leaving town if I'm gonna get busted. The Triad has got people all over the state on the payroll, man. I get busted, the boys'll hear about it, y'know, like yesterday. I won't make it to the South Carolina border, fer Chrissakes.'

'That's what you want, a guarantee the law'll let you out of town without a hassle?' I asked with surprise.

'Once I'm loose, I'm okay,' he said. 'I got some friends in Phoenix. I'll take a moniker. But I can't take a chance, see, some dumb flatfoot, pardon the French, turns me up down here.'

'Why don't you drive?'

'It's their car, their credit cards. I left the car in a downtown parking lot with the cards locked in the dash, sent them the keys. I'm breaking as clean as I can. Hell, I was even afraid to tap my bank account, y'know? It's all set up by the company.'

'So you're tapped out, too?'

'I got a small stash, get me where I'm goin'. Look, I'm not askin' for anything except a ride and some company to Jacksonville. They can put me on the plane, that's it. Am I on the suspect list, Kilmer?'

'Hell, I think I'm even on the suspect list.'

'I need some cover, man, to break out. Whad'ya say?'

The crowd noise surged and I was compelled to look down in the pit. The little dog, the hog dog, had the old warrior by one ear and was dragging it across the pit.

'See what I mean,' Harry cried, forgetting his troubles for the moment.

'What's to trade?' I asked.

'You sure got a one-track mind.'

'Yeah, and right now I'd like to get on that track and get the hell out of here.'

'Like I said, what d'ya wanna know?' he asked.

'Everything you know.'

'It ain't that much.'

'How about narcotics?'

'I don't have nothin' to do with dope.'

'How about Chevos?'

'Look, what do you want? All I'm askin' is a fuckin' ride out of

230

town. This ain't the Inquisition. I can't turn anybody up. That ain't what this is about.'

'Did I ask you to turn anybody up, Harry? You're making me play twenty questions here, that's all. We've never done business before. What's the game?'

'Look, I don't know what you want to know. One thing I *don't know* is who iced these people.'

'Start from the beginning. The first time you came down here from Cincy.'

He thought about it while I watched the activity in the ring. Finally he said, 'I come down here four years ago. It was Tagliani, Costello, Cohen, that's all. I was one of the old man's soldiers at the time.'

'What happened?'

'Nothin'. We was gonna stay at this old hotel out where the Strip is now, but it was rundown. We ended up on this guy's yacht.'

'What guy?'

'I don't remember his name?'

'Was he local?'

'Yeah. A Doomstown johnny. I think he was in the banking business, like a big shot. Look, you wanna know the truth, it was the two guys you were talking to at breakfast.'

'Seaborn and Donleavy?'

'I just don't remember that, I ain't good on names.'

'Did you hear what they were talking about?'

'I never did that. It was none of my business. On the way back, though, Tagliani tells Costello he thinks this guy is gone around.'

'You mean they made some kind of a deal with him?'

'That's the impression I got. In fact, I know it. We all got accounts in his bank.'

'What bank?'

'Seacoast National.'

'You *all* have accounts in the same bank?'

'Sure. We get paid automatically. Every Friday, you can book on it. It goes in automatically.'

'And that's the whole family?'

'Anybody I know about.'

'Did you come down again with Franco?'

'One other time. We stayed on the same yacht. This time there was another guy came out there. Big guy, looked like a football player. Kinda light hair, not blond, but light. I think they called him Zach.'

'Zach?'

'Something like that.'

'Could his name have been Donleavy?'

'His name could have been Mussolini fer all I know.'

'Did you overhear any of their conversations?'

'I told you, it wasn't any of my business, okay?'

'When did you move down here?'

'With O'Brian. I was one of the kid's wedding presents. So I came with them. Nine months ago maybe.'

'The house was already bought?'

'Yeah, that was also a wedding present.'

'So what was the reaction when Tagliani was iced?'

'Well, you know I been through a couple wars. When somebody in the family takes one, the first thing happens, everybody gets together, tries to figure out the who and the why. They did it at Franco's place the next day, the day of the wake.'

'What happened?'

'It ended up nothin'. It didn't make sense. Both Franco and Draganata had got it by then. Everybody else was freakin' out. They din't think anybody even knew who they were. They started talkin' about you.'

'What about me?'

'That you're sweet on Raines' old lady.'

'Who said that?'

'Costello, maybe.'

'So . . .'

'Costello says you're bad luck. There's a big hate on for you over there. It's why I was nervous for O'Brian to meet with you. They say you took down Skeet and then set fire under them in Cincy, which is true.'

'So?'

'So Chevos says maybe he should take care of it and Costello says no, no Fed killing and besides, Nance fucked it up once before and Nance gets really pissed, like bad enough, he could have taken Costello's head off. Couple of us, we had to take them apart. Anyway, it blew over. Later Costello tells Nance he's sorry, it's all blown over, and Chevos says maybe they can use this thing with the Raines broad to bring you down.'

'What'd Costello say?'

232

'He says he'll think about it and Chevos says you're a jinx. He says, "A black cat runs across your path, you kill it, one way or another." That's his exact words and Costello repeats himself. "I'll think about it," he says.'

'Is there paper on me?'

'Not that I heard, just the beef is all. Jesus would you look at that.'

The two dogs were locked together in the centre of the pit. Blood was splashed on the pit walls, the dirt floor, everywhere. The hog dog was no longer a pit virgin. Its face was shredded. I wanted to get out of there.

'Anybody in the mob got a beef against the Taglianis?'

'Not that I heard.'

'Anybody inside got a hard-on for them?'

'Hey, it ain't like that, man. I told ya, everybody's happy.'

'Anything else?' I asked.

'Well . . . there's one more thing I can give you. I heard something about a big coke shipment that's coming in. Mucho kilos.'

'Well, what about it?' I demanded.

'All I know, there was some stuff comin' in from down south. Out of the country. I know this because some of our girls are into snow and it's been short.'

'And . . .'

'And the boat's late. Not to worry, is the word. Could be a storm or something. If it got busted, we'd already know. You guys brag about shit like that.'

'Maybe that's where Nance went, to bring the load in.'

'What about Nance?'

'He's gone underground. We've been looking for him since Monday.'

'I don't know anything about that,' Harry Nesbitt said.

Down below, the fight had gone against the hog dog. The old warrior had it by the throat and was snarling for the first time. You could tell it was almost over for the little pit virgin. His one leg was dangling like it was broken and his throat was spilling blood.

'I'm leaving,' I said to Nesbitt. 'When do you want to leave town?'

'An hour ago.'

'Okay, I'll see what I can do. I mean, I'll do the best I can. I don't know what the hell you gave me for this, but I'll talk to somebody and that somebody'll talk to somebody else and we'll get it together. It may be tomorrow morning before I can swing it. You got a place to flop?'

'Yeah. Early tomorrow, huh?'

'You call me first thing.'

'Seven be okay?'

'Doesn't anybody in this town sleep past dawn?' I said.

But his attention was already back on the dogs. As I started down the tiers towards the door, the referee stepped in and ended the fight.

The little hog dog was finished. He dragged himself by one good leg towards his master and collapsed in the dirt, his tail wagging feebly. He looked up pitifully at his owner.

I turned away again and didn't see the owner take a .38 out of his belt and hold it down between the hog dog's eyes.

The shot startled me. I whirled around and drew my Magnum without thinking. It took me a second or two before I got the gun back out of sight.

Too late.

The giant at the door saw the move. As I got outside I heard his deep voice drawl, 'Hey, boy.'

I kept walking. I walked straight towards Longnose Graves' limo.

'Hey, you with that Heinie pistol. Talkin' to you, boy.'

I stopped a few feet from the limo and turned around. Two friends had joined him. Just as big and just as ugly.

'Want something?' I asked in the toughest voice I could dredge up.

'That was some kind of move there inside,' the giant said. 'Like the old OK Corral.'

'It's a nervous tick,' I said. 'Happens all the time.'

'You needa get it fixed.'

'I'll keep it in mind.'

He moved closer.

'The only firearms we 'low hereabouts go with the house,' he said.

'I was just leaving.'

'You goin' the wrong way.'

Behind me, I heard a car window whirring. I turned. Graves was a shadow in the back seat, a pair of eyes eager for trouble.

234

The bad end of a .38 peeking over the windowsill took my attention away from his eyes.

A voice as soft as baby skin said, 'Let him do his move.'

They thought I was going for a heist.

Before I could say anything, the Mufalatta Kid's pickup roared out of the parking lot and skidded up beside me, raising a small dust storm. When it cleared, Zapata and Mufalatta were there. What the hell was Zapata doing there!

Zapata had his wallet in one hand and a police special in the other. The wallet was hanging open and his buzzer was gleaming for all to see. Mufalatta was behind the door of the pickup, aiming his Cobra at the limo.

'You sure know how to pep up a party,' said the Kid.

46

TITAN DEALS A HAND

The tension was broken by the appearance of another limo. This one was black and I had seen it before, in front of the Ponce Hotel after Draganata was killed. I even remembered the licence plate, ST-1. It pulled slowly towards us until its headlights were shining between us and Uncle Jolly's goon squad. All weapons magically vanished. I heard Graves' window glide quietly back up.

'A lot of limos here tonight,' I said.

'Either one of these is a lot of limos,' the Mufalatta Kid said.

The driver's door opened and a tall, rangy man in a county uniform got out. He wasn't an inch over six six and probably didn't weigh more than two hundred fifty pounds. He walked with a decided limp and there was about him a bug-eyed, almost haunted look. It was a look I had seen many times before, eyes full of fear of what they might see next – or had already seen. He limped towards the front of the car and leaned against the bonnet. He didn't do or say anything, just leaned against the bonnet.

The goon squad turned like robots and marched back inside the arena.

'Luke Burger, the sheriff's man,' said Zapata. 'He's only got one good leg but he can kick the shit out of a rhino with it.'

'What happened to him?' I asked.

'What I heard,' said Mufalatta, 'he was chasing a bootlegger on his hog, lost it going over South River Bridge, took a header over the railing, and went through the roof of some public housing two storeys down. I hear it took them six months to glue him back together. One of his legs ended up three inches shorter than the other.'

Zapata said, 'I also heard Titan covered all the bills his insurance didn't take care of.'

Graves' man sauntered back to his boss's Lincoln and passed a roll of bills through the window.

All of a sudden it was business as usual.

'I had enough of this party for one night,' Zapata said. 'I think I'll just haul my ass outta here. You comin', Kilmer?'

'I think it's time for me to have a chat with Mr Stoney,' I said.

'I'll stick around,' the Kid said, 'I get a bang outta surprises. Take the pickup. I'll go back with Kilmer.'

I walked towards the black Cadillac. Behind me, I heard the big wheel scratch off in the sand. As I neared Titan's car, his man opened the back door.

'Get in,' Titan's crusty voice said from the backseat.

I got in.

'You got more guts than a slaughterhouse floor, doughboy,' he said, 'but a sparrow's got more brains.'

He sat forward, almost on the edge of the seat, his legs tucked close to the black cane, his gimlet eyes glittering like diamonds. When he wanted, his voice had the lilt of Irish flavoured with molasses, a voice you listened to and wanted to believe. It could also be as tough as a cowhand's behind.

'I've heard you're a smart cop,' he said quietly. 'Very savvy, they say. I can believe that. You were a helluva good ballplayer. Too bad about the foot.'

'It was my ankle.'

'Foot, ankle, what's the difference? So you remember me, eh?'

'Hell, Mr Stoney, who could forget you? I remember everything. That was one hell of a summer.'

'It's a dead and buried summer. Best you forget it or move on.'

I didn't respond to his veiled threat, I just listened.

'I know everything that happens in this town, this county. If a cow farts, I know it. I've had my eye on you since you got off the plane. You been havin' quite a time for yourself.'

'Just doing my job,' I said.

'I could get you recalled with a phone call, doughboy. You got yourself way off base.'

'Seems to me that's my business.'

'Don't be a dreamer. Best you forget the past and get on with your work. In the first place, you don't even have the credentials. Besides, she's a happy woman, just gets a little lonely.'

'Did Chief send you to – '

'Chief doesn't know you're here. If he did, I doubt he'd remember you. He's still livin' in 1969. Teddy's death destroyed him.'

'It didn't do a helluva lot for Teddy either.'

'You gonna turn out to be a smartass?'

'I was with him when he died. That kind of thing stays with you.'

'I saw the letter,' he said. He was staring straight ahead, not looking at me or anything else in particular.

I gave him my hardest stare. 'You never did like me, did you, Mr Stoney? You never thought I was good enough for her.'

'I told you what I thought,' he said. 'You were a good halfback until you got busted up. After that . . .'

He let the sentence dwindle away. Fill in the blanks.

'It was all part of watching out for Dunetown, right? Like you're doing now. Sticking your nose in my business again.'

He looked at me and his lip curled up on one side.

'You found your level, doughboy,' he said.

'Just like you, right?'

He sat for a few beats more and then, without looking at me, he said, 'Harry Raines has a brilliant future. It wouldn't do for his wife to be caught screwin' around with a cop.'

'Or anybody else,' I added.

'There ain't anybody else, doughboy.'

'How about Tony Lukatis?'

His eyes narrowed. 'You sure been busy prying into things that don't matter.'

'That makes two of us. Besides, you brought the subject up,' I said. 'Seems to me everybody's awfully concerned about Harry Raines' future and nobody particularly gives a damn about his wife.'

'She ain't runnin' for office.'

'That's all it's about, running for office?'

'Look, don't go making a monkey of yourself. She's vulnerable right now. I'd hate to think you were takin' advantage of the situation.'

'You've got a lot of time invested in him, don't you?' I pressed on.

His eyes continued to twinkle, even in the subdued interior of the limo. He nodded his head sharply.

'Bet your ass I do,' he said.

'I can understand your concern.'

'Hasn't a damn thing to do with that. Chief and Doe are family to me. I won't stand by and see either of them hurt.'

'I wasn't planning on it.'

'Anything else would be tomfoolery,' he snapped. The molasses in his tone had changed to flint.

'Could be there's more to it than that,' I suggested.

'Now what the hell's that supposed to mean?'

'How long do you think you can keep this under the table? How long can Harry Raines play dumb?'

'He ain't *playing* nothin',' the sheriff snapped vehemently. 'If Morehead was doin' his job, none of this would've happened.'

'That's bullshit and you know it. If the *Committee* had done its job, none of this would've happened.'

At my mention of the Committee, he reared back as if I had slapped him. I went on before he could say anything.

'That makes you as much to blame for what's happening here as anybody. I could understand Donleavy and Seaborn being naive enough to swallow Tagliani's line. You're the sheriff, Mr Stoney, lord high protector of Dunetown and all its peasants and all its kings. You should have tumbled to them. Why dump it off on somebody else?'

'Doughboy, I'm beginning to think you're suicidal,' he said softly, and with enough menace that it made me pucker a little.

'Okay,' I said, 'I'll put it on the table. How clean *is* Raines?'

'Don't be silly,' he snapped. 'You think Harry Raines had anything to do with this?'

I said, 'If anybody local sold out to the Taglianis, they're looking down the throat of a RICO case. And that means you, Harry Raines, or anybody else.'

'You have to prove racketeering on the Taglianis,' he said.

'From what I hear, you ain't got doodly-shit on any of them. You're gonna bust out here, just like you did up north. They got you buffaloed, doughboy. Admit it.'

I wanted to tell the crafty old bastard more, but I decided not to. Instead, I said:

'If he's dirty, he's going to get turned up.'

'I said, don't be silly, boy. Harry Raines is as honest as a Swiss pocket watch. You're dreamin' if you think different. Dangerous dreamin'. Harry, Sam Donleavy, me, we all did our best to keep Dunetown clean. Sounds to me like you may be tryin' to put a size two shoe on a size ten foot.'

'On the other hand, if the shoe fits . . .'

I let the rest of the sentence dangle.

'Let me put it to you straight, doughboy,' he said with unmistakable authority. 'You stay away from Doe Raines.'

I didn't answer him. We sat and stared through the shadows for several moments. His jaw was flinching.

'This isn't going anywhere,' I said finally. 'I owe you my thanks. I don't know what you're doing out here, but I'm glad you showed up. A little law never hurt anybody.'

'A *little* law ain't worth a damn,' he said. 'Either you got muscle or you got numbers. You didn't have either.'

I asked it suddenly. I wasn't planning on it, it just popped out, kind of like my gun popping out at the dog fights.

'Is this your game, Mr Stoney?'

He chuckled to himself, a mischievous chuckle, a tsk-tsk chuckle, which made me feel like a wahoo, which is exactly what he wanted.

'I'm gonna give you a little advice, us being in the same game, so to speak. I been at it forty-five years. How about you?'

'Almost ten.'

'People are gonna gamble, doughboy, it's natural. The reason it's natural is because most people are losers and they see themselves as losers and they don't think they'll ever amount to a goddamn so they gamble because in their eyes it's their shot at changin' their luck. So people'll gamble, and a lot of hardass law ain't gonna change it. The same thing can be said of whorin'. Always gonna be whorin' goin' on, doughboy. A man wants to get laid, he's gonna get laid. Now, my job isn't to teach 'em not to gamble or not to get laid; that's a job for a preacher. No, my job is to make sure they don't get hurt bad at it. We all know gamblin' and whorin' can attract some unsavoury characters around it, so for that reason I keep my fingers on things. I like to know who's doin' what. That way I keep things from gettin' outta line, my folks from gettin' hurt.'

'That didn't answer my question,' I said.

'The answer to your question is yes and no. I own quite a few fightin' dogs. It's kind of a tradition in my family. Been fightin' dogs all my life, just like my pap and his pap before him. The Titans've raised pit dogs since before Georgia was a colony. But I don't run the game, Mr Kilmer. That's gaming and that's felonious, and while I can tolerate it and my conscience doesn't have a problem with misdemeanours, it balks when it comes to felonies.'

It was my turn to laugh.

'That's the damnedest bit of rationalisation I've ever heard,' I said.

'Call it what you will, it's the way I keep law and I haven't had a lot of trouble doin' it and I been at it for longer than you've been alive, so that ought to tell you something. Besides, this ain't Cincinnati or Chicago or New York, it's south Georgia.'

'You want to tell me what happened between Nose Graves and Cherry McGee? There was a definite touch of the Bronx to that.'

'Why are you interested?'

'Because Cherry McGee did time in the Ohio pen for helping Tagliani do some dirty laundry. I don't believe in coincidence, Mr Stoney.'

'Mm-hmm. So finish it.'

'So I think Cherry McGee was sent in here by Tagliani to test the waters, find out if there was any local problem. Graves turned out to be a permanent problem for McGee. Then Uncle Franco decided to cool it. Now why do you think he backed off? It wasn't his style.'

'It's your story, boy, why don't you tell me.'

'Maybe he didn't want to attract any more attention. That's a possibility.'

'Obviously not one you favour,' he said sarcastically.

'No.'

'And what's your notion, doughboy?'

'Maybe he was told to back off.'

Titan never changed his expression but his knuckles got a little whiter over the cane.

240

'Now, who might do a thing like that?' he asked.

'I thought you could tell me.'

'Until this very minute, I never thought to connect the two together.'

'It's just a thought,' I said. 'If Franco had been in bed with somebody in Dunetown, that somebody might have told him to cool it before the whole deal went sour.'

'You got a hell of an imagination.'

'Not really. I can't imagine why the man that did McGee in is sitting over in that other limo and he's counting the take from the first fight, and the sheriff is sitting thirty feet away discussing modern romances.'

'I've known Luther Graves since he was a bulge in his mama's belly. What he does, he does honestly. He's like a snake – he only gets mean when you step on him. Like I told you, this is still a small town and it's still my job to keep an eye on it. If it's gonna happen anyway, I like to deal with people who are predictable.'

'You telling me he runs a straight game? Is that what you're saying?'

'However you care to put it.'

'Well, Mr Stoney, it's been your county for so long I guess you can run it any way you want to.'

He looked over at me finally, a smile flirting with the corners of his mouth, his eyes still gleaming under shaggy white brows.

'You probably got a little more brains than I gave you credit for,' Titan said. 'Now I'll ask you a question. Did *you* kill 'em, doughboy?'

'Did *I* kill them?'

I had to laugh at that one. But I stopped when I realised he wasn't kidding. It was definitely something he had considered.

'I can get off right down there,' I said. 'That blue Ford.'

Titan's man was still leaning on the bonnet.

'You avoidin' my question?'

'It's an insulting question, Sheriff. Besides, I was with half a dozen other cops when two of the slayings took place and I was on an airplane flying down here when Tagliani and his party got iced. And besides that, I'm not in the killing business. Thanks for calling off the dogs, if you'll pardon the pun.'

I started to get out of the car.

'Just don't go around here actin' like Buffalo Bill or Pat Garrett or something. I got enough problems on my hands.'

I got out of the limo and leaned back in and offered him my hand. He kept his folded over the gold handle of his cane.

'Thanks for the ride,' I said.

'Take my advice about Doe Raines, one law officer to another,' he said, without looking at me. He pressed a button and the window slid up. The conversation was over.

47

...SO...LONG...

The Kid was sitting in the front seat when I got in my car. As I was about to find out, he was the philosopher of the outfit.

'Okay I hop a ride back to town with you?' he said. 'We don't want you to get lost or something.'

'Where's your pick-up?' I asked.

'I gave it to Zapata,' he answered. 'He put his bike in the back.'

'My pleasure,' I said, cranking up.

'Well,' he said, 'I din't hear no shootin so I guess you two got along.'

'More or less,' I said.

'You sure don't volunteer much,' the Kid said.

'It was kind of a personal thing,' I said. 'I used to know Titan, a long time ago.'

'Oh.'

'How come you showed up out here?' I asked.

'It was Dutch's idea for Zapata to come out. He said you get in trouble when you're out alone. I was following Graves.'

'Very astute of Dutch.'

'No sweat. Is it any of my business what the fuck you were doin' out here?'

'O'Brian's button is running scared. He wants an escort out of town.'

'Did he give up anything for it?'

I laughed. 'I'm not really sure,' I said. 'According to him it's just one big happy family out there.'

'You believe that?' the Kid asked.

'Sure. I also believe in the tooth fairy and the Easter Bunny.'

'Must burn your ass, puttin' in all that work on this bunch and they get wasted all over the place.'

'I don't like murder,' I said, 'no matter who the victims are.'

He was quiet for a moment, then he said:

'My stepfather told me once, you take two violins which are perfectly tuned, okay, and you play one, the other one also plays.'

'No kidding,' I said, wondering what in hell violins had to do with anything.

'The old fart was full of caca,' the Kid went on, 'but he played the violin. Not good, but he at least played the fuckin' thing. I couldn't do it, man. Me and the violin, it was war at first sight. Anyways, I figure he's probably right on that score.'

'Uh-huh,' I said, wondering what he was leading up to. Then he told me.

'He only told me one other thing in my whole life that I remember, and that didn't make any sense to me at the time. Shit, I was just a kid; it was later on I figured it out, what he meant, I mean. Anyways, what it was, I was pissed off, see, because my best friend at the time din't always see things exactly the way I did. The old man says, "Trouble with you, Fry" – he called me Fry cause I was small as a kid; that always pissed me off too – "trouble with you, Fry, you think everybody sees things the same as you." Then he reaches down, scratches his ankle. "My foot itches. That's reality to me. Yours don't. That's reality to you." That's it; he goes back to the sports page.

'So, y'know, I'm maybe eight, nine, at the time, what do I know from reality and itching feet. I figure the old man's temporarily unwired. Twenty years later I'm after this creep in the French Quarter, a three-time loser facing a felony; I get him, he's down for the full clock, right? Son of a bitch is always one step a-fuckin'-way, I can't quite lay my hand on him. I'm thinkin' I know this guy better than anybody, why can't I nail his ass? Then one night I remember what the old fart told me. What I come to realise is that maybe I know this guy's mo, front and back, but I'm not *thinking* like him, instead I'm thinking like *me* thinking like him, see what I mean?'

'So did you catch him?' I asked.

'I would have but the dumb son of a bitch shot himself cleaning his .38. Really burned my ass. But I would've had him.

So what I been tryin' to do, see, I been thinking like whoever's icing all these people here.'

'And what've you come up with?'

'Not a fuckin' thing,' he said.

I sighed. For a moment I thought the Kid had come up with something important. But he wasn't finished yet. 'I don't know the why, see,' he went on. 'If I had a handle on the why, I would nail his ass. Or hers. Y'know, it could be a fancy, ever think of that?'

'Well,' I said, rather pompously, 'once we establish motive – '

He cut me off. 'We're not talkin' motive, man. We're not talking about motive, we're talkin' about where that fucker's head's at. *Why* he's doin' it. Y'see, life ain't logical. That's the myth. Truth is, nothing is real, it's all what we make it out to be. It's the same thing – when his foot itches and we scratch ours, that's when we nail his ass.'

'Okay,' I said, 'if my foot starts itching I'll let you know.'

He chuckled. 'Think about it,' he said.

'And thanks for the backup.'

'It's what it's all about,' he said.

Five minutes down the road my headlights picked up Zapata. The pickup was idling on the shoulder and he was waving at us with a light. I pulled over.

'Kid, you know where South Longbeach Park is, down at the end of Oceanby?'

'No.'

'Then follow me. Don't drag ass.'

'What the hell's going on?' I yelled at him as he crawled back into the pickup.

'There's been a massacre out there,' he yelled back, and roared out onto the highway in front of me. He had a red light on the roof and a siren screaming under the bonnet. I haven't driven like that since I was in high school. Most of the time I was just hanging on to the steering wheel.

It took us thirty minutes to get to South Longbeach. We came in behind the theatre, a grim and foreboding spectre in the darkness, even knowing as little as we did.

This one had drawn the biggest crowd yet, at least a dozen cop cars, red and blue lights flashing everywhere.

The brass buttons were in a semicircle about fifty yards in diameter around the front of the theatre. Nobody got inside the circle, including them. Several men from homicide were stretching a yellow crime scene banner around the perimeter of the movie house and car.

Nick Salvatore, smoking a cherry cigar, was sitting on the fender of his car, looking as sad as a basset hound. Dutch was sitting sideways on the front seat of his car, his legs stretched out into the street.

'It's getting funny,' he said, to nobody at all. Then he looked around and said, 'Is this whole thing getting funny to anybody else or is it just me?'

'What the hell happened?' I asked.

'Somebody tried to top the Saint Valentine's Day Massacre,' Dutch said.

'Right in front of my fuckin' eyes,' Salvatore said, shaking his head.

Dutch was shaking his head too. 'The last three days, that's a year's work for the geniuses in homicide. If we're real lucky, they might turn up a clue by the next census.'

'Who is it this time?' I asked.

'The family man,' said Dutch. 'That's what I remember you saying about him. A big family man.'

'Stizano?'

'And a rather large party of friends. Salvatore saw it go down. He's an eyeball witness, can you believe that. Doesn't anybody see the humour in all this?'

Salvatore ignored Dutch. He was anxious to tell his story again.

'You won't believe this,' he said, speaking very slowly and deliberately, as though he were being recorded, and pointing out little scenes of interest as he described the massacre. 'Stizano, when he comes outta the show, I'm maybe a hundred yards from him, all of sudden it's like . . . like somebody started shaking the ground. They fuckin' keeled over. Now here's where it really gets weird, man. I don't hear nothin', I don't see nothin'. The loudest noise was the slugs, thumpin' into them. Then the glass started going, the box office, marquee. Sweet Jesus, it got fuckin' surreal.'

There were five bodies lying helter-skelter in front of the theatre. Glass and debris everywhere. Several slugs had whacked the car.

'Looks like a bomb went off in front of the place,' I said.

'It was fuckin' surreal, is what it was,' Salvatore intoned.

'Who're the rest of these people?' I asked, pointing at the massacre.

'Coupla shooters, the driver, and another guy I've seen with Stizano more often than not,' Salvatore said.

'Pasty-faced little runt, looks like he died of malnutrition?' I asked.

'That's the one.'

'Name's Moriarity. He's Stizano's number one button.'

'Not anymore,' Salvatore said. His tone changing, becoming almost gleeful.

The scene was as bizarre as any Fellini film.

Stizano lay on his back, staring at the underside of the marquee with a smile on his face and a cigar still clamped between his teeth. His black suit was full of bullet holes. It looked like a rabid dog had chewed up his chest. One of his shooters was five feet away, huddled against the box office on his side in an almost fetal position. His Borsalino hat was knocked down over the side of his face, somewhat rakishly. The bodyguard, whom I had pegged as a one-time Chicago hoodlum named Manny Moriarity, a.k.a. Dead Pan Moriarity, was leaning against the side of the theatre on his knees, his right hand under his coat, and the only expression he ever had, on his face. Two slugs in the forehead, one under the right eye, and his chest was open for inspection. The other gunman, who looked like a body builder, lay face down with his hands buried beneath him, clutching the family fortune. The chauffeur had managed to get around the side of the car and had sat down, made a little cup in his lap with his hands, and tried to stop his insides from spilling out. He hadn't been very successful but it didn't make any difference. He was as dead as the rest of them.

As the little Italian completed his story, the Stick arrived in front of a trail of blue smoke that wound like an eel back down the dark street and, looking at the scene of the crime, said, 'They giving away free dishes?'

'You're very sick,' Dutch said. 'There're five people dead over there.'

'Bank night,' Stick said.

Salvatore repeated his story to the Stick and then pointed across the street to the park.

'Had to be from over there. And, uh, uh . . .'

246

'Yeah?' Dutch said.

'This is gonna sound a little crazy.'

'I'd feel there was something wrong if it didn't,' Dutch said wearily.

'Okay . . . I don't think – judging from the way these people went down, okay – I don't think . . . or what I think is, it was one gun.'

'One gun did all this?' said Dutch. 'This looks like the Battle of the Bulge here.'

'I know it. But, see, uh, they went down just bim, bam, boom, right in a row, like they was ducks in a shootin' gallery, starting with the driver, there, swingin' straight across. Next it was the two gunners, then the button – what was his name?'

'Dead Pan Moriarity,' I coached.

'Dead Pan Moriarity,' Dutch repeated, and smothered a giggle.

'Yeah, him, and finally Stizano. I mean, Dutch, it was *some* kind of fuckin' weapon. Took 'em all out in like . . . ten seconds!'

The Stick was leaning over Stizano, pointing his finger and counting to himself. He stood up, shaking his head.

'I make it eight slugs in Stizano, could be more. Look at him; he didn't know it was coming. Fucker's still smoking his cigar and smiling.'

Stick giggled, a kind of uncontrollable, quirky little giggle, which got Dutch started, only he didn't giggle, he laughed, and the laugh grew to a roar. Then Salvatore broke down and started in and before I knew it, I was laughing along with the rest of them. The harder we tried to stop, the harder we laughed. We were standing there in hysterics when the chief of police arrived.

Chief Walters was fifty pounds overweight and had bloodshot eyes, a nose full of broken blood vessels, and a neck that was two sizes too big for his collar. He looked like a man who sweats easily.

'I must have missed something,' he said, in a fat man's laboured voice, heavy with bourbon. 'What the hell's so funny?'

'You had to be here, Herb,' said Dutch.

'Obviously you weren't,' Walters said. 'Maybe we better talk about this in the morning.'

'We can talk about it right now,' Dutch said with more than a touch of irritation as his smile faded.

'Right now I think I'd better join my people,' Walters said, leaning on the 'my'.

Dutch defused the situation by introducing Walters to me, earning me a damp, insecure handshake.

'Dutch can obviously use all the help you can give him, right, Dutch?' he said.

'Why don't you go over and give the boys in homicide a pep talk,' Dutch said.

'If I can help you in any way, Kilmer, just pick up the phone. I answer all my calls personally.'

'That's wonderful,' I said.

As he walked away he added somewhat jovially, 'At least you can't say we've got a dull town here, right, Kilmer?'

I began to wonder if the whole damn police force had been recruited from some funny farm for old cops.

'Well, you've met the chief,' Dutch said, 'now you can forget him.'

'Twelve in Stizano and this guy with the hat,' the Stick cried out, returning to his self-appointed task of counting bullet holes in dead people.

Callahan was last to arrive, wearing a three-piece grey suit with a rose in his lapel. He got out of his car and looked around. No comment. While we were counting bullet holes and scratching our heads, Callahan vanished into the park and returned five minutes later with a whiskered, filthy relic wearing the dirtiest trench coat I've ever seen. You could smell his breath from across the street.

'Don't anybody light a match,' Salvatore said as they approached.

'Saw something,' Callahan said, explaining the bum in tow.

The drunk sniffed a few times, then wiped his nose with the back of his hand

'D'wanno trouble,' he mumbled.

Dutch leaned over him, his hands stuffed in his pants pockets and an unlit Camel bobbing in his mouth. 'I'll tell what,' he said. 'You don't spit it out, you'll have more trouble than a constipated goose.'

The bum looked offended at first, until it dawned on him that he was, for the moment, the centre of attraction. Suddenly he started singing like a magpie.

'I was down in the park near the pond, see, grabbing forty on a bench, and, uh, first thing I know, see, I hear a lotsa like clicks. Sounded like, uh, m'teeth.' He hesitated and laughed but the laugh turned into the worst cough I've ever heard.

'Keep talkin' pops,' Dutch said. 'You're doin' fine. Just don't cough up a lung before you're through is all I ask.'

The bum's Sterno eyes glittered feebly. 'What's in it fer me?' he demanded. Then, looking around, he said, 'Got a butt?' to everybody in earshot.

The Stick gave him a cigarette, steadying the old man's hand while he lit it.

'What's your name?' he asked.

'J. W. Guttman,' he said proudly. 'My friends call me Socks.' He grinned and pointed to his feet. He wore no shoes but his toes wiggled through holes in a pair of rancid, once white sweat socks.

'Okay, Socks, so you were on your favourite bench down there, you heard somebody's teeth clicking,' Dutch said.

'That's what it sounded like.' He flicked his uppers loose with his tongue and rattled them sharply against his lower plate. '*Tic-tic-tic-tic*, like that.'

'Fine,' Dutch said, rolling his eyes.

'And then all them lights down to the movie start blowin' up. Sounded like the Fourth of Julahrrgh.' He coughed again, cutting off the end of the sentence.

'Did you *see* anything?' Dutch asked him.

He gathered his breath together and sighed. 'Been tryin' to tell yuh – seen, uh, this car.'

'Where?'

'On Pelican Avenue, goin' towards the beach.'

'What kind of car?' Dutch demanded.

'Just a car. They all look alike.'

'Did it have a colour?' Dutch asked.

'Uh, well, it was a dark car.'

'*Verdammt*,' Dutch said.

'Black?' the Stick asked. 'Two-door, four-door?'

'Tol' ya, it was dark. Coulda been – ' He stopped and thought hard for several seconds. 'Blue, right? Sure enough, in the dark there, see, coulda been blue. Dark green, maybe . . .'

He hunched up his shoulders, coughed, shivered, and did a little jig. Something under the stack of rags he was wearing was gnawing on him.

'Anybody know what's he talking about?' Dutch said.

'Maybe he thinks it's a test,' Salvatore said.

'Somethin' else,' J. W. Guttman said, when he had regained his breath.

'Don't make me beg,' Dutch said.

'Had funny wheels.'

'Funny wheels,' Dutch said.

Guttman nodded vigorously. 'That's right.'

'What kind of funny wheels?' Dutch asked, and turning to me, said under his breath, 'I'm beginning to feel like a straight man for this old fart.'

'Big floppy wheels. I could hear them . . . flop, flop, flop, up there on Pelican.'

'What the hell's he talkin' about?' the Stick asked.

'Beats me,' said Dutch. 'Floppy wheels, huh, J.W.?'

'*Popeta, popeta, popeta*. That what it sounded like.'

'Maybe somebody had a flat,' I suggested.

Socks smiled grandly, a man suddenly thrust into the limelight by *tic-tic-tic* and *popeta, popeta, popeta*.

'That's it?' said Dutch.

'It was dark,' J. W. Guttman whined.

'I know it was dark,' Dutch snapped.

The little man cowered.

'Five people get blown away and the best witness we can muster up is a whacked-out dipso,' Dutch said, shaking his head. 'Go back to your bench, Mr Guttman.'

'Socks.'

'Socks.' Dutch started to walk away and Socks grabbed his sleeve. 'Look, Cap'n, how 'bout takin' me in, maybe you could, uh, book me for like a material witness. Cap, I ain't had a square meal since Saint Patrick's Day.'

Dutch took out a tenspot and motioned one of the patrolmen over.

'Take Socks here over to the lunch counter, buy him a decent meal, and stay with him until he eats it,' Dutch said.

'Me?' the cop said in disbelief.

'Who d'ya think I'm talkin' to, God?' Dutch growled. 'Just do it.'

'Right.'

He started to lead Guttman away.

'Cap'n?'

'What is it now.'

250

'Can I get a pack a butts, too?'

'Get him a pack of butts, too,' Dutch said to the policeman.

'Yes, sir.'

'God bless ya,' Socks said, and stuck out his hand. Dutch recoiled in horror. 'Take that thing away from me,' he said to Socks, and to the cop: 'Make him wash his damn hands before he eats; he's liable to poison himself.'

Salvatore and Callahan returned to the fold with half a dozen brass buttons in tow.

'Just did the park. Nothin',' Callahan said, in his Western Union parlance.

'Had to be the car,' said Salvatore.

The Stick was standing across the street, near the entrance to the park, looking back at the marquee. He waved us over and pointed at the front of the theatre. Light bulbs had been blown out across the front of it. Wires hung down, spitting at each other. Several of the letters were blown out.

What was left of the sign spelled 'So— Long————

48

WHO'S NEXT?

The shootout at Longbeach had attracted most of the SOB's and others were on the way. Only Kite Lange and Cowboy Lewis failed to show up for the festivities. While the hooligans were gathering, I grabbed a minute with Stick.

'Anything new on Nance and Chevos?' I asked.

'Nothing on Nance yet,' he said apologetically. 'Kite Lange is staked out with Chevos. We tailed him to Thunder Point Marina. That's where Chevos lives. Nance wasn't with him and never showed. Kite stayed on to keep an eye out for Nance and I came back here. That was an hour or so ago.'

'I wonder how come Stizano didn't make the wake?'

'He did. He and his entourage left early, I guess to catch the flicks.'

'Keeps Nance in the picture,' I said, not trying to conceal my joy.

Charlie One Ear was next to appear, as dapper as ever in tweeds although he had replaced shirt and tie with a turtleneck sweater.

'God, what a mess!' was Charlie One Ear's reaction.

Callahan said, 'Take a look, other end of the park.'

'Why?' asked Charlie One Ear. 'Is it worse down there?'

'Line of fire,' said Callahan, in his abbreviated English.

'Also we got a witness, thinks he saw a car,' Salvatore added.

Charlie turned his back on the police gala in front of the theatre and said, 'Let's get off the firing line, shall we, gentlemen? I've got a bit of news I'd rather not share with the masses.'

Dutch led us to the hot dog stand where he ordered two dogs suffocated by chili, kraut, mustard, and raw onions. The rest of us settled for coffee, which was strong enough to poison a whale. Charlie One Ear ordered tea. We moved down the street for a powwow.

'So far it's a goose egg,' he began. 'Nobody knows anything, nobody's heard anything. I cruised the hotels out on the Strip, spent the afternoon at the track, and didn't see a face that worried me. I got on the horn, checked the network . . .'

He counted them off on his fingers.

'New Orleans, New York, Cincy, Detroit, Saint Looey, Chi, Vegas, L.A. What I got from that was bupkus. As of this minute, I'll stake my pension there aren't any outside guns in this town. At least none I can connect to this little hurrah.'

'Maybe we should just sit back and wait a day or two more,' Salvatore said. 'There won't be anybody left and we can forget it.'

'If this was an outside mob moving in, somebody would know about it,' Charlie One Ear said. 'That kind of information moves faster than a dirty joke at a wedding reception.'

'Any of these insiders of yours try a guess as to the why of it?' Dutch asked.

Charlie One Ear shook his head. 'No, but the word is about. The Taglianis, or what's left of them, are very nervous. Apparently they haven't got the foggiest either.'

Dutch moved away from the group and stood on the curb, shaking his head, then turned suddenly and threw his cup at the wall. Coffee showered all over the sidewalk.

'What a bunch of *sheiss kopfes*,' he growled to himself, 'and I

252

lead the parade. Twelve people! We had eyeballs on them all, they still get shot right out from under us!'

Frustration shimmered around him like an aura. He turned and looked down at me, his blue eyes burning fiercely behind his glasses.

'I'm goddamned embarrassed, if you want to know the truth,' he said. It was one of the few times I heard him use profanity in English.

'Don't take it personally,' I said. 'These people have much more experience taking care of each other than you or I. If they can't keep themselves alive, it's not our fault.'

'Look, I'm really sorry, old man,' Charlie One Ear said, 'but I may have a consolation prize for you. I'm not sure whether it ties in or not, but a chap I know is carrying a rather large snow monkey. He says the coke market's been dry for more than a month, but the local snowbirds are dancing in the street. The word is, the drought is about to end.'

'Harry Nesbitt mentioned that,' I said.

'When's this snowstorm going to happen?' asked Dutch.

'Imminently.'

'Does this snitch know who the importer is?'

'I wish you'd refrain from calling them snitches,' Charlie One Ear said. 'Some of these people take a great deal of pride in working for me. It's rather like a public service for them.'

'Charlie, all canaries sing alike. Does he know who the distributor is or not?'

'He only knows his own street connection.'

'Want a guess?' I said. 'Bronicata. It's his game.'

'That makes sense,' Stick said. 'Unless maybe it's Longnose Graves.'

The Mufalatta Kid broke his silence. 'Nose don't touch hard stuff,' he said.

'Times are changing,' I countered. 'This place is ripe for toot; it's wallowing in heavy rollers.'

'I ain't stickin' up for the dinge,' the Kid said. 'On the line, he ain't nothin' but a shanty-ass, nickel-dime nigger, say. He just don't fuck with heavy drugs, man. Ain't his style.'

Dutch stepped in. 'Any idea how much coke we're talking about here?'

'Rumours vary. I would say fifty kilos, pure.'

'*Gemütlich!*' Dutch rumbled under his breath.

Salvatore whistled softly through his teeth. 'We're talking bucks here,' he said.

Charlie One Ear took a thin, flat calculator from his shirt pocket and started adding it up.

'Let's see. A hundred and ten pounds of stuff, which they'll likely kick at least six, perhaps eight, to one. Let's say roughly eight hundred pounds, which is roughly thirteen thousand ounces, which is roughly three hundred thousand grams. At eighty dollars a gram, that would come to twenty-four million dollars along the Strand. Roughly.'

That stopped conversation for almost a minute. Stick broke the silence.

'Well, that'll cover the old car payment,' he said.

Dutch turned to me again. 'You're the one knows these people,' he said. 'Do you think they'd snuff each other over twenty-four million bucks?'

'Hell, *I* might kill them for twenty-four million bucks, Dutch. The question is, does it make sense? My answer is no, it doesn't. They deal in bigger numbers than that every day.'

Salvatore added his thoughts:

'I agree. It could happen if there was some rhubarb over territory, somebody in the family got his feelings jacked off, personal shit like that. Then, maybe. I don't see them cuttin' each other up over some dope deal either.' He shook his head vigorously. 'That don't come across as a possibility.'

'So we're back to square one, and we got five more corpus delectis on our hands,' Dutch said.

'I'll keep digging, of course,' Charlie One Ear said, and went off to the other side of the park with Salvatore and Callahan to look for car tracks.

They returned ten minutes later. Charlie stood with his hands stuffed in his jacket pockets, rocking on his heels. After a proper dramatic pause he said, 'It's highly likely the damage was done from the other end of the park. We found what could be tyre tracks. Actually it looks like someone may have wrapped burlap or some other heavy material around the wheels so they wouldn't leave any identifying tracks.'

'How far is it from back there to the theatre?' Dutch asked.

'About a furlong,' Callahan said, and when we all stared dumbly at him, he added, 'Two hundred yards, give or take a few feet.'

254

'An Uzi with a good scope could handle that,' said the Stick.

'Isn't that comforting,' Dutch said.

I took Callahan aside and told him about the game at the Breakers Hotel and Thibideau dropping over fifteen grand.

'Interesting,' said Callahan. 'Disaway'll go off, twenty, thirty to one Thursday. It rains, pony wins, Thibideau can buy the Breakers.'

'Maybe I'll come to the races Thursday afternoon,' I said.

'Back gate, one o'clock. I'll wait ten minutes.' And he drifted back with the gang.

Dutch walked over and joined me.

'Twelve people blown out from under us,' he said, 'and all we've done so far is provide airtight alibis for every good suspect we got . . . at least the ones that are still alive.'

'All but one,' I said.

'Who's that?' Dutch asked.

'Turk Nance.'

'You sure got a one-track mind,' he said, drifting off to talk to the Kid and Zapata. I checked the time. It was half past twelve. I sought out Stick.

'How about a nightcap?' I suggested.

'Sure. Want to meet at the hotel?'

'Ever been to a place called Casablanca?' I asked.

His eyes widened. 'I've been to almost every place in town at least once,' he said. 'Once was enough for that place.'

'We'll take my car,' I said, ignoring his comment.

'Done,' he said with a shrug. As we headed for my rented Ford, Stick tossed his car keys to Zapata.

'Take my heap back to the Warehouse, will you, Chino?' he asked. 'And keep it in second under forty, otherwise it'll stall out on you.' And then to me, 'Let's go to the zoo.'

I was about to find out what he meant.

49

CASABLANCA

I didn't talk a lot on the way to the place. I was thinking about the kid's itching foot story, which led me to murder, which led me back to the Kid.

Maybe I was wrong about Nance. Maybe the killer was closer to home. Could it have been Salvatore? or Charlie One Ear? Callahan?

Almost any one of the hooligans could have done the jobs, except Dutch, who was with me when Draganata was slain, and Mufalatta and Zapata, who were at Uncle Jolly's when Stizano got his.

Of the group, Salvatore might have a reason, perhaps something related to his *mafioso* father and Philadelphia. I was thinking about the *why*, not the motive. The itching foot.

I let it pass. I didn't like the idea.

Casablanca was on the downtown waterfront, a scant fifteen minutes from the scene of the crime. I parked on the promenade overlooking the river and we walked down a circular iron staircase to the river level. The Stick and I were quite a pair, me in my narc Windbreaker and boots, Stick in a suit that looked at least a decade old, a tie that defied time, and his felt hat balanced on the back of his head.

The nightclub was perched on the edge of a pier. The windows had been taken out for the summer and replaced by shutters, all of which were open. A rush of music and heat hit us as we entered it.

'Welcome to Mondo Bizarro,' said the Stick.

The place looked like it had been designed by an interior decorator on LSD.

None of the tables and chairs matched.

Gigantic stills from the Bogart film covered most of the walls. Towering up one was a gigantic blowup of Bogart, with cigarette and snarling lip, standing in front of Rick's nightclub in his white tux. Nearby, Peter Lorre leered frog-eyed at a fezzed and arrogant Sydney Greenstreet, while on another wall Claude Raines, dapper in his uniform and peaked cap, peered arrogantly at Conrad Veidt, who looked like he had just swallowed some bad caviar.

And, of course, Bergman. The eternal virgin stared mystically from under the sweeping brim of her hat on the wall opposite Bogie.

It wasn't the movie posters that gave the place its macabre charm, it was the animal heads, mounted like hunters' trophies between the blowups; psychedelic papier-mâché animal heads painted in nightmare colours. There was an enormous purple elephant with pink polka dots and a giant red hippo with mauve eyes. An orange snake speckled with blue dots curled around one of the posts that held up the ceiling, and a lapis lazuli parrot swung idly on a brass ring under a ceiling fan.

The waitresses were poured into tan leather pants tucked into lizard-skin cowboy boots and wore matching leather halters, which just barely earned the name, and safari hats.

Mondo Bizarro was a conservative appraisal.

The crowd was as eclectic as the decor: tourists, college kids, pimps, gigolos, gays, straights, local drugstore cowboys, and what looked like every woman in town, eligible or otherwise.

We took a table opposite the entrance and settled down to watch the Circus Maximus. I wondered if I could even see DeeDee Lukatis in the mob, or whether I would recognise her if I did see her.

It didn't take five minutes for the action to start.

I felt the eyes staring at me first. It started at the nape of my neck and crept up around my ears. I let it simmer for a while and finally I had to grab a peek.

I saw her in quick takes, a tawny lioness, glimpsed between sweaty dancers weaving to a thunderous beat that was decibels beyond human endurance, and through smoke thick enough to be cancerous.

Her sun-honeyed hair looked like it had been combed for hours by someone else's fingers; long hair, tumbling haphazardly around sleek, broad shoulders. Her gauzy white cotton blouse was open to the waist and held that way by that kind of dazzling superstructure that makes some women angry and others dash for the cosmetic surgeon. There wasn't a bikini streak anywhere on her bronze skin, at least anywhere that I could see. Her long thin fingers were stroking the rounded lines of the purple elephant's trunk. Her other hand held a margarita in its palm, the stem of the glass tucked neatly between her fingers.

I watched her glide through frenetic dancers without touching a soul. Did she practise her moves in front of a mirror, or did they come naturally? Not that it mattered.

Could this be DeeDee Lukatis? I wondered. The way things were going, my ego needed a boost.

It took her a long time to get to our table.

She slid into the chair opposite me and became part of it, stroking the stem of her margarita glass with a forefinger as though she could feel every molecule of it.

'Hi,' I said, dragging out my smoothest line.

That's when I found out she wasn't interested in me.

She had eyes for the Stick, who was leaning back in his chair with his hands in his pockets, a cigarette dangling from a lopsided smile.

'Well, what d'ya know,' he said. 'The place has a touch of class after all.'

Her voice, which started somewhere near her navel, was part velvet and part vodka. 'Wow, it can talk, too,' she purred.

Class dismissed. Suddenly I was an eavesdropper.

The Stick had an audacious approach.

'The joint's full of younger, better-looking, richer guys. Why me?' he asked, certainly one of the great horse's mouth lines of all times.

Her smile never strayed.

'I love your tie,' she said. 'I like old, rotten ties with the lining falling out. The suit, too. I didn't think they made seersucker suits like that anymore.'

'They don't. It's older than the tie,' the Stick said.

'Are you going to be difficult?' she asked. 'God, I love a challenge.'

I leaned over to the Stick and said, 'This is some kind of routine, isn't it? I mean, you two have been practising, right?' My wounded ego was looking for an out.

'Never saw her before,' he mumbled, without taking his eyes off her. 'Who are you?' he asked her.

'Lark,' she said.

'That your name or your attitude?'

258

That earned him a big laugh. Her grey-green eyes seemed to blink in slow motion. Her look would have melted the icecap.

'Wonderful,' she said. 'Let's go.'

Just like that. Disgusting.

He jabbed a thumb at me.

'He's got the car.'

She looked at me. Flap, flap with the slow-motion eyelids, then back at him.

'How about a cab?' she suggested.

'Do we call it or can we grab one outside?' he asked.

'No, I meant him with the cab.' And she pointed at me.

'Nifty,' I said. 'Played like a champion.'

'I knew you'd understand,' she said, and slowly opened her hand towards me.

I dropped the car keys in her palm.

I glared at the Stick.

'Be in by one,' I said.

His smile got a little broader. 'Nothing personal,' he said.

'Naw.'

'Next time I'll loan you the suit.'

She was on her feet already. The Stick followed. He walked to the door; she augered her way out.

I snagged one of the safari maidens and ordered a Bombay gin and soda with lime, no ice, and looked for someone who might be DeeDee Lukatis. The place had grown more and more obscure. It wasn't smoke, it was fog. A cold wind had sneaked across the marsh and invaded the warm river air. All of a sudden Casablanca seemed wrapped in gauze.

I was beginning to think it was all a bad idea when I felt a hand on my shoulder. I turned and looked up at a very pretty young woman. She had a model's figure, tall and slender, topped by long, straight ebony hair. Her angular features were as perfect as fine porcelain and required very little make-up. Grey, faraway eyes.

'Hi, Jake,' she said. 'Remember me? DeeDee Lukatis?'

50

A LITTLE R AND R

'I was about to abandon hope,' I said. She sat down. She was wearing a kind of bunched-up looking khaki jumpsuit with a lot of pockets and a First Cav patch on the shoulder. The full-length zipper was pulled about halfway down to her waist, which for Casablanca was conservative.

'I hope you don't mind the little subterfuge with Lark,' she said.

'She's a friend of yours?'

'She works in the bank with me.'

'I'm developing a healthy respect for Mr Seaborn,' I said.

'Mr Seaborn's all right. A little stuffy maybe.'

'There's nothing wrong with his taste.'

'Thank you. I told Lark I wanted to talk to you alone. She agreed to try and lure away anybody who might be with you.'

'Try.'

She laughed. 'Actually, she thought your friend was cute.'

'If that was an act, she ought to get out of the banking business.'

'She's a free spirit. Lark does whatever makes her feel good. I wish I could. I come here twice a week. Lark says it's a good way to get rid of my inhibitions. This isn't even my outfit; I borrowed it from her.'

'You have a problem with your inhibitions?'

She rolled her eyes. 'You don't know what a trauma it was to write that note to you.'

'Well, I'm glad you did.'

She had to lean closer to hear me. The music seemed to be getting louder by the minute.

'I . . . I feel a little dishonest about this,' she said.

'About what?'

'Asking you to meet me. Actually I want to ask a favour.'

'I didn't think you were going to propose.'

She laughed and began to relax.

'I've thought about you often over the years,' she said. 'I was so jealous of you and Doe and Teddy Findley that summer. The three of you were so happy all the time; you just seemed to have everything. I was fourteen; all I had was acne and a terrible crush on you.'

'On me!'

'Crazy isn't it,' she said, lowering her eyes. 'I guess in a way I still do. You never quite get over the early ones.'

I thought about that for a moment or two and shook my head. 'No, I guess you don't.' I said. Then I began to get that feeling on the back of my neck again, only this time it wasn't pleasant. I shifted slightly in my chair and looked around the room, what I could see of it, but this time there was no tawny lioness skulking through the dancers. I saw no faces I recognised.

I gave my attention back to DeeDee.

'So what's the favour?' I asked, to make it easier for her.

'I've heard you're a detective now,' she said.

'Well, not exactly. I'm a government investigator.'

'The FBI?' She sounded startled.

'No, why? The possibility seems to worry you.'

'I don't know.' She hesitated before she went on. 'It's about my brother Tony. I'm very worried about him but I can't go to the police.'

'Why not?'

'Because,' she said, 'he may be involved in something wrong.'

'You mean against the law, that kind of wrong?'

She nodded.

The din in Casablanca had become hazardous to the health. The music kept getting louder, the dancers more frenetic, and the special effects more surreal. The lights went out, strobes reflected off smoke and fog, lasers crackled from one side of the room to the other.

I got that weird feeling in the back of my neck again. This time when I turned I thought I saw someone, but it was a momentary flash through light spasms and haze.

DeeDee shrugged her shoulders as though a cold wind had blown by her.

'I'm sorry,' she said. 'I guess all the noise and – '

'Why don't we get out of here,' I suggested. 'I'll call a cab. We can go someplace and talk over coffee.'

'I have my car,' she said. 'That was part of the deal. Lark would get your buddy and the car, I'd get you and keep mine.'

'Did you rehearse this act long?'

She laughed. The idea of leaving seemed to brighten her. I paid the bill and we elbowed through the crowd and left.

The street was empty except for the eerie gas lamps flickering along the river's edge through the mist.

The hazy figure of a man stepped briefly through one of the halos, half a block away.

Barely audible over the din from Casablanca; a car door opened and closed.

We started towards the circular iron stairway that led up to the promenade. The street echoed with the throbbing of the music. The damp fog settled over us. Our footsteps sounded like horse's hoofs on the cobblestones.

I heard the car start. Then the stick dropped into place. It started to move, slowly at first.

No headlights.

Through the mist I could see the mouth of an alley thirty feet away.

I said to DeeDee, 'Listen to me carefully. When we get to that alley, I'm going to shove you in. Start running. I'll be right behind you.'

'What – ' she started, but the tyres behind us bit into the cobblestone street and squealed to life.

'Let's go!' I yelled, and started running, pulling her beside me.

Headlights pierced the grey swirling world around us. The car was beading in on us. I was almost dragging her as we reached the narrow passageway between two old warehouses. I shoved her in. There were half a dozen garbage pails piled up at the mouth of the alley.

'Down!' I yelled, and shoved her behind the cans.

The car, a black Pontiac, swept by a moment later, its brakes squealed, and there were three shots. I didn't hear them; they exploded against the cans and the wall behind us.

I clawed for my .357 and gave them three back. They smacked into the side of the car and it suddenly backed away from the mouth of the alley.

I looked behind us. The alley was about a car and a half wide, two hundred feet long. No doorways, although there was a loading platform and alcove about halfway down. The loading platform lip jutted three feet into the alley. There was dim light at the other end.

'We're going to run for it,' I said. 'I'll be behind you. If you hear any shooting, keep running. If they come after us in the car, keep running.'

She looked at me, terrified.

'Go, now.' I gave her a shove.

She pulled off her shoes and took off. I went after her. She could move, I'll give her that, even in stocking feet on cobblestones. We were almost to the end of the alley when I heard the rumble of the sedan.

The car had gone around the warehouse and was in front of us. Its headlights burst back on, turning the swirling fog into dancing halos.

'Damn,' I cried, spinning her around. We dashed back the way we had come. The car screamed around the corner behind us. I heard a pop, heard the slug wheeze past my ear, heard rubber tearing at cobblestones. Light flooded the alley.

We ran to the loading platform and I dived up onto the lip, pulled her on top of me, and rolled over against a metal door at the back of the loading alcove.

The driver of the car swerved towards our side of the alley, saw the platform lip too late. Metal screamed against wood. The corner of the platform pierced a headlight, ripped through it, and tore part of a fender away. The sedan lurched sideways, its tyres trying to get a grip on the street as it skidded sideways and raked the opposite wall with its rear end. Sparks showered from its tortured rear end.

The gunner was undaunted by all the action. Three more shots spanged off the metal door behind us.

Among other things, I'm a rotten shot, but my .357 was equipped with phosphorescent T-sights. I swung the heavy pistol with the car, steadied my hand, lined up the little green button on the end of the barrel with the notch in the back sight, and started shooting at the face leering in the rear window. Three slugs splattered uselessly against bulletproof glass.

They were playing hardball. The sedan slammed to a stop and I could hear the driver slapping it into reverse. Before he could let out the clutch I heard a cannon explode at the other end of the alley. It exploded three times. Two shots splatted against the bulletproof rear glass. The third one streaked off the rear bumper, an inch above the gas tank.

Stick's voice yelled down the alley:

'Go for the tyres!'

Followed by another blast that sparked off the cobblestones barely an inch off target.

That whisky-troubled voice was the sweetest sound I have ever heard.

'It's okay,' I told DeeDee. 'It's Stick. We're home free.'

I lined up my little green sights and put two slugs into the left rear. The tyre blew like a hand grenade going off. The driver shifted gears and roared off in retreat, the deflating tyre peeling off the rim and the steel hub shrieking along the street. The hubcap spun off and clattered loudly against one wall.

The ruined sedan ploughed into the garbage cans, showered them into street and river, screeched around the corner, and was swallowed by the fog.

I turned back to DeeDee, who was leaning against the metal door. Her eyes were the size of a full moon.

'Okay?' I asked.

She stared at me for several seconds and then nodded furiously.

'Are you good on numbers?'

'I w-w-work in a b-b-bank, remember,' she stammered.

'B-G-O 3-9-6,' I said.

She repeated it. 'Is that the licence?' she asked.

'Right.'

A moment later the Stick came running up, his .357 in hand.

'You two okay?' he asked breathlessly.

I threw my arms around him.

'Yeah, and damn am I glad to see you,' I said, bear-hugging him. 'Where the hell did you come from?'

'When we left the palace there was a joker standing up the street under a light,' Stick answered. 'So we stopped at the edge of the park for a couple of minutes, just in case.'

'So that's what that was all about,' Lark pouted as she brought up the rear. 'I thought it was love.'

Stick gave her that crazy look of his. 'It was both, darlin',' he said. 'I doubled up.'

'Whatever that means,' she said.

'It means we're still alive,' I said, 'for which we'll be eternally grateful.'

'Just part of our twenty-four-hour service,' he said gleefully. 'Keeps us on our toes.'

I helped DeeDee off the platform and she sighed and fell up against me. I could feel her heart thumping against my chest.

'C'mon, we'll follow you love,' Stick said, pulling me up the alley by the arm. 'Dutch is right. You're dangerous when you're out alone.'

51

DEEDEE

At DeeDee's suggestion, she and I went back to her place. It was ten minutes away, in the restored section of town not far from where Della Norman and Tony Logeto had died a few days ago.

On the way she asked, 'Shouldn't we report this to somebody?'

'I'm one of the somebody's you report it to,' I said. 'Besides, the car's probably registered to some nonentity. By now they've either dumped it in the river or dropped it at some body shop. We'll never see it again.'

'You seem to know an awful lot about these things.'

'It's what I do.'

'I thought you just did investigative work.'

'Sometimes it upsets people.'

'*Upsets* people!' she cried. 'Is that what you call it?'

The house was tucked among shaggy oaks, a two-hundred-year-old Revolutionary house that had been meticulously restored, as had the others on the street. It was like stepping into the eighteenth century. The inside was just as authentic. It was a museum piece, filled with bric-a-brac, old etchings and maps, and antique furniture that was as authentic as it was uncomfortable. There wasn't a cushion in the living room.

'This was my inheritance,' she said. 'Dad didn't have much, but he bought this house for a song when it was a falling down wreck. He and Tony did most of the restoration work themselves. It took them years.'

'Does Tony live here with you?'

'Sometimes,' she said vaguely. We made small talk for ten or fifteen minutes, trying to talk past the awkwardness of the situation. Finally I got Lark's phone number and she went off to make coffee.

Lark answered the phone after eight or nine rings. Her voice was still sultry, but not quite as pleasant as earlier in the evening.

'Hello?' she said tentatively.

'I'm sorry to bother you,' I said. 'DeeDee gave me your number. I need to talk to the Stick. It's very important.'

'Who?'

'Mickey.'

'You could have waited just about two minutes more, you know,' she said, 'just two little minutes.'

'This'll take about thirty seconds.'

'Trash. The spell is broken.'

A moment later Stick's whisky tenor rasped its hello.

'Sorry to bother you,' I said, 'but there's something I didn't tell you back there.'

'Yeah?' His interest was lukewarm.

'I got a good look at the shooter in the car. It was Turk Nance.'

'Is that supposed to be a surprise?' he replied.

'Just thought you'd like to know,' I said.

'Breakfast,' he said. 'I'll meet you at the hotel at nine. We'll grab some groceries and go hunting.'

'You sound out of breath. Have you been jogging?'

'Fuck off, Kilmer.'

Click.

DeeDee returned with the coffee. We sat on matching high-back deacon's benches, facing each other across a rock maple serving table.

'Okay,' I said. 'Where were we?'

She stirred cream into her coffee and tasted it before she answered my question.

'I haven't seen or heard from Tony since Saturday. It's really uncommon for him to go more than a day or two without a call.'

'Maybe he's out of town,' I suggested.

'He said he'd be back Sunday night or early Monday.'

'That's only a couple of days.'

'I have this dreadful feeling something's wrong,' she said, then after a moment of thought, added, 'Maybe I should start from the beginning.'

'That would help.'

266

'Tony's been in trouble before.'

'Oh?'

'Three years ago. He and this friend of his, who's a shrimper, were caught smuggling marijuana.'

'How much?'

'A lot. Two or three hundred pounds.'

'That's a lot.'

'He was sentenced to two to five years. It could have been worse, but it was his first offence.'

'How much time did he do?'

'Almost a year.'

'Has he been clean since then?'

'Clean?'

'Out of trouble?'

She nodded.

'Why did he do it? I mean, was there anything other than the money?'

She toyed with her coffee, thinking about the question.

'He wanted something he couldn't afford,' she said finally. 'All the money in the world couldn't buy it.'

'Doe Findley?'

'Raines.'

'Right, Raines.'

'So you know about that?'

'That's all I know.'

'It was the same with Tony and Doe as it was with you and me, except you never gave me a second look. I was always the caretaker's ugly little kid.'

'You don't know that,' I said. 'I happen to be a one-woman man.'

'Still?' It was a gentle pass and I passed it gently.

'Still.'

'That was my ego talking. Anyway, I think Tony's been in love with Doe since the first time he ever saw her. I don't blame her for what happened. Harry Raines was busy running around the state politicking for the gambling laws. She was lonely and Tony was always around. It just happened.'

'So he decided to make a quick killing and take her away from all that?'

'No, it was over before he got in trouble. But in his mind, I think Tony feels if he has a decent car and money in the bank . . .

oh, I don't know. Maybe he was just rebelling against the whole system, getting even for things he never had. He never really talked about it. When he went to prison, all he said was that he was glad Dad died before it happened.'

'And you think he's mixed up in dope again?'

'That's what I'm afraid of. He left Saturday morning. We went to dinner Friday night and he told me he had this job to do, that it was absolutely safe. "Not to worry," he told me, "I'll be back for Sunday brunch." I haven't heard from him since.'

'He didn't say what the job was?'

She shook her head. 'Things have been rough for him this past year. I offered to help, but he turned me down. I think he was desperate.'

'Did he say anything about narcotics?'

'All he said was, "After this, we'll be as good as the rest of them." He wouldn't say any more.'

'Did he drive when he left?'

She nodded. 'A white Mustang. I think it's a '79. But it looks brand-new.'

'How about the licence?'

'I'll get it for you.'

She got up and rooted through a large mahogany desk, leafing through papers until she found a duplicate of the car registration. She handed it to me, along with a photograph from her wallet. It was a colour Polaroid of a tallish, dark man, handsome, but a bit too intense, who looked to be in his early thirties and was built like a lifeguard. He was sitting on the edge of a swimming pool with his legs in the water.

I remembered him and said so.

'I thought perhaps you might check around. Maybe somebody knows or has heard something,' she said. 'I don't want to do anything official. Do you understand?' It was more of a plea than a request.

I nodded. 'Sure, I can do that. Is that all?'

'I'd just like to know he isn't . . .'

She didn't finish the sentence. She began to tremble. I moved over beside her and put an arm around her. The more she tried to stop trembling, the worse it got.

'I'll check around first thing,' I said, trying to comfort her. 'Don't worry. I'm sure he's all right. It's been five days. If anything had happened to him, you'd know it by now.'

I wasn't sure that was true, but it sounded good and she bought it. She was suffering a delayed reaction to both her brother's disappearance and the action in the alley. I gently massaged her neck with two fingers, stroking the tight muscles that ran from the base of her skull to her shoulders. After a while she loosened up. She shifted, turning towards me, and curled up.

I massaged her neck until my fingers got stiff, and she talked about a time that linked us to the past, but in different ways.

'It's funny, the things I remember about Doe from our school days,' she said, and giggled. 'Did you know,' she went on, as if sharing a secret, 'that the maids used to iron Doe's underwear? I know that sounds silly, to remember something like that. But when I heard it, I thought, That's the way it should be. That's the way a princess gets treated. That's what she is, a princess. Her father is the king and she lives in a castle on the bay and nothing bad ever happens to her. I know that's not true, though. She lost Teddy.' She paused and then added, 'She lost you.'

'That's not quite accurate,' I said. 'She didn't lose me.'

'Oh, yes,' she said with a nod, 'she lost you.'

I didn't disagree. There wasn't anything to disagree with. We had different points of view.

'I used to dream of being Doe,' she said. 'When we had a picnic, Doe always carried the flag and the rest of us cleaned up the trash. It's just the way it was. She never asked to be treated special; nice things just happened to her. I suppose it's always that way with the rich.'

She said it almost wistfully and without malice, like it was an undeniable fact of life, and I suppose it was, until life inevitably caught up with even the rich. For the flash of a second I considered telling her what really happened to Teddy, but I didn't want to burst her pretty balloon. She seemed to have control of her memories. Perhaps that's why she recalled them with such innocence and without angst. She had learned the difference between memories and dreams.

She dozed off that way. It felt good there, with her curled up in my lap. I thought I might relax for a few minutes before going back to the hotel, to make sure she was sleeping soundly. I leaned back and thought about Tony and DeeDee Lukatis, always on the outside looking in, close enough to savour the sweet life, but never close enough to taste it. I thought about Tony Lukatis, who tried to make the dream come true and ended up in jail

269

instead, and DeeDee, harbouring a futile high school dream for all those years. I fell asleep thinking about them and realising that in the end, DeeDee, Tony, and I were not that much different.

I had the same old dream again that night, only this time Tony Lukatis was running on the ridge.

52
NUMBERS GAMES

I awoke to soft sunlight, filtering through gauze drapes, and the smell of fresh coffee. Sometime during the night DeeDee had slipped a pillow under my head and draped a blanket over me, but I still felt like I'd been stretched on the rack.

She was wearing a plain black silk dress and her long hair was gathered in a bun at the back of her head, quite a departure from the previous night. Either way, she was a knockout. She put a tray with orange juice, toast, and coffee on the table in front of me.

'Thanks,' I said. 'What time is it?'

'A little after eight. This should give you enough strength to go back to the hotel and clean up before you meet . . . what's his name?'

'Mickey Parver. Everybody calls him Stick but don't ask why, it's too early to talk.'

The juice was ice cold, the coffee strong and hot, and the toast wasn't burned. I wolfed it down while she sat across from me and had her second cup.

'I want to thank you for last night,' she said. She sounded almost embarrassed.

'For what, almost getting you killed?'

'I mean later, after that. It's the first time I've slept in days. And thanks, too, for . . . listening to me ramble.'

'Better watch out,' I said. 'Your inhibitions are showing again.'

'I only wish there was some way I could repay you.'

There it was, the perfect opening. It was time to play cop

again. I sipped a little more coffee. It was tough coming out with it.

'Maybe there is,' I said finally.

She was pleased at the prospect. 'Really?' she cried. 'What? Anything!'

I sipped at my coffee for a moment or two, trying to phrase it just right, but that never works. No matter how I put it, it was going to come out wrong in the end.

'You might want to think about this,' I said.

'Think about what?'

'What I'm about to ask you.'

Her smile started to fade.

'You know a man named Cohen who banks at the Seacoast?' I asked.

'Yes. Not personally, just as a customer of the bank.'

'Does he come in often?'

'Usually every day. Why?'

'Do you handle his account?'

She cocked her head like a puppy hearing an unfamiliar sound.

'No,' she said. 'Mr Seaborn handles it personally.'

There it was. The connection. My pulse picked up but it still didn't prove anything. 'Is that customary? I mean for the president of the bank to handle an account personally?'

'He does it on several major accounts, if that's what the customer wants. What's this about, Jake?'

'I need some information,' I said. 'It will be kept totally confidential, I promise you that. There's no danger of anyone ever finding out where it came from. It will only be used by me to dig up some background information.'

Her forehead furrowed into a deep frown.

'What is it? What do you want?' she asked. Her tone was becoming more formal.

'I need the access number for the bank's computer, and Cohen's account number or numbers.'

She was shocked. For two full minutes she stared at me in disbelief, then she lowered her eyes to the floor.

'So,' she said, 'we both wanted something.'

There was no response to that. It was true.

'If it's at all risky . . .' I said, but her stare killed the sentence while it was still in my mouth.

'Isn't giving out that information a felony?' she asked.

'Only if you're caught.'

'Seems to me somebody said that to Tony once.'

I was prepared to take whatever abuse she might throw my way. It was a rotten thing to ask, a rotten position to put her in. Had it not been for her concern over Tony and my promise to try and help, I could never have broached the subject. I'm sure all of that was racing through her mind.

'Look,' I said, 'if you don't trust me, forget it. I'm still going to get a line on Tony for you, if it's possible.'

'Thanks for telling me that, anyway,' she said. She stared at the floor some more. I decided to push it.

'There are laws that make it possible to put people away,' I said, 'people who deserve to be put away, if we can prove their money is earned illegally. I believe Cohen is a money man for the Mafia. That's who tried to kill us last night.'

She looked up sharply, her concern tempered by curiosity.

'It isn't the first time they've tried to put me away,' I said. 'I have a bullet hole in my side as a memento from their last try.'

She kept staring without comment, making me work for it.

'Would you like to hear how they make their money? Or what they do to people who get in their way?'

'I got a hint of that last night,' she said, getting up and taking the tray back to the kitchen. When she returned, she said, 'Come on, I'll take you to the hotel.'

She didn't say anything else. She got her things together and checked the door to make sure it was locked when we left. Just a couple of normal folks heading off for the daily grind. In the daylight her street was like a picture from an eighteenth-century history book. I almost expected to see Ben Franklin strolling by with a kite or Thomas Paine ranting on the street corner. It didn't seem possible that Front Street was only a few blocks away.

DeeDee didn't say a word on the way to the Ponce. When we got there she turned to me, her face tortured with anguish and anxiety.

'I know how to reach you,' I said. 'I'll call, even if I don't hear anything definite.' I started to leave the car.

'Jake?'

'Yeah?'

She sat for a minute longer, then shook her head. 'I can't do it,' she said. 'I owe a lot to Charles Seaborn, and somehow what you're asking seems like an affront to him. When Tony got in all that trouble, some of the directors at the bank wanted Mr Seaborn to fire me. They felt it gave the bank a bad image. He stuck by me through it all, never said a word or asked anything more of me than I usually gave. I didn't even know about it for months. Lark found out and told me. I'm sorry, but what you're asking . . . I'd feel as if I'd done something to him personally.'

'My mistake,' I said. 'I never should have asked.'

'I'm glad you did,' she said. 'I'm glad you felt comfortable enough to ask me. I'm just sorry I feel this way.'

'Loyalty's a rare commodity, don't apologise for it,' I said. 'I'll be talking to you.'

'Thanks again,' she mumbled as I got out of the car. I watched her drive away and went into the hotel. The Stick was sitting in the lobby reading the morning paper.

'This is a terrible hour to be getting in,' he said drolly. 'What'll the neighbours think?'

'You know what you can do with the neighbours,' I snapped.

'Uh-oh. Get out on the wrong side of the bed?'

'I never got into bed.'

'Ah, that's the problem.'

I glared at him and suggested breakfast in the room to save time. 'I need a shower,' I growled.

We went to the room and I ordered food I needed more than the toast and coffee DeeDee had provided. Then I got Dutch on the phone and gave him a quick report on the night's activities, not wanting him to hear it from anybody else. In the excitement at the movie theatre I had forgotten to tell him about my meeting with Harry Nesbitt. I started off with that, finishing with the shoot-out at Casablanca.

The latter got him fuming.

'I'll have Kite pick up that son of a bitch Nance now,' he growled.

'Won't do any good. He's probably got a dozen people who'll swear he was six other places at the time.'

'So what do we do, ignore it!'

'For the time being,' I said. 'When we get him, I want to get him good – and I want it to stick.'

'What do you want to do about Nesbitt?' Dutch asked. 'It doesn't sound like his info on Nance was too swift.'

'Maybe Nance went around the bend,' I said. 'I can't imagine Costello or Chevos pulling a stunt that stupid the way things are.'

'Why not?' the Stick cut in. 'If he'd nailed you, they could've written you off as another victim.'

'I made a promise to Nesbitt and I'd like to keep it,' I told Dutch. 'Can we find a couple of honest cops who'll smuggle him down to Jax and stick with him until his plane leaves?'

'I'll take care of it,' Dutch said. 'Let me know when you hear from him.'

'Thanks. Stick and I are working on some other things. I'll catch up with you later.'

He rang off and I gave Stick the licence number of the black Pontiac. He called the DMV while I showered and shaved.

The licence plates were hot, stolen a few hours before Nance and company came calling on me.

'Shit,' I growled, 'the way this day is starting maybe I ought to go back to bed and start over.'

A bellhop who didn't look a day over fifteen showed up with breakfast. The phone rang and I answered it, trying to eat, talk, and put fresh clothes on at the same time.

'Good morning, darling.' Doe's voice was as soft as lambskin and husky with sleep. 'Sleep late?'

I looked over at Stick, who was back into his newspaper, then turned my back to him and dropped my voice an octave.

'Yeah. A late night. A lot happened.'

'I thought about you all day and all night.'

'Me too,' I mumbled.

'It was torturous being with Harry after the other night.'

I made a dive for the safe spots, but stopped before I got there. I thought, Why does it scare me when it's what I want to hear?

'That's understandable,' I answered.

'Are you under the covers? I can hardly hear you.'

'My partner just stopped by for breakfast,' I half whispered.

'Ah, so that's it,' she purred. 'Well, I'll let you go. I just wanted to hear your lovely voice before I got up. I want to lie here and think about you. Please make it happen again soon. God, how I miss you.'

'Well, that's good,' I said awkwardly.

She laughed. 'What a silly thing to say,' she replied. 'I'll be staying at Windsong for a week or so, alone. Harry's staying at the townhouse. I'm coming out here after the party tonight.'

'Party?'

'Babs' cocktail party, you goose. If you miss it, she'll kill you –

274

that's if I don't do it first. See you at six. Thank you for coming back, Jake. I love you, my sweet.'

'Uh, yeah, me too.'

She hung up.

I cradled the phone and turned around to finish dressing. A minute crept by before Stick said, without looking up from his paper, 'You really got it bad. You can hardly talk to the woman.' Before I could protest, he held his hand up and closed his eyes. 'Please, don't insult me by telling me that was your insurance man.'

'That's right, it was my insurance man,' I said with mock irritation.

'She wants to crawl all over your bones, right? It's always like that the morning after.'

'How come you reduce *every*thing to a cliché? Maybe this is different.'

'It's different all right. I'll give you that in spades, friend. It is unique. Her old man owns the town, her husband runs the town, you'd like to put him in jail, at least for murder if nothing better pops up, and you tell me it's different! That's the understatement of the year.'

'It's only a problem if I make it a problem.'

'You've *already* made it a problem, putz! What in the fuck do you call a problem if this isn't one?'

'Dunetown. There's a problem.'

I finished dressing and ate another piece of soggy toast.

'Okay,' I blurted, 'it's a problem. She's rooted too deep, man. I haven't been able to get her out of my mind for twenty years. I keep thinking it was the best shot I ever had. I want another crack at it. I'm stuck on what could have been instead of what is.'

'Aren't we all,' Stick said, surprisingly bitterly. There was another pause before he added, 'I think I missed something. The part about the price you have to pay. Or did you leave that out?'

'I don't know the price. That's the big question.'

'I don't know what could have been,' Stick said. 'Want to run that by me?'

Now there was a rueful occupation – thinking about what could have been. But if I couldn't trust Stick, who the hell could I trust? Suddenly I heard myself laying it all out for him, starting from the day Teddy and I became football roommates at Georgia and ending on the day I got the kiss-off from Chief. I didn't leave out anything; I threw it all in – heart, soul, anger, hurt, all the feelings that my returning to Dunetown had dredged up from the past.

'Jesus, man, these people really fucked you over!' was his response.

'I've never quite admitted that to myself,' I said. 'I look at Raines, I think, That could have been me. Every time I turn around the past kicks me in the ass.'

'You're one of the ones that can't stay disconnected,' he said seriously. 'It's not your nature. But you've been at it so long you can't break training, you're afraid to take a chance. Like in Nam, when you're afraid to get too close to the guy next to you because you know he may not be around an hour later. It's an easy way to avoid the guilt that comes later, being disconnected is.'

'Is that all it is, Stick? Guilt?'

'Like I told you the other day, it's guilt that gets you in the end. Shit, you're overloading your circuits with it. You got guilt over the girl, you got guilt because you want to pin something on her husband, guilt because you're losing your sense of objectivity, guilt because of her brother. What is it about Teddy? You keep circling that issue. You talk about him all the time, but you never pin it down.'

I finally told him the story. It was easy to talk to him; he'd been there, he knew about the madness, he understood the way of things.

There were days when time dulled the sharp image of that night, but they were rare. A lot of images were still with me, but that one was the most vivid of all. It was a three-dimensional nightmare, as persistent as my memories of Doe had been. The truth of it was that Teddy Findley didn't die in combat or anywhere near it. He might have. There you have it again, what might have been. Teddy and I didn't have a rough time in Nam until a few weeks before we were scheduled to come back to the World. Until Tet, when the whole country blew up under us. Hundreds of guerrilla raids at once. Pure madness. They pulled us out into Indian country and for the next six weeks we found out what Nam was all about. We got out of it as whole as you can get out of it and finally got back to Saigon. Teddy was a little screwy. He scored a couple of dozen Thai sticks and stayed stoned for days on end. He started talking about the black hats and the white hats.

'I got this war all figured out, Junior,' he said one night. 'What it is, see, we've always been the white hats before. We're supposed to be the good guys. But over here, nobody's figured out what we are yet. Are we the white hats or the black hats?' He said it the way the good witch in *The Wizard of Oz* said, 'Are you a *good* witch or a *bad* witch?'

There was this compound in Saigon run by the military. They called it Dodge City because the man in charge was a major named Dillon. It looked like Dodge City, a hell-raisers' paradise, a place to blow off steam; a couple of blocks of whorehouses and bars controlled by the military for our protection. But the MP's couldn't be everywhere. Sometimes things went a little sour. One night we smoked enough dope to get paralysed and we headed down to Dodge and we ended up in a whorehouse. It was nothing but a hooch divided up by screens. You could hear GI's humping all over the place.

'Let's get about five or six of 'em,' Teddy said. 'Have a little gang bang.' It wasn't for me. I wasn't that stoned and I still had a little Catholic left in me. So he went behind one screen and went into the next stall. He started kidding me; it was like being in the same room.

'How's the foreplay going, Junior?'

'Will you shut up!'

'Having a problem?'

'Yeah, *you*!'

He started to laugh and then the laugh turned into a scream and the scream turned into a muffled cry that sounded as though he was underwater. I jumped up and smashed through the screen.

The girl was gone already. It was a fairly common trick. She had a single-edge razor blade held between her teeth when she kissed him, cut off his tongue with the razor and, while he was gagging in his own blood, slit his throat for closers. He died in my arms before I could even yell for help. I don't remember what the girl looked like; all I remember is that it could have just as easily been me instead of Teddy.

'I knew what it would do to Doe and Chief Findley, finding out he died like that,' I told Stick, finishing the story. 'I forged a set of records saying he was killed in action and I forged a recommendation for a Silver Star and the Purple Heart for him. The captain didn't give a shit. He acted like he didn't even notice it.

'Then I wrote the letter telling them how Teddy had died in action, that it was quick, no pain. I don't know which is worse anymore, Teddy's death, or the lie. Reducing it all down to a fucking piece of paper like that.'

Stick sat there for a long time after I finished, smoking and staring at his feet. It was not a shocker; that kind of thing was common. Just another day in paradise.

Finally he started shaking his head. 'Man, you have really done a number on yourself, haven't you? What's the big issue here? You told a lie and made your best friend a hero. Big fuckin' deal.'

'It's what it represents. Somehow Nam should be more important than that.'

'Nam was a fuck-up. It's like a scar on your belly. You cover it up and forget it; you don't paint it red, white, and blue. You're one of those steel-covered marshmallows, Kilmer old buddy. You're a sitting duck for the vultures. You know what I say? Forget the lie part. Stick to the story; nobody wants to hear the truth anyway. Shit, pal, I say fuck the obstacles, go for it. Could be your last chance.'

He lit a cigarette and went back to his newspaper, and then threw in, 'Just put her old man in the joint, that'll solve all your problems.'

'That's a shit thing to say.'

He dropped the paper on the floor and looked up at me. 'I'm just being honest. The perfect solution for you is to have Raines turn out to be the brains behind the killing and Nance the actual shooter. That way you nail 'em both in one whack. You get even and you get the girl. It's the perfect ending.'

'Incredible,' I said. 'Those are great options.'

'You just figured out the price,' he told me.

'Yeah, business as usual,' I said, and there was a lot of acid in my tone.

'If it's business like last night,' Stick said, 'count me in every time.' It was obvious that he had said all he had to say about my personal problems.

'Thanks for sparing me your tales of conquest,' I said.

'Speaking of business, I got a little for you. Let's get to the number one problem, okay? I don't like to brag, anyway. I was up and at the Warehouse by eight. We got good news, we got bad news, and we got some in-between news.'

'Gimme the good news first,' I said.

278

'The good news is that Kite's finally got Nance in view. The bad news is that he didn't make contact until about three A.M. Otherwise he might have been a witness to your little party over there on the waterfront.'

'It'd be nice to know what he'd been doing for the past three days,' I said.

'Kite's working on it. Also Charlie One Ear has some information on who owns what in town and Cowboy Lewis is hot on Cohen's trail this morning. So what got your day off to such a lousy start, besides the fact that your head's not screwed on right?'

'First of all, I hurt a very nice lady,' I said.

'What'd you do, turn her down?'

'Worse, I asked her to break the law.'

'Oh, is that all? Murder, bank robbery, what?'

'The banks computer code and Cohen's bank account numbers,' I said.

He didn't bat an eye. I might have said I asked her to get me a glass of water, for all he seemed to care.

'Did she do it?'

I shook my head. 'The lady has more integrity than I have,' I said.

'Well, Lark hasn't got any such notions,' Stick said, with that strange smile of his. 'Here's the rest of the good news.' He reached into his shirt pocket, took out a slip of paper, and handed it to me. There were two numbers written on it. Lark had drawn a smiling face behind the second one.

'Are these the bank's computer access numbers?' I asked excitedly.

'And the numbers for the Tagliani account.'

'This is incredible! Are you sure they're correct?'

'I trust the lady all the way.'

'The lady's got one hell of a memory,' I said.

'There's a little more to it than that. Guess who the computer operator at the bank is.'

'You're kidding!'

'She has a master's degree in mathematics and computer technology from Emory University. I may be in love. A dame looks like that with all those smarts, shit, I might even think about early retirement.'

I was impressed with the information, but even more impressed that he had asked for it.

279

'How the hell did you know I was after these numbers?' I asked him.

'Lark told me you went to Casablanca to meet DeeDee, so I figured you must be after something,' he said. 'It wasn't hard to figure out what it was. Hell, I can put one and one together and get two almost every time.'

'Now that I've got them, I'm not sure what to do with them,' I said.

'Have you forgotten I spent six months slaving over a computer when I joined the Freeze? I know what to do with them.'

'Can you access the code and get into the bank's main terminal?'

'I can hack into anything,' he said with a grin. 'I'm the magic man, remember?'

My palms got sweaty thinking about what we could come up with. For the first time since arriving in Dunetown, I felt we were getting close to something important. The information wouldn't stand up in court, but it could lead us straight to the bad seeds.

'You want to tell me what you want, specifically?'

'I'm not sure. But I am sure Cohen's the bagman and he deals only with Seaborn at the bank. DeeDee did tell me that. They're using the bank for a washing machine, I know it. That bank account should tell us something.'

'I agree with you about Cohen. Lark says he usually makes cash deposits once a day. Big ones.'

'Does she know how much?'

'No, but she checked the daily deposit tape once out of curiosity and it was in six figures.'

'What! Jesus, Stick, we're on to something. Just maybe we can get them this time.'

I whistled through my teeth and we laughed and slapped each other on the back and acted like a couple of high school kids. If Lark was right, Cohen could be moving as much as half a million dollars a week or more through the Tagliani accounts.

'It had to be shielded in some way,' Stick said. 'That kind of money activity attracts the Lepers like a petunia attracts a hummingbird.'

I said, 'It also means Seaborn has to be involved.'

'So you want me to go fishing?'

'Yeah. What I'm really looking for is a Hollywood box, some kind of payoff account.'

280

'That the tax boys won't tumble on to?' the Stick said.

'Right.'

'That's been tried before by experts.'

'Well,' I said, 'there's always somebody who thinks he has a better mousetrap.'

53

FLOTSAM AND JETSAM

Dutch Morehead had a hunch.

When we arrived at the Warehouse, he was sitting with his feet on the desk under the two holes he had put in the ceiling the night before.

'Did y'see this?' he asked, tossing us the morning paper.

The article was on page 7, circled with a ballpoint pen:

MAN BELIEVED VICTIM
OF SHIPWRECK

The story, datelined Jacksonville, went on to say that an unidentified white male had washed ashore twenty miles north of the resort town the night before. Local police speculated that he was aboard a trawler believed to have burned at sea three days earlier. Charred wreckage of the boat had been floating up along the coast for two days. An autopsy was planned and there were no other details. The item was about three inches long.

'Don't we have enough trouble?' the Stick said.

'I already talked to the boys down there,' was Dutch's answer.

'I guess we don't,' the Stick replied.

'I got this hunch,' the Dutchman said. It was obvious he was feeling proud of himself.

'Shit!' the Stick said. 'Now what?'

'The Coast Guard got the name of the ship off some of the wreckage. It sailed out of Maracaibo nine days ago with a crew of four. Maracaibo is right around the corner from Colombia, and Colombia spells cocaine to me. The Department of Natural Resource boys have been picking up bits and pieces of it since Monday morning. Then this morning another stiff floated up.

This new one is a black guy. Both of them are full of bullets, Jake. Twenty-twos.'

'What's that got to do with – '

'I'm not finished yet,' he said. 'The labels in this black dude's shirt and pants say he's from Doomstown. Designer jeans, a two-hundred-dollar shirt, five-hundred-dollar boots. And one other thing – he has a shiv mark, from here to here.' He drew a line with a thumb from ear to mouth.

'I'll be damned,' Stick said. 'Stitch Harper?'

'Fits him like homemade pyjamas. He also had an empty holster on his belt,' said the Dutchman. 'Now what sailor do you know dresses like that and packs heat?'

'Who's Stitch Harper?' I asked.

'One of Longnose Graves' top honchos.'

'If it's Stitch Harper,' Dutch said, 'we just might have us a whole new scenario working. And I'll know in an hour or so. I got photos of both victims comin' in on the telex.'

'Okay, let's hear the theory,' I said.

The way Dutch had it figured, Longnose Graves was bringing several kilos of coke by boat from Colombia to Doomstown. Graves bragged the information to Della Norman and she bragged it to her new boyfriend, Tony Logeto, who, in turn, passed it on to the rest of the Taglianis. Somewhere east of Jacksonville Beach, someone from the Tagliani clan hijacked the shipment, killed the crew, and burned the boat. If that's the way it happened, it was a clever scheme. It did Graves out of several million dollars' worth of snow and at the same time made him a loser to his people.

'I think,' Dutch concluded, 'that Graves is on the warpath. Add to all this his old lady gettin' snuffed in bed with Logeto, you got to have one angry mobster on your hands.'

The idea had a lot of merit and I told him so. If Dutch's theory was true, the most likely person to have pulled off the hijacking was Turk Nance, which could account for Nance's whereabouts for the past few days.

'The way I see it,' Dutch said, 'it's either Costello or Graves who's behind all the killing. And right now Graves is the only one with a motive.'

'We don't have anything to move on,' Stick said.

It was true – it was all ifs and maybes. I decided to play devil's advocate.

282

'Supposing that Costello is *real* greedy,' I said. 'Maybe he decided to scratch out everybody except the ones he needed, which would be Tuna Chevos, who controls the waterways, Lou Cohen, his financial wizard, and Bronicata, who's the narcotics pipeline to the street. Maybe they got together, made a front-end deal to waste all the rest of the family, ruin Graves' credibility, and split the town up three ways.'

'It's not as strong as the case against Graves,' Dutch said. 'He's fighting for his life and he's got a revenge motive to boot.'

'Either way, we need that dope,' the Stick said. 'Without the coke, all we got is speculation.'

One thing we all agreed on: If the dead black man wasn't Stitch Harper, or somebody from Graves' gang, Dutch's hunch would be colder than an Alaskan picnic. We decided to table all further discussion until the pictures arrived.

While we were waiting, I went looking for Charlie One Ear. He was sitting in his cubicle, dressed in his best with a cigarette bobbing at the end of a fancy holder, touch-typing a report at about a hundred and twenty words a minute.

'You do that like you know what you're doing,' I said.

'My mother believed in the broadest kind of education,' he said.

'Do me a favour, will you?' I asked. 'I'm trying to get a line on a Tony Lukatis, thirty years old, dark . . .'

'I know Lukatis,' he said. 'Did time in Little Q. Pot smuggling.'

'That's him.'

'Is he in trouble again?' Charlie One Ear asked.

'His sister's a friend of mine,' I said. 'She thinks he may be involved in another – '

I stopped in mid-sentence. My stomach was doing slow rolls.

'My God,' I said, and ran back to the telex room with Charlie a few steps behind me. Dutch was sitting beside the machine, leafing through some reports.

'These things are embarrassing,' he said as we entered the room. 'If anybody else read them, they'd swear Salvatore and Zapata were illiterate.' Then he looked up at me and said, 'What's wrong with you?'

I handed him the Polaroid of Tony Lukatis.

'Know him?' I asked.

He took a look. 'Sure, that's Tony Lukatis. He did a deuce for smuggling grass. Titan nailed him.'

'Titan? I got the impression he more or less tolerated pot.'

283

'Smoking, not smuggling,' Charlie One Ear said. 'What's this all about?'

'The white guy that floated up with Stitch Harper, it could be Lukatis,' I said.

'Why?' asked Dutch.

'Hunch,' I said. 'He's been missing since Sunday. His sister thinks he may have been involved in smuggling.'

The first photo rolled off the tube twenty minutes later.

'Stitch,' Dutch said, 'or what's left of him.'

Crabs or sharks or both had done a lot of damage to the black man's face but there was enough left to tell who he was. The white man was not as lucky. He was missing a foot, his face was nibbled to bits, and he was badly bloated. I hoped the dead man would be someone else, anybody else. I remembered DeeDee's picture of Tony, pleasant, dark, good-looking kid. And I was thinking about DeeDee, to whom life so far had been one bottom deal after another. First her father, now the brother she adored, warts and all. I didn't hope for long.

'It's Lukatis,' Dutch said.

'You're sure?' I asked.

He nodded. 'There isn't much, but there's enough.'

I turned away from the photo. I knew I would be the one to tell DeeDee. And now something new was gnawing at me.

Who was Tony Lukatis working for? Longnose Graves or the hijackers?

54

OBIT

The Quadrangle was a grassy square formed on three sides by old brick warehouses that dated back to the Federalist period, and bordered on the fourth by the river. Cobblestone walks criss-crossed the park; a sundial at its centre gleamed under a broiling, bronze sky. In one corner of the green oasis was a large oak tree, knobby with age, that shed what little shade there was, although nobody had sought its comforting shadows yet. There was hardly a breath of wind.

It was five to twelve when I got there. The park was beginning to fill up with pretty young girls in cotton summer dresses and men who looked awkward and uncomfortable in their business suits, most of them with their jackets tossed over their shoulders. A hot dog stand was doing record business. It was a pleasant enough place to enjoy lunch, despite the heat.

The Seacoast National was on the ground floor of one of the buildings. Facing it on the other side of the Quadrangle was Warehouse Three, where I was to break bread with Sam Donleavy the next day. The third building, which ran lengthwise between them, facing park and river, turned out to be an old, one-storey counting house that was now a maritime museum.

I sat on a concrete bench near the corner of the bank, so I could watch both entrances, and waited for DeeDee. I didn't have to wait long. At about five after she and Lark came out, a striking pair that turned heads like waves as they walked by.

She eyed me uncertainly as they came towards me, as if she wasn't sure whether we were still speaking. I broke the ice.

'I thought maybe we could get back to being friends and forget business,' I said.

Lark took the hint.

'Hot dogs and Cokes, anybody?' she asked brightly. 'I'm buying.'

DeeDee and I both ordered one of each and Lark slithered off towards the hot dog stand, stopping conversation all along the way.

'You were right this morning,' I said. 'It would've been a dishonest thing for you to do and I'm sorry I asked.'

'What's the difference,' she said, still edgy. 'You got the numbers anyway. Your friend convinced Lark it was the patriotic thing to do.'

'Obviously he has more of a way with women than I do,' I said jokingly.

'Oh, I wouldn't say that,' she said, without looking at me.

We started walking and I took her by the arm and guided her under the large oak, away from the noonday sun worshippers. She turned suddenly and faced me, looking up straight into my eyes and sensing my anxiety.

'There's something wrong,' she said. 'I can tell.' And then after a moment she added, 'It's Tony. Something's happened to Tony!'

I nodded and said awkwardly, 'I'm afraid it's bad news.'

Her eyes instantly glazed over with tears. Funny how people know before you ever tell them.

'Oh my God,' she said. 'He's dead, isn't he?'

I nodded dumbly, trying to think of something to say, some gentle way of putting it when there wasn't any.

'Oh no,' she said. Her voice was a tiny, faraway whimper.

She sagged against me like a rag doll with the stuffing punched out of it. I put my arms around her and stood under the tree for a long time, just holding her. I could feel her body tightening in ripples as she tried to control the sobs; then the ripples became waves of grief that overwhelmed her and suddenly she started to cry uncontrollably. I lowered her to the grass and sat beside her, clutching her to me, rocking her back and forth, as if she were a child who had just lost her first puppy dog.

I saw Lark, walking back across the square, engrossed in a hot dog. When she saw us, I waved her over. She knew what had happened before she got to us. She stared at me, her eyebrows bunching up into question marks. She didn't say anything, just sat down next to DeeDee and began to rub her back, trying to fight the tears captured in the corners of her own eyes.

As we sat there I looked over at the bank and caught a glimpse of Charles Seaborn staring out the window. He stepped back into the shadows when he realised I saw him. I looked back at the third-floor windows of Warehouse Three. I don't know what I expected, perhaps Donleavy sending semaphore messages across the park to the banker. The windows were empty, like blind eyes staring sightlessly out of the old building. All the power that had once ruled Dunetown seemed focused on this grassy flat, only now it seemed to be replaced by fear.

We sat under the tree for fifteen minutes, trying to console DeeDee. Finally she got the courage to ask what happened.

'A boating accident,' I lied. I didn't seem to have the guts for the truth at that moment. For the first time since Nam, I felt desperately sorry for someone on the bad side of the law.

Regardless of what Tony Lukatis had done, I knew what demons had taunted him to his death. Doe, the promise of Windsong, the easy life, the same demons that had taunted me, distorted my values, left me emotionally barren after Nam. I remembered the day I wrote the letter to Doe and Chief. It was like history repeating itself, except this time I couldn't escape behind a letter. DeeDee was here and I had to face her grief, to touch it, to feel her tears against my face.

Finally she started asking the inevitable questions, questions for which I didn't have answers yet.

Where? When? Did he drown? Probably. Was he doing something wrong when it happened? I wasn't sure. Where was his body now? I didn't know. Was it terribly painful? No, I said honestly, I didn't think so, it was very quick.

'Look,' I said. 'There's something I have to do. I'll tell Seaborn what happened. Take her home, Lark. Call the doctor and get her a sedative. I'll be over as soon as I can get there.'

We took her to her car and Lark got behind the wheel. DeeDee sat motionless beside her, staring through her tears at nothing.

'Damn, damn, *damn!*' she cried vehemently, her anger suddenly spilling over. 'Damn them all!' And she covered her face with her hands as Lark pulled away.

Seaborn's spidery fingers were dancing along the edge of a barren desk the size of a soccer field. He was trying to look busy when I tapped on the door and entered the room without being invited. He was startled, his eyes widening like a frightened fawn's.

The office was big enough to comfortably accommodate the enormous desk and was as barren as the desktop. Behind the highback desk chair, facing the door, was an oil portrait of a stern-looking man with devilish eyebrows that curved up at the ends and unsympathetic eyes. I guessed from his dress that the man in the painting was Seaborn's old man. There was one other picture in the office which I assumed to be Seaborn's family. Otherwise, the room was as sterile as a spayed bitch. He started to object when I entered but I cut him off.

'DeeDee Lukatis' brother has been killed,' I said. 'Lark is taking her home. I told them I'd tell you.'

'My God,' he said, 'how frightful. What happened?'

'Boating accident,' I said, perpetuating the new lie. 'He was in the water for a couple of days. The predators made quite a mess of things.'

His face turned grey contemplating what I had just told him.

'What can I do?' he said, half-aloud, as though asking himself the question.

'Well,' I said, 'a little tenderness and understanding would help.'

287

'Of course, of course,' he said. Seaborn seemed to have trouble saying anything once. After a moment he cautiously asked, 'Did this have anything to do with . . . uh, the, uh . . .'

'Murders?' I said. He winced at the word. 'Why would you think that?' I asked.

'Her brother's been in trouble before, you know,' he said, as though letting me in on a secret.

'I've heard,' I said. 'I can't answer that question. Right now I'm more concerned about DeeDee than why her brother died.'

'Of course, of course,' he repeated. And then, 'What is she to you?'

'Just a friend,' I said. 'We all need them, you know.' I left him sitting in his vast, sterile office, wiping the thin line of sweat off his upper lip.

As I left the bank, a frenetic little man with sparse black hair and hyperactive eyes scurried past me, hugging his briefcase to his side. Lou Cohen, making his daily deposit.

Death didn't change anything in Doomstown. It was business as usual.

55

DEAD HEAT

Driving out to the track, I kept thinking that it seemed like an awfully festive thing to be doing after the events of the morning. For the first time in years I felt connected to someone else's pain. I could feel DeeDee's, like psychic agony, but there was little I could do about it.

A cloud as dark as Tony's future followed me most of the way to the track, then obliterated the sun and dumped half an inch of rain in about thirty seconds. It was one of those quick, drenching summer showers that come and go quickly, but it made a mess of the traffic at the racetrack gate and made me a few minutes late arriving.

Callahan was waiting at the back gate, with his customary flower decorating a tan silk suit and his cap cocked jauntily over one eye. Here was a man who dressed for the occasion.

288

'What's the latest body count?' he asked dryly as we headed for the grandstand.

'I've lost count,' I said, not wishing to get into the Tony Lukatis thing. 'What's happening today?'

'Disaway's going to win,' he said matter-of-factly. 'Little storm drenched the track down just enough.'

'Will it bring down his odds?' I asked.

'Doubt it. Hasn't shown anything his last two times at bat. Players don't trust him.'

'Are you going to put some money on him?' I asked.

'Never bet the ponies,' he said. 'Rather give my money away.'

The stadium and grounds were exquisite. The grandstand, with its gabled roof and tall cupolas at the corners, was Old South to the core. It could have been a hundred and fifty years old. Callahan led me on a quick walk through the premises.

The place was jammed. The parking lot was almost full and people were milling about the betting windows, worrying over their racing forms, studying the electronic totalisator boards, which showed Disaway paying $33.05 to win, almost fifteen to one.

'He has to beat Ixnay,' said Callahan. Ixnay was the favourite, paying only $3.40 to win. 'The eight horse,' he continued. 'Two horse, Johnny's Girl, is favoured to place. Then it's nip and tuck among the field.'

We went from the betting rooms to the paddock. Disaway and the rest of the horses in the first race were on display. He was showing good temper, standing with his legs slightly apart, his nostrils flared, checking out the crowd. Judging on looks, I would have had my money on Disaway. The other horses in the first race didn't look like they could carry his feed bag.

'Good-looking horse,' said Callahan. 'Too bad he's got such tender feet.'

'Who's riding him today?' I asked.

'Scoot Impastato's up,' Callahan said.

'I thought he was through with Thibideau,' I said.

'Who knows,' Callahan answered vaguely. 'Maybe he needed a ride.'

'Why would he do that?' I asked. 'He seemed so dead against him the other day.'

Callahan looked at me like I had just spit on his shoe.

'How would I know? Why do you do what you do? Why do

jockeys jock? Hell, they get fifty bucks a ride, a piece of the purse if they win. Rainy days, when the track's muddy, it's easy for a horse to go down doing forty miles an hour. Jock can get trampled to death.'

'You mean like today,' I said.

'Not too bad out there now,' Callahan said. 'Sun'll cook off most of the standing water. When it's real muddy, shit! I'll tell you, racing in the mud is one piss-poor way to make fifty bucks. But it's a ride, what they do. Thibideau probably said, "I'm sorry, kid, here's an extra fifty", old Magic Hands is up. Kid knows the horse, Thibideau wants a winner. He made peace.'

After the paddock we went to the top tier and he walked me through the private club section, series of tiered rooms protected from wind, rain, and sun by tinted glass, with royal-blue velveteen sofas, low-cut mahogany tables for drinks and snacks, and TV monitors to provide close-ups of the race for the privileged. Red-jacketed waiters, all of whom seemed to be elderly black men, solemnly served refreshments. The place seemed to brag its elegance, a fact I mentioned to Callahan.

'The sport of kings,' he said. 'These are the aristocrats. Owners, breeders, money people. All part of it, all part of the show.'

From the elite of the club we went down among the commoners at the rail. The crowd was already four deep. Callahan, I learned, had a box in the club section, courtesy of the track, but he preferred to be as close to the horses as he could get.

'Like to feel 'em go by,' he said, adjusting his field glasses, checking out the infield, then the gate. 'When betting starts, we can get next to the wood.'

He handed me a programme and I checked out the charts. There was a list of the stewards, headed by Harry Raines, and some track information that surprised me. According to the programme, taxes took fourteen percent of the pari-mutuel's first ten million, eight percent of the next ten mil, six percent on the next fifty, and five percent on everything over that. Obviously the state was getting fat, a fact which certainly vindicated Raines.

The infield was as impressive as the stadium. A large pond with a fountain in the centre had attracted herons and other water birds to it. Gardens surrounded the pond and there was a granite obelisk at one end.

'What's that?' I asked, pointing to the large marker.

290

'Remember me telling you about Justabout at chow the other morning?'

'You mean the ugly horse?'

Callahan nodded. 'First big winner to come off this track. Ran his first heat here, ran here most of the next season. First two years he won forty-two races. Ugly as he was, he was so good he once got a standing ovation for coming in second. The crowd figured he'd been racing so much he was tired. Just before the season ended last year; he got trapped against the rail going into the far turn, tried to break out, bumped another kid, went down. They had to destroy him, so the board of stewards decided to bury him out there.'

At exactly ten minutes before post time a horseman in a red cutaway and a black hunter's cap led the horses out onto the dirt parading them around the track and in front of the stands. There was a ripple of applause, now and then, and a lot of chitchat among the horseplayers as the Thoroughbreds went by. Disaway was acting a little frisky, jogging sideways and shaking his head.

Callahan was right about the railbirds. Ten minutes before the first race, half of the crowd around us seemed to rush off en masse, waiting until the last minute to get their bets down. We moved up against the rail and across from the finish line, a perfect position.

The odds on Disaway changed very little, as Callahan had predicted. Five minutes before post time they dropped from $33.05 to $26.20, still a hefty long shot as far as the bettors were concerned.

As they started putting the horses in the gate, Callahan gave me the binoculars.

'Watch Disaway, the four horse. He's acting up a little but I don't think he's nervous. Anxious to run. Looks good, lots of energy.'

I could see him jogging sideways and throwing his head about as the handler tried to lead him into the stalls. Magic Hands was leaning over his shoulder, talking into his ear. A moment after the horse settled down and strolled into the gate.

I turned around and appraised the clubhouse with the glasses. Raines was in the centre box, alone, looking stern, like Patton leading his tanks into combat.

'There's Raines,' I said, 'centre stage.'

Callahan gave him an unsolicited compliment. 'Raines is a

291

tough administrator. Built a rep for the track; well run, clean, profitable.'

'Aren't they all,' I suggested.

'Hah! I got out of college,' said Callahan, 'got a job working for the vet at a little track. Florida. Assistant track doctor. Track was dirty. Shit, they switched blood samples, dosed horses . . . crazy. Saw two horses die that summer, one with heaves. Terrible. Pony just lies down, gags for air. Like watching him suffocate only takes hours. Don't want to kill him because you keep hoping he'll turn around, make it. I decided to make a stink how bad it was. Got me fired. Told me I'd never work at a racetrack again. So I became a cop, went back, cleaned their tank. Heads up, they're coming out.'

I gave him back his glasses just as the bell rang. I could see the horses charging out of the stalls, a blur of horseflesh and wild colours; mauve, pink, orange, bright blues and greens, seemed to blend together in a streak of colour, then the line began to stretch out as the field moved for position. The crowd was already going so crazy as the eight horses pounded towards the first turn, I couldn't hear the announcer giving the positions.

'How's he doing?' I yelled, unable to make one horse from the other on the backstretch.

'Off the rail and fourth going into the turn,' Callahan yelled. 'Got a bad break coming out of the gate . . . making up for it . . . Scoot's laying it on . . . on the outside now, moving into third. Scoot isn't letting him out full yet . . . passing the three-quarter post . . . Scoot still holding him back running him to win, all right. Not gonna let him out until the stretch . . . there he goes into third place . . . he's moving for the inside now . . .'

I could see the horses clearly as they came around the clubhouse turn. Disaway was running hard, challenging the two horse, Johnny's Girl. I could feel the excitement of the crowd as they started down the last five hundred yards.

Callahan continued his running commentary.

'He's on the rail now . . . pushing for second. He's a nose out of second place now . . . and Scoot's letting him out! Look at that horse go! Damn, does he like that mud . . .'

Disaway nosed past the two horse and challenged the leader. I could feel the thunder of their hoofs as they stormed towards the finish line, the jockeys' livid colours splattered with mud.

292

Callahan's voice began to rise as he, too, was caught up in the excitement of the finish.

'Disaway's going for it. They're neck and neck coming down the stretch, and there he goes, he's pulling away, he's got the lead by a head and romping.'

Suddenly Callahan stopped for a second, and then he cried out, 'Jesus!'

As they approached the wire, Disaway suddenly swerved away from the rail and headed diagonally across the track, his left front leg dangling crazily as he made the erratic move, the two horse behind him tried to cut inside but it was too late. They collided, hard, neck on neck. Disaway was thrown back towards the rail as the two horse went down, chin into dirt, rolling over its hapless jockey. Disaway was totally out of control and Impastato was trying vainly to keep him on his feet, but the three horse was charging for the wire and they hit with a sickening thud. Scoot Impastato was vaulted from the saddle, spinning end over end into the rail, followed immediately by Disaway. The rail shattered and Disaway, Impastato, the three horse and jockey, and the horse behind it all went down in a horrifying jumble of legs and torsos and racing colours and mud.

The crowd shrieked in horror.

Then, just as suddenly, it was deathly still.

From the infield I heard a voice cry out, 'Get him off me, please get him off me!'

One of the horses was trying to get up, its legs scrambling in the dirt.

One of the three jocks was on his knees, clawing at his safety helmet.

The two horse and rider were as still as death in mid-track.

Sirens. An ambulance. People running across the infield.

The place was chaotic.

'Let's get the hell over there,' Callahan said, and we jumped the rail and headed for the infield.

56

RAINES GETS TOUGH

It was a bizarre sight: Disaway was spread out on an enormous metal table, three legs askew, its head dangling awkwardly over one side, its bulging eyes terrified in death, its foreleg split wide open and its muscles and tendons clamped back, revealing the shattered bone. The vet, whose name was Shuster and who was younger than I had pictured him, a short man in his mid-thirties who had lost most of his hair, was leaning over the leg with a magnifying glass, and Callahan, dressed in a white gown, was leaning right along with him. Both gowns were amply blood-stained. I walked to within three or four feet and watched and listened, keeping my mouth shut and eyes and ears open.

So far, two horses were dead, a third might have to be destroyed, and two jockeys were in the hospital, Scoot Impastato with a fractured skull and a broken leg.

'I've never seen a break quite this bad,' Shuster was saying.

'The other horses could've done some damage when they ran over him,' Callahan answered.

'I think not. The pastern bone broke inward here . . . and here. No chips or other evidence of impact. This is what interests me. See? Right here and then down here, at the bottom of the break.'

Callahan leaned closer and nodded.

'Yeah. Maybe it splintered when the bone broke.'

'Maybe . . .'

Shuster took a pair of micrometers and leaned back over the carcass.

'Less than half a millimetre,' he said. He took a scalpel and scraped something from the edge of the fractured bone into a test tube.

'Calcium?' Callahan said.

'We'll see.'

'Butes did this,' Callahan said.

'I'd have to agree. The horse was coming up lame. He should have been scratched.'

294

'What was the trainer's excuse for dosing him?'

'Runny nose.'

'Yeah, ran all the way down his leg.'

'I couldn't argue,' Shuster said apologetically. 'It's a perfectly legitimate excuse.'

'Nobody's blaming you. This isn't the first time a pony with a bad leg has been buted up.'

The door opened behind me and Harry Raines came in. His kelly-green steward's jacket seemed out of place in the sterile white room, but my rumpled sports jacket didn't add anything either.

A barrage of emotions hit me the instant he entered the room. In thirty-eight years I had never made love to another man's wife, and suddenly I was standing ten feet away from a man whom I had dishonoured and towards whom I felt resentment and anger. I wanted to disappear, I felt that uncomfortable when he entered.

I had a fleeting thought that perhaps he knew about Doe and me, that maybe one of the Tagliani gang had anonymously informed on us. Too many people either knew or had guessed about us, Harry Nesbitt had made that clear to me. I almost expected Raines to point an accusing finger at me, perhaps draw an 'A' on my forehead with his fountain pen. I could feel sweat popping out of my neck around my collar and for an instant I blamed Doe for my discomfort, transferring my anger and jealousy to her because she had married him.

All that in just a moment, and then the feelings vanished when I got a good look at him. I was shocked at what I saw. He seemed not as tall as when I had seen him at the track two days earlier, as if he were being crushed by an invisible weight. His face was drawn and haggard, his office pallor had changed to a pasty grey. Dark circles underlined his eyes. The man seemed to have aged a dozen years in two days.

Is he really the success-driven robot others have made him out to be? I wondered. He looked more like a man hanging over a cliff, waiting for the rope to break.

Quite suddenly he no longer threatened me.

My fears were unfounded. He didn't pay any attention to me at first. He was more concerned with the dead horse. When he did notice me, he was simply annoyed and somewhat perplexed by my presence.

'What are you doing here?' he asked, looking at Callahan as he said it, as if he didn't think I knew the answer.

'We're working together,' was all the big cop told him.

Raines said 'Oh' and dismissed it from his mind. He turned his attention back to the business at hand. 'I don't mean to push you, Doc. Did he just break a leg?'

'Two places. He was also on butes.'

'What!'

'He had a cold.'

'According to who?'

'Thibideau.'

'Damn it!' Raines snapped, and his vehemence startled me.

'Uh, there could be something else,' Callahan said. He came over to us and took off the gown. 'There's a crack in the pastern leading out of the fracture. It appears to be slightly calcified, which means it's been there a while. Couple of days, at least.'

'So it wasn't a cold.'

'I'm telling you this because Doc here can't say anything until he finishes his tests. But I'd say this animal was on Butazolidin because he was gimpy after the race on Sunday.'

'Where did you get that information?'

'The jock, Impastato. But he didn't have anything to do with this I don't think. He quit Thibideau yesterday because he'd been made to break the horse out at the five-eighths and the horse was strictly a stretch runner, which is another reason he lost Sunday.'

'The trainer's Smokey Barton, right?'

Callahan nodded.

'He'll go to the wall for this.'

'It's done a lot,' Callahan said.

'Not at this track,' Raines growled. 'Not anymore.'

Shuster went back to work and Callahan nodded for me to follow him out of the room. We went outside and leaned against the side of the building in the hot afternoon sun. Callahan didn't say anything. A few moments later Raines came out.

Callahan said, 'Mr Raines, I think we need to talk.'

Raines cocked his head to one side for a beat or two and then said, 'Here?'

'Preferably not.'

'My office then. We'll go in my car.'

He drove around the track without saying a word and parked

in his marked stall. We took the elevator to the top floor of the stadium, then headed down a broad, cool hallway to his office. It was a large room, dark-panelled and decorated completely in antiques, down to the leatherbound volumes in its recessed book-cases. Ordinarily the room would have been dark and rather oppressive, except that the entire wall facing us as we walked in was of tinted glass and overlooked the track. The effect was both startling and elegant.

His desk was a genuine something-or-other and was big enough to play basketball on. Executives in Doomstown seemed to have a penchant for big desks. This one was covered with memorabilia. It sat to one side and was angled so that Raines could see the track and conduct business at the same time. The view was breathtaking.

There were three paintings on the walls, two Remingtons and a Degas, all originals. There were only two photographs in the room, both on his desk. One was a black and white snapshot of an older couple I guessed were his mother and father. The other one was a colour photograph of Doe, cheek to cheek with a black horse who must have been Firefoot.

I had a hard time keeping my eyes off her.

'Is this going to call for a drink?' Raines asked.

Callahan hesitated for a moment or two and then said, 'I could do with a bit of brandy, thanks.'

'Kilmer?'

'Sounds good to me,' I said.

The wet bar was hidden behind mahogany shutters that swung away with a touch. Raines took down three snifters that looked as fragile as dewdrops and poured generous shots from a bottle that was old enough to have served the czar. The brandy burned the toes off my socks.

'Have a seat and tell me what's on your mind,' he said in a flat, no-nonsense voice.

The leather sofa was softer than any bed I'd been in lately. He sat behind his desk with a sigh and pinched his eyes.

I was beginning to like him in spite of myself. I had remembered him as just another football jock, but Raines had about him the charisma of authority, even as weary as he seemed to be. He domineered the office, not an easy thing to do considering the view.

'This thing with Disaway,' said Callahan, 'it goes a little deeper than splitting a foreleg because of Butes.'

Raines swirled his brandy around, took a whiff, then a sip, and waited.

'Disaway was favoured to win a race this past Sunday – '

'He dragged in eighth,' Raines said, cutting him off.

'Yeah, right, well, we have what I would call very reliable information that the race was fixed for Disaway to lose. Would you say the information is good, Jake?'

'I'd say it's irrefutable,' I said.

The muscles in Raines' jaws got the jitters.

'I can't tell you exactly how it was done,' Callahan went on. 'Probably cut back his feed for a couple of days and overworked him a little, raced him a little too much, then probably gave him a bag of oats and a bucket of water a couple of hours before the race and he was lucky to make the finish line. But there's no doubt that he was meant to lose. Money was made on it.'

'By who?' Raines demanded.

Callahan hesitated for several moments. He was in a tight spot. To tell Raines about the recording was to admit that there was an illegal tape in Tagliani's house.

'I'm sorry, sir,' Callahan said, firmly but pleasantly, 'I can't tell you that. Not right now. The thing is, it worked as a double. He lost so big Sunday, his odds were way up for today's race.'

'He went off at about eighteen to one,' Raines said. He took another sip of brandy but his dark eyes never left Callahan's face.

'That's right, but he was posting $33.05 until a few minutes before post time. According to your man at the hundred-dollar window, a bundle was laid off on him just before post time and his odds dipped to $26.00 and change.'

'Do you know who placed the bundle?' Raines asked.

Callahan shook his head. 'It was several people, spread across both windows.'

'Who was responsible?'

'Could've been anybody from the groom to the owner. Thing is, sir, we can't prove any of this. Except we know the loss on Sunday was fixed.'

'We can prove the horse was dosed with Butes,' Raines said angrily.

'Yeah,' said Callahan, 'except it isn't against the law in this state.'

'Well, it's going to be,' stormed Raines. 'I've always been

298

against the use of Butazolidin on any horse up to forty-eight hours before a race. I know horses, Callahan.'

'I know that,' the big man answered.

'But I don't know the kind of people that fix horse races and you do. I need some proof to use on Thibideau so this won't happen again.'

I decided to break in at this point. Callahan was playing to close to the vest.

'Mr Raines, Pancho here's reluctant to discuss this because it involves some illegal evidence gathering. I trust you'll keep this confidential, but the fact is, we *know* the race was fixed, but we are powerless to say anything about it. The proof is on a tape which is nonadmissable.'

He stared at both of us for a few moments, toyed with a pipe on his desk, finally scratched his chin with the stem.

'Can you tell me who was involved?'

'A man named Tagliani,' I said. If he knew the name, he had either forgotten it or was one of the better actors I had ever seen in action. There was not a hint of recognition.

'I don't think I'm familiar with – '

'How about Frank Turner?' I said. 'That's the name he was using here.'

I could see Callahan's startled look from the side of my eye but I ignored it.

The question brought a verbal response from Raines.

'Good God!' he said. 'Is this fix tied up in some way with the homicides in town?'

It was obvious that he had bought the soft-pedal from the press just as everyone else in town had. Just as obviously, he was totally in the dark about who Tagliani really was and the ramifications of the assassinations.

'Not exactly.' Callahan answered, still trying to be cautious.

I decided it was time to let the skeleton out of the closet. I told him the whole Tagliani story, starting in Ohio and ending in the Dunetown morgue. I told him about Chevos, the friendly dope runner, his assassin, Nance, and their front man, Bronicata. I told him about the Cherry McGee-Longnose Graves war, a harbinger of what was to come. The more I talked, the more surprised Callahan looked.

Surprised was hardly the word to describe Raines. He was appalled.

I was like a crap shooter on a roll. The more aghast they got, the more I unloaded. I watched Raines' every muscle, trying to decide whether he had truly been misled by Titan and the others, or whether he was one of the greatest actors of all time. I decided he had been duped. Whatever had been weighing on his mind earlier in the day probably seemed insignificant compared to what I was telling him. I saved my best shot until last.

'I'm surprised Titan, Seaborn, Donleavy, or the fellow who owns the newspaper and TV station – what's his name?'

'Sutter,' he said hoarsely.

'Yeah. He's handling the cover-up. I'm surprised one of your associates didn't tell you before this,' I said.

Pause.

'They've known about it for several weeks.'

Callahan looked like he had swallowed his tongue.

Raines got another five years older in ten seconds.

I'm not sure to this day whether I was venting my anger towards the Committee, Chief, and the rest of the Dunetown crowd, or telling the man something he should know, whether it was a petty move on my part because I wanted his wife, or a keen piece of strategy. That's what I wrote it off as, even though it was still a reckless thing to do. Whatever my motives were, I knew one thing for sure: A lot of hell was going to be raised. Some rocks would certainly be overturned. I was anxious to see who came running out.

By the time I was finished, he knew I knew who was in the Committee and the extent of its power and I did it all by innuendo, a casual mention of Titan here, of Seaborn there, none of it incriminating. I stopped short of that.

I was having a hell of a time. It was the Irish in me: don't get mad, get even. I was doing both.

'Anyway,' I said, summing it all up, 'the fix wasn't part of this other mess, it's just indicative of what was happening here. Uh . . .' I tried to think of a delicate way of putting it. '. . . A change of values in the city since the old days.'

His cold grey eyes shifted to me and he stared at me for several seconds although his mind still seemed to be wandering. Then he nodded very slowly.

'Yes,' he said sadly. 'That's well put, Kilmer. A change of values.'

It was then that I realised how deeply hurt he was. Bad enough

300

to find out you have been lied to by your best friends, but to get the information from your wife's old boyfriend went a little beyond insulting. I stopped having a good time and started feeling sorry for him. A lot of Harry Raines' dreams had been destroyed in a very few minutes.

Pancho Callahan stared out the window at the racetrack. He had less to say than usual – nothing.

Raines got up, poured another round of brandy, and slumped on the corner of his desk.

'I appreciate your candour,' he said, stopping to clear his voice halfway through the sentence. 'I understand about your . . . previous ties to Dunetown. All this is probably difficult for you, too.'

He wasn't doing bad at the innuendo himself. A lot of information was bouncing back and forth between us, all of it tacitly. I almost asked him what had been troubling him.

Instead, I dug it in a little deeper.

'It hasn't got anything to do with old ties, Mr Raines,' I said. 'I'm an investigator for the government. I came to help clean up your town. I've been here four days and I only know one thing for sure. Everybody of importance I turn to for help, kicks me in the shins instead. Callahan wouldn't have told you all this. He wouldn't be that inconsiderate. I, on the other hand, have never scored too well in diplomacy. It doesn't work in my job.'

I stopped talking. The dialogue was beginning to sound defensive.

Raines looked at Callahan. 'Can you confirm this?' he asked quietly.

Callahan nodded slowly.

'My God,' Raines said again. And then suddenly he turned his attention back to Pancho Callahan.

'The blame rests squarely with the trainer,' Raines snapped, almost as if he had forgotten the conversation moments before. It was as if it had given him some inner strength. The weight seemed to be gone. Fire and steel slowly replaced it, as if he'd made a final judgment and it was time to move on. 'I'll have Barton's ass. I'll get him out of here along with that damn Butazolidin.'

Callahan chimed in: 'Seems to me, sir, we're talking about two different things here. Buting up the horse today and fixing the race on Sunday. They're connected this time, but they're two different problems.'

'Yes, I understand that,' he said. He braced his shoulders like a marine in parade and ground his fist into the palm of his other hand.

'We talked to the jockey . . .'

'Impastato,' Raines said, letting us know he knew his track.

'Right. Impastato got chewed out by Smokey Barton for letting Disaway out at the five-furlong post – he usually goes at the three-quarter. Anyway, it was Thibideau who told him to run the race that way.'

'That happens; it's not uncommon,' Raines said, attempting to be fair.

'No. But it's usually not done in a race where the horse is favoured and the track is right for him.'

'I agree,' said Raines, who was turning out to be nobody's fool, 'but it's not enough to prove the race was a fix.'

'No, but there's something else. The last race Disaway ran, Impastato says the horse was shying to the right going out of the backstretch. Started running wide.'

'Look, I'm sorry, Callahan,' Raines said impatiently, 'but I need to know where you got this thing about the race being fixed. I can't go to the stewards and tell them I heard it around the track.'

'You can't take it to the stewards at all . . . or the Jockey Club,' Callahan said, looking at me for support.

'And why not?'

'We can't prove any of it,' I said. 'You're a lawyer. All of this is expert conjecture. You could get your tail in as big a crack as ours would be.'

'My tail's already in a crack,' he growled.

Callahan said, 'What Jake means is, we can't prove the horse was burned out so he wouldn't run well. We can't prove Thibideau put the final touch on it by opening him up too early. We can't even prove it was Thibideau. Fact is, we can't even prove for sure the horse has been running with a hairline crack in his foreleg.'

Raines' anger was turning to frustration.

'Why don't you just spell it out for me,' he said.

'Okay,' said Callahan. 'The way I see it, they couldn't bute him on Sunday because there's a little kick to Butes; the horse might just have done the job anyway, and he was favoured. The fix was for Disaway to lose. They had to bute him today because he was going lame after the workouts, and today was his day to win. So Disaway ran like a cheetah, couldn't feel the pain in his foreleg until he went down. What I think is that Thibideau set up the loss on Sunday. Smokey's only sin was not pulling the pony because he was going lame. Hell, you could run a lot of trainers off the track for doing that.'

'Then I'll run 'em off,' Raines said angrily. He finished his second brandy and stood with his back to us, staring down at the track. 'An owner's greed, a trainer's stupidity, and two horses are dead. One jockey may never ride again, and another is lying in pain in the hospital.' He turned back to face us.

'To my knowledge, there's never been a fix at this track, not in almost three year.'

'Well,' Callahan said, 'it was well thought out and impossible to prove. Would've worked like a Turkish charm, too, except the leg was weaker than they thought, which is always the case when a horse breaks a leg in a race.'

'Then just what the hell *can* I do?' Raines roared, and for a moment he sounded like Chief Findley.

Callahan finished his drink and stood up.

'About this one? Nothing. Thibideau lost his horse; he's paid a price. The other two horses and jockeys? Don't know what to say. It'll go down in the books, just another accident. I don't think – see, the reason we told you this, it isn't the last time it's going to be tried. I know how you feel about the track and the horses. It's something you need to know.'

Raines sighed and sat back in his chair and pinched his lower lip.

'I appreciate it, thanks,' he said, But he was distracted. His gaze once again was focused somewhere far away.

'Mr Raines, it wouldn't help us – Callahan here, myself, and the rest of Morehead's people – for you to talk about this fix business. Not for just now. Maybe a day or two, okay?'

He could hardly refuse the request and didn't.

'I respect your confidence,' he said, without looking at either of us. 'Will forty-eight hours be enough?'

Callahan looked at me and I shrugged. 'Sure,' I said, 'that'll be fine. We'll be checking with you.'

We left him sitting there, staring out at the track he had created and which he obviously loved and cherished and felt protective of, the same way Chief felt about Dunetown. I felt sorry for him; he was like a schoolboy who had just discovered some ugly fact of life. Callahan didn't say anything until we were outside the building and walking back around the infield to the car.

'You were pretty tough in there,' he said.

'Callahan, do you ever get tired of dealing with pussyfooters?' I asked with a sigh.

'All the time,' he said, looking down the track where they were repairing the infield fence.

'That's what just happened to me. I got the feeling Raines is anything but. But he's surrounded by a bunch of pussies.'

'It's your business to tell him?'

'Nobody else was going to do it. Time somebody played honest with the man.'

'Did that all right,' he said. 'Just wonder what Dutch is going to say.'

'I wouldn't worry about Dutch,' I replied. 'I'd worry about Stoney Titan.'

After a moment Callahan said, 'Yeah . . .' and seemed awed at the prospect.

I didn't tell him what else had happened, that I was measuring the man to see what kind of stuff he was made of.

I wasn't sure I liked the answer.

57

FLASHBACK: NAM DIARY, THE SECOND SIX

The 77th day: We know this village is a VC hideout. We go by the place, there's this pot of rice cooking, enough for maybe a hundred people, and there's some old folks around, a dozen kids, two or three younger women, that's all.

'They sure are skinny, to eat that much,' Jesse Hatch says as we walk by.

Flagler's replacement is this kid from Pennysylvania, handles a .60-calibre like it was part of his arm. He learns fast too. We call him Gunner. He says he used to hunt all the time, poaching and everything, summer and winter, since he was maybe eight, nine years old. Nothing scares him. He achieved 'aw fuck it' status before he ever got to Nam.

Anyway, we go back tonight to see if maybe the village is a gook shelter and there was activity all over the place. What we got is Gook City. We flare the place and hit it from both sides, only there's a stream on the back side of the village and they get on the other side and we are pinned down. There are green tracers going all over the place, rounds bouncing off shit, kicking around us.

We're pouring stuff into the hooches, just shooting the shit out of them, and all of a sudden one of them goes off. They must've had all their ammo stored inside because it was the Fourth of July – squared. Grenades, mortars, tracers, mines. Everybody's freaking out, running around. Then Hatch catches one in the leg from the other side of the stream and he goes over the side into the water and he panics and starts yelling that he can't swim and Carmody is yelling, 'Shut up, for Christ sakes' only it's too late and Jesse catches a couple in the head. Carmody and me, we go over the side and drag him back. But I knew he was finished. It was like trying to lift a house.

Carmody keeps saying, over and over, 'Why did he yell, why the fuck did he yell. Fuckin' stream was only three feet deep.'

But it was dark and everything had gone wrong and Jesse couldn't swim. Hell, I don't know why I'm apologising for old Hatch, look what it cost him.

The 105th day: *The lieutenant's beginning to act weird. It started a couple of weeks ago when we lost Jesse Hatch. It's like he has a hard time making up his mind about anything.*

Last night I go by his hooch and I say, 'C'mon, Lieutenant, let's have a beer.' And he just sits there, looking at me, and then he says, 'Let me think about it.' Think about having a beer?

Today he says, 'My luck's going bad. I shouldn't have lost Flagler and Hatch.'

'You can't blame yourself,' I say to him.

'Who'm I going to blame, Nixon?' he says, only he says it with bitterness. He's lost his sense of humour, too.

The 122nd Day: *We got separated from our outfit and we were two days out in the boonies. We come up on this handful of gooks. Ten of them, maybe. We just break through some brush and there they are, twenty feet away plus change.*

Everybody goes to the deck but the lieutenant. I don't know what happened. He just pulls a short circuit and stands there. This one VC has his AK-47 over his shoulder, he rolls backwards and gets one burst off. Carmody takes three hits. He's lying there, a few feet away from me, jerking real hard in the dirt.

It's the shortest firefight I ever saw. It's over in about ten seconds. Everybody is shooting at once. We are on top of these people and Carmody is the only one gets hit. One of the gooks jumps in the river and Gunner just goes right in after him, takes him out with his K-bar. Just keeps stabbing him until he's too tired to stab anymore.

I take the lieutenant in my arms and hold him as tight as I can and keep telling him it's going to be all right. I hold him that way until he stops shaking and I feel him go stiff on me.

It doesn't seem possible. A month to go, that's all he had. I don't know why I thought the lieutenant was invincible. You'd think I'd know better after four months out here.

The 161st Day: *It's almost six weeks since Carmody took it. I wish the hell I would have time to thank the lieutenant. If he had just come around for a minute or two. Shit, you just take too much for granted out here.*

I've been acting squad leader ever since. They made me a sergeant. Doc, Gunner, me, we're the only old-timers left. Jordan beat the rap and rotated back to the World. The night before he left we got him so drunk, shit, he was out cold. So we tie him to the back of his PT-boat and drag him back up to the base, which is about eight or nine kliks. He almost drowned. By the time we got to the base, he was sober. So we got him drunk all over again. He was a wreck when he got on the chopper to Cam Ranh. I'll bet he's still got a hangover. Something to remember us by.

Can you beat that, five months and I'm an old-timer.

I never even told the lieutenant I liked him.

The 188th Day: *I got called down to Dau Tieng today, which is division HQ, and I talked with this captain who seems to run the whole show in this sector. He tells me I'm recommended for a Silver Star for this thing up at Hi Pien. It was a rescue mission and I guess I looked pretty good that day.*

He asks me how I feel about the war. Can you imagine? How does anybody feel about the war, for Christ sakes.

'I've had better times,' I said. 'Like the time I had my appendix out.'

306

The captain has real dark eyes, like he needs sleep and could use a week or two in the sun, and he got a kick out of that.

'I mean, how do you feel about the war politically,' he says.

'I don't know about that,' I say to him. 'I'm not interested in political bullshit. I'm here because I was sent here. I don't even know what the hell we're doing over here, Captain. Right now it looks like all we're doing is getting our ass kicked.'

'Does that concern you? I mean, that we seem to be getting our ass whipped?'

'You some kind of shrink or something?' I ask him.

He laughs again and says no, he's not a shrink.

So I say to him, 'Nobody's over here to lose.'

Then he asks me how old I am and I tell him I'm twenty-one and he says to me, 'You're a damn good line soldier.'

'I'll tell you, Captain, I'm almost a short-timer. I got six months left to pull and I got two objectives in life. Get me back whole, get my men back whole. I don't think about anything past that. There isn't anything past that. You start thinking about what's past that and you're a dead man.'

'I'm going to field commission you,' he says, just like that.

'Shit no,' I says. 'Don't do that to me, Captain. Gimme a break. What do you want from me?'

'I need a lieutenant on that squad and you're the best man for the job.'

'Look, gimme six stripes, okay, that way I outrank anybody else on the squad. I'll stay right there, do the same shit I been doing, but I don't want a goddamn bar, man. Bars get you killed. I'm walking away from this, Captain. I'm not dying in this swamp. You hand a bar on me, it's like a fuckin' hex.'

So he gives me six stripes and a night on the town, which is kind of a joke, and the next day I'm back at Hi Pien and nothing is changed. It's the same old shit.

The 231st Day: We had this nut colonel who came up on the line. He was an old campaigner, you could tell. He knew all the tricks and he just ignored them. He didn't even make a lot of sense when he talked. I don't think he was wrapped real tight anymore.

Later in the day he was going to grab a medevac out and we're standing on the LZ on top of this knoll and he takes a leak right down the side of the hill, and just like that the VC start popping away at us. I don't know where they came from, and he's laughing, and I'm

307

telling him, 'Colonel, you better watch out, we seem to have Charlie all over the place.'

'Piss on 'em,' he says.

All of a sudden 9-millimetres were busting all around us. They must've busted fifty caps and the ground around his feet was churning up like little fountains. He finished, zipped up, and shot them a bird. Then the Huey comes in and he climbs aboard and they dust off. I thought, There's a guy needs to get off the line, bad.

'That crazy son of a bitch'll get somebody killed,' Doc says. 'He doesn't give a shit anymore.'

'What the hell're they gonna do with him?' I say. 'He's too crazy to send back to the World.'

'I don't know, send him to the crazy colonel place,' Doc says, and we all laugh about that.

The 256th Day: *Gunner was over in Saigon for a week of R and R and he meets this ordinance guy and they hang out and get drunk and raise some hell. Anyway, the ordinance guy shows Gunner how to take the timer out of a hand grenade and when Gunner comes back, he sits around every night, taking the timers out of M-4's and then loading them into ammo packs. He puts five or six to each bag.*

A couple of nights later we're sitting on this LZ and the VC jump us. Gunner says follow him. He leaves the bags behind, we give them about thirty metres, hole in, and when they take the position we start a counter. Next thing I know there's hand grenades going off all over the place, gooks screaming, all this chaos. Then we went back and jumped them and took the position back. We wasted about twenty. Half of them only had one arm.

We did this a couple of times, moving off LZ's and what have you. Gunner keeps a couple of bags of these grenades around all the time now. Every time we move out we leave a couple behind. It's like our trademark. Fuckin' monkeys never learn. It works like a charm every time.

The 289th Day: *We had this ARVN assigned to us. I don't trust Vietnamese, not even the southerners. They have a tendency to run when things get hot. I know that's a generalisation, but over here, sometimes generalising keeps you alive. Anyway, this ARVN scout was on point and he runs into a sniper. One lousy sniper but this crud leaves the point and comes running back to report. What it was, he didn't have the guts to cream the fucking gook.*

So he comes running back and the sniper pops off three men, one, two, three, just like that. We get up there and I get around behind the sniper and I empty half a clip into him.

When we get back to base I radio upriver and tell them I'm sending this creep ARVN back to them, I can't use him.

'Keep him,' they say. 'It's politics.'

Poli-fuckin'-tics. Jesus! Politics my ass.

Tonight we're camped out in the bush, he heads back into town to see his lady friend. I take off my shoes and follow him. He's going to the river to hop a ride and I jump him before he gets to the dock and slit him ear to ear with my K-bar, just drop him in the fucking river.

That's one son of a bitch isn't getting any more of my people killed.

The 292nd Day: *This time when I went down to Dau Tieng, it was the captain and this lieutenant named Harris, who looked like he didn't take shit from anybody, and we met in this bar which everybody jokingly calls the Cafe Society. I figure it's about the ARVN. They probably found him, he's some asshole's brother or something. It doesn't even come up.*

'You know the trouble with this war,' the captain says. 'We get these people for a year. Just when they're getting good enough to stay alive and take a few tricks, they go home.'

And I says to myself, Uh-oh.

The lieutenant says to me, 'You got a real handle on what it's all about, Sergeant.'

And I laugh. I don't know what's happening two miles away and I say so.

'I mean out on the line,' the lieutenant says.

'Oh, that,' I says.

'Ever hear of CRIP?' he asks me.

I had heard some vague stories about a mixed outfit made up of North Viets who had defected to our side and called themselves Kit Carson scouts, plus infantry guys, some leftover French Legionnaires, and, some said, even some CIA, although you could hear that about anything. What I heard was that they were pretty much assassination squads. Our own guerrillas, like the Green Berets and the SEALS, which is like the Navy berets. Anyway I said no, because what I heard was mostly scuttlebutt.

'It's Combined Recon and Intelligence Platoons. Special teams. We keep them small, four or five people. You know how that goes, everybody gets so they think like one person. You move around pretty

much on your own, targets of opportunity, that sort of thing. I think it would be just up your alley.'

'I got ten weeks left,' I said, and I said it like You must be nuts.

But it was funny, I was interested in what he was saying. I mean, this lieutenant was recruiting me, asking me to do another tour, and I was listening to the son of a bitch. And he went right on.

'We have a low casualty rate because everybody knows what they're doing. You go out, you do your thing, you come back, everybody leaves you alone.'

'That's about what I'm doing now,' I said.

'That's what I mean, you're perfect for CRIP. We need people like you.'

I'm getting a little pissed. 'What's in this for me, Lieutenant? Just sticking my ass out there to get whacked off for twelve more months? Shit!'

He says, 'So what's back home? You work eight hours, sleep eight hours. Shit, Sergeant, all you got left is eight hours a day to live. Tell me this isn't better than bowling.'

I told him I'd think about it and I got shacked up for two days and went back down to the squad.

The 312th Day: *We had this kid, a replacement, his first time on the line. I don't even remember his name. Anyway, we're rushing this hooch and there's a lot of caps going off and the kid twists his ankle and down he goes and he starts screaming. We all just stay down and all I'm thinking, as many times as I told this kid, 'You go down, keep your mouth shut no matter how bad you're hurt,' and he's losing it all.*

They zero in on him but Doc gets to him first and he's dragging this kid by the feet, trying to get him behind something, away from the fire.

I hear the round hit. It goes phunk, like that.

I was hoping it was the kid but no such luck. Doc took one round, dead centre.

Then the kid freaks out and runs for it and they just cut him to pieces too.

What a waste, what a goddamn awful fucking waste.

Later on, the GR's come in with their body bags. Doc is lying beside a tree. He looks like he's taking a nap and I'm sitting beside him and this guy comes up with the bag and plops it down beside Doc and zips it open.

God, how I hate that sound. I hate zippers.

'Don't put that on him,' I say, and I grab that goddamn green garbage bag. 'Don't put that fuckin' bag on him.'

'Hey, easy, pal, okay,' the gunner says. 'He's gone. We lost him. Let them take him back.'

You can't cry, you know. Nobody cries up here. You cry, everybody thinks you're losing it. Doc had eight days. Eight fucking days to go. All that time, all that experience. All stuffed in a fucking garbage bag.

The 343d Day: *Ever since, I been thinking a lot about Carmody and Flagler and Jesse Hatch. Doc Ziegler. Some of the others. The lieutenant's right; it is kind of a waste, spending a year on the line and then leaving it just when you really get so you know what you're doing. I've never been a pro before at anything. But I know how to fight these motherfuckers. I feel like I'm doing something positive, accomplishing something. You know, in my own way, doing something to turn this thing around, getting even for Jesse and Doc and the lieutenant, all the rest of them.*

And one more thing. I wouldn't want to tell them this, or anybody else. I like it. I'm going to miss it . . . getting a gook in my sights, squeezing off, watching the fucker go down. Shit, man, that's a jolt. That's a real jolt. There's not another jolt in the world like it.

58

PYRAMIDS

There were a couple of wrong turns before I found DeeDee's street. A red Datsun Z sat in the driveway and there were kids playing hide-and-seek in the yard next door. From the outside of the house, everything appeared normal. Obviously death had not made its presence known to the neighbourhood yet.

Lark answered the door and ushered me inside. The house was dark, oppressive, silent. The rituals of passage had not yet begun. There were no flowers, no covered food dishes from the neighbours, no mourners sitting silently, trying not to stare at the casket.

Lark sat on one of the hard, uncomfortable antiques, her hands folded in her lap, looking at the floor, unsure of how to act in the presence of tragedy. I could tell it was a role uncommon for her, that she was accustomed only to the good things in life. Tragedy thus far had passed her by.

'Dee's sleeping,' she said, after moments of strained silence. 'The doctor gave her two shots before she quieted down. I don't know how long she'll be under. A couple of hours, at least.' She paused, fiddling with the hem of her skirt. 'Mr Seaborn called. Thanks for telling him. He seemed to be honestly concerned.'

'I'm sure he is,' I said, trying to think of something more significant to say. 'I just came by to see how she's holding up.'

'Hard to say,' Lark said. 'I don't know what's going to happen when she wakes up. She was in shock when the doctor got here.' She looked up at me suddenly and asked, almost with desperation, 'Was Tony breaking the law when it happened? I think Dee's more worried about that than anything. Not for herself. She doesn't want people to remember him . . . badly.'

'I can't say for sure,' I said, 'but it's possible.'

'How did he die?'

'I'm not sure about that either,' I said, and trying to avoid telling her a bald-faced lie, I added, 'He could've drowned. Apparently he was in the water for some time. He washed up near Saint Somethings Island, wherever that is.'

'Saint Simons,' she said. 'It's south of here, about fifty miles.'

'They're doing the autopsy there,' I said.

She shuddered when I said the word. Then she looked up suddenly. 'I almost forgot,' she said. 'Mickey was by. He said if I saw you to tell you he needs to get in touch. He says it's very important.'

'Do you have my number?' I asked, getting up to leave. I had really wanted to see DeeDee and had little else to say to Lark. She nodded. 'I'm staying at the Ponce.' And she nodded again. 'Well,' I said, 'if I can do anything . . .'

'You did the toughest thing of all,' Lark said. 'It was nice of you, telling her that way instead of . . .'

The sentence seemed to die in her mouth, as if she were unsure how to finish it. I put my arm around her and hugged her until I felt the tension begin to ease. It was a hug I could use, too, just feeling someone close to me, to share a moment of caring with.

'You ought to have somebody here with you,' I said.

'No, not yet. Dee wouldn't want that.'

I left and drove back to the warehouse. The Stick's black Pontiac was lurking in front. Inside the converted supermarket reading a computer printout.

'You're back early,' he said. 'Did'ya get my message?'

Obviously he had not heard about the events at the track and I wasn't in the mood for details. It was only midafternoon but I felt like my cork had been pulled for the day.

'I'm dead,' I said casually.

'A lot of people are having that trouble these days,' he drawled. 'How are things at the track?'

'There was an accident,' I said. 'Three horses went down.'

'What!'

'One of the horses split a foreleg in the stretch and took two other nags down with it.'

'Are the jockeys okay?' he asked.

'Busted up but they'll live. Lost two of the horses.'

He whistled through his teeth, but that seemed to be the extent of his interest.

'And how are things at the bank?'

'I thought you'd never ask,' Stick answered with a smile. 'I tumbled on to how they're using the bank to wash their money. The bad news is, as far as I know, what they're doing is legal.'

'Impossible!' I snapped.

'Well, to some extent it's legal,' he said, amending his original comment. 'The account Cohen uses is in the name of the Abaca Corporation. According to Charlie One Ear, Abaca owns Thunder Point Marina, Bronicata's restaurant, the Porthole, the Jalisco Shrimp Company, etcetera. I checked the account and there are daily deposits, but never more than a couple of thousand dollars.'

'That's inconsistent with what Lark told you.'

'Hang on,' he said, 'I'm not through yet. I only had that one account number, so I decided to check the daily tape. That's a chronological list of all the deposits made at the bank each day. Lo and behold, there're ten deposits for ten grand each, all within seconds of each other.' He made a grand gesture with his hands and smiled. 'Pyramids,' he said.

'Pyramids?'

'Cohen has this thing for pyramids.'

'I don't understand.'

'It's simple, once you tumble on to it. Cohen puts a hundred G's in, Abaca shows a deposit of only ten grand. It only gets complex when you start trying to decipher the whole system.'

'Well, try, 'cause you've lost me,' I said.

'First, let's assume that Seaborn is in collusion with Cohen. Cohen is using the bank as a washing machine. The whole point is to move a lot of cash through the bank without making the IRS suspicious, right?'

'Uh-huh.'

'That's where the pyramids come in. What happens, let's say Cohen makes his daily deposit . . . ten grand, for the sake of discussion. The deposit goes into the Abaca Corporation. That's the base company, okay? But the computer is programmed to immediately dispense that money, by percentage, into several other accounts. It never appears as a ten-grand deposit because the computer spreads it over ten other accounts *before* making the deposit.'

'Does it always go into the same accounts?' I asked.

He shook his head. 'There's a code designation on the account number that tells the computer what set of accounts the money goes into and what percentage goes into each. Then each of those accounts is spread over five or ten other accounts. So what they got is pyramids.'

'So every dollar that goes into the bank is diverted into so many other accounts, you don't see any big sums going anywhere and it doesn't wave any red flags at the Lepers,' I said.

'Exactly,' he said. 'If you weren't looking for something, you'd never tumble over it. Thing is, they seem to be using these accounts for legitimate purposes. Payrolls for Triad employees, accounts payable and receivable for the Bom Dia restaurant, Jalisco Shrimp Company, Thunder Point Marina . . . the Seaview Company, Hojan and Rajan, whatever that may be . . . hell, there could be a couple of hundred accounts. This Cohen is a genius. If he had to, he could probably legitimately account for most of the money going into these pyramids.'

'There's got to be a reason for going to all that trouble,' I said. 'There's got to be some skimming accounts, or payoff accounts.'

'Yeah, I agree,' he said. 'But what are they? We're looking at one pyramid off another here. Creative bookkeeping compounded by creative computer technology. So maybe some of these accounts are payoff accounts or skim accounts; there's no way to tell which ones.'

Stick was right. The system, although devious, was not illegal. What was illegal was using the bank to channel illegal monies from gambling, prostitution, narcotics, and whatever else, into legitimate accounts and then siphoning off some of those accounts without reporting the income to the IRS. The big question was how they were doing it.

'We'll never unravel it all without a key list of *all* their accounts,' said the Stick.

I said, 'Stick, we're close to nailing them. Cohen must have this defined somewhere. It's far too complex to keep in his head.'

'Probably in a computer of his own,' said Stick. 'And there's no way we can access a private terminal.'

'Then one damn thing is for sure,' I said. 'We've got to keep Cohen alive. He's got the key to the puzzle.'

'Wanna put 'em under protective custody?' Stick said. 'I can't think of anything else to do. We're baby-sitting 'em around the clock now.'

'Yeah, and so far it hasn't helped any of them,' I said.

There was one other possible answer. We could offer to put Cohen in the witness protection programme if he would cooperate with us. And I know what my answer to that proposal would be if I were Cohen. I'd tell me to get stuffed.

59

THE COCKTAIL HOUR

I suppose the most spectacular view in town comes with the tallest building – that's if you have the money to make the view worthwhile. Babs Thomas had them both and the taste to do it right. The penthouse was like a glass box surrounded by gardens. Glass walls everywhere: the living room, bedrooms, kitchen, even the bathrooms. Floor-to-ceiling drapes provided whatever privacy was necessary, although the only danger of eavesdroppers seemed to be from low-flying aircraft.

The penthouse was lit by slender tapers, an effect both unusual and stunning, since the glass walls reflected every flickering pinpoint and then re-reflected it, over and over, bathing the rooms in a soft, yellow glow.

There were at least thirty couples there, Babs' idea of a few friends, all of them old-monied and well pedigreed. I assume only a death in the family would have been a suitable excuse for missing the soirée. That or, as in the case of Charles Seaborn, the bank examiners.

Babs, a vision in yellow silk wearing a white hat with a brim wide enough to roller-skate around, swept over to me as I entered, pulled me into a neutral corner, and filled in my dance card for me, advising me on who was worth talking to and whom to skip.

My top priority was to meet the remaining members of the infamous Committee.

Arthur Logan, the lawyer, was forty and looked sixty. Poor posture made him appear almost humpbacked, his face was pinched into a perpetual frown, and his eyes were paranoically intense and busy, like a man who expects to hear bad news at every turn. Ten minutes of conversation proved him to be as senile in mind as in body, a man so fanatically conservative that even Calvin Coolidge would have found him an anachronism. His wife, also singularly unattractive, appeared to have lost her chin somewhere along the way. She complimented him by smiling and keeping her mouth shut.

On the other hand, Roger Sutter, the big-shot journalist, was just the opposite, the epitome of the young man on the go. His handshake was painfully sincere, his gaze intense, his attitude open. He talked to me for five minutes before he figured out I wasn't there to invest money in Dunetown, then his gaze became less intense and began to wander from one female rear end to the other. His wife, who let me know she was the best tennis player at the club thirty seconds after we met, was busy flirting with the men in the room.

Charming.

No wonder the city had fallen prey to Tagliani. Dutch had said it the night I arrived. Dunetown had been entrusted to wimps. Were they involved with Seaborn and Cohen?

316

Doe caught me by surprise. I was ordering a drink when I felt a hand on my shoulder. I turned and she was standing there. My knees started to wobble again.

The big surprise was that Chief was with her.

He sat, tall and erect in his wheelchair, and while time seemed to have taken its toll, the old man still looked like everybody's grandfather ought to look, his white hair cresting a craggy face that was indomitable.

I knew the Findley background well. I should have, it was a story I had heard repeated often enough. Chief's greatgrandfather, Terrence, a bonded Irish collier, had escaped to Dunetown in 1823, won a waterfront tavern in a card game and parlayed that into the city's first million. After that it was cotton, banking, real estate, God knows what else. The same flint that had fired old man Terrence had also struck wit and wisdom in every crevice of Chief's face and his eyes were as fiery and intense as ever. Only his body seemed to be failing him.

'Hello, Chief,' I said. 'Been a long time.'

'Yes,' he said, 'and a sad one.'

I knew the breed well enough to know that Chief would not mention Teddy or my unanswered letter. Apologies come hard and infrequently to men like that; they're not prone to admitting mistakes. Or maybe Chief just didn't see it the way I did; maybe he had just closed the book on that chapter.

'Doe tells me you're in government service,' he said, with obvious sincerity. 'That's quite admirable.'

That was the end of our conversation. A moment later someone pushed past me to pay homage to the old warrior, and then someone else, and someone else, until I was gradually edged out of the circle. Doe eased her way to my side. I could feel the sexual electricity humming around her. Time had not changed one thing – they were still the lightning people.

'Where's Harry?' I asked.

'He cancelled out at the last minute. There was an accident at the track. Some horses were killed.'

'I know, I was there.'

'It must've been just horrible,' she said, then added hurriedly, 'Albert's coming in ten minutes to take Chief home. I'll meet you out on the terrace after he leaves.' She turned abruptly and wormed her way back into the circle of sycophants.

Suddenly I was alone and staring across the room at Sam

Donleavy. I shouldered my way towards him through the crowd, catching snippets of conversation along the way. The women cheeped like sparrows, while the men sounded more like trumpeting elephants. Donleavy seemed relieved by my company.

'It's hot in here. Let's step out on the terrace and get some air,' he suggested.

Lightning was playing in the clouds south of the city and the wind was jangling a delicate glass wind chime near the door. You could feel rain in the air.

'We still on for lunch tomorrow?' I asked, by way of starting the conversation.

'Looking forward to it,' he said. 'I heard about the Lukatis boy. A damn shame.'

'Yeah,' I said. 'A tough break for his sister.'

'Do you think it's tied in to these other deaths?'

'I wouldn't know. The body's down south of here. The autopsy will be done there.'

'I see. Look, I want you to know that any help you give us in cleaning up this mess will be greatly appreciated. Things have been happening so fast it's hard to assimilate them.'

'Yeah,' I said, 'the pace has been breezy.'

'I suppose you're accustomed to such things.'

'Not really. Murder is always ugly, no matter where it happens or who the victim is.'

'Yes, I suppose. At any rate, if you need any help at all from me, just ask.'

'Thanks,' I said. After a decent pause I asked, 'Did you know Tagliani?' I tried to make it sound casual.

'Yes. But as Frank Turner.'

'Were you social friends?'

'Not at all. I met with Turner on a couple of occasions to help him get oriented, but that was some time ago.'

'And to size him up?' I suggested.

He stared at me intently for a few seconds, then nodded slowly. 'That, too.'

'So you knew him personally?'

'Not really; it was all business. I haven't seen him to talk to since he moved here.'

'When was that?'

'I couldn't say accurately. About three years ago.'

'Did you meet here in Dunetown?'

He nodded. 'The first time we were supposed to meet at the old Beach Hotel, but it didn't suit him, so we switched the meeting to Charlie Seaborn's yacht. The second time he had his own boat down here.'

'What did you talk about?'

'Development ideas, other money interests. Later he put us on to' – he waved a hand vaguely in the air – 'several others . . .'

'Bronicata, Chevos,' I said.

'Yes, only not by those names. You've got to remember, he came very highly recommended. He had development resources, excellent credit references, all in the name of Frank Turner.'

'And you never suspected who he really was?'

His face clouded up. 'Of course not,' he said. There was a touch of indignation in his tone but he tempered it quickly. 'Look,' he went on, 'we were looking for developers here. It was obvious the track was going to change things, and Turner talked an excellent game. He seemed very civic-minded. His development ideas were sound. We had no reason to doubt him.'

'I wasn't accusing you of anything,' I said.

'I know that. I just want you to understand, this is all very new to us. At worst we were guilty of naiveté.'

Babs Thomas appeared in the doorway, tapping her foot.

'The party's in here,' she said sternly. 'You two can talk football, or whatever you've found so damned interesting, some other time. And you, Sam, have a phone call. I think it's Charlie. You can take it in the bedroom.'

'Damn!' Donleavy said. 'I'm sorry. We can finish this over lunch tomorrow.'

'Just one other thing,' I said. 'Do you happen to remember the date Tagliani came here the first time?'

He thought about it for several seconds, then took out a business card and scrambled a number on the back.

'No, but I've got an old date book at home,' he said. 'Here's my number. Give me a call about quarter to eight and I can give it to you precisely. Don't wait until eight or you'll be out of luck. Dutch Morehead usually calls me then. We talk once a week, keeps me in touch. He's very prompt and we've been known to talk for an hour or more.'

I thanked him, pocketed the card, and we started back inside. As Donleavy hurried off to take his call, Stonewall Titan materialised from behind a potted plant.

'Hello, doughboy,' he said. 'Don't miss a trick, do you? Just pop up everywhere.'

'I was thinking the same thing about you,' I said.

Titan looked at me, the candles igniting sparks in his narrowed eyes.

'You've done it again, raised more hell, ain't you, son?'

'What do you mean?' I asked.

'I mean your conversation with Harry at the track. That was a damn fool thing to do.'

'Time somebody levelled with him.'

'You're a bad penny, doughboy,' he growled. 'You show up back here and within four days we got somethin' akin to twelve homicides.'

He slashed at a potted plant with his cane.

'I haven't had *two* unsolved goddamn homicides at the same time in this county in forty damn years. Now I got twelve!'

Donleavy came out of the bedroom, made his apologies, and left to await Dutch's weekly call, waving good-bye as he did. It was seven fifteen. In another forty-five minutes we could all leave.

'I'll give it to you again,' I said. 'I didn't cause the homicides and murder isn't my game. It's not why I came here and it isn't why I'm staying.'

'I mean *altogether* I haven't had twelve unsolved homicides since I been sheriff,' he said, ignoring my comments. 'You understand my concern when we have twelve in the space of a couple of days?'

'Sure.'

'Sure? What do you mean, sure?'

'I mean sure, I understand your consternation.'

'Hot damn, college boy. Consternation. Well, listen close, because my consternation tells me you know one helluva lot more about what the hell's goin' on than I do, and since this is my county, I think it's time we shared whatever information you might have.'

I smiled. 'And what would I get out of it?' I asked.

'Your ass, in one piece,' he said flatly.

I laughed. 'What're you going to do, Mr Stoney, put out a contract on me?'

'It may be funny to you, doughboy – '

'That's not what I'm laughing about,' I said, cutting him off. 'I've been under the impression we were both on the same side.'

He ignored my comment and went right on making his point.

320

'I'm not without considerable influence where it means something,' he said. 'I could have your tail bent till it hurts by just raisin' a question or two about your conduct of this investigation.'

'I'm sure you could.'

'What the hell's goin' on? What are you after, Kilmer?'

'I'm looking for RICO violations, Mr Stoney. You know that. Now, I could be wrong. Tagliani may very well have inched in here without anybody knowing who he really was. But I've got to know that for sure.'

'No matter who gets hurt, that it?'

'I don't give a damn whose tombstones I have to kick over to get to the truth.'

'Or who's bed you sleep in?'

'Who are you really worried about, Mr Stoney? Who are you trying to cover?'

'The integrity of my county,' he snapped.

I shook my head with disbelief. 'You mean what's left of it, don't you?'

'You can be an irritatin' son of a bitch.'

'Probably. I didn't come here to run for Queen of the May.'

His tone became more condescending.

'I don't wanna see things blown out of proportion, okay, doughboy? People make mistakes. It's natural. We ain't all perfect.'

'I'll buy that,' I said. 'I just want to make sure that's what they were – mistakes.'

'I'm tellin' you they were.'

'Sheriff, I'll tell you everything I think. Not what I know, because I don't know that much. I think the same gun killed Tagliani, Stinetto, and O'Brian, possibly an American 180. I think the same gun was used to kill Stizano and his bunch and Draganata, probably an M-15 equipped with a grenade launcher. Whoever used them has a military background and killed Logeto and Graves' girlfriend, Della Norman, using a garotte that was fairly common in Vietnam. I think it was all done by one person.'

Titan pursed his lips and cocked his head to one side. 'Not bad for someone who's game ain't murder,' he said. 'Why?'

'If I knew that, I could give you the killer.'

'Humph,' he snorted.

'Now I've got a question to ask you. Who busted Tony Lukatis on the pot charge?'

'Why?'

'He's dead, that's why.'

'I know that. They're doing an autopsy down in Glynn County right now. So what does Tony's previous record have to do with anything?'

'Just curious.'

'The drug enforcement boys nailed Lukatis and his buddy.'

'Did they both do time?'

He paused for a second or two and shook his head. 'The shrimper turned state's and got a suspended sentence.'

'Was Lukatis running marijuana for Longnose Graves?'

Titan looked shocked. 'Hell no,' he stormed. 'Graves doesn't run dope. He may have a lot of faults but that ain't one of them. Far as I know, Lukatis and his friend were freelancin'.'

'Where were they caught?'

'On Buccaneer Island, where the South River empties into Buccaneer Bay. Why are you so interested in Lukatis?'

'Just trying to keep all the lines straight,' I said. 'He and at least one of Graves' men were killed at the same time. Don't you wonder why?'

He leaned forward and said, 'I'll find out why when it's necessary.'

'You know what I think, Mr Stoney?' I said. 'I think you want to neutralise me and I'm not sure why. Like I said, I thought we were both on the same side.'

'I told you last night, I enforce the law my own way,' he said. 'Be advised.' He turned abruptly, elbowed his way through the chitchat, paid his respects to Babs, and left. She breezed back over.

'You're just the life of the party,' she said. 'So far you've talked to Chief Findley, Stoney, and Sam Donleavy, and all three of them have left the party.'

'I do seem to have that effect on people, don't I?'

'Well, darling, Doe is still here. All is not lost.'

'I keep telling you – '

'And I don't believe a word of it,' she said, finishing the sentence, and went off to attend to something.

I stepped out onto the terrace but the rain had started, its first big drops splattering me, so I stood under an awning, watched

322

the thunderclouds gather around the penthouse, and listened to the wind give the chimes a nervous breakdown and the rain grow to a steady downpour.

Doe moved on me slowly, stopping here and there to chat as she came through the room. Finally she stepped outside and stood there, staring up at me.

'I've called you and called you today,' she said, somewhat sternly.

'I don't spend a lot of time around the hotel,' I said.

'Come back to Windsong with me tonight,' she said in a half-whisper.

'You're crazy. What do you plan to do about Harry? He's – '

'He won't come out there. He stays at the townhouse during the racing season. He doesn't like to make that long drive twice a day. Are you going to make me beg you, Jake?'

'Don't be silly.'

'I'm spoiled, Jake,' she said with a laugh. 'Nobody's ever denied that.'

'Nobody ever complained either.'

'I want to make love to you again. I want it tonight. I don't want to wait a minute longer.'

'It's getting too touchy,' I told her. 'Even Titan knows all – '

'I don't care about Stoney. He's my godfather; he should want what's best for me and if he doesn't, the hell with him. We're talking about you and me and tonight. That's all I care about. I want you. I want to make up for twenty years.'

'In one night?'

She laughed again. 'Well, it's a start.'

Bolts of lightning were duelling around us and the full fury of the storm lashed rain under the awning.

'Let's get inside,' I said.

'Not till you promise.'

'Promise what?'

'When you leave here you'll come out to Windsong.'

'I have to make a stop on the way,' I said, thinking about DeeDee Lukatis. I wonder whether Doe knew that her ex-lover was dead. If she did, she was handling it very well. I decided that if she didn't know, somebody else could tell her.

'How long?' she demanded.

'An hour.'

'Don't be late,' she said, wheeled away, and dodged back inside.

I waited for a minute or two before going back in. It was a futile gesture. Babs was watching intently from across the room, like the linesman at a tennis match. I nodded and smiled my way back to her.

'It's not what you think,' I said.

'Please,' she said, rolling her eyes, 'you don't have to tell me a thing. I have two perfectly good eyes in my head.'

'Don't make it sound like some damn intrigue,' I said.

'Darling, I just love intrigue. It's what makes life worth all the trouble.'

60

MIRROR TRICKS

Before I left the hotel, I stopped by my room and called Sam Donleavy. He was pushed for time, he explained, since Dutch would be calling shortly, but he assured me that he would locate the book and bring it to lunch the next day. I said that was just fine. Then I dug the company car out of the hotel garage.

A familiar black Pontiac was crouched under the trees in front of DeeDee's house when I got there. The Stick answered my ring.

'Just the two of you here?' I asked.

'Yeah, I brought over some dinner. Lark needed a little relief. She's stretched out there taking a nap.'

'That bench is worse than the rack,' I said.

'She was too tired to notice.'

'How's DeeDee?'

'Still out. The doctor must've given her enough sec to knock an elephant on its ass.'

'Good, the more sleep she gets the better. I'm afraid she's going to be in for it from the homicide cops, once they finish the autopsy.'

'She doesn't know shit.'

'You know it and I know it,' I said. 'But the turkeys from the murder division also don't know shit.'

'I'll handle them,' he snapped.

'Stop acting like Humphrey Bogart. They'd be dumber than I think they are if they didn't talk to her.'

'What do we do about the pictures that came in on the telex? They'll be out here flashing them around.'

'Burn them. She can't ever see him, Stick, not the way he looks now. She'd have nightmares for the rest of her life.'

'You're beginning to sound like a concerned friend.'

'I'm trying. This is one tombstone I'm sorry I kicked over. Besides, Tony's death isn't going to be handled by the local cops. It's out of their jurisdiction.'

'Where'd he wash up?'

'Saint Solomons Island.'

'That's Saint *Simons* Island.'

'Well, they've got him down there, and it's their problem.'

'Five gets you ten they dump it up here anyway.'

'If it relates.'

'*If?*' Stick said.

'Let's wait and see on that one,' I said.

'There's something else bothering me,' the Stick said.

'What's that?'

'Nance,' he said. 'He's moving around like a wolf on the prowl. Lange and Zapata are taking turns with him.'

'I've been keeping my eyes open,' I said.

'Why don't we lean on him? We can bust his ass, at least, let the fucker know he can't go around taking potshots at federal agents.'

'He'd be on the street in thirty seconds. Costello'd see to that. I want the full clock on that son of a bitch when he goes. Life with no parole. There's no percentage bringing him in and then having him walk. All that is, is frustrating. Besides, I don't think he was ordered to put me on ice, I think he got a wild hair up his ass and decided to just do it. Nesbitt told me he took a lot of shit because he missed me that time in Cincinnati.'

'Well, Zapata and Lange are all over him. He can't go to the john without Chino washing his hands when he's finished. Hopefully, he tries for you again, they'll clean his pipes.'

'As long as he's in view, we're okay.'

I changed the subject to the cocktail party and gave Stick a brief rundown on my talks with both Donleavy and Titan.

'Donleavy says the Committee passed on Tagliani because they're all naive,' I said, summing it up.

'It's possible,' he said. 'What's the problem with Titan?'

I didn't want to discuss Doe Raines, so I shrugged. 'Beats the hell out of me,' I said.

'I almost forgot,' Stick said, taking a sheet of paper from his pocket. 'I did a little more work on the computer.' He unfolded a readout sheet and handed it to me. 'Here's a rundown on the eight main accounts and their subaccounts. There's eighty-six different accounts there, Jake. And that's like the tip of the pyramid, man.'

'Thanks.'

'So what do we do with them?' he asked.

I looked over the printout. About a third of the accounts were corporate.

'Can you access corporate information on that gadget?'

'Sure.'

'I'd like you to check all the corporate names on this list and see if any of them were incorporated in Panama.'

'Panama? The country Panama?'

'The country Panama.'

'Do I get to know why?'

'Ever heard of the Mirror Rule?'

He shook his head.

'You haven't been doing your homework, Stick. Panama, the country, will not divulge any information about Panamanian corporations, not to anyone for any reason. You can't even get a list of officers or stockholders unless the company wants you to have it. So a Panamanian corporation is automatically indemnified from any kind of examination or investigation except by authorities of Panama itself.'

'That's real interesting,' the Stick said.

'It is if you incorporate in Panama. Because then you can have funds from an American bank transferred to a bank in the Virgin Islands.'

'Where does the Virgin Islands fit into all this?'

'The Virgin Islands, although it's a US territory, has its own revenue service. They don't like the Lepers, so they don't corporate with them.'

'The IRS can't get the info on Virgin Island bank accounts, that it?' Stick asked.

'Exactly. And the bank account in the Virgin Islands is a mirror account of the corporate account in Panama. So it's possible to transfer money from a US bank to a bank in the Virgin Islands and then into a Panamanian corporation without the IRS knowing about it.'

'You think that's what Tagliani was doing?'

'It could explain how the payoff accounts work. If there's a Panamanian corporation on this list, it could be a transfer account.'

'And the payoff would go straight through the computer and into the Panamanian bank account, without ever showing up as a deposit,' Stick said, with a touch of wonder.

'And so could their skim,' I said.

'You think Seaborn knows about this Mirror Rule?' Stick asked.

'If he doesn't we ought to have him jailed for incompetence. It's international banking law.'

'Which means Seaborn's involved.'

'That's a little touchy right now. There's nothing illegal about transferring money to Panama. But there is if it's igg.'

Stick smiled. 'The old ill-gotten gains. What would we do without them?'

'The question is, does Seaborn *know* it's a scheme to wash dirty money? Maybe not. He could be that naive.'

'Well, if he didn't know, he probably does now.'

'Right. And since we haven't heard from him, we can at least assume that he might be withholding information.'

'Where the hell did you find all this out?'

'I may not file reports, pal, but I sure as hell read them. This dodge is used a lot by the Mafia. Using the bank's computer to pyramid their accounts, now that's a new wrinkle.'

A phone rang somewhere in the back of the house. Stick bolted, trying to catch it before it woke someone up. He was too late. Lark stirred on the wooden bench, opened one eye, saw me, waved a limp hand in my direction, and managed a feeble smile.

'Go back to sleep,' I said. 'Stick and I will hold the fort a while longer.'

Wrong again, Kilmer.

Stick came out of the kitchen with a crazy look in his eyes.

'What's the matter with you?' I asked.

'You're not gonna believe this, Jake,' he said.

'Try me.'

'Somebody just put a bullet in Harry Raines' head.'

61

G-A-L-A-V-A-N-T-I

It took us less than ten minutes through heavy fog to get to the scene of the crime, and a familiar scene it was. Harry Raines had been shot down in the centre of the Quadrangle, no more than a hundred yards from Charlie Seaborn's bank.

It looked like every police car in Dunetown was there. Red and blue lights flashed eerily through the thick fog, like silent fireworks. A small crowd had wandered up from the riverfront clubs and restaurants to see what all the fuss was about.

It took a couple of minutes to locate Dutch in the mist. He was standing with couple of plainclothesmen, studying a chalk form drawn on the cobblestone walk. Yellow police scene ribbons had been suspended around the area. Dutch informed us that the ambulance had come and gone already.

'He's still alive!' I said.

'Yeah, but not by enough to matter much. One shot, right here.' He tapped his forehead an inch above the right eyelid. 'Bullet's still in there.'

'My God,' a hoarse voice whispered, and it was a second or two before I realised it was mine.

'We got a couple of ear witnesses,' Dutch said, leading us away from the chalk-marked form on the walkway.

'Ear witnesses?' the Stick said.

Their names were Harriet and Alexander although, for reasons that elude me, Alexander preferred to be called Chip. They were in their mid-twenties and two weeks away from their wedding day and she had lost his engagement present to her. The girl was as fancy as a plain girl can make herself. The boyfriend, short and stubby, with a badly trimmed moustache, seemed far more concerned over the missing necklace than the shooting.

'We stopped off here on the way to dinner because, see, this is where we met,' he babbled, probably for the fifth or sixth time. 'But it was so foggy, we went on down to the Porthole to meet our friends for dinner . . .'

'You couldn't see your hand in front of your face,' Harriet said, nodding vigorously.

I was getting edgy, listening to their routine.

'Like it is now,' Chip said. 'This wasn't half an hour ago.'

'Yes,' I said. 'I got that – go on!'

Harriet continued her extravagant nod. 'Like it is now,' she repeated.

He glowered at her and continued his story.

'And that's when her necklace was gone,' Chip said. 'It was a cluster of diamonds on a gold chain. Eight diamonds. They added up to a full carat.'

'Can you please get on to the details!' I demanded.

'We're sorry about the necklace,' Dutch said tersely. 'Can you finish your story.'

'Yes, well,' he said, 'so we excused ourselves and came back up here hoping maybe we could find it.'

'That's when the man got shot,' Harriet said, nodding even more exuberantly as she got in the big one. Chip's bubbly cheeks turned scarlet at being upstaged.

'Did you see anybody?' I interjected.

They both shook their heads.

'Did you hear them? Did they say anything?'

'I'm not sure,' Chip said firmly.

'Well, they did say something,' Harriet piped up again, 'or at least one of them did. He said, "You're finished."'

'You're not sure, Harriet,' Chip said curtly.

She nodded her head vigorously.

'Would you recognise the voice if you heard it again?' the Stick asked.

Chip said, 'We weren't paying much attention. We heard somebody on the walk, the footsteps stopped – '

Harriet jumped in, stealing his thunder again. 'And there was "You're finished" and Bang!' Big nod.

Chip's face twisted in anger. 'Harriet! May I please tell the story?' he said.

'What else is there?' I asked.

'Harriet screamed and the killer ran away,' he said, glaring at his future wife to keep her quiet.

'Nobody's dead yet,' Dutch growled.

'Well, you know what I mean,' the kid said nervously.

'Which way did this person run?' I asked.

'We couldn't tell,' Chip said. 'You can't really tell because of the buildings, uh, the sound . . .'

'Accoustics, is that what you're talking about?' Stick asked.

'Exactly,' Chip said, and he started the nodding routine.

It was true. With fog so thick you could hardly see your feet, and with the three buildings forming a kind of box, it was impossible to tell where sound was coming from.

'Did you find the body?' I asked.

They shook their heads in unison.

'No way,' Chip said. 'We ran back over to the bank because there were some lights on in the back, but nobody came to the door, so I went to the phone booth and called the police.'

I asked: 'This person who ran away after the shooting, could you guess whether it was a man or a woman?'

'Man,' they said simultaneously.

That was all they had. It was too foggy to waste any more time there. Stick and I left our cars in the parking lot and headed for the hospital with Dutch. The lights in the back of the bank were dark when we left.

There were a couple of blue and whites parked at the hospital emergency entrance and one car that could have been an unmarked police vehicle. The long, beige hallway inside the emergency doors was empty, as was the emergency operating room. Raines was in ICU, which was on the second floor.

Four uniformed cops and two plainclothes detectives held the unit captive.

'You taking this one on?' one of them asked Dutch.

'It's personal,' was all the big Dutchman said in return.

The chief surgeon and the resident were there but noncommunicative. They were waiting for Raines' personal physician. An intern with the trauma unit, however, confirmed what we already knew and added a few details: that Harry Raines had been shot once in the left forehead by a large-calibre weapon, that it had been held close enough to cause heavy powder burning, that he was beyond critical and, as far as the intern was concerned, was moribund.

'He's a lot more dead than alive,' the young doctor said. 'If he lives another hour, the Catholics'll probably sanctify the whole wing.'

'How's that?' Dutch asked.

'Because it would be a miracle,' the young doctor said.

330

'Any idea what kind of gun did it?' I asked.

'I don't know about things like that,' he said. 'That's police work.'

The intensive care unit was a fairly small room with curtained cubicles around its perimeter for patients and a control bank of machines and monitors at its core. Every cubicle was monitored by closed-circuit TV. There were three nurses on duty, all of whom seemed very busy. The two doctors retired to an empty cubicle and pulled the curtain behind them.

I could see Raines, in the tiny black and white TV screen, half his face bound up in bandages, muttering to himself.

'Do you have a tape recorder in that war wagon of yours?' I asked the Stick.

'Yeah, minicorder. A Pearl with a voice activator.'

'Get it fast,' I whispered, and he was gone, returning in less than five minutes with a recorder no bigger than the palm of my hand.

'Fresh batteries and a fresh tape,' he said. 'You gonna try and tape Raines?'

'Yeah. Keep the jokers at the door busy for a minute or two.'

When I could, I slipped behind the curtain into Raines' cubicle and hung the tape recorder over the retaining bar by his head. His lips were moving but his words were jumbled. He was the colour of clay, his unbandaged eye partially open and rolling crazily under the lid.

As I came back out of the cubicle, a small whirlwind of a woman in a dark grey business suit burst into the room. She was about five one, on the good side of forty, could have dropped ten or fifteen pounds without missing it, looked colder than a nun's kiss, and was meaner than Attila the Hun. She took over like the stormtroopers in Paris, snapping orders in a voice an octave deeper than nature had intended, punctuating every word with a thin, manicured spear of a finger. I could hear the arctic air whistling through her veins as she snapped orders to the four men with her. I stood back and watched the performance.

'You two get into hospital blues,' she said. 'You, get on the door. Nobody gets in unless I say so. And you, sit by that control desk.'

Then she saw me.

'Who are you?' she snapped icily, jabbing the spear under my nose.

'I could be the doctor,' I snapped back.

She looked me up and down. 'Not a chance,' she said.

'The name's Kilmer. Federal Racket Squad.'

'Out,' she barked, tossing her thumb over her shoulder like an umpire at home plate. 'He's mine.'

'And who the hell are you?' I demanded.

She stuck her tiny, bulldog face as close to mine as she could get it without standing on her toes and said, 'Galavanti. Honore Galavanti, G-a-l-a-v-a-n-t-i. Oglethorpe County DA. I've got my own people with me. I don't need you, so out.'

'Not so fast,' I challenged.

'Listen, here, uh, what was your name again?'

An act. This was a tough lady, but then she would have to be. It would take a tough lady to get elected DA in Stonewall Titan's macho court.

'Kilmer. K-i-l-m-e-r.'

'Oh, yeah. Scram.'

'Aren't you pushing this DA thing a little far?' I said.

She glared at me for several moments and said, 'They told me you'd be trouble.'

'Who's they?' I asked.

'Everybody that's met you,' she snapped back.

Then she saw the tape recorder on the retaining bar beside Raines' head.

'What's that?' she demanded, spearing the air with her finger again.

'That is a tape recorder.'

'Listen to me – '

I pulled her to one corner, away from the nurses, who were trying not to listen, and said, 'Won't you step into my private office? I think maybe we should talk.'

I led her into another empty cubicle and sat her down on the bed.

'Leave the recorder where it is. Anything that's on it is yours. All I want to do is hear it. If he says anything before he checks out, we share.'

'You sound like his checking out is a fait accompli,' she said.

'He's got a bullet in his brain.'

'His doctor should be here any minute.'

'The man's the colour of wet cement, his fever's rising like fresh bread, and his blood pressure's about two over two. Unless

God's on his way here, forget it. You've got a hot potato on your hands, lady, any way you cut it. That's the most powerful man in town dying in there. Somebody's gonna go to the dock before it's over and your case is going to rely on a homicide squad, which if I'm any judge at all, collectively couldn't put their socks on in the dark. Off hand I'd say you need all the help you can get.'

That slowed her down a little. I could almost hear the gears clicking inside her brain.

'What have you got to offer?' she said after a minute or two of hard thought.

'Some ideas, a few hunches. All I need is a day or two to see if they wash.'

'So what do you need me for, Kilmer?'

'Look, Gavalanti – '

'It's Galavanti,' she said. 'The "l" comes before the "v", like in "gal".'

'Sorry . . . , Galavanti. You've got twelve homicides on your hands. Thirteen if we lose Raines. Sooner or later you're going to have to deal with all these cases.'

'What're you driving at?' she demanded.

'Maybe I can put them right in your lap.'

'You know who's behind all this?'

'I'm getting close,' I bluffed.

She laughed. 'God, have I heard *that* line before,' she said. 'That the first thing they teach you at the police academy?'

'What have you got without me?' I asked.

'Zero-zero at this point,' she admitted.

'Ms Galavanti, I haven't laid eyes on you before tonight. Twelve homicides and this is the first time you show your face.'

'Don't be naive. That man over there's being touted for governor.'

'I think if you're smart enough to be DA of this county, you're smart enough not to pay any attention to what the newspapers are saying. You keep in touch with Titan and Morehead and everybody else in town that counts. You know all about the Tagliani connection.'

'You think this shooting is connected to the others?' she asked cautiously.

'Seems likely, doesn't it?'

She pursed her heart-shaped mouth while she mulled over what I said.

'I'm also smart enough to know you Feds are after something and murder's not it,' she said finally. 'Whatever happens, the villains in this piece will go to federal court before I get a crack at them.'

'Maybe not . . .' I said and let her fill in the rest of the sentence.

'All right, Kilmer, what's your offer?'

'Before this is over, some RICO cases could be coming down. Between you and me, if murder's involved, too, I'd be glad to turn the culprits over to you on the homicide charges before I take them to federal court.'

'Why are you being so good to me?'

'Two reasons. Murder puts them away for a lot longer than racketeering and we can always go after them after you get finished.'

'And the other reason?'

'I want a little straight talk in return.'

Suspicion put a frown on her face. 'About what?' she asked.

'Tony Lukatis,' I said.

'What about him?'

'Did you prosecute his case?'

'Yes,' she said with a shrug, 'although it's nothing to brag about.'

'How come?'

'It was open and shut. We had a corroborative witness.'

'His partner?'

'That's right. Gil Winslow.'

'I heard the DEA made the arrest. Wouldn't that make it federal?' I asked.

'Titan's people were there. They took the credit.'

'So Titan turned the case over to you for prosecution?'

'That's right. Listen, if you're looking to make trouble for Mr Stoney . . .'

'I'm not looking to make trouble for anybody who doesn't deserve it,' I said, and hurried on. 'So Stoney took credit for the bust and put the case together. And he provided the turncoat witness.'

She nodded suspiciously. 'If you want to call Winslow that.'

'I don't mean this to be insulting, but didn't the boat belong to Winslow?'

'Mm-hmm . . .'

334

'Wouldn't it make more sense to lay it on him, confiscate his boat, take him off the water?'

'None of my concern,' she snapped. 'Look, Kilmer, what happened, the case came to me with Winslow. His testimony was that Lukatis had the scheme and the finance. Lukatis knew where a ton of pot was hung up in the Bahamas. He offered Winslow fifty thousand dollars' guarantee against a split if Winslow went over there and brought the stuff in.'

'On Winslow's boat?'

'That's right.'

'How much?'

'One ton.'

'Who's idea was it to land on Buccaneer Island?'

'I don't know,' she said earnestly.

'What was the other side of the coin? Lukatis must've had a story.'

'Yes. He claimed it was Winslow who approached him.'

'And the front-end financing?'

'Lukatis' story was that Winslow did it all; he just went along to help,' she said, then her mood became hostile and suspicious. 'How come you're so interested in this? Are you going to do something stupid – like try to overturn the verdict in the Lukatis case?'

'Hardly,' I said. 'Tony Lukatis is dead.'

Her reaction told me she didn't know about Tony Lukatis yet. That made sense, since the homicide was being investigated outside her jurisdiction.

'What happened?' she asked.

'We're not sure yet,' I said. 'Our guess is that he tried another dope run and it went sour.'

'Where?'

'South of here. We should have the autopsy report by now. He may have been in it with Longnose Graves.'

'What? Never!'

'How come you're so sure he wasn't?'

She held up one finger and said, 'Graves isn't in the trade,' and then a second, 'and if he were, he wouldn't go near Tony Lukatis.'

'Why?'

'Because Mr Stoney wouldn't like it?'

'And Graves and Titan get along, that it?'

'An uneasy peace, but it seems to work for the sheriff. That's not my business, anyway, Kilmer.'

'You could make it your business.'

'Not and stay in office. We're getting off the subject anyway.'

'If Lukatis financed the Winslow run, I'd like to know where he got the hundred grand or so in front money it took. That's what we're talking about, hot off the boat.'

'He was financed by his connection,' she said with a shrug.

'Did you prove that in court?'

'It's what Winslow testified.'

'So he was the main witness?'

'Yes. And the arresting officers.'

'Do you think Lukatis was really the guilty one?'

It was an insult, a question I was sorry I asked as the words were coming out of my mouth. Her expression said how big the insult was. She looked shocked and angry.

'I'm sorry,' I said hurriedly. 'I withdraw the question.'

'It was a strong case and a good one and I did the best I could with it, which is how I handle every case, Mr Kilmer. I talked at length with Tony Lukatis. He was arrogant and uncooperative.'

'Which is the way anyone might react if they felt they were being double dealt,' I said.

She hesitated for a moment and then shrugged. 'I suppose so,' she said. 'Anyway, all this is a matter of public record.'

I said, 'With any luck, I'm going to make you a hero.'

'I've heard that song before.'

'Not in my lovely alto,' I said.

She hesitated a moment longer. 'God, would I like to trust you,' she said, half-aloud.

'What've you got to lose? Besides, we've got a deal. You told me what I wanted to know.'

We started to leave and a new face appeared in the ICU. He was tall and so painfully thin that he looked amorexic. He was wearing a tuxedo and there was a panicked expression on his face. He stared at us and at the cop sitting at the control unit.

'Who are all these people?' he said, motioning to us, but looking at the nurses.

'I'm District Attorney Galavanti,' she said, and pointing to me, 'This is one of my people.'

'Can we please clear the area,' he said, taking command again. 'I'm Dr George Hanson, Mr Raines' personal physician.'

336

'Yes, sir,' she said. 'There's just one thing. I have a small tape recorder on the bar near Mr Raines' head, in case he should say something . . .'

'Oh my good God,' Hanson groaned. 'I can't believe this is happening.' He scurried away to confer with the resident and the surgeon, who came out of their cubicle when they heard him. They held a whispered conference as Hanson peeled off his tux jacket and slipped into a robe offered by one of the nurses. We left the unit.

'Thanks,' I said on the way out. 'We may end up with zip, but we could score.'

'Like I said, Kilmer, I'll believe it when it happens.'

We stepped out into the hall and came face to face with Stonewall Titan and Doc Raines.

62

DEATHWATCH

She looked like one of those wide-eyed French mimes you see on the stage. Tiny, fragile, vulnerable, terrified, and none of it an act, if I was any judge. This was a woman who was running out of control. A stone in the road could throw her over the edge.

The DA excused herself and got out of the line of fire. Dutch and the Stick had moved back down the hall, out of earshot.

'How is he is he all right?' she babbled, making one question out of two. Titan looked at me as if I had bubonic plague. His nostrils flared like an angry mule's.

'Don't you ever light anyplace?' he growled.

'Jake, how is Harry?' Doc demanded, ignoring Titan.

I steered her into a small waiting room adjacent to the ICU. Titan scurried along behind us, his cane tapping along the linoleum floor like a blind man's. I pushed the door shut behind him. She stared at me with her saucer eyes, waiting.

'He's dead, isn't he?' she said.

'No, but there's very little hope,' I said.

'Oh, God,' she cried out. 'Oh, God, I did this to him.'

'What are you talking about?' I said.

'That's pound foolish,' Titan added.

She started to sag. I took her by the shoulders and put her in a chair. She sat there with her hands between her knees and began to shake.

'Better get a doctor in here,' I said to Titan, and he left to look for one.

'What did you mean, Doe?' I asked, kneeling in front of her.

'I do love Harry, I do. He's a fine person and he's been a good husband,' she said in a whimper.

'I know it.'

'Maybe if I'd been more honest . . .'

'You had nothing to do with it, Doe. Don't go off on some guilt tangent.'

'Why did this happen?' she asked, as tears burst from her eyes.

'I don't know.'

'Was it something to do with the horses?'

'I doubt it,' I said. 'Did he tell you where he was going tonight when he cancelled out of the party?'

She shook her head. 'He called me from the track, told me about the accident, and said he was staying in town.'

'He didn't say why?'

'No. It was fairly common – not the accident, his staying in town.'

'Look, we'll find out who did this, I promise you.'

She nodded but she was close to shock. Nothing was getting through to her.

'Where was he shot?' she asked.

'Down at the waterfront, in the Quadrangle.'

'Oh,' she sobbed, 'his favourite place in the world.' She stared around as if expecting some psychic cloud to drift into the room and erase her pain. 'It was his idea. We donated the land for it.'

I took her hands between mine and rubbed some warmth into them.

'Jake, I feel so . . . rotten.'

'Titan's right, that's pound foolish. Nothing good can come from that kind of thinking.'

But she wasn't listening. She began to rock back and forth and moan like an injured animal

'How did Harry sound when he called you?' I pressed on. 'Was he angry? Sad? Confused?'

'He just sounded like Harry. He was funny about keeping

338

things from me if he thought they would be upsetting. My God, listen to me, I'm talking like he's dead already. Oh, Jake, I'm sorry.'

She lowered her head into her lap and started sobbing. A moment later Dr Hanson and Titan came in. Sam Donleavy was with them. She jumped up and rushed over to him.

'I'm sorry. I just heard,' Donleavy said. 'I've been on the phone half the evening. I drove in from Sea Oat as fast as I could.'

Doe turned quickly to the doctor.

'How is he?' she said, in a voice that was shrill and ragged at the edges.

He looked at me sternly and said, 'May I speak with Mrs Raines privately?'

'He's a friend,' she said.

He didn't like that very much but it wasn't the proper time to argue the point. He said, 'Doe, we're going to do the very best we can but I'm afraid that's not very much. Harry was shot in the forehead. They've done a scan and the bullet is lodged in the rear of the frontal lobe. It's inoperable.'

She fell against him, her arms limp at her side.

'I'm going to give you something to relax you,' he said, but she started shaking her head violently.

'No, I'm not going to sleep through this. I've been protected enough in my life. I'm not a child, George.'

'It won't put you to sleep, it will just take the edge off things a little.'

'I want the edge. I want to feel it all. Don't you understand? This isn't your problem or Mr Stoney's, it's mine. He's my husband and I will make whatever decisions are necessary here. I can't do that stoned out on a cot.'

'Let her handle it her way,' Donleavy said quietly.

Hanson was uncomfortable. He patted her shoulder. 'As you wish,' he said.

'May I see him?'

'Of course,' Hanson said.

'I'll come along,' Donleavy said, and followed them into the ICU.

The minute they were out of the room, Titan turned on me, his teeth showing.

'Keep out of this,' he hissed, jabbing his finger in my face. 'The one thing she don't need right now is you.'

'That's up to her,' I hissed back.

'I'm telling you, back off. Get out of her life. I blame all this on you, you and that bunch of stumblebums of Morehead's. This never should have happened – '

'Forget it!' I barked back. 'You can't blame Morehead. Your mighty committee screwed up. That's how Tagliani got in here.'

'Damn you,' he said in a threatening whisper. 'We ain't smart college boys like you hotshot federals. So they got in! Morehead's job was to keep this element in line if they *did*.'

'Screw you, Titan,' I said vehemently. 'You're just like the rest of these assholes who want to pass the buck to somebody else.'

'I don't give a hoot owl's cross eyes what those wop bastards do to each other,' Titan said, his voice rising to a shriek. 'They want to kill each other off, that's goddamn good riddance, I say.'

He was trembling with rage, the rage of a man whose power had been compromised.

'That ain't what I had to say to you, anyway,' he went on. 'I'll try appealing to your sense of honour, if you got any. Don't give the town reason to wag their tongues, doughboy. She surely don't need such as that at this time.'

'Doe and I are old friends. Did it occur to you that I may be able to help?'

'Keep away from her!' he screamed.

'Mind your own fucking business,' I said softly, and left the room.

'What was that all about?' Dutch asked as I joined them.

'Titan got a little out of line,' I said.

'Titan doesn't get out of line,' Dutch said.

'Wrong,' I said. 'He just did.'

We hung around for fifteen or twenty minutes. It was obvious that Raines' time was running out, but the doctor was playing his prognosis close to the chest. Doe stayed in the unit with Raines while Titan and Donleavy were knee to knee, palavering in the waiting room probably deciding who would replace Raines in the political structure. There were several uniformed police hanging around and there was nothing further we could do, so we moved on after I scribbled a brief note to Doe with some phone numbers on it and left it with a nurse.

It had cleared up outside. A warm summer wind had blown away the storm, leaving behind a beautiful, starry night. Dutch, Stick and I drove back to the park in silence, each of us in his own way trying to make sense out of what appeared to be a senseless holocaust plaguing Doomstown.

There was still a light fog hanging over the park, like a wisp of cloud, but I could see across it to Warehouse Three, on the opposite side. Cobblestone walkways crisscrossed the park like an asterisk, intersecting at its centre. One of them dissected the park and ran straight to the river's edge; another ran between the bank and Warehouse Three.

Plainclothesmen and uniformed cops were still examining the scene and had extended their yellow control ribbons around the entire park.

Raines had met his assailant about halfway between the back of the park, where Dutch's ear witnesses were searching for the lost necklace, and the river. I stood next to the chalked form on the walk and looked back and forth. Chip and his fiancée had been less than thirty yards away when Raines was shot.

'I wonder what direction Raines was walking in and where he was going,' I mused aloud.

'His Mercedes is parked down behind the bank,' Stick offered.

I walked the fifty yards or so down to the river's edge. What had once been a dock had been converted into a small fishing pier. The dark river swirled past its pillars, gurgling up small black whirlpools. The river walk ran from River Road, where it turned and coursed up an embankment to the highway above, along the riverbank, and behind three warehouses that had been converted into office buildings.

'Findley Enterprises is in Warehouse Three, next to the park, and Costello and Cohen have their offices in One. That's three buildings down on the end,' Dutch offered.

I looked up and down the river, then back towards the museum and the spot where Raines was shot.

'Any ideas?' said Dutch.

I had a lot of ideas, all of them pure guesswork, none of them provable, and none I cared to share at that moment.

'Not really,' I said. 'How about you two?'

'Let's say Raines parked his car over at the bank and started across the park towards the Findley office,' Stick said. 'That young couple was twenty, thirty yards away, talking. The killer must have heard them. Seems to me whoever did the trick had to know the park pretty well.'

'And knew which way Raines was coming, so he or she knew exactly where to wait,' Dutch conjectured.

'And was pretty desperate,' I concluded.

'How so?' said Dutch.

'To shoot him down with witnesses a few yards away,' I said. 'I call that taking a chance.'

We walked back towards the bank, looking on all sides of the walkways, but found nothing else of interest. The locals had obviously worked the place over. I stood at the shooting site for a moment or two more.

'Could've been Nance,' said the Stick. 'Could've come down from Costello's office, waited until Raines parked his car, started across the park, done the deed, and run back to Costello's office.'

'Maybe,' I said. 'A lot of maybes, as usual.'

'Why don't we talk this out over a piece of pie and coffee,' Dutch said. 'This caught me in the middle of dinner.'

'Suppose it wasn't Nance,' I said. 'Suppose it was somebody who was so desperate they had to take a chance and blitz Raines on the spot. What would they do?'

'Run in the opposite direction from the witnesses,' Dutch said. 'Down towards the river.'

'Yeah,' I said. 'And if they were real desperate, they might have ditched the weapon.'

'In the river,' Stick said.

'Exactly,' I agreed.

'George Baker,' both Stick and Dutch said in unison.

'Who's George Baker?' I asked.

'The best black-water diver in these parts,' said Dutch. 'If there's a gun in the river, he'll find it.'

'Think it's worth a chance?' I asked.

'Are you kidding?' said Stick. 'George'd leave a movie queen's bed to go diving. It's how he gets his jollies.'

'Then let's get him,' I said.

'How about pie and coffee?' Dutch implored.

'Let's see if we can dig up Baker first,' I said.

63

BLACK-WATER DIVE

Stick found Baker at home watching television. The diver, excited by the prospect of finding the murder weapon, promised to keep his mouth shut and be on the pier at first light. Coffee and pie brought Stick, Dutch, and me nothing but endless speculation. We packed it in early and I went to bed after checking the hospital and being told that Raines' condition was 'guarded'.

At five thirty A.M. I was back at the park with Stick, huddled over the river's edge in fog thicker than the previous night, sipping black coffee from a plastic foam cup and listening to George Baker describe what he and his partner were about to do. Baker was a big man with a barrel chest, hulking shoulders, a neck like a spare tyre, and black hair cut shorter than a buck private's. A telephone man by trade, he was a black-water diver by avocation and an auxiliary policeman, whatever that was, for the hell of it.

'It's dark down there,' he said dramatically as he pulled on his wet suit. His patois, a blend of southern colloquial and old English, was as descriptive as it was archaic. He sounded like the hawker for an old medicine show.

'Yessir, dark and dangerous. Don't take much more'n a Mexico minute for a man to perish under these waters. A man cannot afford errors of the mind, for you don't make any miscalculations, least not more than once. Why, sir, I dive in waters so dark, even a torch will hardly cut their swarthy depths. The bottom is either sugar mud, which is shifty and quicksandy, or it's covered with old, rusty cables, the likes of an octopus, and old boat propellers, tin cans, and other such various obstacles from time past when this here was a pier for mighty ships of the sea. Why, say, at high noon, it's so dark at the depths of fifteen feet, I must, by needs do everything by the touch of these here fingers.'

He wobbled ten fingers at us, just in case we didn't know what a finger was, and stared at them himself with awe.

'Yessir,' he said, 'sometimes there ain't nothin' twixt me and the Almighty but a measly ol' fingerprint.'

The bottom, Baker told us, sloped away from the bank for about thirty feet, then dropped off sharply into the channel. He would use what he called his 'tender system', a ball of twine that he ran from pillar to pillar and used as a guide under water. His buddy diver, a scroungy-looking young man identified only as Whippet, who I later learned was a bootlegger by trade, kept track of his progress by means of a tie line around Baker's waist.

'If I get in trouble,' said the master diver, 'Whippet will endeavour to pull me up, careful but sure, in hopes that I will survive whatever calamity might befall me.'

Baker also had a theory, derived from looking for more than just a few murder weapons in his time.

'A man most likely will throw the gun out in the water, such as flingin' a baseball,' he said, 'whereas a lady, who don't normally have much truck with guns, will tend to just drop the weapon straightaway, so as to get it out of hand as quick as is possible. I will operate from the edge of the channel in, thereby usin' the tide to my advantage.'

'If I were guessing,' I volunteered, 'I'd say he or she dumped the gun fast, as soon as they reached the end of the walk. There were witnesses who heard the shot from fairly close by.'

'Thank you, sir,' Baker said formally. 'I'll keep that in mind.'

Fully dressed with mask and tanks, he could have modelled for a Hollywood monster, an enormous black bulk peering like an owl through his face mask. He clambered down the side of the fishing pier, vanished into the fog, and a moment later splashed into the water fifteen feet below us.

'If you got somethin' t'do, might's well get on with it,' Whippet said, stuffing snuff under his lip. 'This'll most likely take a while.'

Stick and I groped our way through the fog, found a coffee shop, and took on breakfast. Charlie One Ear arrived shortly after, with him the autopsy reports on all the victims up to and including Tony Lukatis and Stitch Harper.

'The same gun killed Tagliani, Stinetto, O'Brian, Harper,' he told us. 'A .22. All of them shot to hell and gone except for Lukatis. He was only shot once, back of the head, with a .357. A .223 removed Stizano and his people.'

'Coup de grâce,' I said.

344

'What?' Charlie One Ear asked.

'Just thinking out loud.'

'So what else do you think?' he said.

'What I've always thought. We got an M-16, probably with a forty-millimetre grenade launcher mounted on it, that takes care of the Stizano massacre and Draganata. We got an American 180, sounds like a dentist drill, fires a hundred eighty rounds in six seconds, which takes care of the Tagliani kill, O'Brian, and the boys on the boat. The rope trick was used on Logeto and Della Norman. And we got a .357 that was used to put the insurance shots into Stinetto, Tagliani and Lukatis. Not that big an arsenal for all the damage that's been done to date.'

'How about Harry Raines?' Charlie One Ear asked.

'We won't know for sure until they get the slug out. Dutch says it was probably a .38 or close to it. That means it could be .357 or even a nine-millimetre. They're all about the same diameter.'

'And Nance shoots a nine-millimetre Luger, right?' Stick asked.

'Nance didn't shoot Harry Raines.'

He looked at me with surprise.

'How do you know that?'

'Instinct,' I said. 'Really logic. First of all, he's not a contact killer. He likes to work from a distance. Second, he's a planner. He wouldn't ice his mark in a fog with two people twenty yards away. It's too risky. Nance is a pro. He's only made two mistakes that I know of.'

'What were they?'

'He missed me twice,' I said.

Dutch and our breakfast arrived at the table together. He had found us there to tell us that Harry Raines was dead.

'About forty-five minutes ago,' the big man said, sinking into the booth beside me. 'I been up all night. It's a sad, sad thing. Doe Raines is a wreck and Stoney Titan is blaming everybody but the President. Donleavy finally stepped in to make the arrangements.'

I listened but didn't hear any more. I was thinking about Doe and the devils that had shown themselves to her in the hospital, devils that could twist her mind into a private hell if they were not dealt with and quickly. Strange how lovers and family always assume the guilt of death. Both DeeDee and Doe had lost loved

345

ones in the same day and both were assuming guilt for the loss. I still wondered if Doe knew or cared that Tony Lukatis was dead. She had bigger things to deal with now.

'Does Chief know yet?' I asked finally.

'I dunno, that's probably Mr Stoney's chore,' said Dutch. The death of Harry Raines didn't seem to spoil his appetite. He ordered a breakfast that would have given me indigestion for a week.

'I can't believe it,' Dutch said. 'Sam Donleavy and I were talking about all this as it was happening.'

'What time did he call you?' I asked.

'I called him,' he said. 'About five past eight.'

'Where?'

'He lives in the condos out on Sea Oat, just before you cross over the bridge to the Isle of Sighs.'

That gave Sam Donleavy an airtight alibi. I had talked to him at quarter to eight. Even the Stick at his best could not have driven the distance from Sea Oat to town in less than fifteen minutes. To drive both ways in twenty minutes was literally impossible.

'I've got something for you, Jake,' Charlie One Ear said, breaking into my reverie. 'Stick asked me to check out the Tagliani bank accounts. Three of those companies are foreign.'

'Incorporated in Panama?' I said.

'Now, how'd you know that?' asked Dutch.

'A psychic flash,' I said. 'Which are they?'

'The Seaview Company, which owns the hotels; a company called Riviera, Incorporated, which does maid and janitorial service for the hotels and other clients; and another called the Rio Company, which is some kind of service outfit, although we couldn't find out much about it. The Thunder Point Marina and the Jalisco Shrimp Company are both owned by Abaca Corporation, which is a local company. The restaurant is a proprietorship.'

'Bronicata the proprietor?'

'Yep.'

'All makes sense,' I said. 'They need a few legitimate businesses as part of the washing machine.'

Charlie One Ear, encouraged by my enthusiasm, left to see if he could dig up more facts.

Dutch's beeper started bugging us and he went to check it out. He returned, both amused and surprised.

'What now?' asked Stick.

'Everybody seems to be turning their cards up,' he said. 'Nose

346

Graves made a wreck out of the Jalisco Shrimp Company not twenty minutes ago. Nobody's hurt but he spread the place all over the county. What's left is burning.'

'Shit!' I said grimly. 'It's starting.'

'What's starting?' said Dutch.

'What I've been afraid of,' I said. 'Open warfare. If it's not stopped, Harry Raines won't be the only innocent victim. I've seen a gang war up close, in Cincy. It isn't pretty. It'll make the Tagliani massacres look like a harmless warm-up.'

That put a crimp in the conversation for a moment. Then Dutch reached in his pocket and took out the tape recorder I had hung on Harry Raines' bed.

'I almost forgot,' he said. 'I retrieved this for you.'

'Anything on it?' I asked.

'I haven't checked,' he said.

'Do you know Graves did the Jalisco job for sure?' the Stick asked Dutch.

'Absolutely. That was the Mufalatta Kid on the horn,' Dutch said. 'Seems we did something right for a change. The Kid was shagging Graves and watched the whole thing happen.'

He gathered up our bills. 'I'll let the city pay for these,' he said. 'Let's go have a talk with the Kid.'

'Where is he?' asked the Stick.

'Baby-sitting on Longnose Graves' doorstep,' Dutch said, and his Kraut face broadened into the biggest smile I had seen since I got to Doomstown.

64

LONGNOSE GRAVES

The usual twenty-minute drive across Dunetown to Back O'Town took the Stick less than fifteen. He turned off the siren six or seven blocks from the scene and flew dead-stick the rest of the way in. Dutch smoked two cigarettes, back to back, without taking them out of his mouth once they were lit. He didn't say anything, just sat stiff-legged, puffing.

'Go a block past the club and pull in behind the drugstore

across the street,' Dutch told Stick as we neared the end of the journey. 'Kid doesn't want we should turn him up to Graves' bunch.'

'Gotcha,' Stick said. He wheeled in behind the drugstore, stopped, braked, turned the car off, and was outside on his feet before I could pull mine out of the floorboards. All Dutch said was, 'Phew. He never drove like that with me before.'

'He never drove any other way with me,' I said. 'You're damn lucky.'

The drugstore was an antique, like the ones I remember from childhood, like Bucky's was, in downtown Dunetown, before it became Doomstown. It had a marble fountain top and wire-rung chairs and smelled of maraschino cherries and chocolate instead of vitamin pills and hair spray. A grey-haired black man behind the counter sized us up and nodded towards the Kid, who was sitting back from the front window, sipping something pink that looked medicinal. He was watching a two-storey row house, which stood alone in the middle of the block. A vertical neon sign over the front door of the place said that it was the Saint Andrew's African Baptist Church.

'I didn't know he was the Reverend Graves,' I said.

'Used to be the church,' Mufalatta said. 'When they moved to their new place, the sign ran the wrong way, so Nose bought it. He still calls the place the church.'

'Doesn't that upset the Saint Andrew's African Baptist congregation?' I asked.

'Naw, he's head of the choir,' the Kid said, and left it at that.

'Who's around?' the Stick asked.

'Two carloads of 'em just went inside,' Mufalatta said. 'Man, are they feelin' high. You never saw such grins in your life.'

'How did they waste the shrimp company?' I asked.

'Just drove in, two cars of 'em, pulled up to the front door, got out, and checked to make sure the place was empty. Then they doused it with Molotov cocktails and tossed a couple of sticks of dynamite in the front door as they was leaving. Man, the place went sky high.'

We all stood there, staring across the street at the church, wondering what to do next.

'If we're going to arrest him, don't we need a warrant?' I asked.

'Arrest them? Arrest who, man? Graves?' was the Kid's

amazed response. 'The four of us are gonna sashay in there and bust Nose Graves and maybe eight of the meanest motherfuckers south of Jersey City? Us four? Shit, man. Death with honour, *si*; death by suicide, bull*shit*.'

'Then why don't I just go in and have a talk with him,' I suggested.

Mufalatta looked at me like I was certifiable. Dutch chuckled deep in his throat, like he had just heard a dirty joke. The Stick didn't do anything; he stood there and pro and conned the idea in his head. He broke the silence.

'Why?' he asked.

'He's being suckered,' I said. 'Maybe we can stop this craziness before anybody else dies.'

'Do tell,' said the Kid. 'And you think he's gonna give a royal shit what you think, man?'

'What've we got to lose?' I said. 'Stick and Dutch, keep an eye on our front and back doors. The Kid and I'll go in and gab with Graves.'

'Absolutely crazy as shit,' the Kid said.

'I'll second that,' said Dutch.

'Hell, why not?' the Stick said. 'Sometimes crazy shit like that works.'

Dutch sighed. 'Let's get some more backup over here,' he said.

'Why?' I asked. 'This isn't the gunfight at the OK Corral. We just want to talk.'

'The man just blew up a business,' Dutch reminded me. 'If he knows he was seen doing it, he's not gonna be too receptive to any chitchat with the cops.'

I shrugged. 'Then we won't tell him yet,' I said, and walked out the front door and across the street with Mufalatta legging it beside me.

'This is crazy, man,' he said. 'This guy had no fuse at all, okay? No fuse, man. You light him up, he blows all *over* the fuckin' place. They will hear it in West LA. Shit, they will hear it West Fuckin' Ber*lin*, is what they'll do. You hear me talkin', man? Am I just makin' my gums bleed for fun?'

'I heard you, Kid,' I said. 'He's got a short fuse.'

'No fuse, brother. None. N-o-n-e. None!'

We entered the church.

'Okay, okay,' Mufalatta said as we walked into the dark

349

stairwell. 'Just let me get us to the man, okay? Let me do that because, see, I think in this case I have a gift of communication which you don't.'

'How's that?' I said.

'Because you're a thick-headed, fuckin' honky, that's why, and this man don't even trust high yellows.'

'Get us to the man,' I agreed with a nod.

We walked up a short flight of steps to the main floor of the building. It was a cathedralled room with a pulpit at one end and pews shoved back in a semicircle to form a large dance floor. The room was tiered. On the second tier there were low-slung tables surrounded by large cushions. The colour scheme was cardinal red and devil black. Four stereo speakers the size of billboards were booming almost visible sound waves. The music was so loud it hurt my Adam's apple. Not a ray of sunshine penetrated the once sacred interior.

Two black giants were sitting in wooden chairs at the top of the stairs. They looked both of us up and down, then one of them said rather pleasantly, 'Sorry, gents, no action till four o'clock.'

'It isn't that way, man,' Mufalatta shouted. 'We're here to talk with the man.'

The two giants exchanged grins, then laughed loud enough to drown out the music. One of them yelled, 'What you gonna do, turkey, ask him to boogie?'

'Yeah,' I said, taking out my wallet and letting it fall open to my buzzer. 'Here's our dance card.'

'Shit,' the Kid said. 'There goes diplomatic relations down the fuckin' toilet.'

The big guy doing the talking looked like I was waving a pretzel at him. He looked at Mufalatta, then me, trying to put us together, then pointed at me. 'You stay right there, both a you,' he said, and to his partner, 'Keep an eye on them.'

He turned and lumbered across the dance floor, up into the shadows. The other giant stood and glared at us alternately, his eyeballs clicking back and forth. Obviously he was a man who followed orders to the letter. When you're that big, you don't have to think.

There was a minute or two more of musical torture and then the music magically stopped.

'Up here,' Ape One yelled down. 'Do them first.'

'On the wall,' Ape Two said. 'I'm gonna toss you.'

He patted us down and took a .357 and a switchblade knife away from Mufalatta. All I had that looked threatening was a nail file, which he studied for several moments.

'It's a nail file,' I said finally.

'No shit,' he said. 'I thought it was a toothpick.'

Ape Two led us across the hardwood floor and up into the far corner of the room to the only booth in the place. Inside the booth was a round table and behind it, a hand-carved chair big enough to suit the Queen. Graves was sitting in the chair with one leg draped over an arm. He was dressed like a Brazilian banker, in tan linen with a dark brown handkerchief draped from his jacket pocket and a brown striped tie. Like Zapata, he wore sunglasses in the dark.

Several of his lieutenants slipped back into the shadows. They didn't go anywhere, they just became part of the ambience.

Graves leaned forward and pulled his glasses down slightly, peering over them.

'Well, what do you know, it's the dog lover.'

I smiled. The Kid didn't do anything.

'You shouldn't do that,' Graves said in a whispery rasp. 'Come in a man's place flashing all that shit around.'

Mufalatta smiled. 'Well, what it was, King Kong and Mighty Joe Young there didn't think looks was enough to get us an audience.'

Graves smiled. He was a handsome man. Whoever had done the job on his nose had done him a favour.

'Who the fuck are you?' he said quietly.

'Feds,' I told him.

He whistled softly through his teeth. 'That's bad,' he said. 'Am I drafted?'

'Yeah, the marines can hardly wait,' Mufalatta said.

'So, say your thing, man. What's it about?'

'Can we keep this between just a couple of us?' I asked.

Graves looked at Ape Two.

'They's totally clean,' the black giant grunted.

Graves leaned back and waved his hands. 'Okay,' he said, 'give us some air. You men drink?'

'Not right now,' I said.

'You the talker, dog lover?' he asked, nodding towards me.

I said I was.

'So talk.'

351

I didn't know how I was going to start or exactly what I was going to say. I had to wing it. Graves was no fool. If we were there because of the morning raid on Chevos' shrimp company, we would have come in force with warrants. We wanted to talk and he was all ears.

'Things come to me,' I said. 'Because of my business I hear things.'

'And what's been comin' at you, man?' the lean, ebony mobster said, still smiling.

'It comes to me that a Cincinnati gangster named Tagliani and his outfit came down here to set up shop. They wanted the Front Street action, but they knew they had to get past you, one way or another. They may have had some local help moving in here – that's up for grabs right now – but one person Tagliani definitely did not have help from was Stoney Titan, and since you and Stoney have a deal, they couldn't ease you out. It comes to me that the Taglianis decided to try the water, find out just how tough you were, so they sent an Ohio hoodlum named Cherry McGee in to test you. He couldn't take you, so Tagliani managed to frame you and after you did your clock, you came out and blew McGee up, along with a couple of his pistols.

'Meantime, they started taking over, squeezing in here and there. They started dealing heavy drugs, mostly cocaine, to service the big rollers from out of town, which, it comes to me, is not your style. They also had big money, and that's where they started hurting you. They were squeezing you out because they had the financing.

'So it comes to me that you decided to make one big move, a coke connection in South America that would net you maybe twenty, thirty mil on the street plus bite a big hole in their trade.

'Then, last Sunday, Tagliani hijacked your load, killed your people, and burned the boat, which left you without your goods and owing the connections that fronted you. So, it comes to me you declared war and started wasting Taglianis. And then when Harry Raines got hot under the collar over all the shooting, you put him away.'

I paused for a moment and then said, 'That's the way it comes to me.'

He took off the sunglasses and bored holes in me with cast-iron eyes.

352

'Dog lover, you're so full of shit you're contagious,' Graves murmured, without humour. 'Comes to you, my ass.'

'I said that's the way it comes to me, I didn't say that's the way it was. But that's how it could be played, if enough people wanted it done that way.'

He leaned back and toyed with the glasses. Now I had his interest.

'Okay,' he whispered, 'how do you think it was?'

'Well, here's the way it wasn't. I don't think you killed any of the Tagliani clan, except maybe McGee and some of his gang. And I don't think you put Harry Raines away. Not only that, but I can probably prove you didn't.'

'That's damn nice of you, brother,' he said. 'What do you want me to do in return, marry your sister?'

'I want you to call off your guns, right now. Before the shooting really starts and a lot of people who don't have anything to do with this get wasted.'

'You want we should stand in the middle of the boulevard and invite that fuckin' Nance to have target practice on us, that it?' his voice rasped.

'I'll take care of Nance,' I said. 'I got more reason than you. He's tried to kill me twice.'

For some reason that impressed Graves. He said, 'I'm not real clear on what it is you're offering me to do for what.'

'If you hang up your guns, I'll see to it that the Taglianis do the same. Then all you have to do is sit back and let the Feds put the rest of the Tagliani clan away and it'll be all yours again.'

'And the Feds're just gonna leave me alone, right?'

'That's the way it'll work out,' I said.

'And what it is, you're just doin' this because you're a fine, upstanding dude that does good work, right? Shit, man, what you take me for? I wasn't out pickin' cotton when the brains was handed out.'

'Look, I know about your deal with Mr Stoney and I don't – '

'I ain't got no deal with Mr Stoney,' he said. 'He don't deal, man, don't come grubbin' around with his hand out lookin' for part of the action, shit. That ain't his style. Me and Mr Stoney have an understanding. If I fuck up, I get hammered. If I don't, everything's velvet.'

'What I'm saying is, I'm after Tagliani. I don't care how you and Mr Stoney run the town. It looked pretty good to me in the old days.'

'You talked to Mr Stoney about all this?'

'He'll figure it out by himself,' I said. 'Personally, I think you're getting suckered into this gunfight with Tagliani.'

His smile vanished, but the voice didn't change.

'I don't get suckered, dog lover. That ain't my style.'

'You want to listen?' I said bluntly.

He put his leg back on the floor and leaned over the table towards me. 'Okay,' he said, 'we've come this far. Just don't piss me off.'

'They need a fall guy for the whole enchilada.'

'Who needs?'

'Maybe Chevos. Maybe Costello. Maybe even Bronicata, although I doubt it. Whoever knocked over eleven Taglianis so far this week. Somebody had to go down for it and they're setting you up to be the guy.'

He leaned back in his chair, made a church steeple of his fingertips, and stared up at the dark ceiling. There was a lot to sort through, most of it guesswork on my part, and very little of it, if any could be substantiated.

Without looking down, Graves whispered:

'Also I didn't kill McGee. Man, I was gonna whack that little cocksucker off but somebody else did the job for me.'

That one caught me by surprise, although I did my best not to show it.

'I've had my people killed in this thing,' he said. 'Hard to forget.'

'So why get more killed? It'll just get harder to forget. I understand people went down on both sides.'

Pause.

'That's true,' he agreed. Then still looking at the ceiling, 'I take the fifth on that cocaine shit. That's federal. Put that motherfucker back in the file.'

'You're clean on that one too,' I said. 'If somebody else lifted the load, you're not guilty of violating anything. Whoever stole and brought it in, that's the guilty party.'

He looked down at me and smiled. 'You could be in the wrong game, dog lover,' he said. 'You oughta be a fixer.'

'I used to be,' I said.

'Well, shit, how about that.'

'Can we talk about Leadbetter?' I asked. I wanted to know about the dead police chief. That was another coincidence I didn't believe in. Mufalatta was staring at me, open-mouthed, as I pushed it as far as it would go.

'What about him?'

'Was he giving you any trouble?'

Graves shook his head very slowly. 'Him and Mr Stoney,' he said, entwining two fingers, 'like that.'

'Do you know why he was killed?'

'I heard it was an accident,' he said.

'There's one other thing,' I said. 'Did Tony Lukatis ever do a job for you?'

'Shit, don't be a jiveass. I hardly knew the little motherfucker.'

'You didn't like him then?'

'I didn't think about him one way or the other.'

'So he wasn't working for you on the Colombia run?'

'If there was a Colombia run, he wouldn't have been workin' for me, nohow. Okay?'

'Okay.'

'So what the hell's the plan, baby? Do we wait for you to tell us the truce is on or what?'

'I need a couple of hours,' I said.

'To do what?'

'Cool the situation down. Just stay low, that's all you got to do.'

He stroked his jaw with a large, rawboned hand that sparkled with a diamond ring as big as the house I was born in. He started to chuckle in that whispery, gravel voice of his.

'I don't believe this, y'know. I mean, me trustin' a fuckin' honky Fed. What's your name, man?'

'Kilmer. Jake Kilmer.'

'Like the poet?'

'You read poetry?' I said.

'Why not,' he said. 'I got class.'

65

SHOOT OUT IN BACK O'TOWN

'Okay, you got a deal,' Graves said, offering me his hand. 'We'll stay cool until you get Nance and the rest of them off the street. But they come lookin' for trouble, Kilmer, forget it. I ain't standing still for any motherfucker.'

A phone rang somewhere in the darkness of the church. It kept ringing persistently until it was finally answered. A voice in the darkness said, 'It's for somebody named Kilmer. Is that either one of you?'

I stood up, followed by Graves' hard glance.

'I hope this ain't some kind of stand-up, 'cause if it is, man, you go down first.'

'Probably my broker,' I said, and followed a vague form back to the cash register. The phone was on the wall, an old-fashioned black coin-eater.

'Kilmer,' I said.

It was Dutch. 'Get your ass outa there now,' he told me.

'We're doing fine here,' I said.

'Kite Lange just called central from his car. He's following Nance and two carloads of Tagliani gunsels, and they're headed your way.'

'Call in some blue and whites.'

'I've done that but you got maybe a minute to get out of there before shooting's likely to start.'

'Goddamn it,' I said, 'Nose has agreed to a cease-fire!'

'Then you better get your ass out here and tell that to your buddy Nance, cause he's about to come around the corner.'

I slammed down the phone and stumbled through the darkness back to Graves' table.

'We got a problem,' I said as calmly as I could. 'Nance is on his way with two cars.'

An S&W .38 appeared in Graves' fist. There was a lot of movement around us. The gun was a beauty, a Model 19 with a four-inch barrel, Pachmar grip, the cocking spur shaved off. Not fancy, all pro.

'What the fuck's goin' down here?' he hissed.

'That was our partner. One of our people spotted Nance and his bunch heading this way. Police cars are coming. Just stay inside, keep your heads down. Let us handle it.'

'You ain't goin' nowhere till this gets unwound, dog lover.'

An explosion ended the conversation. The front door erupted and yellow flames lashed up the stairwell, followed by bits and pieces of wood and glass that seemed to float lazily in the updraft.

The place shook like an earthquake had hit us.

The Kid dived sideways, out of Graves' line of fire, and pulled me with him. Graves couldn't have cared less about us, though. He dashed towards the door.

Handguns started popping down on the street. Then a shot-gun bellowed and somebody screamed.

The Kid turned a service table on its side, smacked a leg off with his elbow, grabbed it like a club, and motioned me to follow him to a side door.

Another explosion. I looked back and saw a gaping hole in the side of the room. Light slashed through smoke and fire, showing me several men with guns, heading towards the front stairs, fire be damned. More gunfire. Another scream. Hand-guns were popping off all over the place. I could hear several sirens shrieking out on the street.

Heavy artillery boomed behind the door just as we got to it. The Kid kicked it open and came face to face with one of Turk Nance's goons. His Remington twelve-gauge had just blown a hole through one of Graves' men, who was tumbling down the stairs behind him. The Kid jumped back inside as the hoodlum swung the shotgun up. Mufalatta pulled the door shut, and dragged me to my knees beside him as the riot gun blew a six-inch plug out of the centre of the door. The Kid counted to three and then slammed the door open again, right into the gunman's face. The shotgun barrel slid through the hole it had just made in the door. The Kid grabbed the barrel with one hand, pulled the door shut again, and wrenched the weapon from the gunman's hands. He reached through the hole, grab-bed a handful of the hoodlum's shirt, pulled him against the shattered door, and slammed the butt end of the table leg into his chest. The gangster fell away from the door, gagging, and the Kid charged out, swinging the table leg like Lou Gehrig, and almost took off the goon's head. The gunman hit the stairs halfway down, bounced once, and piled up in the doorway.

We followed him down the stairs. The shotgun was an 870P police riot gun loaded with pellets, an awesome weapon. At the foot of the stairs we peered cautiously around the corner of the door. One of Nance's cars was parked twenty feet away. They saw the Kid's black face and every gun in the car opened up.

We jumped back as the doorjamb was blown to pieces.

'There's one of 'em outside the car on the other side,' the Kid said. 'I'm gonna squirrel the son of a bitch and get us a little breathin' room.'

Squirrelling is a useful trick. Fire a shotgun or any projectile weapon at less than a forty-five-degree angle into anything solid, and the bullet or pellets will ricochet exactly eight inches off that surface and stay at that height. That's just low enough to go under a car. The Kid got the shotgun ready, leaned around the corner, and cut loose twice.

Kow-boom! Kow-boom!

Forty-eight pellets sang off the sidewalk and showered under the car, tearing through the ankle and shin of the man on the other side. He went down screaming. The Kid took advantage of the hiatus to put another blast through the rear window. The car took off, with the wounded thug hanging on to the window.

Outside all hell had broken loose.

At least two of Nance's shooters and one of Graves' men were down in the street.

Pedestrians were cowering behind parked cars and in alleyways.

The church was in the middle of a block with Gordon Street in front of it and Marsh Street behind. Empty lots on both sides. It was under siege. The front of the place was aflame, as was a police car sitting sideways in the middle of Gordon Street on blown-out tyres.

Both ends of the street were clogged with blue and whites.

The mob car slammed on its brakes as it neared Gordon, and the human cargo hanging on to the door was vaulted end over end into the street. He lay there clutching his ankles until a volley of gunfire from the church stilled him. The Nance car spun around and started back our way. As it did, Dutch Morehead pulled his Olds out of Marsh Street, into the lot, jumped out, and dashed for cover. The Kid shot off a rear tyre and most of the rim as the sedan roared past. The Nance car lost control, tried to swerve out of the path of the Olds, slammed into the front end of the Dutchman's car, vaulted over it, and slid to a grinding halt on its side.

Nance's men started crawling out of doors and windows. Cops swarmed up from Marsh Street and were all over them.

The other car was nowhere to be seen. Then it suddenly burst backwards out of an alley beside the drugstore and into Gordon Street, spun around on screaming brakes, and careened into the lot as the Stick's black Pontiac roared out of the alley in pursuit. Longnose Graves dashed from the door of the church and emptied his pistol into the fleeing car.

As Nance's car passed our doorway, showering dirt and debris towards us the Mufalatta Kid sent one burst into its rear window. He could handle a shotgun, all right, but it didn't slow down the escaping car. It cut left into Marsh, glanced off a police car, sideswiped a brick wall, and was gone, with Stick growling off after it.

Fire trucks and ambulances arrived. More confusion.

The church was burning out of control. Graves' people tumbled out into the street, coughing and rubbing their eyes. A fast body count showed three of Nance's men dead to two of Graves' gunmen.

Graves was not in the roundup.

Dutch said, 'He must've slipped us in the confusion.'

I didn't believe that. I went back to the side door and ran upstairs. Smoke swirled through the church. Flames were snapping at the far end of the room.

Graves was sitting on his wooden throne, tie askew, suit and face smoke-smeared, a bullet hole high in his left chest, his .38 aimed at the floor. He looked up with surprise as I stumbled through the smoke to the booth.

He raised the pistol and pointed it at my head. His rasping voice said, 'Shit, dog lover, you don't know when you're well off.'

'Why don't you get out of here while you can,' I said.

'I ought to kill you on general principles,' he said.

'What's stopping you?'

His finger squeezed and an electric shock sizzled through me. The hammer clicked harmlessly.

'Out of bullets, poet,' he said, laughed, and threw the gun at my feet.

66

BODY COUNT

Dutch and I piled into the Kid's car and followed the ambulance to the hospital. It was like a front-line medcorps unit. Doctors, nurses, and attendants raced in and out of doors in bloodstained robes, while several of the wounded lay on stretchers in the hallway, waiting their turn in the emergency room.

'How bad is this one?' a hawk-faced nurse asked as they wheeled Graves in, a blood bottle stuck in his arm.

'Bullet in the chest and bleeding,' the attendant said.

'Room three,' she snapped officiously, and then to Graves, 'Do you have hospitalisation?'

Graves looked up at her and managed a smile.

'I'm on welfare, lady,' he whispered. And they wheeled him away.

Kite Lange and Dutch filled us in on the particulars. Dutch had hardly finished his phone call to me when Nance and his sidekicks had whipped into the street. One car had gone in from Morgan Street, across the empty lot to the side door. Nance had driven straight to the front of the church, gunned down one of Graves' men, and thrown a stick of dynamite through the front door. Then all hell exploded. Lange, coming in close behind, rammed Nance's car and ruined his own in the process. Nance had headed up the alley beside the drugstore only to run into Stick coming towards him, slammed into reverse, and backed out. We knew the rest of the story.

'My car's a wreck,' Lange moaned.

'Your car was already a wreck,' said the Kid. 'We'll go to the city dump tomorrow and get you another one.'

Dutch was as busy as a centipede with athlete's foot, assigning cops to the wounded and trying to get a final count on dead and injured. Miraculously, only one cop had been hurt in the mêlée. He had broken a toe jumping out of his burning patrol car. A quick count showed two of Graves' men dead, three shot or burned, and the boss himself fighting for his life. Five more had been arrested at the scene.

'We may be missing one or two more,' volunteered the Kid. 'I think there was thirteen of them countin' Graves.'

Nance had not faired well either. Three were dead, two more hanging on for dear life, two had minor wounds, and three were in custody.

'One of 'em looks like he got struck by lightning,' Dutch said. 'The whole top of his head's stove in.'

'That was me,' the Kid muttered.

'What'd you hit him with, a meat cleaver?' asked Dutch.

'Table leg.'

'That's gonna look great on the report,' Dutch said.

'Anybody see how many there were in the getaway car with Nance?'

'Three or four,' said the Kid.

'Not bad,' I said. 'This may have been Waterloo for both gangs. They've got to be running out of hoodlums about now.'

'Let's hope Stick nailed Nance and the rest of his bunch,' Dutch said.

'If anybody can, he can,' I said.

I was right – and wrong.

A few minutes later an ambulance wheeled into emergency, followed by the Stick. The ambulance held three more of Turk Nance's gunmen, one of whom had literally lost his head in the shooting.

'That was me, too,' Mufalatta murmured again.

'You had some day,' Lange said.

No Nance.

'They headed for the interstate bridge,' Stick explained. 'I radioed ahead, had the bridge sealed off. They tried to go cross-country and hit a delivery truck. Nance was AWOL. I don't know what the hell happened to him, but I've put an all points out on him.'

'We got the little s.o.b. this time,' Dutch said. 'We can nail him with murder, arson, creating a public nuisance, discharging firearms in the street . . .'

'Yeah,' I said, 'all we got to do is find him.'

'How about Nose?' the Kid asked. 'What do we charge him with? He was just protecting his ass.'

'Concealed weapons?' Stick suggested.

'There wasn't anything concealed about them,' Dutch said. 'I don't know what we're gonna do about Nose. There's gotta be something we can stick him with.'

'One thing for certain,' Stick said, 'it's sure as hell gonna attract a lot of people.'

It did. Within thirty minutes Chief Walters, Titan, Donleavy, and several other dignitaries were in the emergency clinic, all asking questions. I had better things to do. I asked the Stick to run me back to the park to get my car and check on the progress of our black-water diver. As we started to leave, Titan grabbed my arm.

'What the hell happened over there?' he demanded.

'Ask Dutch,' I said. 'I'm busy.'

'I'll bet my pension you shook up this ruckus,' he said, his voice beginning to rise. He sounded like a dog whining.

'That's right. I attacked all twenty-five of them with my nail file,' I said, and walked out.

A few doors down from emergency, a bronze casket was being loaded through the morgue entrance into a hearse. Doe Raines was standing alone, watching the procedure. I walked down to her. She was wearing a severe black suit and a black hat and was carrying a black purse. As usual, she was dressed impeccably for the occasion.

'I'm sorry,' I said. 'If it's any consolation, I really think Harry was one of the few people in this town who wasn't involved in this whole mess. His only sin was naiveté.'

She looked up at me. She was drifting aimlessly through a bad dream. Her make-up, heavier than usual, could not cover the grief lines around her eyes. Her voice, low and husky with sorrow, sounded like it was coming from someplace far, far away.

'It's been ghastly,' she said in a tiny voice. 'The newspapers in Atlanta and New York have been calling. TV stations. I don't know what to say.'

'Let somebody else do the talking. Let Donleavy do it. Besides, when they get down here they're going to find a lot more to interest them than you.'

'I've done a lot of thinking,' she said. 'Can we talk a little later on? I'll be at the funeral home until seven. Can we have a drink after that?'

'Sure.'

362

'I'll be at the townhouse,' she said. 'It's on Palm right up the street from the hotel. The Breezes.'

'I'll see you about seven thirty,' I said.

'Yes, thank you,' she murmured, shifting her attention back to the hearse.

I watched her drive away, remembering what DeeDee had said, about Doe being a princess and everything always working out well for her.

The Stick drove back to the park like a human being, apparently having had enough action to hold him for an hour or two. The fog had lifted and a warm drizzle had started. We found Baker empty-handed.

'I have just about cleared the shelf,' he said. 'But I been thinking, this killer might just have thrown the gun up *under* the pier. For one thing, it would not have made as loud a sound such as throwing it out in the river would have.'

'What's under there?' I asked.

'One helluva mess,' Whippet said around his chewing tobacco.

'It's liken I told you, sir,' Baker said. 'Cables, old rope, ship propellers, just a lots of junk. The weapon could have slipped down amongst all that there, but it might be stuck close up to the surface of it also. I'll certainly give her a try.'

'Thanks,' I said.

I looked at my watch. It was barely one o'clock but it seemed like days since dawn. I sat down under a tree to think while the Stick went off for hot dogs and Cokes. Then I remembered the tape recorder. I took it out and rewound it. There was an hour's worth of tape, all of it full, none of it worth the bother. The Stick came back and we listened as we ate.

We could hear Raines' voice, muttering, sometimes yelling in agony. Once it sounded like he was giving football signals. Another time he said Doe's name very distinctly, but nothing before or after it. Nothing else was intelligible.

I looked at Seaborn's window several times but if he was there, he wasn't showing himself. Someone had already placed a black wreath on the side door of Warehouse Three.

'What next?' the Stick asked.

'I'm going to sit here for a while while Baker plumbs the murky depths,' I said.

'It's swarthy depths,' said the Stick. 'He's plumbing the swarthy depths.'

363

'Right, swarthy,' I said.

We watched Baker's air bubbles playing on the surface of the river while I mentally catalogued the events of the previous six days. Ideas were forming slowly. There's a thin line between what is logically true and what is fact, what can be proven and what can't. Most of my ideas were logically true. Proving them was going to be touchy. I decided to go for broke, throw the long bomb, and break up the ballgame. It was a risky plan and I ran it by the Stick to get his opinion. He loved it. I knew he would. It appealed to every perverse bone in his body.

'Do me a favour,' I suggested to Stick. 'Check out the gun stores in town.'

Facing Nose Graves had been nervy. Now it was time to try something really rash.

67

MONEY TALK

It was nearly five when I went to the bank. It was closed but I had been watching the place for two hours and I knew Seaborn was still there. Now I could see him, through the double glass doors, sitting back in his office behind that massive desk, talking frantically into the phone.

I tapped on the front door. A bank guard, swaybacked by time, shuffled slowly up, tried to talk to me through the door, and gave up. I could have driven to Key West in the time it took him to open the door. He fiddled with his keys, took two or three stabs at the latch before he got the key in, and finally got the door open a sliver.

'We're closed,' he said, in a patronising voice that sounded like it was squeezed from a balloon. 'Open at nine in the morning.'

'I've got an appointment with Mr Seaborn,' I said. I was getting almost casual about lying.

He looked me up and down, sizing me up. 'I'll check with the president,' he said. 'What was the name?'

'Kilmer. It still is.'

'Huh?'

'Never mind,' I said.

He closed and locked the door and shuffled across a wide, cold, marble lobby to the office in the back. I could see his stooped frame, silhouetted in Seaborn's doorway. Finally he turned and slue-footed back to the door. He didn't have a fast bone in his body.

He opened it another sliver.

'The president says he's busy and – '

I had my wallet out and I flashed my buzzer as I shoved past the old gentleman. 'The hell with protocol,' I said. 'This is business.'

Seaborn looked up wide-eyed when I entered the office. I closed the door behind me and leaned against it. He looked out the window, then back at me, his face doing every number in the books as he tried to change his expression from fear to anger.

'What do you mean by this?' he demanded. 'This is the second time in two days you've intruded on me without – '

'I didn't intrude on you yesterday,' I said, without waiting for him to finish. 'I came to tell you your secretary had a death in the family.'

'What are you doing here now?'

'I thought we could have a little talk, Mr Seaborn, just you and me.'

'About what?'

'About Franco Tagliani, who called himself Frank Turner. About Lou Cohen's banking habits. About Harry Raines, who got himself killed right over there.' I nodded towards the window. He followed my gaze, but looked up instead of out, towards the top floor of Warehouse Three. The sun was getting low and it was dark enough for lights but there weren't any. Nobody was home. The boss was dead.

Seaborn's nervous fingers rippled up and down the desk as if it were a concert piano.

'I hardly knew Mr Turner,' he said. 'And I don't know anything about poor Harry's death.' He paused for a minute and then said, 'Perhaps I should summon my lawyer.'

'You could do that. Or you and I could have a private little chat. Just the two of us. That's if you want to cooperate. Otherwise, you don't have to call your lawyer, I'll leave. Somebody else will come back; that's when you'll need your lawyer.

That's when they read you your rights and all that stuff you see in the movies.'

He turned ash grey.

'What is it, then?' he said, in a faltering voice that was rapidly losing what little character it had. He looked back over at the warehouse.

'There's nobody over there,' I said. 'The place is closed. Another death in the family. So what's it going to be? Talk? Or lawyers?'

'Ahem. We can . . . certainly . . . start . . . uh . . .'

'Look here, Mr Seaborn, there are some things I know, and some things I think I know, and some things I'm strictly guessing at. I think maybe you can eliminate some of my guesswork.'

He didn't say anything. He sat there like a man with his head in the guillotine, waiting for the blade to drop.

'I repeat,' Seaborn said, putting a little strength back in his voice. 'I knew the man as Turner. He was just another businessman. We were actively soliciting new business and capital into the community, that's no secret. And he made us a very attractive offer.'

'No strings attached, right?'

He paused for a minute and said, 'Right.'

'Who proposed the banking arrangements?' I asked.

'What do you mean?'

'This is what I know, Mr Seaborn. I know that Tagliani did his banking with you. I know that Lou Cohen was the bagman for the operation and made all the cash deposits directly to you. I also know that a lot of that cash came from pimping, gambling, and narcotics and that classifies it as *ill-gotten gains*, which is dirty money and that means we can confiscate it, and any other money made through the use of it by anybody connected to them.'

'I don't know where his money came from,' Seaborn said.

'Cohen made enormous cash deposits to you almost every day. You didn't find that odd?'

'It's not my business to question my customers,' he said.

'It's your business to report all deposits over ten thousand dollars to the IRS, isn't it?'

That stumped him. He looked out the window again. I followed his gaze. I could see Stick down on the pier, talking to Whippet.

'I assure you,' he said, after a long pause, 'that there was nothing illegal in his banking transactions. It would be a violation of confidence to discuss it any further.'

'At least three of the accounts are Panamanian mirror accounts,' I said.

'Still none of my business and perfectly legal,' he said, too quickly.

He was feeling stronger and putting up a pretty good fight. I only had two cards left to play.

'What about the Rio Company?' I said.

'What about it?' he said. 'It's one of their corporations. They have dozens. I really don't know for what purpose. I was not Cohen's confidante, I was simply his banker.'

He seemed sincere enough. So I played my last ace.

'How about the pyramid accounts?' I asked.

This time he jumped as if a flea had bitten his ass.

'I told you, I don't know anything about their business,' he said, almost in a whisper.

I reached in my pocket and took out the tape recorder, punched the play button, and sat it on the edge of the desk. The heart monitor was beeping a monotonous background to Harry Raines' strained breathing. He was muttering, then a pause, then he cried out, 'Doe!'

Seaborn's eyes bulged. His Adam's apple was doing a little dance.

I turned the player off.

'He said a lot before he died,' I lied.

Seaborn's tough shell began to peel away. He stared at the recorder as if it were a black widow spider crawling across the desk towards him.

'We were talking about what I know,' I said. 'I know you called Sam Donleavy at Babs Thomas' party a little after seven. I know you were in the bank because your lights were seen by two witnesses. I know that when Harry Raines was shot, he was either walking from his office in the warehouse towards here, or from here towards his office. It's illogical to think he was meeting somebody in the park, it was too foggy. Whoever shot him was either waiting for him or caught up with him.'

His fingers starting playing on the desk again.

I said, 'He came here and braced you about Tagliani. You broke down and before it was over, you told him the whole story.

367

He threatened to expose you and when he left you went out the back door of the bank, followed him, and shot him.'

His face turned purple. 'You're insane!' he screamed. 'I don't even own a gun. And I didn't have time to run after him. I was still sitting right here when – '

He stopped babbling and fell back in his chair.

'When you heard the shot,' I said.

He sat dead still for a full minute, then his face went to pieces and he nodded.

'I swear to God I don't know who shot Harry,' he said, almost whimpering. 'I've done nothing illegal. There was nothing illegal in the way Cohen's money was handled.'

'It's a subterfuge,' I said.

'You're guessing,' he said. 'Besides, that's not what Harry was so angry about.'

'He was angry because you'd gotten into bed with the wrong people, right?' I said.

'That's as good a way of putting it as any,' he said.

'What did you tell Sam Donleavy on the phone?'

'I told him . . . I told him Harry knew everything. I couldn't help it. Harry came here and he was insane with anger. Abusive. He could always intimidate me with that cold stare of his, anyway. I don't know why he suddenly got so upset. Then yesterday he went crazy. I told him everything. I tried to make him understand how it happened, that we didn't know who Turner really was until it was too late. He was screaming about trust and loyalty.'

'What did Donleavy say?' I asked.

'He talked to Harry.'

'Raines was here when you called the Thomas woman's apartment?' I said with surprise.

'Yes.'

'And . . . ?'

'Sam had to go out to his place and wait for a phone call. He said he'd call us when he got there. About forty minutes later he called back.'

'Did you talk to him?'

Seaborn nodded. 'Yes. He told me he had to talk to Dutch Morehead at eight o'clock and that he would ask Harry to come out to his place and they'd have it out. He said he felt Harry would be reasonable, that we'd done nothing really wrong, nothing illegal. Then he talked to Harry.'

368

'Did Raines say anything?'

'He just listened for a minute and then said, "All right, I'll see you there." Then he hung up and left. He didn't say anything else to me, just turned around and stalked out of here. That's the way Harry Raines was. He couldn't forgive anything. Mister Perfect. All he ever cared about was his career, his goddamn career. He wouldn't have been anything if he hadn't married Findley's money.'

'And you were sitting here all by yourself when he was shot,' I said.

He nodded.

'That's your alibi, is it? Mister, if I were the jury, you'd have one foot strapped in the chair already. You have a motive, you had the opportunity, and you haven't got an alibi.'

His shoulders sagged. He looked out the window again and then dry-washed his hands, like a funeral director pitching for the solid copper casket. Sweat twinkled on his upper lip and across his forehead.

'I didn't kill Harry Raines,' he repeated. 'Neither did Sam. He was miles away when it happened. We don't know who killed him or why. I assumed it had something to do with these other killings.'

'I'm sure it does, in some way or another,' I said.

The phone rang, startling both of us. He stared at it for several rings, then picked it up as if he were afraid it would burn him.

'Hello? Yes . . .' He looked over at me wild-eyed and mouthed the word 'Sam'.

I held out my hand and he gave me the phone.

'Sam, this is Jake Kilmer.'

Silence. Ten or twenty seconds of silence. When he finally answered he was quite pleasant.

'Sorry about our lunch date, old man,' he said.

'It's been a pretty grim day all the way around,' I said. I looked up at the warehouse. The lights in the corner office were on. 'Where are you now?'

'As a matter of fact, I'm in my office. You can see it from Charlie's window. The river corner.'

'Do you have a minute or two now?' I asked.

Another silence.

'I was planning to go over to the funeral home,' he said. 'But I can take a few minutes.'

'I'll be right over,' I said. I gave the phone back to Seaborn.

'He hung up,' Seaborn said, with surprise.

'I'm sure he found out what he wanted to know.'

'What do you mean?'

'He wanted to know who you were talking to.'

Seaborn looked over at the warehouse. His face caved in.

'What do we do now?' he said, almost to himself.

'Go home, Mr Seaborn,' I said. 'You can't do anything here, so go on home.'

He stared at the big, bare desktop for a second and then said, 'Yes, I suppose so.'

We left the bank together. Seaborn went to his car; I returned to the pier.

Baker was sitting on the edge of the concrete dock sipping coffee from a thermos.

'No luck, eh?' I said.

He shook his head. 'I'll make one more attempt before dark,' Baker said.

'I appreciate your effort, Mr Baker,' I said, then to Stick, 'Did you find out what I wanted to know?'

'Nothing to it. A silver-plate S&W .38, two-inch barrel, black handles.'

'I'm going upstairs,' I said. 'You got the number?'

'Yep.'

'Give me fifteen minutes.'

'You got it.'

As I turned to leave, he said, 'Jake?'

'Yeah?'

'Love your style,' he said with a grin.

68

THANK YOU, MA BELL

Number Three Warehouse was a three-storey brick building dating back to the late 1700s with nothing between it and the river but the narrow cobblestone walkway leading behind it from the park. A small sign over the wreath told me the company was closed because of Harry Raines' death. The door was unlocked.

I remembered coming there with Teddy and marvelling at how clean and polished everything was. Nothing had changed. The brass hand railings and doorknobs were dazzling and the wood looked oiled and elegant. There was about the place, as there is with most old buildings, that kind of musky odour that comes with age and care.

Donleavy's office occupied most of one corner of the third floor, overlooking both park and river. He was wearing his dark blue mourning suit but had taken off the jacket and was in his shirt-sleeves. The air conditioning was off and he had the office windows open; although the rain had stopped and the sun had peeked out before dropping to the horizon, it was still warm and muggy in the office. His smile was sad but sincere and his handshake was so vigorous it was almost painful.

'That was quick,' was his greeting. 'Sorry it's so hot in here. The air conditioning's been off all day.'

I told him I could live with it and peeled my jacket off too.

'I'll just put on the answering machine so we won't be disturbed,' he said.

'Would you mind leaving the line open,' I said. 'I don't have my beeper with me. I had to leave this number.'

'No problem,' he said amiably.

From his window I could see the park below. A small group of people clustered around the spot where Harry Raines was shot and a couple of pretty girls sat on one of the park benches, giggling and knocking shoulders. The river sparkled brightly in the dying sun.

On the other side of the park was the darkened Seacoast National Bank. It reminded me of DeeDee Lukatis, her own grief all but forgotten in the wake of Harry Raines' death, and the bitter irony that linked Doe and DeeDee with death. Altogether, a sad view on this particular day.

'The last twenty-four hours have been insane,' Donleavy said with a sigh.

'Yeah,' I said, watching George Baker appear over the side of the pier, pull off his face mask, and start talking to Stick. 'It's been one thing after another.'

He followed my gaze down to the waterfront.

'I hear they've been diving down there all day,' he said.

'We're looking for the gun that killed Harry Raines.'

'What makes you think it's in the river?' he asked.

'Logic,' I said.

'Logic?'

'Sometimes it's all we have to go on. A young couple was nearby and heard the shot. She screamed. I figure the killer ran in the opposite direction, towards the river. Not knowing who else might be nearby in the fog, he tossed the gun in the river.'

'Any luck so far?' he queried, showing only mild interest.

'Not yet,' I said.

'You say "he". Are you sure the killer is a man?'

'Figure of speech,' I said. 'It could be a woman.'

'Humph,' he said, and dismissed the subject of murder temporarily. 'I was thinking,' he said. 'Perhaps these mobsters had phony credit profiles. Maybe that's how they got by us. It's not uncommon, you know.'

He reached into a small refrigerator, took out a couple of Cokes, popped the tops off them, and handed me one.

'It's possible,' I said, although it was obvious I didn't believe it.

'Well, I'm jumping ahead of you,' he said. 'You should be doing the talking.'

'Did you ever find that book with those dates?' I asked.

His eyes rolled with embarrassment.

'My God,' he said, 'with everything that's been happening, I completely forgot it. I'll make a note to myself to dig it up.'

'That's all right,' I said. 'I may not need the information after all.'

Baker slid down over the side of the pier and dropped out of view. Good man, he was making one last effort.

'Do you think Harry's death is connected to these other killings?' Donleavy asked.

'It seems likely, doesn't it?'

'I wouldn't know. I don't know much about police work.'

'I thought maybe being a lawyer . . .' I said, and let the sentence hang.

'I went to law school but I never practised law,' he said. 'Harry asked me to come on board straight out of college. I've never really worked anywhere else.'

'Well,' I said, 'let's just say I'm not real big on coincidence. It happens, but it isn't logical, it's the long shot. Logic is simply using all the facts you have in order to draw a conclusion.'

'Seems to me there's a danger in that,' he said. 'You tend to look only for the evidence to prove the conclusion.'

'I suppose,' I said, noncommittally. 'Anyway, logically speaking, Harry Raines' death would seem to be connected to the Tagliani massacres.'

'That's a rather gruesome way of putting it.' He shuddered.

'Gruesome work,' I said. 'Murder always is.'

'Why would they want to kill Harry?'

'It's the way things happen. One thing leads to another. One murder leads to another.'

'So you think these mobsters did it all,' he said, making it a statement rather than a question.

I looked back at him. The park was growing dark.

'No,' I said.

'But you said – '

'I said I thought they were connected. I don't think the same person killed the Taglianis and Harry Raines.'

'Oh. Logic again?' he said. His mouth was iron-bent in a smile.

He opened a walnut cigar box on his desk and offered me one of those thin cheroots, the kind riverboat gamblers in costume dramas always seem to prefer, accepted my refusal with a shrug, and peeled the wrapper from his own.

'So what does logic tell you about all this?' he asked as he lit the cigar.

I sat down on the windowsill.

'First, I'd say Raines was obviously coming over here when he got shot,' I said.

'That certainly seems logical,' Donleavy said. 'He was probably parked in the company lot.'

'He was parked behind the bank.'

'Well, he still maintains his office here. Maybe he was coming over to get something.'

I went on. 'Second, all the Tagliani killings were well planned. Daring, perhaps, but infinitely well planned and executed. That isn't logic, that's fact. Logic tells me Raines' death wasn't. It has all the earmarks of a sudden move, even a desperate one.'

'How so?'

'Because the killer couldn't plan on it being foggy, so he must have decided to *use* the fog, and that means the killer had to know exactly where Raines was going to be and the exact moment he was going to be there. As our witness said, "You couldn't see your hand in front of your face."'

'Perhaps he followed Harry,' Donleavy suggested.

'Yeah, except our ear witnesses only heard one person, which leads me to believe the killer was waiting for Raines.'

'Interesting,' Donleavy said, contemplating the tip of his cigar for a moment. He then added, 'Look, Jake, I may as well tell you, Harry was on his way out to my place. He was very angry. He and Charlie Seaborn had words. I called Charlie just after I talked to you. Harry was there. I told him I thought at worst we were guilty of poor judgment and he agreed to come and talk it out, once and for all.'

'Did Raines have a bad temper?' I asked.

'Only when he felt threatened. He couldn't stand being intimidated, by anything or anybody.'

'How about Seaborn? How upset was he?'

He chuckled. 'Charlie's easily upset, a worrywart. But he certainly wasn't distraught enough to kill anybody.'

'Perhaps there was a problem beyond just bad judgment,' I suggested.

'What do you mean?'

'Ever hear of the Rio Company?' I asked.

His expression didn't change.

'The what?' he said.

'Rio Company,' I repeated.

He shook his head. 'No, should I have?'

I explained to him about the Panamanian Mirror Rule and Virgin Island accounts and that whole rigamarole. Donleavy was a lawyer, I was sure he knew what it was all about. I guess I wanted to make sure he knew that I knew.

'The Rio Company is what we call a Hollywood box,' I said. 'It's like a street on a sound stage, all front with nothing behind it. It's usually used as a payoff.'

'A payoff? For what?'

'Favours, hush money, politicians, illegal lobbies, bad cops. They have a lot of palms to cross in their business.'

'Doesn't cash work anymore?' he said, laughing.

'This isn't the old days,' I said. 'We're not talking about a few Ben Franklins here and there, we're talking about hundreds of thousands of dollars a week. The trick is how to hide it. The Hollywood box is one good way. They pay off their graft with dirty money and use the banks to clean it along the way.'

'And this Rio Company was used for that purpose, eh?' he said.

I nodded.

'Are you implying that Charlie Seaborn was involved in all this?' he said, his face clouding with concern.

'I'm not implying anything. But his bank is being used as the instrument. He helped set up a rather elaborate subterfuge to help make it work. And a lot of the money that went through those accounts is what is called ill-gotten gains. It can be confiscated under the RICO act. I'm not sure how deeply involved Seaborn is. He may be guilty only of stupidity. But he could be on the sleeve.'

'The sleeve?'

'The take, part of the payoff. He could be getting a piece of the Rio Company – that's if he knew what he was doing and Tagliani felt it necessary to put him on the sleeve. I don't know the answer to that yet.'

'What do you think?'

'I don't think he was.'

'Why?'

'Too much to lose. I think Seaborn's indiscretion was that it looked good for the bank and good for the town and he didn't think about the consequences. Seaborn's a small-town banker. It probably never occurred to him that what he was involved in was illegal until it was too late to get out. That's the way it usually happens.'

'Who else was getting paid off?' Donleavy asked, leaning across his desk. 'What cops? What politicians?'

'I'm working on that.'

'Any ideas?'

'A few.'

'Care to share them?' he asked. 'I assure you, I am as interested in resolving this mess as you are.'

'I'm sure you are,' I said.

He was leaning on the desk now, staring intently at me.

'Any more logic?' he asked, still smiling.

'I've been thinking a lot about Raines' death,' I said. 'Trying to narrow down the possibilities.'

'Have you come up with anything?'

'Yeah,' I said. 'Logic tells me that there's only one person who could have killed Harry Raines.'

'And who's that?' he asked eagerly.

'This is going to sound crazy,' I said.

'Try me.'

'It seems to me the only person who could have killed Harry Raines was you.'

'Me!' he gasped, and started to laugh. 'Well, except for the fact that I was at my place on Sea Oat Island twenty miles from here and couldn't have done it, how did you come up with such a notion?'

'Yeah, I know,' I said. 'You have two alibis, me and Dutch. And yet, I have this thing about the logic of the situation. According to Seaborn, you were the last one who spoke with Harry Raines before he was killed. He left Seaborn's office without even saying good-bye and he was gunned down two minutes later. That makes you the only one who *could* have known exactly where he was going, and when.'

'Now how would I have known that?' he demanded.

'When you talked to Raines, you must have told him to come here, not to your condo. You knew he'd walk straight across the park. All you had to do was go down and wait for him.'

His eyes were beginning to bob like fishing corks on the sea. His white shirt front was stained dark grey with sweat. He jumped up.

'Christ, I think you're serious,' he said angrily.

'Deadly so,' I said.

'You're out of your mind, Kilmer,' he snarled. 'My God, talk about trying to prove a preconceived notion! Barring the fact that I *couldn't* have done it, what reason would I have had for killing my best friend? A disagreement over an error in judgment? Don't be ridiculous.'

I could have given him a lot of stereotyped reasons – greed, power, fear of Raines – but they would have been simple answers. They didn't cover the abstractions.

He sat back down, put his feet on his desk, and glared at me over the end of his cigar.

'Well?' he challenged.

'Let's forget the obvious and deal with the abstractions,' I said.

'What the hell do you mean, abstractions?' he said.

'Look, I understand you, Donleavy,' I said. 'There was a time when I could've been in the same boat, doing things the way I was told to do them, or expected to do them, running the show in the same old ways, with an occasional pat on the head. I also know that in the end I would have had to make a name for myself, to prove I was worth the trust, that I wasn't just somebody's lover or best friend.

'The thing is, you were smarter than I was. You had it figured out from the beginning. You knew the power was given and you knew it could be taken away. I learned that lesson the hard way. Hell, I never did know the rules.

'You were given the power, the day-to-day business of running Findley Enterprises. You got it from Raines who got it from Chief, and you ran it the way it was always run, the way the Findleys had run things since Oglethorpe was governor. But sooner or later, Donleavy, you had to prove your value, not only to everyone else, but to yourself. You had to prove you weren't a sycophant, just another jock with a rich friend. And not just *any* rich friend. Harry Raines lived by the rules. He managed the Findley businesses brilliantly, got himself elected a state senator, moved a mountain by swaying public opinion in favour of the pari-mutuel laws, and looked like a shoo-in to be the next governor. A tough act to follow. You had to show Dunetown that Sam Donleavy could move a mountain or two himself.'

'Big deal,' Donleavy snapped. 'Since when is ambition a crime?'

'There's nothing wrong with ambition,' I said. 'It's all in how you handle it.'

'And just what do you know about how I handle things?'

'I know that Raines was a clone of the old guard. I think when the opportunity presented itself, you saw yourself as a harbinger of the new. Dunetown was growing, and suddenly you had a chance to revitalise the town – before the track was even finished. After all, tourist trade was booming; the city was growing faster than flies in a dung heap. What you needed was to pump fresh money into the system that had been passing the same old tired bucks back and forth for centuries. Then a windfall blew your way. A chance to develop the beach with new hotels, condos on the waterfront, subdivisions in the swamplands. Dunetown to Boomtown, courtesy of Sam Donleavy.

'Except the dream turned into a nightmare. Dunetown

became Doomstown, because the opportunity was spelled T-a-g-l- i-a-n-i – '

'You're ploughing old ground,' he snapped, cutting off the sentence.

I ignored him and kept ploughing.

'And when you found out you were in bed with La Cosa Nostra, you had to make one helluva decision. Tell Raines? Risk his wrath? Or ride it out? What did you have to lose? Tagliani was reclusive, his people were running legitimate businesses, everything was coming up threes for you, so why rock the boat, right, Sam?'

He hadn't moved. He was twisting the cheroot between his lips, staring straight into my eyes.

'So far nothing you've said is incriminating, immoral, or illegal,' he said.

'Right. But you forgot one thing – the Golden Rule of Findley. They didn't give a doodly-shit whether it was immoral, illegal, incriminating, irregular, or anything else. The unwritten rule of Findley was that Harry was going to be the next governor and your job was to cover his ass, not grease your own. You fucked up, Sam. When you made your deal with Tagliani, you jeopardised Harry Raines' political career and padded your own, and that was an error Raines would never forgive. It was imperative that Tagliani's real identity be protected, not for him, but for *you*. You needed to keep that power until you established your own power base. Then the war with the Taglianis broke out and you ran out of time. Like I said, the power is given and the power is taken away.'

'Nobody has taken anything away from me!' he said, rising up as though he had grown an inch.

It was time to go for the jugular.

'That's a lie,' I said. 'You committed the big sin. You betrayed Raines' trust. He knew Seaborn was too naive to get as deeply involved as he was on his own, and he really didn't have any hold over Seaborn, anyway. But you? You he had by the short hairs. Harry was the only person in the world who could destroy you, and he was going to do it. It wasn't the killer who said, "You're finished" to Harry Raines down there in the fog; it was Harry Raines, saying it to you. So you shot him.'

His expression didn't change. He blew a thick stream of blue smoke out into the room and watched it swirl away in the breeze from the windows, and then he laughed in my face.

378

'Nobody'll believe that hot air,' he sneered. 'You couldn't get that story into small claims court if you had Clarence Darrow, John Marshall, and Oliver Wendell Holmes on your side.'

I ignored him. I said, 'The irony of all this is that Raines might still be alive if it weren't for a horse with a game leg and his crooked owner. It was the death of the horse, the shock of learning that a race had been fixed and Tagliani knew it, that woke Raines up.'

The phone gave me a breather. Its buzzer startled Donleavy. He snatched it up, said 'Hello,' paused, and then handed the receiver to me.

'Kilmer,' I said.

It was the Stick. 'You were right,' he said. 'I dialled the other number.'

'Any other news?'

'Not yet. Baker's doing his best. You want me to come up now?'

'That sounds good, thanks,' I said. I gave the phone back to Donleavy.

'Now that your course in Psych 101 is over,' Donleavy said, slamming down the phone, 'maybe you'd like to tell me how I'm supposed to have gotten here from Sea Oat. Did Peter Pan fly me over?'

'You never went home,' I said. 'You came straight here from the Thomas cocktail party.'

I took out the card he had given me the night before, the one with his home phone number on it, and picked up the phone. One of the dozen or so yellow lights on its base lit up as I dialled the number. When it started to ring, the light beside it gleamed.

He stared down at it dumbly.

'Pick it up,' I said.

He hesitated for a moment and then lifted the phone.

'It's called call-forwarding,' I said, the two of us staring at each other across the desk. 'Courtesy of Ma Bell. If you want to forward your calls to another number, you punch in a code on your home phone, followed by the new phone number. The calls are forwarded automatically. Obviously you use it all the time; your home phone's on it right now. That was your home number I just dialled.'

He wasn't talking. The muscles under his ear were jerking with every heartbeat. He tapped the ash off the cigar without taking his eyes off me. I went on:

'When you left the party last night, you came here instead of going home. You knew Raines was in Seaborn's office; you had talked to him when Seaborn called you at Babs' party. You also knew Raines would intimidate Seaborn enough to get the whole story. You probably had your gun there in the desk, or in the car. After I called you, you called Seaborn's office again, told Harry you'd meet him over here. Then you went downstairs and took the walkway through the park towards the bank. When he came up on you and said, "You're finished," you knew your career was flushed, so you shot him. The girl screamed, you ran back towards the river, dumped the gun, and came back here in time to get Dutch's call.'

He sighed and shook his head. 'Well,' he said, 'I must admit you've got quite the imagination. But I can see why you don't practise law. You couldn't get anywhere with that outrageous bunch of circumstantial bullshit.'

The office door opened and the Stick meandered in, his hat perched on the back of his head as usual.

'Who the hell are you?' Donleavy demanded.

'He's with me,' I said, and to the Stick, 'Did you get it?'

He smiled and took a package out of his jacket pocket. It was a Baggie containing a very wet nickel-plated S&W .38, with black rubber pistol grips. I looked at it. There was a number scratched on a piece of tape on the side of the bag.

'The number of your .38 – is it 7906549?' I asked Donleavy.

'What .38?' he demanded.

'The one you bought on February third of last year at Odum's Sport Shop on Third Street,' Stick said. 'Mr Odum remembers it very well. The only thing he had to look up was the exact day and the serial number.'

'This is hard evidence,' I said. 'There's nothing circumstantial about a murder weapon.'

'That gun was stolen from me months ago,' he squealed.

'Tell it to the judge,' I said.

'Let me see that,' he demanded.

'When we get downtown,' I said. 'You want to book the man, Stick?'

'Delighted,' he said, grinning. 'What's the charge?'

'Murder in the first,' I said. 'Let's go all the way.'

Stick took off his hat and peered into it. He had a list of rights printed on a card taped to the inside of the crown and started reading them to Donleavy.

380

'You have a right to remain silent – '

Donleavy swatted the hat out of his hands. 'The hell with that,' he snarled, reaching for the phone.

I laid a forefinger on the receiver. 'You can make your call from the tank like everybody else does,' I said.

The Stick took out a pair of cuffs and twisted Donleavy rudely around. 'Normally we wouldn't need these,' he said quietly in Donleavy's ear as he snapped on the cuffs. 'That was a mistake, doing that thing with my hat. Your manners are for shit.'

'Hell,' I said, 'we all make mistakes. Look at poor old Harry, he wrote his own epitaph: "Here lies Harry Raines. He trusted the wrong man."'

Donleavy was smart enough to keep his mouth shut. We escorted him downstairs and turned him over to two patrolmen in a blue and white and told them we'd meet them at the station.

'What do we do now?' Stick asked.

'Pray,' I said.

We didn't have to. George Baker came running across the park as we started back towards our cars. He was still in his wet suit, although he had changed his flippers for boots.

'Gotcha a present,' he said, and handed me an S&W .38, black handles, two-inch barrel. It was wrapped in a cloth to protect whatever fingerprints might be on it. I checked the registration. It was Donleavy's gun.

'I assure you, that's the weapon,' Baker said proudly. 'It has not been underwater long enough to gather rust.'

'Thank you, Mr Baker,' I said with a smile. 'You just saved my ass.'

'Well now, sir, that's a compliment which I will certainly not liken to forget.'

I gave Stick the Baggie he had given me in Donleavy's office, the one with the other S&W silver-plate .38 in it.

'Where did you get this one?' I asked Stick.

'A friend of mine on Front Street,' he said.

'Beautiful,' I said.

'That was one helluva play up there,' he said. 'Remind me never to play poker with you.'

'I don't play poker,' I said.

'Love your style, man,' said the Stick.

69

MURDER ONE

I was feeling great when we got to the county courthouse. The stately brick antique stood alone in the centre of a city square surrounded by ancient oaks big enough to pass for California redwoods, and palm trees, which seemed somehow cheap and out of place beside them. The old place seemed to groan under its burden of history. One story had it that Button Gwinnett had drafted his amendments to the Declaration of Independence in one of its second-storey offices. Another that, on Christmas Eve, 1864, in a secret meeting in one of the courtrooms, Sean Findley, Chief's great-great grandfather, had turned Dunetown over to General Sherman without a shot, after Sherman agreed to spare the city from the torch. It was a story Teddy loved to tell, although the way he told it, old Sean's role in the surrender came off more selfish than patriotic. Others apparently thought so too. The old man was assassinated on the front steps of this same courthouse as he was being inaugurated as Dunetown's first postwar mayor.

So much for history.

The DA's suite was on the first floor, protected by a frost-panelled door and little else. The door to Galavanti's office stood open. The tough little district attorney was poring over a sheaf of legal documents as thick as an encyclopedia, her Ben Franklin glasses perched on the end of her nose. I leaned on the edge of the door and rattled my fingers on the jamb.

'Hi, kiddo,' I said. 'Send anybody to the chair today?'

She glowered at me over the top of her glasses.

'I'm not your kiddo, Mr Kilmer,' she said. 'We're not that familiar. How about the Harry Raines tape?'

'A bust,' I said. 'Nothing but a lot of rataratarata.'

She narrowed her eyes as if she didn't believe me and said, 'I should have guessed that would happen.'

'Now that's no way to talk to someone who just laid the

biggest case in the county's history right in your lap,' I said.

She leaned back, still staring warily at me.

'And just what case is that?'

I paused a little for effect, then said, 'The State versus Sam Donleavy.'

She leaned forward so quickly that her chair almost rolled out from under her.

'You busted Sam Donleavy?' she said, her tone sounding like I had just accused Billy Graham of indecent exposure.

'He's being booked right now,' I said, as casually as I could make it.

'On what charge?'

'First-degree murder.'

She jumped up, all five feet of her, and stood with her mouth dangling open.

I held up a forefinger and repeated the news: 'Murder one.'

She gulped. I had never heard anybody gulp before, but she definitely gulped.

'Who the hell did he kill?'

'How about Harry Raines for starters?'

'Oh my God!' she said, and the 'God' stretched out for several seconds.

I walked into her office and dropped the Baggie-cased .38 on her desk.

'I'd feel better giving this to you than the Keystone Cops down in homicide. It's the gun Donleavy used to do the trick. We dug it out of the river about half an hour ago.'

'Harry Raines,' she said with awe, staring at the .38.

'Donleavy has an alibi but it won't hold water,' I continued.

She hadn't caught up with me yet.

'Harry Raines?' she repeated, still staring at the gun, as though she expected it to say something back.

'You may have a little trouble proving premeditation,' I went on. 'I don't think the idea occurred to him until about thirty minutes before he did it . . .'

This time she heard me and cut me off in midsentence. 'That's plenty of time,' she said quickly. 'Hell, if he gave it five minutes' thought, that's premeditation enough for me.'

'If you can make it work in court, that's okay by me.'

'Why did he do it?'

I gave her the basic details as quickly as I could, including background on the pyramid accounts, the Hollywood boxes, and Seaborn's questionably benign role in the matter.

'So the motive was fear of exposure by Raines,' she said. 'Seems to me he was on borrowed time, anyway. Tagliani would have surfaced sooner or later.'

'By that time Donleavy hoped to establish such a strong power base of his own that he could override his "error in judgment". That's what he likes to call it.'

'What do you call it?' she asked.

'Graft,' I said. 'Besides, as I told Donleavy, murder leads to murder.'

'You mean he killed somebody else?' she asked, her eyebrows flirting with the ceiling.

'Accessory,' I said.

'Before or after the fact?'

'Both. Ike Leadbetter.'

'Ike Leadbetter! Ike *Leadbetter*!'

'Yeah, you remember him, don't you? He used to be chief of police.'

'Leadbetter's death was an accident,' she said.

'Only because you couldn't prove otherwise,' I told her.

She closed one eye and gave me her sternest look. 'Don't get uppity with me,' she said.

'Dutch Morehead thinks it was murder and I'm inclined to agree. At first I figured Dutch was angry and wanted to make a case out of the Leadbetter drowning. It wasn't Tagliani's style to kill a police chief, particularly when Tagliani was on the dodge. And there weren't any other likely suspects. Then I thought better of it.'

'Oh? How come?'

'I don't believe in accidents any more than Dutch does. Not in this town. Not when the police chief is the victim.'

'Why was Leadbetter killed?' she asked.

'Look, Ms Galavanti, if one person in this town was likely to make Tagliani, it was Leadbetter. He had done some time on the force in Atlantic City before coming here, so he was more than just a little familiar with LCN and how it operates.'

'You think Leadbetter recognised Tagliani?' she said.

'Right, and Leadbetter went to Donleavy with it, the natural thing to do. After all, Donleavy was Harry Raines' personal choice to head the Committee. Donleavy was facing exposure himself, so he panicked and took it to Tagliani, who had Leadbetter burned. That's when Rio was set up and Tagliani put Donleavy on the sleeve.'

'And had him on the hook forever,' Galavanti said.

'You get an A in the course. Want to try Cherry McGee next?'

'Cherry McGee? How about the Kennedys and Anwar Sadat,' she said. 'Let's not leave anybody out.'

'You want to finish the story for me?' I said.

'Go ahead, you're doing great,' she said. 'Except that Long-nose Graves killed Cherry McGee and his hoodlums.' She paused for a moment, then added, 'Didn't he?'

'Nope.'

'Humph,' she said. 'I'll admit we tried everything but prayer to hang it on Graves.'

'And couldn't,' I said, 'because he didn't do it. At least Graves says he didn't and I'm inclined to believe him.'

'Why?'

'I kind of like him.'

'Well, that's one hell of a good, legitimate reason,' she said caustically.

'Why would he deny it?' I said. 'Everybody thinks he did it anyway, and he wanted to. Somebody beat him to it.'

'Any ideas?' she asked, then, waving her hand vigorously in front of her face, said, 'How silly of me, I'm sure you do.'

'Same cast,' I said.

'Are you saying Tagliani killed his own man?'

'Cherry McGee and Graves were in a Mexican standoff and Donleavy was on the spot again. He had to stop all the shooting before Raines got nervous. When Tagliani couldn't nail Graves, he eliminated McGee. McGee was a hired hand, he wasn't family. Tagliani couldn't have cared less.'

She whistled softly through her teeth. 'Can we prove any of this?' she asked.

'Donleavy and Seaborn may break down and unload it all,' I said. 'But if you're as good as they say you are, it doesn't make any difference. Donleavy can only hang once, and most of the Taglianis who were involved are probably dead.'

She looked at me like she was waiting for a second shoe to drop. Finally she said, 'Well?'

'Well what?'

'Well, what do you want out of all this?'

I said, 'Cohen, alive and spilling his guts. Then I'll have my RICO case. It would help me a lot if you got a court order to freeze the pyramid account until we can get into it. I'd like to know nobody's going to push the erase button on the computer before we get there.'

'I'll take care of that in short order,' she said, running in high gear, her eyes as bright as a Mexican sunrise. 'Nobody's going to believe this,' she said, standing up and flipping her glasses on the desk.

'There is one more little favour . . .' I began.

She eyed me slyly. 'I knew it,' she said.

'Did either Winslow or Lukatis have any priors?' I asked.

'I wish you'd let me in on this thing you have about Lukatis.'

'It's personal,' I said.

She pondered my question a little longer.

'Yes, there was a case on the books against Winslow,' she said finally.

'For what?'

'Controlled substance.'

'What happened to it?'

'Dead-docketed.'

'For . . .?'

'Lack of evidence.'

'Ah, good old lack of evidence,' I said.

'Look,' she said, 'if I don't have the goods, I can't go to the grand jury. My buck and wing is terrible.'

'I'm not blaming you,' I said quickly. 'Was it dropped before or after the trip with Lukatis?'

'I really don't remember.'

'Guess.'

'You son of a bitch.'

'Well?'

'Probably after.'

'Beautiful. And Titan asked you to drop the case, right?'

She had to think about that one for a while.

'Not exactly,' she said. 'He just didn't come up with the goods for an indictment.'

'Fair enough,' I said. 'Okay, we're even, kiddo. By the way, I suggest you push for a no bond on Donleavy. If I'm right, he probably has half a million dollars waiting for him in Panama. If he gets on the street, he'll turn rabbit.'

'Over my dead body,' she snapped.

'Don't say that,' I groaned. 'We've got enough of them already. Who knows, kiddo, you just might ride the Raines case into the governor's mansion.'

I winked at her as she scurried by and headed for the booking desk.

70

NANCE SHOWS HIS STRIPE

The Breezes reeked of money. The conservative, two-storey town-houses were Williamsburg grey with scarlet trim, and the walkways wound through ferns and flowering bushes that looked almost too good to be real. Some intelligent contractor had left a lot of old oaks and pines on the development and there wasn't a car in sight; the garages were obviously built facing away from the street. The lawn looked like it had been hand-trimmed with cuticle scissors.

There was a combined exit and entrance in the high iron-spike fence that enclosed the compound. It was divided by an island with a guardhouse and around-the-clock guards. The one on duty, a tall black weightlifter type, was starched into his tan uniform, and his black boots glistened like a showroom Ferrari.

He looked at me through no-shit eyes and shifted his chewing gum from one cheek to the other. He didn't say anything.

'My name's Kilmer, to see Mrs Raines,' I said.

He checked over his clipboard, leafing through several sheets of paper, and shook his head.

'Not on the list,' he said.

'Would you give her a call? She probably forgot. It's been a rough day for her.'

'I got a "no disturb" on that unit,' he said.

'She's expecting me,' I said, trying not to lose my temper.

'There's no Kilmer on the list and I got a "no disturb" on that unit,' he said, politely but firmly. 'Why don't you go someplace and call her, tell her to call the gate and clear you.'

I showed him my card and his eyes stuck on the first line – 'Agent – US Government' – and stayed there until he looked back up.

'My brother's a city cop,' he said, looking out the window at nothing in particular. 'He's taking the Bureau exams in the fall.'

'Fantastic. You know what's going on up there at Mrs Raines' place, don't you?'

'You mean about Mr Raines?'

'Yeah.'

'Terrible thing.' He looked back at the buzzer and asked, 'This official?'

'What else?' I said in my official voice.

'They got tough rules here, buddy. Nobody, not *nobody*, goes in without a call from the gate first. It's in the lease.'

'Like I said, she's expecting me; probably forgot to give you the name with everything else that's going on. Why don't I ride through?'

'Hell, I'll just call her,' he said. 'Guest parking is to the right, behind those palmettos.'

I pulled in and parked in the guest lot, which was so clean and neat it looked sterilised. When I got back, the guard had his grin on.

'A-okay,' he said, making a circle with thumb and forefinger. 'You were right, she forgot. First walk on the left, second unit down, 3-C.'

I thanked him and headed for 3-C. The place was as quiet as the bottom of a lake. No night birds, no wind, no nothing. Pebbles crunched under my feet when I reached the cul-de-sac. It was a class operation, all right. Each condo had its own pool. There wasn't a speck of trash anywhere. Soft bug-repellent lights shed a flat, shadowless glow over the grounds.

Three-C stood back from the gravel road at the end of two rows of azaleas. It seemed as though all the lights in the house were on; the place looked like a cathedral on Christmas Eve. I pressed the doorbell and chimes played a melody under my thumb. Chains rattled, dead bolts clattered, the door swung open, and she was standing there.

The events of the last twenty-four hours had taken their toll. Her eyes were puffed, her face drawn and sallow. Grief had erased her tan and replaced it with a grey mirror of death. She closed the door behind me and retreated to a neutral corner of the room, as though she were afraid I had some contagious disorder.

'I'm glad you're here,' she said, in a voice that had lost its youth.

'Glad to help,' I said.

'Nobody can help,' she said.

'You want to talk it out?' I suggested. 'It helps, I'm told.'

'But not for you, is that it?'

I thought about what she said. It was true, there were few people in the world I could talk to. A hazard of the profession.

'I guess not,' I said. 'Nobody trusts a cop.'

'It's hard to realise that's what you do.'

I looked around the place. It was a man's room, no frills, no bright colours. The colour scheme was tan and black and the antique furniture was heavy and oppressive. The walls were jammed with photographs, plaques, awards, all the paraphernalia of success, squeezed into narrow, shiny brass frames. The room said a lot about Harry Raines; there was a sense of monotonous order about it, an almost urgent herald of accomplishment. A single flower would have helped immensely.

Oddly, Doe was in only one of the pictures, a group shot obviously taken the day the track opened. The rest were all business, mostly the business of politics or racing; Raines in the winner's circle with a jockey and racehorse; Raines looking ill-at-ease beside a Little League ball club; Raines with the Capitol dome in Washington soaring up behind him; Raines posing with senators, congressmen, governors, generals, mayors, kids, and at least one president.

'Didn't he ever smile?' I asked, looking at his stern, almost relentless stare.

'Harry wasn't much for smiling. He thought it a sign of weakness,' Doe said.

'What a shame,' I said. 'He looks so unhappy in these photographs.'

'Dissatisfied,' she said. Resentment crept into her tone. 'He was never satisfied. Even winning didn't satisfy him. All he thought about was the next challenge, the next victory, another plaque for his wall. This was his place, not mine. I'm only here because it's convenient. As soon as this is all over, I'm getting rid of it. I'm sick to death of memorials, and that's all this house is now.'

'How about you, did you satisfy him?'

'In what way?' she asked, her brow gathering up in a frown.

'I mean, were you happy together?'

She shrugged.

'We had all the happiness money can buy,' she said ruefully, 'and none of the fun that goes with it.'

'I'm sorry,' I said, feeling impotent to deal with her grief. 'I'm sorry things have turned so bad for you.'

She sat down primly, her hands clasped in her lap, and stared at the floor.

'Oh, Jake, what happened to it all?' she said, without looking up. 'Why did it shrivel up and die like that? Why were we betrayed so? You, Teddy, Chief, all the things that had meaning for me, were nipped out of my life.'

'We all took a beating,' I said. 'Poor old Teddy got the worst of it.'

'Teddy,' she said. 'Dear, sweet Teddy. He didn't give a damn for the Findley tradition. In one of his letters from Vietnam he said that when you two got back, he was going to buy a piece of land out on Oceanby and the two of you were going to become beach bums. He said he was tired of being a Findley. It was all just a big joke to him.'

'We talked about that a lot,' I said. 'Sometimes I think he was halfway serious.'

'He was serious,' she said, sitting up for a moment. 'Can't you just see it? The three of us out there telling the world to drop dead?' She looked up at me and tried to bend the corners of her mouth into a smile. 'You see, I always knew you'd come back here, Jake. Sooner or later Teddy would get you back for me. Only what I thought was, it was a glorious fantasy, not a nightmare. Then Teddy died and the nightmare started and it never ended and it keeps getting worse.'

She picked at a speck of dust for a moment and then said, 'The gods are perverse. They give lollipops to children and take them away after the first lick.'

I wanted to disagree with her, but I couldn't. What she said was true. It's called growing up. In her own way, Doe had resisted that. Now it was all catching up to her at once and I felt suddenly burdened by her sadness. Not because of Raines' death

– there was nothing to be done about that – but because of what they didn't have when he was alive; because the bright promises of youth had become elusive; because the promises of the heart had been broken. I remembered Mufalatta's story about the two violins. She was playing a sad tune and my violin was answering.

'Harry knew from the start that he was second choice,' she went on. 'I never deceived him about that. But I tried. In the beginning we both tried real hard. Then Chief got more and more demanding and Titan started talking politics and Harry started changing, day by day by day, and pretty soon I was just part of the territory to him. Just another plaque on the wall. I wanted the commitment, Jake. Oh God, how I wanted that. And now I want him back. I want to tell him I'm sorry, that it was all a . . . a . . .'

She shook her head, trying to find a way to end the sentence, so I ended it for her.

'An error in judgment?' I suggested.

She looked up at me and said, 'An error in judgment? What a cheap way to sum up a life.'

I was trying to think of a way to tell her about Sam Donleavy, but I didn't have a chance to get around to it.

'I can't stay here, Jake,' she said, staring at the pictures on the wall. 'Every place I look I see him.' She looked at me. 'Drive me out to Windsong, will you please? Get me out of here.'

'Let's go,' I said. I could tell her on the way out.

She did whatever women do before they leave the house – it seemed like an eternity of puttering around – then we left and walked back to my car. We didn't say anything but she clung to my arm so hard it hurt.

The security guard flagged me down as we drove towards the island.

'You got somebody waiting for you?' he asked.

'Why do you ask?'

'There's this black sedan down to the right. Pulled up just after you went in. He's been down there ever since.'

I squinted through the dark and could see the car, half a block away, sitting on our side of the street. It cculd have been one of Dutch's hooligans, but I didn't recognise the car.

'Can you tell how many there are?'

'Just the one,' he said.

'Maybe he's sleeping one off,' I said.

'Yeah, well, just thought I'd mention it,' the guard said.

'Thanks.'

'My pleasure.'

I pulled out of the security drive and turned left, away from the parked car. It pulled away from the curb without showing any lights and fell in behind us. I drifted, letting it pull closer. As usual, my gun was in the trunk.

'Hook up,' I told Doe.

'What?' she asked.

'Your safety belt. Hook it up, and hang on.'

She groped for the belt and snapped it across her lap.

'What's the matter?' she asked, urgency creeping into her voice.

'We've got company,' I said, hooking up my own belt. 'Just hang on. It'll be like the old days in the dune buggy.'

I waited until the car was ten feet behind me, then slammed down the gas pedal and twisted the steering wheel. The car leaped forward, its tyres tortured by the asphalt, and then spun around. I hit the brakes, straightened it out, and left rubber all over Palm Drive as I headed in the other direction.

The other driver was faster than I figured. He swerved and hit my left rear fender. I lost control for a moment, spun wheels, hit gas and brakes, trying to get it back, leaped over the banquette, missed an alcove of garbage cans and Dempster Dumpsters, and wasted about thirty feet of the fence surrounding the compound. My car came to a grinding halt, its ruined radiator hissing crazily.

I fumbled with the keys, got them out of the ignition, jumped out, and ran back towards the boot. The other car did a wheely and headed back towards me, stopping ten feet away. I was still struggling with the boot latch when I heard Turk Nance say from behind me:

'You need driving lessons.'

While we were looking for him, Nance had followed me.

Doe was out of the car and beside me.

'Get back in the car,' I said as quietly as I could

'What's going on?' she squealed.

Too late. Nance was standing in front of me, his Luger at arm's length pointed at my face, his reptile eyes dancing gleefully, his tongue searching his lips.

I reacted. Without thinking. Without figuring the odds. Without thinking about Doe.

It was like an orgasm, a great flood of relief. All my frustrations and anger boiled up out of me into a blind, uncontrollable rage. Nance was more than just a psychotic who had killed people I knew and who'd tried to kill me. He was every broken promise, every shattered dream, every pissed-away value in the last twenty years of my life.

I didn't think. I grabbed the gun by the barrel and twisted hard, heard the shot and felt the heat surge through the barrel, burn my hand, and howl off down the street. I hit him, knocked him into the alcove of garbage cans, hit him again, kneed him, thrashed him back and forth, from one wall to the other, and then hit him again and kneed him again. He started to fall and I held him up and kept hitting him. I could hear Doe screaming my name hysterically but I couldn't stop. Every punch felt good, every kick. He started screaming, trying to get away from me. His shirt tore and he fell to his knees and scrambled towards the street like a crab. I slammed my foot down on his ankle to stop him, twisted it, and hit him in the back of the head several times with my fist until my hand was burning with pain. I dragged him up and kicked him in the small of his back and he vaulted in a clean diver's arc into the garbage cans.

It wasn't enough. I snatched up a garbage pail lid and slammed it down on his head, three, four, five times, until it was a mangled wreck, then threw it away, dragged him to his feet, and jammed my knee into his groin again. I grabbed a fistful of his shirt, held him, and hit him half a dozen more times, short, hard shots, straight to the face. I hit him until he was a bloody, limp rag.

Doe was leaning against the wall, her hands stifling her screams, her eyes crazy with fear and shock.

'Stop it, Jake, for God's sake please stop it!' she cried.

I dragged him up and threw him across the bonnet of the car, picked up his Luger, and jammed it into his throat.

The entire exhibition had taken about thirty seconds.

'You fucking Mongoloid!' I screamed in his ear. 'That's three strikes. You're out.'

'No, no, no!' Doe screamed.

The security guard was in the street, blowing his whistle, not sure whether to pull his gun or not.

'Call this number,' I yelled to him, and barked out the number of the Warehouse. I repeated it.

'You got that?' I demanded.

'Yes, sir!'

'You call it now, tell whoever answers that Jake Kilmer wants company and not to waste time getting here.'

'Yes sir.' He dashed back inside the security house.

Nance wasn't alone. Nance was never alone. Nance was a company man; he liked people around.

'Run back inside the compound,' I told Doe.

'But – '

'Do it now. This creep isn't alone. Just get inside and stay there until – '

Headlights ended that sentence. The car moved towards us from a block away. I gripped the Luger in two hands and blew out a headlight. The car picked up speed and stopped an inch in front of mine. I aimed at the other light and a voice behind me said: 'Drop it, or the girl goes down.'

Nance tried to gargle something through swollen, bloody lips. I dragged him off the bonnet and threw him on the ground, dropped the clip out of his gun, and threw it at him with everything I had. It hit him in the side and clattered harmlessly across the sidewalk.

A moment later something just as hard hit me in the back of the head. The street turned on end. Doe spun around me like a doll on a merry-go-round. The lights went out.

71

FLASHBACK: NAM DIARY, END OF TOUR

The 556th day: *We been on the ass of this crazy schoolteacher named Nim who's been raising hell up and down the river and has maybe a hundred slopes tagging after him now. HQ says he's getting to be some kind of God to these people and to terminate the cocksucker posthaste. I mean, there's five of us on this CRIP team, right, and we're gonna bust this crazy bastard and a hundred or so nuts that are hanging out with him?*

So I tell HQ I need about fifty, sixty first-class hunters, Kit Carsons'll do fine, but I ain't running up against this fuckin' army of Nim's with a five-man team, I don't care how good we are, and I'll tell you this, we're the best they got down here, goddamn it. Between the five of us, I'd say we got probably three hundred fuckin' scalps. Not bad for six months on the line, five guys. Corrigon, French Dip, Squeak, Joe Fineman, and me. Five guys, one head. We're charmed. We got this daily bet, we start off with a bill apiece and each add a twenty every day we're dry. First one gets his kill, takes the pot. It ain't ever gone over eight hundred, that's four days.

So anyway, we go down to meet the riverboat today and pick up this bunch of sharpshooters HQ sent down, and the boat crew says the war's gonna be over any day now and I say, 'Sure, I've heard that before,' but the team, they all buy it and they get a couple jugs of Black Jack from the black market guy on board and while I don't put up with drinking out here I figure, what the hell, we got all these wild-eyed slopes from HQ, why not, they deserve it. So the rest of the team, they get juiced up to the eyeballs and I have to sit guard all night to make sure this asshole Nim don't come crawling up on us, blitz us all. The slopes are okay in the daylight, face-to-face, that kind of fighting. I don't trust them at night when I can't see them, so I sit up.

All night I keep thinking about the cease-fire and about what that Lieutenant, what was his name, Harris? said, that night in Dau Tieng, about going back to the World and bowling every night and all. Shit.

Turns out it was a false alarm, about the cease-fire, I mean.

Another day of grace.

The 558th day: *It was beautiful. Last night we catch up to Nim just before sunset and we blitz the shit out of his whole fuckin' bunch. We have them boxed in and we have a fuckin' field day. The Carsons are crazy motherfuckers. They cut heads, drink blood, I mean really rubber room crazy. We get in close enough, the team is having some real sport. We all managed to acquire these Remington pumps from the juice man upriver and so the deal is, this time we have to use shotguns to win the pot. So anyway we load up with rifle slugs; it's about an inch around and weighs about three ounces and it's rifled so you get a little spin on it and when it hits anything solid, it fuckin' blows up. You hit one of those motherfuckers dead centre, the body being mostly water, it's like shooting a fuckin' watermelon. We call them splashers.

Anyway, it was like shooting skeet. So I take the pot. We just put it up this morning, six hundred bucks. Nine scalps. A good day's work. The only problem is, this Nim and about twenty of his gooks got away from us.*

So this morning we track them into this little valley with a hump in the middle, looks like a tit in a cake pan. Lots of trees, I call in some air and we do a little macing. It's hotter than a whore's mattress and we spread out around the perimeter and we give the fuckers a little while and that gas starts mixing with their sweat, next thing you know one of these Kit Carsons, he stands up, starts sniffing the air like a hyena, points down in the bush, here comes about fifteen of them, beating the shit out of themselves because of the mace, crying. The Kit Carson, he up and blows the first one away, just like that if you please, and then he tells the rest of them to get their hands behind their heads like good little gooks. Man, they took a beating, all covered with mace burns, their eyes all bugged out. Whipped dogs, man, they got as much fight left in them as a guppy. So we figure we're lookin' at, what, five, six of them that are left maybe. Fuckin' Nim ain't in the group.

I got this American 180, a neat little submachine I won in a poker game with some civilian types up in Saigon, shoots .22's but, like, thirty rounds a second. You could drill a hole in a brick wall with this motherfucker. That's what it sounds like, a fuckin' dentist drill:

Brrrttt, brrttttt.

Like that. Jesus, what a nice piece of work. Two of these, the Alamo would have never fallen. So what it is, you learn to do things quick over here, know what I mean? You move fast, shake 'em up, they'll tell you anything you want to know. The thing is, you don't spend a lot of time thinking, you just do it, see. I call one of these little bastards over, he gets about four feet away, I give him a burst.

Brrttttt.

He hits the dirt, jerks once, it's all over. I call out the second one, ask him where this fucker Nim is, he starts thinking about it . . .

Brrttttt.

Another one down. The third one I point at tells us all of it. The slopes don't call me Monsieur Morte for nothing. What it is, there's this pool at the foot of the hill and Nim's holed up there in a cave. I call the air back and this time he comes in and lands and the pilot, who is this fuckin' rosy-cheeked bastard about twelve years old, he jumps out, says, 'Where's the lieutenant?' and I tell him there ain't any lieutenant, I'm a sergeant and I'm in charge and what's his problem, and he says the cease-fire is tonight and it's official, all that shit, and he wants to call the whole thing off. 'What the hell,' he says, 'it's only a few more hours,' and I say, 'Lissen, you fuckin' wimp, we been following this little cocksucker for days and we're goin' in there and get the motherfucker, so let's get on with it.' He gets the colour of a goddamn beet and he says, 'I'm putting you on report. What's your name, mister?' and I say, 'Just tell them Monsieur Morte insulted you, that a Pall Mall'll get you a kick in the ass and that's all it'll get you,' and he says, 'Don't give me any of that Wild West shit, what's your name?' and I say, 'Parver, P-a-r-v-e-r,' and I spell it for him and then I say, 'And either you're gonna fly that fuckin' bird or one of us will. We're goin' over that hump and my people ain't wadin' through a lot of fuckin' mace to get there.'

Anyway, before it was over, we were in the chopper and we go over the hump and the pool's down there, like the gook says, and there's little grey wisps of mace, still hanging in there, like stringy strands of cotton. So we drop a string down and three of us drop into the pit there, we beat it over to the cave and we look in and this fuckin' Nim is sitting maybe twenty feet from the cave entrance. What a mess! His legs are crossed at the ankles, he's naked as a fuckin' flounder. His body is covered with these scorched sores, his eyes are swollen shut, and he's foaming at the fuckin' mouth from all the mace, like a goddamn mad dog. Fuckin' forty-five-year-old schoolteacher thinks he's Fidel Castro, or something, and the fucker's still breathing but blind as a bridegroom. All of a sudden he starts reaching around for his weapon, which is an M-16 and you know where he got that, the little bastard, so I step in behind him and

Brrttttt.

Lights out, spook. Then, and I don't know why I did it, maybe it was because, you know, it's the last day of the fuckin' war, you want to try to get in as much as you can, I take Fineman's machete and lop that fuckin' slope's head off, swock, just like that, pretty as you please. Fineman almost pukes, can you believe that? All he's seen, for Christ sake. I throw the trophy in this ammo bag, take it back for the rest of them to see. What the hell, they have a right. Call it spoils of war.

The last day: This time the scuttlebutt's true. We get back to the river and it's all over. Everybody's cheering, singing songs, drinking, and the black market man is giving away booze. I never thought I'd live to see the day. They're settin' off rockets and flares, shooting up shit, like the Fourth of Fuckin' July, and all I'm doin', I'm sittin' there thinkin' about what that lieutenant said, about bowling. Only he didn't talk about what happens when it's over, maybe none of us thought it ever would be. Thing is, we're goin' back to the World, man, whether we like it or not. It's all over. No more fuckin' grace.

ZAPATA SAVES THE DAY

The call came in at 8:04.

The Warehouse was already babbling with activity. Dutch was quizzing Lange, Cowboy Lewis, and Pancho Callahan. Charlie One Ear took the call.

Callahan was doing most of the talking.

'*We all showed up at city pier together, no more than thirty minutes ago,*' *he told Dutch.* '*Kite there was following Bronicata, and Cowboy was on Chevos. I had Costello. Zapata was there, too, doing something, I don't know what. All of a sudden all four of us are watching each other and the three of them are tooting out into the bay on Costello's boat.*'

'*Cute. So right now we're standing on empty, that it?*' *Dutch said.*

'*Well, Zapata powdered. I don't know where he went. One minute he was there, the next minute he wasn't.*'

'*We woulda followed Costello and them but we couldn't find a rowboat to rent,*' *Kite Lange said.*

'*Hilarious,*' *said Dutch.* '*You auditioning for the* Comedy Hour?'
Charlie One Ear burst through the door.

'*What's bugging you?*' *Dutch asked.*

'*A security guard over at the Breezes just called. That's where Harry Raines and his wife lived. He says Jake Kilmer and the Raines woman were attacked leaving the place and were shoved in a car at gunpoint.*'

'*When?*' *Dutch roared.*

'*About two minutes ago.*'

'*Jake Kilmer was with Doe Raines?*' *Dutch said.*

'*That's what the man said. It's a late Eldorado, cinnamon-coloured, too far off to get a licence. They headed east on Palm.*'

'*Did you get an APB out on that?*' *Dutch demanded.*

'*You want to stop every Cadillac in town?*' *Charlie One Ear asked with surprise.*

'*How the hell many cinnamon Eldorados do you think we got in town?*' *Dutch yelled, snatching up the phone and calling central radio.*

The Stick was next to appear in the doorway.

'What the hell's going on?' he asked.

'It appears that Nance and his bunch have lifted Jake Kilmer and Harry Raines' widow,' Pancho Callahan said.

'Nance kidnapped them?'

'It don't sound like no scavenger hunt,' said Lange.

Charlie One Ear said, 'It sounds straight. Jake's car is still out there. Apparently it's permanently imbedded in the security fence. The security man checked the licence for me. I've got a blue and white on the way to make sure somebody isn't giving us the finger.'

'Speaking of fingers, right now we ain't got a finger on anybody in the mob, that right?' Stick exclaimed.

'Chino and Salvatore are still on the range somewhere. Shall we try to raise them?' Charlie One Ear replied.

Dutch slammed down the phone. 'Okay,' he said. 'There's gonna be a lot of pissed-off Cadillac owners in town, but maybe we'll luck out and nab them before they get too far.'

Five minutes later Zapata answered his page. Stick snatched up the phone.

'Chino, it's Stick. Where the hell are you?'

'Outside one of these strip joints on Front,' he answered.

'What are you doing there?'

'Watching Silo Murphy, the one they call Weasel.'

'You got Murphy in sight right now?' the Stick said.

'Yeah. He didn't go on the boat ride so I stuck with him. Salvatore's still trying to get a line on that fuckhead Nance.'

'I'm on my way,' said Stick. 'If he leaves, follow him and keep me cued through central. What's your number?'

'Car seventy-three. What's goin' on?'

'Ten minutes. Tell you when I get there,' said Stick. He slammed down the phone and headed for the door.

In Dutch's office the rest of the SOB's were also wrestling with the problem.

'How about the traffic chopper,' suggested Cowboy Lewis. 'Maybe we can run down Costello's cruiser.'

'Good idea, get on it,' said Dutch. 'So where do we stand right now?'

'Salvatore and Zapata are still on the street,' said Charlie One Ear. 'Mufalatta's on the range rounding up the rest of the Graves gang. The rest of us are here.'

'Where'd the Stick go?' demanded Dutch.

'*He's checking on Chino,*' said Charlie One Ear.

'*Not anymore,*' said Callahan. '*He just went out the door like his underwear was on fire.*'

'*Sheiss, what next!*' cried the Dutchman.

I came around with elephants thundering in one ear and out the other and the bitter-salty taste of blood in my mouth. I was stretched out on a fairly comfortable Naugahyde sofa. Doe was sitting beside me, bathing my aching head with a wet cloth.

'Oh, thank God!' she said as I opened my eyes.

'You okay?' I asked.

'I'm fine. It's you they knocked out.'

'Where are we?'

'I'm not sure. They blindfolded me,' she said. 'We're near the water, though, I can smell it.'

My nose had been knocked out of commission along with half of my other senses. I couldn't have smelled my hair if it was on fire.

'How long did it take to get here?'

'Twenty minutes, thirty maybe. I've never been very good about time and I don't have a watch on.'

'My God, how long have I been out?'

'Another ten.'

'They must've hit me with a poleaxe.'

'Actually it was a little black stick one of them had strapped to his wrist.'

'Just a plain old-fashioned sap,' I said. 'Just like me.'

I sat up slowly, so my head wouldn't fall off, got my feet on the floor, and sat very still to keep from vomiting. Eventually the nausea went away. The room was small and tidy and looked like a doctor's office, without the medical journals and four-year-old *National Geographics* strewn everywhere. The only light in the room came from a table lamp made from a wooden anchor with 'Saint Augustine, Florida, 1981' hand-painted on it. The room had two windows, both heavily draped, and there was a TV monitor camera mounted high in one corner.

I decided to see if I could stand up. That brought some activity from the other room. The door opened. I could tell from the silhouette that it was Nance. I didn't realise how badly I had beaten him until he turned sideways and the light from the other room fell across his face. Both eyes were swollen to slits, he had bruises and gashes down both sides of his face, he was limping, and there was a cut that had swollen to the size of an egg on the corner of his mouth, surrounded by a blue-grey bruise that spread almost to his ear. He was a wreck. I felt better when I saw him.

'Hi, Nance,' I said. 'Been a real shitty day for you, hasn't it?'

He made animal noises in his throat and started towards me but a hairy paw against his chest stopped him. Arthur Pravano, the one they called Sweetheart, stepped past him.

'Don't make any more trouble,' he said to Nance. Sweetheart leaned on the doorjamb and stared at me.

'Well, well,' I said, 'the pool's getting full.'

'You talk awfully big for a man with his balls in the ringer,' said Nance.

'Go on outside,' Pravano said, and Nance bristled for a second, then turned and vanished from the doorway.

'You ought to do something about him,' I said, 'like give him a brain transplant for Christmas.'

'Big-mouth Fed,' he said, shaking his head. 'You got about as much time left as an ice cube in a frying pan.'

'No less than you,' I replied, although I was sorry the moment I said it. They were all in up to their eyeballs. Murder, kidnapping, arson – all could be proven, regardless of whether or not we broke down Cohen, Donleavy, and Seaborn and opened up the pyramid. They were all smart enough to know you can only hang once. One or two more murders couldn't have bothered them less, so I cut the smart talk and hoped that Doe wouldn't figure it out too.

'So why are we here?' I asked.

'It's a scientific experiment,' Pravano said. 'We want to see how long it takes for a Fed to wet his pants.'

'There's a lady in the room,' I said.

'She's got rotten taste,' he snarled.

'Your dance partner's no trophy winner,' I snapped back.

He let it pass. 'Don't try nothing spectacular, okay, to impress the lady, like the thing with Turk back there in town. Keep away from the windows. Don't make no racket, bust up the furniture, start no fires, that kind of shit. We got people outside and people watching that.' He jerked a thumb towards the monitor. 'You fuck with that, I'll let Turk come in and blow off your goddamn balls, if you got any.'

He left.

'Who was that!' Doe cried.

'One of the seven dwarfs,' I said, and tried a chuckle. It sounded more like a dirge.

Zapata was sitting sidesaddle on his Hog, smoking a Fatima and watching the traffic go by when Stick got there.

'*He's in that strip joint over there, drinking Scotch and checking crotch,*' *the Mexican said. '*What the hell's going on?*'

'*Costello and his bunch ditched the boys. They're out pleasure cruising on Costello's boat.*'

'*I know. I been watching this Weasel 'cause I heard him and Nance were, y'know, kinda tight, if that psycho has any friends. Anyways, he don't go on the boat. So I figure maybe he's gonna meet Nance and I shag him. He comes over here. Is that what it's all about?*'

'*Dutch wants to have a talk with Weasel,*' *Stick said. '*Let's go over and see can we ease him out of there without starting a riot.*'

The girl on stage was all legs. Legs and purple hair with a white streak, front to back, dyed on one side; a punk stripper who looked about as sexy as a stuffed flounder. Weasel Murphy was sitting at the bar, as close to the action as he could get without getting his nose caught in her G-string. A pair of worn-out speakers were thumping out a scratched version of 'Night Life' as the punker peeled off her bra and let her ample bosom flop out. The Prussian army could have marched in and Murphy would have missed it. He had eyes only for the Purple People Eater.

'*Wanna just put the arm on him?*' *said Chino.*

'*Dutch says try to avoid a ruckus,*' *Stick said.*

'*What do we do?*'

They sat down at a table the size of a birdbath near the door to think it over. Purple People Eater was snapping her bra like a slingshot in Murphy's face. He stuffed a five-dollar bill in the tip glass and she kneeled down in front of him, pulled her G-string down to the bar, and let it snap back. He tucked a twenty in the string, dead centre. She ended her performance by seducing an imaginary pony, complete with squeals of delight and instructions to the invisible animal. Murphy was wired so tight he was humming.

One of the B-girls slid a chair over to the table and sat down backward. The runs in her hose looked like black varicose veins. This one had orange hair, no streak. It looked like it had been cut with pruning shears. She ran a finger along the brim of Stick's hat.

402

'Love it,' she said. 'I didn't think anybody wore those anymore.'

'It was my grandfather's,' Stick said. 'How'd you like to make an easy twenty?'

'We're not allowed to do that,' she said coyly. 'Just have a drink with the customers.'

'You don't even have to do that,' said Stick. 'See that dude at the bar, the one who's sweating so hard?'

'You mean the one that looks like a possum?'

'Close enough. See, what's happening, we got this bowling club and we just voted him in but he don't know it yet.'

'You're into bowling?' she said. She made it sound like child molestation.

'Yeah. Anyway, see, we're gonna put the snatch on him, take him out to my boat. The rest of the guys are out there waiting and we're gonna surprise him, tell him he's in, y'know.'

'Sounds like a real great party,' she said, and yawned.

'What we'd like, see, all you have to do is get him out the side door there, onto Jackson Street. We'll take it from there.'

'This ain't some kidnapping or something?' she said suspiciously. 'I mean, I ain't goin' to the freezer for some snatch job.'

'Look at him,' Zapata said. 'His own mother wouldn't kidnap him.'

'So how do I get him outside?' she asked.

'For twenty bucks, you can write the script. When he goes through the door, you get the double saw.'

She thought about it for a minute.

'He's a big spender,' she said. 'The boss might get pissed with me.'

Stick took out a twenty and wrapped it around his little finger.

'When's the last time the boss laid twenty on you for walking to the door?'

She eyed the twenty, eyed Murphy, who was catching his breath between acts, and looked back at the twenty.

'I'll see what I can do,' she said.

'The Jackson Street entrance. The twenty'll be right here on my pinky.'

She giggled. 'Pinky! Jesus, I haven't heard that since I was in the fourth grade.'

Stick and Zapata went outside and Stick pulled his car around the corner and parked near the door.

'This seems like a lot of time and money when we could just bust his ass and haul him in.'

'Dutch doesn't want a fuss.'

'Yeah, you told me. How do we do this? We just cold-cock the son of a bitch or what?'

Stick took out a pair of thumb cuffs.

'When he gets outside, bump into him and knock him into me. I'll grab him from behind, get his arms behind him, and thumb-cuff him, throw him in the car.'

'My hog's around the corner.'

'I'll see you out at the Warehouse.'

'Okay, but it seems like a lot of hassle.'

They waited about five minutes, then the door opened and the orange-haired punker and Murphy came out. He was wrapped around her like Kudzu around a telephone pole. Zapata bumped into them and the girl stepped back and Stick grabbed both his elbows and jerked them back, slid his hands down Murphy's arms to his wrist, and twisted both of Murphy's hands inward. Murphy hollered and jerked forward and as he did, Stick snapped the tiny cuffs on his thumbs, twisted him around, and shoved him into the back seat of the car. The girl saw the wire-caged windows.

'Goddamn it, you're the heat, you goddamn lying –'

Stick dangled the twenty in front of her. She snatched it out of his hand and stuffed it down her bosom.

'Better than busting up the place, ain't it?' Zapata said as Stick tipped his hat, jumped into his car, and sped off.

'He's like that,' Zapata said, walking towards his hog. 'Impetuous.'

'What d'ya mean, you snatched Weasel Murphy?' Dutch bellowed after Zapata had finished his story.

'He said you wanted we should hustle Weasel outta that joint and bring him out here on the QT. So that's we did. He shoulda been here by now, he got two minutes' head start on me.'

'Maybe it's the international Simon Says sweepstakes,' Kite Lange said.

'Will you stop with the wisecracks, Lange,' Dutch grumbled. 'Things're bad enough without you imitating Milton Berle. What I wanna know is, where the hell's Stick and Murphy?'

'Perhaps I should put out an all points on Parver's vehicle,' Charlie One Ear suggested.

'Why don't we just bust everybody in town,' Callahan said. 'We can put them in the football stadium and let them go one at a time.'

Dutch buried his face in his hands. 'What is it, is the heat getting everybody?' he moaned. 'I shoulda known when I was lucky, I should of stayed in the army.'

73

CHRISTMAS CREEK

The thirty-horsepower motor growled vibrantly behind him as Stick guided the sailboat out of the mouth of South River and into the bay. Buccaneer Point was two miles away. Five miles beyond it was Jericho Island, where a sliver of creek, two or three hundred yards wide and a quarter of a mile long, sliced the small offshore island into Big Jericho and Little Jericho. Stick set his course for Jericho.

Clouds played with the face of a full moon and night birds chattered at them as the sleek sailboat cruised away from land, its sails furled, powered by the engine. Stick flicked on the night light over his compass. It was 8:45. He would be there in another fifteen minutes. He checked his tide chart. High tide was at 9:57. The bar would be perfect.

Weasel Murphy was crunched down against the cabin wall, his thumbs still shackled behind him.

'I already told you,' the rodent-faced gunman said arrogantly, 'I don't know nothin' about nothin'.'

'Right,' said Stick.

'I get seasick; that's why I didn't go along on the boat. You can't understand plain English?'

'You start getting sick,' said the Stick, 'you better stick your head over the side. Puke in my boat and I'll use you for a mop and throw you overboard.'

'Fuck you,' Murphy growled, but his arrogance was less than convincing.

'Cute,' Stick said. 'I admire your stuff.'

'How many times I gotta tell you,' Murphy said, 'I don't know nothin' about snatching no Fed, or the Raines dame. That's all news t'me.'

'Where's Costello heading on that schooner of his?'

'I told you, I don't fuckin' know! They was just goin' out to have

dinner and get away for a few hours. We was all tired of looking up some cop's nose every time we turned around.'

He shifted slightly.

'Where the hell are we going?' he demanded.

'Up the lazy river,' Stick said.

'You're a full-out loony, you know that. You need about fifty more cards to fill out your deck.'

'Big talk from a man who can't even scratch his nose,' Stick said.

'Look, these things are killing my thumbs,' Murphy said. 'Can you at least loosen them a little? My whole damn arm's goin' to sleep.'

'I want to know where Kilmer is and where Costello's going. You just tell me that, we turn around and head for home.'

'Shit, man, how many ways can I –'

'You already have,' the Stick said. 'You're beginning to annoy me. If you won't tell me what I want to know, keep your mouth shut or I'll put my foot in it.'

They went on. The only sound now was the bow of the boat slicing through the water, and the occasional slap of a wave as it rolled up into a whitehead and peaked. Stick was using running lights although occasionally he snapped on a powerful searchlight for a look around. Otherwise he watched his compass and smoked and said nothing.

At 9:05 he passed the north point of Big Jericho, swung the trim boat in towards land, and followed the beach around to the south. A minute or two later the moon peered out from behind the clouds and in its grey half-light he could see the mouth of Christmas Creek. He turned into it, cut back the motor, and switched the spotlight on again. He swept it back and forth. Murphy straightened up and peered over the gunwale. A large heron thrashed its wings nearby and flapped noisily away. Startled by the sudden and unexpected sound, Murphy slumped down again.

Then he heard the sounds for the first time.

A sudden whirlpool of movement in the water near the boat.

'What'sat?' he asked, sitting up again. 'Hey, there it goes again. You hear that?'

The Stick said nothing.

The sounds continued. There seemed to be a lot of turbulence in the water around the boat. Then there was a splash and something thunked the side of the sailboat.

'Don't you hear it?' Murphy croaked, staring wide-eyed at the circle of light from the spotlight. The Stick still didn't answer.

Stick had stopped in an all-night supermarket on the way to the boathouse and bought a large beef shoulder. It had been soaking in a bucket of warm water near his feet. Now he took it out, laid it on the rear bulkhead, and slashed several deep gashes in it with a rusty machete. Blood crept out of the crevices, seeping slowly into the seams between the boards.

There was a loud splash near the stern, then another, even louder, just beyond the bow. Fear began as a worm in Murphy's stomach, a twisty little jolt. He began to look feverishly at each new tremor in the water, but he could see nothing but swirls on the surface of the creek.

Then he thought he saw a grey triangle cut the surface ten feet away.

'What was that?' he asked.

The worm became a snake. It crawled up through his chest and stuck in his throat. His mouth dried up.

'This is a little nature trip, Weasel,' Stick said, taking a grappling hook from the bulkhead storage box and burying its hooks in the beef shoulder. He wrapped a thick nylon fishing line around it several times and tied it in a half hitch. 'Ever hear of Christmas Creek?'

'I told you, I get seasick. I don't have nothin' to do with the fuckin' ocean.' His voice was losing its bravura.

Stick saw the bar dead ahead, a slender strip of sand, barely a foot above water.

'Well, you're right in the middle of it. This is it, this is Christmas Creek,' Stick said. 'One of the local ecological wonders.'

There was another, more vigorous splash off the starboard bow and this time Murphy saw it clearly, a shiny grey dorsal fin. It sliced the surface for an instant and then disappeared in a swirl.

'Good Christ, those're sharks,' Murphy gasped.

'I was about to tell you,' said Stick. 'This is a breeding ground for grey sharks and makos, and this is the month for it. That's why they're so fidgety. I'd guess there are probably, oh hell, two, three hundred sharks within spitting distance of the boat right now.'

The first shark Murphy actually saw breached water three feet away, rolled over on its side, and dived again.

It was half the length of the sailboat

'Sweet Jesus,' Murphy muttered to himself. He was still trying to maintain his tough façade, but his eyes mirrored his growing fear. He dropped back on the floor of the cockpit and cowered there.

'This bloody piece of beef here will drive them crazy,' Stick continued. 'I thought I'd just give 'em a snack, let you see one of the wonders of the world.'

Murphy hunched down lower.

'C'mon, fella, watch the show,' said Stick. He reached down and pulled Murphy up and slammed him against the bulkhead. He threw the piece of meat overboard, holding it by the nylon cord. It had hardly hit before the creek was churned into bubbles. The water looked like it was boiling. The frenzied killers streaked to the bloody morsel. Their tails whipped out of the water. Fins seemed to be slashing all over the creek. The creatures surfaced in their frenzy, their black marble eyes bulging with excitement, their ragged mouths blood-smeared from ripping at the beef shoulder. A great, ugly mako breached the surface, twisted violently in the water, then suddenly lurched into the air as a large grey disembowelled it, the attacker thrashing its head back and forth as it tore a great chunk from the other shark's belly. More blood churned to the surface. A half dozen more sharks converged on the mako, ripping it to shreds. Then one of them turned and charged the sailboat.

Murphy screamed, a full-fledged, bloodcurdling scream.

The big grey turned at the last moment and scraped down the side of the sailboat.

All Murphy saw was insane eyes and gleaming teeth.

Within seconds the hook was empty. Stick pulled it back in.

'Lookit that, they even gnawed at the hooks,' Stick said with a chuckle.

'What're we doin' here?' Murphy whispered, as though he were afraid he would disturb the predators.

'I'll tell you, when these bastards are horny, they're downright unreasonable,' Stick rambled on.

He swung the sailboat in a tight arc, pulling as close to the sandbar as he could. He knew the creek well; knew, too, that the bar dropped off sharply on its north side, sharply enough to get in tight. Stick grabbed the back of Murphy's shirt and hauled him to his feet.

'What the hell are you doing? Lemme alone, lemmee . . .' the mobster howled.

The boat nudged the bar.

Stick threw him over the side.

Murphy shrieked. He landed on his side in the soft sand, rolled over, still screaming, scrambled to his feet, and sloshed through ankle-deep sand in the middle of the bar. He stood there, his hands behind his back, his eyes bulging with fear, watching the fins circle his diminishing island.

408

'For God's sakes, what'd I do? I didn't do nothin'! Get me off of here. Jesus, Mary, and Joseph, please, get me offa here!'

Stick leaned towards him. 'Now listen good, Weasel. The tide's coming in. This bar lies very low in the water. Another five, six minutes, the water will cover it. At full tide, in about forty-five minutes, it'll be up to your waist. Do you get the drift?'

Murphy looked around, wide-eyed. There were sharks all over the place, circling the tiny island as if they could smell him.

'Here, I'll give you a break,' Stick said. 'You won't have to look at them.'

Stick turned the spotlight off.

'No-o-o,' Murphy moaned.

The moon dipped behind the clouds. Murphy was rooted to his spot. He was beyond fear now, afraid to move in any direction. He squinted into the darkness but it was too dark to see anything.

But he could hear them.

'Get me offa here, please,' Murphy pleaded. There was no bravura left.

Stick replied, 'The tide's coming in, Weasel. In two or three minutes you'll feel it around your ankles.'

Murphy's feet squirmed beneath him. He had trouble catching his breath. He was overwhelmed with fear. Then he felt the first cold, wet fingers seeping through the soles of his shoes, down through the shoelace holes, around the tongues of his expensive brogans, clutching at his feet.

Murphy suddenly started to babble. He couldn't talk fast enough. His words tumbled over each other and he started to stutter:

'They'regointoThunder Point! To Chevos' p-p-p-place! They went outontheboat to celebrate . . .'

'Celebrate what?'

'Costello's the new capo di capi.'

When are they coming in?'

'They're due to get to the marina about t-t-ten . . .'

'How do you know that?'

'That's when I'm supposed to be back. I g-g-got a coupla hours off 'cause I get seasick.'

'Who's going to be there?'

'It's everybody. It's the wholegoddamnw-w-works, except maybe for Nance. I . . . I sweartoG-G-God I don't know where he is. Please, oh, God, please get me offa here. That's all I know. All I know, I swear on my mother's eyes, I don't know another f-f-fuckin' thing. *Jesus, man, I'll p-p-pay you. What d'ya want? You want my car? I got a brand-new Chrysler convertible it's yours. Damn it, please . . .'*

'*That's better, Weasel. Okay, start walking this way.*'

'*I can't, not in the dark, don't do . . .*'

'*Just walk towards my voice.*'

'*I can't m-m-move!*'

'*I'll keep talking and you keep walking and if you don't lose your cool, you'll make it over here. But you better stop fuckin' around, Weasel, because the tide doesn't stop. It's gonna get deeper and . . .*'

'*I'm walkin', I'm walkin'. Can I have the light, can I please have the fuckin' light?*'

Murphy was dragging one foot after the other through the sandy water. Each step seemed to take him deeper.

'*I'm going wrong!*' *he yelled at the darkness.* '*The water's up to my shins!*'

'*I warned you about the tide, Weasel. Just keep coming. You're doing fine, but don't stop. If you stop, they'll be on top of you in another five minutes.*'

Murphy took another step and the water swirled around his knees. He began to get sick to his stomach. He started running, lost his balance, and fell face down in the cold salt water. He scrambled frantically, trying to get his knees under him, but with his hands shackled behind him he had trouble. He swallowed a mouthful of water, then got his head up, coughing and gulping for air.

'*Where are ya?*' *Murphy screamed when he finally regained his footing.*

He heard the sailboat's motor, then realised it was moving away from him!

'*Hey!*' *Murphy screamed.* '*H-e-e-e-y!*'

The sound of the motor grew dimmer and dimmer. The thrashing of the sharks was drawing closer. The water was almost up to his waist.

The last human voice Murphy heard was the Stick's, far off in the blackness of night. The man's singing! Murphy cried out to himself.

'*Up a lazy river, by the old mill run . . .*'

74

GOODBYE HIT

An hour crept by. It seemed like four or five. At first the TV monitor discouraged conversation. I figured the room had to be bugged. After I got my wits together I decided to give it a test. I looked straight into the camera and said, 'Would it be too much to ask for a glass of water?' Nothing had happened, so I kicked on the door. Sweetheart Pravano answered my summons. He was still wearing the battle scars from the fight at the Warehouse; a mouse on his right eye and a four-inch gash in his jaw. He glared at me when I made the request and shut the door in my face but a minute or two later a young kid, who was wearing both suspenders and a belt, as well as an empty shoulder holster under his arm, brought us each a glass of ice water. Then they left us alone.

'What do you think they're going to do with us?' Doe asked.

'I don't know,' I said, quite honestly.

During the remainder of that hour Doe and I talked quietly but steadily. I explained who Tagliani was, although she seemed to have a vague notion already. I also told her Tony Lukatis had been slain hijacking the cocaine shipment, which she didn't know, although the information didn't seem to upset her too much.

'So you knew about Tony?' she said. 'That was over such a long time ago. Poor Tony. He wanted so desperately to make something of himself, to be more than . . .' She tried to explain the Lukatis' obsession, but it wouldn't come out.

'I can understand that,' I said. 'He just picked the wrong way to do it.'

'Was he involved with these people?'

I shook my head. 'I don't think so,' I said, but didn't take it any farther. I still didn't know who he *was* involved with.

'I guess I was the cause of all that, too,' she said, and started to cry. 'I caused it all.'

'No, that's not true,' I said. 'You were a pawn in the game, like a lot of us.'

'It was all over between us before he ever got in trouble,' Doe went on, purging the memory of Lukatis. 'He wouldn't accept that. He kept calling, sending me cards, leaving little gifts. Then I saw him one day and he told me things were going to be different. He called it his big score. I had no idea he was going to . . .'

She let the sentence drift off. She was having a lot of trouble finishing sentences.

That's when I told her about Sam Donleavy. Her shoulders sagged as the story unfolded. Tears welled in her eyes. The shock of disbelief pulled at her face, like the heavy hand of time. I took her in my arms and held her as tightly as I could and let her sob it out.

Then I heard the throb of heavy engines outside. There was a lot of yelling and laughter, people entering the other room. A few minutes later there was what sounded like an angry exchange, although I couldn't tell for sure who was talking to whom, or what the rhubarb was all about. Then the door opened.

The lights of Thunder Point Marina twinkled like stars on the bay a half mile away. Stick hunched down in the cockpit of the sailboat, his hat pulled down over his eyes so the wind wouldn't blow it off. There was a strong wind coming in from the southeast and the sails were full, billowed out like shrouds above him in the darkness. He had the sheets pulled in as tight as he could and the boat was keeled low in the water. The waves bounded past his elbow like a river on a rampage.

For ten minutes he had been watching Costello's yacht as it sailed into the inlet from open water and headed for the marina. Now it was pulling into the dock.

He set the tiller, tied it down, reached under the seat, and pulled out a waterproof bag. First he took out the .357 and checked the chamber. It was loaded with controlled-expansion treasury rounds. Then the 180, his little jewel. He checked the silencer and snapped a 180-round drum into the chamber, mentally ticking off his firepower as he did. He turned on the laser scope and watched the little red dot dance across the swollen sails. Next came the M-16, the old standby, fully loaded with a thirty-shot clip. He took a forty-millimetre grenade from the bag and inserted it in the grenade launcher under the barrel. Finally he got the ammo bag, which held two drums for the 180, six clips for the 16, six grenades, and five quick-loads for the Magnum.

Not bad. Seven grenades and 786 rounds of ammo.

412

He mentally counted the enemy: Costello, Bronicata, Chevos, and two other gunmen on the boat. Nance, Sweetheart Pravano, and at least three others he could think of inside the marina, and two guards with sawed-off shotguns on the dock.

Thirteen. About sixty rounds per man plus the grenades. Piece of cake. He'd been up against a lot worse.

He adjusted the night sight on the M-16 and checked out the deck of the yacht. There they were: Costello, Chevos, Bronicata, Drack Moreno, all the heavyweights but Nance and Pravano, who had to be inside somewhere, and Cohen, who was probably home in bed.

Beautiful, he thought. The timing couldn't be better. Just one big happy family.

That was fine about Cohen. Cohen belonged to Jake. The rest of them were his. He started smearing black shoe polish on his face.

This time it was Dutch who snatched up the phone when it rang. He was waiting for the call. It was Cowboy Lewis, patched in from the police helicopter.

'We spotted 'em, Dutch. Costello's barge is pullin' in to the private dock on the back of Thunder Point Marina right now.'

'You sure it's him?'

'It is unless he cloned that boat of his. Ain't another one around here like it.'

'How far away are you?'

'Half a mile, maybe.'

'Can you get down low enough to check the parking lot for that cinnamon Eldorado without getting your kiester blown off?'

'We'll have to use lights.'

'Okay, but be careful. We're heading out there anyway, just in case. I'm tired of sitting on my duster back here.'

'See ya,' said Lewis.

Stick trimmed his sails and slid quietly past the end of the dock. The two guards were leaning against the side of the yacht, bullshitting.

Stick studied the layout. The marina was to his left, separated from the private dock by a concrete wharf and twenty feet of water. A walkway led from the dock up to the house.

A hundred metres maybe, no more, from dock to house.

Plenty of trees for cover plus a terraced lawn that led down to the water.

Two big lights on a pole at the end of the dock. Fuck it, no problem.

The house itself was one-storey. That was good. No high ground for them. He swept the house with his night scope, planning his attack. From left to right, he made the kitchen, with a sliding panel out to a terrace; the main room, big, with a cathedral ceiling; a bedroom with a large picture window overlooking the water, and a circular waterbed in the centre of it; and a smaller room at the end of the house. At first he thought that room was dark, then he saw a sliver of light streaming through the drapes. That's where they had to be. And they were here. He knew that because Nance was here.

He counted heads.

Three in the kitchen, including Bronicata.

Five in the living room, including Moreno and Pravano.

Chevos, Nance, and Costello in the bedroom.

Eleven, just as he had figured. He still had the touch.

Behind him, out over the bay somewhere, he heard a chopper whop-whop-whopping. He ignored it. He swung around, headed straight for the pier, and pulled in his sails. He tied down the tiller, slung the ammo bag over his shoulder, grabbed the 180 and M-16, and clambered over the cabin to the front of his boat, stretched out on the deck, and got the submachine gun ready. The sailboat sliced through the water and sailed into the orb of light from the two big dock lights.

The door opened and Costello was standing there.

He looked like Yankee Doddle Dandy: white slacks, a blue blazer, a red silk scarf flouncing around his neck.

'Well, well,' I said, 'it's Captain America.'

By that time I was ready to take on the Russian army.

'You just never give up, do you, Kilmer?' he said, in that flat, no-nonsense lawyer's voice of his.

'Offhand, I'd say your little bubble has blown sky high,' I said.

'You talk big for a man who could be sixty seconds from his own funeral,' he said. 'Notice I said could be. I'm all that's standing between Nance and a bullet in your head.'

I ignored the threat. 'You're going across, Costello. First murder, now kidnapping. I've been wrong about you. I thought you were smarter than the rest of these wahoos. You just wear cuter clothes.'

Doe was hanging on to my hand like a drowning woman.

'Why don't you let her go?' I said. 'This is between us boys.'

414

'I didn't have anything to do with this,' he said. 'I've been out on the water for the past four hours. My cuffs are clean.'

'I can hardly wait to see the look on the jury's face when you run that one by them.'

He pulled a chair over and sat down in front of us.

'The monitor's turned off,' he said. 'So we can talk straight. First of all, Nance and you have had this hard-on for each other for a couple of years. I'm not responsible for his actions. And from the looks of him, you could be looking at a case of police brutality, anyway.'

'And what's the lady here guilty of, holding my coat while I did it?'

'I'll admit that bringing you two out here was bad judgment on somebody's part, but we can work all this out.'

'Good, I'm glad you see it that way,' I said. 'If you'll just arrange for a ride back to town, we'll be leaving.'

'Not quite.'

'You're skating on no ice, Costello. You may not be guilty of kidnapping, but holding us against our will sure as hell makes you an accessory.'

'I'm just trying to arrange a negotiation here,' he said, holding his hands out at his sides and smiling. 'So everybody comes out happy.'

'There's no way that can happen.'

'You're all bluff, Kilmer. Right now you couldn't lick a postage stamp in a court of law and you know it.'

'I've got Donleavy cold for murder one,' I said. 'And I've got Seaborn and his bank against the wall. Before it's over, they'll both be singing like Pavarotti.'

'I never had anything to do with either one of them,' Costello said. 'I may have said hello once or twice.'

'Oh, I get it. It's Save Costello's Ass Week, that's what we're talking about here? Okay, here are my terms. You give us Nance for murder and kidnapping, Cohen and his books for violation of the RICO acts, Chevos for smuggling and accessory to murder, and you become a friendly witness for the Fed. I'll see if maybe we can't get you off with five to ten.'

'Dream on,' he said with a laugh. It was his last.

The chopper was bearing in, coming closer.

Whah, whah, whah, whah . . .

Christ, he thought, just like the old days.

The guards didn't even hear the boat until it bumped the dock. He was ready.

'What the hell's that?' one of them said. They both turned towards the boat.

The laser's red pinpoint settled over the heart of the first one. He still had his shotgun over his shoulder.

Brrddtttt.

He went down like an elephant stepped on him. The other one started to scramble. He didn't have time to yell; he made a dash for the trees. Stick squirrelled a burst into the sidewalk, twenty metres in front of him. A dozen rounds whined off the walk and tore through his legs. He went down on his face. The second burst finished him.

Stick jumped ashore and ran towards the house. He blitzed the two big lights as he ran. The chopper was getting louder but Stick was committed. He didn't need any air for this one. This one was a piece of cake. Piece of fuckin' cake.

He dropped behind a tree, twenty yards from the door to the main room, swung the M-16 up, and checked the kitchen and the living room one more time. Bronicata was leaning over a large pot, sipping something from a spoon. The other two were standing next to him.

The five were still in the living room, gabbing. No women, thank God.

He swung the M-16 around and launched a grenade into the centre of the big room.

It happened fast.

Chevos opened the door and said, 'There's a helicopter coming in from the bay, flying pretty low.'

'Probably some businessman coming home late for dinner,' Costello said.

I could see through the door into a bedroom. Nance was sitting on a large, round waterbed, holding an icepack against his jaw. Beyond that there was a large, high-ceilinged room with half a dozen or so goons, and beyond that the kitchen. Bronicata was cooking something. Just a nice domestic get-together. The boys' night out.

Suddenly the living room erupted in a garish orange flash. The explosion followed an instant later and blew the room to pieces.

After that everything happened so fast, I remember it almost like a series of still pictures.

416

Sweetheart Pravano was lifted four feet off the ground and thrown against the wall. His face was gone.

Another hoodlum went out the back window head first as if he had been bounced off a trampoline.

Another fell to his knees in the middle of the room, clutching a bloody mess that had been his chest a moment before, and fell forward screaming 'Mother!'

Bits and pieces of furniture were thrown around the room like dust.

In the kitchen Bronicata was almost knocked into his soup pan.

The explosion blew Chevos face forward into the room.

I grabbed Doe, twisted her around, and went to the floor on top of her.

Costello was knocked off his chair.

An M-16 started chattering.

Bronicata did a toe dance in the kitchen while his pots and pans exploded around him, then fell across the hot stove as if embracing it.

His two pals were slammed against the wall and riddled.

In the other room Nance whirled and dropped to his knees behind the bed.

Chevos was on his knees, a .32 in his fist, his glasses hanging from one ear, hissing like a snake.

Costello rolled over and shook his head.

The smell of gunpowder flooded the room.

Nance turned towards me, his smashed face curdled with hate, his Luger in his hand.

I dragged Doe to her feet and pushed her out towards the far corner of the room, away from the doorway.

The Luger roared and I felt the round twirl through my arm and hit the wall beyond. I knocked Chevos' glasses off, grabbed his arm, and twisted him around, turning his gun hand down and away from his body.

The M-16 thunked again and the waterbed erupted. Geysers of water plumed up from it. Nance dived face down on the floor, huddling by the bed.

Costello pulled a .38 and leaped for the corner, grabbing at Doe.

I got the .38 away from Chevos, shoved him out of the way, jumped across the room, got a handful of Costello's jacket, and threw him against the other wall. It didn't stop him. His lips curled back and he swung the .32 up. I shot him twice in the chest. He fell back against the wall and dropped to his knees. The gun bounced out of his hand. His knuckles rested on the floor. He stared at my belt buckle, then his mouth went slack and dropped open.

The window beside me burst open. The drapes crashed down and then I heard the dentist's drill, an inch from my ear, hum its tune.

Brrdddtttt.

So much for Chevos.

I stuffed a handkerchief inside my jacket. The bullet wound burned. I could smell the almond odour of arsenic. The Stick jumped through the window with the grace of a dancer, the 180 submachine gun in one hand, the M-16 in the other. He held a finger to his lips and pointed towards Nance's room.

We heard footsteps run across broken glass and debris and smash a window. Stick jammed the 180 under his arm, pulled a .357 out of his belt, tossed it to me, and dived through the doorway into the bedroom, the 180 chattering back in hand as he went.

'He's heading for the water,' Stick yelled, and went over the windowsill and into a garden behind the place. 'Stay with the girl. He's mine.'

A shot whined between us and smacked the windowsill. Stick hunched down and took off in a crouch, jumping this way and that, threading his way through the trees. He didn't make a sound.

I went back into the other room. Doe was facing the wall with her hands over her face. I led her outside, to the side of the house away from the shooting.

'Stay right here, don't move,' I said. 'You'll be safe here. I've got to check the rest of the house.'

She nodded but her eyes didn't like the idea.

I went back inside.

A quick check turned up ten bodies in the house. Nobody had survived. The bomb, or whatever it was, and the burst from the M-16 right after it, had killed five gunmen in the living room and three in the kitchen.

There was a shot outside.

A muffled burst of M-16 fire.

418

I checked the .357 and half ran, half stumbled out the back door. Another burst, down near the water.

I started after them.

Nance was out on the dock. He started to get aboard the yacht. I heard the *pumf* of the grenade launcher and the back end of the yacht erupted. Nance was blown back onto the dock. He got to his feet, kept running away from Stick. The big luxury boat started to burn. In the light of the flames, I saw Nance scramble aboard a sailboat at the end of the dock, her sails furled loosely around the boom.

The Stick was hunched near the bowline. He moved away from me, towards the shadows on the far side of the sailboat. Then suddenly he leaped over its side.

His machine pistol was chattering.

Nance got off three shots before he started his dance. He went up on his toes, spun around, slapping his body as if bugs were biting him. His hands flew over his head, and he fell backwards on the deck like a side of beef. One foot kicked halfheartedly and he went limp.

I picked up the M-16 and ran out onto the dock. The Stick was walking awkwardly towards the stern, where Nance was lying.

'Stick!' I yelled.

He turned and crouched in a single move, then his shoulders drew up suddenly, his knees buckled, and he fell over on the deck.

I jumped aboard the sailboat and ran back towards the stern, where he was lying. I was ten feet from him when he raised up and lifted the 180. For a second I thought he was going to shoot me. I just froze there. He swung it up, to my left, and squeezed off two or three bursts. The bullets chewed a ragged line up the mast. Bits and pieces of wood flew out of it, followed by streams of white crystals. They poured out of the bullet holes in the shattered mast, sparkling like snowflakes, were caught in the wind and whisked away, out over the bay and into the darkness. Stick sighed and his head fell back on the deck.

I leaned over him. His eyes were turning grey.

He flashed that crazy smile.

'Wasn't it . . . one helluva . . . blast,' he said, in a funny, tired, faraway voice, 'while it lasted? Huh, Jake?'

'It was one helluva blast.'

His lips moved but he didn't say anything.

'You did it all, didn' you? Took on the whole Tagliani clan?' I said.

He didn't answer. All he said was, 'Burn . . . boat, 'kay?'

The Stick winked, then sighed, and it was all over.

Up near Chevos' compound, I could hear sirens and see red and blue reflections through the trees. People shouting. Doors slamming.

I turned Nance over. Half a dozen slugs had removed most of his chest. He wouldn't be soaking any more slugs in arsenic. The look frozen on his face was pure terror, the mask of a man who had died in fear. That's one I owed that I'd never repay.

I checked over the mast. It was on hinges, the kind that can be lowered for repairs and going under low bridges. I examined it closely, then picked up the machine pistol and racked the mast with gunfire. I started at the base and let the .22-calibre slugs tear it to pieces. As the slugs ripped up the birch pole, the shining white crystals sifted out, sparkling as the wind caught them and tossed them, twinkling, out over the water. I kept shooting until the gun was empty. The powder poured out. I sat down next to Stick and watched twenty-five million dollars' worth of cocaine dance on the wind and dissolve in the sea. It took a while.

I rolled Nance's body off the deck and watched it splash into the bay. Then I carried Stick ashore and fired a grenade into the engine of his sailboat. The back end of the sleek craft exploded, then burst into flames, I threw the M-16 and the 180 as far out into the bay as I could fling them and headed back up the hill to see what was happening.

75

VOTE OF CONFIDENCE

I laboured back up the hill towards the big cottage, lit now by the roving searchlights of a chopper that hovered a few feet above the roof. There were a lot of red and blue lights flashing, by now standard procedure every time the SOB's showed up anyplace.

A small fire was burning in one of the rooms and I could hear the throaty blast from a fire extinguisher. There was a lot of smoke and broken glass around the place. As I passed the kitchen window I got a brief look at the inside of the house. I could see down the length of the five-room cottage. I didn't stop to count bodies, I knew the score already.

The chopper swung away from the house and dropped down in a corner of the parking lot, throwing shards of glass and dirt in little waves below it. Cowboy Lewis jumped out and dashed out from under the whirring blades.

I found Doe in the back, standing with Dutch. Her eyes were the size of pancakes and she was trembling. I'm sure she was as confused as she was stunned by the sudden explosion of activity and by the destruction. I walked straight over to her and an instant later she was huddled against me, burrowing into my chest with her nose, like a puppy.

'What in hell happened?' Dutch asked as the rest of the group began to gather around us. He sounded like he was in shock. I realised it was the first time I had seen all of the hooligans together at one time. All but one.

'Nance lifted Mrs Raines and me off the street in front of her townhouse,' I answered. 'Stick hit the place and got us out. Just that simple.'

I looked back down the hill.

'We need to get somebody down there,' I said. You could hardly hear my voice. 'Stick's lying at the bottom of the hill.'

'Is he dead?' Salvatore asked.

'Yeah,' I nodded.

'Aw, shit,' Cowboy Lewis said. 'Aw, *shit!*'

He started down the hill and Dutch tried to stop him. 'We got an ambulance on the way, Cowboy,' he said gently.

'I'm gonna get him. Fuck the ambulance.'

'I'll go along,' Charlie One Ear said, and followed him through the smoke.

Callahan strolled out of the wreckage looking startled, with Kite Lange behind him carrying the extinguisher. 'All dead in there,' he said incredulously. 'Every last one of 'em. I count ten. Biggest total yet.'

'Why in hell would they kidnap you?' Salvatore said.

'Costello wanted to make a deal. He was willing to turn up Nance and Chevos and dump Sam Donleavy and Charles Seaborn if I'd get him off the hook.'

'Otherwise?'

'He was going to kill us.'

Dutch squinted his eyes and looked down his nose at me.

'How's that again?'

I had started another lie. I was getting pretty good at it by now.

'Let me give you the scenario, okay? Nance and Chevos were going to throw in with Bronicata and Cohen, get rid of the rest of the family, and take over the town. Nance was the official shooter. I don't know the reasons – what difference does it make anyhow? There's none of them left to disagree. Any problems with that?'

Dutch humphed and shuffled his feet around a bit.

'How about Nance?' Mufalatta asked.

'He's floating around in the bay,' I said. 'Stick's last official act.'

'We got the weapons? Any of that?' Dutch asked.

'They fell in the bay,' I said.

They all looked at each other, then back at Dutch, and then at me.

'How about the toot?' Zapata asked.

'In the mast of the sailboat that's burning down there,' I said. 'By now it's either in the bay or turned to charcoal.'

I looked at each of the hooligans in turn, waiting for comments. Only Dutch spoke up.

'It ain't gonna work,' he said. 'There's holes in it.'

'Fuck the holes,' Salvatore said.

'It'll work,' I said.

'How about Titan? Chief?'

'I'll take care of that.'

'It's some story,' Dutch said, shaking his head.

'The only one I got,' I said.

Cowboy came back up the hill with Stick over his shoulder. He laid him on the grass away from the building and started to take off his Windbreaker.

'Don't do that,' I said. 'Don't cover him up.'

He hesitated for a moment before nodding. 'Whatever you say,' he replied.

'Anybody else got any problems with the story?' I asked.

'What story?' Cowboy asked. 'I missed it.'

I repeated it for Cowboy and Charlie One Ear. Charlie One Ear raised his eyebrows and greeted the outcome with a wry smile. But his answer was instantaneous.

422

'No problem,' he said. Then one by one they all chimed in. No problem, they agreed.

'I've got to get the lady home,' I said. 'Anybody got a car I can use?'

Half a dozen sets of car keys were offered. I took Dutch Morehead's sedan. It was the only one I was sure was clean.

As we were walking away, the Mufalatta Kid said, 'Hey, Kilmer?'

I turned around. 'Yeah?'

'We're gonna need to replace Stick. Think about it, huh?'

'Thanks. I'll do that,' I said. And smiled for the first time in a couple of hours.

76
RETURN TO WINDSONG

When we got to the end of the lane leading to Windsong, Stonewall Titan's black limousine was parked in the drive. Luke Burger, the sheriff's man, was leaning against the bonnet of the car. He didn't take his eyes off me from the moment I stepped out of the car I had borrowed from Dutch.

I started towards the house and he said, 'Just a minute there. Gonna have to pat you down.'

'Don't even think about it,' I said, without looking at him or slowing down. I'd had enough of hard talk and tough people for a long time. I put an arm around Doe, led her across the long, green lawn to the house, around the porch, and up the front steps to the door. Warren, the family retainer, opened it before I got a hand on the doorknob, as if a psychic doorbell had rung inside his head. He was older and greyer and arthritis had slowed him down, but he was as starched and precise as ever.

'Good evening, sir,' he said with a smile, as if it were twenty years ago and I was dropping by for dinner. Then he looked closer at both of us and added, 'Gracious, are you all right?'

'We're okay,' I said as we went into the broad entrance hall. I had feared coming back to this house with its ghosts, long gone. But now I had too many other things on my mind, and so there was only curiosity. I figured the years would have distorted my memory of the place, but there were few surprises. I doubt that a single picture, vase, or stick of furniture had been moved in two decades. It was like a museum, preserving the past for future generations of Findleys, generations that would no longer carry the name, which had died with Teddy. Warren led us through the sprawling entrance hall with its twin curved staircases at the far end, and into a sitting room large enough to accommodate a legionnaires' convention.

Chief and Titan were waiting there. It was a room cloyed by nostalgia, all wicker and antiques, its tabletops choked with framed pictures of every size and shape – laughing pictures of Doe and Teddy as children, teenagers, college kids, and finally adults, if in fact they had ever grown up.

The old man looked up from his wheelchair with almost orgasmic relief when Doe came into the room. He held out his arms and she rushed into them, as if she had just returned from a long trip. Titan stood in front of the dormant fireplace, smoking a short, stubby cigar which he held between two fingers like a cigarette. You could almost feel the relief in the room, like a warm breeze seeping through the shuttered windows.

Chief was the first to speak. He looked at me over Doe's shoulder.

'Thank you,' he whispered. 'You're a brave man.'

'Not really,' I said. 'It was my stupidity that got us into trouble in the first place.'

Doe said, 'We're back, Daddy. That's all that matters.'

'We'll make it up to you, son,' Chief said, hanging on to her as if he were afraid the tide was going to rush in and carry her away.

'You don't owe me anything,' I said. 'It was Stick who bailed us out.'

'Stick?' Chief said.

Both he and Titan tried to cover their surprise, but they were not very good actors.

'A cop. You probably know him better as Mickey Parver,' I said, when it had sunk in.

'What happened out there, doughboy?' Titan asked. 'There hasn't been much in the way of radio communication for the last two hours.'

'We were too busy to bother,' I said curtly.

424

I gave them a sketchy report on what had happened from the time we left the Breezes until the shooting was over.

'Costello, Bronicata, Chevos, and Turk Nance are all dead, along with nine of their gunslingers,' I said.

'My God,' Chief whispered, clutching Doe even tighter.

'The four of them were behind the Tagliani killings,' I went on. 'My guess is that Nance did most of the work, although we'll never know for sure.'

Titan looked up as if a bee had stung him, then said, 'Well, I'll be damned.'

'It will all work out because Parver didn't make it,' I said. 'He went down saving me and Doe.'

Titan stared at me. A long minute crept by before he said, 'What do you mean, it will work out?'

'I mean for the record, it will work out.'

'I thought you just said Costello was behind it all, doughboy,' Titan said cautiously.

'I think I can sell the idea. Who's around to argue, right?'

Doe looked at me with curiosity.

'I don't understand,' she said.

'We don't need to talk about this right now,' Chief said.

'Talk about what? You couldn't get me out of the room now if you tried!' she protested.

'Let it pass,' Titan said, looking at his feet.

'No!' Doe said. She stood up. 'What is this all about?'

Chief said, 'It's nothing, baby. Just business.'

'What kind of business?' she persisted.

I said, 'The business of murder.' I wanted her to know. I wanted all the dark corners swept clean, once and for all.

'Tell her,' said Chief. He was too old and tired to argue.

'The thing is, we know better, don't we, Mr Stoney?' I said.

Titan turned his back to me and stared into the empty fireplace.

'Parver was an agent of the Freeze, the same outfit I'm in, but he was assigned to Dutch Morehead and his squad,' I said. 'Stick claimed he didn't know anything about the Cincinnati Triad until my boss, Cisco Mazzola, tumbled on to it a month or two ago. It went by me at the time. I've never been much on filing reports. That was one of my mistakes.'

'You mean you're capable of making a mistake?' Titan asked caustically.

'Oh, I made a lot of them,' I said. 'We all did.'

'For instance?' Titan asked.

'For instance, I had a five-man team in Cincinnati for three years working on the Tagliani case. There were pictures, newspaper clippings, snitch reports, and a link analysis on the Triad in our confidential files. Stick had spent six months studying our computer reports before he came here. He knew all about Tagliani and his bunch. Stick made the Triad right after he got here. Had to be. The question is, who did he take the information to?'

Nobody said anything. Doe still looked confused.

'No takers?' I said. 'Okay, I'll try. I think he came to you, Mr Stoney. You're the logical one, not Dutch. You're the one with the iron hand. You represented the law on the Committee. And you asked Parver to kill Tagliani.'

Titan turned around and glared hard at me from across the room.

'Now why would he do a damn fool thing like that?' Doe said, getting defensive.

'Two reasons I can think of. To protect Harry Raines' career, and to break the Triad's back.'

'Hah,' said Titan. 'I'm not a miracle worker.'

'You're only just finding that out,' I said, and before he could respond, I went on. 'I think you honestly believed that by getting rid of Tagliani, you could run the Triad off, the old "get out of town before sunset" routine. But it was a risky move. Then you found out I was coming down here and the whole story would come out, so you cut Stick loose in desperation. You knew the press would buy anything they were told. You could write the killing off as some kook slaying and, that failing, you could let Graves be the fall guy. As long as it couldn't be proved, Graves didn't give a damn. He never even denied chilling Cherry McGee, even though it was Tagliani who had the job done. And Stick cased the setup by hijacking Graves' cocaine shipment. That provided the final motive, if one was needed at all.'

Titan sneered at the idea.

'I'll admit, it was a rather naive notion on your part,' I said. 'It's understandable, though. You thought you were still playing by your rules; if you need to get rid of someone, do it the quickest way possible, like framing Tony Lukatis because he

426

was a potential threat to Raines. Or suggesting that Stick use him on the hijacking run and then get rid of him. Graves' people and Tony were both shot with the same gun – Stick's. Aw, hell, I guess when you've run a town for forty years, playing God comes easy.'

Doe, still confused, looked at me and said, 'Who's side are you on, Jake?'

'Nobody's. I'm just a simple cop trying to do his job. It's really none of my affair anyway, except I contributed to it.'

'How?' she asked.

'By convincing myself that Nance was the killer because I wanted him to be. For a while I even tried to build a case against Harry, because I wanted you. We all did a little God playing.'

'That's good thinkin', doughboy,' said Titan. 'There's only one thing wrong with it.'

'What's that?' I asked.

'It wasn't my idea. I didn't ask Parver to do a damn thing. It was his idea all along.'

'Why? What did he want out of it?' I said.

'Not one damn thing,' Titan said. 'Besides, if what you say's true, how come it didn't stop at Tagliani?'

I didn't have an answer for that, and still don't. I shrugged my shoulders. 'I don't know. It's moot, anyway. None of this can ever be proved.'

Chief finally spoke up. 'Then why bring it up?' he said sternly.

'Yes,' Doe said, 'why bring it up?'

Suddenly I was no longer the hero. Not even to Doe. I was the enemy, to be disposed of as prudently and quickly as possible.

'Because it's his game now,' said Titan. 'Right, doughboy? What do you want out of it?'

I thought about it for a moment, looking at Doe, standing beside her beloved Chief, as I now knew she always would. At Titan, with his bulldog jaw jutting out at me. I don't think it occurred to any of them that in the end, they had not only lost their precious town, but had cost Harry Raines his life. They would never stand accountable for their actions – that's one of the perks that comes with power.

'The same thing Stick wanted,' I said. 'Nothing.'

I turned and walked out.

77

EULOGY

Driving away from Windsong, I felt a sense of relief, not so much in leaving the place but because I had feared coming back to that house with all its ghosts, and now the fear was gone. If there were ghosts in Windsong, they were ghosts of the past, keeping alive a memory of laughter and youth and a time that was as sweet as the remembered taste of hot dogs and burnt marshmallows, the smell of campfires on the beach. If I had learned nothing else in coming back to this house, I had learned to treasure those moments of my life, not trample them in despair. And if that fleeting time, twenty years ago, was to be the only green summer of my life, at least it was mine. Nobody could ever take that away from me.

Cisco blew in the next morning, raising merry hell.

It was easy to lay the Tagliani massacre off on Nance, Costello and Chevos; there was nobody of consequence left to argue about it. Costello had kept Cohen at arm's length, so Cohen was in the dark. Since they were part of the conspiracy, Titan and Chief also had to go along. Besides, people hear what they want to hear. A hero cop is always good copy.

To Dutch and the rest of the SOB's, it was a state secret, never to be shared outside the team. As for Cisco, he kept mum, too, although he was still bugging me for my report two months later. I never filed it. So what else is new? But he wanted to know. He wanted answers to all the questions. And though I didn't answer a lot of them, and couldn't answer some, one thing kept bugging him until he finally put the question straight to me.

'You didn't get emotionally involved in this thing, did you, Jake?' he asked, over one of his breakfasts of garbage and vitamin pills.

'What do you mean?' I replied.

'I mean, you didn't have something going with the Raines dame, did you?'

I thought about that for a long time before I said no.

I don't really think that was a lie. Looking back, it should have

428

been obvious to me all along that a dalliance with a football player could never last, anymore than one with a lifeguard. For me, the patterns of Dunetown now fit together like the pieces of a jigsaw puzzle. Chief had erased me from Doe's life, just as Titan had erased Tony Lukatis; Harry Raines had filled the spot left by Teddy Findley, just as Sam Donleavy had taken the place once reserved for me. In the end, when the puzzle was complete, the picture was all sound and fury, and the irony was that Tagliani, who was never really a part of it, was the catalyst that brought it all tumbling down. Uncle Franco had come to Dunetown seeking the same kind of things we all want. He thought he could buy respectability. All he bought was the long, dark, forever tunnel. The one with no light at the end.

Looking back on it now, I think maybe the Stick, in his own way, was looking for the same things too. I'll never know the answer to that, but I'd like to think that he wanted to put some sense of order back in his life, to find something of value to replace the values he had lost in that faraway place all of us would like to forget and never will. Or maybe he had simply lost that dream forever. Maybe he was just doing what he did best, the best way he knew how. Whatever he wanted, I hope he found it. I hope death is kinder to him than life and, like all our fallen comrades, he is in some special place reserved for those who stalked the rim of hell and never come back.

One thing for damn sure, Stick had one fine sendoff. He was buried in that beat-up hat of his. The hooligans were the pallbearers and there was an honour guard and Dutch read a eulogy that had everybody weeping. And there was a bugler playing taps and another, off somewhere in the cemetry, echoing its sad eloquence. Everybody was there but Doe. Beautiful Doe, elusive to the end. But DeeDee Lukatis was there, and Lark, and Cisco. And Chief Findley and Stonewall Titan showed up. Salvatore even wore a tie.

SHARKY'S MACHINE

For my wife, Candy,
with love and affection always

ACKNOWLEDGMENTS

To these special people for their love, encouragement, and support before and during the writing of *Sharky*:
to my mother and father; to my children, Cathy, Bill, Stan, Melissa, and Temple; to Carol, Temp, and Julie; to my dear friends, Marilyn and Michael Parver, Carole Jackowitz, Mardie and Michael Rothschild, Leon and Judy Walters, DeeDee Cheraton and Ira Yerkes, Arden Zinn, and Larry and Davida Krantz for 'The Nosh'; to three generous and indulgent editors from the past, Al Wilson, Howard Cayton, and especially Jim Townsend; to Delacorte's Helen Meyer, a legendary woman; and my new friends, Ross Claiborne and Bill Grose for their dazzling enthusiasm; to my editor, Linda Grey, whose warmth and kindness made it easy and whose brilliance made it better; but most of all, to my dynamic and unerring agent, and devoted friend, Freya Manston, who made it all come true.

*Our deeds will travel with us
from afar,
And what we have been makes us
what we are.*

GEORGE ELIOT

PROLOGUE

Chapter One

NORTHERN ITALY, 1944

It had been dark less than an hour when Younger and the two sergeants finished loading their equipment on the three mules and prepared to head north towards Torbole and the rendezvous with La Volte. The young captain was excited, his eyes flashing as they smeared boot black on their faces. He was like a football player just before the first whistle blows, charged up, fiery with nervous energy. Harry Younger was perfect for this kind of cloak and dagger stuff; it was like a game to him. You could almost hear the adrenalin pumping through his veins. When they had the mules ready, Younger took out his map one more time and spread it on the side of an ammo box strapped to the flank of one of the mules and held his flashlight close to it. He went over the details once more and everybody nodded. The paisanos stood back from the group and smoked American cigarettes and said nothing.

When he was finished, Younger smacked his hands together and then ran one hand through his crew cut several times and pulled his cap down over his head. Then he took Corrigon by the arm and led him away from the group, off by himself.

'How ya doin', buddy-boy?' he asked Corrigon.

'Four-o,' Corrigon said, but there was an edge in his voice.

'Sure you're okay?'

'Yeah, yeah, fine, sir.'

'You're not gonna choke up on me, are you, chum?'

Corrigon smiled. 'I wouldn't dare,' he said.

'That's m'boy. Look, it's a piece of cake, Corrigon. I've done this, shit, half a dozen times. You been in here for two days, right? Not a sign of a fuckin' Kraut anywhere around. Don't think about what might go wrong, think about how simple it's gonna be.'

'Yeah, sure,' Corrigon said. *Will you knock off the pep talk, for Christ's sake!*

'I'll make you a bet. I'll bet we all come outa this with Silver Stars. I know this La Volte, see. He's got every fuckin' paisano guerrilla in north Italy up his sleeve. It'll be a little Second Front, up here. They'll kick the Krauts in the ass and we'll be across the Po before Christmas.'

'Yeah, right, right.' Corrigon tried to sound enthusiastic.

'You know why I picked you for this end, Corrigon? Hunh? Because Pulaski and Devlin there, they been sluggin' it out all the way since Anzio. If anything goes wrong, we're between you and the Heinies, if there *are* any. And we been in here now two days and not a sign, not even any recons overhead. Hell, buddy, God lost his galoshes in here. Nobody's gonna bother us.'

Corrigon was beginning to feel a little better. *You oughta be a coach*, he thought. *You'd have the whole team playin' with broken legs.*

'Feel better?'

Corrigon nodded. 'I'm okay, Captain. Believe me.'

Younger laughed, his all-American smile flashing through the blackface. 'What the hell am I pumping you up for? Look, two days, we'll be back in Naples. I'll swing a seven-day pass for all of us out on Capri and the drinks'll be on old Bud Younger.'

'You're on,' Corrigon said.

Younger slapped him on the arm. 'Don't break radio silence until you're set up. You won't hear from us unless there's trouble. When you're ready, give us a call and we'll be back at you. We won't be a mile away from you when they make the drop.'

'Right.'

Younger walked back to Pulaski and Devlin and said, 'Okay, let's saddle up.' They started off to the north into the black night.

'See you in a couple hours,' Younger said jauntily and then the darkness swallowed him up. Corrigon didn't move for a couple of minutes. He felt suddenly lonely. Fear tickled his chest. Then finally he turned to the two paisanos and swung his arm and they started off towards the lake. Fredo led the way with Sepi bringing up the rear, a tight little group walking almost on each other's heels. In less than an hour they reached the bluff overlooking di Garda. They lay on their stomachs on top of the ridge and Corrigon

14

could hear the wind sighing across the lake and feel its cool breeze on his cheeks. Somewhere down below, a hundred yards away perhaps, water slapped against a shore.

'Garda,' Fredo whispered, pointing down the opposite side of the slope. 'Yeah, *si*,' Corrigon whispered. It would have been nice, he thought, if just one of these Eyeties could say something in English besides 'cigarette' and 'chocolate.' But then, why should he complain? The only Italian he knew was 'fig-fig' and a couple of cusswords.

Typical army. Three guys behind the German lines and they can't even talk to each other.

Corrigon took out his binoculars and scanned the darkness. Here and there small diamonds of reflected light shimmered on the rough surface of the big lake. A wave of fear washed over Corrigon and then it went away. He reached into the breast pocket of his field jacket, took out the rice-paper map, and spread it on the ground beside him, holding a tiny penlight over it. Fredo looked at it for a moment or two and nodded vigorously, smiling with a row of broken teeth,. and pointing to a spot on the northeast shore of Lago di Garda. It was almost exactly on the perimeter Younger had laid out for him.

'Phew,' Corrigon murmured with relief.

'*Buono*?' Fredo asked. Corrigon nodded. '*Si*, very *buono*. Uh, the flares, uh, la flam, flame, uh ...'

'*Ahh, si*,' the guerrilla answered and nodded again as he reached into the khaki duffel bag and took out one of the railroad flares. He was a nodder, this Fredo. The flare was eight inches long with a short spike attached to one side and a pull fuse on the bottom. There were twelve in the bag. Fredo and his companion, Sepi, knew exactly what to do. They had been rehearsing all afternoon, ever since Captain Younger had dropped in and made contact with La Volte. Fredo tapped Corrigon's shoulder and pointed down at his wrist.

'Ten to eight,' Corrigon said.

Fredo puzzled with it a minute and then smiled again. 'Den, den,' he said, wriggling ten fingers in the corporal's face.

'Yeah, right, *si*, ten more minutes.' He pointed to the duffel bag and then down the hill towards the lake and Fredo and Sepi moved out without a sound. Corrigon

15

listened for a full two minutes and heard nothing. They were good, no doubt about that, like cats tiptoeing on sand.

He snapped open the khaki cover on the radio and cranked it up, then spoke softly into the headset.

'Spook One, this is Spook Two. Do you read me. Over.'

The radio crackled to life, much too loud, and Corrigon quickly turned the volume down. Sweat broke out in a thin line across his forehead, smearing the black shoe polish on his face. His hands were wet. And they were shaking.

'Spook One to Spook Two. Reading you loud and clear.'

'Spook One, we're set up. No trouble so far,' Corrigon said.

'Roger, Spook Two, and we're affirmative also. Any signs yet?'

'Negative. We got' – he looked at his watch again – 'seven minutes.'

'That's roger and we're in synch. Out.'

'Out,' Corrigon said and cradled the headset. He was lying on his stomach, chewing unconsciously on his thumb, wondering what the hell he was doing there, when he heard a sound beside him. An electric shock of fear shot through his chest and he reached for his .45 and turned on the penlight. Fredo grinned back at him.

Corrigon sighed with relief. 'All set? Uh, okay?'

'*Si*, oh-kay.'

He snapped off the light and lay with his eyes closed, listening. He thought, What the hell am I worried about? It's a fairly simple operation and these guys do it all the time. The sector was isolated, no major roads anywhere near. Why would there even be any Germans around? He began to relax.

At first it was hardly a sound. It was a low rumble, like distant thunder, then it built, growing into the deep, solemn throb of four engines, coming in from the south.

'Now,' he whispered sharply and Fredo and Sepi were gone. The roar grew and then burst overhead, so low he could almost feel the slipstream of the B-24 as it passed overhead.

Pop, pop, pop, pop, pop, pop, one after another the flares sizzled to life as Fredo and Sepi ran along the two lines they had set, pulling the fuses, marking a twenty-yard strip between Corrigon and the lake. Corrigon threw the shoulder strap of the radio over his shoulder and ran down the hill after them. The plane wheeled hard and started back down the run towards him, its engines whining at full speed. It was then Corrigon realized the wind wasn't coming off the lake at all. It was coming from behind him, blowing streams of smoke from the flares out over the lake.

'Holy shit!' he cried aloud. The plane was almost on top of them, roaring down the lakeside. He was vaguely aware of the engines backfiring as he slid the radio off his shoulder and knelt beside it, frantically cranking up the generator.

'Spook Two, this is Spook Two to Angel. Go around, go around, the wind's . . .'

Too late. The bomber rumbled overhead. A second later he heard the faint *fump* as the first chute opened, then another and another . . .

It was then that Corrigon became painfully, terrifyingly aware that he had not heard the engines backfiring. It was gunfire. Gunfire from Spook One's position half a mile uplake.

There were flashes jarring the black sky, the rapid belch of a German burp gun, a faint agonized scream, the hollow crack of a grenade. Fredo and Sepi, etched in the ghoulish red glare of the flares, turned sharply and ran back down the line, kicking over the flares and throwing sand on them.

The first parachute, a grey ghost with its heavy load swinging below it, plopped into the lake. It sank immediately.

'Spook One, Spook One, what the hell's going on?' Corrigon yelled into the radio.

'Bandits, we got band . . .'

An explosion cut off the transmission. Fire swirled up into the black sky and vanished. Then a machine-gun chattered, no more than twenty yards away, and Fredo, running, leaped suddenly into the air. His back arched. Tufts flew from his ragged jacket. He fell on his face, arms outstretched in front of him, rolled over on his back, and lay still, his feet crossed at the ankles. Sepi turned and started back towards Fredo.

'No!' Corrigon cried. It was too late. The machine-gun chattered again. Bullets stitched the ground around Sepi's feet, snapping his legs out from under him. He screamed and fell, skittered along the ground, started to get up to his knees, and was blown back into the air, dangling for an instant like a puppet, then dropping in a heap as the earth around him burst into geysers of death.

There were still flares burning behind Corrigon, but there was no time to bother with them now. Farther up the shore more explosions rent the night, more flames licked the sky. A burst of gunfire tore the radio to pieces. Corrigon veered, started running, hunched over, towards the safety of darkness. He slung the tommygun under his arm, firing several bursts behind him as he ran. He was almost to the top of the hill, almost outside the shimmering red orbit of the flares, when he felt something tug at his shirt, felt fire enter his side, boring deep and burning his insides.

He staggered but did not fall, dove to the ridge, and rolled over the top as a string of bullets chewed up the crest of the hill behind him. Pain flooded his body, seared his lungs, filled his chest.

'AHHHH, G-O-D D-A-A-A-M-N!' he screamed and crawled back to the ridge, laying the tommygun on the ground, pulling it against his cheek. Below him, shadowy figures moved towards the remaining flares. He squeezed the trigger. The gun boomed in his ear, shook him, jarred the pain deep inside him, but he kept firing and screaming. One of the figures whirled and fell, then another. A third turned and ran back towards the darkness, and Corrigon swung the gun, saw the bullets strike, saw the figure dance to his death. He kept firing, raking the three bodies until the barrel was so hot he couldn't hold it anymore. He struggled to his feet, pulled the rice-paper map from his pocket, and stuffed it in his mouth, feeling it dissolve in saliva as he started to run.

He did not know how long he ran, only that each step was worse than the last and the pain in his side seared deeper with each one. Vomit flooded his mouth; he spat it out and kept going. His mind wandered back in time and seized on an old chant from his Boy Scout days, 'Out goes the bad air, in comes the good,' and it became a cadence that kept him going.

Darkness gobbled him up. He tripped, staggered, fell, felt cruel stones bite into his knees, and ignored them. 'Out goes the bad air, in comes the good,' lurching back to his feet and running on. 'Out goes the bad air, in comes the

18

good,' running through a black void with his eyes closed and then he smacked headlong into a wall and his forehead burst open like a tomato and he bounced backward and landed in a sitting position and madness seized him. He pulled his .45 automatic from the holster and in a rage fired over and over again at the wall, and then for no reason at all he started to giggle. Sitting there with his side shot apart and his head split open and a pistol jumping in his hand, lost in the middle of an alien land and alone, totally alone, with death snapping at his ankles, Corrigan laughed and the laughter turned to sobs. Once more he got to his feet, felt the wall, staggered along it to a corner and, turning, felt the gritty rust of a latch. He lifted it and went through the door, and leaned on it, closing it behind him.

Silence. And it was blessed. He felt for his penlight, but it was gone. Then his fingers touched the cold metal of his Zippo lighter. He took it out, snapped the flint, and held it high over his head. He was in a shed of some kind, abandoned except for spiders busily weaving webs in the corners. He walked to the opposite side of the small room and sat against the wall, facing the door.

The pain in his side hit him in waves, subsiding, then washing back through him and subsiding again. He heard himself groaning and he snapped the carriage on his .45 and ejected a bullet into his lap and put it between his teeth.

You're crazy, Corrigon, crazy as shit, sitting here in the dark actually biting on a bullet.

But it helped and finally, as he leaned against the wall trying to make peace with the fire inside him, he passed out.

When he regained consciousness, he was bathed in sweat, the bullet still between his teeth. He looked at his watch. Ten-o-five. Two hours.

Then he heard the voices. Low, cautious. At least two of them, talking rapidly. He strained to make out words. The beam of a flashlight filtered through the cracks of the shed. They were nearer now, at the door. He heard the latch lift from its rusty hook.

Corrigon sat straight up. He held the .45 in both hands and aimed it at the door and waited, biting down hard on the bullet, blinking the sweat out of his eyes. The flashlight beam fell on his face. He squeezed the trigger and the pistol plinked. Empty.

19

Corrigon's shoulders sagged. He lowered the gun to the floor and spat out the bullet and raised his head towards the ceiling, closing his eyes and waiting for it to come.

The flashlight beam lowered and picked out the gun.

'*Americano*,' a voice said.

'*Si*,' came the answer.

'*La ferita è molto sanguinosa. E gravemente leso.*'

'Ummm,' said the other one.

'*E morto?*'

'*No.*'

'*Buono.*'

Buono? That was *good*. What were they saying? Something about blood, death. A jumble of words he could not understand.

One of them was very close now, leaning over him. Then he said, very slowly, 'You are lucky, *amico*. That the gun was empty. I would not want to kill you.'

Corrigon opened his eyes.

The Italian lowered the flashlight and in its reflection, Corrigon could see the two men. The man who had spoken to him was tall and lean with grey hair and a jawline like granite. The other one was younger and shorter and had shoulders like a football player.

'My name is Francesco. *Capisce?* Francesco.'

Corrigon managed a feeble smile.

'Hi, Francesco,' he said in a voice hoarse with pain and exhaustion.

'That is Dominic. He does not capisce English.'

'*No capisce*,' Dominic said and smiled from embarrassment.

'That's okay, I no capisce Italiano.'

'*E ufficiale?*' Dominic said.

'He says, Are you an officer?' Francisco said.

'Shit, I'm a goddamn corporal.'

Francesco turned to Dominic. '*No. Sottuficiale.*'

Dominic shrugged. Then he held up a tommygun. '*Abbiamo udito colpi e trovato una mitragliatrice.*'

'We heard the shooting and we found this gun on the hill.'

'I think it's mine,' Corrigon said, then: 'Who are you?'

'Farmers.'

'Not partisans?'

20

'*Non siamo guerriglieri, ma siamo simpatizzanti.*' Dominic said.

'He says, we are not guerrillas, but we are sympathetic to the Americans.'

'*Grazie.*'

Everybody nodded.

'Do you know La Volte?'

Francesco looked puzzled. '*La volte? The Fox.* What is that?'

'Shit,' Corrigon said, 'I'm too tired to go into it.'

Dominic said, '*I tri altri sono morti.*'

'*Si,*' Francesco said and, turning to Corrigon, told him, 'The other three *Americani* are dead. I am sorry.'

'Ah, Jesus.'

'Pray for yourself. It is too late for them. What are you called?'

'Corrigon. Johnny.'

'*Buono*, Jah-nee,' Francesco said and he took a dagger from a sheath in his boot. Corrigon's smile vanished and he stiffened. 'Easy,' Francesco said, 'I must cut the shirt. There is much blood.'

Corrigon lay back and listened to the blade slicing through the cotton shirt. He felt a finger probe his side and it exploded with pain. He decided to think of something, of Major Halford calling him in, giving him the pep talk, telling him Harry Younger thought he was ready for a mission. 'It's really fairly simple,' Halford had said, 'just drop in, make the connection, supervise the drop and get out.' *Sure, nothing to it, Major. Like falling into a bear trap.* And Younger, all full of piss and vinegar, dreaming about all the broads lining up to rub his Silver Star. Only now it would be a Purple Heart. Posthumously.

And where was the big shot La Volte when all the shooting started?

'Hey, Jah-nee,' Francesco said. 'You are lucky. It just went in one side and out the other.' He whistled softly through his teeth. 'Just like that, eh, paisan? Lots of blood, but it could be worse.'

He reached into a first-aid kit on his belt and took out a small cylinder and a bandage roll. 'You have, how you call it, uh, a nose cloth, *capisce*?'

21

'Handkerchief?' Corrigon asked.

'*Si, si.*'

'Back pocket, left side.'

Francesco took it out, tore it into two strips, and made patches of them. He sprinkled grey powder on the entry and exit wounds. 'Penicillin,' he explained. Then he and Dominic bound up the wound.

'Our town is Malcesine. About three kilometres. Can you walk?'

'How far's that?'

'Two miles maybe.'

'I'll do an Irish jig for two miles to get outa here,' Corrigon said.

The two Italians helped him to his feet. The pain swelled back through him, but he clenched his teeth and tried to ignore it.

'Tough guy, eh, *amico*?' Francesco said.

'Yeah, sure, tough guy, that's me,' he groaned. I'll tell you what I am, he thought, I'm a simple, dumb, dogface, eighty-two-dollars-a-month-plus-combat-pay-corporal from Clarefield, Pennsylvania, and I used to drive a delivery truck for my brother-in-law's brewery and it makes about as much sense me being here as it would to put army shoes on a fucking French poodle but I ain't *so* dumb that I buy that shit about you two being farmers when you have knives in your boots and penicillin on your belts but I'm not gonna argue with anybody right now so let's stuff all the Dick Tracy bullshit and get the lovin' hell outa here fast and maybe, later on, when we can put our feet on the table over a little pasta and vino somebody will tell me what happened back there and why everything went to hell so fast.

But Corrigon hurt too badly and was too tired to think much more about it. All he knew for sure was that Captain Harry Younger and Sergeant Joe Pulaski and the other noncom, Devlin, were dead and Major Halford's operation had bought the farm. And right now four million dollars in gold was lying on the bottom of Lake Garda.

Chapter Two

HONG KONG, 1959

The morning sun blazed off the wings of the plane from Tokyo as it banked sharply over the edge of the bay and began the long descent to the runway that jutted out over Victoria Harbour. In the back of the crowded DC-6 tourist section the stewardess, a beautiful Oriental woman who spoke flawless English, picked up the interphone and began her final announcements:

'Welcome to Hong Kong. In a few minutes we will be landing at Kai Tak Airport terminating PanAm flight twelve. Hong Kong means "Fragrant Harbour". The city is divided into several districts. At the front of the plane on your left is Kowloon Peninsula. Kowloon means "Nine Dragons" and was named eight hundred years ago by the boy-emperor Ping, who believed that dragons lived in the eight mountain peaks surrounding the harbour. His prime minister reminded him that there were really nine dragons, since the ancient Chinese believed that all emperors were dragons. The modern section at the tip of the peninsula is Tsimshatsui, the modern shopping centre of Hong Kong harbour.

'Hong Kong Island is at your immediate left and beyond it is the South China Sea. On the far side of the island is the harbour of Aberdeen . . .'

The man in the dark grey suit in seat 19B tuned her out. He took off his sunglasses and pinched the bridge of his nose. He had been flying for almost twenty-one hours with only three stops and his eyes and neck ached. Although he felt cramped in the tourist section, it was safer, less conspicuous than flying in front, where the passengers somehow seemed noisier and quicker to strike up conversations. Tourist section provided anonymity.

He took out the passport and checked it one more time. It identified him as Howard Burns of Bridgeport, Connecticut. It was a good alias, one he had used sparingly. Only Casserro knew about it. The passport was over a year old

23

and well-used. He had told Casserro, 'Get me something with a little mileage on it, nothing new,' and as usual old Chico had come through.

The man who called himself Burns was of medium height and slender with a few grey streaks in his close-cropped black hair. He was dressed inconspicuously in a business suit and wore dark glasses, and he had slept most of the way from Tokyo, awakening once to eat a warm snack. His food had been cold when he got it, but he ate it without complaint to avoid attracting attention to himself.

He shook off the effects of the arduous trip and, reaching into his suit jacket pocket, took out a small pill which he casually swallowed without water. The amphetamine was mild, just strong enough to get his juices running again. Then he settled back and began ticking off details in his mind, hitting only key words: Peninsula Hotel on Kowloon Causeway. George Wan, Oriental Rug Company, phone 5-220697. Star Ferry to the island. Causeway Typhoon Shelter, Wharf Three. Twelve noon. Brown and tan Rolls-Royce.

Simple. No wrinkles. He settled back, feeling secure as the plane bumped down and taxied to the terminal. He moved casually through customs, his only luggage a small carry-on bag with a change of shirt, socks, and underwear and toilet articles. No pills, not even aspirin. Once inside the terminal he went to the money exchange and traded five hundred dollars for twenty-five hundred Hong Kong dollars. Then he went outside and found a taxi.

The drive to the Peninsula Hotel took only fifteen minutes. The manager, a short, stubby Oriental in a silk brocaded cheongsam, checked him in and presented him with an envelope.

'You have a message, Mr. Burns. I believe it is a package. May I have the porter get it for you?'

'I'll do it myself,' Burns said in a flat, brittle voice.

The manager rang a bell and the porter appeared and followed Burns across the lobby to the cluttered office of the concierge, where a small, middle-aged woman sat reading what appeared to be the morning paper. Burns tore open the envelope and removed a receipt and a key. He gave the receipt to the woman and received a new attaché case, which he refused to let the porter carry.

24

His room was on the fifth floor. It was old and elegant and faced the harbour. Across it, like a jewel shining in the morning sun, was the island of Hong Kong.

'Very nice,' he said and got rid of the bellman with a tip.

He sat on the bed and unlocked the case. Inside were a long-barrelled .22 pistol equipped with a silencer, a nylon cord four feet long, and a pair of latex surgical gloves. In the pocket at the back of the case were six bullets and a physician's envelope containing two pills. There was also a roll of cotton swabbing.

Excellent, Burns said to himself. So far nobody had missed a beat.

Burns put on the surgical gloves and then removed the cylinder and silencer of the gun and checked it with the precision of a toolmaker, examining the barrel and firing pin before reassembling it and dry-firing it twice. It was clean and freshly oiled, although not new. Satisfied, Burns loaded the six bullets into the cylinder and replaced the gun. Then he took out the nylon cord and, wrapping it around both hands, snapped it sharply several times. He doubled the cord, tied a squareknot midway between the ends, and put it back. He put one of the pills in his suit pocket and placed the other back in the envelope, took off the gloves and dropped them in the case, locked it and put it in a drawer.

He checked his watch. Eight-forty. He opened the carry-on bag and from his leather toilet kit took out a small travel clock. He set it for 11:15, then called the operator.

'I'd like to leave a call for eleven fifteen, A.M.,' he said. 'That's two and a half hours from now.'

'Yes, sir,' said the operator, 'eleven-fifteen A.M.'

Then Burns loosened his tie and lay back on the bed, folded his hands across his chest and fell immediately to sleep.

At 11:25, Chan Lun Chai closed his antique shop, put a sign on the door announcing that he would be back in ten minutes, and stepped into sweltering Cat Street. Shimmering heat turned the crowded confines of the old Morlo Gai shopping district into dancing mirages as he threaded his way through the crush of Chinese nationals, tourists, and sailors, towards the phone booth half a block away.

25

A heavy-set Englishman, overdressed for the heat, his tie askew, and sweat pouring into his shirt collar, was bellowing into the phone while his wife, who was almost as tousled as he, waited outside the booth with her arms full of packages.

Unperturbed by the heat, Chan stood nearby, studying the window of a jade shop. He was short and wiry, a man in his mid-thirties, dressed in the traditional black mandarin jacket and matching pants. Only his glasses, which were gold-rimmed and tinted, seemed out of place.

Finally the Britisher left the booth fuming. 'Really! They say you can't make reservations for the Chinese Opera. Have you ever heard of such a thing? No reservations at the opera!' They trundled off through the crowds towards Ladder Street.

Chan stepped into the booth and looked at his watch. It was exactly 11:30. Seconds later the phone rang. He answered in a slow, quiet, precise voice:

'Royal Oriental Rug Company.'

'May I speak to Mr. Wan, please?' The voice on the other end was sharp and irritating, like the sound of firecrackers exploding.

'Which Mr. Wan?' Chan said.

'George Wan.'

'This is George Wan speaking. May I help you?'

'This is Mr. Johnson.'

'Welcome to Hong Kong, Mr. Johnson. Did you get the package?'

'Excellent. Everything's satisfactory.'

'I am pleased,' Chan said.

'How about tonight?'

'It is all arranged.'

'Good. I should be back to you in three hours. Maybe four.'

'I will be here. May I suggest the sooner the better. It may be difficult, locating the object you seek.'

'I understand,' Burns said. 'I'll try to call back by two-thirty.'

'*Dor jeh*,' Chan said, 'which means "thank you". *Joy geen*.' And he hung up.

The shower and shave did not help much. Burns still felt

26

sluggish, his senses dulled by time lag and lack of sleep. After talking to Chan he went into the bathroom and took the pill from his pocket, popped it in his mouth, and washed it down with a full glass of water. He was hardly out of the room when it hit him, a dazzling shot, like a bolt of lightning, that charged through his body, frazzling his skin. He felt as though he were growing inside his own shell, that his muscles and bones were stretching out. He became keenly aware of sounds, the hum of the elevator and the muffled roar of a vacuum cleaner behind a door somewhere. His entire body shuddered involuntarily as he waited for the elevator.

Leave it to the Chinks, Burns thought. Whatever it is, it's nitro, pure nitro.

By the time the Star Ferry was halfway across the harbour, he felt ready again, his eyes bright and clear, his reflexes quivering like rubberbands stretched to the limit. He got out of the cab and let the hot breeze tickle his skin, watched the concrete skyline of the Central District draw closer. The buildings seemed to soar, telescoping up from their foundations and dominating the two mountain peaks at either end of the island. His heart was thundering and he felt a keen, familiar sense of anticipation and his penis stirred between his legs. Without thinking, he began rubbing his hands together. The exhaustion that racked him was jarred, splintered, purged from his body, like torn pieces of paper thrown to the wind. He got back in the cab.

The driver moved expertly off the ferry and down through the crowded slip, blowing his horn and ignoring the catcalls and shaking fists of the crowds of pedestrians. He turned left onto the Causeway, a wide boulevard, and then drove swiftly, due east towards the shelter, passing through Wanchai, the garish night-club colony with its neon signs of exploding invitations to the mid-day trade, and away from the skyscrapers of the Central District. A minute or two later the driver leaned his head back towards Burns but kept his eyes on the highway.

'Typhoon Shelter ahead, san. You have a place?'

'You know sampan three?'

'*Hai*.' The driver nodded.

'*Hai*, that's "yes"?' Burns asked.

'Yes, *hai*.'

27

'How would you say "no"?'

'*Um*.'

'*Um*, hunh? *Um, hai, um, hai*,' Burns repeated several times and began laughing and patting his knees like a drummer keeping rhythm with the words. Abso*lute* nitro!

The taxi turned off the Causeway and wound down a curved road towards the waterfront. The Typhoon Shelter was a triangular cove protected on the inland sides by tall concrete abutments. The driver stopped. Burns got out and looked down at the harbour. The cover was choked with sampans. Hundreds of the small flat-bottomed boats bobbed in the water, their mid-sections protected by hoods made of rice mats, their pilots standing at the tillers in the stern, beckoning to the tourists and calling out prices. Several of the sampans had woks in the bow and chests filled with beer and soft drinks, like floating delis. The wind carried the smell of cooking fish and shrimp up to the abutment.

Burns was overwhelmed by the sight. This was the China he had envisioned.

The driver stood beside him and pointed to a wharf directly below them at the bottom of the concrete stairs. Sampans hovered around it.

'Sampan three,' he said.

'Great. What I owe you?'

'Seven dollars,' the driver said.

Burns gave him eight and said '*Dor jay*', and the driver, smiling at his awkward attempt to say thank you, bowed and replied '*Dor jeh*', and was gone.

Burns walked to the eastern wall of the shelter and waited. At 12:05 a brown and tan Rolls, polished like a mirror, pulled up. The man who got out was tall and beginning to show the signs of overeating. He wore a white linen suit and a flowered sport shirt open at the collar. His receding hair was blondish and he wore a thick moustache and dark blue sunglasses. He walked with a cane of finely polished teak with an ornate dragon's head handle carved out of gold. The man stared down towards sampan three for several moments and then descended the concrete stairway. The Rolls drove away.

Burns waited for a full ten minutes, watching the roadway leading to the stairs and scanning the entire abutment

When he was sure the man had not been followed, he too went back to the stairway and down to the wharf.

The big man stood on the pier, haggling with an ancient and toothless crone who stood at the rear of one of the boats. A small child sat at her feet playing with an empty soda bottle. They appeared to be arguing.

'*Gow, gow,*' the woman yelled in a voice tortured with age.

The big man shook his head. '*Tie goo-why. Laok.*'

The old woman glared at him with anger. '*Laok. Laok! Hah! Um ho gow gee aw!*'

The big man laughed. Burns stepped up behind him and said, 'Why fight with the old crone? There's plenty of other boats around.'

The heavy-set man jumped and turned quickly, startled by the words. He stood close to Burns and the two men stared at each other for several moments. Finally the big man smiled, very vaguely, then said, 'She is telling me I am cheap, to stop bothering her. It is a game we play, *senhor*. She wants nine dollars, I offer six. I pay her seven and tip her two.' He spoke with an accent that seemed part Spanish, part German.

'*Gay doa cheen,*' the old woman yelled, '*um goy?*'

'*Chut,*' the large man replied.

She grumbled. She looked wounded. She chattered and pointed to the child. Then finally she motioned him aboard.

'Are you taking a sampan?' the large man said. 'Perhaps we can share a ride.'

'Sounds okay to me,' Burns said.

The big man offered his hand. 'I am Victor DeLaroza.'

'Howard Burns.' They shook hands.

'I am going to the Tai Tak,' DeLaroza said. 'It is the finest floating restaurant in the city.'

'What a coincidence,' Burns said. 'So am I.'

'Excellent. Are you a visitor?'

'Yeah,' Burns replied.

'Well, perhaps I will be able to recommend some dishes.' DeLaroza took seven Hong Kong dollars from his pocket and gave it to the woman. She counted it and glared at him. '*Aw tsung nay,*' she muttered. DeLaroza laughed. 'She says she hates me. When I tip her, she will tell me she loves me.'

Burns stepped into the sampan and walked to the seat in the mid-section. He was hunched over and walked with his

29

hands on the sides of the tenuous skiff, and he turned cautiously before he sat down. DeLaroza followed, walking upright with ease and sitting beside him.

'You do that like a champ,' Burns said to him.

'*Ho!*' the old woman cried out and cackled.

'She tells me "good",' DeLaroza said. 'I was like you at first, overly cautious. She is the oldest of the old. *Jung-yee Pau Shaukiwan*, the grandmother of Shaukiwan.'

'What's a Shaukiwan?'

'Shaukiwan is the Chinese settlement, a floating village around on the southeast side of the island. You have never seen greater poverty.'

The old woman stood at the rear, moving the scull with arms as thin as twigs, expertly guiding the sampan around the hundreds of other boats and moving it towards the open water of the harbour. Ahead of them, to the west, was a great three-storey junk, its pagodalike awnings stretching out over the water and its garish red and yellow trim gleaming in the sun.

'That's Tai Tak,' DeLaroza said. Behind him the baby started banging the empty bottle on the bottom of the boat.

'Hell of a place to babysit,' Burns said. 'What happens this thing, you know, dumps over?'

'She and the child will probably drown. He is her grandson. She watches over him while her daughter works in one of the whore-houses in West Point, the old city. When he is a little older, they will sell him.'

'Sell him!' Burns was shocked. 'Sell their own kid?'

'It will be better for him. He will be sold to a good family, possibly even British or American.'

'Jesus, don't they have any feeling for the family?'

'Life is harsh on the harbour,' DeLaroza said, and then, 'I almost bought the boy myself.'

Burns turned to him and stared for a moment at one corner of his sunglasses. Burns never looked anyone directly in the eye. Then he looked back at Jung-yee.

'It's all right, you can speak freely. She does not understand English.'

'You're crazy,' Burns said flatly.

'A little, I suppose.'

'You got pretty fat and sassy there, uh, uh . . .'

'Victor. V-i-c-t-o-r. I am Victor, you are Howard.'

30

'Yeah. Anyway, you learned a lot out here, only a coupla years, too.'

'You haven't changed much at all,' DeLaroza said.

'Yeah, well, a little grey hair maybe. Fifteen years is a long time, right? I wouldn't recognize you. Not at first anyway. The weight, the hair. You done something here too, around the eyes.'

'It is called a stretch. They pull the skin tight to the ears on both sides. Gets rid of the wrinkles. I do not have the proper bone structure for a face lift, but . . .' He let the sentence dangle.

'The accent's good too, pal,' Burns said. 'Now what's this about buying the kid? Some kind of guilt thing?'

'No, loneliness. And pride. I am building an empire and there is no one to carry on the line. When Victor DeLaroza dies, then what?'

'So what, that's what. When you die, who gives a damn?'

'They have a saying here. If a dragon smiles on you, you have luck. If two dragons smile on you, you have love. And if three dragons smile on you, you are immortal.'

'Quite the philosopher there, ain't you, Vic, old boy? Well, goes with the new look. We got a saying too. You can't take it with you.'

'Exactly. That is my point.'

'You got a lotta time. So far the dragon's been pretty good to you.'

'So far only one dragon has graced me.'

Burns did not answer immediately. DeLaroza took out a cigar, snipped off the end, and lit it with a small gold lighter. He puffed it until the end glowed evently. Then he turned abruptly to Burns, offering him one.

'I don't smoke. That a real Havana?'

DeLaroza nodded.

'I got a lotta pals, business pals, right? Gonna drop millions down there, that fuckin' Batista runnin' out like that. Castro's closing up the casinos, now the word's out he's gonna take them, just *take* 'em.'

'Castro is an enigma.'

'I don't know about that,' Burns spat out. 'He's a goddamn Commie thief is what he is. We oughta go in there, blow the whole dingo outa the pond with an A-bomb, you ask me. Start over.'

31

Burns's sudden vehemence startled DeLaroza. Then just as quickly the American's mood changed and he started to laugh. 'You hear about Castro going to a costume party. Stuck out his tongue and came as a haemorrhoid.' He laughed even harder at the foul joke and the old woman, caught up in his gaiety, laughed with him. 'Listen to that old crone,' Burns said and laughed even harder. DeLaroza puffed on his cigar. 'Anyway,' Burns continued, 'you got the golden touch, Victor.'

'We may be expanding again,' the big man said.

'How's that?'

'It is becoming more and more profitable to manufacture products out here in the Orient – Hong Kong, Singapore, Japan. Then assemble them in the States. There are certain tax advantages.'

'You thinking of opening up something in the States?'

'It's obvious to me now. In another year or so it will be obvious to many.'

'Well, you got the instincts there, Victor. I'll give you that. Fifteen years, you ain't made a mistake yet. I thought you were nuts, movin' out here from Brazil. What did I know?' He paused, then added, 'Don't you ever wanna stop, sit back, listen to the grass grow, drink a little vino?'

'Not yet. The bigger it becomes, the more challenging it is. We may have to go public. It is all becoming too big for one man. Too cumbersome.'

'Sell out, then.'

'Perhaps. Get out of all this, try something new, different. Something small.'

'Look, I don't care, see? I mean you do what you do. That's your end of it, I got no complaints, no complaints at all. Me, I'm here to do what I do, see? I figure, you used the Pittsburgh drop, it had to be something serious. I got here in three days, pal. Think about it. Had to get things set up, a passport, like that. I was twenty-fucking-one hours on the plane. I don't even know what day it is, flying up and down and around, across datelines, that kinda shit. You know what? I was on Wake Island for four hours, can you beat that? I went out, looked at the monuments and all. I never been this way before, Europe but never over here. For all I know, I get back, it's gonna be the day before I left. You just be careful, that's all. You get too greedy, you'll be like

32

the monkey, you know, kept puttin' his paw in the jar, bringing up a peanut, finally he puts it in there, grabs a whole fistful of peanuts and he can't get the fist out and he won't drop the peanuts and you know what. He got the old blasteroo, that's what.'

'I shall keep that in mind.'

'So what's the problem? What am I doin' here?'

Burns was beginning to sweat. He took off his coat and draped it over his lap.'

'You remember Halford, the major in Firenze?'

Burns thought for a moment.

'Vaguely.'

'He was in charge of Stitch. Tall man. Very straight, tough. Very smart.'

'Yeah, sure I do. The paisanos called him, what was it?'

'*Gli occhi de sassi*. Stone eyes.'

'Right. A very suspicious man. He didn't believe shit. What an asshole.'

'You know him. Four days ago I saw Halford, on a restaurant like the one out there. In Aberdeen Harbour. He is a colonel now, a full colonel.'

'Is that what's got you goin'? Hey, I hardly recognized you and I was *looking* for you. Is that what this is all about?'

'He recognized me. I am sure of it.'

'Ah, c'mon.'

'We were not five feet apart. I was paying the check and I turned to leave and he was just sitting down at the next table and we stood there and stared at each other and I swear, for a moment he almost said something. Then I got out, very quickly. But as we were pulling away in the launch I looked back up and he had come outside. He was at the rail, watching me.'

Burns said, 'Humh.'

'I have been terrified ever since. It is frightening, to be afraid to walk on the street. My company is in Mui Wo, on the island of Lantau, to the west of here. Only occasional tourists come over there, to visit the silver mines. And yet I have been afraid to go outside. Today, coming here, my stomach hurt. I sat in the back seat of the car looking out the window, looking at every face.'

'Take it easy.'

'It has been a nightmare.'

33

'So far you did everything right. You didn't try anything. No phone calls. Didn't try to get a line on him, right? Nothing to set anybody off?'

'No. I followed the plan. I contacted you and waited.'

'Okay. Good for you.'

'There is a danger. He may have reported it to someone.'

Burns said nothing. He stared straight ahead, his brain clicking off the options, the odds. Finally he said, 'Okay, we got to go on the assumption he didn't. I mean if he did, it's too late anyway. So we got to figure he's here on vacation, okay? Was he in uniform?'

'Yes.'

'Okay, nine, ten to one he's on a furlough. So it's a fluke. Maybe he got a little shot, see? Thought to himself, Hey, I know that guy. But it's fifteen years. You changed a lot. What were you then, anyway? I don't see him putting it together. I don't see that at all. Maybe, if anything, he's probably still trying to put his finger on it.'

Burns thought some more.

'Thing is, if he's on vacation, he's too busy having a good time. He's outa the element right now. He's thinking, maybe. Maybe even he's touched it around the edges. But it's a long shot, he made you. I promise you. What we gotta do, we gotta locate him fast and then. . . .' He snapped his fingers and smiled. DeLaroza stared at him and a chill passed through him. Burns went on:

'Okay, okay. You relax, see? You forget it. We have a good lunch, you go back over there to whatever, Mooey Pooey, whatever you call it, lay low another day. By tomorrow it'll be over. You don't worry, see? This is my end of it. This is *my* business. I'm glad you didn't panic. Anytime there's trouble, I handle that. What I don't want, I don't want amateurs fallin' in the soup, know what I mean?'

'Yes. Thank you.'

'Forget it. My problem. It's done. Besides, I may be needing to call on you one of these days. I may have to make a big withdrawal.'

'What happened?'

'Well, you know, this and that and the other thing. Some friends of mine, *used* to be friends of mine, they may have tumbled on to our little freelance thing down there in Brazil. It could be just I've got the butterflies like you. But

34

just in case . . .'

'How much?'

'I dunno. Couple hundred thousand maybe.'

'It will be no problem, my friend.'

'Good. One more thing. About Halford. I want a good description. And I'm gonna need money, Hong Kong dollars.'

'How much?'

'I dunno yet. Could be, maybe fifty thou Hong Kong. How late can you do business with the bank?'

'Up to six is no problem at all. It will come out of the box. The president of the bank and I are friends. We play golf together.'

'Ain't that sweet? Six is okay. I'll probably need to make the tap about five. Deliver it to my hotel. In a shoebox, wrapped up like I bought some shoes, had them delivered. You call me at five, I'll give you the tally. Where's the bank?'

'Right around the corner from the hotel. The China Bank, behind the old Supreme Court building just before you get on the Star Ferry in Kowloon.'

'No problem. You ain't five minutes away.'

'Right.'

'Okay, how about Halford? What's he look like?'

'His full name is Charles David Halford and he is a full colonel,' DeLaroza began, and then described the military man.

'That's beautiful. Look, you can forget it, okay, Victor? Now, what are we gonna have for lunch?'

'Well, I would suggest starting with shark's fin soup and then either the Shanghai crab or empress chicken . . .'

At 2:30, Burns made his call from a public phone booth in the lobby of the Excelsior Hotel, directly across the causeway from the Typhoon Shelter. Chan answered.

'Royal Oriental Rug Company.'

'Is Mr. Wan there?'

'Which Mr. Wan?'

'George.'

'This is George Wan.'

'It's Johnson again.'

'Yes sir. Do you have the information yet?'

'Yeah. An eagle colonel, U.S. Army, name of Charles

35

David Halford. H-A-L-F-O-R-D, Halford. Six-one to two, hundred-eighty pounds, white hair cut short, one of those curled-up-type moustaches. I'm guessing he's down from Tokyo or maybe the Philippines. I don't think he's here permanently. That's all I got.'

'It is enough.'

'I was planning, I'd like to be outa here tonight, know what I mean? Can it be handled that quick?'

'I feel certain, if there are not complications. Call back each hour. If there is no answer, I have nothing to report.'

'That's fine, just fine. Did you make the shipping arrangements?'

'Uh, yes, uh, you understand, there is a risk in moving the object about. There will need to be an additional charge for, uh, packing and insurance.'

'Of course. You get too greedy, I'll let you know. *Dor jeh.*'

'*Dor jeh.*'

There was no answer at 3:30. At 4:30 the line was busy and Burns began to get nervous. Another hour would be pushing the bank deadline. He waited a minute and tried again. The phone rang several times before someone answered.

'*Jo sun,*' a high, whining voice said.

'Is this the Royal Oriental Rug Company?' Burns asked.

'*Um ying gok yun,*' the voice said.

Jesus, he can't speak English, Burns thought.

'George Wan? You know, George Wan?' he said, speaking the name slowly and distinctly.

There was a disturbance on the other end, a flurry of Chinese words spoken in anger and then:

'This is George Wan. Hold a moment, *um goy.*' Then he heard him snap out a stream of Chinese, followed by another flurry. Finally: 'I am sorry. This man was using the booth for business calls. I had a small problem with him. Is this Mr. Johnson?'

Burns paused. Then: 'Where do you work?' His voice was flat, harsh, and suspicious.

'Royal Oriental Rug Company. It is George Wan, believe me.'

'Okay, what've you got?'

'The eagle colonel Halford is with military intelligence.

36

He comes from Korea by way of Tokyo and is on rest leave. It required many calls. I had to prevail on a friend in Japan in the Yakuza and . . .'

'Forget the road map, okay? I don't care where he came from, how he got here, all that. You got to understand, George, you and me we're in the same business. You don't have to jack up the price with all these details. All I want is essentials.'

Wan paused, then he said, 'Yes. Halford is at the Ambassador Hotel on Nathan Street in Kowloon. Everything is arranged for tonight.'

'You got the shipping thing set up?'

'*Hai, nin.*'

'I'm changing signals a little. It'll be two.'

'Two?'

'Yeah, two.'

'But I don't understand, who . . .'

'Think about it, George. You can figure it out. I said I wanted shipping *and* insurance, see?'

This time the pause was longer. 'That could make things very difficult for us, Mr. Johnson. It will really not be necessary to . . .'

Burns cut him off. 'Look, you come over on my turf, you got a job to do, we do it your way. This one we do my way. What happens afterwards, that's your problem. Whatever it's worth, okay?'

'I see,' Wan said. 'It will take a moment . . . uh, the price will . . . uh, I will have to ask sixty thousand Hong Kong dollars.'

'That's a little high, but I ain't arguing. You know where to pick it up?'

'*Hai.*'

'Five-thirty, it'll be there. Now, where do I go?'

'You have something with which to write?'

'I don't write anything down. You gimme the details once, I'll give it back to you word-for-word.'

'It is a place known as the House of the Purple Azalea in New Kowloon . . .'

Colonel Halford had fallen asleep on the balcony outside his room. He was still weak from dysentery. His nerves were shot. He was burned out. And even though his mental and physical condition were improving each day, it was easy to drift off in the hot afternoon sun.

As usual, he dreamed.

Violent nightmares.

The dreams were never the same, but they were alike. Unrelated scenes, spliced together into subliminal nonsense rhymes.

Fagments of fantasy and reality, leaping back and forth through time.

He was in Italy. An olive grove, standing beside a long conference table under the trees, talking to a group of American and Italian officers, but the words were gibberish, like a record played at triple speed, and he was interrupted by the sound of trumpets, and then bells, and sticks beating on pans. Everyone began to run so he ran too, blindly through the grove, past great numbers of soldiers lying dead on the ground, out of the grove to the rim of a high, steep hill and there, looking down, saw hundreds of North Koreans charging towards him and there was gunfire and explosions and men fell all around him screaming but the bullets passed through him and he felt nothing and then the Koreans reached the crest of the hill and ran past him as though he were invisible and he picked up a gun and fired over and over again but it was impotent. He ran after them, back to the conference table and now there were Americans and Italians and North Koreans standing at the table, judging him, pointing all around him to the bodies of the soldiers swinging from tree limbs. And he looked at them and he knew them but he could not put names with their faces and when he tried to speak to them, the words that came out of his mouth were foreign to him.

He awoke in a sweat. For a minute it was difficult for him to breathe. He stood up and took several deep breaths and stood watching the sampans and junks gliding lazily through the harbour. Below, the street was alive with the sounds of civilization and he began to relax.

He tried to ignore the dream, to concentrate on other things.

He thought about the man he had seen on the floating restaurant the other day and tried to place his face. He was sure he knew the man. Perhaps from Honolulu when he was stationed at Pearl. Or from the days in Tokyo, before

38

Korea. But the mental walls were still there, separating Halford from his subconscious.

He began to think about tonight. Perhaps he should not have accepted the invitation. The last time, in Tokyo, he had been embarrassed. The young girl had tried so hard, been so understanding and, ultimately, comforting. He was not sure that he wanted to risk so soon again the anguish of an emotional need he could not satisfy physically.

When he had left Tokyo for Hong Kong and terminated his three-month, twice-a-day therapy with Captain Friedman, it was like cutting an umbilicus. Friedman had recommended the four-week leave. 'Get out of here, try some of the things we've been working on,' he had told the sceptical Halford. 'Look, it's going to be like going to camp by yourself the first time. Scary, but exciting. You're going to be okay, Charlie. Thing is, don't be afraid to *try*. Remember what Bishop Chamberlain said in the seventeenth century: "It's better to wear out than rust out."'

An hour out of Tokyo old fears had begun chewing at his gut again, but he owed it to the doc to at least try. And he had to admit, in two weeks things had improved.

Then there was Kam Sing, who had gone to such trouble contacting his cousin here, arranging 'something special' for him. Yes, tonight he would have to try again. For months, Kam had been a faithful collaborator in Korea and he could not risk insulting the man who had become his friend.

He went into the bathroom and splashed water on his face and then fixed himself a Scotch and started to dress for dinner.

Burns had time for only an hour's nap before the phone jarred him awake.

'Seven forty-five, Mr. Burns,' the hotel operator said.

'*Dor jeh*,' he said.

'*Dor jeh*.'

A moment later the alarm went off. He closed up the travel clock and put it in the toilet case. The pill had worn off and he felt even worse than he had that morning. His mouth was fuzzy and his eyes burned. He took a quick shower, shaved, and put on a clean shirt, clean socks, clean underwear, and threw his dirty clothes in the carry-on bag.

He took the attaché case out of the drawer, examined its contents once more, and went down and checked out. Then he walked two blocks on Nathan Street to the Imperial Hotel and took a cab to the airport. There he checked the bag, confirmed his reservations on the 11:45 P.M. flight to Tokyo and then took another cab to the House of Eagles on Min Street. He had to hand it to old George Wan. The place was no more than ten minutes from the airport. The House of Eagles was a flashy third-class night club which, were it not for the sign in both Chinese and English, could have been in Miami or North Beach or on Sunset Boulevard. The decor was early joint, imitation leather, fake silk drapes, candles in used wine bottles. Three of the five girls were Caucasians and the bartender looked like an ex-sailor from Brooklyn. The place was almost empty. As Burns sat down at the bar one of the Oriental girls walked up to him and ran her hand across his neck.

'Are you from Hong Kong?' she asked.

'Nope.'

'Ah, American. *Aw chung-yee may gock yun.* That means "I love Americans".'

'Not tonight, I got plans.'

'Plans can be changed.'

'Maybe tomorrow I'll come back.'

The girl's smile vanished and so did she. Burns ordered a glass of plain soda water and asked where the bathroom was.

The restroom was filthy. Soiled paper towels littered the sink and floor, and the entire room seemed coated with grime. Burns entered one of the two booths and locked the door. He opened the attaché case and took out the surgical gloves and put them on. He loosened his belt, lowered his pants, and tied the cord around his hips using a simple bow-knot, then pulled his pants back up and buckled them. The knot was directly under the zipper. He took the other pill and put it in his suit pocket and put the cotton swabbing in one of his pants pockets. Then he took out the pistol and checked it once more before reaching around to his back and slipping it in his belt.

He buttoned his coat and flushed the toilet and went back to the bar.

The glass of soda was waiting for him. He slipped the pill

into his mouth and washed it down with soda water. The rush was almost instantaneous. His body seemed to vibrate with electrical charges. Life surged back into his feet, his hands, his fingertips. New strength flooded his worn-out body, adrenalin pumped through his brain. His eyes began to clear. The sounds in the room amplified, were crisper, more distinct. With the rush came an anticipation so keen that he began to fantasize as he mentally ticked off the steps he was about to follow.

He looked at his watch. It was 9:20, time to go. When he got up to leave he was aware for the first time that he had an erection.

The house on Bowring Street sat back from the road among hundreds of dwarf azaleas, an old Chinese one-storey mansion, weathered and ancient, its tiled pagoda roof scarred by the years, its azaleas, perfectly shaped, blooming in small step terraces down to the kerb.

The house was deceiving, for it was shaped like a U and only the south wing faced Bowring. A wall circled the entire block. It was nine feet high and had a single opening, a mahogany door nine inches thick with brass hinges embedded in the wood. The door had no latch. It could be opened only from the inside with a special key. The top of the wall was littered with broken glass.

Behind it was a garden almost three hundred years old, a garden that was weeded and trimmed and pruned every day and was so immaculately manicured that it was rare to find even a single blossom on the ground. A small stream curved through it with benches at intervals where lovers for the evening could sit and talk or perhaps just touch each other. Each of the interior rooms of the house had a frosted-glass panel that opened onto the garden.

In the front of the house, over the door, a lamp hung from an ornate brass serpent that seemed to curl from the wall. There were no other lights. The windows of the house had been blacked out for years.

The place was as still as a painted landscape.

Halford stood in front of the house for several minutes after the taxi left. He smoked a cigarette and walked to the corner and back. The old fears gnawed at him and the sounds of Min Street beckoned him away from the house.

41

But something else drew him to it, something Captain Friedman had said to him early in their therapy, a quote from Spinoza: *So long as a man imagines he cannot do something, so long as he is determined not to do it; then it is impossible for him to do it.*

Finally he went up the cobblestone walk and rang the bell.

The door was opened almost immediately by a woman, an ageless and splendid Chinese woman, tiny but erect and commanding, her greying hair pulled tightly away from a face that was unwrinkled and smooth as a rose petal. She was elegantly dressed in a formal cheongsam and wore a tiara of small, perfectly shaped diamonds. If she was startled by Halford's gaunt appearance, by the sunken eyes peering from black circles and the caved-in cheeks, she did not show it. She bowed deeply to him.

'Welcome to my house,' she said. 'I am Madame Kwa. You must be Colonel Halford. We are honoured by your presence and thank you for being so punctual.'

'After twenty-four years in the army, madame, I doubt I would know how to be late.'

'You forget time here, Colonel. At the House of the Purple Azalea there is no time, only pleasure.'

She ushered him into a small room in the south wing. The lights were low and soothing and the room was decorated with antiques from several Chinese dynasties. There were gold, teak, and silver and the furniture was deep and soft, covered with satin and linen. There was music somewhere, as elusive as an old memory, and the imperceptible presence of perfume. She brought Halford a drink, offered him opium, which he refused, and seated him facing a wall covered by a scarlet silk curtain.

'And now, Colonel,' she said, 'permit me to introduce my young ladies to you.'

The lights in the room lowered and went out. The silk curtain drew back on soundless runners. Behind it was a plate-glass window and behind that, darkness. Then a spotlight faded in and a young woman sat in its glow. Her hair was woven in a pigtail that hung over one shoulder and she looked out through the glass with narrow almond-shaped eyes that were the deepest brown Halford had ever seen.

42

She wore gold slippers trimmed in white and a white mandarin sheath split almost to the hip. On her left arm, over the bicep, the numeral 1 had been tattooed in bright colours. She smiled.

'This is Leah, the number one girl,' said Madame Kwa. 'She is nineteen years old and was trained in geisha houses before she came to me. She has perfected the Twenty-one Pleasures of the Chinese Wedding Night and she speaks English, French, Portuguese, Japanese, and three dialects of Chinese, and can recite more than a hundred love poems, including those banned by the cabala priests of Israel . . .'

One after another, the lights illuminated the women of the house, each a beauty in her own way, each with some special love secret from the ages, each with her number tattooed in small colorescura numerals on her arm. Halford's fears evaporated. He was entranced. He was aware of old stirrings, old needs. But he was waiting now for one girl in particular, because the cousin of Kam Sing had told him as he was leaving the cab, 'Wait for number nineteen. Kam Sing says the number is very special. You will understand.'

And now Halford understood, for the light revealed a young woman whose beauty stunned the Colonel. She was small and delicate, her skin the colour of brushed leather and hair coal-black, hanging straight to her waist. She looked not at him, as the others had done, but at the floor, and Halford was drawn to her instantly.

'This is Heth,' Madame Kwa said. 'She is special to all of us. She is only eighteen and she came to me when she was nine from deep in old China. She speaks Chinese and Japanese and some phrases of English. She has observed the mysteries of love from all the other ladies and she has mastered the ancient secret of the String with Twelve Knots. It is said that her tongue is like the wings of a butterfly.'

Halford was moved by the obvious vulnerability of this beautiful creature and by the sadness in her enormous eyes.

'Yes,' Halford whispered, 'it must be her.'

Madame Kwa smiled. 'You have made the choice of the wise men,' she said. 'The gods will envy you.'

'How do I talk to her?' Halford asked.

'It will not be necessary. She will communicate with you, Colonel, and you will have no trouble understanding.'

Burns stood in the shadows at the end of the alley watching the house on Bowring Street. He had disposed of the attaché case in a convenient storm sewer. He waited until he was certain the street was empty and then crossed swiftly to the mahogany door, which was propped open by a stick.

He moved the stick, stepped quickly through the door, let it click shut behind him, and stood with his back against the wall, waiting until his eyes were accustomed to the darkness of the garden. It was empty. He moved swiftly across the stream and stood in the shadows under a cherry tree thirty feet from the corner room of the north wing of the house. Again he waited.

The room was small and comfortable, its floor covered with a llama rug, its walls decorated with yellow and red striped satin. It contained a large wooden tub big enough for two people and a massage table covered with a mat of goose feathers. Beside it was a smaller table covered with urns of oils, powders, and creams. There were no lights, only scented candles.

Heth led Halford by the hand to the room and she slid the door shut behind them.

'You wait,' she said in her tiny, melodic voice.

She walked across the room to the door leading into the garden. But a foot or two from the door she stopped. Her hand reached out and, like a hummingbird poised before a honeysuckle bush, it fluttered for a fraction of a second before it found the door and slid it open.

Halford was stunned. Now he understood her vulnerability, the sadness in her incredible eyes, why Madame Kwa had said, 'She is special to all of us.'

Heth was blind.

'You see,' she said turning in his direction, 'gar-den.'

Emotions he had forgotten swept over him, desire, feeling, longing. He walked across the room and held her face between his fingertips.

'Yes, I see,' he said gently. 'I see for both of us.'

Heth smiled and her fingers moved over his body, as soft as cobwebs swaying in the wind.

44

Thirty feet away, Burns watched from the shadows, saw Halford framed in the doorway, watched as he touched the girl's face, saw her respond, her fingers moving over his body, the buttons on his shirt opening as if by magic as she removed his clothing.

The girl was great.

She led Halford to the tub and her hands moved down, unbuckling his belt, unlacing his shoes. She knelt before him and removed his shoes and pants and, reaching up, slipped her hands inside the waistband of his shorts. Her fingertips flirted with him, touching and yet not touching. She finished undressing him, leaning forward and breathing softly on him, letting her lips brush against him. She began an almost imperceptible chant in Japanese. She touched his face, felt the rigid line of his jaw, his quivering lips, and slipped two fingertips inside his mouth, tapping his tongue. Her own tongue flittered over his chest and sucked at his nipples. She took his hand in hers, helped him undress her, guided them over her breasts, her stomach, and down to hair as soft as rabbit's fur.

His fears vanished. He was hypnotized, overcome by a sensuality more complete than any he had ever known. His manhood was restored.

Burns moved silently across the garden and stood near the door, heard her soft chant, the sounds of water splashing, the murmur of soft laughter. He took the cotton swabbing from his pocket, wrapped a strip around one hand, held it in place with his thumb, and slipped on one of the surgical gloves. He repeated the action with the other hand. He unzipped his pants and took out the nylon cord, wrapped it several times around each hand, and tested it again, pulling it taut. The knot was centred perfectly. He eased himself to the door and looked in.

They were out of the tub. Halford lay on his back on the table, facing away from Burns, who stood watching, behind him.

Heth covered her hands with warm oil and began massaging Halford, her strong fingers kneading the muscles in his legs and chest. She stroked his arms and placed them at his sides. Then she got up on the table, straddling him, settling down on him, moving against him, leaning over him. Her butterfly tongue teased his stomach, moved lower,

45

and her mouth enveloped him.

Halford was unaware of the new presence in the room, an obscene presence moving stealthily across the llama rug, the nylon cord dangling between latex-sheathed fists.

But Heth was aware. Her keen ears amplified each creak in the floor, the rustle of clothing, a different rhythm of breathing in the room. She reached out to the smaller table. Her fingers found a short silk string with twelve knots tied in it, each about an inch apart. She slipped her hand under Halford and began to insert the string. Halford, lost in fantasy, hardly felt it. His pulse was hammering, his breath was laboured and quick.

The tempo increased. Faster. Faster. Faster.

Halford gasped. His blood, charged with lightning, surged through his body. His head rose off the table. His body went rigid. At that moment Heth ripped the string from inside him and Halford cried out. He exploded.

As he did, Heth dropped her legs over the side of the table and clamped them under it. Her arms enveloped it and she grasped one wrist with the other hand.

Halford was caught in a human vice.

Burns dropped the nylon cord around his throat. His hands snapped apart.

The knot in the cord bit deep into the hollow in Halford's neck. Ecstasy turned to pain. His temples erupted. His breath was cut off, trapped in his throat. His tongue shot from his mouth.

Burns snapped the cord again, tighter this time.

Halford began to shake violently. Spasms seized his body. It began to jerk against Heth's. She tightened her grip. He tried to scream, but the cry was crushed in his throat. He looked up, saw the grotesque inverted face above him. He tried to utter one last word, a syllable, distorted and guttural, which died in his mouth:

'Wh-a-a-a-r-r-ghh . . .'

And then his windpipe burst. He shuddered convulsively. His breath surged from him like wind squealing from a punctured balloon.

He went limp.

Heth released her death grip. She lay across Halford's body, her arms and legs dangling over the sides of the table. Tears burned her cheeks.

Burns stepped back, unwound the cord from one hand, and pulled it free. He dropped it on the table beside Halford's body. Sweat bathed his face. His breath came in short gasps.

The girl struggled to a sitting position. She cried soundlessly.

Burns reached behind him and took the pistol from his belt. The girl made no move. She was looking towards him but not at him. It was then that Burns too realized she was blind, understood what Wan had meant when he had said it would not be necessary to kill two: There was no way the girl could identify him. He hesitated for a fraction of a second but then, like a programmed machine committed to one last act, he stepped behind her and held the pistol at arm's length an inch from her head. She followed the sound, turning her head, as if to look back over her shoulder.

'The door,' he said in his brittle voice. She took the bait, turning back instantly.

The gun jumped in his hand, thunked, and her head snapped forward. He held her hair in his other hand and pulled her head instantly back up. *Thunk.* He lowered her across Halford's body.

Burns laid the pistol beside the nylon cord, walked quickly out of the room, crossed the garden, and went out through the gate. He stripped off the gloves, wrapped them in the cotton swabbing and walked back down the alley towards the storm sewer.

A moment after the door clicked shut, two figures emerged from the shadows of the garden and entered the room.

Burns was the first passenger on the plane. He walked to the rear cabin, found a pillow, sat down, buckled his seat belt, and settled back. By the time the flight for Tokyo roared down the runway and eased into the night sky he was deep in an untroubled sleep.

Chapter Three

ATLANTA, 1975

The face was malevolent, its mouth wrinkled and shrivelled with age and frozen in an evil leer, its taunting eyes flickering feebly as they stared through the window of the pub. Outside a cold fall wind raced across the courtyard that separated the two-storey shopping mall from the mirrored skyscraper, sweeping leaves before it as it moaned through the open plaza. They skittered along the pavement, dancing past the grinning apparition and swirling away into darkness.

A few blocks away the chimes of the cathedral began tolling midnight, striking the last seconds of Allhallow Eve. Pursued by the clock, ghosts and goblins, saints, sinners, black magicians, and lords of the underworld raced across the moon-mad sky, and fire-eyed birds darted to the safety of skeleton trees. The last chord sounded. The piazza was quiet. A blanket settled over the city. Devilment ended. Halloween was over.

But not quite.

Evil muses were still at play, concocting one last monstrous trick.

The door of the pub called Kerry's Kalibash opened and a man in a scarred leather jacket stepped out into the chilly night air, carrying with him briefly the sounds of merriment, of laughter and music and ice rattling in glasses. The door shushed shut behind him. The man was tough-looking, with grey hair and dull eyes. He stood, shoulders hunched, and stared across the plaza at the twenty-storey building, watching the blinking lights of a jet jog across the mirrored façade. It was a stunning structure, floor after floor of mirrored windows reflecting the distant skyline. The man turned as he stared up at the penthouse where lights glowed mutely.

He had followed the woman there. Somewhere in this building was the man he had wondered about, hated, for thirty years. As he watched, there was a movement in the

48

shrubs near the pub behind him. He seemed hypnotized by the soaring building, by the kaleidoscope reflected in its face, by the bullet-shaped elevators that shot up and down the outside wall. A couple left the pub, laughing and wrapped in each other's arms, and walked towards the parking lot.

The hidden figure froze against the wall. *Son of a bitch*, he thought, *too open, too dangerous. Not neat and planned like Hong Kong. But it had to be done now.*

The couple vanished into the parking lot. The figure moved again. He came straight towards the back of the man in the leather jacket. As he approached him he raised his left arm. He was holding a pistol with the ugly black cylinder of a silencer attached to the end of the barrel. The gun was only a few inches from the back of the man's head when the gunman said softly:

'Corrigon.'

The man in the leather jacket whirled and stared straight into the barrel of the pistol, now only two or three inches from his eye. A strange look crossed his face, a crooked grin of recognition and relief.

He saw the weapon only an instant before it flashed, before he heard the curious little *pwuit* the silencer made, before he felt the brief, fiery pain tear into his head, rip through his brain, and explode against the back of his skull.

His fingertips went numb. Then his hands. Then his arms. He lost the feeling in his legs and feet. His mouth filled with bile. He was falling and didn't know it. Streaks of light cascaded down towards him from the building, showering past him like antic stars. Then they diminished and died. He heard a scream, a tight and anguished cry trapped in an agonized throat. Then all was darkness and silence except the relentless wind crying across the open plaza.

The last thought the man in the leather coat had was that the scream he heard was his own.

BOOK ONE

Chapter One

At 5:25, Sharky pulled his battered Volkswagen into an alley two blocks off Peachtree and a block behind the bus station and parked near a Dempsey Dumpster. He was five minutes early.

The cold December wind swirled dust along the alley and rattled litter against the buildings. It had dropped ten degrees since the sun went down. Sharky's heater was shot and one of the windows would not close all the way. He breathed on his hands to keep them warm.

At 5:30, he got out of the car and stood with his back to the door, stamping his feet. He buttoned the top button of the plaid lumber jacket. Dirt hit his eyes and mouth and filtered through his beard.

'Shit,' he muttered, leaning forward and shaking the dust from the thick growth on his face, then turned suddenly towards the rear of the car. A newspaper whirled from behind it and flattened against the Dumpster.

Sharky was nervous. He reached inside the jacket, fingering the brown manila envelope stuffed into the waist of his Levis.

No sign of High Ball Mary.

He kept his eyes moving. If High Ball were setting him up, now would be the time. A quick shot in the head here in the dark and High Ball would be six hundred dollars richer. And there wouldn't be much Sharky could do about it.

To his right, in the darkness against the building across the alley, Sharky sensed movement. Then he heard a low, deep chuckle.

'Whatsa matter, honk, got the chills?'

The son of a bitch.

'High Ball?' Sharky said.

'Who else, baby? Got the price?'

'Think I'd be freezing my ass off out here if I was short? Let's get back in the car and deal, I've had enough of this goddamn wind.'

'I like it better in the open, man. Take a little taste o' the lady here and you won't give a shit how cold it is.'

'Bullshit. I'm gettin' outa the wind. You wanna freeze your balls off, stuff your lady.'

'*Ooo*-weeee, ain't we testy this evenin'!'

Sharky got back inside and turned the interior lights on so High Ball could check out the car. He lit a small A&C cigar and held his hands around its glowing end.

High Ball strolled across the alley, hands in the pockets of an expensive full-length fur coat. He was wearing a wide-brimmed Borsalino snapped down over his forehead, yellow platform shoes, and cream-coloured wide-flare pants. He moved cautiously to the car, walking around the far side, leaning over with his hands still stuffed in the pockets, looking in the back seat. The gold earring that had earned him his nickname, Mary, glittered in the light from the dome. Finally he got in.

'You think I got J. Edgar Hoover stashed back there?'

'That fairy's off, man. Where you been?'

'The ghost lingers on.'

'Turn the fuckin' lights off, turkey. This ain't a goddamn floor show.'

Sharky turned the switch and the lights died.

'I tell you, honk, I'm gettin' my coat dirty in this garbage can.'

'It beats walkin'.'

'You score with this shit, man, you can get yourself some uptown wheels.'

'Where's the merchandise? I get nervous sittin' here.'

'How about the green, baby? No green, no sheen.'

'I ain't showin' you shit till I taste your stuff.'

'Oh, ain't we mean!' Mary took a small glassine bag from his pocket and held it up by his fingertips. He shook the white powder in the bag. 'Lookit here, turkey, how 'bout that? And fifteen more where that came from. Sixteen grams, m'man, a generous o-z of super snow A hundred trips to the mooooon. Cut it three for one at least. Forty-eight bags at sixty per . . . lessee, that's uh . . .'

'Twenty-eight hundred and eighty geezoes, High Ball. Cut the bullshit and get it on. Open up.' He felt the anxiety building in him as he wet his middle finger and dipped it into the bag, drew it away with several grains stuck to it, and tasted it. His jaw tightened from the bitter taste. Good shit.

A car entered the alley at the far end and rolled slowly towards them.

'What the fuck's this?' High Ball growled. Fear and anger flooded his eyes. 'What the fuck we got here?'

'Cool it, for Chrissakes. It's just a car.'

'Crank up and move someplace. Too crowded here.'

The car moved past them.

'Man, you're on a string,' Sharky said.

'Fucker's stoppin'.'

The car stopped, then backed up, pulling up in front of the Volkswagen and boxing it in. A large figure got out and loomed in the darkness, moving towards Sharky's side of the car.

'I'm takin' the train, turkey,' High Ball snapped. Sharky could feel the tension crackling in the air.

'Stay cool, okay? I'll handle it.'

'You ain't holdin', man. I can't stand a toss.'

'I said I'll handle it.'

The large man appeared at the window on Sharky's side, a flashlight in his hand. Light flooded the interior of the car.

'Goddamn,' High Ball snapped.

'What the hell . . .' Sharky started to say, then his eyes met those of the fat man at his window.

Tully! Jesus Christ, that stupid shit!

Tully's eyes met Sharky's.

'Sharky!' he bellowed, 'Jesus, I didn't . . .'

'Shut up!' Sharky yelled.

'Motherfucker!' High Ball screamed. 'You wired me, you motherfuckin' goddamn pig!' The glassine envelope flew out of his hand. White powder billowed like a cloud in the interior of the car. Mary was already going out the door. Sharky grabbed his collar, but the black man twisted away and slid out sideways, landing on the balls of his feet, a small pearl-handled .25 calibre revolver appearing suddenly in his fist. He was hissing like a snake. Hate turned his eyes red.

Sharky hit the door on his side with his shoulder and shoved hard. It flew open, knocking Tully backward into the street. Sharky rolled out as Mary fired his first shot. The gun popped like a firecracker and the bullet breezed past Sharky's cheek as he fell, and hit the rim of the door, whining off down the alley.

Mary was already halfway to the corner when Sharky bounced back on his knees and reached under the front seat, feeling the cold grip of his 9mm Mauser automatic. He pulled it out and laid both arms across the front seat, steadying his gun,

'Freeze, Mary . . .'

Too late. The wiry black man slid around the corner, his Borsalino flying off into the gutter. Sharky leaped across the front seat, yelling back at Tully as he did.

'Call it in, call it in . . . you goddamn moron. He's headed south on Spring towards Harris.'

Tully struggled to his feet, his face chagrined and confused as Sharky ran to the corner. Sharky stopped for a second and peered around. Mary, halfway to the next corner, slowed, aimed the .25, then realized it wouldn't carry that far, and cut diagonally across the street. A car slammed to a stop as he raced in front of it. Sharky went after him, cutting through the traffic. Cars screeched to a stop all around him.

Jesus, Sharky thought, *five-thirty. The middle of rush hour. Neat. Real neat.*

The pusher reached the corner and turned towards Peachtree Street. He fired an off-hand shot across his chest as he ran. The bullet smacked a telephone pole eight feet from Sharky. Sharky kept going, closing the distance on the pusher, who was hampered by his cumbersome shoes.

Half a block away five-thirty traffic choked the main thoroughfare. Pedestrians crowded the street corners, waiting for buses. Mary was panicky. He had to get lost in the crowd or get some transportation fast. He ran into the thick of it with Sharky closing in. As he started across Peachtree a black Cadillac drove in front of him, so close it brushed him. He jogged in place for a moment, then ran around the rear of the Caddy and dived headlong across the hood of the Buick behind it, sliding up against the windshield and falling on his hands and knees on the other side.

The astonished driver slammed on his brakes as Sharky ran up, jumped up on the hood in a sitting position, and swung his legs around, dropping to the other side.

The light had changed. Traffic was moving out. On the opposite side of the street a city bus began to pull out into the free lane in front of it. High Ball threaded through traffic, ran in front of the bus, slammed his hand against the grille, and reached the door. He aimed his gun through the glass at the driver.

'Open up, motherfucker,' he demanded and the driver opened the door.

Through the window on the driver's side, Sharky saw the wild-eyed pusher waving his Saturday night special in the terrified driver's face. Then Mary saw Sharky and fired a shot past the driver's nose. It smacked through the window and hit the street between Sharky's feet, rocheting into the fender of a nearby car.

Sharky aimed his automatic at the dealer and Mary dove out of sight towards the rear of the bus. Sharky pulled out his wallet and holding it towards the driver, flashed his shield. He ran to the door. The driver pushed the handle and the door hissed open.

'On the floor,' Sharky yelled and dove aboard. The driver rolled out of the seat as Mary fired another shot. It screamed off the chromium rod near the driver's seat and went through the windshield with a splat.

Inside the bus, pandemonium. Women and children screamed, dropped behind seats, spilled packages. An elderly woman sat speechless in her seat, clutching a shopping bag to her bosom, staring straight ahead.

Sharky leaned against the wall between the front stairwell and the first seat as Mary fired another shot. He was gasping for breath. It had all happened too fast. Now he was in a box. A Mexican standoff in a crowded bus with a madman loose in the back. High Ball hunched behind the wall separating the seats from the stairwell at the rear exit. He shoved on the door but it was activated by stepping on the bottom step while the driver pressed a release button in front. Mary kicked frantically at the door, then turned and fired another shot towards the front of the bus. More screaming.

'You goddamn pig motherfucker,' Mary screamed, 'I'm taking me some hostages! I'm killing me some fuckin' kids back here, you don't open the goddamn door.'

Sharky took a fast peek over the divider in the front of the bus and ducked back quickly as Mary's gun roared and the bullet sighed overhead and cracked through the windshield. Everyone behind Mary was on the floor. There was no time to negotiate. Mary was in a killing mood and had to be stopped fast. Sharky had soft-nosed loads in his pistol. There was little chance they would go through the pusher and hit someone behind him. He had to take the risk.

Sharky reached over to the busdriver's coin changer and clicked a dozen tokens out of it. He knelt and threw them across the bus behind the driver's seat. Mary took the bait. He stood and fired two more shots into the driver's seat. As he did Sharky rose up, throwing both arms over the retainer, and squeezing off a single shot. It hit Mary in the cheek. The right side of his face burst open. Blood gushed down his face and onto his chest. The shot slammed him back against the wall at the rear of the stairwell.

The elderly lady, less than two feet away, continued to clutch her shopping bag and stare straight ahead.

Mary looked surprised. He shuddered as blood poured out of his face. He started to raise his gun hand again.

Sharky lowered his aim an inch or so and fired twice more. The automatic jumped in his hands. Two more holes appeared in Mary's chest, less than half an inch apart. He moaned, turned sideways, and fell on his knees on the bottom step, his hands between his legs and his forehead resting against the door. Sharky stepped over the driver, who was huddled on the floor with his hands over his ears, and pushed the release button. The door opened and Mary pitched out head-first.

Sharky opened the front door and jumped out.

Two uniformed cops were eight feet away, leaning across the hood of a Chevrolet, their service revolvers trained on Sharky.

'Hold it right there.'

Sharky held his I.D. high over his head and strode towards the rear of the bus.

'Sharky, Central Narcotics,' he yelled. 'Get an ambulance.'

'I said, "Hold it right there," ' the cop yelled again.

Sharky threw the wallet at him. It bounced off the hood of the car and spun around, opened at his shield.

'I said, "Call a goddamn ambulance," ' Sharky said and kept walking. He reached Mary's still form lying face down in the street and stood over him, his gun aimed at the back of the dope dealer's head. He slid the .25 away from the body with his foot, then slipped it under High Ball, and rolled him slowly over.

The dealer looked straight up at the dark sky. Blood rattled in his throat. The eyes turned to glass and rolled up in his head. Sharky stuck his gun in his belt and reached down, pressing his fingers into Mary's throat. Nothing.

One of the two cops was shouting into his radio mike. The other joined Sharky and handed him his wallet. 'What the hell's going on?' he asked.

'I just retired a junkman. Better have your partner call the ME too.'

People pressed in from all sides. Horns blared as the traffic built up. Inside the bus, passengers crowded to the windows, pressing their faces against the cold glass. The elderly woman suddenly opened her mouth and screamed over and over at the top of her lungs. A flashgun went off, blinding Sharky.

'What the hell was that?' he yelled.

'Somebody took a picture.'

'No pictures, goddammit! No pictures!' Sharky barked.

'Too late,' the cop said.

More noise. More confusion. A siren was shrieking nearby.

Sharky leaned against the bus. He felt suddenly tired, disgusted, used up, sick to his stomach. 'Ah, shit,' he said, half aloud.

He leaned over High Ball Mary's body, his fingers feeling the coat lining. He felt the bags, then a zipper, and pulled it open. Inside, in small pockets sewn into the lining of the coat, were fifteen one-gram bags of cocaine.

Chapter Two

He arrived at the station at 9:45, fifteen minutes before his appointment. Jaspers's secretary was a hard-faced, sour-tempered policewoman named Helen Hill, a competent officer turned mean after eight years tied to a desk. She was less than affectionately known in the House as the Dragon Lady.

'Sit over there,' she snapped, pointing to a hard oak chair without arms. She glared at his scruffy exterior for a moment, then ignored him.

The outer office was spartan. Nothing to read, no pictures on the wall. The Dragon Lady got up once, poured herself a cup of coffee from an urn on a table near the door, and sat down again. She did not offer Sharky coffee, a drink of water, the time of day, or a kind word. Finally he got up and helped himself to a cup.

'Don't you ask?' the Dragon Lady growled.

'May I have a cup of coffee?' Sharky said with a mock smile. He sprinkled half a packet of sugar into the cup, stirred it with his finger, licked it off, and returned to his seat. The Dragon Lady ignored him. He slurped his coffee loudly and stared at her. She continued to ignore him. The minutes crawled by. Fifteen minutes seemed to take an hour, at least. At exactly ten o'clock the phone on her desk buzzed.

'Yes, sir? Yes, he is. Yes, sir.' She hung up. 'All right. You may go in now,' she said, without looking at him.

He plopped the half-empty cup in the middle of her desk. 'Thanks,' he said, 'for starting my day so cheerfully.' She glared at him as he knocked on the door. A voice inside said, 'Come.'

Captain Jaspers was a tall, angular, emotionless man in his early fifties. A scar as thin as a fishing line stretched from in front of his left ear down to his jawline. His black hair was streaked with grey. Cold, dead eyes hid behind glasses set in gold frames. His attire was as rigid as a uniform, dark blue suits, white shirts, drab ties, black lace-up shoes. His Timex watch had a grey cloth band. He wore no other jewellery.

To Sharky's knowledge, Jaspers had no friends in the department. His only confidant was the new police commissioner, Ezra Powers. Jaspers was a ruthless officer with little regard for his men, a rigid and stern disciplinarian, quick to demote or suspend the men in Central District, which was his command. Five years earlier when Sharky was assigned to a blue-and-white, his partner had been Orville Slyden, who had been flopped from detective third grade to patrolman and given six-and-six, six weeks' suspension and six weeks at reduced pay, for taking a handout. Later Slyden had been proven innocent, but Jaspers refused to restore him to rank. It was the captain's contention that anyone even suspected of such an infraction did not deserve to be a detective. It was Slyden who had given Jaspers his nickname, The Bat. 'He's a fuckin' vampire,' Slyden had said and the name had stuck, although nobody ever called Jaspers that to his face.

Jaspers's predecessor had been a thoughtful and highly respected man who had risen slowly and painfully through the ranks. He had committed suicide after learning he had terminal cancer. According to a persistent rumour of the House, Jaspers had loaded the gun for him.

The office was barren. A spotless desk with nothing on it but a telephone and a letterbox. A table behind the desk contained a police squawk box, nothing else. Two uncomfortable chairs. A single photograph on the wall of Dwight Eisenhower shaking hands with Jaspers, who wore the uniform of an army major. Neither of them was smiling. There were no ashtrays; Jaspers did not approve of smoking or drinking.

He did not look up when Sharky entered the room; he jabbed a finger towards one of the chairs and continued reading a file that lay in front of him. Sharky sat down. Another five minutes died. Finally Jaspers closed the cover of the file and took a newspaper out of his desk drawer. He held it up with a flourish for Sharky to read. Jaspers thrived on these little *dramatis momenta*. The headline read:

'UNDERCOVER COP KILLS DOPE
PUSHER ON CROWDED CITY BUS'

Beside the story a photograph showed a scruffy, bearded, and weary Sharky, gun in hand, leaning over High Ball Mary.

'I saw it,' Sharky said.

'When you blow your cover, you certainly do it extravagantly,' Jaspers said. His voice was a dry, brittle rasp.

'Well, I had a little bad luck.'

'You had a *lot* of bad luck.'

'The way it happened, I was –'

'I *know* the way it happened. Anybody who can read knows the way it happened.'

'The story in the paper isn't quite –'

'I read your report, what there was of it.'

'Yes, sir, uh, about that . . . Lieutenant Goldwald thought we should leave out some . . .'

'I know what Goldwald thought. I've already finished with Goldwald.'

'Could I just give you my end of it? Sir.' Sharky said.

'No. I know all I need to know. I know you went into this meet with, uh, what was his name? Uh . . .'

'Creech. Percy Creech. A/k/a High Ball Mary.'

'Yes, Creech. You went in there solo. No back-up. No surveillance team. Six hundred dollars of department money in your pocket. You set up this buy with a very dangerous pusher and kept the details to yourself. A real grandstand play, Sharky. And then to get involved in a chase through the most crowded section of town. At rush hour. A shoot-out on a crowded city bus filled with women and children. Just what else would you like to add to that?'

'Everything was rolling smooth until that goddamn Tully . . .'

'I'm not interested in Tully,' Jaspers snapped, cutting him off. 'Tully was an accident. Accidents happen. You should anticipate, *anticipate*, problems.'

Sharky's face began to redden.

'He's a moron . . .'

Jaspers cut him off again.

'Are you deaf?'

'Pardon?'

'Deaf. Are you deaf? I said I am not interested in Tully. Tully was a mistake. It's what happened *after* Tully that concerns me. You forgot everything. You panicked, forgot every regulation. You ignored the rules. Pro-*ced*-ure. There is pro-*ced*-ure to be followed.' Jaspers sat back in his chair and stared across the desk at Sharky, who felt suddenly like a grammar school boy called before the principal. It was humiliating and Sharky could not abide humiliation.

'Look, do I have any say at all? I mean, do I get to tell my end of this?'

'Don't be insolent,' Jaspers snapped.

'Insolent! Insolent, shit.' He stood up and walked to the edge of the desk. Jaspers's face was scarlet with rage. 'Lemme tell you something, Captain. I spent three months on that goddamn machine. Three months setting it up, kissing that miserable bastard's ass so I could make that buy.'

'Sharky!' Jaspers roared.

'No, I'm gonna finish this. This wasn't any ordinary coke buy, y'know. Creech was leading me upstairs, to his man. We were talking coke in pounds. Pounds! He couldn't handle that big a thing; he had to go to the supplier. That's who I was after, High Ball's connection. I had to. It couldn't leak out, see. One leak – '

'How dare you?' Jaspers was enraged now. 'What in God's name possessed you? A gunfight on a crowded bus.'

Jesus, is that all that mattered? The bus? Sharky started to explain what happened. That he had taken a chance and looked at High Ball Mary, that everyone behind the pusher had dropped to the floor, that he was using soft-nose bullets. It wasn't some irresponsible snap decision; he didn't have any choice. But he said nothing. *What the hell, all The Bat cared about was the goddamn bus.*

'This kind of press is disastrous,' The Bat was saying.

'Press? For Christ's sake, what was I supposed to do, kiss his ass and wave goodbye?'

'I ought to break you. For insubordination alone. I ought to give you six-and-six and put you back where you belong, in a blue-and-white on Auburn Avenue. You'll never learn, will you? You have no respect for anyone.'

'Captain, look, it happened too fast. All of a sudden there we were on a bus full of Christmas shoppers and he was bonkers, totally around the bend, threatening to kill kids and all. I had a clean shot and I took it. What the hell else is there to say about it?'

'Three clean shots, apparently.'

'Okay, I hit him three times. I didn't want to take a chance that maybe he squeezes one off and wastes some old lady on the way home to dinner. Or some kid. I took him out. Isn't that the way it's supposed to work?'

Jaspers drummed his desk with his fingers. He glared at Sharky. God, how he despised these young hotshots. Headline hunters.

'I don't want any more headline hunting,' he said.

'That's what it's going down as, hunh? Headline hunting? Everybody's scared shitless of the papers.'

'You've tried my patience with your insubordination, Sharky.'

'Captain, I'm asking to be treated fairly. No more consideration than we give to some bum in the drunk tank, that's what I'm asking for.'

'I'll give you hell and call it whatever you want to call it. Right now you're about as useful to Narcotics as a paraplegic.'

'I don't . . .' Sharky started to say something and stopped. He stared at the cold eyes. The bottom of his foot began to itch. He tried grinding his foot into the carpet. The itch grew worse. He tried to ignore it. Tears began welling up in his eyes. *Christ,* he thought, *the son of a bitch is going to think he's got me crying.* Sharky sat down, unzipped his boot and pulled it off, frantically scratching the bottom of his foot. His big toe stuck through a hole in his sock.

Jaspers stared at him, appalled.

'What in God's name?' he stammered.

'My foot itches,' Sharky said. 'It's driving me crazy.'

Jaspers threw the paper in the wastebasket. He stood up and leaned across his desk. 'Put that shoe on,' he said. 'Put it on and stand at attention.'

Sharky put his boot back on and stood up.

'I'll tell you what's going to happen, Sharky. As of eight A.M. today you are no longer attached to the narcotics section. As of eight A.M. you are in Vice.'

Sharky looked at him in disbelief.

'Vice!'

'Vice. Report to Lieutenant Friscoe.'

Sharky stared at him for several moments. He looked around the room, struggling to keep his own anger in check.

'Sir, will you please just look at my sheet? I think I deserve that much. Eighteen months on the street, eighteen collars, all hard drugs. I dumped eighteen goddamn pushers, one a month, and fourteen got the basket. The DA knows . . .'

'Shut up.'

'I beg your pardon?'

'I said, "Shut up." '

'Sure. Yes, sir. I'll just, uh, yeah, keep my mouth shut, sit over there in public library watching the freaks jack off.'

'Somebody has to do it. You think you're too good for the Vice Squad, that it?'

'I got eighteen months out there. That's got to be worth something to Narcs. Even on a desk I can be a lot of help down there.'

'You're lucky I don't send you over. I've busted better men than you for a lot less. I had the mayor on the phone half the night. The commissioner calling me at six-thirty in the morning. What kind of a nut is he? everybody asks. I'm giving you a break. I want you out of sight for a while. No more headlines. No more grandstanding. *Out of my sight.* I don't want to pick up the paper and see your shaggy . . . my God, look at you. When's the last time you shaved? Had a haircut?'

'You, uh, there aren't a lot of dope deals on the make out there for guys in Brooks Brothers suits and Florsheims. Sir.'

'Clean yourself up. Get a shave, a haircut, some decent clothes. Buy some decent socks, for God's sake. Friscoe wants a man for something he's got working and you're it. I don't know what it is, I don't care. But I want you to understand one thing. Do you understand the term *low profile*?'

'Sure. Of course. Yes.'

'*Sir.*'

'Sir.'

'Fine. Because from now on the first order of business for you is to maintain a very, very, *very* low profile. L-o-w. Clear?'

Sharky nodded.

'Good. Now get out of here.'

Chapter Three

It was noon when Domino headed across the windy plaza towards Mirror Towers. The cathedral clock began tolling the hour and as it did she shuddered unconsciously. It wasn't the wind. Or the cold. It was something else, the reflection in the building of the street behind her perhaps. Or the chimes solemnly striking twelve.

She shuddered again. What was it her mother used to say? *Someone's walking on your grave.*

She shrugged off the feeling and entered the building, walking through its wide, stark lobby to the private elevator in the corner. The security guard stood at leisurely attention. He smiled and touched the bill of his cap.

'Hi, Eddie,' she said brightly.

'Miss Domino,' he said. 'How's it going today?'

'Just great,' she said as she stepped into the glass-and-copper bullet attached to the side of the building. Eddie unlocked the up button with a key and pushed it. Then he picked up a wall phone and pressed a button. 'Miss Domino's on her way up,' he said.

The doors of the elevator swished shut and it shot up the side of the building, stopping at the twentieth floor. Five miles away, the skyline of the city was a sparkling cluster in the haze.

The elevator opened on a reception room that was almost as stark as the lobby, except that the two-storey ceiling was supported by a dozen Plexiglas pillars. The interior of each pillar was lit by a single spotlight recessed overhead. Within each was a single toy, and each of the toys was unique. Electronic toys, stuffed toys, toys that moved, that sang, that walked and danced and spoke by means of tiny tape loops hidden deep inside them. Each was the prototype for a production model and each performed its eerie function silently within the towering glass rectangles that dwarfed the reception desk at the far end of the uncomfortably quiet room. To Domino, the collection of dolls, animals, trolls, and other creatures was almost too real. She walked past them without looking, her heels echoing on the tile floor.

At the reception desk a husky Oriental man, his ice-cube eyes concealed behind heavily tinted glasses, was operating the complex pushbutton switchboard. Music whispered from a tiny transistor radio at his elbow.

She made a pyramid of her hands and bowed low from the waist.

'*Jo sun*,' she said.

The guard-receptionist repeated the gesture.

'*Jo sun, dor jeh*,' he said.

He pushed a button under the desk and a door slid soundlessly open nearby. 'He awaits you,' he said and she was gone.

She stepped into a lush botanical garden, a giant two-storey terrarium filled with rare plants and shrubs from all over the world: dracaena sanderianas, maidenhair ferns, dwarf azaleas, Chinese fan palms and amazon lilies, saffron pepper trees, butterfly gardenias, and six-foot ferns, all flourishing under an enormous sun dome. In one corner a circular stairway wound up through the foliage to the penthouse above.

She skirted the dense, moisture-laden foliage and peered past the greenery, through a heavy window into the office beyond. Pieces of Mayan and Chinese sculpture crouched under soft lights on Oriental rugs.

In the centre of the office a man sat behind a broad desk cluttered with curios, a large, heavyset man, bald as a crystal ball, with a full red beard that was turning grey. He wore gold-rimmed bifocals and his large hands lay flat on the desk in front of him. He was wearing one ring, on his left hand, a platinum and jade design that covered one entire joint of his little finger. His silk mandarin shirt had three entwined dragons brocaded in red and gold across the chest. He stared at her for several seconds and then smiled and pushed the button that opened the door between the greenhouse and his office.

She stopped several feet in front of his desk, stared down at him, turned slightly, raised her chin, and arched her back and glared at him over her shoulder.

Incredible, he thought.

She had high cheekbones and a full, almost arrogant mouth. Her thick black hair was bobbed at shoulder length and had been tousled just enough by the wind. Her neck was long and slender and the hollow place in her throat, between her collarbones, was as soft and delicate as the petal of a flower. She was slender, long-legged, narrow-waisted, and her breasts were as firm and as perfect as an artist's sculptured fantasy.

She wore a Halston dress, its simple, straight lines flattering every curve, every line, its muted rose-grey accentuating the shades of colouring in her skin, her hair, and her eyes. She was young. Haughty. Superior. Elegant. Untouchable. And totally desirable.

'Well?' she said and raised an eyebrow.

He leaned back in his chair and, with a flourish of his hands, said, '*Você é bela.*'

She raised the other eyebrow and half closed her eyes. '*Muito obrigada.*'

'Pardon me,' he said. 'Of course, you are fantastic. *Muito prazer em revê-la.*'

She looked perplexed and shook her head. 'Now you lost me. You know how limited my Portuguese is.'

'It means simply, "I am glad to see you",' he said.

'That's all, hunh? Just glad to see you?' She struck another pose. She unbuttoned the top button of the dress. Then the second. The dress opened slightly. He watched her breathe. She was superb. He had known women in every country, of every race, he had known legendary beauties, the whores of the world, and had once lived for a short time in a very famous house in Bangkok where he had made love to two, sometimes three women at a time. None of them could match her beauty, her intelligence, or her incredible talents.

He laughed out loud.

'Is something funny?'

'Just a thought,' he said.

'I'll give you ten dollars for it.'

He laughed harder. 'What extravagance! It is not worth more than a penny.'

She reached into her purse, took out a penny, and tossed it into his lap.

'There.'

'All right. I was thinking, I have worked hard all my life; I have built corporations on every continent. I have made

68

millions and millions of dollars, created cartels. I have done all this and I was thinking, I could have become just as rich running a whorehouse with you in Hong Kong.'

She threw her head back and laughed until small tears appeared at the corners of her eyes. She walked close to him, her perfume flirting with his nose. He wanted to reach out, to touch her, but he did not rush things. She touched his cheek.

'Victor, you are the most fascinating man I have ever met,' she said warmly.

'And the most generous?' he asked.

'Well,' she said, 'there was this gentleman from Kuwait...'

Victor DeLaroza scowled.

'He was extremely grateful...'

The scowl deepend. 'Oh?'

'But not nearly as much fun as you are.'

'Thank you.'

'You're welcome.'

'Did he ever take you to Paris for the weekend? Shopping?'

'No, he never did that.'

'And did he ever arrange for the most famous couturiers in the world to open their salons especially for you?'

'No, he never did that either.'

'Did he ever take you sailing on a Chinese junk?'

She was laughing again. She shook her head. 'Unh unh.'

DeLaroza leaned back and grinned. 'You see, gratitude has its limitations.'

'My gratitude to you has none,' she said and reaching down, unbuttoned the top two buttons of his shirt, slipped her hands inside, and caressed his chest, her fingers pinching his nipples. He closed his eyes, reached out to run his fingers along her satin-sheathed thigh, but it was gone. She had already moved away, as elusive as a dragonfly. She crossed to the windows and looked back at him.

'And now you make toys,' she said.

'You always say the word *toys* with a very patronizing attitude,' DeLaroza said. 'I do not just make *toys*. I create masterpieces. Do you know I once made a tiny Rolls-Royce, it was a foot long, a perfect replica. The wheels moved, the pistons worked, the engine worked, even the radio worked. It was exact to the most infinitesimal detail.

The gentleman I made it for sat on the floor in this office and clapped his hands together like a child when he came to get it. It cost twelve thousand dollars, a fourth of what the real thing costs. He paid for it in cash.'

She shrugged. 'Big deal,' she said.

He mimicked her. 'Big deal. That is all you have to say, "Big deal"? It was a very big deal to him. And to me. Besides, everyone loves a toymaker. It carries with it a unique kind of respect. Who can fault a man who spends his life making children happy?'

The question hung in the air. Domino did not hear it. She was looking at the ground, twenty storeys below, at two boys rough-housing in the plaza, their arms wrapped around each other as they battled back and forth. She shuddered again.

'Is something wrong?' DeLaroza asked.

'It's nothing. I just remembered something. It's really quite silly.'

'It could not be that silly, to have such an effect on you.'

'You remember the last time I was here? Halloween night?'

A small fear crept into his chest.

'Of course. I never forget one of your visits.'

'As I was leaving, these two men were on the other side of the plaza. I saw them from inside the building. One was very drunk. He was so . . . so limp . . . and the other one was trying to get him in the car . . .'

DeLaroza was no longer listening. The fear grew and crept deeper into his chest. He pressed his knuckles together until they were white. *Good God*, he thought, *did she see something? Was this the beginning of blackmail?* His eyes narrowed for just a moment. Old paranoias swept over him, rising up again from the past, nightmare creatures nibbling at his heart. He suddenly felt cold and alone.

'. . . Guess I just felt sorry for him. I had a feeling I had seen him before. He was wearing this old leather jacket, way out of style.'

'Did you tell anyone about this?' DeLaroza asked casually.

'What's there to tell? That I saw a drunk being shoved into a car?'

'Then why does it bother you so?'

'I wish I knew. It's like . . . like some kind of instinct. I can't put my finger on it. Am I being silly? Do you think I'm silly?'

'I think,' said DeLaroza, 'that you are far from silly.' He shrugged off the feeling. This was not the time to deal with it. 'Look at you,' he said, 'when you came in here you were, uh – how do you say it? – *acima* . . . high. Up. Now you seem so sad.'

She turned back to him and smiled again. 'It's all gone. And you're right, I am up. What did you call it?'

'*Acima.*'

'*Acima.* That's me.'

'And why? Do you have some special new trick for me?'

'No. It's something more selfish.'

'So? Everyone has the right to be selfish at times. What is it?'

'I knew you'd understand. You particularly would understand.'

'Hmm. What is this all about?'

She came back across the room and sat on the corner of his desk.

'Victor . . . I think I've fallen in love.'

He stared at her for a moment, then said, 'Think?'

'I didn't plan on it. It just sneaked up on me. It surprises me. But then, of course, I adore surprises.'

'And you have not been in love before?'

'Oh, many times,' she said and laughed. 'But not recently.'

'Then I am happy for you. And who is the lucky gentleman. It is a man?'

'Oh, yes, a very special man.'

'Aha, and do I know him?'

'Of course.'

DeLaroza took out a large Havana cigar and started to peel away the cellophane. He needed time to sort out his thoughts. He found her news upsetting. She took the cigar away from him, snipped off the end and lit it, twirling it between her fingers so it burned evenly. Then she handed it back to him.

'*Obrigado,*' he said.

'You're welcome.'

He took a deep drag and blew the smoke out slowly. His face had grown sad.

71

'Have I upset you?' she asked.

'No. I am concerned, not upset. You know, of course, that he is going to make his announcement Monday night at the opening of *Pachinko*!'

'Yes.'

'To continue this love affair at this time could be very risky.'

'Love affair?' she said. The words hung in the air as though she were listening to them in instant reply. She frowned.

'Well,' he said, 'call it what you wish. Infatuation?'

'Trite. Trite words and trite phrases.' She was scowling at him.

DeLaroza chuckled. 'Far be it for me to accuse you of being trite, my dear,' he said.

'Thank you,' she said.

'It is just that I know both of you so well,' DeLaroza said. 'I've known Donald for sixteen years and you . . . for two . . . .'

'Almost three.'

'Yes, almost three.'

His gaze moved past her, settling on the foliage outside his office. Three years. At their first meeting he had acted on what he thought at the time was an impulse. A very lucky one, he had come to realize, although totally out of character for him. The first time he had ever seen Domino she was standing in a fleamarket in Buckhead, staring intently at an antique Morris chair. A stunning woman, though her clothes were not quite right, her hair a little too long, and yet . . . And yet.

He had ordered Chiang to turn the Rolls around and go back. He had found her, still contemplating the chair.

'The chair is overpriced,' he had told her. 'You should be able to purchase it for half what they are asking.'

She smiled at him. 'I'm not very good at that kind of thing,' she had told him.

'Then I shall act as your agent in the matter.'

Her education had begun that day. Now even he had to marvel at what Domino had become. And now, too, in retrospect, he understood that meeting her that day had not been mere impulse. Domino had fitted his plans perfectly.

'Hello,' she said.

72

DeLaroza looked back at her. 'Sorry,' he said. 'I was thinking about the fleamarket.'

She laughed. 'I still owe you twelve dollars for the Morris chair,' she said.

'I consider that one of my better investments.'

'You were saying?'

'Uh . . . what was I saying?' he was slightly embarrassed that he had forgotten his point.

'You were saying that you know both of us very well.'

'Oh, yes. Perhaps love was too strong a word. There is a need there, for both of you.'

'Of course. I guess it really isn't fair to say we don't love each other. I love Donald. And I love you.'

'You love power, my dear. It is your passion.'

'Maybe I'm just turned off by the lack of it.'

'My point is, after Monday night you will become a luxury Donald can no longer afford.'

A half-smile played briefly over her face.

'You know I'm really surprised that you're sharing the spotlight of your beloved *Pachinko!* – even with the next president of the United States.'

DeLaroza looked away from her. She was quite astute. *Pachinko!* was DeLaroza's grandest achievement, an amusement park like no other in the world. It had taken years to conceive and build it. But Donald Hotchins's announcement at the opening of the park was part of his plan. Even Domino was part of it. DeLaroza did nothing without a plan. He finally waved a hand in the air.

'It will be a delicate situation,' he said. 'I hope you can handle it. I admit if anyone can, you can. But the Chinese have a saying: The peacock should not strut when the tiger is about. There will be many tigers about, waiting for him to make a mistake so they can devour him. It could destroy him.'

'Then I'll have to be very clever.'

'You can be that.'

'I'm sorry. Am I hurting you? I wouldn't hurt you.'

'Of course not. I know you would never hurt anyone knowingly. It is just that I seem to have – how do you say it? – bit off my nose?'

'Cut off my nose to spite my face. It's a stupid saying.'

'Yes, but true. I will not see you again, will I? That is

what you are really saying to me, is it not?'

'Of course I'll see you. We'll all be good friends.'

'Not business acquaintances.'

The remark stunned her, as if he had slapped her. 'Is that what it's been to you?' she said. 'I hoped it was more than just business. You're very special to me. Don't you know that?'

He watched the smoke curl towards the ceiling, swirling in and out of the pools of light from the recessed lamps. 'Yes,' he said finally, 'I do.' She reached out and touched his hand with her fingertips. 'You are quite something,' he said. 'You have what we call in Brazil *beleza inexplicada*. A quality that cannot be described.'

'Thank you.'

'Does he know about you? All about you?'

'No. Is that really necessary?'

He shook his head. 'But if he should find out?'

'Someday I'll explain it all to him.'

'No, no, you will not, my love. It is a thing you will never be able to do. But that is your problem.' Then: 'So this meeting was all for talk, eh? Conversation. I will be disappointed this last time.'

She moved closer to him, so close he could feel her warmth. She leaned over him and her breasts touched his chest. She brushed her lips across his eyelids. It made him tremble.

'No,' she said. 'You're very special to me. You've been very good to me and I know what makes you happy, Victor. I want our last private meeting together to make you happier than you've ever been before. A very special night. Tonight you will come to my apartment at eight o'clock and I'll give you your farewell present, *mui bita*?'

'Yes,' he said. 'I understand.' He sighed, staring at her open blouse, at the tinted edges of her nipples, feeling her perfume hypnotizing his senses. Her fingers moved lightly across his neck and drew his head to her, his cheek against her breast.

'And why are we waiting until tonight?' he asked, his voice trembling.

'Because,' she said, and her voice was a husky, inviting, ageless whisper, 'I want you to think about it. All day long. It will be much sweeter that way.'

74

He closed his eyes, turning his head so her dress fell away from her breast, and he was tasting the tartness of her hardened nipple.

'You are a masterpiece,' he whispered. 'On Ipanema, you would steal the beach away from the sea.'

'You should have been a poet, Victor,' she said softly.

'You *are* a poet, my dear.' But even at that moment the old fear crawled back inside him again and the horror of what had to be done was like an angry voice hissing in his ear. And he could not ignore it.

Chapter Four

The Vice Squad was located deep in the bowels of the main station house, a windowless, airless, cramped, messy space hardly big enough to accommodate the sixteen men who called it home. It was a forgotten hole, away from normal traffic, a place nobody had to pass or see or contend with. Prison-grey pipes rattled overhead. The place was too hot in the winter and frigid in the summer.

Barney Friscoe sat in a closet of an office, a short, chunky lieutenant with eternal five o'clock shadow and thinning brown hair, dressed in chinos, Adidas, a Wings Over America tee-shirt, and a yellow windbreaker. His cluttered desk looked like a combat zone. As Sharky entered the cubbyhole, he stood up, peering over the reading glasses that were perched halfway down his nose and smiling in a row of crooked, off-colour teeth. He offered Sharky a hairy paw.

'Welcome to Friscoe's Inferno,' he said. 'You're Sharky, right? One o'clock, right on time. I hardly recognize you without all that hair on your face. Grab a chair there, throw that shit on the floor. You had lunch?'

Sharky shook his head, nodded yes to the question, and moved a pile of debris from one of the two battered chairs in the small room.

'Jesus,' Sharky said, 'what'd you do to deserve this?'

'Dirtiest digs for the dirtiest squad. Oh, well, nobody gives a shit. We don't spend any time around here anyhow.' He waved outside the office at the bullpen where half a dozen desks were jammed together in a space hardly big enough for four. On the corner of one was an antiquated coffeemaker. Sugar and powdered milk formed pools around it and a dirty communal spoon lay forgotten nearby.

There were two men in the outer office. One of them, a hard-looking black man in his forties with a deep scar over his left eye and streaks of grey in his tight-cropped afro, wore a tan corduroy three-piece suit. The vest was open and his tie was pulled down to his collarbone. He stared coldly at Sharky then turned back to a battered Royal typewriter and began pecking out a report with two fingers. The other, an older man built like a refrigerator, was on the phone.

'That's Livingston and Papadopolis out there,' Friscoe said. 'Livingston's the one with the tan.'

'He got something against me?' Sharky asked.

'Not that I know of,' Friscoe said. 'The Bat sent your sheet down. Looks like you got the shit stick handed to you. That was a nice machine you had workin' there until that dimwit Tully fucked it up for you. He was down here a while. You cut off his head, he wouldn't be any dumber than he is with it on.'

'I've been told to forget it.'

'Probably the best thing to do. What's gonna happen with Tully, Tully's gonna end with his toes up one of these days. He's too stupid to stay alive. It's still tough, y'know. Nobody likes to take the gas pipe when they been workin' a thing as long as you were. Anyways, I got something down here you can maybe get your dick into. So far what we got is odds and ends, see? Nothing ties together yet. But it's lookin' pretty good. Here and there.'

'You're a little vague,' Sharky said.

'Paranoid,' Friscoe said.

'Oh,' Sharky said and laughed at Friscoe's candour.

'What it is, every once in a while one of my boys turns up something sounds interesting. Not the usual stink finger, hands-up bullshit but something maybe we can make a little mileage outa. What happens, I don't wanna give anything away, see what I mean? What I don't want, I don't want Homicide or Bunco or some lace doilie outfit workin' special for the chief stealin' my melons, okay? Fuck that shit. I figure it starts here, I wanna keep it here. The other thing, I don't make a habit, see, of goin' down to the DA with my dick in my hand. Unless we make a heavy case, we don't nail it down, I flush it. We got a machine goin' and we can't put it together, it goes down the toilet.'

He slurped coffee and kept talking. Sharky found himself breathing for him.

'Just so's you know the territory down here, let me tell you, here's how I feel about Vice. I got sixteen years in, almost seventeen. I been on foot in the boondocks. Did a two-year trick in a blue-and-white. Had one partner snuffed

77

out from under me and another one, he tried to drive through a warehouse wall, ended up in a wheelchair. I got out lucky with a bad back. I been in Bunco, six years in Robbery, I did a short tour in Homicide and I was in the IA for about two minutes before I ended up here.'

Sharky laughed. He could just see Friscoe in Internal Affairs in his sneakers and sweatshirt, investigating complaints against his fellow officers.

'Internal Affairs,' Friscoe went on, 'I told 'em to stuff it. I got to deal with snitches every day. I'll be damned if I'm gonna snitch on my own, see what I mean?'

Sharky nodded. There was a rumour you could not even be interviewed for the IA unless you'd been born out of wedlock.

'Anyways, I personally don't give a rat's ass what the public does,' Friscoe growled. 'Some guy wants to stick his dick in a coffee grinder, who am I to argue, okay? It's his dick. Personally I got better things to do. I could care less some shirt salesman from Dubuque comes inta town, wants to pay out fifty, a hundred bucks to get laid, get a little head, shit, why not? Live and let live, I say, but it's where they put you. The Bat, the commissioner, the chief, whoever puts you where you are. Like I say, I got almost seventeen in, so I don't growl too loud. Mainly we got misdemeanours down here. Hooking. Pandering. Freak show. It takes a lotta time, effort, to make a misdemeanour case, okay? I mean, nobody's sucker enough if he pays some chippie fifty to gobble his pork, he's gonna show up in court and testify against her. He's gonna head for the hills first.'

'So what's the answer?' Sharky asked.

'So we make a case against somebody for trickin' it's gotta be the cop makin' it and that means he had to make a deal and money has to change hands. What we really look for is felony. Extortion. A and B. Juvenile crimes. The worst. But it's rare. Mostly what we do, we answer complaints and do what we can to keep the streets clean. If we get a handle on something good, it's gravy on the potatoes. You want some mud? It's strong enough to play fullback for the Falcons.'

'No thanks.'

'Another thing. We got that fuckin' DA Hanson comin' up for re-election so he's got all the Baptists, the bluenoses,

Billy Grahamers fired up right now. . . . The schmuck hasn't done anything but indict homos and jack-off artists for two years, but he's makin' a lot of noise right now so he'll look good to the PTA, that kinda shit. To listen to him, see, you'd think you can't take a breath of fresh air downtown without gettin' the clap.'

Sharky broke up again, but Friscoe went right on, ignoring the laughter.

'Anyways Hanson is keepin' me busy just on routine, shakin' up the ladies on the street, bustin' the massage parlours, movie pits, hourly hotels. What I want, see, I want to zero you in on this thing we got a handle on, let you loose, see what you can do. I give you Arch – that's Livingston – and Papa and anybody you can dog-rob outa some other department. That's your whole army.'

Sharky nodded. 'I've heard stories about both of them.'

'Whaddya hear, good or bad?' Friscoe asked.

'Both. Depends on who you listen to. The guys I listen to say they're in sudden death playoff with the best there is.'

Friscoe beamed, obviously pleased. 'Livingston there, he's got thirteen in. Best goddamn street cop in the House. He's cautious but lotsa smarts upstairs, right? College guy like you. Papadopolis, a hell of a cop. Papa doesn't give a shit. He'll stake out the governor's toilet you tell him to. Been shot three times; don't even remember where the scars are. And that's your machine. Oh yeah, one other thing. You gotta understand the politics of the House, see. All of us down here, in the cesspool here, we either don't know the politics, see, or didn't give a shit. Or maybe what it was, we were too hard-headed. That's what happens, you don't suck ass, play by the book, all that shit, you end up down here in the fuckin' leper colony. I been hearin' about you, the last two, three years. The word's been around the department head's on you, okay? Some say you're a hardhead. Others say you're dynamite on the street. Thing is, I give you maybe three, four years, you'll walk.'

'To where? I'll have eight years in. Where the hell do you go after sinking that much time in the cops?'

'I dunno, but y'see, Sharky, you're too goddamn contrary to suck up to the system and too smart to live in it. I heard this morning, from this buddy of mine in IA, he calls me before I got a cup of coffee in me, tells me The Bat's getting ready to flop you out of detectives and give you a six-and-six. Even upstairs they figure you got a raw deal. I mean, the way I look at it, what do they want? Maybe you should've given the creep a ticket to Detroit and cab fare to the fuckin' airport, right? So I go up to see Jaspers and I tell him I gotta have some help and could I have you since I heard he was bustin' you outa the narcs. The Bat thinks it over a minute or two and finally says, "Okay, but tell him to keep out of my hair." And then he says something real strange. He says, "Tell him to keep his shoes on in my office." What the fuck was that all about?'

'My foot itched.'

'And you took off your shoe and scratched it, that it?'

'Right.'

'Bad form. Very bad form. You gotta understand about The Brat, about them all. Shit, look, it's a lotta fuckin' crap protocol up there, see? That's what I'm talkin' about. You're a third- or second-grade detective, you're a maggot to them. Takin' off your shoe, that makes sense to you, but to a creep like The Bat, it's death warmed over. That's what I mean, I see you walkin' a coupla years from now. You gotta roll along and take the punches, let the big shots grab the big collars, keep your face off the front page, don't make waves. That kind of thing. Otherwise what happens, you end up down here. Me, I should give a shit. Two years I make captain, probably get assistant in charge of Criminal Investigation, some nice job to go out on. Another two years I take my retirement and fuck it. But you, you're gonna kick ass a lot and get kicked a lot. It's what always happens you got a guy who's smart, savvy, don't mind taking a chance or two now and then.'

'You sure paint a rosy picture.'

'Truth. I deal in truth. What comes from bein' a Boy Scout my younger years. Point is, see, it takes me a long time to say something, but I'm glad to have you down here, okay?'

'Thanks, lieutenant.'

'It goes for Arch there and Papa. Arch, he was the first black cop on the force. And he didn't suck ass, didn't eat any shit. The ones that followed him, they, y'know, stuck their dick in the air see which the way wind's blowin', kissed the right asses, moved on up there. Fuckin' Uncle Tom shit, but Arch, he didn't bow down nowhere along the line. So here he is, best fuckin' street cop on the force bustin' hookers and library freaks.'

'What happened to Papa?'

'Papa was in Bunco workin' under a shitass name of Shaushauser, a fuckin' Nazi. He's dead now. Rest his soul, all that shit, but he had it comin'. Anyway Papa brought down two, three big scams and this Shaushauser he takes the collars and even ends up with a citation. One day Papa has enough. He's in the locker room with Shaushauser and suddenly he starts playing handball, only Shaushauser's the ball. Bim, bam, bim, he takes the lieutenant off the wall a couple times, ties his feet in a knot, goes about his merry business. Shaushauser goes to the hospital, Papa does a ten-and-ten, a year back in uniform, and then down here. That's what I mean about the system, Sharky. You can't beat the motherfuckers, so you either give in or walk. I see you walkin', all I'm sayin'. Anyways, it ain't gloryland here, but it's better than what you had, you ask me. You know what they say – Fuck around with frogs you end up with warts on your dick.'

'I think it's "Lie down with dogs and get up with fleas." '

'Right, just what I said. Now let's get goin'. Hey, Papa, hang up the phone goddammit, we got business. Arch, get your ass in here. We can't wait until the day after tomorrow you finish that report. And somebody bring the tape recorder. Let's put some goddamn wheels on this machine.'

Chapter Five

The man who arrived at one o'clock at the private suite in the Regal Hotel was short and unkempt. He needed a shave, his greying hair was frazzled and uncombed, his fierce grey eyes ringed with circles. He wore a pair of baggy slacks, a mismatched sports jacket, and his tie was a disaster. He carried a cheap plastic snapshut briefcase under his arm and a copy of *The New York Times* he had brought with him on the early morning flight from Washington. And he was hyper; energy vibrated around him. He sucked noisily on an empty pipe, walking in tight little circles waiting for someone to answer his knock.

His appearance was deceiving. Julius Lowenthal, former advisor to two presidents and a gnawing antagonist for a third, had once been described by a Pulitzer Prize-winning journalist as having the appearance of a burlesque comic and the mind of a Borgia.

One did not court Lowenthal's services; he offered them. On this morning he was about to meet Senator Donald Walden Hotchins, Jr.

He was greeted at the door by another political curiosity. Physically, Charles Roan was Lowenthal's alter ego: a tall, husky, pleasant man with an ebullient personality, boundless energy, and a taste for three-piece tailored suits. He was an open, buoyant man, unlike the caged lion that was Lowenthal. As Hotchins's campaign manager Charley Roan had overcome two major drawbacks: he was a former All-American football player – a jock – and he had been Hotchins's room-mate in college. Sixteen years earlier, when Hotchins had challenged one of the strongest old-line machine politicians in the state for governor, his appointment of Charley as campaign manager had been regarded as a joke. Nobody laughed any more. Roan had been the architect of a remarkable success, had guided Hotchins through two terms in the statehouse, a term as governor and finally had helped him defeat the state's senior senator. It was Roan who had discreetly let it be known to Lowenthal that Hotchins needed him.

The suite was modest, a living room furnished with comfortable but undistinguished hotel furniture, a bedroom with a king-size bed, and a small kitchenette. Only a few of Hotchins's closest confidants knew he maintained the suite. The senator was standing near a window when Lowenthal entered the room. He smiled and limped across it with the aid of a highly polished shillelagh, a tall, lean, handsome man, well-tanned, with blond hair and penetrating blue eyes. He was casually dressed in flared slacks and a dark blue sports shirt. He shook hands with Lowenthal.

'How's the foot?' Lowenthal asked.

'It's okay. Occasionally it acts up when the weather's bad.'

Lowenthal smiled. 'Can you run on one leg when the weather's bad?'

'He can run on his hands if he has to,' Charley Roan said.

'I appreciate your coming,' Hotchins said. 'Do you think I'm crazy?'

'Sure I do,' Lowenthal said. 'Anybody who runs for public office is crazy. Anybody who runs for this office is mad as a hatter.'

Hotchins smiled. 'Okay, welcome to the tea party. How about some coffee?'

'Cream and sugar,' Lowenthal said. 'I stayed in the airport motel in Washington last night and sneaked out. I don't think anybody knows I'm here. Once the press finds out, the cat's out of the bag. I'd like to forestall that as long as possible.'

'You can stay here. Nobody knows about this suite but a few of us. My press secretary, Pete Holmes, is at a luncheon. He'll be along in an hour or so. He's very good at handling the media.'

'So I've heard.'

'Well,' Roan said, rubbing his hands together, 'what do you think?'

'What do I think?' Lowenthal said raising his eyebrows. 'What do I think about what?'

'I think what Charley means is, What do you think of our chances?'

Lowenthal stuffed tobacco into his battered pipe and lit it, almost disappearing in a nuclearean smokecloud. He waved the smoke away with a hand.

'I think if you can survive until the convention, once you've made the announcement, you've got a chance. I also think that is one big *if*.'

'I'm not a pussyfooter, Julius,' Hotchins said. 'Are you interested in working with us?'

'That's why I'm here, Mr. Senator.'

'Great. That's great!' Roan said and slapped his hands together. Lowenthal felt a moment of annoyance before remembering that exuberance was one of the prices one paid for youth. 'I took the liberty of talking to Bob Fitzgerald at the National Committee yesterday,' Lowenthal said. 'I hope you don't object. I realize it was a bit unorthodox going ahead before we talked, but the timing seemed right to me. I operate on instincts, been living with them a long time. Usually don't take time to question them, I just go.'

'And how does Fitzgerald feel about us?' Hotchins asked.

'Well, you got to remember that Fitz is an old party bull. He's been chairman of the NC for ten years. He's tough, probably the best machine politician this country's seen since Tammany. He's like an odds maker. He adds it all up and then he makes his bet.'

'And?' Hotchins said.

'And he's still betting on Humphrey.'

'Humphrey!' Roan bellowed. 'Jesus Christ, he's already been whipped once. Does he want to hand the election to Ford?'

'The way he sees it, it's going to be a free-for-all in New Hampshire, Wisconsin, West Virginia, and all the early runners are going to burn out in the stretch. We're talking about a lot of money and a lot of endurance. Hubert can afford to wait it out until May, maybe even June, then jump in at the last minute after all the shooting's over and walk off with it.'

'So,' Hotchins said, 'what it's going to take is a long-distance runner with a lot of money.'

'That's it,' Lowenthal said.

'And he's writing us off, right?' Roan said.

'He thinks Carter's going to be the man in the South. And he doesn't even give *him* a chance. He doesn't think either one of you has a chance nationally. Doesn't think you have the clout. You've stepped on too many toes. The

84

insurance companies, the lobbyists, nuclear power. You've kicked a lot of ass, Mr. Senator.'

Hotchins smiled. 'And there's still plenty of kick left in my good foot,' he said.

'But that's where the money is,' said Lowenthal.

'We got the money,' said Roan.

'We're talking big money. *Big* money.'

'We have *big* money. And we have stamina.'

'How about Carter?' said Lowenthal.

'Well, how about him?' Hotchins said.

'He's going to run. I talked to his people last week.'

'We can take Carter,' Roan said. 'He hasn't got the charisma Hotch has.'

'And he's soft on some key issues. I know Jimmy. We get along fine. I like him. But we can take him,' Hotchins said. 'We can beat him right here in the back room before he gets started. I guarantee it.'

Lowenthal nodded. 'I agree. I think you can. But you're going to have to beat him out of the gate and that means starting the race too soon. It's dangerous.'

'He'll have to do the same. It's a question of who comes out first. And we're coming out next Monday,' said Roan.

'Next Monday!' Lowenthal looked shocked.

'We'll lock the state before Jimmy gets out of bed,' Roan said. 'Then hit New Hampshire like the blizzard of '88.'

Lowenthal shook his head. 'You'll be on oxygen before spring,' he said.

'No way,' Hotchins said and the intensity of his retort surprised Lowenthal. 'I can hop faster and farther than any of them can run on two legs. I've been training for this for too long. Let 'em think we'll burn out. Let Fitzgerald think so.'

Lowenthal nibbled on his pipe. He was seeing a new side to Hotchins. Tough. Obsessed. A man who did not consider losing. Maybe he could do it. Maybe he just had the fever to do it. He decided to try another approach, another test. 'Let me put it this way,' he said, 'You know how the National Committee works. They control party finances. They can also play hell with the convention, with delegates' votes, simply by screwing with the convention rules. They browbeat, cajole, threaten, blackmail, call in favours – there are a hundred ways they can steal committed votes.

You could go all the way to the wire and see it vanish in a two- or three-ballot donnybrook.'

'They tried it on Kennedy and got their ass handed to them,' Roan said.

'And Harry Truman,' Hotchins added. 'Talk about stamina. He whistle-stopped Dewey to death. We can do the same thing. To Carter, Udall, Frank Church, even Humphrey if we have to. We know all this. The question is, Do we need the committee?'

'Academic question,' Lowenthal said. 'We don't have 'em, so why worry about it? Fitz'll fight you all the way to the final ballot. I know him. I've been up against him before. He wants a winner; that's the name of the game this year. And he doesn't think you have a chance in hell. Look, you're running, okay? You need money. If you're a good party hack, they back you. If you're a maverick, played by your own rules, voted against a few big party bills – which you have – they run out of money just when you need it. So you can forget the committee for money *and* support. And it can get very lonely out there if the party strongarms are against you. They'll throw everybody in the party at you in the early primaries. They may even quietly support some weak sisters to split the vote, throw it into a runoff. Make you spend more money. And what Fitz is looking for is for you to run out of breath in the stretch. He plays for longevity. Longevity is what counts.'

'We'll be waiting for him in New York come July,' Hotchins said, with more than just confidence. The way he said it, it was a statement of fact.

Lowenthal shook his head and chuckled. 'Well, if confidence alone could win it, you'd be on the way to Washington right now,' he said. 'But I must tell you, I don't agree with this plan to announce on Monday. Hell, at least wait until after the New Year.'

'We can't,' Roan said. 'Carter's getting ready himself.'

Lowenthal shook his head. 'It's Christmas. Nobody gives a damn about politics right now.'

'They will,' Hotchins said.

'Damn, you're determined!' Lowenthal said.

Hotchins fixed himself a cup of tea and put half a spoonful of sugar into it. He stirred it slowly, looking at Lowenthal with his crystal blue eyes.

'What's your interest in me, Julius?' he asked.

Lowenthal smiled. 'Plain and simple? You're a maverick and I like that, always have. I've been watching you for years. We believe in the same things.' Then: 'So much for idealism. Now we'll get to the bottom line. You have style. You have a hell of a war record. But the big thing is, I don't think Humphrey can beat Ford and I think you just might. Ford's the weakest incumbent president the Democrats have ever run against, but that doesn't mean he's a pushover. He can shake the Nixon thing. He's already done a pretty good job of that. My personal opinion is that a dark horse is going to take him. And they don't come any darker than you right now.'

Hotchins and Roan both laughed.

'Besides,' Lowenthal said, 'maybe, just maybe, you could make one hell of a president.'

Hotchins smiled warmly. Then he laughed out loud.

'I'll be a son of a bitch,' he said. 'That's one hell of an answer.'

'Good,' Lowenthal said, 'now let's get to the nut-cutting fast. You got any secrets. Anything in the closet we ought to know about? Any illegitimate kids, bad friends, vices that may upset the little old ladies in Nebraska?'

Hotchins smiled to conceal a tiny shock that hit him in the stomach. A picture of Domino flashed past his eyes. 'Of course not,' he said casually.

'We've been through this before,' Roan said. 'If there was anything, it would have been turned up by now.'

'Not like this time. This time they'll be all over you – into your business deals, your war record, your family life. *Both* parties in the beginning. I don't want any surprises popping up at the last minute.'

'What else?' Hotchins said, killing that conversation.

'What's your net worth?'

Hotchins thought about that for a few moments. 'I suppose I'll show close to a million dollars when my CPA finishes the audit. But most of that's on paper. Investments, stock in trust to protect me from conflicts of interest.'

'How much liquid?'

'Less than two hundred thousand dollars.'

'Our credit position is very strong,' Roan said. 'We can tap several banks. I'd say we can raise a million, maybe

87

more to start with.'

'Not enough.'

'What is enough?' Hotchins asked.

Lowenthal tapped dead ashes out of his pipe. Then he said, 'Two million, minimum. It could go higher depending on how rough it gets. And no big contributors. It could hurt you later. It also could be illegal.'

Hotchins stared at the lawyer. He had to be careful with Lowenthal. No matter how tough he might talk, Lowenthal was known for his integrity. It was one of the traits that gave him credence and had ever since he had first appeared on the political scene during the Kennedy campaign. But Hotchins was thinking, *Illegal?* It was only illegal if they got caught and he knew DeLaroza well enough to know Victor would never get caught. Hotchins's big concern was two million dollars. Was his finance minister prepared to raise that kind of money? He thought he knew the answer.

'We've got it,' he said suddenly. 'And without that son of a bitch Fitzgerald. I don't want his money. I don't want him until we get to New York. Then I want him with his hat in his hand, begging to get on board.'

He limped to the window and looked down at the street, at the little people scurrying back to their offices and after-lunch Alka Seltzers. The voters. They *were* little people to him, humiliated by the routines of life, badgered by the banks and the mortgage companies and the institutions, running one step ahead of failure. His contempt for the common man was a deeply guarded secret, a flaw which could destroy him. And looking down at them he felt a deep rage that his future lay in their hands. But the emotion passed quickly.

'So it's Humphrey we have to beat,' he mused aloud.

'Hubert's a fine man,' Lowenthal said. 'And a hell of a campaigner.'

'He had his chance in '68,' Hotchins said, and there was a snap to his voice, like a whip cracking. To Hotchins, he was a loser, a failure, like the little people below, a man who smiled in defeat and cried in public. Happy Warrior, hell. But he said nothing, for he sensed Lowenthal's respect for the Minnesota senator.

Lowenthal walked over to him. 'Look, you got a lot going for you. You're handsome, honest, got a great record.

You're a war hero; you left a foot in Korea and came back with the Distinguished Service Cross and a Purple Heart. You took a little nothing business and an SBA loan and parlayed it into a national franchise. You're a lawyer, a soldier, a businessman. Got a great family. Mr. Clean. And it's all beautiful and great. What it gets you, it gets you into the gate, period.

'After that, it's a balls-out race. What I can do for you, I can bring in some real heavyweights. Joe McGuire, Angie Costerone, John Davis Harmon. They'll come aboard if I'm aboard. I can work the demographics, tell you how to get the Chicano vote in L.A., the blacks and Puerto Ricans in New York, the Irish vote in Boston, the Polish vote in Chicago, deal with the unions, the city machines, the state hacks. We can do all that. But it won't mean a damn unless we come off big. You got to open up your campaign like a winner and run like one. When we announce we have to take the biggest hall in the state and fill it with the kids, the senior citizens, blacks, reds, yellows, greens, pinks, Wasps. We want bands and noise and, uh, what we can't do, we can't come out with *bupkus*. You know *bupkus*? It's Yiddish. It means nothing, zilch. A quiet noise. You sneak into this campaign and Fitz figures he's got you dead already. You come out big, with me and McGuire and the rest, it's gonna scare him to death.'

Hotchins grinned. He was going to come out big, all right. That, he could guarantee.

Phipps Plaza was one of the city's more elegant shopping centres, located a few minutes from Victor DeLaroza's office, its parking lot three storeys deep and under the mall. At two that Thursday afternoon there were only a few cars on the lower level. One of them was a brown Rolls-Royce which sat facing the exit ramp, its motor mumbling softly.

Hotchins guided his Buick down the ramp and parked beside it. As he got out of his car the rear door of the Rolls swung open and Hotchins got into its elegant interior. DeLaroza was sipping a cup of espresso, an enormous Havana cigar smouldering in his fist. He grinned as the senator sat beside him and he pressed a button in the arm-rest near his elbow. A window rose silently between the front and back seats.

'*Bom dia*,' DeLaroza said.

Hotchins shook his hand warmly. 'I feel like I'm in the CIA,' he said, 'sneaking around parking lots just to have a chat. You should have come to the hotel. I want you to meet Lowenthal.'

'All in time,' DeLaroza said. 'I still put a high price on my privacy. When it becomes necessary for me to become a more public person, then I will deal with that problem at the time. So, what is so urgent?'

'Lowenthal's in.'

'Excellent, excellent!' DeLaroza cried.

'And he's bringing in McGuire, Casterone, and Harmon with him.'

'Ah! Even better. That is splendid news. More than you had hoped for, eh?'

Hotchins's voice became flat and hard. His eyes narrowed. 'I was counting on it,' he said. 'Lowenthal is like an ace in a poker game. Without help he could be beat by a pair of deuces.'

'An interesting analogy. And who are these deuces?'

'Fitzgerald and Humphrey.'

'So, the National Committee has made its choice.'

'Yes.'

'It is no surprise, my friend, right?'

'No. And I like it this way,' Hotchins said. 'When the convention's over, we'll have Fitzgerald at our feet. That's what I want. I want them all to line up and kiss my ass.'

DeLaroza's eyebrows arched as he listened to Hotchins's venom spill out. He said, 'I am sure Fitzgerald is aware of this threat.'

'Sure he is. They're going to fight us hard and dirty. That's all right. It'll make the victory that much sweeter. I tell you, Victor, I can taste it. *Taste* it.' Hotchins's eyes burned with almost sensual delight as he spoke.

'Easy, my friend. Save that energy, it is a long time between now and July.'

But Hotchins's ardour could not be stemmed. He had contained himself in Lowenthal's presence, not wishing to reveal his need. Now he let go, savouring what he felt was a sweet victory.

'I can feel it in my bones,' he said. 'Lowenthal's commit-

90

ted. He's excited, enthusiastic. And he's a brilliant tactician. Just what we need to go up against the committee. Now we can beat 'em, I know it. We can grind the sons of bitches under.'

DeLaroza stared at the senator and puffed on his Havana. Somewhere within the immaculate framework of the Rolls an exhaust fan quietly sucked the smoke from the rear compartment.

'You remember a movie with Brando called *One-Eyed Jacks*?' DeLaroza said.

'Why? What's the point?'

'You remind me of a one-eyed jack. The rest of the world sees only half your face. They see the veteran hero, the warm family man, charging windmills, tilting with the political machines. How many people ever see the other side, the hidden face of the jack?'

'Why, what do you see there?' Hotchins asked cautiously.

'A barracuda. A competitor with big needs, big hungers. It is what attracted me to you, Donald. That is why you will win. It will not be because of Lowenthal or Casterone or any of the others. You will win because you have an instinct for the jugular and that will surprise them.'

Hotchins leaned forward in the seat, tense and suddenly uneasy. They had never talked this openly before. Finally he said, 'Takes one to know one, right, Victor?'

'Oh, I am not a barracuda,' DeLaroza said. 'The barracuda is selective. It picks its victims to appease its appetite. I am a shark, Donald. I will eat anything that comes in my way.'

'Sounds like a warning,' Hotchins said.

'No. I want to make sure you are aware that I too have big appetites. And I also go for the throat.'

Hotchins pondered the comment for a few moments and then laughed. 'All right,' he said.

DeLaroza laughed with him. He puffed on the cigar again, then said, 'Now, what are the complications?'

It was Hotchins's turn to raise his eyebrows. 'Complications? Who said anything about complications?'

'My friend, there are always complications.'

Hotchins rubbed his hands together but said nothing.

'I would guess,' said DeLaroza, 'that it is money.'

'You're a mind reader.'

'Not really. The last thing one always discusses is the price.'

Hotchins's blue eyes grew colder. He looked DeLaroza hard in the eyes. 'The price is two million dollars.'

The big man said nothing for a few minutes. He puffed on the Havana, savouring the taste of the smoke on his tongue, letting the smoke ease from his lips, watching it race towards the concealed exhaust vents. Then he said, 'Is this Lowenthal's estimate?'

Hotchins nodded.

'He's low,' DeLaroza said.

'Low?'

'Yes, low. According to our computer, it will take four point six million. That is, of course, considering all the variables. Possible run-offs, et cetera. Add on a ten per cent contingency, over five million.'

Hotchins chewed his lips. He looked out the window of the car, staring around the tomblike interior of the parking lot. A Honda pulled in and stopped and a hassled suburban wife lifted a crying child from the car, then dragged him along behind her towards the elevators.

'I know what you are thinking,' DeLaroza said, 'you are thinking how could Lowenthal make such a sizeable error. Correct?'

'It crossed my mind.'

'It is simple. The last time he was involved in a campaign was '68. In '72 his man lost in the primary, *but* principle was involved. We cannot fault him there. The point is, it is eight years since he was involved in a campaign that went all the way. Inflation. New Methods. The cost of television, newspaper advertising, all rising every day. Many things could account for the discrepancy. He is not an accountant. His political acumen is beyond value. With his friends, you have a package worth more than a million dollars. You probably could not buy them for that.'

'You can't buy them at all,' Hotchins said.

'I would tend to doubt that. It is naïve, but also immaterial. We have them, that is what is important.' He paused, then mused aloud, 'Five million dollars. A lot of money.'

'Yes,' Hotchins said. 'Now we have some strong bank commitments and . . .'

DeLaroza held up a hand. 'Donald . . . *Donald*, wait. I said a lot of money. I did not say *too much* money. You have relied on my financial advice for what – sixteen years now? Are you getting nervous because the price is going up?'

'It has to be done carefully,' Hotchins said. 'You know the rules of disclosure. If Fitzgerald can turn up anything – '

'Please,' DeLaroza said, 'do not tell the hunter how to load his gun.'

Hotchins stopped. Then he patted DeLaroza on the knee. 'Sorry,' he said.

'The money is my problem,' DeLaroza said. 'There is this other thing.'

'It can wait,' Hotchins said quickly.

'No, I think not.'

'It can wait!'

'No.'

The muscles in the corners of Hotchins's jaw quivered, then grew rigid. The flat, hard tone returned to his voice. 'It is personal, Victor.'

'It is a dangerous thing now. Before it was merely risky. I could understand it. I know that kind of hunger. But . . .'

'It's still *my* business.'

'I have never risked five million dollars on you before, Donald.'

'Ah, so now I find out where the strings are.'

'Have there ever been strings attached before?'

'No. But I knew there must be a price. Sooner or later there had to be a price. I guess now is as good a time as any to settle that.'

'You are getting off the subject.'

'This *is* the subject.'

'You are getting angry,' DeLaroza said.

'You're damn right. We're getting into my personal life – '

'You have no personal life any more.'

'Half the politicians in Washington have mistresses.'

'Half the politicians in Washington are not running for president.'

'Jesus!'

'Donald, we are friends. After all it was I who introduced you to the woman. I saw the need. Understood it. But now

93

it must wait until after the election.'

'You think she's going to wait around until after the election? Hell, you know her better than that, Victor. Besides, it's not just me, it's the idea of me that fascinates her.'

DeLaroza nodded. 'I am glad you realize that,' he said.

'It would be a sign of weakness, asking her to sit in the wings until the election's over.'

'My friend, when you are in the Oval Office, you will have anything you wish. Women will be at your call.'

But I need her now, Hotchins thought to himself. 'I'm not talking about women,' he said, 'I'm talking about her.'

'Are you in love with her?'

'Possibly. No, not really. Not in the dramatic sense. But in a way I . . . hell, I don't know. Don't push me. *Don't push me.*'

DeLaroza scowled. He was on dangerous ground and he knew it. Now was not the time to start pulling the strings. And yet, the issue was crucial to him. 'Am I to believe that you would risk something like this for a piece of ass?' he said.

Hotchins glowered at him, his face red, anger boiling in his eyes. 'What was that?' he demanded.

DeLaroza shook his head violently and waved his hand in the air. 'I am sorry,' he said quickly. 'That was a foolish remark. Forgive it.'

They sat without speaking and the minutes crept by. Finally DeLaroza said, 'We will drop it for now. I did not mean to cause harsh words. I was speaking as one friend to another. Just promise me that you will consider it. Think about it. Will you do that?' It annoyed him to patronize Hotchins, but he sensed two egos keening the air like duelling swords.

'Sure,' Hotchins said, 'I'll think about it.'

More silence.

Hotchins felt boxed in, but the furies began to settle down inside him. Perhaps DeLaroza was right. And yet he had never known anyone like her. Her sexuality had given him a new vigour, a vitality that he had missed for years. It was not a motivation; it was fuel for the motivation. And yet if giving her up was part of the key to winning . . .

'Let us get back to the money,' DeLaroza said. 'We have

. . . commitments from individual contributors for almost a million dollars. I can call them in today. In the meantime I can make the funds available through my own accounts. Immediately if necessary. Oh, don't worry, it will be done properly. Nothing would ever appear as a loan.'

Hotchins held up a hand. 'I trust you, Victor. I am sure it will be done in a way that's above . . .' He started to say 'suspicion' but quickly changed it to 'reproach'. He sank back in the seat. His shoulders drooped and he sighed. 'I'm sorry too,' he said. He held out his hand and they shook.

'There will be many anxious times,' DeLaroza said. 'I sometimes forget that we are both emotional men.'

'It's forgotten,' Hotchins said. 'Look. I've got to get back. It's hard for me to get away at all these days, even for a few minutes. They want an itinerary when I go to the bathroom.'

'Get used to it,' DeLaroza said. 'Your private days are about over.'

'I'll be in touch,' Hotchins said. 'Thanks.'

He left the car and DeLaroza settled back. The smile vanished from his face. He sat deep in thought for several minutes. *Yes, his private days are over,* he thought, *and so are mine.* Thirty years of living in shadows and now, in a few short days, the recognition he had needed for so long would be his. He had built an empire and was about to create a king and now, finally, he would have what he deserved – applause. An ovation! The plan to emerge from his self-imposed cell of secrecy had started forming in his mind when he met Hotchins. It had taken sixteen years to gestate. Sixteen years. And now the blood hammered in his temples. Four more days.

He pressed the button, lowering the window between the front and back seats of the car. Chiang, his chauffeur-bodyguard, handed him a cassette. Another addition to the *Gwai-lo* file. It was time to discuss matters with Kershman.

Gerald Kershman was sprawled face down on the bed, his hands and feet bound to the corners by velvet cords. Sweat stung his eyes and he gulped for air as the strips of leather bit into his already tortured flesh. He turned his face into the silk sheets that muffled his cries of pain. The naked young man standing over him with the cat o' nine tails was hard and lithe; his blond hair tumbled in sweaty ringlets over his forehead.

Finally Kershman turned his face towards the youth. 'Enough,' he gasped.

The blond, who was in his late teens, lowered the whip and stood over him. Kershman took several deep breaths and shivered involuntarily and then relaxed. 'Untie me,' he said.

The young man freed him, and Kershman, his back and rump slashed with red welts, struggled from the bed soiled with his own semen and grimaced with pain as he sat on the edge. He was a small, fat man with thick, contemptuous lips and froglike eyes. Black hair curled obscenely on his shoulders and back. He reached out to the night table near the bed with chubby, trembling fingers, feeling for his thick glasses and putting them on with some effort.

'Okay I get dressed now?' the youth asked.

Kershman stared at his naked body for a few more moments and nodded. He wiped the sweat from his face with a towel and watched as the young hustler slipped on a pair of red bikini briefs and arranged himself. 'You really love it, dontcha?' he said. 'I never seen nobody eat up a beatin' like that before.'

'Shut up,' Kershman groaned. He got up and walked towards the bathroom, a silk bathrobe trailing from one hand.

'Hey,' the blond said, 'how about my bread?'

'You're not through yet,' said Kershman. 'Come in here.'

He lay face down on a massage table in the opulent bathroom and pointed to several bottles of ointment and balm in a tray attached to the table. The boy spread them on carefully, chattering aimlessly as he did. Kershman turned his face away from the youth. Tears edged down the side of his nose. They were tears of humiliation, not pain. The blond completed his task and Kershman eased himself off the table.

'All right,' he said, 'you can leave now.'

'The bread, the bread,' the hustler said, snapping his fingers at Kershman. The small man looked at him and hate filled his eyes. His lip curled viciously.

'You snap your fingers at me one more time,' he said,

'and I'll have them broken, one at a time.'

'Hey,' the blond said. He stepped back, balling up his fists.

'Your bread,' Kershman said wearily, 'is on the dresser.'

The younger man went into the bedroom and emptied the contents of a brown manila envelope, eagerly counting the bills. His eyes lit up. 'Jeez, thanks,' he said, 'ya want me to come back again tonight?'

'I don't want to see you again,' Kershman said. 'You show your face around this building again and you'll regret it.'

The hustler looked at him for a moment and then grinned. 'Wotsa matter, doll, was I too rough on you?'

Kershman stood in the bathroom doorway, regarding him through thick glasses that distorted his already bulging eyes, his mouth still trembling from the combination of pain and ecstasy. He said, 'If it makes you feel any better, you were magnificent. I happen to prefer one-nighters.'

'Sure, honey, that's cool. Different strokes for different folks, right?' He pulled on his leather jacket and left.

Kershman struggled into his clothes and left his apartment, taking a private elevator down one flight to the eighteenth floor of the Mirror Towers, where the giant computer awaited him. There were only three entrances into the sprawling computer complex which consumed most of the eighteenth floor. One was by private elevator from Kershman's apartment, the second a private elevator between DeLaroza's office and the console room. The third was by the exterior elevator, which had to be programmed to stop as it descended from the top two floors. Special keys activated the computers and the elevators.

Only three other people worked in the computer complex, none of whom really understood its complexities or the maze of interlocking information it contained. They were simply technicians.

It was a little after 2:30 when Kershman's elevator opened and he entered the main console room, the nerve centre of the complex. A young woman wearing a white uniform was stringing a spool of tape on one of the computer banks.

'Anything unusual?' Kershman asked.

'Not really,' she answered brightly. 'We have to complete the annual audit on WCG and L today. I'm running the totals now.'

'Fine,' Kershman said and went into his private office. The audit on West Coast Gas and Light Company, when complete, would require Kershman's final personal touch, since DeLaroza planned to have its directors apply for a rate increase.

It was a measure of Kershman's financial genius and tenacity that while still an undergraduate at the University of Pennsylvania's Wharton School of Business he had once appeared at the office of the president of Ticanco, one of the world's largest conglomerates, and asked for an appointment. Although he was told it would be impossible, Kershman had appeared at the office every morning at precisely 8:30 and remained there until five in the afternoon. After twenty-six consecutive working days, he had exhausted the executive's resistance and was finally ushered into his office.

'You have two minutes,' the man said sternly. 'If you can't state your business by then you're wasting your time as well as mine.'

'Oh, I can do it in one sentence,' Kershman replied confidently. 'I can show you an absolutely foolproof method that will save you eight million, three hundred thousand dollars in corporate income taxes this year. Are you interested?'

The actual saving was a little under seven million dollars, but it had earned Kershman, an orphan from the slums of East Saint Louis, his tuition and a generous living allowance for the remainder of an educational odyssey that included two more years at Wharton, three years at Harvard, where he earned a doctorate in corporate finance, and a stint at Georgetown Law School, where he received his degree in international law. After completing his studies with distinction at all three universities, Kershman had refused a generous offer from Ticanco, to go to work instead for the Internal Revenue Service where during the next three years he designed an infinite variety of schemes for beating the income tax laws. By the time he was thirty-three Kershman was earning six figures a year as a consultant for several corporations.

To Kershman the world became a giant financial chess

board and he took Machiavellian delight in developing methods for circumventing the international trade agreements and treaties which were its rules. In 1968 Kershman had proposed to one of his clients that within a few years the Arab nations would use their control of oil to dominate prices all over the world. Kershman, a Jew, had negotiated a dangerous and volatile deal with two Arab nations which, in exchange for enough guns and ammunition to supply their armies, would provide to the company Kershman represented crude oil at a low fixed price for fifteen years. The arms were delivered by boat to Turkey and from there were shipped overland by caravan to the Mid-east. The oil was sold to a refinery in Jakarta, shipped to a refinery in Yokohama, and re-sold as surplus to the Y and D Oil Company in Philadelphia. By 1975 Y and D had grown into one of the largest U.S. gasoline companies, with its own coast-to-coast chain of filling stations. It constantly undersold all competitors by two or three cents a gallon.

Y and D was owned by Victor DeLaroza. He was amazed by Kershman's ability, as well as by the alacrity with which a Jew had dealt with Arabs. In the seven years that had followed the oil deal Kershman had become the financial architect of DeLaroza's tentacled empire, carefully constructing a maze of contracts, stock transfers, holding companies, and silent corporations throughout the world which concealed the ownership of more than three hundred corporations, controlled the prices of three major industries, and had on its payrolls (including several heads of state) more than a hundred thousand people. Only Kershman and the electronic brain on the eighteenth floor understood the complicated corporate polygamy he had created, although two men were being groomed to succeed him if the need should arise.

In exchange DeLaroza had insured Kershman's loyalty by providing him with an opulent cocoon, an outrageous lifestyle which Kershman could never have achieved personally a salary of two hundred thousand dollars a year, stock equity in several key corporations, an executive jet, homes in Tokyo, London and on Crete. To satisfy Kershman's gluttonous appetite for gourmet food, there were open accounts in the world's greatest restaurants and a personal chef from the Cordon Bleu who created exotic dishes in Kershman's own kitchen when he was not travelling. And there were bonuses, each one unique, among them an awesome pornography collection that included five priceless volumes stolen from the personal collection of King Farouk by the same thief who had stolen a Picasso from the Musée de l'Art Moderne, a Rembrandt from the National Gallery in Washington, and three Van Goughs from the private collection of a Greek shipping magnate.

Finally, to protect Kershman from the danger of scandal-making indiscretions, a one-time film actor named Tod Donegan, whose sexual deviations had destroyed a promising film career, had been hired as Kershman's Judas Goat, to cruise the gay haunts and deliver to the financial wizard young lambs for his sexual slaughter and – although he secretly despised the less than attractive Kershman – provide the service himself when Kershman so desired.

The protective shell provided by DeLaroza had done its job. Kershman had become a pathologically private man, terrified by normal social situations. He had no close friends and seemed irresistibly drawn to the sordid side of life. His need to occasionally escape the cocoon was fulfilled by playing fantasy roles. He cultivated bizarre relationships, subtly exploiting them in order to bolster a veneer of superiority that covered a battered and confused self-image. One was an alcoholic veterinarian who worked for the humane society. Kershman frequently visited him on those days set aside for the extermination of unwanted animals. Kershman often achieved orgasms watching the puppies and kittens in the final spasms of death. Another was a self-defeated police detective to whom Kershman represented himself as a journalist for several foreign news agencies so he could accompany the policeman on assignments or buy him lunch and listen to the gruesome details of some particularly shocking police case.

Kershman had just poured a cup of tea when the red light near his phone began blinking. It meant that DeLaroza wanted him. He picked up the receiver and punched 0. DeLaroza answered immediately.

'Can you come up here right away, Dr. Kershman?' he said softly.

'Of course,' Kershman answered. He went into the console room and unlocked the private elevator to DeLaroza's office. He punched out an intricate code in a hidden keyboard and the car rose two storeys.

DeLaroza was seated behind his desk pondering over an open briefcase.

He nodded and handed Kershman the cassette from the meeting with Hotchins. 'Add this to *Gwai-lo*,' he said.

'Right away.'

'Are you totally current with the laws regarding political contributions?' DeLaroza asked.

'Of course, sir. The full disclosure laws . . .'

'I don't care for a review,' DeLaroza said, 'just make sure that everything we do with the *Gwai-lo* file from now on will stand the most rigid investigation.'

'I've always been extremely careful on that file,' Kershman answered.

'I want to move five million dollars into the campaign account. We'll start with a million. I'd like it in today if that's possible. The rest of the money will be made available to you during the next ten days or so in cash from my personal accounts.' He shoved the briefcase across the desk. 'Here is the first million. Any problems?'

'No, sir. I would suggest we make them all personal contributions. Keep them low, no more than fifty thousand per individual, range from thirty to fifty I would say. We can backdate the contributions and arrange for Jefferson Trust to loan this million, using the pledges as security. That way it will not appear as if all the contributions were made in a short period of time. I'll rearrange the accounts and –'

'Doctor.'

' – we can reimburse with bonuses spread out over –'

'Dr. Kershman?'

Kershman, who had been momentarily entranced by his evaluation of the ploy, stopped. 'Yes?'

'I'm not interested in how. I assume you know exactly how to handle that. Just keep me informed on the progress. I would like to know which of our people we are going to use, so I can brief them personally.'

'Right.'

'I think that should do it,' DeLaroza said.

'May I ask, sir,' Kershman said, 'are we going to move on the final phase of the *Gwai-lo* project?'

'Yes. The cassette is self-explanatory. I may add some personal notes to the file later today.'

'Well,' Kershman said, his thick lips rolling back in a fat smile, 'may I say I am delighted?'

'It's been a long time, hasn't it?' DeLaroza said.

'Yes sir. I was hoping it would be this election.'

DeLaroza smiled and leaned back in his chair. Not even Kershman knew that he had been planning this move for more than sixteen years. He felt a sudden surge of excitement. His fingertips tingled.

'He's ready,' DeLaroza said. 'He'll never be readier.'

Chapter Six

'Jesus,' Friscoe bellowed as he swept debris into one corner of his desk, shoving into a single disordered pile case reports, file folders, bits of paper, a half-eaten Swiss cheese on rye and a cardboard container of coffee with what looked like penicillin floating on top. 'I wish to hell we could get the goddamn clean-up committee down here. What we got here is the makings of a bubonic plague.'

He was stringing a reel of tape on the Sony which now sat on the cleared space on his desk.

'What we got, Sharky, is about two hours of phone taps here, spread over about three, four weeks. It's all legal – Judge Alvers gave us the flag. Now before we get into this good I want you to listen to this take just so's you'll get an idea of the range of this little operation. We got each take tagged on front, so you'll know who, what, and where. The rest, it speaks for itself.'

He turned on the switch and adjusted the volume. The tape hissed for a moment and then Livingston's voice came on.

LIVINGSTON: This tape is PC-1, a recording of a telephone conversation between the subject, Tiffany Paris, made from the phone in her apartment, Suite 4-A, the Courtyard Apartments, 3381 Peachtree Street, Northwest, November 22, 1975, one-ten P.M., and two male callers, the first identified as Neil, n.l.n., and the second Freddie, n.l.n., also referred to as Freaky Freddie.

Click.

TIFFANY: Hello?

NEIL: What's happening?

TIFFANY: I'm dead. That joker last night belongs in the zoo.

NEIL: Yeah, well, his money's as green as anybody else's. Guess who I've got on the phone?

TIFFANY: I'm too tired for guessing games, Neil.

NEIL: Freddie.

TIFFANY: Freaky Freddie?

NEIL: Freaky Freddie.

TIFFANY: Don't tell me. What's on his mind?

NEIL: Now what the hell you think's on his mind?

TIFFANY: Oh not now. I'm just not ready for him. I haven't even had a bath . . . .

NEIL: Hey, you know the score. When he's ready, he's ready, and right now he's ready.

TIFFANY: I've got to get my head on straight. Tell him . . . have him call back in twenty minutes.

NEIL: Now! Twenty minutes, he'll beat off and save the money.

TIFFANY: Christ, Neil –

NEIL: I said it's now, baby. Now straighten your head up and let's get it on.

TIFFANY: (Groans) Okay, five minutes, stall him for five.

NEIL: I'll give you three.

Click.

LIVINGSTON: Tape PC-2, same subjects, one-thirteen P.M.

Click.

TIFFANY: Hello.

NEIL: You ready?

TIFFANY: I guess. This won't win any prizes.

NEIL: I'm looking at a bill-and-a-half, not any Academy Awards. I'm patching you in now.

Click.

FREDDIE: H-h-h-hello?

TIFFANY: (Very softly) Hello Freddie.

FREDDIE: I, uh, h-h-how you b-b-been?

TIFFANY: Just fine, and you?

FREDDIE: Okay.

TIFFANY: Freddie, guess who I've got here with me?

FREDDIE: (Excited) I d-d-don't know. I g-g-give up.

TIFFANY: My photographer friend.

FREDDIE: Y-y-you mean the one w-w-with . . .

TIFFANY: The redhead, Freddie, with the big tits.

FREDDIE: Oh y-y-yeah.

TIFFANY: She's shooting for *Penthouse* this time.

FREDDIE: *P-P-Penthouse?*

TIFFANY: She looks really wild today. She's wearing a silver, uh, lamé jumpsuit.

FREDDIE: W-w-with z-z-zippers?

104

TIFFANY: All the way down the front. Why don't you just relax Freddie? Lay back and relax and let it happen, baby. You have some music on?

FREDDIE: B-B-Berlioz.

TIFFANY: Perfect.

FREDDIE: Are the z-z-zippers p-p-pulled down?

TIFFANY: Give me time, honey.
The zipper goes all the way down the front.
And . . .
she's zipping it down,
now . . .
real slowly,
down . . .
down . . .
It's spreading open, Freddie. I can
just see.
Oh, wow, I can see the edge . . .
of her nipples.
The suit zips aaaall the way down
and under, you know?
When it's open, Freddie,
you can see it all.

FREDDIE: W-w-what else?

TIFFANY: You know what I'm wearing, Freddie?
She brought it. It's black,
silk, very thin silk,
with beige lace
across my tits . . .
and on the bottom, too. Just under my hair.
And you know what's under it, Freddie?

FREDDIE: W-w-what?

TIFFANY: A white garter belt
and white stockings.
Sheer white stockings.
Her zipper's pulled down
below her stomach . . .
I can just see . . .
I can see the edge of her hair,
bright red,
curling over the slit in the zipper . . .

FREDDIE: The p-p-pop-p-poppers, d-d-don't forget . . .

TIFFANY: Oh, wait until I tell you about that.

She has this, this special little inhaler.
It has two little tubes,
one for each nostril.
She's breaking the poppers,
putting them in the tubes . . .
and . . . she's
waving it . . .
waving it under my nose.
Oh! Oh, my God, Freddie . . .
I'm tingling . . .
tingling all over. Even my skin is
tingling . . .
and my tits are hard . . .
hard like you, Freddie.
My pussy
feels like it's going to . . .

FREDDIE: C-c-cunt . . . say *c-c-cunt*, I love it
w-w-when . . .

TIFFANY: My cunt
is burning up.
It's throbbing . . .
It feels like it's . . . it's
vibrating
and getting wet.
I'm getting ready and
she's beginning to shoot,
she's straddling me.
Can you hear it, Freddie, the camera?

Sound of camera discharging.

FREDDIE: Oh yeah . . . I hear it . . .

TIFFANY: She's making me
spread my legs. And she's
kneeling
in between them . . .
leaning over.
Her knee is so close
I can feel the heat of her body. I . . .
I'm going to just
move down a little . . .
maybe just, touch it against her . . .
But she's moving away, her knee
is moving away.

I can't stand . . .
Oh Freddie, she's pulling down one of the
straps
on the . . .
the . . .
oh, oh . . . on the negligee, sliding the lace
over my nipples.
Back and forth.
Jesus, I'm hard.
It feels . . .
I feel . . .
like I have a volcano between my legs . . .
shivering
ready to explode,
with hot lava.
She's got the negligee down.
My tits are free.
They're so hard and pointing up at her.
And now she's
taking my hand . . .
putting my fingers in her mouth,
sucking them
She's leaning over . . . her tits . . .
are rubbing mine.
God.
Oh, God, Freddie,
she's taking my fingers, putting them on our
tits
making me squeeze them,
together,
and putting my other hand,
moving it down,
down,
Freddie . . . I'm touching it. All warm and
wet,
swollen,
swelling up.
Oh, yeah, she's doing me . . .
with her hand on mine.
I can't tell who's doing . . .
doing what to who.
She's zipping the jumpsuit down . . .

It's taking her forever.
Um . . . okay . . . I can see it,
I can see the top
of her cunt.
She's slipping out of it, taking it off.
Jesus.
She's moving up on me.
Her cunt . . .
Oh, God, Freddie, her cunt is just . . .
just kind of brushing my tits.
And it's so soft . . .
sooo soft,
like feathers, Freddie,
and my tit is wet from her.
I want to come, Freddie . . .

FREDDIE: Not y-y-yet, *no!*

TIFFANY: She's sitting down on me.
My nipple is . . .
God, it's inside her.
She's moving,
back and forth
and my
tit
is fucking her, Freddie . . .
Oh, yeah,
oh yeah,
I'm so hard, Freddie,
my clit is standing up . . . like your cock.
Are you hard, Freddie, good and hard?

FREDDIE: Y-y-yes . . .

TIFFANY: She's rolling over on her side.
Taking my hand,
putting my fingers inside me,
moving them . . .
in and out . . .
in
and out . . .
and she has my other hand
on her cunt.
I'm stroking her
and she's moving
back and forth

faster
faster
and I'm moving my hand in and out of
me
with her.
She's rubbing me
she's right on it and rubbing . . .
everybody's together, moving together.
Jesus, Freddie, she's getting off,
she's moving real fast and
her mouth,
her mouth is wide open.
She's
going
to come, and so . . .
so . . .
so . . .
Freddie, I can't wait. Don't make me
wait.
She's coming, Freddie.
She's coming.

FREDDIE: Oh yeah,
oh yeah,
oh yeah . . .

TIFFANY: Here it comes, Freddie,
here it comes, Freddie.
Ohhh, Freddie,
ohhh, Freddie.
Ohhh,
ohhh,
Freddie . . .
Freddie . . .
Freddie . . . Freddie, Freddie, Freddie,
Freddie . . .
Oh, oh, oh, oh, oh, *Oh, Oh, Oh* . . . AHHH!

Freddie cried out with her, a pinched, tight squeal,
caught in the constrictions of his throat, and ending in a
whimpering sigh.

Pause.

The tape was quiet except for the sounds of their laboured
breathing and an occasional sigh.

TIFFANY: Jesus, that was good.

109

It was *really* good. How about you Freddie? How was it for you?

Pause.

TIFFANY: Freddie?

More heavy breathing.

FREDDIE: (Groans) Oh, God.

TIFFANY: Tell me about it, Freddie. I could get off again, you know that, if you just tell me how it was.

Still no answer.

TIFFANY: Freddie?

FREDDIE: Uhhh . . .

TIFFANY: You know what I'd like? I'd like you to be here right now. Deep inside me. Make me feel like a woman again. Can you do that?

Can you get me off, Freddie?

FREDDIE: I w-w-want to t-t-try . . .

TIFFANY: Great. Because it's building again, Freddie. All for you.

Friscoe switched the tape recorder off. 'Well, enough of that,' he said, 'the rest is X-rated.'

Sharky sat in stony silence, staring at the machine. He was repulsed, yet strangely turned on by the intensity of the woman's performance and by the eroticism of the phone conversation. He was embarrassed, but he shielded his feelings.

'If that Freddie has any problems, that's pretty good therapy,' Arch Livingston said. 'Look at Sharky, he's struck speechless. Bet you never heard anything like that before, did you, speedy?'

Sharky shook his head.

Friscoe was laughing. 'Little dirty tricks there, Sharky,' he said. 'That one there, that's an odd-ball situation. Tell you the truth, I'd like to get a look at old Freaky Freddie. He's the kind, sounds like he gives freaks a bad name. It's what we call an ear job, A hunnerd-and-a-half ear job. Normally, see, what happens this Neil – he's the pimp, okay? – he lines up the johns, makes the deal, then calls the girl. It's strictly a one-way street, from the john to old pimpo deluxo to the hooker. She never calls Neil or the john. I don't even think she knows his phone number. And

110

neither do we yet. Anyway, it's a very cautious set-up. Probably the neatest phone-and-fuck operation I've ever run into.'

Friscoe ran the tape forward; its garbled squeal filled the room. He stopped several times, seeking a particular take.

'How, uh, did you get on to this?' Sharky said finally.

Livingston smiled. 'Believe it or not, a snitch.'

'One of the johns?'

Friscoe shook his head. 'Naw, don't I wish? You think any of these bimbos gonna say anything, put their balls in the wringer? Shit, no. It was this old campaigner we call Mabel the Monster, been street trickin' must be ten years now. Her heels are so round she has to hang on to the lamppost keep from fallin' over backwards. What happened, back there late in November we had some kind of religious convention in town. Shit, on Saturday night we had about a thousand Jesus freaks runnin' all over town screamin' and hollerin' like a grizzly bear with his nuts caught in the door jamb. So, about seven o'clock the goddamn switchboard lights up like it's the Fourth of fuckin' July and then The Bat calls in, and the chief, and finally the commissioner himself. It seems the whole Peachtree hooker line turned out in force. Musta been, we counted thirty-two pros working the two blocks between the Regal Hotel and the Towers. So we go over, drop the hammer on about twenty of 'em, and poor old Mabel turns up in the line-up. Usually, see, she's quiet as a lamb. She's been nailed so much she oughta be payin' rent down at the pound. Only this night, Jesus, we had a fuckin' maniac on our hands. So Papa there, he takes her in the backroom, waltzes her around a bit, and turns out she's pissed, see? She says we're pickin' on the low-renters and turning a deaf eye on the high-rolling ladies. For a while Papa can't get anything specific outa her and then he offers to let her walk, she gives him something we can hang our hat on, and she comes up with a name and address. Bingo, we got Tiffany.

'We figure, the last three weeks or so, we got – how many, Arch? – ninety-one phone calls on tape, eighty per cent is jobs. She's turnin' four tricks a week at five and six bills a pop and you gotta figure it's at least a hundred g's a year, tax free. Still, *still* misdemeanour, but, you know, *big* misdemeanour. Worth workin' on. Then three days ago, we

111

turn up this take I'm gettin' ready to play for you. Now it's a new ball-game because we got what looks like a shake-down. A fat one. And that's a felony extortion, baby,' Friscoe smiled and licked his lips.

'Also,' Livingston said, 'we got a joker popping up in the deck.'

'We'll come to that in a minute,' Friscoe said.

'Wouldn't the IRS love to get a piece of this action?' Sharky said.

Livingston cringed. 'Wouldn't they though? And fuck it up for everybody else, as usual.'

'All those assholes are interested in is their own chunk of the kiwash,' Friscoe said. 'They don't give a diddly shit about anybody or anything but their own shitass little back-yard. They're as much help as a broken leg.'

'Maybe we could lean on Tiffany, get to Neil. He knows everything that's happening,' Sharky said.

'You're jumping the gun,' said Friscoe. 'Just listen to this here take. There's a lot happening. We move too soon now and we could blow the whole machine right down the fuckin' toilet, believe me. Just hook an ear on this.'

He turned on the recorder.

LIVINGSTON: This is tape PC-74, tape recording of a telephone conversation between the subject, Tiffany Paris, Suite 4-A, the Courtyard Apartments, 3381 Peachtree Street, Northwest, December 15, 1975, three-thirty-two P.M., and a male caller identified as Neil, n.l.n.

Click.

TIFFANY: Hello?

NEIL: It's me.

TIFFANY: Oh, thank God, I was afraid it was —

NEIL: Hey, calm down, calm down.

TIFFANY: He came by here, no call, no nothing, just showed up at the door. Anybody could have been here. My mother —

NEIL: I said calm down. It's taken care of. It won't happen again.

TIFFANY: But it never happened before . . . it was like that . . . terrible little man following me that ti —

NEIL: Bag it, Tif.

Friscoe turned the machine off for a moment. 'That bit there. We think what happened, some john probably took it on himself to bypass Neil, call in person. Blew her mind, see.'

'What's that about somebody tailing her? Was that one of your people?' Sharky asked.

'No. We haven't figured that one out yet. Anyway, moving along here we get to the meat.' He switched the machine back on.

NEIL: Listen to me. I talked to him, eye-to-eye, read him the facts of life. It won't happen again, believe me.

TIFFANY: It really upset me. The man that was following me that time, the one in the leather jacket, I know he was a cop and –

NEIL: He was not a cop. He was some shitass little conman looking for a buck. Besides, he vanished, right? When's the last time you saw him?

TIFFANY: He was following Domino, too, Neil. She told me –

NEIL: Shit!

TIFFANY: I still think Norman sent him. He was so angry and he made those threats.

NEIL: Norman did *not* send him. And Domino's forgotten about it. Norman's back in Texas, playing with his oil fields. Drop it. Now, I mean it.

'Here we go,' Friscoe said, 'now listen close.'

TIFFANY: He told me, he was going to do something to my face. You try forgetting something like that.

NEIL: Tiffany, the son of a bitch was a pussycat. Those fat shmucks have to show the hair on their chest, make a little noise. You know, they think they got balls as big as the Ritz. One look at the stills and he coughed up his fifty grand and rolled over like a pet dog and that was that. The other guy, maybe he wanted a free piece, who knows?

TIFFANY: Domino told me she thought he was following her too –

NEIL: Domino forgot it, goddammit! She's cool and you better . . . Jesus. That was back in October. You gonna carry that around the rest of your life?

'Who's Domino?' Sharky asked.

'She's the joker Livingston was talkin' about,' Friscoe said. 'All along we figured it was this Neil and Tiffany, period. Now we know he's got another one in his stable. Listen . . .'

TIFFANY: Anyway, I think it's too soon to try it again.

NEIL: You let me decide that.

TIFFANY: Can't Domino do this one?

NEIL: Keep Domino out of this. What Domino and I do is none of your business. She ever bang your ear about what's happening with her? Hell, no, she doesn't.

TIFFANY: How come I get the dirty deals?

NEIL: (Pauses) Let me ask you, since when is twenty-five g's a dirty deal? It's passed. And this time we're going for bigger stuff, maybe a hundred big ones, Tif. You want to sneeze off your half of a hundred grand?

Silence.

NEIL: Now are you set up for tonight? I don't want you getting ants in your pants around Domino, got that straight? These two tonight, they're worth a bloody fortune. Diamond merchants from Amsterdam. They're throwing out fifteen hundred for the night. I don't want you doing a sad-ass on me. They may be back and that's big money for everybody.

TIFFANY: I'll be fine.

NEIL: Good. They'll pick you two up about eight-thirty in a limousine. Have a good time.

TIFFANY: Thanks.

NEIL: Later.

Friscoe switched the recorder off.

'Okay, there it is,' he said. 'The way we put it together, this Neil and the Tiffany broad took some Texas oil million-aire named Norman for fifty grand. They had pictures, who the hell knows what else? But they stuck it to him and now it sounds like they're getting ready for another round, only this time they're sniffin' after a hundred g's. Christ, that's just plain greedy.'

'You got any idea who?' Sharky asked.

'Not the foggiest. But whoever it is, the way I see it, we let it start to come together, then we step in and maybe we can bust the whole lot.'

'Who's this Domino?' Sharky asked.

'Another lady in the stable. All the while we figure it for a twosome, now all of a sudden up pops the devil and we got another one in the act.'

'You think maybe she's got a scam working too?' Sharky said.

'Why not? It seems to be the season for it.'

114

'Then let's go after her too,' Sharky said. 'Do we have a line on her.'

'Yeah. Livingston and Papa dutched them the night they went out with the boys from Holland,' said Friscoe, 'then followed Domino home.'

'We should all live that good,' Livingston said. 'A Caddy limo the size of a 747 picks them up. They hit Nikolai's Roof for dinner, dancing afterwards at Krazz. The bill for the four of them must have been five hundred bucks.'

Sharky whistled. 'Maybe we're in the wrong business,' he said and grinned. 'I wonder if she'd give me about ten dollars' worth?'

'Yeah,' Papa said, 'for ten bucks she'll goose ya.'

'On your pay you can't even afford to smell it,' said Friscoe.

'Maybe she'll take a dollar down and a dollar a week,' Sharky joked.

'Look,' Friscoe said, 'I agree we need to go after the Domino broad too. I already got the office from Alvers. After I played that performance between Tiffany and Freaky Freddie, he was ready to give me permission to bug her church pew.'

Sharky's mind was humming. He had survived on the street for eighteen months with instinct and little else. Now every nerve ending was telling him that this Domino would provide a key, although he was not sure why. Perhaps because it had taken almost four weeks for her name to pop up. It seemed to him she was being well shielded and there had to be a reason.

'What we need,' he said half to himself, 'is a first-class wireman. Somebody who can do it right. The apartment. The phone. The whole shooting match.'

'Yeah, well, that's tough shit,' said Friscoe. 'All we got is what's down here in the dump. One lousy tape recorder and maybe a little help from the phone company to tap into her phone.'

'I want the whole place,' Sharky said.

'Good luck,' Livingston said.

'I got just the guy for the job,' Sharky went on. 'He'll love it. It'll be a challenge.'

'Who is this genius?' Friscoe asked.

'The Nosh,' Sharky said.

'Who the fuck is The Nosh?'

'Larry Abrams. He's got everything we need. Voice-activated recorders. Mikes the size of your fingernail. FM pre-amps for the pick-up. Let me tell you, The Nosh could plant a bug in a hummingbird's ass.'

'So where do we find this wonder boy?' Friscoe asked.

'Right here in the House. He's in OC.'

Friscoe rolled his eyes. He shook his head. 'Forget it,' he said forlornly, 'Organized Crime is D'Agastino's outfit. That cheap guinea wouldn't loan us the dog shit on his shoes.'

'The hell with D'Agastino,' Sharky said. 'The Nosh and I go back long before either of us was on the force. I can sneak him out long enough to get it done.'

Friscoe thought about it for a few moments, then shrugged. 'Look, it's your machine, see. We all figure, maybe you can bring something into it we can't. We've all been . . . you just get jaded after a while. You wanna do some dog-robbing here in the House it's okay with me. If the shit hits the fan, well . . . we'll all duck.'

Sharky was thinking about The Nosh. Little Larry, fiddling around in the workshop in his garage, inventing gadgets that only he would ever use. He chuckled thinking about it.

'I tell you what we're gonna do. We're gonna be all over this Domino. Before we're through we'll know what she's *thinking*. Because The Nosh and I, we're going to put more wire in her place than an AT and T substation.'

Chapter Seven

Sharky guided the grey Dodge Charger down through a squalid warehouse district known as the Pits and parked in front of a bleak, washed-out two-storey brick building. He switched off the engine.

Livingston, sitting beside him in the front seat, slid down and lit a plastic-tipped cigar. 'Welcome to Creepsville,' he growled.

From the outside the building looked deserted. Weeds pushed through cracks in the sidewalk, water stains streaked its sides, a sign, ravaged by time and weather and barely readable, announced: For sale or lease. B. Siegel and Sons. The building had no windows, although here and there along its grimy face large squares of new brick indicated where several had been sealed up. Midway in the building was its only opening, a scarred, grim, ugly door with a single window covered with steel mesh. It was electrically operated and everyone entered and left the building through this single forbidding portal.

'Looks like something you'd see in Russia. The *bad* part of Russia,' Livingston said.

The building housed the Organized Crime Division, known as the OC, which was run by a pompous, taciturn political opportunist, Captain D'Agastino. Inside, a maze of computers, readouts, photo lines, and electronic gadgetry connected the building, like a giant umbilicus, to the FBI.

'D'Agastino runs this place like the fuckin' CIA,' Livingston said. 'He doesn't do zilch for us out on the street, him and that bunch of élitist shits.'

'Bunch of assholes, you ask me,' Papa volunteered from the back seat.

They fell silent. Livingston stared up at the sky thick with black, swarming clouds and blew a smoke ring which wobbled through the air like a flat tyre and fell apart against the windshield.

'Gonna rain like a son of a bitch,' he said.

More silence.

117

Sharky stared straight ahead, toying aimlessly with the steering wheel.

'Thing is,' Livingston said, 'I don't trust any of those turkeys in there.'

Silence.

'Do you trust any of them, Papa?' he asked.

'Shit,' Papa said with disgust.

Sharky picked lint from his suede pullover.

Livingston finally looked over at him.

'And this Abrams, he's a buddy of yours, hunh?'

Sharky nodded. 'Yeah.'

'Well, uh, how come you're so thick with somebody in the goddamn OC?'

There it was, the big question. Sharky had felt it coming. They were testing him. And why not? He was the new kid on the block and already he was captain of the ball club and bringing in his own pitcher.

Livingston blew another imperfect smoke ring, watched it fall apart. 'I heard that bastard D'Agastino won't even consider you for the OC unless you'd turn in your own mother. You hear that, Papa?'

'Anything you heard, I heard worse. I heard you gotta pass the bad breath test just to get in the door.'

Sharky started to burn, but he held his temper in check.

'What've you heard there, Sharky?' Livingston said.

'Not much.'

'Not much, hunh.' More silence. Finally: 'Wanna tell us about this Abrams?'

Sharky did not answer immediately. What could he tell them? That he and The Nosh, which is what he had called Abrams since they were kids, were born across the street from each other, grew up together, fought together, had even broken the law together? Should he tell them about Red Ingles or the night the transmission fell out? Shit. In high school Sharky and The Nosh had befriended a grizzled, solitary alcoholic named Red Ingles who lived up the street from them. Ingles had a singular talent; he souped up cars. Boy, did he soup up cars. Ingles souped up cars the way a piano tuner coaxed perfect pitch from the strings of an old baby grand. The chromium touch, Sharky called it. Ingles worked in his backyard, a backyard cluttered with battered old wrecks that looked as if they might fall apart if you slammed the door too hard.

But under those tarnished, dented hoods, engines gleamed with stainless-steel carburettors, chromium headers, and glistening valve lifters. Ingles usually worked on two cars at a time, interchanging parts and tuning one against the other until the engines hummed in perfect harmony. Then he gave The Nosh and Sharky five dollars apiece and told them to 'take those Jessies and blow them mills out good'. And he would settle back with his jar of still whisky while they drove out to the river, poised fender to fender on hidden dirt roads, motors straining underfoot, and then took off, the engines whining and shivering in their mounts, speedometers inching up to 150 and 160 as they skimmed over the dirt, skittering at the very edge of disaster with that reckless and wonderful sense of indestructability reserved for the young.

They never asked what Red did with the cars. They didn't have to. At night they sneaked down to his place and lay under the shrubs, watching him negotiate with heavy-set men in galluses and sweaty felt hats, passing the fruit jar back and forth as they argued and cursed and ranted. Finally Red would smile and slam his hand down on the fender of the car in question and the good old boys would count out the price. In the morning the cars were gone. Sharky was certain that Red Ingles was the sole supplier of transportation for every moonshiner in North Georgia.

Then Ingles had made them an offer. He needed trans-missions, tough transmissions. He would pay them seventy dollars for every working Corvette transmission they delivered to him. The Nosh was delighted. 'I can drop a Vette transmission in fifteen minutes flat,' he confided to Sharky and they went into business. They put roller skate wheels on a piece of plywood and once a week they borrowed the rumpled pick-up Sharky's old man used at the hardware store and they cruised the dark streets, looking for prospects. When they found one, The Nosh rolled up under the car and dropped the transmission while Sharky sat behind the wheel of the pick-up, ready to sound the horn in case of trouble. They were the toast of Grady High. The Nosh, barely five feet tall, became a ladies' man while Sharky, already a cocksman of some renown, became the Beau Brummel of Ponce de Leon Avenue. Then one night the owner of a brand new Stingray appeared suddenly and unexpectedly while The Nosh was toiling under his car. It was too late to blow the horn. The owner flicked a speck of dust off the trunk, kicked a tyre, climbed in, revved up, and took off with his tyres chewing up the pavement.

But no Nosh. He was caught under the Vette, his jacket hung up on the transmission, and he went right with the car, rocketing along on his plywood platform. When he finally tore himself loose, the platform flew out from under the Vette, sparks showering from the tortured roller skate wheels. It screamed down the street, hit a curb, and splintered, the wheels soaring off into the night while the Nosh was launched end over end into a fishpond.

Sharky ran to his side. A dazed, soggy Nosh staggered from the pool. And at that moment, with an anguished clatter, the transmission fell out of the Corvette. They ran to the pick-up and took off down the street while the teary-eyed Corvette owner ran after them, hands waving wildly overhead.

'I don't ever want to take a ride like that again,' The Nosh said.

'Right,' said Sharky.

'Besides, I feel sorry for that guy.'

'Me too.'

'There's got to be an easier way to make a buck.'

'Yeah.'

And they quit.

So how come I'm so thick with The Nosh? Sharky thought. It was basic. They had grown up together, exchanged bloody noses and embarrassed apologies, got laid together, and had joined the cops together. Their roots went deeper than blood or family.

'I'll tell you,' Sharky said, 'we been asshole buddies almost since the day we were born. And I don't give a damn if he's in the OC, the PDQ, or the screw-you, it's okay with me.'

Livingston puffed on his cigar. Papa cleared his throat but said nothing. Finally Livingston nodded. 'Well, it ain't much detail, but it's sure clear as hell.'

After a moment, Papa said, 'Where did he get that crazy monicker?'

'It's Yiddish. Means to nibble, eat between meals. The Nosh is one hell of a nibbler. He can also fix plumbing, do carpentry, fix radios, cameras. Shit, he can do just about anything. And he just might be the best wireman that ever came down the pike.'

Between puffs Livingston said, 'Does he walk on water?'

Sharky laughed. 'Probably. One of his ancestors did.'

'Well, I just got to wonder, okay? I got to wonder how in hell he ever got tied in with that mother-humping piece of camelshit, D'Agastino.'

'Like I said, he's the best wireman in the country. Maybe D'Agastino needed him.'

'I don't care if he can bug running water. If he ain't white, Christian, six-feet tall, and don't wear pin-stripe suits and look like a goddamn stockbroker, he's in the wrong outfit.'

Sharky pointed towards the door of the OC. 'Does that look like a six-foot stockbroker to you?' he asked.

Larry Abrams, The Nosh, came out of the building, a short, boxy little man, a hair over five feet tall and almost as wide, wearing faded jeans, a blue work shirt, a suede jacket, and carrying a black tool box almost as big as he was. His thick black hair was longer than regulations permitted; he was wearing glasses a quarter-inch thick and his crêpe-soled hiking boots were as muddy as they were ugly. The Nosh was grinning; he usually was.

Livingston looked shocked. '*He's* in the OC!'

'Jesus,' Papa said, 'there ain't much to him is there?'

Livingstone watched the little man approach the car. 'Amazing,' he said, 'everything in the world that fuckin' D'Agastino hates. He's Jewish, he's too short, his hair's too long, he's overweight, his shoes are dirty, he's smiling, he's dressed like a janitor, and he looks human.'

The Nosh leaned against the door of the car. 'Hey, Shark, what's up?'

'Any problems with D'Agastino?'

'Nah. I told him I had to go over and do a trick for the FBIs. That's the magic word in the fortress there. You say *FBI*, everybody wets their pants.'

'Hop in.'

The Nosh crawled into the back seat and Sharky introduced him around.

'Where we headed?' the Nosh asked.

'Moneyville. Lancaster Towers,' Sharky said.

The Nosh whistled through his teeth. 'Who we after?'

'A very pretty lady,' Livingston said.

'Aww,' the Nosh said, 'I hate to pick on pretty ladies.'

Livingston turned sideways in his seat so he could look at Abrams as he talked. 'Me too, but this lady happens to be a very high class hooker whose pimp just shook fifty g's out of a Texas oilman. We think she may be involved in a new scam and this time the stakes may be even higher. What we'd like is to wire up her place like a Christmas package and see what we can turn up.'

'What kind of set-up?'

'Nobody's been inside yet. You know the Lancaster Towers?' said Livingston.

'I've driven by it, never been inside.'

'Okay, what we got is twin towers, twelve storeys each, an east tower and a west tower. They're connected at the third floor by a terrace that runs between them. Swimming pool, bar, that sort of thing. The parking garage is below ground-level, three storeys, with a gate that's activated by one of those plastic coded cards. Visitor parking on ground level. Both buildings have security guards. She's in 10-A, facing the east wing. We been checking her number for the past hour or so and her machine answers.'

The Nosh nodded. 'She could be up there doing a number.'

'We considered the possibility,' Sharky said.

The Nosh said, 'We can give the door a rattle. If she answers, we tell her we're checking the TV cable, something like that.'

'Sounds good,' Livingston said. 'We also have the security guards. I'd like to keep this in the family, but I don't see any way to get past them without showing our hand.'

The Nosh smiled and opened his tool chest. It was meticulously arranged. Wire, diodes, phone-jacks, screws, nuts and bolts of all sizes, miniature amplifiers, microphones, and tape recorders, all were neatly fitted into the case. A tray on top contained tools of all kinds and, arranged neatly in one corner, two Baby Ruth bars, a box of Good'n' Plenty and a coconut Twinkie. The Nosh opened a drawer and took out a bundle of business cards. Leafing through them, he stopped and smiled. 'Here we go,' he said. 'We're from the elevator inspection department. That's city.

Suppose we, uh, suppose we're doing a stress check on the elevators. We'll be in and out for the next couple days.'

'What's a stress check?' Papa asked.

'Hell, I don't know,' The Nosh said, 'but it sounds good.' They all laughed.

Papa stared at the candy bars. 'I got a weight problem,' he said. 'You got a weight problem?'

'I can put on a couple pounds driving past a deli,' The Nosh said.

'I gain weight readin' recipes,' Papa said.

'Wanna split a Baby Ruth?'

'Love it.'

He cut one of the candy bars in two and gave Papa the larger piece. Livingstone turned back to Sharky. 'It's love at first sight,' he said. 'They'll be engaged before the weekend's over.'

'Here it comes,' Sharky said as raindrops began pummelling the windshield.

'You mind I ask you a personal question?' Livingston said to The Nosh.

'Shoot.'

'How the hell you ever get in the fuckin' OC?'

The Nosh giggled. 'It was because of the Feds,' he said. 'I was workin' radio maintenance down in Central and one day this FBI named Weir shows up and he's lookin' for somebody can really do a number on an automobile, so they loaned me to him. What it was – you remember that Mafia guy, Degallante, retired down here about a year ago?'

'Sure,' Livingston said, 'he got deported.'

'Well, not exactly. That's what the Feds are puttin' out. What really happened, the FBIs figure Degallante is not really retired. He's down here maybe to get his foot in the door and they wanted to pin something on him, only they were striking out all over the place. So they decide maybe if they bugged his car he might, y'know, be doin' business there and they could get something on him. A big black Lincoln limo. I hung around the Lincoln place until they brought the car in for service and I wired it front to back. The first tape we pulled, you wouldn't believe it,' and he began to giggle. 'What it was, the old bastard had his son-in-law giving him head in the back seat.'

There was a moment of stunned silence before everybody laughed.

'No shit, there he was cruising down the interstate and his daughter's husband is blowing him. Well, Weir takes the tape out to Degallante's place on West Wesley Road and they're all sitting around the living room finessing each other out and Degallante is telling them how he's not connected anymore and he's retired and they can get lost and then Weir turns on the tape recorder. Thirty seconds and the old man throws up all over the floor and Weir tells him what they're gonna do, they're gonna give copies to *The New York Times, Time* magazine and *Playboy*. A month later he was back in Sicily and the whole family was with him and that's the way it really happened.'

'So how did you get in the OC?' Papa said.

'Weir told D'Agastino and D'Agastino drafted me. I got a workshop in the basement. He never sees me, I don't see him. We're both very happy about the arrangement.'

Sharky turned into Lindburgh Drive and headed towards Peachtree Street. The two white buildings loomed through the rain like stark, windowed tombstones.

'How much time we gonna need?' Sharky asked The Nosh.

'Not long. We give the place a quick wash, decide where we want the buttons, then plant 'em. I want to see the roof first, maybe set up a listening post up there. I'd say fifteen, maybe twenty minutes and we'll be out.'

'You're on,' Sharky said.

'Papa and I can recognize her,' Livingston said. 'How about I stay in the car so I can spot her when she comes in? Papa can ride the elevator, slow her down if he has to.'

'That's the play, then,' Sharky said.

They parked the car. Sharky, Papa, and The Nosh entered the building. The security guard, a large white-haired man with a wasted body lost in an oversized uniform and a seamed face, was sitting in a small office reading *The National Enquirer*. The Nosh laid the card on the desk in front of him.

'I'm Friedman, city inspection department. We're doing a stress check on your elevators,' he said. 'We'll be in and out of the place here for the next couple of days.'

124

The guard looked at the card and reached for the telephone. 'I better check the main office,' he said.

'You didn't get the letter?' The Nosh said quickly.

'I didn't get no letter,' the guard said, his hand resting on the phone.

'Well, your main office got the letter. We already checked with them.'

'Hell,' the old man said. 'I sit here on my duster all day, nobody tells me shit.'

'Ain't it the truth. We're always the last ones to know, right?'

The guard relaxed. He had found company for his tarnished ego. 'Sure is the way. The workin' man is always the last one to know anything. Well, I go on Social Security in six months. After that they can all dip their wick in the mashed potatoes for all I care. You need any help?'

'Is the door open onto the roof?'

'Yep.'

'Then we're in business. Tell you what, we'll leave Johnson here in the elevators. That way, if we have to shut down for a minute or two he can calm down the residents.'

'I appreciate that. I get enough crap as it is. People ain't happy if they ain't bitchin' about something.'

'Keep the card so the night man'll know we're here, okay? Don't want anybody takin' a shot at us.' The Nosh winked at him.

'Gun ain't loaded anyway.'

They got on the elevator.

'There's a guy got the wrong end of the chicken all his life,' Papa said. He looked at The Nosh. 'You coulda been a pretty good conman.'

'He *is* a pretty good conman,' Sharky said.

They got off at twelve. Papa said, 'Keep in touch,' as the elevator doors hushed shut. Sharky and The Nosh went up to the roof, surveying it through a hard, slanting rain. 'Over there,' said the Nosh, 'that concréte blockhouse.' They ran through the rain to the concrete shed in the middle of the roof and entered it. It was a single room, fairly warm and spotless. Fluorescent tubes flickered overhead, shedding uncertain light on a row of humming motors. On the wall facing the motors was a bank of power and water meters.

'Perfect,' The Nosh said.

'What are we doin' up here?' Sharky asked.

'What we're gonna do, we're gonna set us up a listening post in here, okay? The mark is only two floors down so we can use wireless mikes.' He opened the tool chest and took out an object no larger than a button which was attached by a single wire to a rectangular box about the size of a disposable cigarette lighter. A pin protruded from the back of the button. It looked like a drawing pin.

'This is the mike,' The Nosh said, 'and the little box is the amplifier. We pre-set the amplifier to a specific frequency and it can be picked up by this miniature FM tuner.' The tuner lay in the flat of his hand. 'Then I plug this cassette deck into the tuner. It's voice-activated. When anybody down there talks, the tuner picks it up, the recorder turns on automatically, and it's all on tape.' The cassette deck was also miniaturized. 'I made it myself,' The Nosh said. 'Real simple. Only one circuit.'

'You could put the whole works in your pocket,' Sharky marvelled.

'Each mike has its own tuner and recorder. If she walks from room to room talking, one recorder cuts in when the other one cuts off. We'll plant the mikes in each room.' He pointed to a button on the tape decks. 'This is a monitor button. Push it down and you can listen continuously. I also have a set of earphones I'll leave up here which will help with the monitoring.'

'Amazing,' Sharky said. 'Will it pick up anything else?'

'Yeah, stereo, radio, like that. Not walking or normal room noises. But don't worry. Later on, see, we can go in with a dip filter and erase the background noise. What we do, we dip in there and set the filter for the voice frequency, then – '

'Nosh?'

'Yeah?'

'You're telling me more than I want to know.'

'Right.'

He took out three tuners and recorders and fitted them together and placed them in one corner of the room behind the motors. 'One more thing,' he told Sharky. 'I got you a dozen or so cassettes and they're clearly marked so you don't put 'em in backwards. The tapes're good for ninety

126

minutes a side. There's a beeper on each tape which sounds off thirty seconds before the end.'

'Right.'

'Okay, let's go down and see what we got on ten.'

Sharky removed a walkie-talkie from a case attached to his belt. 'This is Zebra One, we're leaving topside.'

They found 10-A next to the elevators. Sharky rang the bell. Nothing. He rang it again and they waited. Still nothing. He knocked sharply on the door.

'Okay,' The Nosh said, 'let's do it.'

He took a case from the tool chest and opened it. It contained a set of stainless steel needles varying in length from one to six inches. He studied the lock carefully, then selected one of the needles and, holding it between his thumb and forefinger, eased it into the keyhole, twisting it slowly as he did. It caught for an instant and The Nosh gave it a quarter-turn, felt it slip farther until it caught again. Another quarter-turn and the tumblers clicked. He smiled, stood up, and opened the door.

They moved in quickly and quietly, closing the door behind them, waiting, listening. There was not a sound. 'Okay,' Sharky said, 'check it out.' They went swiftly through the apartment, peering into each room. Empty. They returned to the small entrance hall by the front door and studied the layout. The living room was directly in front of them. On either side of it was a bedroom and bath. The dining room was immediately to their left and the kitchen was adjacent to it. A balcony connected the living room and the master bedroom to the right.

Sharky curled his tongue against his teeth and whistled softly.

'I'll give her one thing,' he said. 'She's got class.'

The living room was done in beige and cream with pale mauve walls. A large Olympus beige-on-cream sofa faced them. It was several feet in front of the french doors, which opened onto the balcony, and half the width of the room. Two brown and beige striped Savoy chairs faced each other on each side of the sofa. A Porto Bello coffee table in antique white sat in front of the sofa and between the chairs. The vicuna rug was grey. There were plants all over the room, beside the french doors,. in the corners and hanging from the ceiling, tall nephrolepis ferns, bottle

127

palms, begonias, columnea, and spider plants. The stereo sat in a lowboy against one wall with the speakers in the ceiling.

The dining room had mirrored walls and a large smoked glass table with chromium and silk chairs.

'Shit, the furniture in here cost more than my house,' The Nosh said.

'You take that bedroom and I'll check out the master,' Sharky said. 'We may run out of time.'

The bed was king-sized and covered with a llama blanket. The wall behind it and the ceiling were mirrored. The rest of the furniture was white wicker with pale green cushions. An enormous Norfolk pine filled one corner of the room and several hanging baskets dominated the corner facing it. Sharky checked the drawers in the night tables. One contained s small bottle of pills, a vial of white powder, a silver cigarette case, and three vibrators of various sizes, one of which was shaped like an egg. Sharky tasted the powder, opened the cigarette case, smelled one of the cigarettes, and examined the pills.

'Hey Shark, c'm'ere,' The Nosh called from the other room.

He put the pills back in the drawer and closed it. The other room contained a massage table over which was a light bar with four sunlamps aimed at the table. The two windows were stained glass. A pair of lovebirds cooed and kissed each other in a tall wicker cage that hung among the flowering baskets that dominated the room. A small marble-topped table covered with vials of oils and body creams sat beside the massage table. In one corner there were perhaps a dozen multi-coloured pillows of all sizes arranged on the floor and against the wall. Tropical fish peered bug-eyed from an enormous gurgling aquarium against the other wall. The fish stared at them, then darted soundlessly through dancing seaweed.

'It's Disney World, Sea World, and Jungle World, all wrapped up in one,' The Nosh said with delight. 'I could let the kids loose in here for hours.'

'The table in there by the bed has some first-rate machine-rolled Colombian grass, Quaaludes, poppers, and some coke that must've cost a bill-and-a-half on the street.'

'You ever get the feeling we're in the wrong business?'
The Nosh said.

'Only when I'm awake,' said Sharky. 'Let's get it on.'

'The plants are perfect,' The Nosh said. He took one of the button-mikes and slipped the pin into the stem of a broad-leafed calathea plant in a corner of the room. The mike faced the massage table. He ran the wire down along the stem of the plant, securing it with a roll of green tape. Then he pushed the aerial down into the soft earth and brushed loose dirt over it. He opened one drawer of the tool chest and took a small tube of green paint from among many multi-coloured vials and dabbed the mike until it blended into the plant. He stood up and smiled.

'That's it. This room is fixed.'

'What if she waters the plants?' Sharky asked. 'Won't it hurt that equipment?'

'Nope. All the stuff is coated with silicone. It's waterproof. Let's hit the living room.'

He stood in the centre of the room and snapped his fingers several times, checking the ambient sound. 'Not bad,' he said, 'not bad at all. All the furniture, plants, that shit, deadens the room. We won't get too much bounce. But we gotta keep away from those speakers in the ceiling.' This time he chose a ficus tree and jabbed the mike into the trunk, close to the dirt. He dabbed it with brown paint, whistling softly to himself as he buried the amplifier. Sharky stood on the balcony, trying to look down at the parking lot, but he could barely see it.

'Hey, Shark,' The Nosh said, 'you remember the time I bugged the teachers' lounge at Grady and we caught old man Dettman screwin' the phys. ed. teacher?'

'Are you kidding? That's how I passed geometry.'

'I was just thinkin' how at the time we thought they were such degenerates. She was a real hunk, Shark. A real hunk.' He smoothed dirt over the amplifier. 'Lookin' back, I can't say I blame old Dettman.'

'Maybe we should've worked out a trade-out with her. Who ever uses geometry anyway?'

'What was her name?'

'Old Torpedo Tits.'

'No, her real name?'

129

'Jesus, I don't remember.'

There was no way to see into the parking lot. He went back into the living room. 'Old Torpedo Tits,' The Nosh said, heading into the master bedroom.

Down below, a blue Mercedes 450SL drifted into the complex and stopped in front of the east tower. Sharky's walkie-talkie came to life.

'Zebra One, this is Zebra Three,' Livingston said. 'You got company.'

'Okay Nosh, she's back,' Sharky said. He pressed the button on his box. 'Zebra Two, this is Zebra Three. We need a little time.'

'You got it,' Papa said.

A porter came out of the building, running through the rain, and held the door for her. She got out, a long silk-sheathed leg preceding her. She stood an inch taller than the porter as she slipped him a dollar.

'She's heading for the lobby,' Livingston said. The Nosh was on his knees, dabbing paint on the mike. 'I'm wrapping it up,' he said.

Sharky started to leave the room, then went back to the night table. He opened the drawer, took one of the joints from the cigarette case, and dropped it in his pocket.

'Let's hustle, brother.' The Nosh was checking out his case.

'I'm missing a paintbrush,' he said. 'It's gotta be right around these plants somewhere.'

'Shit,' Sharky said.

Papa had seen the blue Mercedes pull up in front of the apartment, watched as she got out carrying a large Courrèges bag, tipped the porter, and then walked through the rain. He pressed several buttons on one elevator and sent it up, then waited in the other one. She entered the building, smiling at the security guard, walking with her chin slightly raised, looking straight ahead with azure eyes that glittered with life. She was taller than he remembered and very straight and as she approached the elevator she looked straight at Papa, but her gaze seemed to go through him, past him, off someplace beyond him. Papa was suddenly embarrassed, not from tension, but because she was probably the most stunning creature he had ever seen.

Jesus, he thought, *no wonder she gets six bills a pop.*

She stopped, hesitating a moment at the elevator that was already going up. 'Going up,' Papa said. 'We're just checking this one out.'

'Thank you.'

A voice like down feathers.

She stood beside him.

The back of Papa's neck got very warm. 'What floor?'

'Ten, please.'

He pressed the button and the doors closed. The elevator started up. Papa shifted slightly so his body shielded the control buttons and, reaching out very cautiously, he pressed the stop button. The elevator glided to a halt.

'Oh, no!' she breathed.

Papa pressed the button on his walkie-talkie.

'Say, uh, up there, uh, this here's Johnson. I got a passenger, uh, and, uh, like the power just cut off.'

'Is something wrong?' Delicately.

'Nah,' Papa said, 'they just shut us off there for a second. Don't you worry none, little lady.' His walkie-talkie came alive. It was Sharky's voice.

'Uh, yeah, sorry about that, Johnson, we, uh, just had to, uh, reset the flatistan up here. Uh, it's okay now, uh, you can crank it up again.'

Papa pushed the ten button and the elevator started up again.

'Sorry about that,' Papa said.

She smiled at him, looking directly into his eyes.

'It's perfectly all right.'

Hardly more than a whisper. Papa felt a thrill like he had not felt for many years.

'Nice weather,' he stammered for lack of something better to say.

She laughed. 'Yes. I love the rain.'

Beautiful, Papa thought, *nice weather all right. There's a typhoon outside.*

The elevator slowed to a stop and the doors slid open. Sharky and The Nosh were standing there. Domino looked first at The Nosh and then at Sharky. She stared at him for a fraction of a second and then her lips parted very slightly in a smile.

'Hello,' she said as she walked past him.

Sharky was immobilized, nailed to the floor, stunned as

131

though he had been clubbed. It was more than her elegance, her beauty, something else. A softness he had not expected, a vulnerability he sensed, in her eyes and the softness of her voice. The Nosh had to pull on his sleeve to get him into the elevator. Her scent was still there. He watched her until the doors closed.

'Okay,' The Nosh said, 'we're in business. We go back on the roof, check everything out, and then maybe we swing by Taco Bell, grab a quick burrito supreme.'

Papa smiled. 'You got my vote.'

But Sharky did not hear either of them. He was like a statue, staring at the closed door. In just a few seconds Domino had claimed a new victim.

Chapter Eight

DeLaroza was hunched down in the rear of the power launch. A forgotten Havana twirled unlit between his fingers. He stared straight ahead, a man hypnotized by his own thoughts, as the boat moved towards the northern end of the lake.

Suddenly his concentration was jarred by a speedboat which charged from a nearby inlet, skipping like a stone across the choppy surface of the lake. He watched through cold eyes as the boat arced wide around them and sped south, its engine buzzing like an angry bee, the driver perched on his haunches at the stern.

By the time the surly north wind had whipped the speed-boat's wake into frothy whitecaps, DeLaroza was deep in thought again, repeating over and over a single word:

'Gowmanah . . . gowmanah . . . gowmanah . . .'

It was a form of Shinto meditation he had learned in Japan. In a few seconds the intrusion was forgotten. He was entranced, his mind cleansed.

Once his concentration was purged, he dealt with the problem at hand as he dealt with all problems. His method had been developed thirty years before in Brazil, where he had spent five years and a fortune becoming Victor De-Laroza and developing a personality that fitted the man he created. These had been the difficult years, the dangerous years just after the war, when his constant companions had been paranoia and fear. It was the Jews he feared most, for they could have become the unwitting instrument of a cruel and ironic joke. The Nazis had come to Brazil, seeking anonymity, trying to rebuild their failed dream. And behind them came the Jewish commandos, cold, efficient, zealously checking every record, perusing all newcomers, methodically rooting out war criminals. And always there was the gnawing fear that they might tumble onto him by accident. He was a man wary of every footfall, suspicious of all strangers. The fear of surprise was a worm in his gut. To avoid surprises, he learned to predict them before they happened. His reflexes became as swift and deadly. He lied when necessary, bribed when expedient, arranged murder when he had to, a ruthless survivalist, as he moved on to Hong Kong, where he *was* Victor DeLaroza, the international businessman who destroyed competitors, sucked up companies, and built his empire.

His method was always the same. First, cleanse the mind of all emotional or personal considerations – they weakened logic; second, feed the facts into the mental computer; third, consider all alternatives, options, dangers. Once this was done, logic released the solution from his brain.

Sitting in the rear of the launch, he considered the facts. He was safe, safer than he had been for thirty years. They had lured Corrigon to Atlanta and eliminated him, and with him the last danger of recognition. His partner was about to leave the country but DeLaroza no longer felt he needed him. In Yokohama friends in the Yakuza were waiting to take care of that problem. Hotchins was no longer the dark-horse candidate. With Lowenthal and his people on the team Hotchins would become a serious contender and eventually the favourite.

Now only Domino posed a threat. No, more than a threat, she was dangerous. She could connect DeLaroza to Hotchins and possibly Corrigon to DeLaroza. Unwittingly she could tie the noose that would hang them all.

Those were the facts. The logic? Hotchins did not love the girl; he was obsessed by her sensuality. But he had made his decision clear that morning and although he had promised to consider giving her up, DeLaroza knew *all* the hungers that go with power. Like all self-made men, Hotchins was fiercely protective of his independence. In the end he would deal with the Domino situation emotionally and DeLaroza knew he could press the issue no further.

For he also knew Hotchins's passion to become president. The conclusion was obvious.

His mind made up, DeLaroza leaned forward, cupping his hands against the chill breeze, and lit the cigar.

'Chiang,' he called to his bodyguard and the Chinese turned to him. In addition to his powerful build Chiang had a scar running from his hairline down the right side of his face, across his eye to his jaw. The eye dropped from the old wound, half-closed, and the pupil had turned almost white. It added another dimension to his imposing size. 'We must put the cover over the seats back here,' DeLaroza said in Chinese. 'It is too cold for open riding.'

Chiang nodded and DeLaroza knew it would be done before the day ended. DeLaroza had saved Chiang from a prison in Macao almost ten years before. Now no task was too menial or too demanding: Chiang had devoted his life to DeLaroza.

Twenty miles north of the marina the lake narrowed and the current became stronger. A mile or so ahead there was a steady rumble as the river emptied into the lake. It was a desolate area and rarely travelled. The launch slowed, swung easily around a tree-scarred peninsula. A cove emerged in front of them and at its far end, partially obscured by tall pines, the curious geometry of a Chinese junk appeared. Its polished stern rose high above the water, sloping gently towards the bow. Its tall masts were partially obscured by spidery burnt-orange sails which were furled tightly against them. The cabin was slightly astern, its roof bordered by a frieze of temple dogs and dragons that curled around the cornice.

Chiang guided the launch expertly alongside a small pontoon dock that was lashed to the side of the junk and quickly tied it down. Then he helped DeLaroza out of the launch. The big man slowly mounted the jacob's ladder to the deck and stood for a few moments admiring his treasure. The deck and cabin glistened with teak oil that had been hand-rubbed into every crevice and pore. The paint, although old, was perfectly preserved. He called her *Psalm-Lo*, The Three Devils, after the legend of the dragons.

DeLaroza looked at Chiang and pointed below decks.

'*Hai*,' Chiang answered.

DeLaroza knew that the three Orientals who manned the junk despised the *Gwai-lo*, the foreign devil, who was living on board, although they would never say anything to DeLaroza. They had been his servants, his bodyguards, his soldiers, for many years. Each was a master of karate; each was an expert at Tai Chi, the Way of the Peaceful Warrior; each had a deadly proficiency with the dagger and the *yinza*, a small steel disc the size of a silver dollar with twelve barbs around its perimeter which when scaled with the flick of a powerful wrist could pierce the skull and drive deep into the brain. And each of them religiously followed the ancient rituals of his ancestors. To them the *Gwai-lo* was a coward who killed without honour.

DeLaroza went below. The cabin was divided into three sections. Below the foredecks each member of the crew had his own quarters and behind them, towards the stern, was the galley. To the rear, under the lofty stern, were two bedrooms, one decorated in modern décor, the other with antiques smuggled out of Kowloon to avoid the new laws that prohibited the removal of historic artifacts from the crown colony. The living room was a museum: teak and rosewood chests with sculptured gold handles and hinges; sofas and chairs covered with thin-striped silk from the finest shops on Pearl Street; hand-painted mandarin screens dating from the dynasty of the boy emperor, Ping, eight hundred years ago; delicate Royal Doulton porcelain figures, jade statues, and Lalique crystal.

Against one wall was a mahogany cabinet with glass doors and inside, displayed against purple velvet, were several ancient weapons: a jewel-encrusted samurai sword; an awkward blunderbuss with an ornate buttplate and a curious swirling hammer; several daggers, their worn blood gutters hinting of dark deeds from the clouded past.

DeLaroza stood quietly in the darkened room looking for – who was he now? His partner had had so many names through the years that DeLaroza sometimes had difficulty remembering who he was from day to day. Howard? Yes, Howard Burns, that's what he again called himself.

At least I have been consistent in my own alias, DeLaroza thought.

The junk moved gently in the water. The screens muffled the sounds of the lake, the water slapping against the hull, the dock nudging the side, timbers groaning underfoot. But the cabin was still.

And yet DeLaroza knew he was there, could sense that deadly presence and smell the odour of death that seemed to exude from his partner's every pore.

'Howard?' he said, peering into the dark corners of the cabin.

There was no answer. But there was a stirring, a shifting of shadows, and then he saw the eyes, gleaming, alert, cold, the eyes of a snake. Burns moved into the light filtering through the portholes and DeLaroza sensed that he was in the presence of a man verging on madness. His gaunt face reflected a lifetime of killing. His thin, veined fingers were taut. A muscle in his jaw jerked with the beat of his pulse. He had a stubble of grey beard and the nostrils in his hawk-like nose twitched, like a predator sniffing out his prey.

In one hand he held a .22 calibre Woodsman, its long, slender barrel encased in the ugly silencer.

Burns said nothing. He moved slowly into the centre of the cabin, his eyes darting feverishly.

He stepped closer to DeLaroza and held the gun an inch from his heart, his eyes afire with rage.

'Bang,' he shouted and an icy hand squeezed DeLaroza's heart. 'You're an inch from being dead,' he said. 'Next time don't keep me hangin' like that. I ain't heard shit from you in almost a week.'

DeLaroza stared down at the gun. 'Don't make jokes,' he whispered.

'You think I'm joking?' He waved the pistol around, backed into the shadows. 'You think I'm *joking*? Stuck out here with these goddamn slant-eyed creeps of yours. They don't ever talk. Move around like mice. Half the time I can't hear them, don't know where the hell they are. I got the willies. They're all the time doin' this weird slow-motion shit, moving around on one leg, like a bunch of faggot ballet dancers. The TV ain't worth a shit. All I get on this fuckin' radio is static . . .'

He lashed out suddenly, smashing the pistol into the loudspeaker of the radio, which flew off into the corner and crashed in the shadows. An instant later the hatch opened and Chiang stood above them, glaring down, his fingers stiff at his side. Burns aimed the pistol at the Chinese.

'Get outa here. Tell that gook to get lost or – '

DeLaroza held a hand towards Burns and turned quickly to Chiang. '*Jaaw hoy! Jaaw hoy,*' he said quickly and the Chinese disappeared. He turned to Burns. 'Easy.'

'Don't tell me easy,' Burns roared. His face flushed, his eyes danced from corner to corner, back to DeLaroza, over to the hatch door. 'They're pushin' me around the bend, them gook monkeys of yours.'

'When they move like that, what you call slow motion, they are practising Tai Chi, the Way of the Peaceful Warrior it is called.'

Burns wiggled the gun under his nose. 'They come around me, fuck with me, I'll make peaceful warriors outa them.'

'To attack them is like attacking water. When you strike them, it is like striking air. They cannot be hurt and they cannot be stopped when they are committed. They can kill with one finger. And they have been ordered to protect you at all costs.'

'I protect myself. Me and Betsy here is all the protection I need. The bullets are soaked in garlic, know what that means? It's poison inside you. You die screaming for your mother.'

A shiver rippled through DeLaroza.

'Please. Everything is good. Believe me, I've been very busy, very busy. I do not want to use the mobile radio; it could be dangerous. From now on I'll come every other day . . .'

'From now on! How the hell long? . . .' Burns's shoulders slumped. He dropped the gun with a clatter on a polished rosewood chest and rubbed the knuckles of one hand furiously into the top of his close-cropped hair. 'It was only gonna be a month, gettin' this show on the road. Christ, I been here what, eight weeks? Nine? Don't fuck me over, you got it? *Don't fuck me over.*'

'Nobody is fucking you over, Howard. It takes time to get passports, visas, make the proper arrangements. Your wife is safe, we moved her to Canada, then across to the coast, and then on over to Yokohama. Nobody knows. Even the FBI lost her. It was done perfectly, as promised.'

'Yeah, well, it ain't perfect with me. Twice you ask me to do a job for you, twice in what? – the thirty years I've known you? Both times I come through.' He snapped his fingers. 'Just like that. Quick, right? Clean, right? Everything down to a tee. Now you got this thing to do for me, it's a month of Sundays already.'

He paced the room on the balls of his feet, tense and alert, like a prize-fighter stalking his opponent. His nerves were stretched out like violin strings. DeLaroza could almost hear them keening.

'This ain't my turf, okay. I don't even know where the hell I am, out here, some fuckin' lake, eighty miles from nowhere. Nothin' to do all day but listen to those fuckin' monkeys doin' that slow-motion shit. It's a . . . I'll tell you what, it's a goddamn bad dream come true is what it is. Get me outa here. Get me outa here, Victor.'

Madness burned in Burns's eyes. There was hate there, and fear. DeLaroza could see it. He was a different man from the cool killer in Hong Kong.

'You and this nut idea, wantin' to put your fuckin' mug in every paper in the world. Lemme tell ya, pal, I didn't mind doin' that job for you in Hong Kong, I could unnerstan', see, how you could go a little off the wall when you seen that Colonel from Italy. But suckin' Corrigon in, plantin' that seed in his brain, and bringin' him down here, right in your own fuckin' back*yard*, that was crazy. Suppose he told somebody else, hunh? Suppose he wrote it down some-wheres to cover himself? You ever think of that?'

'There was no reason for him to do that. You think he *knew* we were setting him up?' DeLaroza said.

'After thirty years, a guy gets prison wise, learns a lot. I'm just sayin' we coulda left it alone. We didn't have to wiggle the finger, get him down here and kayo him just so's you could come outa the closet after all these years. Shit, you got the fuckin' tenderloin, you gotta have it all?'

'You do not understand what it was like, all those years, all I have done, and no recognition for any of it.'

'I unnerstan' this, pal, all that what you done you're so proud of? It started with the rip-off. I don't care if you made fifty billion, see, you couldna done it without the four mil we took off Uncle Sam. Any way you slice it, you and me we're both thieves. And a gonif's a gonif. A genius gonif, maybe, but a gonif all the same. You ain't changin' that by puttin' your fuckin' picture in the papers.'

'There is no way for you to comprehend what it has been like for me. All these years, hiding my face, letting others take the credit, give the interviews . . .'

'Hey, I been in a closet myself there, seven years now. Don't tell me what it's like, livin' with your face to the wall. All I'm sayin' is that pushin' over Corrigon, that wasn't necessary. I done it, okay? but that wasn't part of our deal, see, that was a personal gift, me to you, got that?'

'Howard, for thirty years I have lived in fear of the day Corrigon got out of prison. Wondering whether I might turn around in an airport one day and find myself face to face with him.'

'He wouldna recognized ya, not after all that time.'

'I never would have been sure. And if he had recognized me, you would have suffered too.'

'Yeah, yeah, yeah, yeah, ya made the point. Okay. Look, whaddya want from me, anyways? Ya think it was easy, phonyin' up my own death a *second* time? My old lady still ain't made sense outa the whole thing. Point is, it's done, okay? Corrigon is kaput. Now I want outa here!'

'Very soon, now, I promise you.'

A thin line of sweat formed at the edge of Burns's brow. It began to inch down his forehead. He wiped it with the back of his hand.

DeLaroza walked cautiously to the chest and picked up the gun by the barrel. Burns turned as fast as a humming-bird, took two steps, reached out, and grabbed the pistol, twisting it sharply in towards DeLaroza's body and snapping it out of his hand.

'Don't touch my piece. You got that? That clear? Nobody touches my piece.'

'Of course, of course.'

Burns slid the gun back under his arm.

'I was just, uh, you see this chest is six hundred years old – '

Burns cut him off. 'Fuck the chest. I don't give a shit, Moses stored the tablets in it. When am I movin', gettin' outa this fuckin' scow? Away from them Chinks?'

'A few more days.'

'Shit!'

'Just a few more days, Howard.'

'Too long!'

'It's the passport, Howard. It's going to be clean, no strings. You will never again have problems. This is all being done right for you.'

Burns leaned against the wall and breathed hard through his nose. He wiped his mouth with his hand, pinched his nose several times.

'Too old for this kinda shit, anyhow,' he said.

'I know, I know.'

140

Burns looked up at him and said quickly. 'It don't mean I lost my touch. I mean, don't go blowin' smoke rings up your ass, you think I ain't what I used to be.'

'I didn't say anything about that, Howard.'

'I like things to happen quick. No bullshit, see? I'm on the run. You don't get that, do you there, Victor?'

'Of course.'

No, he didn't understand. Victor had it made, all the aces. But him, he had spent years developing one cover, losing it, and now he was starting again dodging from rock to rock like a fox with the hounds snapping at his heels. DeLaroza had offered a chance, a chance to get out for good. But the closer it got, the more terrified he became. His insides were burning, his guts grinding with turmoil.

Burns sighed and leaned against the bulkhead, breathing deeply through his mouth. Tears gathered in the corners of his eyes.

'Easy, my friend. I promise you, you're almost out.'

'Yeah, yeah, I hope so. Hope so.'

'Have you, uh . . . you aren't taking . . . pills?'

Burn's eyes jumped back and glared at DeLaroza.

'So what. What if I did? Yeah, I had a little shot there, took a red, one stinkin' red to get started this morning. Any of your business?'

'Of course not, I – '

'You're big time, ain't you, Victor. Get all that nookie, that's your reds, Vic, hunh? Right? I pop a red, get a little shot, you get your ashes hauled. Same dif, same dif.'

He rubbed a wrist with the palm of his hand, then shook the hand as though it might have fallen asleep.

'Feelin' better,' he said. 'I just got the willies, okay? I'm tellin' you, Victor.' He lowered his voice, stepping so close to DeLaroza the garlic on his breath almost brought tears to the big man's eyes. 'It's them fuckin' gooks is what it is. Could you, maybe tell 'em to knock off that slow-motion shit while I'm here? It's makin' me whacko. I'm off the wall, see?'

'I'll have a talk with them. It is a discipline, Howard. A thing they must do each day. But I will tell them to do it in the forward cabins, not in front of you if it upsets you.'

'It upsets me, okay. Upsets the shit outa me.'

DeLaroza nodded.

'Y'see, I ain't used to this. Cooped up here and all. Not used to it at all. Goddamn, I'd lose a few bucks, win a few bucks. Maybe catch the Jets, watchin' Namath throw that ball. See what I mean, I gotta have some action, not sit here, listen' to the fuckin' water grow.'

DeLaroza moved away from him, sat down in a chair on the opposite side of the cabin and lit his cigar, which had gone out. *Now was the time*, he thought, but he had to handle the situation carefully. Perhaps it was too volatile. Perhaps Burns was too hyper.

'You mind?' Burns said.

'I beg your pardon?'

'The cigar, do ya mind? It smells like a fuckin' cowturd burnin', Victor. Jesus, it's close enough in here.'

'I'm sorry.'

'Yeah, okay. It's I don't like boats, see? All I need is to get seasick. Puke my guts out, that's all I need.'

'It's just a lake.'

'I don't like *boats*!' His voice rose again, near hysteria.

'I understand, I understand.'

'Jesus, I don't like to be this way, y'know.' Burns shook his head. 'I like everything easy, no hassle. Slick ice. I'm sorry, okay?'

'Of course. I was thinking . . .' He paused, trying to word the proposition just right.

'Yeah?'

'We have a situation. Something has come up. If you, uh, felt up to it. It could, uh, you could stay busy for a day or two. No. No, it's not a good idea. Forget it.'

'Forget what? You ain't told me anything to forget.'

'A bad idea.'

'You wanna tell me about it? Let me decide?'

'It's the girl.'

'What girl?'

'I told you about the girl. Domino.'

'The one you and Hotchins share. That one?'

'It is not exactly like that. He knows nothing about the woman and me.'

Burns laughed hard. He sat down next to DeLaroza and slapped his knee several times. 'That's rich, that is. You and him fuckin' the same broad and he's not in on it. I'll tell you

142

somethin', Victor. You got some kind of funny balls, you do.'

'The problem is not funny.'

'It is to me. You ever hear of Angel Carillo? Big don in Philly, maybe *the* big don in Philly. No? Well, you don't read much, because Angel makes the headlines now and then. He had an arm, name of Donny Duffield, Irish punk but a good arm. Very quick. He did a hit, it was no planning. He'd just go out, do it, go have a beer. Anyways, Donny introduces Angel to this broad which Donny has been punchin' since high school. A real looker. And Angel gets a thing for her, starts takin' her out, buyin' her shit, clothes, jewellery, the old wham bam. Sets her up in this cushy apartment. And all the time Donny is giving her the old squirtaroo on the side. I mean Angel is maybe gettin' it once, twice a week; Donny, he's over there dippin' in morning, noon, and night. You know those goddamn micks, got a hard-on thirty-six hours a day. So Angel finds out about it and he muscles Donny down to the old ice house there and he says to him, "Whaddya mean, you're fuckin' my girl?" And Donny says, "Whaddya mean, 'your girl'? I was fuckin' her long before you." And Angel says, "Yeah, but she's my girl now." And he takes out the old stiletto and whacko, clean as a whistle, he takes off Donny's cock and balls. "Okay," Angel says when he's through, "you want her, you got her." And like that he gives her back to Donny, who has to piss through a hole in his belly. Funny, hunh? What a sense of humour.' Burns leaned back in his chair and laughed again.

DeLaroza rubbed gooseflesh from his arm. 'I really don't see the analogy,' he said.

'You don't make the connection, hunh?'

'I seriously doubt that Donald Hotchins would castrate anyone.'

'Ah, what ya mean, you take me literally there. No, I ain't sayin' he'd do it in so many words. But what's the dif between him and Angel Carillo? They both of them are heavy hitters there, Victor. You don't take from them. Angel, he does his own cuttin'. Hotchins gets it done for him. Maybe in a different way, see. But the end result, that's the same. Like they say, don't fuck with Matt Dillon, he's got the biggest gun. I was you, I'd back off.'

'That is not the problem. I cannot tell him about her. That she is a prostitute, I mean. After all, I introduced them. There is too much at stake here.'

'So let him dump on her. Lemme tell you something, partner. You better stay outa the picture. You better be the man that wasn't there, you know what I mean?'

'I just give advice.'

'And money,' Burns said viciously.

'Yes, money. This man is going to be the next president.'

'I don't get you, Victor. What's in all this for you? Takin' these chances. You were afraid Corrigon would make you, somebody else could too. All this so you can call the White House when you get the urge? Big deal.'

'It is what I want. What do you want? To walk free, yes? To put the past behind you. I have done that already. We have played a different kind of game, you and I.'

'I played the only game I knew. The spots, there, they come on the leopard.'

'Well, you will get what you want, finally.'

'I'm still busy cleanin' up, Victor. I'll never walk free again. The onus was on me before I ever met you. It started when I was a kid. You think they ever let you off the hook? Shit, the only way you get out, they take you away feet first, throw roses in your face. All they gotta do, somebody sees my face one time and every pistol in the fuckin' country's after me. You think them years in Nebraska was easy, livin' like a goddamn shirt salesman? All I want is to be covered until I get lost again, see what I mean? Go someplace, sit in the sun, get freckles. I'm fifty-six, I ain't got all that much time left. But I wanna use what I got. I want the rest of it to be good, see? It ain't gonna be easy now, keeping the Feds *and* the Family from tumblin' on to me. Thing is, what's all these millions you parlayed for us gonna do for me; I can't enjoy it, right?'

DeLaroza toyed with the cigar.

'There's something else about all this,' he said.

'Oh, yeah? How's that?'

'She knows something. She saw you with Corrigon that night. She was leaving my place.'

'She saw me hit Corrigon?'

'No. After. Putting him in the car.'

'But she saw me?'

'I do not think, honestly, that she can recognize you.'

'Ho ho. Bullshit there.' Burns's eyes narrowed. His breath hissed through clenched teeth. 'She saw me. She saw me.'

'It was dark. It could have been –'

'She saw me.' Burns stood up and paced the cabin. He rubbed his wrist again and then snapped his hand. 'Okay, so they turn up Corrigon. Sooner or later they'll probably turn him up, know what I mean? Maybe even figure out who he is. Then they put his picture in the paper. She recognizes *him*, see. She leads them to the scene. Your front door. And then she starts doin' the mug books. Maybe she didn't see me, but then maybe she saw enough there, to make me from the pictures.' He turned and stood over DeLaroza. 'See what I mean? She could put me together with Corrigon at your front door and there goes the fuckin' ballgame. You got *that* picture there?'

DeLaroza nodded.

'I was, uh, I didn't want to worry you,' DeLaroza said.

'Oh, you didn't, hunh? Gonna let me sit around, wait till the building falls in one me?'

'It is both of us.'

'I did the hit. Just like in Hong Kong that time. It was *me*!' Burns bellowed. 'I'm the one they'll come squat on. You may go down the toilet there, Victor, but I get the gas pipe.'

'Well,' DeLaroza said and let the sentence hang.

'We got a saying in the rackets. The rope only has one noose. You know what I mean, Victor? I only got one neck. How many times you think they can stretch it? How come you wait so long to gimme this piece of news?'

'I just found out.'

'When?'

'At noon.'

'Jesus. I don't believe you. I don't fuckin' believe you. Here we got this broad can hang us both higher than the church steeple, you're still gettin' a little. You just finished tellin' me you don't know how to handle this here with Hotchins, you're dippin' the wienie. Jesus Christ!'

'It was not like that. I talked to her. Told her to step out of Hotchins's life. She is a threat to his future.'

145

'Well, I'll bet she lapped that up with a fork all right.'

'No, you are right. She did not lap it up with a fork.'

'What do ya need, a picture book? They'll get ya every time. Ask Adam. Ask John the Baptist. Ask Samson, Ask 'em all, man. She's got a meal ticket. He goes to Washington, she goes along for the ride. Besides, that ain't the question here. You know what the question here is, Victor. Can she put it on us? Can she finger me for chilling Corrigon? And if the answer is maybe, that means the answer is yes.'

DeLaroza said nothing. He wanted desperately to light his cigar. Outside, the first deep rumble of thunder rolled across the sky.

'Listen to that. It's gonna rain like a son of a bitch,' Burns said. He fell quiet. The juices were beginning to run. He felt the first nibble of excitement, the first surge of lust. His palms tingled. He licked his lips.

DeLaroza went up the steps and opened the hatch door leading to the cabin, watching the storm clouds race angrily across the sky. He lit the cigar, letting the hard, cold wind carry the smoke out across the lake.

'You know where she lives?' Burns asked.

'Yes. In fact, I, uh, I am going there tonight.'

Burns shook his head. 'Unreal,' he said.

'It is something special. A goodbye. I have known this woman for a long time,' he said. Then, after a pause: 'Too long, maybe.'

Burns smiled but there was no mirth in the grin. Then he said, 'Not *too* long. *So* long. Get what I mean?'

DeLaroza turned and looked back at him. 'What do you mean?' he said.

'What do you mean, what do I mean? You know what I mean. Don't act dumb, because I know you ain't dumb.'

A sudden flash of lightning jarred DeLaroza. A second later it cracked like a whip snapping in the trees nearby. Burns seemed to draw strength from it. His eyes lost their coldness and began to beam with exhilaration.

'You're gonna be right there,' Burns said. 'So you can case out the situation for me. You're in the catbird seat there, Victor, because we ain't got a lot of time. Now do you know what I mean?'

DeLaroza did not answer. His lower lip began to tremble. He was thinking about tonight, about making love to her.

Burns was totally calm, the killing machine, lubricating itself with visceral oil.

'You did good, Victor,' he said.

'I don't understand.'

'Sure you do. You didn't come out here to feed me all that bullshit about my passport, that crap. You came out here to put the edge on the knife. Right?'

DeLaroza fell quiet again. He stared down at the cigar.

'I ain't pissed about it, Victor. In fact, I gotta hand it to you. In your own sweet way you're just like me. You'd kill your own mother for a two-point safety. You worked it out nice. It's one and one makes two, just that simple. You're here because the chippie has to take a hit and I'm the one's gotta do the job. Ain't that right, Victor?'

DeLaroza stared at the floor. Finally he nodded very slowly.

'Lemme hear you say it there, partner.'

DeLaroza continued to stare at the floor.

'Lemme hear you say it,' Burns said flatly. 'Say it out loud.'

DeLaroza remained quiet.

'Say it.'

DeLaroza started to speak. His lips moved, but the words died in his mouth. He coughed, trying to clear his throat.

'Say it!'

The voice was hoarse and seemed far away. 'Kill her,' DeLaroza said.

Burns grinned. 'See how easy it is when you try.'

Chapter Nine

The ant was as big as an elephant. It crawled across the ceiling and Sharky watched it, wondering what it was doing on the roof of a twelve-storey building and why it even wanted to be there at all.

Sit and wait. Boredom. The curse of the stakeout.

At least Livingston had provided him with what Arch called his stakeout kit – an army cot, blanket, hot plate, and several packets of instant soup and coffee. It helped. They had also left a car on the street below near the exit of the apartment parking deck in case he had to tail her.

But he had nothing to read. After all the stakeouts Sharky should have remembered something to read. And he would be there until Papa relieved him at eight A.M.

He lay on the cot with the blanket under his head and the earphones on and watched the ant scurry across the ceiling and start down the wall. The recorder for Domino's living room whirred quietly on the floor near the cot. The radio was on. Led Zeppelin boomed in his ears.

She was moving around, singing to herself, the recorders for the bedroom and massage room cutting on and off as she went from one to the other. She was in the master bedroom when she made the phone call.

'Hello, is Mister Moundt there, please? . . . Hi, it's Domino . . . Fine, and you? . . . Oh, you do? Wonderful. I was afraid it wouldn't get in. . . . Thank you, that's so sweet. It's for tonight. I hope it wasn't too much trouble. . . . Wonderful, I'll be by in a few minutes. Bye.'

Good. He could pick up a paperback or some magazines. He pulled on his suede pullover, smoothed back his hair, and walked down to the ninth floor, making sure the elevator he took did not stop at ten. He did not want to end up in the same elevator with her. He walked through the cold drizzle to the stakeout car, a blue Chevy, got in and waited. A few minutes later the gate swung open and the blue Mercedes pulled out.

He followed her down Peachtree Street, staying several car lengths behind her. When she turned into the lot at

Moundt's he drove past, u-turned, and ambled back, giving her time to enter the store.

Moundt's was a gourmet supermarket, possibly the best in the city. It had two entrances, the main door on Peachtree Street and another through the side that led past a snack bar. He got a cup of coffee, stood in the doorway, watching her as he sipped it. She was in the rear of the store, talking to Moundt, a tall, grey-haired, amiable man who seemed to know her well. He gave her two cans which she put in her shopping cart.

Supposing she makes you? Sharky thought. *Remembers you from the elevator?*

He went to the fruit department, got some white seedless grapes and half a dozen hard apples, then cruised the store, staying two or three rows away and well behind her. He reached the paperback rack and, keeping his back to her, looked for a book. He selected a thick novel by Irwin Shaw, then turned cautiously, and looked back over his shoulder.

She was gone.

He moved towards the checkout counter, peering over the tops of the aisles. As he reached the end of the aisle she stood up. She had stooped down to get some crackers and now, suddenly, they were face to face, an aisle apart.

He left the basket, went back up the aisle, aimlessly searching the counters as though he had forgotten something. She was facing the other way when he came back and he pushed his cart hurriedly to the checkout counter.

An elderly lady got there at the same time. He smiled, reluctantly, and motioned her in front of him.

Goddamn, she must have fifty dollars' worth of stuff in that cart.

He watched her put the items on the checkout counter. It took forever. Sharky waited. Then he casually turned sideways and looked back over his shoulder towards the store.

Domino was standing there, right behind him, three feet away.

Well, shit!

She smiled at him, blue eyes crinkling at the corners. *His nose is broken. How interesting.* 'We seem to be following each other,' she said pleasantly.

Do something, stupid, don't just stare at her. He smiled back. 'Looks like it, doesn't it?' he said.

'You live in the neighbourhood?'

'No,' he said, then realized it was a stupid answer and added quickly, 'I like to shop here.'

'Me too. It's my absolute favourite.' *I'd like to reach up and just touch him, there between the eyes.* 'Are you going to be working in the building for long?'

'Well, uh, I, uh, yes, a couple of days.' *Neat, Sharky. Why don't you give her an itinerary? Show her your shield. Take out the old pistol and spin it on your finger, do a couple of John Waynes for her. Back out of the conversation. You're blowing it. Putting it all in your mouth. Foot, socks, shoe, the works.*

And she thought, *He's interesting. Trim and hard, almost skinny. Faded green eyes, very warm. And that flat place across the bridge of his nose. He'd be pretty if it were not for that.*

He was staring into her shopping cart.

'Shark's fin soup?' he said with surprise.

'Have you ever tried it?' *I'm glad he's not pretty. Good God, what are you doing? Getting off on his broken nose!*

'I'll be honest with you,' he said, 'I never heard of shark's fin soup.'

His eyes wandered. She was wearing a tee-shirt with *ice cream* written across the chest in dribbling letters, as if it were melting, and tight Italian jeans that hugged her ass and a fur jacket that looked like it would have cost him a year's salary. There was no doubt about it – she was something special.

'It's quite a delicacy,' she said, 'Mister Moundt ord – '

She stopped, aware that he was not listening, that he was looking, no he was *lost* in looking at her. And she liked it. It seemed open and honest and it felt good to her and she looked him over again, admiring the way he held himself, loose, like an athlete, and confident.

She looked back at his eyes and a moment later he looked up and knew he had been caught.

He's blushing! I haven't seen anyone blush since college. She turned it on, staring hard into his eyes. The lady at the checkout counter was almost through. *Do something. He'll be gone in a minute or two.* 'I think you should try it,' she said.

'Try what?'

'Shark's fin soup.'

She's making a pass, Sharky. 'Well, I, uh, yeah . . . you know, one of . . .'

'I mean today.'

'Today.'

'Um hum, today. About six o'clock.'

'Six o'clock today?'

'I'm making it for a friend. I'll be finished cooking it by about six o'clock.'

She bored in with the blue eyes and he just stared at her, half-smiling.

'10-A,' she said.

'10-A.'

'10-A, six o'clock.'

'Right. 10-A, six o'clock.'

What the fuck!

She smiled. 'Splendid.'

He sat on the edge of the cot and nibbled grapes and tried to read, but his eyes kept wandering to the tape recorder. Finally it clicked and he slipped the earphones over his ears and shoved the monitor button, heard her close the door, followed her footsteps into the kitchen, listened to the rattling of paper bags, the refrigerator door opening and closing, pots slamming about, heard her singing to herself, filling in forgotten lyrics by humming.

She went into the living room and he could hear her shuffling through record albums. She put one on and the softness of a guitar took the edge off the hollowness of the room. A moment later Joni Mitchell's plaintive voice came on singing the plaintive lyrics to 'Harry's House'.

Sharky's mind wandered back to a high school picnic and a girl in a bright yellow bikini that barely covered her swelling breasts and she had turned out to be, what was her name? Mary Lou? Mary Jane? Mary-something-or-other, who had suddenly grown up, and remembering her, he made up aimless lyrics to a nothing song:

'Baby did I lust for you,
Da da da da da da da,
And everybody else did too,
Dadadada da da da . . .'

151

He heard the sound of water running in the bathtub and he forgot the yellow bikini bathing suit and Mary-something-or-other and thought about Domino taking off the tee-shirt with the melting ice cream, envisioned her slipping off the tight Italian jeans, pictured her in his mind, naked, and he closed his eyes.

She poured bath oil in the tub, turned, and looked at herself in the full-length mirror and, singing along with Joni Mitchell, slowly stripped off the shirt, let it fall away from her shoulders, turned sideways, and studied her breasts, was pleased that they were still firm, curving up and away from her body, reached up under them and traced the curve with her fingertips, sliding her fingers out to the nipples, and squeezed them gently, watching them grow hard at her touch. She unbuttoned the jeans, pulled them over her hips, let them fall to the floor. Her panties had pulled down too, and she looked at her hair curling up over the top of them and ran her hand across the flat surface of her stomach, let her little finger slip down under the band, enjoyed the softness, and finally edged them down and stepped out of them, running her hands down the insides of her thighs, letting her thumbs ripple across the thick black down.

The beat of the music began to change to the blues and she hummed as Joni Mitchell sang:

> 'The more I'm with you, pretty baby,
> The more I feel my love increase,
> I'm building all my dreams around you
> Our happiness will never cease.'

She tested the water with a toe, slipped down into its oily warmth, let it envelop her, and lay back with her eyes closed, caressing her legs, her thighs. Her thumb found her belly button, lingered at its edge while the rest of her fingers slid down between her legs and she slowly pinched thumb and fingers together, lightly, slowly, and she thought about the elevator man, about his trim, hard body, the rugged face, the shattered nose.

> 'We'll find a house and garden somewhere
> Along a country road a piece,

A little cottage on the outskirts
Where we can really find release,
'Cause nothing's any good without you.
Baby, you're my centrepiece.'

And while Domino prepared herself for Victor, thoughts of the elevator man kept intruding. Intruding. Intruding . . .

She opened the door on the first ring and stood facing Sharky, her chin slightly raised, an arrogant, almost impish look on her face, her thick black hair, not quite dry yet, hanging damply about her ears. She wore no makeup. She didn't need it and she knew she didn't. She was wearing a scarlet floor-length kimono, silk, trimmed in brilliant yellow and split up both sides almost to the hip. There was nothing under it, nothing but her; he could tell by the way it stayed with her, moulded to her breasts, her hips, her flat stomach. Her eyes sparkled mischievously. The sweet odour of marijuana drifted past Sharky.

She smiled and said, 'Well, I just lost a bet with myself.'.

'How come?'

'I bet you wouldn't come.'

'I can always go back.'

She stepped back, swung the door wide and leaned against it, cocking her head to one side. 'No,' she said, 'no, I don't think so.'

He went past her, into the familiar living room, looked around, and feigned surprise. 'Very elegant,' he said, nodding his head.

She closed the door and came very close to him, staring up at his face for several seconds, then said, 'Thank you.'

She had set a place for him on the smoked-glass table. A linen placemat with delicate silverware, Wedgwood china and a tall, fragile wine glass. 'If you'd like to wash up, you can go in there,' she said, pointing to the bathroom. The door to the massage room was closed. He went into the bathroom and washed his hands. Patches of mist lingered in the corners of the mirror and the room was warm with the memory of her bath and smelled vaguely of bath oil.

When he returned, she was pouring white wine into two glasses. She motioned for him to sit down. Soup steamed in the bowl.

There was a record playing, a soft ballad sung almost off-key by a Frenchman.

'That's a very pretty song,' he said. 'I don't think I've ever heard it before.'

'It's called "The Dreams In Your Soul". It's my favourite song. That's Claude DuLac. He's very popular in France but it's hard to find his albums over here. Americans don't appreciate romantic singers anymore, do you think?'

'No, I agree with you.'

I'm glad you like it.

'I'm . . .'

'Yes?'

'Nothing.'

You're getting pushy. Don't rush it.

He swirled a pat of butter into yellow patterns on the surface of the soup. She raised her wine glass towards him.

'*Bon appétit,*' she said.

'Thanks.'

The glasses pinged as they touched. She leaned forward on her elbows, holding her wine glass between her fingertips, and stared at him again, the blue eyes digging deep.

'I have to ask you something,' she said, very quietly, almost confidentially.

Jesus, does she know? Does she suspect? 'Fire away,' he said.

'How did you get that?' she asked, pointing towards his nose.

'What?'

She reached out and ran her middle finger very delicately down between his eyes, lingering for a moment where his nose flattened out between them. 'That,' she said.

'Oh, that.'

'Um hum,' she said, adding, 'If it's something unromantic, like you got it caught in an elevator door or something, lie to me.'

'The first thing they teach you in elevator school is not to get your nose caught in the door.'

She laughed and the laugh became a smile and stayed on her lips.

'Well, when I was in high school there was this bully named Johnny Trowbridge and he hit me with a brick.'

She paused and then laughed again. 'Really?'

154

'Really.'

'And what did you do?'

'He was about, uh, three feet taller than me, so I went to the Y and I took boxing lessons for six months and then I beat the living bejesus out of him.'

She was laughing hard now and she shook her head. 'Did you really?' she said, 'did you really do that?'

'I really did it. Acceptable?'

'Oh, yes. Oh, absolutely. If it's a lie, don't change it.'

It was a lie, although a bully named Johnny Trowbridge had hit him with a brick and he had taken boxing lessons and a year later he'd kicked the shit out of Johnny Trowbridge. But his nose had been broken in an alley behind the bus station when he was a rookie cop. A drunk had scaled the lid of a garbage can straight into his face with uncanny accuracy.

She sighed. 'I'm so glad we got that settled.'

'What?'

'The business about your nose.'

'Does my nose bother you?'

She shook her head very slowly, staring at it. 'No. It gives you character.'

'Thanks.'

'Eat your soup before it gets cold.'

Upstairs on the roof the tapes were whirring, recording their conversation. He could envision the rest of the machine listening to it in Friscoe's Inferno. He knew what The Nosh would think. But how about Friscoe? Livingston? Papa? And The Bat! The Bat would have a coronary. He would sit in his office and his face would turn red, then blue, and he would clutch his heart and make a face like a fish out of water, and he would fall dead on the floor. *I may have to erase this tape.*

He raised the spoon to his lips, sipped the soup. It was unreal. Fantastic. Soup wasn't the right word for it. It was nectar. He held it in his mouth a moment, savouring it, before he swallowed.

'Well?' she asked.

'It's . . . incredible.'

'Incredible good or incredible bad?'

'Good? Hell, it's . . . historic.'

'Historic'! What a wonderful choice of words.

155

'Of course I'm not an expert. Is your friend Chinese?'

'No, but he lived in the Orient for years.'

Is he the mark? Is the dinner tonight part of the set-up? Sharky decided not to push it. 'Do you pick up strays in the supermarket very often?' he asked.

'Only in Moundt's. I would never pick up a stray in just *any* market.'

He laughed.

'Actually I felt kind of sorry for you. You looked so forlorn, wandering around, trying to decide what to buy. I can usually spot a bachelor in the market. They can never decide between what they want and what they need. In the end it's a disaster.'

She leaned forward and stroked the broken place on his nose again. He felt chills. It was like school days again. He was reacting like a kid. But he liked it. *You can keep your finger there for the rest of the night,* he thought. *You have fingers like butterfly wings.*

'You know something,' she said. 'I don't know your name.'

'That's right, you don't.'

'What is it?'

'Sharky.'

'Sharky what? Or is it what Sharky?'

'Just Sharky. How about you?'

He reached out and ran his finger down between her eyes, felt the tip of her nose.

'D-D-Domino.' *My God did I stutter?*

'Domino?'

'Um hum, just Domino. Like just Sharky.'

He smiled and nodded and took his hand away and she wanted him to leave it there. 'That's fair enough,' he said.

It went on that way. Small talk and jokes. And occasionally they touched, no – brushed, as if by accident. They flirted with subjects, never getting too personal, keeping it light.

'Did you ever play football?' she asked. 'You look like you played football.'

'I thought about it in college, but I wasn't good enough.'

'Where did you go to college?'

'Georgia.'

'What did you study?'

156

'Geology.'

'Geology?' she said, surprised.

'Sure, geology.'

'Why geology?'

'I like rocks,' he said.

'Okay, so why aren't you a geologist?'

'Well, it was like, uh, there wasn't a lot happening in geology when I finished.'

'You spent all that time and then just . . . forgot it?'

'It made my father happy. He took out an insurance policy when I was born, and when I graduated from high school, he handed me the cheque. It was a dream of his, that the kid should go to college. So he deserved it.'

You're a nice man, Sharky, she thought. *Naïve, maybe, but what's wrong with that?* 'That's a generous thought,' she said.

'Look, I like my old man. He was always good to me. It was something I could do back, make him happy. What the hell.'

'I liked my old man, too,' she said, without thinking, then wondered whether she should have brought it up.

'What was he like?'

She could make up a story. She was used to that. Something glamorous, something they wanted to hear. She didn't.

'He was a mining engineer. Well, actually he was a roustabout, you know. He loved brawling and whoring and drinking with the boys. Mister Macho, that was old Charlie. The word was invented for him. Itchy Britches, mom called him. We went wherever the action was. I grew up in one temporary town after another. They were always either too muddy or too dusty. Mom still says the saddest thing about losing Dad was that he died so ingloriously. He really would have liked to go out in a blaze of glory like Humphrey Bogart in some old movie. Instead, he died in a miserable little town called Backaway in Utah. He came home one afternoon, got a beer and the paper, sat down in his favourite chair, and died.'

She seemed weighed down by the memory. Sadness crossed her face, very briefly, like shadows on a cloudy day, then it passed.

'Well,' Sharky said, 'I'm sure he would have been proud

of you. It looks like you're doing pretty well.'

She closed the subject quickly.

'I'm independently wealthy,' she said, smiling. 'A rich aunt.'

Sharky laughed and raised his glass.

'Okay, here's to rich aunts.'

She sat with her chin in her hand and stared at him again, then shook her head. 'I just, uh, I don't believe it. I mean, a geologist working as an elevator man?'

'I'm not an elevator man. I'm an engineer. An elevator man is an old guy with spots on his uniform who never stops in the right place. You know, he's always too high or too low.'

She was laughing. 'Yes,' she said. 'You always have to step up or step down.'

'Besides,' Sharky said, 'I once knew a dentist who quit and became a mechanic.'

'A mechanic?'

'You know, in a garage. It's what he got off on.'

'And you get off on elevators?'

'Well, you know, I'm not going to do this for the rest of my life. It keeps me off the street.'

She felt warm towards him. Secure, comfortable. And she wanted him, wanted his arms around her, stretched out on the floor listening to DuLac, free and easy, just letting it happen. It was something that had been missing from·her life for a long time. She had given up on it. *It's a silly notion*, she thought. *A nowhere notion.* But it was a nice feeling.

And Sharky felt the same way. *I want you*, he thought. *Here. Now.* But he let it pass. Even a one-time shot wouldn't work. No future. In a week he might be putting her in the slams. And yet, he didn't want to leave it.

'Tell you what,' he said, 'I'll come back again before I leave, okay? Maybe I'll be lucky, catch you on a day when you're having a whale stew or barracuda steak.'

This time she didn't smile.

'How about·just plain steak?' she said. 'I can handle that.'

'Any time,' he said.

'Then come back,' she said and touched his cheek.

And Sharky realized that for a few minutes he had forgotten why he was there because he wanted to come back.

Chapter Ten

Chiang drove the black Cadillac Seville up into the plaza
and circled it slowly, observing the entrance to the apartment and the location of the security guard, then he turned
back into Peachtree Street, went half a block to a side
street, and parked. He sat immobile, staring straight ahead,
awaiting his instructions.

DeLaroza looked at his watch. Seven forty-five. Three
hours, he figured. Domino could perform a miracle in three
hours.

DeLaroza's mind was still in a turmoil. The day had been
eventful, exhausting. But now his thoughts were on Domino.
I want you to think about it all day long, she had said, *it
will be much sweeter that way.* And he had. Images of her
had flashed continually through his mind, images of other
times, when he had introduced her to a world reserved for
the gods and the very rich.

Burns was right. He was concupiscent, a man driven by
his lust as others are driven by fame.

Now it would end. But not before tonight.

They walked back to the apartment and DeLaroza stood
in the shadows while Chiang entered, standing in front of
the night guard, his bulk concealing the front door as he
haltingly tried to explain that he was lost. The guard, confused by his broken English, concentrated on every word
while DeLaroza slipped into the building and trotted to the
stairwell. He did not want to risk being seen on the elevator.
He walked up to the tenth floor, preparing himself for her
pleasures as he climbed the steps, cleansing his mind.

Gowmanah

remembering her in Paris, flaunting h r sensuality until
even the fag couturier was bewitched by her

gowmanah

remembering her at Quo Vadis, where even the arrogant
waiters stopped and looked when she made her entrance

gowmanah

remembering her in the bathhouse in Tokyo and the four
geishas, flocking around her, bathing her, caressing her

breasts while he sat forgotten in an adjoining tub
gowmanah . . .

The pressures of time slipped away. DeLaroza was prepared for whatever Domino had to offer.

She too had prepared herself for his arrival. It was to be her game, her rules tonight. She answered his first ring and DeLaroza stepped back in awe when she opened the door.

Her eyes were sketched into delicate almonds by the subtlest of eye-liners. A dust of shadow accentuated her high cheekbones. Her black hair was pulled to one side and pinned behind her ear by an azalea blossom. Her form-fitting gown of white gauze was split almost to the hip on each side and trimmed in gold. She wore no shoes, no jewellery.

The scent of flowers surrounded her. Behind her the room shimmered in the glow of candles, revealing freshly cut daffodils and the coffee table bearing wine and other delights. A recording wi is ered Chinese love songs. She stepped back into the cool, dim fragrance and he could see her body through the thin cotton. Her skin seemed to glow in the dark, to provide its own radiation. The chocolate points of her breasts held the gauze at bay and he could see the thick black triangle of hair where her trim legs joined.

She put her hands together and bowed her head.

'Welcome, Cheen Ping,' she said, 'to the lair of the Third Dragon.'

Sharky listened, heard the doorbell ring, heard her open the door but her remarks were lost among the tinkling bells and the Oriental music on the stereo. What was that? Something about dragons? There was movement, a rustling as though she perhaps had removed his coat.

'*Dor jeh.*' A deep voice. Mature. But what was he saying?

'There will be only three courses to dinner,' she said and her voice was soft. Melodic. Almost . . . subservient? 'And before each you must satisfy your innermost desires so that you may enjoy the meal to its fullest.'

God *damn!* Sharky lit a cigar, held it between his teeth, and pressed the earphones so he could hear better. Was this the same woman he had followed to Moundt's? Who had joked with him about being an elevator man? Served him soup and wine and seemed hypnotized by his broken nose?

'Only two courses, Ho Lan Ling. I am afraid three might be more than enough.'

He heard her laugh. *Well, shit*, Sharky said half aloud, *they're off and running in Peking!*

She led DeLaroza to one of the Savoy chairs, stood behind him, began massaging his temples. Her touch was so light he hardly felt it. She pressed her thumbs in the middle of his forehead, held the first three fingers of each hand just inside the depression of his temples, and began rotating them in circles, widening the circle until her fingers moved over his eyelids. He sat with his hands resting on the arms of the chair. Her fingertips relaxed him. His head grew light under her touch. He eased into the chair. The music filled his head.

She poured him a glass of dry white wine and offered him a white pill on a satin pincushion. He washed the pill down with the wine, watched her do the same. She opened a long, shallow antique box, removed a pipe from it. Its porcelain stem was eight inches long and the rosewood bowl was well worn and scorched black. Then she took a piece of what appeared to be black putty and rolled it between her thumb and forefinger into a perfect ball. The Quaalude began to work on him, he felt his organs being stroked as though her hands were inside him. The room was a warm, protected place for him. She knelt beside him, humming in harmony with the music, put the ball in the bowl of the pipe, and held a match to it. As it glowed red, she offered him the pipe and he took it, drawing deeply, feeling the smoke burn his throat and lungs. He took it deep, holding it in until he thought his chest would burst. She turned the stem to her own mouth, drew deeply herself, closing her eyes, letting her head fall back. Then she offered the pipe back to him.

The first rush of opium engulfed him.

His body began to vibrate. He seemed to be sinking into the pillows.

The music engulfed him.

His skin was caressed by invisible feathers. His groin began to swell.

Domino lay back in a bed of pillows she had arranged at the foot of the chair, the Quaalude and opium etching her desire, defining her prurience. She felt another presence outside of herself, like a second skin, shimmering, protecting her and caressing her. The dress slipped down between her legs, rested against her hair and she felt its weight along her vulva. Her thighs began to tighten and relax. Tighten and relax.

The chimed music filled her head, flowed down through her throat and filled her chest. Her nipples grew until she thought they would pierce the gauze that enslaved them. The music began to flow again, down through her stomach, deep inside, and finally into her vagina. Her body spasmed, very lightly, and again. She stared at DeLaroza through eyes already fogged with passion. Her mouth was open. She was beginning to breathe in a long pattern, inhaling to the count of seven, holding to the count of seven, exhaling to the count of seven. It enhanced the music inside her. She put her hands on her stomach, searched lazily, lightly, for her navel, found it and brushed her fingertips around and into it. She looked at DeLaroza and the swelling between his legs excited her even more. She crossed her chest with her hands and began moving them up her sides, exploring her armpits while the palm of her hands grazed her nipples. She rose to meet the hands but they were elusive, rising as she rose. Her nipples swelled to meet them finally – the touch. The thrill shot through her, like electricity, firing sparks into her breasts, her stomach, her neck, into her vagina, her rectum. She caressed her neck, slid her fingers under the gauze dress, savoured the roundness and then felt the dimpled ridges of her nipples. She held them gently between her fingers, began to squeeze them. DeLaroza now was breathing with her, his erection straining against his zipper.

She took one hand from under the dress and moved it down between her breasts to her stomach, slid it over her thigh, reached the bottom of the skirt, and pulled it up, slowly. Her hand disappeared under the skirt, slipped along her thigh, brushed over her hair and moved back down.

She began to rock up and down to the rhythm of her breathing, rising up to meet her hand as it grazed her thick patch. She let her hand slip between her legs, her finger probing, closed her eyes, stretched her head back, and gasped, then began rocking and breathing faster and faster and faster . . . .

Sharky listened to the sounds. First her singsong humming, then the breathing. He tried to picture the man. Deep voice. Probably large, not fat, but large. The voice was mature. A man in his forties, possibly early fifties. And there was a trace of accent or perhaps the *lack* of an accent. An Americanized foreigner. German?

Then he envisioned Domino. Naked.

The Big Man was touching her, kissing her, possibly going down on her. The Big Man's hands caressed her, stroking her tits. He was touching her now, his hand stroking the dark fur between her legs. Now she rolled him over and got up on her knees and straddled him and he was hard and he reached out for her.

Only it wasn't the Big Man anymore, it was Sharky, reaching out for her, touching her.

He pulled the earphones off and dropped them on the bed. His pulses were jumping in his wrists. He wiped sweat off his forehead with a corner of the blanket. He felt guilty, embarrassed, humiliated. And then he began to question his feelings. Guilty? Of what, getting a hard-on listening to a beautiful woman screwing another guy? Hell, who wouldn't? Embarrassed? For whom, by whom? There was nobody else there but him. And why should he be humiliated? They were not even aware he was listening; they certainly were not trying to humiliate him. He lit another cigar. And thought again about Domino.

As Domino began rocking faster, she began chanting, at first very faintly.

'Hai . . . hai . . . hai . . . hai . . .'

She felt her lips swell and open, her fingers slide down across her trigger, felt it harden and grow under her touch, just as DeLaroza was growing. Her finger slid inside her, was entrapped by the moist muscles which tightened around it, held it, then released it. She rocked faster, increasing the tempo of her cries.

'Hai . . .hai . . . hai . . .'

DeLaroza gripped the arms of the chair until his knuckles were swollen white. His pulse thundered in his temples and the muscle under his testicles jerked in spasms.

He was hypnotized by her fingers, grazing, brushing, their whispered touch urging her lips up through the forest of her sex. Her cries urged blood up into his swollen penis. He slid down in the chair. His legs stiffened.

She was rocking in a frenzy, her redolent musk torturing his nose, her hair weaving frantic patterns across her face as her head jerked back and forth.

'Hai . . . hai . . . hai . . . haihaihaihai*haihai*. H-h-h-*aaaaiii.*'

She stiffened, her head thrust back among the pillows. Her body jolted in the spasms of orgasm. DeLaroza was on the edge of madness. He too began to spasm and as he did, she rose slowly, tantalizingly to her knees before him, shuddered, zipped down his pants, freeing him, and, with a tiny animal cry, let her face fall across his lap. Her mouth enveloped him, her tongue brushed him, the moist membranes of her mouth closed on him, and an instant later he too exploded.

The meal was prepared by the chef of the finest Szechuan restaurant in the city, who arrived at precisely nine o'clock, assisted by two busboys, and moved silently into the kitchen, where he set up and awaited her command. Domino sat at the head of the table. She was no longer the servant, now she ruled like an empress, clapping her hands once at the beginning of each course and twice when they were finished, the busboys appearing and disappearing as silently as time passing. DeLaroza sat at the opposite end of the table, eating slowly, savouring every bite, smiling, and nodding approval after each course. They ate in silence, in the manner of Chinese royalty, devoting their full attention to the food.

It was spectacular. The courses were small, to prevent overeating. And while Domino had prepared only one course, the shark's fin soup, she had planned the entire meal, selecting the most succulent dishes from the menu of the Princess Garden restaurant in Hong Kong. It was truly a meal fit for an emperor: *t'ang-t'su-au-pien*, a salad whose main ingredients were fresh lotus roots, sesame seed oil, and soy sauce; *chow fan*, a mound of rice concealing bits of egg, shrimp, ham, peas, and onions, all deep-friend in peanut oil; *hasi-tan*, a side dish of deep-fried bamboo shoots and water chestnuts served over noodles; and Peking duck, basted in salad oil and roasted until the skin crackled, th :n served as three different courses. First, the skin was presented, dipped in thick soybean paste, sprinkled with onions, and wrapped in Chinese pancakes. Next the bones were offered, boiled into a gravy with cabbage and mushrooms and served with the *chow fan*. Finally, the meat itself, juicy, spicy, hot, and sliced into thin strips. The dessert – sliced bananas dipped in batter and deep-fried, then immersed in ice water that froze the outer crust into a glaze while the bananas remained steaming hot – was the perfect conclusion.

When the meal was over and the chef and his assistants had departed as silently as they had come, she served absinthe, smuggled in from Ecuador, and they smoked a joint of pure Colombian grass the colour of cinnamon. It warmed and mellowed them, stirring the libido again. They stared dreamily across the table at each other. Not a word had passed between them for more than two hours.

Finally she left the table and went back to the massage room. DeLaroza lit a cigar, leaned back in his chair, fully content, awaiting whatever surprises she would offer next.

His thoughts began to wander. To Hotchins. To the campaign.

To Burns.

The thought of Burns chilled him and he closed his eyes, summoning his mantra to purge the devils from his mind.

Gowmanah

thinking about her, lying before him among the pillows . . .

Gowmanah

stroking herself, turning herself on, performing for him . . .

Gowmanah

visualizing her undressing, revealing her immaculate body . . .

Gowmanah

and it was simple. `Once again, Eros commanded his mind.

He heard her clap her hands and, turning, saw her

silhouetted against a dozen or more candles, her body oiled and glowing. He obeyed her command and went to her. Feather fingers stripped him, eased him down among the pillows on the floor, spread warm oil over his body, massaging him from head to foot, subtly caressing his genitals, stroking him, her tongue teasing him to fullness. She knelt over him, resting on her knees, her spiderweb plume brushing against him, her moisture preparing him. He began to throb and she shifted, rolling to her side beside him and reaching to the small table beside her, picked up a mirror, and placed it on her stomach.

She had prepared four long rows of cocaine on the mirror, carefully chopped and arranged in narrow files, each one about five inches long. Beside the rows were a short piece of glass straw perhaps four inches long and a spoon of pure Andean gold brought from Cuzco, the capital of the Inca empire, in southern Peru, its handle delicately hand-carved in a sculpture of Virgo, the Inca goddess of coca, the minutely detailed headdress containing the tiny bowl of the spoon itself.

He turned and lay between her legs, her tuft against his chest, took the straw and; holding one nostril shut, moved the straw up one row of coke, inhaling sharply. He snorted deeply through the other nostril. The coke hit him in a rush. His groin surged. The tartness of the drug burned his throat. He slid the mirror towards her, slipped down, buried his head between her legs.

She lay the mirror beside her, turned slightly, snorted the second row, let it sizzle through her body, felt it charge up deep into her sinuses. She lay back down, shuddering as the cocaine surged through her senses, touching every organ with life.

DeLaroza rose up on his elbows, retrieved the mirror, and, using the straw as a pusher, filled the spoon with the powder. She bent her legs slightly at the knees. Venus rose towards him, lips apart and moist, inviting him, enticing him. He held the spoon between her legs, lowered it until it almost touched her. Her ringlets rose towards his hand and parted and he lowered the spoon, touched her vivid heart-shaped opening, tapped his finger against the side of the spoon, watched the minute crystals sprinkle as he moved the spoon along her waiting lips.

Her eyes were closed. She began to shudder.

He moved the mirror, slid up between her legs, rose up above her, overpowered by her lust. She was his erotic master, orchestrating his orgasm. He felt godlike. He was Priapus, son of Dionysius and Aphrodite, who fornicated for eternity without losing his erection, and he roared with desire as he surged against her.

The cocaine felt like ice, first numbing her membranes, then suddenly setting them afire. She cried out, feeling him against her, rising up to meet him, her senses screaming for satisfaction.

'Ohhh . . . my God!'

Sharky lay on the cot smoking a Schimmelpenninck, staring up at the smoke hanging near the ceiling like strands of cotton candy, his thoughts jumping to Domino, envisioning her. He dropped the cigar on the floor and put the earphones back on, heard her peculiar breathing pattern starting again.

Seven in, hold seven, seven out.

And he joined her, closing his eyes, letting his own fantasies take control.

He was lying among the pillows in the massage room. She was standing over him, her long legs dominating him.

Thick black swansdown inviting him as she stared down . . .

Stared down between her breasts, smiling . . .

He reached up, touching the soft skin behind her knees, stroked it, then pressed lightly.

She lowered towards him, an agonizing vision in slow motion.

Seven in, hold seven, seven out.

She stretched out over him, not quite touching him. Her nipples brushed his, her lips hovered over his, her thick tuft teased his shaft. Their lips brushed together, tongues searching, touching, melding into one.

He kissed her neck, her throat, the bulge of her breasts, her nipples, and felt her settle against him, moving against him, like a wave washing over him.

He could wait no longer. He reached down, lifted her by the hips, and together they stared down between their bodies, moving, touching, and moving apart until neither of them could stand the agony any longer and as he poised her over him and they both looked down at what was waiting and he reached between them, brushed his hand across her silken mound, she moaned, 'Ohhh . . . my God!' as he rose up and felt her against him. Open and waiting, she sucked him inside. . . .

DeLaroza rose high above her and then plunged down, the power, grasping, taking, and she felt him inside her, only her eyes were closed and now her fantasy took over and it was not DeLaroza entering her, it was Sharky, for now she no longer wanted the lust of power, she wanted to get and to give, to join him, not be his for the taking. She felt his hard, muscular stomach, his lean chest, his neck, taut and straining, his arms with their pinion fingers stroking, gentling, hardening her, and his mouth against hers, lightly at first, then crushing against hers.

Her breathing pattern shortened.

Five in, five hold, five out.

She counted faster as her breathing quickened. He was breathing with her, thrusting with her.

Two, two, two.

Two, two, two.

two, two . . . two, two . . . two, two . . .

One, one.

One

One!

'Ahhh!'

She cried out again and again. Her body stiffened. Volcanoes sputtered, rumbled, spat fire, and erupted inside her. Hot lava engulfed her, warmed her, flooded through her head, her throat, her chest, her stomach. Her vagina burst and words tumbled from her lips that made no sense, a disconnected alien vocabulary surging from her throat.

DeLaroza popped the amyl nitrite tube and passed it back and forth between them, felt her instant response, the renewed assault on her senses. She was an errant star, lost in space, as it hit again and again and again. The mountain below his testicles swelled and slammed between his legs and he too convulsed and erupted. . . .

In his post on the roof Sharky heard them, felt the same

168

urgent rush, the same mountain between his legs, the same volcanoes blowing apart, the same fervid explosion in his groin and, crying out, he came.

DeLaroza lay beside Domino for only a few minutes, then got up, showered, and dressed. When he returned to the room she was still lying on the table, although she had covered herself with a robe. He was anxious to leave. With his orgasm DeLaroza had closed the book on Domino.

He leaned over the table and she looked at him with smoky eyes, smiling. 'Magnificent,' he said. 'You exceeded your promise. I shall never forget tonight. When next we meet, it will be as old friends. The past is erased.'

'Thank you,' she said softly, 'for everything. For showing me the world and its treasures. You have been a dear friend. *Joy geen.*'

'Goodbye to you,' he said and kissed her, knowing it was the last time he would ever see her. Then he closed the door. In his mind Domino was already dead.

She lay alone for several minutes before the tears came and then she cried softly to herself, not so much because she would miss him, but because it was an ending and endings always saddened her.

Sharky did not hear them. He had pulled off the earphones and dropped them beside him on the cot. The last twenty-four hours had burned him out. He had killed a man, been chewed out royally by The Bat, been transferred to Friscoe's Inferno, assigned to this machine, bugged an apartment, and had not only been attracted to a suspect but joined her vicariously while she made love to another man.

Great, Sharky. You aren't even hitting the slow pitches.

His nerves were stretched to the breaking point. Everything seemed amplified. The buzzing fluorescent tubes overhead, the humming motors, the wind whistling at the crack in the door, all agitated his skin. He scratched his arms and neck.

I'm cracking up, he thought. *Standing in the doorway of the rubber room.*

He remembered the joint he had lifted from the drawer earlier in the day. He put on his jacket and went out into the

169

icy air. Leaning against the wall of the utility room, he lit up and took two deep hits, holding the smoke in his lungs as long as he could before exhaling. The high came quickly, soothing his tattered nerves. He closed his eyes, let the cold wind wipe his face.

He thought more about Domino, surprised that he felt no ill feeling towards her, that he did not condemn her open sensuality, her need to embrace pleasure, and he understood why. He had the same needs, the same desires, and for the first time in his life he accepted them without guilt.

He wanted Domino. Period.

'So what?' he said aloud and then chuckled.

He appraised the situation. She had done nothing illegal tonight. No money had changed hands. There wasn't even any *talk* of money. Hell, there was hardly any talk at all. She had entertained a friend and how she entertained him was her business.

Unless, of course, the man below was the mark and tonight was part of the set-up. If so, the tapes would prove she knew him. Intimately. They would provide the connection.

He would have to identify the mark. He could call in Livingston, have him follow the guest when he left her apartment. But that would take time. So he would do it himself.

He returned to the dim interior of his listening post. The tape recorder to the master bedroom was spinning.

Jesus, he thought, *they're not going at it again!*

He held one of the phones to his ear. There were *two* women speaking now.

He put the earphones on, pressed them to his ears, concentrating on the voices. One was talking, the other was singing. And the shower was going.

Of course, the television was on. Virginia Gunn, Channel Five, was giving the weather report. The shower stopped. He heard her come into the bedroom, heard the click of a remote unit, and the television went off.

Silence.

The recorder stopped.

The mark was gone. He had left while Sharky was out on the roof.

'Shit!'

He went back out on the roof, knowing it was too late. He looked over the parapet, down at the parking lot, but there was no activity. He went to the other side of the roof and stared down into darkness. The wind rattled the treetops below him. Overhead the storm clouds moved silently away and the cold stars mocked him.

He went back to his solitary room, dropped wearily on the cot, then stretched out, and before he could decide on his next step, Sharky fell into a deep, dreamless sleep.

Chapter Eleven

Sharky was still asleep when Papa arrived to relieve him at 7:48 the next morning. He jerked awake when he heard the door open. Reaching under the blanket he had used for a pillow and grabbing his 9mm automatic, he flipped the blanket off and sat up quickly.

Papa stopped short, appraised the situation through bored eyes and smiled.

'Easy there, Roy,' he said, 'it's only Gabby Hayes.'

Sharky sagged, letting his gun hand drop between his legs.

'I musta died,' he said.

'Why not? Tough day,' Papa said.

'I was jumping outa my skin last night.'

'Any action?'

Sharky put his gun under his arm. 'Lots of action, very little dialogue. Nothing we're interested in.'

'Who was the trick?'

Sharky looked up at him and an embarrassed grin played on his lips.

'You're not gonna believe this,' he said.

'Fell asleep,' Papa said. 'Missed him.'

'How the hell did you know that?'

'Done it myself,' Papa said smiling. 'Fifteen years. I fucked up every way you can fuck up. Arch, too. Friscoe. Nobody hits a thousand. You got the tapes.'

'Shit, if there's twenty words on the goddamn tapes I'll eat them.'

'Answer me something, okay, Sharky?'

'Sure.'

'Why we staked out? We got the tapes, why not check 'em, you know, every three, four hours, see what's doin'?'

'I figure if they go after the mark and somebody's here, on top of it, we can maybe nail them while it's happening. We're four hours late, we could come in on our ass.'

Papa nodded. 'Okay, I buy it. Go home.'

'Yeah, I feel like I was born in these clothes.'

Sharky reached down to retrieve the used tapes. Then he noticed that the fresh tapes in the machines to her bedroom

172

and the living room had advanced.

'Well, I'll be damned,' he said. 'I slept through something here.'

He rewound them and listened. The machine to her bedroom had been activated by the television set, *The Today Show*. She was moving around in the background, opening and closing the closet doors, obviously getting dressed. The tape ended abruptly when she turned off the television. The radio had activated the machine for the living room. Once again he heard her in the background. A disc jockey's fast patter was interrupted by music and traffic reports. Then:

'Okay, all you pillow pounders, it's Doctor Dawn here on Z-93 and it's a c-o-o-o-old Friday morning out there. Seven-twenty-nine and here's one to get you on your feet. ELP, Emerson, Lake, and Palmer and – '

The radio cut off. The tape went dead, then cut back on. She was opening the door, leaving the apartment. It closed and the latch clicked. The tape ended.

'I'll be a son of a bitch,' Sharky said.

'Early starter,' Papa said.

'I don't believe it. She got out on us.'

'She'll be back.'

'Yeah, but we should be on top of her right now. For all we know, she could be – '

'Go home. Forget it for a while. See ya at six.'

'Okay,' Sharky said. He wiped the sleep out of his eyes and stuffed the tapes in his pocket. 'There's some fruit in the bag there, also a book to read.'

'Got my own,' Papa said, taking a worn copy of *The Guinness Book of World Records* out of his coat pocket.

'You read that on stakeout?' Sharky said.

'Easy to put down, if I gotta move,' Papa said.

'You got a point there,' Sharky said, walking to the door.

'Hey, Sharky?' Papa said.

'Yeah?'

'Car keys?'

Sharky tossed them to him. 'Maybe at six o'clock I'll be back with the living,' he said and left.

He flagged down a passing patrol car and had them drop him off at Moundt's, thinking she might be doing some early morning shopping. The place was deserted. He had a cup of

173

coffee and called The Nosh.

'I got some weird tapes for you, pal,' he said.

'X-rated?' The Nosh asked sleepily.

'You better believe it.'

'Where are you?'

'Moundt's, on Peachtree. I got to get home, get a shower, and change clothes. I don't have a car.'

'Can you give me thirty minutes? I need to walk through the shower myself.'

'I'll be here. Listen, on the front end of one of these tapes there may be something I can use, a name maybe. But there's heavy interference from the record player.'

'Don't sweat it,' The Nosh said. 'We'll lift the music out.'

'Beautiful,' Sharky said. 'See you when you get here. Take your time.'

It was almost dark and the damp, cold wind hinted of more rain. A man walked leisurely past the exit gate from the parking deck of the Lancaster Towers. He was wearing dark glasses and a long blue overcoat, his dark, close-cropped hair hidden under a plain cap, an undistinguished-looking man taking an early evening walk.

A vintage Buick pulled up to a post near the exit gate and the driver slipped a plastic card in a slot in the post. The exit gate swung open and the Buick pulled out. The gate remained open for twenty seconds and then swung shut. The pedestrian was inside when it closed, standing in the shadows near the wall. He took off the dark glasses, studied the interior of the garage. It was empty. Burns smiled to himself. That was the most dangerous part of it, getting in without being seen.

He walked briskly to the east tower elevators and pressed the up button, holding a handkerchief over his nose and mouth, prepared to fake a sneeze if someone was in the elevator. His right hand extended down through the vent in the right-hand pocket of the raincoat. He held a .22 Woodsman, pointing at the floor. The elevator doors opened. It was empty. He stepped in and pushed the button for the twelfth floor. He was lucky. It went straight up without stopping.

174

He got out, looking up and down the hallway. Empty. He moved swiftly to 12-C and rang the bell. Nobody answered. He picked the lock, stepped into the apartment, and closed the door quietly behind him. He listened, the ugly silenced snout of the .22 poking between the buttons of his coat. He heard only the sound of his own breathing, nothing else. The apartment was dark and smelled musty. He moved rapidly from room to room, checking closets, even looking under the beds. He relaxed. It was empty. He holstered the .22.

He felt a sudden urge to relieve himself and swore under his breath. Age and tension conspired against his kidneys. He went to one of the bathrooms and urinated.

He returned to the living room and took a pair of surgical gloves from his pocket, pulled them on. He pulled an easy chair over to the large picture window facing the west tower. He propped open two slats of the venetian blinds with two wooden matches, making a small peephole about six inches long and two inches high, and leaned forward and peered through it. He had a perfect view of Domino's apartment, two floors below in the opposite tower.

He took off the raincoat and spread it out on the floor beside him. The coat had three special pockets sewn in the lining. From one he drew the twin-barrelled carriage of a twelve-gauge shotgun, from the other its well-worn stock. He snapped them together, cocked both hammers, slipped his fingers inside the trigger guard and barely touched the two triggers. The hammers clicked a fraction of a second apart. He slid the rubber buttplate back and removed two shells from a special pocket. He popped the shotgun open, loaded both barrels and snapped it shut.

From the third pocket he took a small pair of opera glasses and a device that looked like two long tubes soldered together. He slipped them over the end of the short-barrelled shotgun and tightened them in place with a thumbscrew. He laid the shotgun on top of the coat.

He put the opera glasses on the windowsill and took a small plastic bag from his shirt pocket and laid it beside them. It contained two red pills. He went to the kitchen, got a glass of water, brought it back and put it beside the pills. The excitement was starting. He scanned Domino's windows with the opera glasses. It was dark. He smiled. Plenty of time. He put the glasses back on the sill, and leaning forward with his elbows on his knees, he waited.

In his post on the roof Sharky too waited. He had returned at 5:30, clean, refreshed, wearing jeans, a turtleneck, a leather jacket, and sneakers.

'Not back yet,' Papa reported, smacked him on the back and left. He settled down with his book, aware that he was rereading passages several times and concentrating more on the tape recorders than his book. He finally put it aside. He had been thinking about Domino all day. He had been thinking a *lot* about Domino.

He could go down there when she came home and lay it all out for her, give her a chance to cooperate in exchange for immunity.

And she would probably tell him to get stuffed.

Or blow it out his ass.

Or maybe tell him she didn't know shit. And just maybe she didn't. In which case she could blow the whistle on them to Neil and flush the whole machine.

The thing was, at that moment, Domino was clean. They had absolutely nothing on her but an association with a man they knew was a shakedown pimp.

Forget it, Sharky.

The machine in the bedroom suddenly turned on and he grabbed the earphones. It was the phone ringing. After the third ring her recording machine came on.

'Hi, this is Domino. I'll be away from the phone for a little while. Please leave your name, a short message, and your phone number, and I'll get back to you as soon as possible. Wait for the beep tone before you start. Goodbye and have a pleasant day.'

A second later the beep sounded, followed by:

'Hi, it's Pete. Look, I'm running a little late. No problem. I'll call you back in fifteen, twenty minutes. So long.'

Pete? A new name for the catalogue. Perhaps the big man from last night. *No*, he thought. *Different voice. Maybe it's her trick for tonight. In which case, since it's almost ten to eight, she's cutting it a little thin.*

The machine in the living room turned on. She was coming in the door. She closed it, turned on the radio, and went into the bedroom. He heard the bed groan under her weight, heard Maria Muldaur's voice:

> '. . . 'til the eve-nin' ends,
> 'til the eve-nin' ends . . .
> . . . Mid-night At The Oasis,
> Send your camel to bed. . . .'

The phone rang again. She caught it on the second ring. *Eager Pete*, he thought. But he was wrong.

'Hello . . . hello . . . ?' A pause, then an exasperated, 'He*llo*?' She slammed down the phone. Sharky lay on the cot, waiting for her trick to arrive.

Burns cradled the phone gently and smiled, the mirthless, ugly grin of anticipation. He shook one of the reds out of the plastic bag and washed it down with water. He put his raincoat on, put the glass back in the kitchen, swung the chair back to its original position. He sat down with the shotgun between his knees, waiting for the speed to start.

It surged through his blood and his heart began pounding. His scrotum pulsated. He closed his eyes, taking the ride up, letting the red carry him along until his nerve endings were keening with excitement.

He was ready, his senses sharpened, his guts buzzing with anticipation.

He stood up and put his hand through the pocket vent and took the shotgun, aiming it at the floor. He buttoned the coat and started towards the door and stopped.

Jesus!

The fuckin' matches.

He went back, took the two matchsticks down, and straightened the venetian blinds.

I'm gettin' too old for this, he thought. *Well, this is the last one. Just don't get careless now.* He hated the thought of giving it up. It was like having his last piece of ass, knowing it was all over. The speed raced along his nerves, like fire burning along a fuse. He shook his shoulders, closed his eyes, and let his head fall back for a moment. He was getting hard and he sighed with ecstasy.

Oh, yeah. Jesus.

Was he ready.

He took the stairs to the third floor, walked across the connecting terrace. The wind rattled the plastic pool cover and he jumped, the shotgun coming up. His eyes burned fiercely, then he relaxed and kept moving. He entered the stairwell of the west tower and listened.

Nobody. Just the wind, moaning through the shaft. He climbed the stairs, thinking about what was coming, reached the tenth floor, and cracked the door. The hall was empty.

He closed the door and ticked the steps off in his mind. He cocked the shotgun. Unbuttoned the bottom buttons of the raincoat. Double checked the location. Apartment 10-A was between the door and the elevators. On the right.

Perfect. Twenty, maybe twenty-five feet, no more.

He took several deep breaths. His pulse battered at his temples.

Four apartments on the floor. The one across from her, 10-D, was being repainted for a new tenant. No one was home in either of the other apartments at the corners of the hall, he had called both numbers. He was lucky tonight. Tonight was definitely his lucky night.

He went through the door and walked to the elevators, pushed the down button and waited. One of the elevators arrived. He stepped in, pushed all the buttons between ten and the ground, and stepped back out. The doors closed. He pushed the down button again. The other elevator arrived and he repeated the manoeuvre.

He held his thumb across both hammers of the shotgun to make sure it did not discharge accidentally and walked to the door of 10-A.

He rang the bell and then swung the barrels of the shotgun up through the opening of the raincoat.

They were playing a golden oldie, 'Long Time Comin'' by Crosby, Stills, Nash, and Young when the doorbell rang.

'Coming,' she said. There was gaiety in the voice. She sounded happy. Was it part of the act?

Sharky heard her take the chain off the door, turn the latch.

The two muffled shots came almost as she opened the door.

Thumk thumk.

Almost together and no louder than a fist hitting a refrigerator door.

There was a cry, not loud, like an animal whimpering.

A sound like gravel hitting the wall.

Something fell, heavy, on the floor.

He heard the door close.

Shotgun. A silenced shotgun.

He forgot the earphones. They ripped from his head as he bounded for the door. He had his automatic in hand before he reached the stairwell. He bulled into the stairshaft without precaution. Below him, several floors down, someone was running, taking the steps two or three at a time.

'Hold it!' he yelled. 'Police, hold it!'

He followed the sound, taking the steps six at a time and hanging onto the railing to keep from falling. Several flights below him he saw a shadow flee across the wall. He kept going. A door opened and slammed shut.

What floor? What fucking floor?

He reached four, flattened himself against the wall, pulled the door open, and held it open with his foot as he swung around and leaped into the hall.

Empty.

He went to three, swung the door open and went through head first and low, almost on his knees, the 9mm held in front of him in both hands. He was outside on the terrace and he jumped quickly into the shadows, letting his eyes grow accustomed to the darkness.

He listened. The wind flapped the plastic pool cover. He started moving through the shadows towards the door on the other side of the pool. His reflexes were ready, but his mind was jumping back and forth. *What had happened on the tenth floor. Was she all right? What the hell was going on?*

He remembered his walkie-talkie. As he ran to the east tower he pulled it out of the case on his belt.

'Central, this is urgent. Contact Livingston, Papadopolis, and Abrams and tell them Zebra Three needs them at base immediately.'

The walkie-talkie crackled. 'Ten-four.'

He reached the other door, pulled it open and waited a second, listening, before he went through.

Nothing.

He waited and listened.

Nothing.

He went back on the terrace, checked it quickly, and then returned to the west tower. Both elevators were on the bottom floor. He went up the stairs. His mouth was dry and he was gasping for air when he reached ten. His heart felt as though it was jumping out of his skin. The hallway was empty. He went to 10-A and rang the bell, then pounded on the door. He stepped back and smashed his foot into the door an inch or two from the knob.

The door opened halfway and hit something.

He went in and slammed it shut with his elbow.

The first thing he saw was a scorched pattern of tiny holes near the ceiling. Blood was splattered around the holes. The second pattern had chewed a piece out of the corner of the entrance hall where it led into the living room.

A small marble-topped table lay on its side, a vase of freshly cut flowers spilled out on the floor.

She lay beside the table. Her face was gone. Part of her shoulder was blown away. The right side of her head had been destroyed. She was a soggy, limp bundle, lying partly against the wall in front of the door, blood pumping from her head, her neck, her shoulder. A splash of blood on the wall dripped down to the body. Her hands lay awkwardly in her lap.

Sharky clenched his teeth, felt bile sour in his throat, and swallowed hard and cried out through his clenched teeth.

'No. Goddammit, no!

'No.'

'*No!*

'*Go-o-od damn it . . . no!*'

BOOK TWO

Chapter Twelve

It was another country, another world, a place ripped from the past and sown with the fantasies of a mastermind.

The gardens, a tiny paradise stitched with walkways and encompassing almost three acres, stunned the eye with colour. Purple, yellow, and fuchsia azaleas were in full bloom, surrounded by hundreds of small pink and red camellia blossoms. Beds of iris, their praying flowers streaked with lavender and pastel blue, lined the pathways and grottoes, and small lotus trees and lush green moss covered the cliffsides and stream-fed alcoves.

Only a chest-high fence which prohibited pedestrians from straying off the path tainted the landscaped beauty. There was good reason for the fence. At the far end of the garden, hidden from the bountiful and lush sprays of colour by a sixty-foot-high cliff, was an arroyo, a tortured place that split the cliff in half. It was foreboding, a stark and shocking sight compared to the beauty of the gardens. There were no flowers here. Steam rose from between the rocks. A chill breeze blew down through its crevices.

Halfway up the cliffside, almost hidden by red clay banks, boulders, and scattered foliage, was a dank and ominous cave.

Within its depths yellow eyes glittered evilly, accompanied by a sibilant warning, an intermittent hissing that sounded like air rushing from a giant punctured tyre. The creature lurking in the cavern was more sensed than seen. But its presence feathered the nerves.

One heard the other creature before seeing it, a half-growl, half-cry that drove icicles through the heart. A moment later it appeared, moving cautiously around the edge of the cliff, a towering myth, at once terrifying and majestic, like some primordial sauropod. It was a dragon, a golden dragon, each scale of its lutescent skin gleaming as it reared back on its hindlegs, stretching a full forty feet from its fiery mouth to the tip of its slashing, spiny tail. Green eyes flashed under hooded lids. Five ebony claws curled out from each padded foot. As it opened its fanged jaws a

183

stream of fire roared from its mouth and rolled upward.

The dragon moved like a cat on the prowl, sensuously, slowly, sensing its prey nearby.

The yellow eyes inside the cave followed the dragon's every move. It began to hiss again, a dangerous sound that reverberated off the cavern walls.

Then it moved. Slowly it slithered from its hiding place and emerged, an enormous two-headed snake, its sinuous muscles sheathed in blood-red skin, the nostrils flat and piglike in its ugly snouts, its forked tongues flicking from two moist mouths as it slid up through the rocks seeking a vantage place high in the grim landscape.

It moved with chilling grace towards its adversary, eyeing the dragon through glistening black beads.

It began to coil, its thirty-foot body curling into a tight spiral. Then it struck, the vicious twin heads streaking from between the rocks, swooping down, its mouth yawning malevolently, then snapping shut, the fangs sinking deep into the neck of the dragon.

The dragon screamed in outrage and pain, twisted its head, and spat an inferno that engulfed the hissing serpent. The viper's body surged forward, wrapping itself around the neck of the dragon while one of its two heads snapped back and struck again. The dragon's shriek joined the hissing of the serpent. The two unearthly creatures were locked in a nightmare embrace.

High above them, from a soundproof booth overlooking the primeval battle, his face shimmering in the red glow of the flames below, DeLaroza looked like a vision from hell. The eerie reflection sutured his features with fleeting scars. His eyes flashed with joy and he clapped his hands together. He was, in that instant, an incarnation of the devil.

'Incredible, absolutely incredible!' he cried out. 'Nikos, you have outdone yourself.'

Seated beside him in front of a large electronic control board, the creator of the scene smiled. His name was Nikos Arcurius, a wiry little man, trim yet powerfully built, his biceps hard and veined, his black hair frosted white at the sideburns, his brown eyes twinkling with the rush of achievement.

The dragon and the snake, coiling, hissing, spitting fire, fought on.

'Enough,' DeLaroza said. 'Save the climax until Monday night.'

Arcurius leaned over the control board and pressed buttons, twirled dials, and the two mammoth creatures slipped apart. The snake retreated back to its cave and the dragon, like a regal legend come to life, stalked back to its hiding place among the rocks.

'It is a masterpiece,' DeLaroza said with awe. He laid his hand on the shoulder of his collaborator. Arcurius leaned back in his chair and surveyed the atrium and then nodded. It was true; it was a masterpiece.

Arcurius was Greek. Abandoned by his parents, he had grown up a street thief and pickpocket. When he was thirteen his quick hands had earned him a two-year sentence in Da Krivotros, a dismal island prison known as The Boxes because of the rows of solitary cells where even the slightest infraction of prison rules resulted in weeks in squalid isolation.

Thrown in with hardened criminals, Arcurius had earned their respect by putting his nimble fingers to a new use, carving puppets in the prison shop. He earned cigarette money and other favours from the prisoners by putting on Sunday shows in the visitors' compound for the wives and children of other prisoners. He was back on the street by the time he was sixteen, first joining a travelling circus, then trying to make a living as a puppeteer in Athens, but by the time he was twenty he was on the run again, fleeing from one country to the next, always with the law snapping at his ankles.

The salvation of Nikos Arcurius came when he signed on as a crewman on a steamer going from Marseille to New York to escape the local gendarmes. In New York his fortunes finally changed. Starting as an apprentice, he moved up quickly to become one of Broadway's most innovative set designers and while still in his twenties Arcurius was lured to Hollywood. There, on the vast sound stages of the big studios, his imagination flourished.

And it was there that he had met a visitor from Hong Kong. Victor DeLaroza was drawn to him not only by his enormous talent but by the candour with which he spoke of his early life.

'These fingers,' he once told DeLaroza, wiggling all ten

in the air, 'belong to the second best pickpocket in Athens. The best one was never caught.'

DeLaroza quickly realized that Arcurius's real genius lay not only in design but in production as well. He put Arcurius to work developing a new concept for toys and together they had revolutionized the industry. The Greek had an uncanny ability for breathing life into DeLaroza's wildest fantasies, designing and building toys of remarkable realism. Small transistor cards hidden inside dolls whose skin felt almost real caused eyes to blink, mouths to open and close, and activated tape loops through which the lifelike creations spoke simple sentences. His animals were marvels of innovative miniaturization. One, a small horse, performed four different gaits, its ingenious insides set in motion simply by the snap of a finger.

DeLaroza's exhaustive marketing skills had turned Arcurius into a household word and his creations, called Arcurions, into the most popular toys in the world, several of them so remarkable that even though mass-produced, they had already become collector's items.

Then DeLaroza had conceived an idea so exciting, so challenging, that he and Arcurius had devoted five years to designing it, another four to building it, and spent more than ten million dollars on the project.

Now, the result of their combined genius sprawled below them. It was to be the instrument by which DeLaroza would emerge from his self-imposed world of secrecy.

Now, with Corrigon out of the way – and tonight, Domino – DeLaroza felt secure at last. Publicity releases would now begin revealing his contributions for the first time. Now he felt he could face cameras for the first time, unafraid.

Now he himself would introduce the world to his grandest accomplishment.

Pachinko!

The most outrageous, the most breathtaking, the most stunning madness of all.

Pachinko!

The ultimate playground.

In the heart of the glass tower DeLaroza had gutted six floors and replaced them with a towering atrium that began five storeys above the ground. It was encircled by a narrow, eight-foot balcony from which spectators could view *Pachinko!* as if they were standing on a precipice looking down on it. Behind them the city of Atlanta could be seen, sprawling out behind floor-to-ceiling windows.

The panorama was staggering. Within the great space, nearly the size of four football fields, DeLaroza and Arcurius had recreated their own version of Hong Kong. A bustling, vibrant, ebullient amusement park and bazaar, as startling as it was ambitious, had been built in the middle of a skyscraper.

The journey to *Pachinko!* began on the first floor where an imported Chinese arch led to four bullet-shaped glass elevators that travelled up the exterior of the building. The arch was guarded on either side by two ten-foot temple dogs, their red tongues curling humorously beneath gleaming, dangerous eyes. A blazing Art Deco sign over the arch announced *Pachinko!* always with the exclamation point. A booth in front of the gate converted American dollars into reproductions of Hong Kong dollars, the medium of exchange for special attractions in the complex. One elevator lifted spectators who simply wanted to observe the spectacle to the special balcony where, for another dollar, they could watch the revellers below. Four other elevators opened on the eleventh floor, the entrance to *Pachinko!*, where two ancient stone posts imported from Macao stood on either side of a long, rambling stairway that led to the main floor, six storeys below. The stairway was a replica of Hong Kong's bustling Ladder Street, a narrow confined alley teeming with shops, cubbyholes and snack-food stalls, and intersected by several other avenues.

DeLaroza surveyed his version of the city. Looking down on the exciting maze below him, he envisioned it crowded with tourists and sightseers, entertained by strolling magicians and acrobats while a travelling Chinese band provided the background music. It was a splendid bazaar, with banners floating over more than thirty shops where everything was sold, outrageously expensive antiques, cheap souvenirs, suits custom-made by Kowloon tailors, Oriental rugs, postcards, imitation Buddhas, cameras, the finest jade. Food stalls offered snacks of sizzling ribs and Peking chicken. Cats strolled the steps.

On the main floor the Greek had created a shallow lake

with a small version of the Tai Tak floating restaurant in one corner, its cuisine presided over by Wan Shu, one of Hong Kong's finest chefs, its garish decks reached by small sampans which carried diners from the main promenade, a winding path where theatres offered karate, judo, and weaponry exhibitions, excerpts from Chinese opera, and puppet shows for the children. There were three night clubs and two other fine restaurants, a recreation of the Man Mo Temple, known as the Place of a Thousand Buddhas, a sixty-foot model of the Shinto Pagoda, an opium den, and a sampan ride through a tortuous series of tunnels under Ladder Street where like-real Arcurions played out some of the most dramatic moments from the turbulent history of Hong Kong. The main street terminated at one end at the gardens with their abundance of rare flowers and beautiful young Chinese guides, who would escort visitors through the enchanting maze, explaining the icons of Chinese mythology found in its grottoes and pavilions. As they ended the tour the guides recounted the legend of Kowloon, the Ninth Dragon, and his battle with T'un Hai, the two-headed snake of the Underworld. Throughout, DeLaroza had insisted on historical, mythological, and architectural integrity.

The grand opening, now only three days away, would attract all three major television networks, radio, magazine, and newspaper reporters from all over the world, leading politicians and British and Chinese dignitaries, all to be flown in on special junkets. Photographs and visitors had been barred from the amusement complex until opening night, for DeLaroza knew that the reaction would be much more excited if an aura of mystery were created about *Pachinko!* So it had remained an enigma, a giant surprise package to be unwrapped the following Monday night.

What better time for Donald Hotchins to make his announcement?

Julius Lowenthal stood a few feet from DeLaroza, his eyes saucers of amazement as he stared down through the glass front of the soundproof control booth at *Pachinko!* DeLaroza turned to him, towering over the weary Washington lawyer.

'Well, sir,' DeLaroza said, 'what do you think of our toy, eh?'

'Toy?' Lowenthal said incredulously.

DeLaroza chuckled. 'Perhaps I should say "playground". Until tonight no outsider has seen it. I have forbidden photographs and all but the most general description.'

Lowenthal shrugged his shoulders in an almost helpless gesture. 'I, uh ... I've lost my tongue,' he said. 'I'm speechless.'

'You do not approve?'

'Oh, my God, of course. It's monumental. A monumental undertaking.'

DeLaroza took him lightly by the elbow and led him out of the booth and along the balcony towards Ladder Street.

'I'm flattered that you let me take a look,' Lowenthal said.

'The least I could do,' DeLaroza said. 'Once again I must apologize for Donald's absence. It is an old and personal political commitment. He will be back tomorrow and you two can get back to business.'

'I've been around politics long enough to understand these things,' Lowenthal said.

'Good. Besides, this will give us a chance to know each other a little better, yes?'

'Of course.'

But Lowenthal doubted it. He had been close to many rich and powerful men during his career but had never really known any of them well, for they were guarded people. Secrecy went with power and money – it was a thing he had learned early on. But he had to admit that DeLaroza was perhaps the most shielded of all. There was nothing but the skimpiest of dossiers on DeLaroza. No pictures, no stories. Lowenthal knew that he had come to America sixteen years before and had become a naturalized citizen four years ago. He had managed Hotchins's campaign finances almost from the beginning and done it impeccably. There was little else available. His holdings and personal worth were unknown, his companies privately held. If this was to be an opportunity for anyone to get to know anyone, it was DeLaroza who would find out about Lowenthal and

189

Lowenthal knew it.

Oh, well, he thought, *what's to know about me?* He had no secrets at all.

'You're taking quite a gamble,' he said as they approached the long, winding steps of the Ladder Street bazaar.

'I suppose so,' DeLaroza said.

'And if the public doesn't bite?'

DeLaroza paused a moment, then said, 'I never consider failure. There is a Chinese proverb – The fish that fears it will be eaten becomes dinner for the shark.'

Lowenthal smiled. 'And you don't fear the shark?'

DeLaroza looked at him and smiled faintly. 'No,' he said, 'I do not fear the shark.'

They turned into Ladder Street and started the long walk down to the main floor, DeLaroza stopping occasionally to chat with shopkeepers. Along the way, they passed two jugglers tossing fire sticks back and forth as though they were playing catch.

'What's the story behind the dragon and the snake?' Lowenthal asked.

'Ah, my favourite legend, although I must say there are many Oriental myths which stir the imagination. The guides in the garden explain it quite poetically. My chef has prepared for us a potpourri of the menu, a preview of its delights. I will have one of the young ladies tell you the story while we eat.'

At the foot of Ladder Street, an elderly Caucasian gentleman with soft, gentle features and snow-white hair sat on a wall playing the violin. He nodded to DeLaroza as the two men passed him.

'That is Mr. Reynolds,' DeLaroza said. 'He has journeyed all over China with a travelling band, played first chair in the Vienna Symphony, played ragtime music with the greats in New Orleans, and he once taught at the Boston Conservatory. I have known him for many, many years and I have no idea how old he is. He is not interested in age. For him, every day is a new experience. He is the leader of our Chinese band.'

'Where did you find him?'

'He found me,' DeLaroza said cryptically and ended that part of the conversation. 'The restaurant is over there. On the other side of the pond. It is a replica of Tai Tak, the finest restaurant in all Hong Kong – at least *my* favourite. But first let me show you one more thing. I think this may excite your imagination more than all the rest of this.'

They walked up a curving pathway to the end, near the outside wall of the building. Lowenthal saw the looming figure before they reached it, seven feet tall, his eyes gleaming slits, his moustaches plunging down to his chest, his fingernails curved like talons.

'Meet Man Chu, the war lord,' DeLaroza said proudly. The giant turned its head and glared down at the two men. For an instant Lowenthal almost held out his hand to shake its menacing fist.

'It's almost real,' Lowenthal breathed in wonderment.

'The definitive Arcurion,' DeLaroza said. 'Nikos does not make toys or robots; he makes people and creatures. Sometimes I find myself talking to them as though they were alive.'

'What is this?' Lowenthal asked.

'The *pièce de résistance*. A thrill ride like no other in creation. This is where the park gets its name. Pachinko.'

The robot stood in front of a hollow stainless-steel ball large enough to seat two people. The door in the front of the ball opened towards the floor.

'Step inside,' DeLaroza said. Lowenthal got into the ball and settled into the soft leather seat. DeLaroza closed the door. The top half was open so that the rider had a clear view out of the round car.

'Now imagine Man Chi, here, firing this ball into that tunnel in front of you. You drop down a chute to the floor below, which is an enormous pinball field. Bumpers, lights, tunnels, mirrors. The car rolls freely on ball bearings, it never turns upside down and the speed is electronically controlled by an operator who sits in the middle of the pachinko board. Once it leaves the chute here, it is on its own. Only the speed is controlled, so it does not fly out of control. Otherwise it bounces from bumper to bumper up to thirty miles an hour at times before it drops through another chute and arrives on the first floor . . . where your attendant hands you your car keys.'

Above the entrance tunnel was a large replica of the pachinko board itself, an electronic grid on which a blip followed the course of the ball, lighting up the bumpers and registering the score on a digital counter.

DeLaroza helped Lowenthal from the ball. 'Now come along,' he said.

He led the way from the entrance to the ride, along a narrow alley and through a fire door. A flight of steps led down to a second door, which opened onto the field itself. Its walls were mirrored. Strobe lights flashed intermittently and the bumpers gleamed gaudily. It was the bumpers that intrigued Lowenthal, for they were like a vast field of strange statues, each in the shape of a Chinese deity.

DeLaroza strode out on the board, and was immediately dwarfed by the jazzy hardware of the giant pinball machine. He pointed first to this bumper, then that, talking continually.

'This is Shou-Lsing, the god of long life. I call him the laughing god. That one, the serene one, is Lu-Hsing, the god of salaries. Over there, that fat one? Who else but the god of wealth, Ts'ai-Shen? And this lady here, this is Kuan-Yin, goddess of mercy and compassion. Forty-two bumpers in all, enough to satisfy even the most masochistic thrill-seeker. The ball makes one complete revolution of the board here at thirty miles an hour before it rolls through that chute up there. The box in the centre is the control-board. One man can control three balls. On opening night, of course, we will shoot them through one at a time.'

He turned and looked at Lowenthal. It was indeed a fitting climax for *Pachinko!*

'Well,' DeLaroza said grandly, 'now what do you think?'

Lowenthal held his hands out at his sides, palms up. 'What can I say? It is the definitive fantasy. Congratulations.'

Obviously pleased, DeLaroza led him back to the main floor of the park.

'And now,' he said, 'we shall enjoy the *crème de la crème*. Wan Shu is waiting. Now that we have excited your emotions, we shall do the same for your palate.'

Chapter Thirteen

Barney Friscoe stormed through the lobby of the Lancaster Towers West with Papa trotting at his side. The security guard watched them enter and came out of his office with his eyebrows arched into question marks.

Papa managed a lame smile. 'Superintendent,' he said, pointing to Friscoe, whose face looked like a volcano about to erupt.

'Everything hunky-dory up there?' the guard said, with a touch of panic in his voice.

'Fine, fine,' Papa said, 'nothin' to worry about. Routine.' They got into the elevator. The guard watched the door shut and finally shrugged and returned to his television set.

'What's this "superintendent" shit?' Friscoe snapped.

'A cover. He thinks we're workin' on the elevators,' Papa said.

'The elevators? Jesus H. Christ, Papa, this better be important, that's all I got to say, pullin' me outa the symphony, right in the middle of Prokofiev. And *Lieutenant Kije* at that! My oldest kid made third chair tonight, you understand that? It's important.'

Papa said nothing.

'A fantastic programme, we got Brahms, we got Schubert, and we got Prokofiev! And there I am, third row centre.' Friscoe, who was wearing a tuxedo, pulled his velvet tie loose and opened the top button of his shirt as the elevator stopped.

'To the right, first door on the right,' Papa said.

Friscoe stomped down the hall, muttering to himself. 'This better be good. This better be fingerfuckin*lick*in' good.'

Friscoe hammered on the door to 10-A.

'Who is it?' Livingston asked from inside.

'It's Little Red Riding Hood, for Chrissakes, who do you think it is? Open the goddamn door.'

The chain rattled and Livingston swung the door partially open. Friscoe charged through it without looking to the right or left. He came face to face with Sharky and The

Nosh. Friscoe stood in front of them, his hands on his hips and his tie dangling like black crêpe paper from his open collar.

'Awright,' Friscoe bawled, 'what the fuck's so urgent you jokers get me outa the symphony right on the dime, when in ten more minutes I could've sneaked out between numbers and nobody woulda been the wiser? I had to crawl over half of Atlanta society to – '

Livingston was tapping him on the shoulder and at the same moment Sharky pointed back toward the door. Friscoe spun around.

'What the hell do you – ' he said, and stopped in mid-sentence.

He saw the bloody pattern near the ceiling, the splash of blood on the wall where the force of the shot had thrown her, the streaks down to the crumpled body below.

A gaunt spider of a man was leaning over her, examining the body.

'Terrible for the blood pressure, Barney, blowing up like that,' the gaunt man said quietly.

'Holy shit!' Friscoe said, half under his breath. He took a few steps towards the corpse and stopped. His face contorted. He swallowed hard, shuddered, looked at Livingston, back at Sharky, and then at the corpse again.

'What the fuck . . . who is it? What happened here?'

Sharky started to speak but his voice cracked and he stopped to clear his throat. Livingston finally spoke up. 'It's the Domino woman,' he said. The words cut deep into Sharky's gut when he heard them said aloud.

'Domino!' Friscoe said.

'Yeah.'

Friscoe's eyes widened. 'So what happened?'

The gaunt man, his hands encased in blood-covered surgeon's plastic gloves, looked up at him. 'Somebody aced the lady,' he said in a voice that sounded tired.

'I ain't blind,' Friscoe bellowed. 'What I wanna know is, what happened?'

'What happened, Sharky's on the roof monitoring the bugs,' Livingston said. 'She got away from us this morning and was out most of the day. About seven-forty there was a call from somebody named Pete saying he would be late and would call back. She came in at seven-forty-four. Two

194

minutes later another call. Whoever it was hung up. At seven-fifty-eight the doorbell rang, she opened the door and' – he nodded towards the corpse. 'Couple more things. She was packing her suitcase when she got hit. It's in there on the bed. Then about fifteen minutes after . . . it happened . . . there was another call. We let the machine answer it. It was this Pete again. I picked it up, but he hung up as soon as he heard my voice.'

The gaunt man stripped off his gloves, put a hand on his knee, and stood up. And up. And up. He was a shade over six-foot-six, thin as a stalk of wheat, his clothes hanging from bony shoulders like rags on a scarecrow. His complexion was the colour of oatmeal, his hair – what there was of it – the colour of sugared cinnamon. The bones in his long, angular face strained against wafer-thin skin. His long needle fingers seemed as brittle as the limbs of a dead bush. Art Harris, one of the city's better reporters, had once profiled him thus: 'Max Grimm, the Fulton County coroner, is a cadaverous stalk of twigs who looks worse than many of his subjects . . .' The description provided Grimm with his nickname, Twigs. At sixty-seven he had been coroner for forty-one years and had managed to stave off compulsory retirement at sixty-five with the excuse that he was suffering some vague terminal disorder and wanted to work as long as possible at the job he had held for almost two-thirds of his life. Nobody believed him, but that was immaterial. He was too good to retire anyway.

His partner in crime was George Barret, head of the forensics lab. Together, they were the Mutt and Jeff of Pathology, the Tweedledee and Tweedledum of crime lab and morgue. Barret stood barely five-five, outweighed Grimm by at least twenty pounds, wore rimless bifocals, and parted his strawberry-coloured hair down the middle like a turn-of-the-century snake-oil pedlar. He was an arch-Baptist who neither smoked, swore, nor drank and was constantly offended by Grimm's penchant for Napoleon brandy, which the coroner nipped constantly from a Maalox bottle. Barret entered the scene from one of the bedrooms carrying an ancient black snap-satchel which his late father, a country doctor, had willed him. Inside were crammed all the mysterious vials, chemicals, and tools of the forensic trade.

In his soft Southern voice he said, in a single sentence virtually uninhibited by punctuation: 'Nothing here, I got all the pictures and measurements I need, oh, hi, Barney, I think we can assume from the tape and what we can – or more correctly, what we can't – find that the killer never ventured beyond the door there.'

Friscoe was a man fighting frustration, pearls of sweat twinkling on his forehead. 'Well, where's everybody else?' he asked.

'What do you mean?' Livingston replied.

'I mean where the hell is everybody else? Where's Homicide? I see the ME there. I see Forensics. Where is everybody else? Here it is an hour and five minutes since it happened and there ain't a Homicide in sight yet.'

'Nobody called Homicide,' Livingston said.

Friscoe's eyes went blank. 'Nobody called Homicide?'

'Nobody called Homicide.'

'Well, uh, is there a reason nobody called Homicide? I mean have all communications between this here apartment house and the main station busted down or what?'

Sharky was staring at the floor. He had said nothing since Friscoe arrived. He was still having trouble putting together an intelligible sentence. The one thing Friscoe would not understand, would not accept, was Sharky's personal feeling and Sharky knew it would be difficult, if not impossible, to put his personal anger aside. He had to be cautious and it was that necessity that kept him from saying anything. Friscoe finally turned to Livingston. 'Arch?'

'Sure,' Livingston said and then suddenly words seemed to die in his mouth, too. It was Papa who finally broke the awkward stammering cadence of the conversation. 'We wanna do it,' he said simply.

'We wanna do what?' Friscoe said.

'We wanna handle this one.'

'What are you talkin' about?'

'He means we want to run with it, Barney,' Livingston said. 'We know more about – '

'Wait a minute! Wait a fuckin' minute,' Friscoe said, and his voice wavered. He held up a finger. 'You all understand, right, that the golden rule, I mean rule number *one* of the holy scriptures according to The Bat, is that in the event of any sudden or unexplainable or suspicious death, *any* death of that nature, Homicide gets notified first. Before anybody even goes to the fuckin' *bath*room, the Homicides are brought in. That's gospel, boys.'

'Listen a minute,' Livingston implored.

'No! I don't believe my ears. Maybe the robust second chorus of *Lieutenant Kije* has temporarily damaged the old ears here, because if what I'm hearing is what I *think* I'm hearing, you're all off the wall. You're all dangerous if that's what's comin' off here. You're as dangerous as a goddamn cross-eyed barber if you're thinking what I think you're thinking.' Friscoe's face had turned red with anger.

'Look, don't take it personal, for Chrissakes,' Livingston said.

'Well I am takin' it personal. How about that? I'm takin' all this bullshit personal. And that's what it is – bullshit.'

'Look,' Livingston said, 'we're all a little, uh, freaked right now.'

'Oh, I can tell that, yessiree. You're all around the bend, if you ask me. You – you're Abrams, that right?'

The Nosh nodded.

'And you go along with this?'

The Nosh nodded again.

'Shit, you're all nuttier than a team of one-legged tap dancers, you wanna know what I think. That's if anybody's interested in what I think.'

The Nosh smiled.

'It ain't funny there, Abrams,' Friscoe roared. 'You got yourself one hell of a pile of trouble. What you think's gonna happen when D'Agastino hears about this? You think I'm going up? Hah! D'Agastino's gonna break eardrums in Afghanistan. That fuckin' wop can outscream Billy Graham.'

'Will you just listen for a min – ' Livingston started to say.

Friscoe cut him off. 'Crazy,' the lieutenant said, 'crazeeee.' He put his hands over his ears.

Livingston looked at Sharky and shrugged. 'What'd I tell you?' he said.

'What'd I tell who?' Friscoe said, still holding his hands over his ears.

'I told him you'd think we were nuts.'

'You are nuts. Absogoddamnlutely nuts. The lot of you. N-u-t-s.'

197

'I thought at least you'd . . .' Livingston started, and then let the sentence dangle.

'Thought what? Thought what?' Friscoe said, his voice beginning to rise again.

'I thought you'd hear us out.'

'What is this here you're layin' off on me, Arch? What's with this heartbreak hotel shit? Jesus, right now, this here very minute you are all up to your ass in alligators. And for Christ's sake, so am I. I ain't even involved in this and I'm in trouble. The Bat's gonna have ass, man. Ten fat cheeks nailed to his fuckin' wall. And you, too, Twigs. You and George there. You know the procedure.'

'I work for the county,' Twigs said quietly. 'Captain Jaspers can go suck a duck egg.'

'That's real cute,' Friscoe said. 'How about you, George?'

'He owes me,' Livingston said. 'I just called in my green stamps.'

'Jaspers won't bother me,' Barret said. 'I can remember when he was pounding a beat. He had difficulty tying his shoes in those days.'

'He still does,' Twigs said. 'Besides, until you arrived, Barney, Arch was the senior officer on the scene. All I am required to do is make a preliminary study of the corpse on the scene prior to performing an autopsy. The officer in charge gets the results. In this case, I believe Sergeant Livingston was the ranking man on the scene.'

Barret smiled. 'I follow the same procedure. Livingston will get my report. If he handles it improperly, it's his problem, not mine.'

Friscoe sat down on the couch. 'Cheez,' he said. He sat for several seconds shaking his head slowly. Finally: 'Okay, okay. Everybody here's gone a little ape. I can understand that. I'll work it out. I'll take on The Bat and get it straightened out.'

'Barney, all we want is the weekend. Sixty hours. What the hell's that? Until Monday-morning roll call,' Livingston said.

'It's nuts, that's what it is,' Friscoe said. 'Look, I said I'd get it straightened out. But right now we got to get some Homicides up here and fast.'

Ironically, it was Papa who exploded. Papa – who rarely said anything and when he did could reduce the Constitution

198

and the Bill of Rights to a single syllable, Papa who rarely showed any emotion – exploding like a wounded bull.

'Fuck 'em!' he roared, jolting the anguished Friscoe, 'Fuck 'em all. Fuck The Bat, fuck Homicide, fuck that goddamn psalm-singin' moron of a DA. Fuck 'em all. Arch and me have been stuck down in that stinkin' garbage pail at Vice for six years. You been there longer, Friscoe. Everybody in the House thinks all we're good for is puttin' the arm on hookers and perverts and wipin' dogshit off our shoes. We ain't a bunch of morons, y'know. Between you, me, and Arch there we got about fifty years in. This here's our caper. We turned it up. I'm the one waltzed that goddamn Mabel around interrogation until my arches fell and that's what started it all, got us into this here spot in the first place, or maybe you forgot that. Now you know what we're gonna get outa all this? More shit, that's what. The rest of the force is gonna come down on us with their wisecracks and insults. It don't make no never mind that Sharky was up there on the roof doin' his job proper. Don't make no never mind that we turned this whole thing up and followed through. Hell, no! All we're gonna hear is that we had a man on the roof when that lady there got her brains handed to her. Well, I'll tell you what – I'm tired of bein' the asshole of the whole police department. Fuck 'em all, Barney. I say we go after this son of a bitch ourselves and when we get him we hang his goddamn balls on Jaspers's wall. I'm tired of bein' shit on.' Papa pulled open the french doors and stormed out on the balcony, his face as pink as a salamander.

Friscoe was flabbergasted. 'I don't understand what's happening to everybody. I've known Papa for ten years. Worked with him for six. That's more in one breath than he's said the whole rest of the time I've known him. What the hell's the fuss? What we got is a hooker suspected of complicity in a felony who got totalled. Big fuckin' deal. It ain't the first time somebody put the zap on a goddamn prostitute.'

'She was a nice lady,' The Nosh said.

'*A nice lady?*' Friscoe said.

Sharky had been sitting on the couch without a word. Now he had to say something. But what? How could he possibly explain that he had met Domino and the strange circumstances of the meeting. Or that he had sensed a vulnerability that had drawn him to her. Or that because he had felt an attraction to her this senseless violence that had snuffed out Domino's life seemed somehow directed at him, too.

'Don't you understand?' he said finally. 'I feel responsible. Whether I am or not, I *feel* responsible.'

Friscoe stared at Sharky and his anger began to subside. 'Okay, I do understand that. Thing is, nobody here's responsible. You were doin' exactly what you were supposed to be doin'. Look here, did you – did *any*body – have any idea she was gonna get shoved over?'

No answer.

'Anybody at all?'

Still no answer.

'Of course not. Nobody's responsible for nothin'. Nobody knew it was comin' down, right? Now I can understand Doc Twigs here goin' a little off the wall. You gotta be a little weird, goin' around sniffin' that goddamn formaldehyde all the time. But not the rest of you. See, no matter what we did, if we wrapped this one up before breakfast, we'd all end up one through five on The Bat's shit list. When he finds out, that's it. And he's gonna find out, make no mistake about that. Anybody wanna argue that point? No, there ain't no argument there. And even, see, even if Jaspers falls deaf, dumb, and blind in the next thirty seconds, we still got one J. Philip Riley to contend with. I'm sure you will all recall that Lieutenant Riley heads up Homicide, but what maybe you don't know is that when God handed out brains this same J. Philip Riley was on the front of the line. And also what maybe you don't know is that J. Philip Riley has got a temper that when *he* blows, The Bat and D'Agastino're both gonna sound like a pair of sopranos in the Sunday school choir. I mean, Riley ain't gonna take too lightly to the fact that a bunch of stand-up comics from Vice just hi-de-ho stepped in and took over one of his homicide cases. That's for openers. For closers I would like to point out that this same J. Philip Riley happens to be a friend of mine and a damn good cop and I ain't inclined at this minute to stick my dick in the meat grinder just because Sharky here feels *respons*ible.'

'That was quite a little speech, Barney,' Barret said in his quiet, funereal voice. 'All they want is the weekend. I happen to know that Jaspers is in Chicago addressing the NAPO convention. He won't even be back until Monday night.'

'That's fuckin' immaterial,' Friscoe snapped.

'I don't think so,' Twigs said.

Friscoe whirled away from him as if he had the plague. 'Just keep your dime out of it, Twigs,' he snapped.

'Why? What you're saying merely points up the fact that Sharky and Livingston, Papa out there on the porch, are right. It doesn't make any difference what you do now, the Bat and Riley are both going to be on the warpath. What've you got to lose?'

'I don't go for breakin' procedure – that's one thing I don't go for. That's suicide!'

'Yeah, Barney,' Livingston said, 'the reason you've been in Vice for almost seven years is because you're so big on procedure. Shit, we haven't followed *procedure* since I been in the squad.'

'This is interdepartmental,' Friscoe said.

Sharky stood up and began pacing around the room. The shock was wearing off and in its place was anger, a welling fury deep inside him. 'Maybe you like it down there in Friscoe's Inferno,' he said, and his voice was brittle. 'Maybe you been lying with the dogs so long you like the fleas.'

'Who the hell do you think you are, to say a shit thing like that to me?' Friscoe said, his face turning blood red.

'I'm just thinking about that spiel I got when I checked in yesterday,' said Sharky. 'Was that all bullshit? About how you and Arch and Papa were down there because you didn't suck ass. Didn't play by the book. A bunch of hardheads. I'll tell you what, Lieutenant, you gave me this machine and Arch and Papa and The Nosh there are along for the ride. Now you want to hand it over to Riley? Shit, maybe you were right. Maybe I should walk. Maybe I should walk right now, right out that door, and go after the son of a bitch myself.'

'You do and I'll bring you down myself. I don't go for headhunting. That's cheap shit and you know it.'

'Look, every minute we sit around here arguin', the son of a bitch is moving farther away,' said Livingston. 'Why not give Twigs and George a chance to tell us what they've picked up? Five, ten minutes more. Like you say, we're up to our asses in alligators anyway.'

Friscoe's shoulders sagged. Defeated, he waved his hand at Twigs. 'Go ahead, for Chrissake.'

Twigs smiled. 'Don't worry about Riley. He's got seven stiffs down there in the icebox and two of them are John Does. He'll probably be grateful for any help he can get at this point.'

'That's a laugh,' Friscoe said. 'Riley ain't happy unless his caseload looks like the casualty report from World War Two.'

'May we go ahead?' Barret asked.

'Sure, why not?' said Friscoe. 'Before this is over we're all gonna be directing traffic on the outskirts of Boise, Idaho, anyhow.'

'What do you remember from ballistics training?' Barret asked.

'You must be kidding,' Friscoe said. 'I been in Vice so long, I can remember when they busted Socrates for pinchin' little boys on the ass. Keep it basic.'

'All right. First, the obvious. The weapon was a shotgun, twelve-gauge, judging from the number of pellets in the shot, and I think we both agree that it was sawed-off. Why? Because the shot leaves the barrel at a muzzle velocity of about eleven hundred feet per second. Up to about three feet the shot is contained; the effect is like a single rifle bullet. After that, the pellets begin to spread. If you want the shot to spread faster, the best way to accomplish your purpose is to saw the barrel off. The effect of a sawed-off scattergun is the same at about three feet as the pattern of a normal shotgun at about eight or ten yards. Now, let's take a look at the scene a minute. Mr. Grimm?'

'Yes, Mr. Barret.'

The gaunt man took a pencil from his inside pocket and drew the point along his hairline at the forehead. 'Singed hair along the frontal lobe here. In fact the hair was burned in places. Also some scorched bits of skin embedded in the wall with the pellets that didn't hit her. The heat from a shotgun blast dissipates very rapidly. So I would say the weapon was three to four feet from the victim's face when it was fired.

'Judging from the destruction, the pattern was already wide, seven to eight inches in diameter. Where it hit the wall there it has already spread to ten inches. That's the kind of dispersal we would normally expect at eight or ten yards. So I would say the gun was fired from the vicinity of the door and that it was sawed off pretty close, maybe eight or nine inches from the firing pin as opposed to a normal barrel length of thirty or thirty-two inches. Mr. Barret?'

'Thank you, Mr. Grimm. As for the weapon,' Barret said, 'if you listen to Sharky's tape recording you will notice that the two shots came almost simultaneously; in fact they overlap slightly. They are too close together for the weapon to be an automatic or a pump or lever action. So what we got is a sawed-off double-barrel twelve-gauge shotgun and one that was very effectively silenced.'

'A *lupaba?*' Livingston asked, and there was surprise in his voice.

'What's a *lupaba?*' Sharky said.

'It's Sicilian for a shotgun of this kind. The classic Mafia execution weapon,' Barret said. 'Certainly a possibility.'

'You sayin' this is a Mafia hit?' Friscoe said.

'I'm saying it's a similar kind of weapon. And I'm also saying that this was no amateur at work. No amateur would have a weapon like that. Certainly not one that was silenced. Besides, this was very well planned.'

'There's another thing,' Twigs said. He knelt and picked up one of the pellets from a plastic bag with a pair of tweezers and held it under Friscoe's nose.

'Smell anything?'

'Yeah,' Friscoe said, 'gunpowder.'

'Anything else?'

Friscoe closed his eyes and sniffed. His forehead wrinkled up. 'What is that – garlic?'

'Exactly,' Twigs said.

'Don't tell me,' Friscoe said, 'the shotgun had spaghetti for dinner.'

Barret smiled. 'Perhaps. It is another Mafia trademark. The *caporegimi*, the Mafia lieutenants, sometimes soaked their bullets in garlic. It infected the wound and also made the wound more painful. It was a tactic used mostly for revenge or official executions. But never in a shotgun. It's quite strange.'

'You're not saying this is some kind of official Mafia hit?' Friscoe said.

'I tend to doubt it.'

'What then?'

'Maybe it's part of his m.o.,' Sharky said.

'That's more like it,' Barret said. 'A habit. Or perhaps even a trademark.'

'So he could be an old-time *caporegime*,' Livingston said. Barret nodded.

'What the hell good is that?' Friscoe said. 'So you've narrowed the field down to a coupla thousand ace hitmen spread out all over the country. Big deal.'

'Profiles, dear Barney, profiles,' Twigs said. 'A few more details. The projectile was upward. You can tell from the way the shots hit the wall. The victim measures approximately 178 centimetres, that's about five-ten. Assuming from the other physical evidence that the killer was standing in the doorway, we can draw an imaginary line from the centre of the pattern through the victim's head to a point where the killer was standing. We can assume he did not shoot from the hip. If he had, the second shot probably would have hit him in his own chin. So he either fired with the piece under his armpit or against his shoulder. From all this we can make a pretty good guess at the killer's height. Mr. Barret?'

Barret had drawn a diagram on a sheet of paper and was punching the keys of a small pocket calculator. 'Five-nine tops. More likely five-seven or eight. Also from the position of the two shots, I would say you're looking for an over-under double-barrel rather than a side-by-side.'

'Pretty common, right?' Friscoe said.

'Yes,' said Barret, 'I wouldn't waste my time trying to trace the gun. The significant thing is that it adds to his m.o.'

'The more you talk, the more I think we better get Riley and company up here fast,' Friscoe said. 'Let Homicide and the OC worry about it – it's their problem.'

'If D'Agastino gets involved you can forget it,' The Nosh said. 'Before it's over, he and Riley will be killing each other. That D'Agastino actually keeps evidence to himself so the OC can get the glory.'

'That's okay. I'll put Riley against him any day. You ain't seen nothin' till you've seen that crazy Irishman mad.'

'Barney, Phil Riley got his job because he deserved it. D'Agastino is a politician. In your experience which gets preference in the official hierarchy, politics – or talent? Riley's going to spend weeks wading through the red tape and then he'll be lucky if the case stays in his department.' Twigs took out his Maalox bottle and celebrated his analysis with a swig of brandy.

'Let's add up what we know about the shooter, shall we?' Barret said. 'I think we're looking for an old-timer, someone with definite habits. Extremely cautious, a careful planner, experienced enough to be sure of himself. I'd say he goes back a ways. The young ones avoid habits. They vary their methods constantly to avoid detection. The older ones are too set in their ways. They follow traditions. They're scared to make changes. They stick with what they know works. So I'd say an old-timer definitely. Late forties, early fifties at least, maybe older. Five-seven to five-nine. Quite possibly a contact killer, someone who likes to work close to the victim, perhaps even psychopathic in that sense. Mafia and possibly an executioner fairly high in the Mafia hierarchy, because of the garlic thing. The use of garlic these days, I would think, is part of his ritual, something associated with luck or tradition.'

'Thank you, Mr. Barret,' Twigs said.

'Thank *you*, Mr. Grimm,' Barret said.

Papa broke into the conversation from the balcony. 'You know what I think?'

'God knows,' Friscoe said.

'The fink was watchin' the apartment. Had to've been. Wouldn't stand in the stairwell all day waitin' for her to come home. Wouldn't be out in the open – too easy to spot. Phone call was probably to make sure she was home. Had to be where he could see lights come on. He was watchin'. From over there someplace.' He gestured towards the east tower.

They all looked towards the other building, at the irregular boxes of light shining through apartment windows. Sharky felt a sudden chill. Goose pimples rippled along his arm and he rubbed them away as surreptitiously as he could. Perhaps the killer had been there, all day, watching as Sharky listened from his perch on the roof. Anger began replacing the sorrow he felt for Domino, worms nudging his instinct for revenge, urging it into motion. He remembered the previous day when they were planting the mikes in the apartment and Domino had returned. He said, 'Papa's right. He had to be watching. It happened too fast to be luck or coincidence. And you can't see this apartment from the street. Yesterday Arch had to warn The Nosh and me when we were up here. We couldn't see her when she came home.'

'You can't see it too good from the swimming terrace, either,' Papa said. 'Which leaves the north side of the building, and that's all residential, a lot of trees and backyards . . .'

'And over there,' Papa said.

They all stood on the balcony, looking across at the east tower.

'He could be sitting over there watching us right now,' said Twigs.

'You kiddin'?' Friscoe said, 'He's halfway to Detroit by now.'

'Makes sense, y'know,' Barret agreed. 'Perhaps an empty apartment?'

'Too chancy,' Friscoe said. 'He's sittin' in there, somebody comes in for a look-see, a prospective tenant, you know. Bingo, he's made. Too smart for that.'

'How about somebody who's out of town?' Sharky suggested.

'Sounds like a lot of crap shootin' to me,' Friscoe said.

'No,' Twigs said, 'it's deduction. And that's what's going to break this one no matter who handles it. You, D'Agastino, Riley, or whoever.'

'There's not enough physical evidence at this point. I agree,' Barret said.

'I think,' said Sharky, 'it's time to have a chat with the security man.'

'Look,' Friscoe said, 'if we *are* gonna do this we can't even tell the press she's dead. We can't even notify her next of *kin*. What the fuck are you going to tell the security man?'

Sharky smiled for the first time since Domino had been killed. 'I'm goin' to con him,' he said. 'How do you think I stayed alive on the street for eighteen months?'

The security guard was in his office watching an old

Randolph Scott movie on television when Sharky appeared at the doorway. He smiled and said, 'Hi.'

The guard nodded back. 'Everything copasetic up there?' he said.

'Yeah, sure,' Sharky said. He lit a small cigar. 'Old Randy was tough, wasn't he?'

The security guard said, 'Don't make 'em like that anymore,' without taking his eyes off the screen.

Sharky blew smoke towards the ceiling and decided it was time for a long shot. 'How long were you a cop?' he asked.

The guard looked up, surprised, 'How'd you know?' he said.

Sharky took out his wallet and flipped it open, baring his shield.

'I'll be a son of a bitch,' the guard said. 'You know somethin'? I had a feelin' all along that story about the elevators was a lot of crap.' He leaned towards Sharky and said very softly. 'What in hell's goin' on, anyway?'

'We need to trust you,' Sharky said. 'What I'm going to tell you is very confidential.'

'Hey, I was nineteen years on the College Park force. I'd still be there only I piled up a blue-and-white chasing some goddamn teenagers and almost lost a leg. Had to retire early.'

'That's tough,' Sharky said. 'What's your name?'

'Jerry. Jerry Sanford.'

'This stays between us, right?'

'Tellin' Jerry Sanford is like talkin' to a grave.'

'Okay. The boys up there with me, we're all a special team from burglary. For three weeks now we've had a cat burglar working the high rent apartments and condos along Peachtree. He's very good, driving us up the wall. He always knows exactly what he's after, who to hit, and who not to hit. He knows when people are out of town. He can pop a double-lock LaGard box easier than opening a can of beans. So far he's been two feet ahead of us all the way. We figure he's got to take this place sooner or later.'

'We got good security,' Sanford said.

'He's hit just as tough.'

'Yeah?'

'Believe me, this guy is first rate. He's into tricks we never heard of.'

'No shit. What'd you say your name was again?'

'Sharky.'

'Tell you, Sharky, Raymond Security is tough.'

'Here's the thing. We figure he does a real number before he hits. Checks out the residents. Maybe even has a method for scoring financial statements. He usually hits apartments or condominiums where the tenants are out of town for a while. Business, maybe, or travelling. He might even call ahead, ask questions about the tenants. But very clever.'

'We don't tell nobody nothin' about our occupants.'

'He's clever, like I said. Maybe passes himself off as a delivery man. A salesman, like that.'

'No solicitations in the building.'

'Maybe a door-to-door thing?'

'Nobody gets by this desk without we check who they're going to see and get an okay from the occupant.'

'How long are you on? What's your shift?'

'I'm on two to ten right now. The graveyard man takes over from ten to six in the A.M. Then the early man does six to two. We revolve the shift every six weeks. I been on the evening trick for a month.'

'How about the other men?'

'First rate, everybody. I'm telling you, Raymond Security is the best.'

'And there hasn't been anyone around? No phone calls?'

'No, sir.'

'Nobody suspicious hanging around?'

'If there was, you'd be the first to know. We've had a couple of people looking at apartments, asking about vacancies. The place stays a hundred per cent full. We got four on the waiting list now. The two empties are bein' renovated. They're both leased already.'

'Which ones would they be?'

'Let's see, there's 10-B west and 4-C east.'

'10-B west?'

'Yeah. They're puttin' in the carpeting now. It goes to an elderly lady. A widow. Very well fixed. The other one goes to a young couple. He's a doctor.'

'Anything temporarily vacant? You know, people away on vacation, anything like that?'

'Sure. But we got the list. Let's see. There's the Cliffords,

9-C east. They're in Florida for the holidays. Go down every year. He's retired. And then there's Mrs. Jackowitz. She's in Hawaii with her daughter. They take a trip every year this time. The daughter's a travel agent. Mr. Jackowitz passed on about two years ago.'

'Where's her apartment?'

'That would be 12-C in the east tower.'

'That would face?'

'West. A and B are on the east side of the building. C and D on the west. Four apartments to the floor.'

'So the Jackowitz apartment is on the twelfth floor of the east tower facing the west tower?'

'Right.'

'And the Cliffords?'

'9-C, east.'

'Both apartments face the other tower, right?'

'Right.'

'And nobody soliciting, no calls, nothing like that?'

The guard shook his head.

'Okay, Jerry, thanks. We'll be in and out for a couple of more days.'

'You want to stake out one of the empties, it's okay with me. I got a passkey.'

'Thanks, we may just take you up on that.' Sharky started out of the office and brushed against a tall corn plant in the corner, its leaves turning brown at the tips. 'You're overwatering your plants,' he said to Sanford. 'You can always tell when the leaves turn at the ends like that.'

'I got the original brown thumb. I already killed one of the Jackowitz plants and two more in here.'

'You go in the Jackowitz apartment?'

'Yeah, I water the plants for her. I hate to do it, too. I don't have the feel for it, know what I mean?'

'Yeah. When's the last time you were in there?'

'Jackowitz? Lessee, it was Sunday. I water them on Sundays.'

'Thanks. We'll keep in touch.'

Sharky started to leave and Sanford suddenly snapped his fingers. 'Hey, I just thought of something. There was a call. I just thought about it when you started talkin' about those plants. It was . . . uh . . . day before yesterday. He was with some plant store. I'll think of it here in a minute.'

'What did he want?'

'It was a new service. Plantland, that's the name of the place. Right up the street. What they do, they water and fertilize plants for people.'

'Did you tell him anything?'

Sanford chewed on his lower lip for a moment. 'What I did – see, I hate takin' care of the plants, like I said. I told him to send them some literature.'

'Who. Send who?'

'Everybody in the place. I was afraid, you know, I'd forget if he sent the stuff to me.'

'Did you tell him the Cliffords and Jackowitz were away?'

'Uh, well, I told him I was having trouble, y'know. I thought maybe he could gimme a tip or two.'

'Did you tell him they were out of town?'

'I didn't say anything *specific*. I told him they were potentials, see. Send the stuff direct to them but that it may be a little while before they get back.'

'You gave him the names and addresses?'

'Yeah, four or five different people who travel a lot, not just them.'

'But did you mention specifically that the Cliffords and Jackowitz women are out of town now?'

'Just so he'd know it might be a while before they got back to him.'

'I see.'

'I fucked up, right?'

'Maybe not.'

'I'll call them right now, check it out.'

'No,' Sharky said quickly. 'I wouldn't do that. If it is a possibility you'd just warn them, right?'

'Oh, yeah. I didn't think of that.'

'Let us handle it.'

'Sure, sure.'

'I'll keep this between us.'

'Hey, Sharky, that's damn white of you. I appreciate it.'

'Any time, Jerry. Any time.'

Forty minutes in the Cliffords' apartment yielded nothing but bruised knees. Barret was a fanatic. He checked everything. Under the beds, in the commode, behind pots and

210

pans in the cabinets, the disposal, the windowsills, under chairs and couches.

Forty minutes later he said, 'Forget it,' and they headed to the Jackowitz apartment on twelve. Barret told Sharky and The Nosh to stand back until he vacuumed the carpeting around the door and dusted the doorknob. He carefully swept the small camel's-hair brush on the brass handle, smoothing out the black powder.

He looked up and grinned.

'What d'ya know,' he said. 'Clean as a new dime.'

'So?' The Nosh said.

'So how many people do you know polish off the doorknob when they enter or leave their place?'

Sharky stepped close to Barret. 'You through here?' he asked.

'Yep.'

'Then why don't you step over there out of the way and let Nosh and me take the door, just in case.'

'Why, indeed,' Barret said and walked ten feet down the hall. The Nosh knelt down and popped the lock with less trouble than it would have taken to open a can of soup. Sharky took out his automatic and, holding his arm close to his side and bent at the elbow, pointed the gun towards the ceiling and slipped the safety catch off. The Nosh took out a snub-nose .38 and leaned back against the wall on the opposite side of the doorway, the pistol nestled in two hands.

'Here we go,' Sharky whispered and The Nosh nodded. He twisted the doorknob slowly and then pushed the door open, jumped inside and fell flat against the wall in the dark room. An instant later The Nosh came through and kicked the door shut behind him. They waited for a few seconds, listening to each other breathe. 'Scares the shit outa me, doin' that,' The Nosh said finally.

Sharky clicked on the light. The apartment was empty. They let Barret in. Barret slipped on surgeon's plastic gloves and went to work. Slowly and methodically he moved through the apartment. The doorknob inside was also devoid of fingerprints. He spot vacuumed the rug, marking each bag of dirt and grit with a small diagram of the room showing the exact location of the sample. He got down on his hands and knees with a flashlight and perused

211

the carpeting. Then he told Sharky to turn off the lights.

'Kneel down here beside me,' he said. The finger of light skipped across the piling of the carpet. Barret moved it slowly back and forth. 'See anything?' he asked.

'You mean the marks there on the floor?'

'Um hmm.'

There were four deep grooves in the rug. Then Barret saw something else twinkling in the rays of the flashlight under the chair. He took tweezers and picked it up. It was a small red oblong pill.

'Look familiar?' Barret said.

'Looks like a red devil to me,' Sharky said.

'Could be, could be. Or some kind of angina medication. Perhaps the woman who lives here dropped it.' He plopped it in a baggie, then turned his attention back to the chair.

'Somebody swung this chair around in front of the window,' Barret said. 'And see here, on the windowsill, those circles. Still damp. It looks like somebody put a glass of water down here.' He looked at it under his magnifying glass. Along the edges of the water ring was a slight red discolouration.

'When's the last time anybody was in here?' Barret asked.

'Last Sunday,' Sharky said.

'Hmmm.'

Barret went over the living room in minute detail, then the kitchen and bedroom.

'Okay,' he said finally, 'here's what we got. Somebody moved the chair. Somebody dropped a pill on the floor. That could've happened a week ago, yesterday, or last month. But the water rings on the windowsill – that was recent. No more than a few hours. Still damp. Also there's water in the sink in the kitchen and one of the glasses is damp. I'd say three or four hours on the outside, or both the glass and the sink'd be dry by now. That red discolouration on the sill could have come from that pill we found on the floor. I took a scraping. The lab'll confirm that. No prints in the apartment, no *recent* prints in the apartment. Everything's latent. Okay, we can expect that. There's also a trace of oil on the carpet in front of the window. Smells like machine oil but I'll check that out. It could have been from a gun if somebody laid one there on the floor. The phone is

212

clean. Some old prints and smudges. My guess is somebody wearing gloves picked up the phone. It's operating, by the way.' Barret went to the window and parted the venetian blinds with two fingers. 'Direct view of the other apartment from here.'

He stopped and for several moments he stared into space, saying nothing. Then he said, 'I think he was in here. Somebody was, and within the last few hours.' He nodded to himself, still staring.

'I have one more idea,' he said.

He took his brush and vial of black powder and went first to the guest bathroom and kneeling down, dusted the handle on the toilet. It was clean. He went to the other bathroom and repeated the procedure.

The loops and whorls seemed far away at first.

Then as Barret dusted them they seemed to jump out at him.

'Well, I'll be a son of a gun,' Barret said with a grin. 'Bingo! We got ourselves a fresh print.' He looked up at Sharky and The Nosh and winked. 'Keep that in mind,' he said. 'Nobody likes to wear gloves when they take a leak.'

Chapter Fourteen

From a table near the railing of the Tai Tak Restaurant Lowenthal watched as a beautiful young Chinese woman dressed in a red silk mandarin dress jumped lightly from the sampan and came up the walkway to the deck of the floating restaurant. She was a tiny flower of a girl, barely five feet tall with an almost perfect body and an ebony ponytail that cascaded over one shoulder.

Wan Shu, the chef of the restaurant, motioned her to the table. He was almost a parody of the stereotyped Chinese, a fat man, Buddha-like, with thin moustaches that drooped down over the corners of his mouth and a perpetual smile on his lips.

'Is Heida,' he said as she joined Lowenthal and De-Laroza, 'from Wanchai section. Three weeks here. Okay?'

'A splendid choice, *p'eng-yu*,' DeLaroza said.

Wan Shu beamed. 'You drink before dinner?'

DeLaroza nodded and turned to Lowenthal. 'What would you like?'

'Would Scotch be irreverent in present company?'

'Hardly. You forget, Hong Kong is a crown colony. There is probably more Scotch consumed there than anything else. Ice?'

Lowenthal nodded and DeLaroza gave the order to Wan Shu in Chinese. He rushed away, snapping his fingers and issuing commands to waiters.

'Where do you live in Wanchai?' DeLaroza asked Heida.

'On Jaffe Road near O'Brien. I live with my mother who sews for Jau Pun in Kowloon.'

DeLaroza nodded. 'I know him well. One of the finest of all tailors in the city. He has made many suits for me. How old are you?'

'I am nineteen,' she said in a high, melodic voice. 'I have gone to the university for one year. I study history. I hope to work for one year here and save my money so I may finish.'

'What're you going to do with the history?' Lowenthal asked.

214

'I hope to be a school teacher, perhaps in the British settlement at Tseun Wan.'

'Very ambitious,' DeLaroza said. 'I assume you know the legend of Kowloon and T'un Hai well, then?'

'*Hai*. My father told me the story many times before he died. It was a special thing between us.'

'Mister Lowenthal here does not know the story. Would you honour us?'

'Of course, *nin*. It is *my* honour.'

'Would you like something to drink first?'

'*Um, dor jeh*. I have had too many Coca-Colas already. I will be fat like T'sai-Shen if I am not careful.'

'Who is T'sai-Shen?' Lowenthal asked.

'The god of wealth and happiness. He is so-o-o big,' she said, holding her arms in front of her in a large circle.

'I doubt that,' Lowenthal said with a smile.

'Should I begin then?'

'Please,' DeLaroza said.

She stood b wing, pressing her hands together in an attitude of p aye·, and then began reciting the myth in her bell-like voice, acting it out in pantomime; moving slowly in place, each gesture a ballet of grace. Lowenthal could not take his eyes off her.

'In the land of my father the most wondrous and ancient of all creatures is the dragon, for the dragon represents both earth and water.

'The dragon has the power of the rains, he puts colour in the cheeks of the flowers. He brings the bountiful rice crop.

'But if the dragon is offended by the misdeeds and dishonour of the emperors, he becomes angry. The rains do not come. It is a time when the earth is like the wrinkled face of the prophet. The crops die in the ground, the rivers become like dusty pathways. The harvest is a time of sorrow and weeping.

'And so, once a year the ministers and lords of the empire honour Chiang-Yuan, the Dragon of the Ten Toes, and it is a great celebration which is called the Feast of the Dragon Door and they adorn the dishes from which they eat, the robes they wear, even their thrones, with the countenance of Chiang-Yuan.

'In the time of Fu Hsi, who was by legend the first of all the great emperors of China, a dragon horse arose from the

Yellow River and presented himself to the emperor. He was sent by Yu-huang-shang-ti, the August Emperor of Jade, and god of all gods, to serve Fu Hsi and give to him the wisdom of the gods. On the back of the dragon horse was a mystical chart from which all of the written language of China was taken. And in the time of Fu Hsi there was peace in the land and it was a time of plenty.

'And so, from that time on, the Dragon of the Ten Toes has been the imperial symbol of all emperors.

'His enemy was T'un Hai, the two-headed blood snake of the dark world, for it was believed that the snake tore the souls of the dead to pieces and scattered them to the sea. Only Chiang-Yuan could save them and lead them to everlasting peace in the kingdom of the Jade Emperor.

'And so it was in the time of the boy emperor Ping, eight hundred years ago. The young king loved Chiang-Yuan and believed that when an emperor died his soul lived on in the body of the dragon. And he believed also that in the eight mountain peaks surrounding Hong Kong there lived eight dragons, each with the soul of one of Ping's ancestors. His prime minister told Ping that there would be another dragon when Ping died and it would live in the high mountain on the western side of the island of Hong Kong and it would be called Kow-Loon, which means "ninth dragon," and Ping's soul would live in its great body and would protect the harbour and the souls of the dead from T'un Hai.

'When Ping passed on, the dragon Kow-Loon appeared on the western peak and its soul was the soul of Ping and Kow-Loon went forth on the island in search of T'un Hai and in the place now known as Tiger Balm Gardens he found the snake of lost souls in a cave. T'un Hai came from the cave and attacked Kow-Loon and they fought for twenty-three days and nights until the earth was scorched from Kow-Loon's fiery breath and the earth was scarred from their battle and the hills fell into the sea. The earth trembled. A great earthquake shook the island and the people escaped to the sea in their sampans and waited until the battle was over and T'un Hai slid into the sea and was never seen again.

'And since that time Kow-Loon has protected Hong Kong and many people still live on sampans so they will be safe if T'un Hai ever returns and there is another great battle and the earth trembles again.'

Heida closed her eyes and bowed her head. The story was over.

'Thank you,' she said.

Lowenthal sat back and stared at the young lady, entranced by the story and by her visual interpretation. 'No,' he said, 'it is I who thank you. I'm very touched by your story. You tell it with great passion.'

'It is only because my father told it to me with passion, for he believed the story, just as he believed that when he died he would ride on the back of the dragon horse to the place where the August Supreme Emperor of Jade resides.'

'And do you believe the story?' Lowenthal asked.

A smile touched her lips. '*Hai.* Of course. I believe it because it is a legend that sings with truth.' She reached inside her blouse and took out a thin gold chain with a gold pendant hanging from it. On the pendant in bas relief was the tiny figure of a dragon, grinning ferociously, his head crouching between his five-toed feet. 'It is always around my neck,' she said, 'even when I sleep. It protects me from T'un Hai.'

DeLaroza thanked her and she bowed and was gone.

'I must say, you make all of this very real,' Lowenthal said. 'I wonder why it is that Easterners have much more interesting and dramatic gods than we Westerners.'

'*You* Westerners,' DeLaroza said with a smile. 'I am a Buddhist. But enough of that. Let us talk about the campaign. Needless to say, I am delighted you have joined us.'

'So far you seem to be doing just fine without me.'

'So far we have played in our own territory.'

Wan Shu arrived with the first of many dishes, what appeared to be tiny chicken wings covered with a clear sauce. 'This looks delicious,' Lowenthal said. 'What is it?'

'Well, it is hardly what we would call *chia-ch'ang-pien-fan* – everyday food – in China. You eat the whole thing, the bones and all. Just chew it well. They are sparrow wings.'

Lowenthal paused in mid-bite and there was a moment when he seemed to be wondering whether to go on or not.

'Please, do not stop,' DeLaroza said. 'Heida mentioned the Feast of the Dragon Door. What Wan Shu is preparing is a meal based on that feast. There will be some rare

217

delicacies, such as these sparrow wings. Also quail, elephant trunk, sturgeon intestines, bear paw, and deer tail, along with more traditional fare. The meal for two hundred guests will cost ten thousand dollars.'

'That's five hundred dollars a meal!'

'Exactly. The banquet originated during the time of the Emperor Tsi Tzu of the Sung Dynasty, about seven hundred years ago. It usually went on for days. I have eliminated some of the more exotic dishes. Peacock tongues, monkey brains, gorilla lips.'

'Gorilla lips?'

'A truly rare delicacy in China. But I don't want to discourage any of the guests.'

'Elephant trunk and deer tails may take care of that.'

DeLaroza leaned forward and winked. 'We won't tell them until *after* they've eaten.'

The sparrow wings actually were quite delicious and Lowenthal finished them with relish. He sat back and said, 'Tell me, what took you from Brazil to Hong Kong?'

'I see you have been checking up on me.'

Lowenthal shrugged. 'There's not much to check up on, actually.'

'I have always avoided publicity. A quirk of mine.'

'Modesty hardly becomes you,' Lowenthal said, motioning to the spectacle of *Pachinko!*

'I am about to change my image.'

He chuckled and then the chuckle became a hearty laugh.

'Fate dictated the move to Hong Kong,' he said. 'I was on holiday in the Orient and visited the plant of a gentleman named Loo who manufactured radios, which also happened to be my business. Mr. Loo was in trouble. His company was undercapitalized and a British concern was about to buy him out. But the British were stupid. They would have engulfed him, eaten him up. Loo's strength was his ability to produce components cheaply. His weakness was assembly and marketing. So I formed a partnership with him. He produced the parts; I assembled and sold them. We were highly competitive and the merger was quite successful. Had I bought Loo out, as the British proposed to do, I would have lost his expertise. A man always works better for himself than for others.'

'And how did you get into the toy business?'

'Fate again. This time an accident of nature. Loo had a side venture, producing toys for the tourist trade, cheap little items. Our electronics plant was seriously damaged in the 1961 typhoon, but the toy company was hardly touched. While we were undergoing repairs I decided to concentrate on toys. Before long it was – how do you put it?'

'The tail wagging the dog?'

'Yes. The Chinese might express it more poetically, but the Americans are more to the point. It was soon after that I met Nikos Arcurius. Now the tail wags many dogs.'

'Where does Hotchins come into the scenario?'

'I decided to move to the United States. This is the marketplace. Also the place to assemble and sell products. My company was the first to make that move. At the time Donald was in the state – Congress?'

'Legislature,' said Lowenthal.

'Right. He was about to run for governor. He sponsored a law that made it advantageous for us to come to his state. We became friends and I offered my business knowledge to the campaign.'

'You are really quite savvy to American politics for a . . .' He hesitated, letting the sentence hang.

'Foreigner?' DeLaroza said. 'The word does not offend me, although I am now an American citizen. I have studied politics all my life. It is not a hobby, it is an avocation. Not only American. British, French, Chinese, German.'

'And what attracted you to Hotchins?'

DeLaroza considered the question for a few moments. 'Aristotle once wrote that law is reason without passion. Hotch is a man of law and a man of passion. I found the combination irresistible. He is also quite honest. In fact blunt at times.'

'Pretty good answer.'

'And how would you answer the question?'

Lowenthal toyed with his wine glass, making small circles on the table top. 'A lot of things. He's a winner. I guess that must be number one. We need a winner badly. He's a self-made man. A lawyer and a businessman. And he's tough. Anybody who can survive four years in a Korean prison camp with his foot blown off is tough. So far he doesn't seem to owe anybody. Somebody once said, "Capitalism gives all of us a great opportunity if we seize it with

219

both hands and hang on to it." I think the man on the street wants to believe that again.'

'An interesting comment. Who said that?'

'Al Capone,' Lowenthal said and they both laughed.

'There are some things I want to make sure of,' Lowenthal went on.

'Anything.'

'Is he clean, Victor? I mean is he *really* clean?'

A vision of Domino flashed before DeLaroza and then it vanished. A danger he hoped no longer existed.

'Is anybody *that* clean, Mr. Lowenthal? Richelieu told one of his bishops once, "Give me six sentences written by the most innocent man and I will find something in them to hang him." I assure you, Donald can withstand any scrutiny.'

'Excellent. Will his wife make a good campaigner?'

DeLaroza nodded. 'And a fine First Lady.'

Lowenthal nodded, but there was still doubt in his expression.

'What else?' DeLaroza asked.

'I am concerned about opening the campaign this soon. I know that you have very carefully designed his strategy, but it is contradictory to the normal campaign strategy, coming out this soon. For one thing the cost will be staggering to keep a bandwagon rolling that long.'

'Cost is not a factor. We can afford it.'

'Also it makes him a public target for that much longer.'

DeLaroza's eyebrows rose. 'At this point he is virtually an unknown quantity. We are not selling a dark horse, we are selling an un*known* horse. That is why we plan to open the campaign here, Monday night. We have some political supporters already on hand. We have tremendous press exposure. Hotch must have a chance to become not only a household word but a face to go with it.'

'I agree with that. But to go on the campaign trail for ten months? It's scary.'

'Just think. Monday he makes his announcement. Tuesday you make yours. Wednesday he will be in Dallas for the opening of the new Merchandise Mart there.'

Lowenthal smiled. 'It'll knock Fitz on his Irish blueblood ass.'

'And send the competition into a panic. Who will throw

down the gauntlet first? Which one will try to follow his lead? The old-timers cannot afford the public exposure for too long. They have already made their views known. They will become boring and die of attrition.'

'There's still Fitzgerald.'

'We have some surprises for him, too. How do you think this Fitzgerald will react when he discovers we do not need his money?'

'He won't believe us.'

'Good. When he finds out it will be too late.' DeLaroza leaned forward and lowered his voice. 'The planning is done already. It is totally computerized. Every state, every county, every city, demographically charted. Voting histories recorded. Voting records of party leaders recorded. Complete dossiers on prospective competitors. We can tell you how much it will cost to have a barbecue in Topeka, Kansas, next year. Availability of assembly halls. Key political dates. Everything you need to know, available with a press of the finger.'

Lowenthal was impressed. 'Well . . .' he started and then stopped.

'And now about you, sir. The Chinese have a proverb – "The beginning of wisdom is calling a thing by its right name." '

'In other words, let's be blunt?'

'Yes, let us be blunt.'

Here it comes, thought Lowenthal. *Now it's his turn.*

'What do you want out of all this?' DeLaroza said.

I'll outlast him, Lowenthal thought, *with word games.*

'I'm an idealist,' Lowenthal said. 'Idealists never want anything for themselves.'

'Hmm. I have always thought that an effective idealist is one who gets what he wants in such a way that the public thinks he is doing them a favour by taking it.'

Lowenthal laughed. He held up his glass to DeLaroza. 'Good shot.'

'We were going to be blunt.'

All right, Lowenthal said to himself, *what the hell.*

'I want to be attorney general.'

DeLaroza settled back in his chair and slapped his hands together. 'Well, sir, that is what I call the beginning of wisdom. And what is the problem?'

221

'I don't think there is any. I'd make one hell of an attorney general.'

'No question about it. And as I see it, no competition. So, will you think about our plan to announce here on Monday? Sleep on it. We can talk in the morning, over breakfast. Donald should be back late tomorrow afternoon, hopefully with Senator Thurston's endorsement, and I am sure it will be the first thing he will want to know.'

Lowenthal nodded and lifted his glass again. 'To sleeping on it,' he said with a smile.

'No, sir. To victory.'

On the sixteenth floor of the Mirror Towers, DeLaroza's holding company, Internaco, maintained a guest apartment, a handsomely decorated suite, its silk-draped windows overlooking the city. There were two keys to the suite. One was given to the guest, the other was kept by the guard. After sending Lowenthal back to his hotel in his private limousine, DeLaroza took an elevator to the apartment. He stood outside the door listening for several moments and then very quietly slipped the guard's key into the lock and opened the door.

Howard Burns, standing in front of the windows, staring out through a cold haze that circled the city in the wind, was captivated by the city lights, which looked like hazy shards in a kaleidoscope. He heard the key enter the lock and the door open. He whirled, crouching as he did. The wine glass clattered off into a corner and the .22 Woodsman appeared in its place, like a coin in a magician's sleight-of-hand trick.

'It's me!' DeLaroza screamed, falling back against the door jamb.

Burns stared at him with a flash of white hate, his hands trembling, his trigger finger twitching in the steel guard. He stood that way for a very long time and then slowly bent his elbow and pointed the weapon at the ceiling. The hand was shaking. 'That's how close you came,' he said nodding to his hand. 'Walk in on me like that, from behind, no knock, no nothin'. Whatsa matter, you *crazy*?'

'I thought you'd be asleep. I thought after . . .'

'Asleep? Who you shittin', asleep? I'm high. I'm up there somewhere. I blew a chippie's head off an hour or two ago. Whadya mean, sleep?'

'I am sorry, I, uh, I don't know . . .'

'No, that's right. Somebody always does it for you. No powder burns on your lily whites, is there? Shit, lookit that, I spilled my fuckin' drink. *You don't walk in behind somebody!*'

'All right, all right.'

Burns went to the wet bar and poured himself another glass of Bertolucci red wine and plunked an ice cube in it. 'I seen that circus downstairs. I sneaked a look on the way up here,' he said.

DeLaroza stepped into the room and closed the door behind him. He wiped sweat from his forehead with the back of his hand.

'You oughta be sweatin', a dumbass play like that,' Burns said. 'Thirty years you stay clean, then all of a sudden you're gonna walk right out there on the trap door and spring the trap yourself. Whaddya want, me to tie the noose around your neck?'

'It's safe now. I have been working for this moment since 1945. The dangers have all been removed.'

'Bullshit.'

'Listen to me, Howard –'

'*Bull*shit. I scratch the colonel in Hong Kong, Corrigon shows up. I scratch Corrigon, there's the dame. Now she's outa the way, who's next, hunh? Who's gonna pop outa the box next? You think somewhere there ain't *some*body's gonna look at that face of yours and start thinkin' and then start rememberin'? Lemme tell ya, partner, I been livin' like that for seven years. A new name, new business, new place. Had to give up everything and live in Nebraska. Neb*raska* for Chrissakes. Shit, they don't even get all the fuckin' television stations in Nebraska. Took me two years to find a bookie. And with all that, see, with the Feds practically feedin' me with a spoon, I was waitin' every time I turned around to see somebody from the old life.'

'It is thirty years for me,' DeLaroza said, 'not nine. Nobody will recognize me. I do not even look like the same man.'

'I'd spot you in a minute, kiddo. That phony accent, red beard, all that fat, that wouldn't throw me.' Burns sipped on his wine, then added, 'You bring it down, I go down with it, know what I mean?'

223

'There is no way to put us together.'

'Oh no? How about those Chinks on the boat? The gook that picked me up tonight? How about the guard downstairs when we come in?'

'They have no idea who you are.'

'Well, they ain't blind, are they? One picture, pow! I'm made. They'll dump me, don't make no difference if I'm in Yokohama, Singapore, or the fuckin' South Pole, I'm a gone gosling.'

'Look, what you did with your life, I cannot do anything about that. I did something else. What you were is your business, what I am is mine.'

Burns turned his back to DeLaroza and stared out the window again. He said, 'This Domino, the one I burned, she was a hooker, you said.'

'A very high class hooker.'

'She have a pimp?'

'Well, I suppose you could call . . .'

'She had a pimp, right? And he didn't know about this Hotchins, this pimp didn't?'

'No. Nobody knew.'

'But he knows about you, right? He knows you knew her and he can tie you two together. All it takes is your name, they'll be knockin' at the door.'

'He will not do that. He will put them on to many others before that.'

'Shi-i-t. I gotta laugh.' He looked over his shoulder at DeLaroza. 'I been in the rackets all my life. Had a couple dozen buttons on my payroll at the time. Know what a button is, DeLaroza? A shooter. Very loyal people. But if the need comes up that one of them has to go quiet, there's only one way.'

'We can't keep killing.'

'Hah, that's my line. One goes, then another, then another. It don't stop. You take out the pimp, it'll be somebody else. Whyn't you leave it alone, keep yourself in the background. You got it made. All the power. All the money. The heavy friends. You're gonna blow it. You're gonna get us both killed.'

'You are getting melodramatic, my friend. That's ridiculous.'

'No, it's experience. Which you ain't got and that's what

224

scares me shitless.'

'You are safe, Howard, believe me.'

'You listen to me, see, because I been around a long time. I know how this system works. You gotta hit the pimp. Your people, well, okay, I can't go whackin' off half the population of China. But the pimp goes. You don't like it, that's too bad. I cover my own ass.'

'You can do it again, this soon?' DeLaroza said and there was a look of shocked disbelief on his face.

Burns smiled. He poured another glass of wine, plopped in another ice cube. 'You think it's real tough, don'tcha? That's funny.' He closed his eyes, remembering the way the room looked and her, her head haloed by the lamp, the perfect target. 'I forgot how good it was,' he said. DeLaroza's arms went numb. Burns kept talking. 'Up close like that, I was Dominic Scardi again, not some name I don't even know. You get your balls off thinking about all the people you control, all the money, all that power. Well so do I, baby. I get off too because I got power, right here in this hand, in this fuckin' *finger* I got it. I hold the vote. Yes, they live. No, they go down. You think that ain't power? When you see it in their eyes? You know what, partner? I had to change my underwear when I got back here. That's right. I shot off in my drawers. I always do. You take a little pill, it makes it even better. Works in two ways. It keeps you on top, see, keyed up, y'know. But it also makes coming that much better.'

He reached in his pocket for the other red devil. His fingers searched the corners of his pocket. It was gone. But where? He had had them both in the apartment. He tried to think back, remember where he had seen it last.

'Is something wrong?' DeLaroza asked. 'Did something go bad tonight?'

'Go bad. Did it ever go bad with me?'

'No, I can honestly say no to that.'

'You there, you're a little off your feed. Kinda sends you up when it happens, don't it?'

'No.'

'Who ya shittin', Victor? You ain't cut out for the real messy stuff. Anyways it's my thing, right? You make the money, I clean the cat box.'

DeLaroza turned towards the door. 'I guess I better get

back downstairs.'

'Don'tcha wanna hear about it?'

'Not really.'

'Boom, boom, just like that. The first shot took her straight on. Gorgeous. She saw it a second before she got it. The second one caught her as she was going down. Three feet, four feet – '

God, I hate him, DeLaroza thought. He was a pariah, a killing machine, enshrouded by death, and the carrion smell of his flesh filled the room.

' – quick and easy. I don't torture people there, Vic. It ain't my style. But the second before I squeezed it off, that's when it felt best. Waitin' just for that fraction of a second when they're between heaven and hell. You think that ain't power?'

DeLaroza said, 'Yes, I suppose so.'

Burn's lip curled back revealing his yellowing teeth. Suddenly there was hate burning in his eyes, too. 'Ya know somethin', Vic old boy? I was thinkin', on the way back over here with that Chink friend of yours. All these years I been hearin' about what a hot shit you are. Big brain. You been pullin' the strings, playin' the big cheese all over the world. You had me believin' all that shit, y'know. But if it wasn't for me, you wouldn't be nothin'. Just another dumb yokel kissin' ass someplace to get a five dollar raise. And when your eyes turned white, when you needed somebody pull the ol' trigger, you hadda come cryin' to me. When the tit was in the wringer, who did the dirty work? Me. And don't you forget it.'

'I never – '

'Don't say nothin', pal. Just put it in your scrapbook. Oh yeah, only one other thing, buddy-boy. There was a cop in the place.'

'A cop?'

'Take it easy. Don't panic. He was on the premises somewhere. I don't know exactly where. He was on top of me, just like that. I can't figure it out exactly. The shots, you couldn't hear twenty feet away. But he come into that stairwell three, four floors above me, like a bat outa hell.'

'Are you sure it wasn't the security guard?'

'Maybe, but that ain't what he said. He said *police.* "Stop, police!" That's the words he used. And he wasn't wearing no uniform. I still can't figure it out. Anyways he was yellin' and runnin', and I kept on rollin', out on the terrace there. I was reloaded already when the motherfucker came out. He was ten feet from me once. A young guy in a suede jacket carrying some kind of 9mm piece. All he hadda do was turn around once there, and pow, right in the gut. He was in a hurry though. I walked away from it clean. Nobody saw nothin', nobody heard nothin', just this fuckin' pig.'

Worms crawled deep in DeLaroza's gut. Burns was paranoid and it crept over him, suffocating him like a blanket.

'*Pachinko!* opens Monday night. Tuesday you go to Vancouver on my JetStar. That night you're on your way to Yokohama. Do not worry about the pimp. I'll take care of that.'

'Did you take care of that bet for me?'

'Ten thousand on Dallas.'

'How about the spread?'

'Seven points.'

'Good. So, the wine's beginning to get to me. Don't catch your asshole on the doorknob, okay?'

'Yes,' DeLaroza said and after he had left the apartment he leaned against the wall and closed his eyes, breathing like a man who had just run a very long way.

227

Chapter Fifteen

It was the hour of the ravens and Sharky's Machine prepared to invade the heart of darkness, seeking among the bookies, gamblers, pushers, strongarms, prostitutes, conmen, muggers and killers, those who could be cajoled or threatened into revealing the secrets of the night people.

Time. Time was against them. The hour was right, but the clock was their enemy. For though Friscoe had joined them (at first reluctantly, then after the discovery of the fingerprints, enthusiastically) they all knew the chase would end with Monday morning roll call. He would not be pushed farther than that.

'Remember,' a wise old cop told them, 'never trust a snitch. They're lepers. Give a squealer a piece of confidential info, he'll try to sell it to your partner twenty minutes later. You got to catch 'em with their hands full, get 'em on the hook, or needing help, then you can maybe trust 'em — for at least thirty seconds.'

The wise old cop was Friscoe, who operated on the theory that no matter how experienced his men were, no matter how much they knew, it never hurt to repeat good advice.

The plan was devised in Domino's apartment: Work fast, dig up what you can, bring in any scraps you get, rendezvous at the Majestic Grill at seven in the morning to begin putting the pieces together.

'Just don't waste time,' Friscoe said. 'If you got a lead and it starts to crap out, get off it, move to something else. What we ain't got, we ain't got time, see, to beat on any dead dogs. Let's see what a night's digging turns up. We ain't got anybody on base by morning, I say we flush it.'

Barret and Grimm headed to their respective laboratories. By ten P.M. Twigs had gathered up the remains of the victim in a body bag and moved it by freight elevator and his own station wagon to the morgue, where he eagerly went to work, prying into its vital organs.

Barret, alone in his lab working under a single lamp, pored over the scraps of physical evidence, beginning with the little red pill.

The Nosh returned to the OC, there to wire the two fingerprints from the top and underside of the commode handle to the FBI in Washington and to begin filtering out whatever voices existed on Sharky's tapes.

Friscoe hastily drafted a vice cop named Johnny Cooper and went in search of Tiffany Paris, hoping to begin an interrogation which might lift the veil of the mysterious Domino.

The apartment was sealed. Sharky would return later to check it out. For now, he would go with Livingston looking for information. The time was right.

Papa, who preferred to work alone, quietly went hunting.

As did Sharky and Livingston, cruising the night haunts, searching out the weak among the vipers.

Disco music thundered at Papa as he entered Nefertiti, the city's most hallowed night spot – at least for that week. Two leads had already gone down the toilet. Now he was looking for Leo Winter, a good old boy with an easy grin whose casual charm had dazzled more than one jury. There was only one problem – Papa had nothing in his pocket. Right now Leo was clean. It would have to be a bluff and Papa was not the best poker player in the world.

The maitre d', sartorially splendid in a cocoa-coloured tuxedo, stood at the inner entrance to the club, dwarfed by a tall image of the Egyptian queen that stared enigmatically down at the lobby through gleaming emerald eyes. He eyed Papa sceptically, starting at the black tie-up shoes, the rumpled suit, the faded blue shirt, and the outrageous tie which did not go with anything else he had on. His patronizing smile never went beyond his lips.

'Sorry, sir, full up in there,' he said. 'Could be thirty, forty minutes before there's any room in the bar. You might like to try a little place up the street – '

'I got a reservation,' Papa said and flashed his shield.

The maitre d' looked distressed. 'Is there going to be trouble?'

'I don't know. Are you expecting some?' Papa said and went into the club.

The interior was outrageous. The decor was Egyptian with music surging from enormous amplifiers hidden in two mummy cases at each end of the large room. Brass palm trees shimmered before its onslaught, hieroglyphics decorated the sconces, and the announcer worked the controlboard with the frenzy of a concert pianist, his booth nestled between the paws of an enormous sphinx that dominated one end of the room. Spotlights roved the club, while the dance floor, illuminated from below, seemed to pulsate with the beat of the music.

The place was jammed but Leo Winter was easy to spot. He was on the dance floor, moving casually with the beat, dancing with a blonde whose gothic chest, wrapped in see-through cotton, jogged in rhythm with the music.

Winter, a triangle of a man with bullish shoulders, hardly any waist, and large hands, was dressed in a yellow leisure suit, brocaded at the collar and open to the waist, a gold chain with a charm the size of a manhole cover bouncing around his neck. As one record segued into another Winter and the woman returned to their table beside the dance floor. His eyes made an alert sweep of the room, passed Papa, then flicked back and lingered on him for a moment. The big cop jerked his head towards the door, turned, and went outside.

He stood near his car in the parking lot, outside the perimeter of light around the flamboyant entrance, with his hands stuffed in his pockets, protecting them against the frigid night wind that had chased away the rain. Winter emerged a few minutes later and joined him, the wind rippling through tight curls on his head. He held his jacket closed with one hand.

'Hi, Cowboy,' he said to Papa.

'How's it going, Leo?' Papa said.

'Right now I'm freezing my ass off. This gonna take long?'

'Depends on you.'

'Uh oh. I got some trouble I don't know about?'

Papa shook his head. 'Information.'

Leo's attitude changed. His body tightened and seemed to grow an inch. He stood with one shoulder towards Papa, staring into the dark parking lot.

Papa said, 'I'm gonna tell you something and you're gonna forget it as soon as I tell you. Then I'm gonna ask you something. Then we'll go from there.'

Leo continued to look into the darkness.

'First off, you know a fancy pros calls herself Domino?'

Leo thought about the question, then said, 'Is this a freebie or can we do a little trading?'

'Leo, I got this big problem. I'm runnin' outa time and I ain't even got started good yet. Can we talk about Domino or not?'

Leo rubbed his shoulder with his free hand then shrugged. 'I've seen her here and there.'

'You know her pimp?'

'You mean, do I know him or are we asshole buddies?'

'I mean, do you know him? That's what I mean.'

'I know him. We're not thick.'

'I got Neil. I need the rest of the name and an address.'

Leo looked down at his foot, tapping his toe gently against the car tyre. 'This Neil, is he in trouble?'

'Maybe.'

'Bad trouble?'

'If he's in trouble, it's bad trouble.'

'You're a regular encyclopedia of facts there, Papa.'

'If you ain't wrap-around pals, what's the difference?'

'Yeah, I suppose there's something to that. Okay, his name's Dantzler. He lives out on Peachtree in The Courtyard.'

The name struck a bell. Papa's mind dug back as he kept talking.

'The apartments?'

'Dantzler lives in a condo.'

'How about Tiffany? What do you know about her?'

'You're really fishin', ain't you, Papa. From here I'd say you don't know shit for sure.'

'If I did, would I be here?'

'You got a point.'

'So?'

'So, Tiffany's Dantzler's old lady. She lives in the apartment complex out there, but mostly she uses her pad for tricks. Whenever Dantzler snaps his fingers, she's up at his place with her legs spread.'

Now Papa remembered why Dantzler's address had ticked off his memory bank. It was the same complex as Tiffany's. 'You mean this Dantzler pimps for his own girlfriend?'

231

'You got it. Real sweetheart, right?'

'Okay, gimme the package on this shmuck.'

'Dantzler's a scam artist. Rich kid. His old man took a bath in real estate about ten years ago, got in the shower, and emptied his brains out with a .45. All Dantzler had goin' for him was a shaky pedigree and a smooth mouth. A pretty boy, y'know? He played off his country club connections and worked some fast deals but he got in trouble with the state over some pyramid scheme he had goin' and he dropped outa sight for awhile. When he came back up, he has this Tiffany in tow, and she's a real piece, not just your everyday low-class honey, know what I mean?'

'And he was pimping for her?'

'More than that. Dantzler's living with her and pimping too, and she's turning three, four-hundred a night tricks with his uptown friends and the fat-wallet out-of-towners. But she doesn't quite have it, okay? Then a couple of years ago Dantzler pops Domino outa the closet. She was like a super version of Tiffany. More of everything and a class act, to boot. At first she was kind of shy and Tiffany got the soreass, but then this Domino sprouts wings, man, a real angel, and she kinda has a soft spot for Tiffany, so they end up tighter than a fat couple in a single bed. Domino won't have anything to do with any of the other street people – didn't want to and didn't. But all of a sudden you see her everywhere, dressed like she come off a magazine cover. Let me tell ya, Papa – this lady, when she walks in a room even the clock stops tellin' time. A very selective lady and smart as a kick in the ass. The way it comes to me, she doesn't like the trade, she packs it in and goes home. Left more than one big spender with his thumb in his ear.'

'But Dantzler was pimping for her?'

'Sure. He's got the connections. He's got the ins.'

'And Domino is independent?'

'You know it. A no-shit lady. Even starts shaping up Tiffany. In fact, the way I get it, Tiffany's got another old man on the side and this Domino covers for her all the time. I mean, shit, man, how long could anybody put up with that little mama's boy?'

'But Domino gives Dantzler a hard time, right?'

'Hey, c'mon Papa, between the two chicks Dantzler must be knockin' down fifteen, sixteen a week after the split and no tax. Does that sound like hard times to you?' He paused for a minute, then said, 'I thought you were gonna give me something I got to forget.'

'Okay, here it is. Somebody put this Domino on ice about four hours ago.'

'*Hunh!*'

'Right in the doorway of her apartment. And from my end of the street it wasn't no amateur hit.'

Leo looked hard at Papa and a scowl crossed his face. 'Are you tellin' me there was paper out on her? You tellin' me that?'

'I'm tellin' you somebody staked out her apartment for several hours and then punched her out with a sawed-off shotgun. Does that sound like amateur night to you?'

Leo whistled softly through his teeth, then shook his head. 'Bad news.'

'If this goes any further there, Leo, I'll be back out and step all over those pretty Mary Janes of yours.'

'Did I tell you it stops with me? Did I tell you that or not?'

'Just so it's clear.'

'You put me in a funny kinda box, Papa.'

'How's that?'

'Let's just say this was a local contract, okay? And it wasn't run past me first. Then I would be very unhappy with some people. Like if a local shooter took this on, I would want to know it's comin' down. And if there was any hotshot freelancers around, I would know that, too. Now I'm not saying I'd have anything to do with that kind of action, okay. What I'm saying is, there are courtesies and out of courtesy it would come to me and I would say no, or maybe I would say it ain't any of my business.'

'What you're saying is the shooter is an out-of-towner.'

'What I'm saying is if the shooter *isn't* an out-of-towner, it's going to hit the fan. I mean there's going to be a shit storm that'll make Hurricane Alice look like somebody sneezed.'

'Could you gimme a guess why it happened?'

'Papa, I never got closer than ten feet to the lady. Couple of months ago I came up a heavy winner in a poker game and Dantzler lost his ass. I took his marker for five bills. I offered to trade it out for a night with Domino and *she* nixed it, not him. Maybe, you know, she thumbed her nose

233

at the wrong guy.'

'You hear anything about Dantzler and Tiffany juicing some tourist recently?'

Leo began to laugh. 'Jesus, you sure want a lot for your nickel, don't ya?'

'Leo, how long we known each other?'

'Too long.'

'Did I ever stand short on you?'

'No, I can't say that.'

'So when I tell you time is short, I mean time is short. We do my problem, then we do yours. Now tell me about this shakedown.'

'A few weeks ago Dantzler shows up with a new Ferrari. And he buys up my marker and generally settles up around town. So I ask him, "What did you do, hit a bank or something?" and what he says is this: "Tiffany and me found ourselves a turkey in a ten-gallon hat." So I says, "Was Domino in on it?" And he says, "Don't I wish! If I could get Domino in on it I could retire." The figure I heard was fifty g's. The way he was throwin' money around, I believe it.'

'So Domino was *not* in on it.'

'I don't know how to say it, but she was a very classy lady. I don't think she'd get her hands dirty in that kind of action.'

'Shit, she's . . . she was a hooker, Leo.'

'You asked me, I'm tellin' you. If I was making book on this question, I would give odds she didn't know a thing about it, and if she did, she would have given Dantzler the long goodbye.'

'Could she maybe have found out about it and given Dantzler some trouble?'

'I see where you're goin' with this. Let me tell you, this Dantzler's got balls the size of a blackhead. Phony paper, pyramids, pimping, that's his style. He don't have the guts to step on an ant – or ask anybody else to. Anyway, even if he had it in mind, you know, he would have known to run it past me and I would have kicked his ass all the way to Alabama for even thinking about it. No, you can scratch Dantzler. He might be able to tell you why he thinks it was done, but he didn't have a thing to do with it. That's my opinion.'

'So I end up exactly nowhere.'

'No, you end up with a travellin' hit man on your hands. If you want to come down on Dantzler, it's going to have to be for something else.'

Papa nodded. 'Okay. I want you to do this for me. I want you to listen around and if you hear anything, *any*thing about this gambit, you give it to me. And if you hear anybody outside the Vice Squad askin' questions about Domino or Dantzler or any of that crowd, you get on the horn to me.'

'You want me to let you know if I get pneumonia from standing out here?'

'You wanna run around half naked that's your problem.'

'Okay, but I got another problem.'

'I'm listening.'

'I got married a couple of weeks ago. Maybe you heard.'

'You got a problem all right but there ain't anything I can do about it.'

Leo laughed again. 'It ain't her, it's her brother. He got dumped for running a red light and they turned up two lids of reefer in the car. It was strictly for personal use. The kid doesn't push dope.'

'Two ounces for personal use?'

'So he smokes a lot, what do I know? He's twenty. You know how it is when you're twenty. You don't do anything in moderation.'

'You need to have a heart-to-heart with the kid.'

'I already did. What it is, they hit him with felony possession.'

'Anything over an ounce, the law says you're pushing.'

'Look, the kid's okay. Anyway, I only been married a month, I'd like to give the old lady a little delayed wedding present, know what I mean?'

'This kid's first time out?'

'He got caught in a little bust here about a year ago. A bunch of kids were selling tax-free cigarettes they brought in from North Carolina. They must have cleared all of twenty bucks.'

'Careless son of a bitch, isn't he?'

'He's not real bright.'

'Okay. I got a pal just off the Narcs. I'll talk to him.'

'Whatever you can do.'

'I can maybe work it out for a suspended sentence. He'll have to do about six months probation or so, cough up a couple of yards for the fine.'

'That's okay. Maybe a little probation'll straighten him out. I can handle the fine.'

'Okay, Leo, we got a deal Just keep in touch. Keep your ear close to the ground for the next forty-eight hours or so.'

'That's cool.'

'And forget you heard anything about Domino from me or anybody else.'

Leo's eyebrows rose. 'Who's Domino?'

A harsh chilling wind had replaced the rain, turning dirt in the gutters into dervishes as Livingston cruised down the dark streets. Beside him, Sharky stared silently through the windshield, his mind assaulted by nightmare demons – the what ifs and maybes, all the ways he might have prevented Domino's death. In the brief time he had seen her, talked to her, listened to her make love to another man, in those few hours she had touched a place deep inside him nobody had ever touched before. He knew it was crazy. But it was a reality he could not escape and the reality tortured him.

'Okay,' Livingston said after several minutes of silence, 'what the hell's eatin' you?'

The question shook Sharky back to the present.

'All of it,' he said. 'The whole thing.'

'Got to kick that monkey, m'friend.'

'Yeah.'

They drove another block without words.

'I got this, this, uh, lump in my gut, like a bad meal layin' down there,' Sharky said. 'Like maybe I'm missing something.'

'Hunch, hunh?'

'Maybe. Yeah, could be that.'

'Really got to you, didn't she?' Livingston said. 'Got to thinkin' about it, right? Wonderin' what a five-hundred-dollar piece was like.'

Sharky felt himself bristling. *It wasn't like that*, he felt like saying, but then he began thinking about it, remembering how he had felt, listening to her making love the night

236

before. He felt cold and he huddled deeper into his suede pullover.

'Yeah,' he said finally, 'she really got to me.'

'I been in Vice a long time, Shark. Too long. Seen lots of fancy tricksters come and go. I done my share of wondering, too. All of us have. I mean, if you *didn't* think about it, it wouldn't be natural.'

'It's more than that.'

'What? You talkin' about duty, that kinda shit? Listen here, you're a cop, you ain't God. You make mistakes just like everybody else. Only trouble is, in our business a man can take an extra cup of coffee, fall asleep at the wrong moment, make a bad guess, it ends up disaster for somebody. You learn to live with it or get out. You're gonna make a fuckin' mistake now and then, you can't afford to, but you're gonna make 'em anyway. Couple of years ago a friend of mine named Tibbets lost a material witness. They had this cat under protective custody in a house off Highland Avenue and it all started comin' down on this guy, y'know, he got the shivers. So one night he goes to the can and hangs himself in the shower. Tibbets is twenty feet away watchin' a ball game. He never got over it, started in drinkin', two months later he blew his brains out. So what did that prove? We had already lost a witness. The court case went down the toilet. Then we lost a good cop and for what? We all human, baby. You start thinkin' otherwise, you're in deep trouble.'

'Keep reminding me of that, will you?'

'Okay. For now just put it aside. She's dead, man. That boat's sailed. What we need to be doin' right now is figure out where we goin', not where we been. Now would you like to hear a thought?'

'Anything at all.'

'These Mafiosi are usually big gamblers. It goes with the territory, y'know. Comes to me that maybe this shooter's found himself some local action. There ain't that many bookies around and if he's a heavy player, maybe we can get a line on him.'

'Terrific. Only trouble is, I wouldn't know where to place a fifty-cent bet on anything right now.'

'Well, I know a few bookmakers. What I'm gonna do,

I'm gonna quietly check with Whit Ramsey on the Gaming Squad, see if any new bookies are operatin'. Maybe we can shake somethin' outa their pockets.'

'Let's get it on then,' Sharky said. 'Pull over to that phone booth. You can touch base with Whit, I'll call Barret and see if he's turned up anything at the lab.'

'That's cool.'

It took Sharky a minute or two to get the night operator and another minute to get George Barret on the phone.

'Sharky, I haven't got much, but I just thought you'd like to know you were right about that little red pill. It's a red devil all right. Seventy per cent speed, thirty per cent nitroglycerine.'

Sharky whistled through his teeth. 'Jesus, that's pure dynamite!'

'I'd certainly agree with you. Blow a normal man straight through the roof. Whoever's using these is flirting with a coronary.'

'Anything else, George?'

'Well, they'd be highly addictive, if that helps. I'd say two or three a day at least.'

'Just a shit kicker, right? No medicinal value?'

'I miss the point.'

'Well, it wouldn't be the kind of thing maybe he'd have a prescription for?'

'Not unless the doctor that prescribed them is a homicidal maniac. No, this is not the kind of thing you would find on the medicine shelf. It's narcotics, period.'

'George, you're a winner. Got anything else?'

'Really, sir. I've just gotten started.'

'Talk to you later.'

He got back in the car. A moment later Livingston joined him.

'Got anything?' Livingston asked.

'Yeah. You ever heard of red devils?'

'Some kind of upper, right?'

'Upper is right. You could launch a rocket with one of them. Our shooter was probably using. And if he was, Barret says he's more than likely addicted.'

'You're gonna have a hell of a time trackin' down every pusher in town that might be peddlin' this shit, ain't you?'

238

'Maybe not. I haven't seen any red devils on the street in a year or two. Too expensive. They go down for about five bucks a pop.'

'Jesus, you can do smack for that kind of money.'

'Different kind of high. Point is, maybe they were specially ordered. That would narrow the field a bit. How about you?'

'I got three names, M'man Ramsey says if these three juicers ain't bookin' him and he's a big player, then he's using a phone contact somewhere else. And I know one of these guys. We grew up together. I can always finger him, so I figure we try to run down the other two first, save old Zipper until last.'

'Zipper?'

'Got a scar down his back at least a foot long. I grew up in a rough neighbourhood.'

'Okay, but first let me try one more call.'

Ben Colter had worked his way through Georgia State University playing 'Melancholy Baby,' 'One for the Road,' and other such classics for raucous salesmen and ageing divorcees in a red-and-black vinyl lounge called Mona's Piano Bar. It was a job he had learned to hate passionately while staring out across the elongated piano six nights a week at faces he later said had only two expressions, drunk and desperate. The day he received his diploma he swore he would never again play the piano, not even in the solitude of his own home. The world had heard his last rendition of 'My Way'.

Retirement from the keyboard, however, was not in the cards for Ben. After serving six months as a rookie on the APD and two years and three months as a patrolman, Colter was promoted to third grade detective and assigned to Captain Vernon Oglesby in Narcotics. Oglesby was a competent officer, but he had a flaw. He was intrigued by intrigue. Because he loved the drama of subterfuge, Oglesby had more men on the street undercover than he had on straight duty. Any excuse at all and Oglesby would put another man out with phony I.D.'s and some new and flamboyant cover.

Colter was made to order for Oglesby. His presence on the Narcs summoned forth one of the captain's most outrageous ideas. Colter's past had caught up with him. He would form a trio and the Captain would arrange for the group to play at the Arboretum, one of the city's more popular uptown bars, there to get the inside on the dope traffic among the better-heeled swinging singles.

Within four weeks, an appalled Colter found himself the leader of the Red Colter Trio, the other two members being a hastily drafted teenage drummer who thought he was Buddy Rich and a guitar player who, as one of the patrons once observed, probably could make better music picking cotton than guitar.

Nevertheless the trio was modestly successful and Ben Colter, to his joy, discovered a marvellous fringe benefit: flesh. The ladies were young, liberated, and among the best looking in town. Hardly a night passed that the latent groupie instincts of some female patron were not vested in Colter's corner. They always had a little Colombian weed and occasionally a snort of coke to share. Ben properly excused his transgressions as part of the job and one night he had experienced his first amyl nitrite popper, later likening the resulting orgasm to a combination of the Mount Vesuvius eruption and the San Francisco earthquake.

Almost as a side benefit of the job Colter became an expert on the latest hip talk, the ultimate styles, the fashionable drugs – pot, Quaaludes, coke, poppers – anything that stimulated bedtime organs, heightening the allure and dulling the uneasiness of the one-night stand. He also was compiling an impressive list of the uptown pushers, those who made their contacts at the crowded Arboretum Bar and delivered their dream cigarettes and nose candy in the seats of the Mercedes, Corvettes, and baby Cadillacs that nightly filled the parking lot.

On this particular Friday night Colter was feeling very lucky indeed. A young woman in a black skintight jumpsuit zipped down the front almost to her navel and bulging with incredible natural endowments was sitting just below the bandstand where for an hour or so she had been staring at Colter without even blinking her eyes.

Colter was stirred. He was also encouraged by her escort, a thirtyish loudmouth who obviously thought he was still in a fraternity. His size indicated that he had probably played either guard or tackle, although what had once been muscle

240

had long since congealed into blubber. For an hour he had been extolling the virtues of the Auburn University War Eagles while quaffing down one bottle of Bud after another, swallowing the contents in a single long, horrifying gulp until eventually the beer took its toll. The War Eagle rose, his face the colour of a bishop's vestments, and headed unsteadily towards the men's room.

Now is the time to strike, thought Colter, and abruptly ended his version of 'Take the A Train' while his two partners floundered hopelessly in mid-chord. As Colter hit the floor a waiter handed him a note.

'Guy says it's urgent,' the waiter said.

The note said: 'Sharky. P-929-1423.'

The *P* was a simple code for phone booth. The call was indeed urgent.

Colter smiled at the jumpsuit zipper and winked, then hurried across the room to the public phones.

Sharky answered on the first ring.

'Sharky?' Ben said.

'Yeah. That you, Ben?'

'Yeah, man. How ya doin'?'

'I've had better days.'

'I heard what The Bat did to you for icing High Ball Mary. That dumb shit. For what it's worth, Shark, I think we lost the best street man we had.'

'Thanks, Ben. How's it with you?'

Ben wasn't listening. The girl in the jumpsuit was leaning over, saying something to one of the other girls at the table.

She's comin' over here, thought Colter. *I know she's comin' over here. I gotta get off the phone.*

'Uh, what did ya say, buddy? It's loud as hell in this place.'

'I said, how ya doin'?'

'Oh, yeah, man. It's a drag, y'know, a real drag.'

She was getting up, looking his way. A bead of sweat popped out between Colter's eyes.

'Ben, I need some help.'

'Okay, name it.'

Here she comes.

'When's the last time you saw any red devils on the street?'

'Red devils,' Colter repeated and then looked frantically

around for fear someone had heard him. 'Red devils,' he said, lowering his voice. 'Shit, nobody buys red devils anymore. Who's gonna lay out five bucks a pop, when you can get good uppers for two bits?'

She had caught the wind and was in full sail, coming straight at him, her course irreversible. He had to get off the phone. The sweat was now dribbling down the side of his nose.

'What I need, Ben, is a line on a pusher, somebody out in your territory who maybe scored very big in red devils in the last two, three weeks.'

'Two or three weeks,' Colter repeated, watching the jumpsuit slink closer.

A customer reached out and took her by the arm. But she looked down, said something terminal, and he dropped his hand.

'Red devils, hunh?' Ben said. 'Lemme see, that could be, you know, three or four shovers I know of. Gimme an hour, I'll see if I can pin it down without blowing my cover.'

'Thanks. Should I call you?'

'Use the squad room drop. Give em a number at . . . eleven o'clock. I'll call in and get it.'

'That's cool, Ben. And thanks.'

'Any time, buddy. Later.'

He hung up. She was three feet away, staring up at him with eyes that looked like they had dust in them.

'Lining up your dance card for the rest of the night?' she said. The voice was perfect.

'I just broke all my plans until after the holidays,' Colter said.

'Aren't I the lucky one?'

War Eagle came out of the men's room with tears in his eyes, wiping his tie with a paper towel. A blast of heat and noise hit him like a tidal wave. His cheeks bulged and he turned and fled back through the door.

'I bet you're gonna need a ride home tonight,' Colter said.

'Nope,' she said, 'he is.'

'I'll call a cab.'

The Nosh leaned intently over the controls of his electronic magic set, a carefully organized series of tape recorders, filters, rerecorders, and other electronic hardware that looked like a small radio station. He was in his glory, punching buttons, twisting dials, hunched under padded earphones as he worked to lift the voices from one of Sharky's tapes.

He looked up suddenly, startled by the appearance in the doorway of Sergeant Anderson. The Nosh felt sorry for Anderson, a man beaten down by life, his hair an ugly tangle of grey, his shoulders sagging under the weight of an unhappy marriage. Anderson seemed always to be around, offering help where it wasn't needed and advice where it wasn't wanted. The squad room was his home. He remained there, night after night, until he was too tired to stay awake or until he ran out of excuses to avoid going home.

The Nosh pulled off the earphones.

'Give you a hand?' Anderson said.

'Nah. Thanks anyway.'

'Coffee or something?'

'Thanks anyway, Sarge.'

'What you up to, anyway?'

'Just giving Vice a hand. A little wiretap operation.'

The tape was still running and a cacophony of sound emerged from the loudspeaker. A combination of soft music and cries of passion.

'What in God's name is that?' Anderson asked.

The Nosh giggled. 'Sounds like a Chinese orgy,' he said.

'Well, I'll be around a while longer if you need anything.'

'Tell you what, Herb. I got a fingerprint report coming in on the telex from the Bureau. If you hear the bell ring, gimme a call, will ya?'

'Glad to,' Anderson said and smiled, grateful for something to do. 'But they won't come in with anything before morning, will they?'

'I tagged *urgent* on it and I got a flash back. They're gonna pull the package for me tonight, if there's anything to pull.'

'Okay,' Anderson said. His curiosity was aroused, but before he could pursue the subject further, The Nosh said, 'If you should run out of the house for anything, you might swing by Grady morgue. Twigs has a tape over there for me.'

The coroner had called a few minutes earlier to report that he had completed the autopsy on Domino. But, he had added, there was little in the post mortem that would help the Machine.

'I'll just go on over now,' Anderson said. 'I need a little air.' And he left.

The Nosh slipped the earphones back on and was immediately lost in his electronic fantasy world. *Somewhere in that Chinese orgy*, he thought, *there's a word or two, something, that'll make sense to somebody*. All he had to do was lift them out, get rid of the background noise. Eagerly he returned to his dials.

Sharky was stamping his feet in a phone booth near the Peachtree-Battle shopping centre when the phone rang. He lunged for it.

'That you, Sharky?' Ben Colter asked.

'Right.'

'I got lucky.'

'Good! Give it to me.'

'There's a pusher named Gerald Lofton, a regular in the place. I got enough shit on this guy to bury him. But I can't move on him yet. There's a lot more where that came from. Anyway, right after you called, Lofton came in and we had a drink together and I moved the subject around to speed. I mentioned a friend of mine in Chicago told me something about red devils and was he hip to them and Lofton's eyes lit up like a church steeple and he tells me red devils are dynamite but expensive. Then he tells me a friend of his just moved – are you leaning on something?'

'I'm leaning on something.'

'Fifty pills. At ten bucks a jolt!'

'Ten bucks!'

'I say this buyer must work for the mint and Lofton tells me he don't know who the big score was, but during the conversation he dropped the name of the connection.'

'And . . .'

'The pusher's a first-class asshole who uses the name Shoes.'

'Shoes? Like on your feet?'

'Right. Shoes. Anyway this Shoes, you gotta watch him. What he does, he plays the redneck joints out near Inman

Park on payday. Does some heavy over-the-counter trade in pills and even some nickel bags.'

'The red-devil buy was made in Inman Park?'

'No. He also has some select clientele out this way.'

'What's he look like?'

'Hell, you won't have any trouble there. Tall, all bones. Has long white hair, almost like a high yellow, only he's white. Dresses like a cowboy. Also he never holds. He usually pays a teenager or some wino to carry the shit for him. He makes the deal, goes out in an alley, puts the stuff in a paper bag, and then the customer picks it up from the decoy. By that time Shoes is half a block away.'

'Neat.'

'Tonight's a good night to dump him. It's payday.'

'Good.'

'What's comin' down, anyway? I thought you got dumped off the dope squad?'

'I did. This is something else. In fact you can do me a favour and forget we even talked.'

'That's cool. One more thing about this Shoes. He was dropped twice in New York state, both felonies. The last time he did a nickel-dime and went thirty-three months before parole. He'd put his own mother on ice to stay out of the slams. But Oglesby doesn't want him busted right now. He's hoping the son of a bitch'll lead us upstairs.'

'Thanks, Ben.'

'Anytime, Shark. Everybody on the squad owes you one. You took a bad rap. Anyone of us woulda done the same thing in your boots. I guess we're all just glad it wasn't us The Bat dumped on.'

'See you in the lineup, Ben.'

Sharky returned to the car.

'We scored,' he said to Livingston. 'You know a pusher does the country-music scene name of Shoes?'

'Nope.'

'Tall. Beanpole. Mulatto-white hair. Dresses like a rodeo rider.'

'Sounds like we could make him in the dark.'

'He just dumped fifty red devils on somebody at ten bucks a hit.'

'Holy shit!'

'Yeah.'

245

'Well, you wanna take him first or visit my friend Zipper?'

Livingston had struck out on the first two bookies. He was obviously losing faith in his hunch. Sharky decided he deserved to run his string out first.

'Let's do your guy first. Mine'll be around till they turn the streetlights off.'

'You got it.'

He turned the red light on and went down Peachtree Street to Spring and then into the middle of the city with his foot on the floor. Sharky casually hooked up his safety belt as they screamed in and out of traffic past the Omni complex, a cluster of tall buildings that included a hotel and a sports arena. Livingston turned into the city viaduct and went down to Hunter Street where he turned again. Six blocks later he pulled up to the kerb. A block ahead of them was a low, squat building joined like a Siamese twin to a three-storey indoor parking garage. A sign flashed on and off over the building, announcing that it was the Lucky Strike Bowling Alley.

'We'll hoof it from here,' Livingston said. They got out of the car and locked it. The street was filled with festive black men in fur coats and Borsalino hats with laughing ladies on their arms. Sharky and Livingston walked towards the bowling alley.

'Let's do this my way, okay?' Livingston said. 'I grew up here. It's my turf. I know every crack in the sidewalk.'

'Whatever you say.'

'Here's the set-up. A long mall with the bowling alley at the end. Twelve alleys all together. When you go in, there's a lunch counter on your right and a concession stand on your left. The mother-fucker running the concession stand owns the place, but you'd never know it. He's uglier than a cross-eyed kangaroo and twice as mean. What I need is for you to get his attention long enough for me to come in behind him and freeze him. He's got buttons under the counter. If he gets nervous, he'll blow the whole play on us. Go down in there, okay? Walk along the alleys until you're right in front of the fuckin' concession stand, then walk straight back to it and lose some time there. Buy a candy bar, anything. If he gets nervous, put him on ice. Stick that 9 mm of yours right up his nose, otherwise he won't think you're serious. When I make my play, gimme some room and do exactly as I say, okay?'

'I got it.'

'Good. Let's give it a try and see what happens.'

Sharky went down the mall and stopped behind the chairs of the middle alley. A tall teenage black gave him a dirty look, then went back to his game. Sharky moved slowly along the alleys, aware of the concession stand to his left but not looking directly at it. When he was in front of the stand, he turned and strolled straight back to it.

The man behind the counter was the size of a warehouse with arms like two sides of beef. Thick lips were wrapped around the short end of a cigar which had gone out hours before. An earring glittered in one ear. He wore a tweed cap pulled down over his forehead and a black tee-shirt with a black-power fist emblazoned in the middle of it.

He eyed Sharky as though he were a cockroach walking across the counter.

'Alley's full,' he said as Sharky leaned on the countertop.

'Got any Good 'N' Plenty?' Sharky said. Behind the man with the earring, Livingston entered a side door and moved quietly towards the concession stand.

The black man leaned on the opposite side of the glass countertop. His eyes were not as bored as he wanted them to seem. One arm dropped to his side, dangling near a drawer under the candy shelf.

'Nope. Try the drugstore for that fancy shit.'

Livingston reached the other side of the counter. 'Easy, Cherry,' he said. The owner's face went blank, then he smiled, a gold tooth twinkling in the front of his mouth.

'Yes, suh,' he said without turning around. 'How they hangin', Sergeant?'

'Hangin' full, babe. What's happenin?'

'Not a thing, not a thing. Just hangin' around, right?'

'Right. That's my friend Sharky. Say hello.'

Cherry kept on smiling. 'Hello, brother,' he said.

Livingston walked to the side of the counter and lifted a hinged section of the countertop and stepped inside. He ran a nimble hand down one side of Cherry's body and up the other, extracting a stubby .25 calibre pistol.

'I got a permit for that, Sergeant.'

'I'm sure you do.' Livingston opened the drawer and ran his hand along the top of the space. He smiled. Cherry smiled.

'Now how we gonna do this, Cherry?' Livingston said. 'You gonna keep that drawer closed and stay over there while I go upstairs, or am I gonna take this whole fuckin' counter apart?'

'Don't do that, Sergeant.'

'Then it's cool, dig?'

'Gotcha,' Cherry said and moved away from the drawer with his hands resting on top of the counter.

'Just stay right there. Sharky and I are gonna go over there by the Coke machine and have a chat.'

They went to the Coke machine and Livingston dropped in two quarters. He gave one of the soft drinks to Sharky.

'See the door over there, about halfway down the first alley?'

Sharky looked over at the door. A red exit sign glowed over it.

'Okay.'

'I'm goin' through that door. You stay here and make sure Cherry don't break the rules. If he gets fancy, bust him up alongside the head and make it good. He's got a head as hard as h.ɔ bowling balls.'

'Got it.'

'Anybody gives you any shit, show them some bronze. Then wait for me.'

Sharky nodded. He went back to the concession stand and watched Arch Livingston walk to the red exit door, his hands loose at his sides, striding on the balls of his feet like a prizefighter.

Sharky smiled at Cherry. 'Just you and me, pal,' he said and Cherry said, 'Right, brother. You and me.'

Livingston disappeared through the door.

Livingston stepped cautiously through the exit door into what was the second floor of the parking garage. The entrance was one deck below on a side street. A noisy car elevator dominated the core of the building, surrounded by numbered parking places. Most of them were full. From somewhere close by, Stevie Wonder's plaintive voice lamented the sorrows of 'Livin' for the City'.

Livingston moved slowly along the rows of cars, holding his .38 down at his side. The music grew louder. He stopped behind a pale green Lincoln. A black man wearing a floppy white hat and a silver grey full-length suede coat sat in the front seat with the door open, beating his knees in time with the music, a .32 Special lying on the dashboard a few inches from his hands.

Livingston moved around the car until he was directly behind the gunman. It was then he recognized him as a young tough named Elroy Flowers. 'Keep your hands on your knees and – '

He never finished. Flowers moved unexpectedly and with the agility of a greyhound, swinging both legs out of the door as he reached for his pistol. It was a mistake. Livingston slammed the car door, smashing Flowers's ankles between the door and the jamb, and swung his pistol in a wide overhead arc down on top of Flowers's head. The felt hat deadened the blow but not enough. The half-conscious gunman grunted, reaching out blindly with one hand and knocking the pistol to the floor of the car.

Livingston grabbed a handful of Flowers's shirt and coat, swung him out of the car, spun him around, and slammed him against the hood. He put the flat of his hand against Flowers's head and shoved him hard into the window of the Lincoln.

The window cracked and Flowers's eyes went blank. He sighed and dropped straight to the floor. Livingston dragged him by his shirt front across the floor and into the car elevator, dropping him face down on the metal floor. He pushed the up button and then jumped off the elevator and ran across the parking deck to the fire steps, taking them two at a time as he raced to the third floor.

The elevator shuddered, groaned, and started rising. On the third floor another black man was leaning against the fender of a cream-coloured Rolls-Royce. He was bigger, more dangerous, than Flowers, a blockhouse of a man in a dark blue suit. He was reading a racing form which he tucked under his arm as the elevator started up. He walked casually towards it. Behind him Livingston stepped through the third-floor door and leaned against the back of a parked car, holding his .38 in both hands and aiming it at the centre of the big man's back.

The big man peered down into the slowly rising elevator and saw Flowers lying on the floor.

'Hunh?' he said. His hand slipped under his coat, reaching for his armpit.

'Don't do nothin' stupid, nigger,' Livingston yelled. 'I got softnose loads in this piece.'

The big man turned towards him but kept his hand inside his jacket.

'Bring it out slow and easy, motherfucker. You do anything sudden, I put a hole in your belly big enough to park that Rolls in.'

The big man continued to stare. His hand stayed inside the coat. Doubt troubled his eyes as he calculated the odds.

'Don't get fancy, man. I'm the heat and I don't miss.'

The rear window of the Rolls glided silently down and a voice that was part silk and part granite said, 'Okay, Steamboat, cool it. I'll talk to the man.'

The back door of the Rolls swung open. The man called Steamboat uncoiled and withdrew an empty hand.

Livingston peered over the .38 into the interior of the Rolls. It was a study in gaudy opulence. The seats were upholstered in mauve velvet with gold buttons. The floor was covered in ankle-deep white shag carpeting. Built into the back of the front seat were two white telephones, a bar and an icemaker. A bottle of Taittinger champagne sat on the bar shelf.

The man who sat in the corner arrogantly sipping champagne matched the decor. He was shorter than Livingston and looked younger, but he was beginning to show the signs of good living. His afro flared out, encircling his head like a halo, and his moustache was full and trimmed just below the corners of his mouth. He was wearing a dark-blue pigskin jacket, rust-coloured gabardine pants, and a flowered shirt open at the neck, the collar flowing out over the lapels of the jacket almost to his shoulders. Gold chains gleamed at his throat, diamonds twinkled on his fingers, a gold Rolex watch glittered from under one cuff. His mirror-shined shoes were light tan with three-inch hardwood heels. A white handkerchief flopped casually from his breast pocket. He stared at Livingston through gold-framed tinted glasses, then looked down at the .38 that was pointed at his chest.

'You mind, nigger?' he said, nodding towards the gun.

Livingston appraised the back seat, lowered his gun, and laughed.

'Shit,' he said, 'I could get you ten to twenty for what you done to this poor Rolls.'

'Get on in, goddammit. All my fuckin' heat's runnin' outa here.'

Livingston got in and pulled the car door shut.

'Been a long time, Zipper.'

'Ain't that the truth. Last time I saw you, you was wearin' a fuckin' monkey suit, sittin' in the front seat of a goddamn patrol car. Bi-i-ig shit.'

'Last time I saw you,' Livingston said, 'you were in Fulton Superior Court apologizin' for boosting car radios.'

'That long ago, hunh? Shit, time do fly. You mind tellin' me what the fuck all this Wild West shit's about, comin' in here, bustin' up my people, wavin' all that iron around? No need for that shit. You here to bust my ass?'

'This is a social call.'

'Shit. What d'ya do when you come on business, kill somebody?'

'Flowers went for his piece, man. You think I'm gonna stand around, let some dumb nigger blow my ass off?'

'He is a dumb fuckin' nigger, no question about that. Good help's hard to come by these days.' He looked through the car window. Steamboat was standing by the front of the car, watching. 'Now Steamboat's a whole nother case, baby. You fuck with Steamboat, you better have your plot paid for.'

'Used to fight, didn't he?'

'Light-heavy. Mean son-bitch. Cat's never been knocked out. Too slow was his fuckin' problem. He was instant death when he was in-fighting but the fast boys would lay out there, cut him to pieces at arm's length. You just let that motherfucker get in one good shot, though. Shit, they'd think they was run over by a goddamn freight train. What you want, nigger?'

'Told ya, man. It's a social call.'

'Un hunh. How long you knowed about this here travellin' bookie parlour of mine?'

'About three years.'

'Aww, don't shit me, nigger. We grew up on the same

251

fuckin' street, man, remember?'

'Look here, brother, long as you keep your operation clean, I ain't interested in bringing' anything down on you. You ain't connected. You strictly cash and carry, don't take no markers, so nobody gets their head stove in, any of that shit. I ain't in any rush to turn you up to some white dude on the Gamin' Squad just so's he can make some goddamn points. I'd rather know what you doin', Zipper, have some motherfuckin' stranger come in here bustin' nigger ass all over town, you dig?'

Zipper thought it over, then smiled.

'How about a little wine there, for old times' sake?'

'Thanks anyway, man. It gives me heartburn.'

'Heartburn! Man, that shit's fifty dollars a bottle. Ain't no fuckin' heartburn in this shit.'

'I'll still pass. I got a partner downstairs starin' down Cherry. I got to get back before they get bored, start hurtin' ass.'

'Okay, so get it on. What the fuck you doin' here?'

'I need some information.'

Zipper sat up as though he had been slapped. At first he seemed surprised, then surprise turned to anger.

'Shee-it.'

'Listen here, motherfucker . . .'

'Sheee-IT, man. What you handin' this nigger? Come in here, think you can . . . god*damn*, hey, Zipper ain't no fuckin' stoolie. Zipper don't rub ass with the heat. Man, you forgot where you came from.'

'You ain't changed a bit, sucker. Still put your fuckin' mouth up front of your brains.'

'Well, you changed, motherfucker. Shit, give a nigger a piece of goddamn tin and a peashooter, motherfucker thinks he's Father fuckin' *De*vine.'

One of the phones rang and Zipper snatched it off the hook. 'Closed for lunch,' he snapped. 'Call back in ten minutes.' He slammed the phone back.

'Look, I ain't interested in your goddamn bookmaking, I told you that. I got a problem and I think maybe you can help me with it. Now, the dude I'm lookin' for is white.'

'Shit,' Zipper said, 'I don't do no business with honkies. Ain't you heard? They's a lotta fuckin' rich niggers in Atlanta now.'

Livingston looked at the floor. 'You tellin' me you don't do business with whitey, I'm tellin' you I'm talkin' to one lyin' nigger. You takin' layoff bets from half the highpocket white bookmakers in town, Zipper, and I know it.'

'Layoff bets? Man, that's different. I don't see none of them turkeys. M'bagman picks up the takes, brings me the bread and the slip. Then he takes back what we lose. All I do, I count the money and put down the bets. I don't know any of them motherfuckers personal.'

Zipper poured another glass of champagne, huffing while he poured.

Livingston looked around the back seat, stared out the window, finally lit a cigar. He said, 'We gonna talk or are you gonna get that fuckin' hard head of yours dragged downtown and let a couple of white cats play good guy-bad guy with your ass?'

'I told you my position. Zipper don't hand out no shit to the fuzz. I don't care we was street brothers fifteen years ago.'

'I ain't here 'cause we ran together,' Livingston said. 'I'm here 'cause you got information I need. And I don't have time to fuck around.'

Zipper looked at Livingston with contempt. 'Know somethin'?' he said. 'You was one bad motherfucker. Nobody shit with you on the street, man. You bust ass. Now look at you. Two dollar fuckin' suit, wash 'n' wear shoes, honkie goddamn haircut. And you want me to turn fuckin' stoolie. I ain't believin' you, now.'

'Listen here, Zipper, and listen good. I ain't interested in your goddamn players. We're talking about murder.'

Zipper looked startled.

'That's right,' Livingston said. 'Murder. Now you keep your fuckin' yap shut until I finish. Cat I'm after is white. He's an outfit hitman, can you dig that? Last night this son-bitch burned a very nice lady. He's a fuckin' lady-killer. And you givin' me all this shit about protectin' his ass?'

Zipper said nothing. He stared into his champagne glass.

'This motherfucker woulda come into town a couple weeks ago. If he is a gamblin' man, he'd be a *big* gamblin' man. Sports, ponies, any national shit. Now you don't know anything about such a cat, okay. But if you do, Zipper, I got to know about it, 'cause man, we talkin' about rough trade here.'

'How come you so fuckin' sure this dude gambles?'

'I'm not. It's a hunch. But right now it's all I got.'

The car was quiet. Zipper cleared his throat. Then the phone rang again.

'Go ahead and talk,' Livingston said, 'I know you're a bookie. What the shit you so shy about?'

Zipper yanked the phone off the hook. 'Hello . . . Yeah, this Zipper. What it is? . . . It's Dallas and seven . . . Well, that's tough shit, turkey. That's the fuckin' spread and ain't nothin I can do about it. . . . Listen here, motherfucker, I don't make the odds. You don't like it, put your fuckin' money back in your goddamn shoe. Now, you want some action or don't you? . . . Well, fuck you too, nigger.' He slammed down the phone.

Silence again.

Finally Zipper said, 'Only one possibility. Only one possibility. Cat can't be your man. Can't be.'

'Who says?'

'I say. He makes book in a fag bar out Cheshire Bridge Road.'

'A fag bar?'

'That's right. This tough-nuts shooter you talkin' about queer?'

'Who is he?'

'Shit, I told ya, nigger. I don't have no truck with any of those fuckers personally. This joint, it's called, uh . . . this stays with us, that right?'

'C'mon, Zipper.'

'This joint is called, uh, the Matador. Got this pansy-lookin' bullfighter on the sign out front.'

'I know the place.'

' 'Bout five weeks ago my bookie friend out there, you know – he does nickel and dime shit out there, nothin' big, mostly local games – anyways, he calls me, says, do I want to take a layoff on the Oakland and Miami game? Fucker took the spread for five grand and lost his ass. Next week he's back again. Motherfucker doubles up, lays out ten grand on some NFL game and a basketball game, and splits. Been goin' like that ever since. Five, ten g's a clip. Right now I'm into him for about five thou.'

'When's the last time he bet?'

'Yesterday.'

'Yesterday?'

'You heard right, yesterday. He bettin' on the playoff. Took Dallas and the points over Minnesota. Ten big ones.'

'Zipper, I got to know who this player is.'

'No fuckin' way.'

'Just the name, man.'

'No motherfuckin' *way*. Shit, I told ya. I don't even know who it is. The bookie deals with the score and I deal with the bookie.'

'Okay, who's the bookie then?'

'C'mon, goddammit. You lean on him, he's gonna know I done it to him.'

'I'll cover your ass. Don't you worry about that. I ain't interested in the fuckin' bookie. I want his mark.'

'You *got* to cover my ass, Livingston. Tell you somethin'. You come down on this little motherfucker, he gonna die on the spot.'

'I'll do it right, man. Who is it?'

'The bartender. Name's Arnold.'

Livingston sighed. 'Jesus,' he said, 'that was worse than pickin' cotton with your goddamn feet.'

'Just don't fuck me over on this, hear? And don't come back with any more of this snitch shit either. I done made my contribution for life.'

Livingston started to get out of the car. 'Shit, motherfucker,' he said, 'my eyes couldn't stand any more of this pussywagon.'

Zipper's eyes flared. 'Pussywagon, *Pussy*wagon! Shit, you fuckin' no-class nigger, this car cost fifty grand. Fifty fuckin' thousand goddamn dollars. Ain't no goddamn Detroit pussywagon. Shit, I don't even scratch my balls when I'm in this machine. You hear me, Livingston?'

But the policeman was gone, down through the fire door towards the bowling alley below.

'Pussywagon, my ass,' Zipper growled, then he leaned out the door. 'Steamboat!'

'Yeah, boss.'

'Take that fuckin' dumbass to the Gradys and get his head stitched up and then fire his ass.'

At four A.M., Friscoe quit for the night. He drove home,

grumbling to himself, angry because he had turned up nothing at all in six hours of hard work. His back ached and his eyes burned as he entered the house, passing up his customary raid on the refrigerator and going straight to the bedroom. He went into the bathroom and closed the door before turning on the light so as not to awaken Sylvia, splashed cold water on his face, and sat on the commode to take off his shoes. He sighed with relief as he dropped them on the floor, then went back to the bedroom and sat on the edge of the bed, bone weary and almost too tired to get undressed.

His wife rolled over and said sleepily, 'Barney?'

'No, it's Robert Redford,' he said wearily.

'Oh, how nice.'

'If he was as tired as I am, you could forget it.'

'What time is it?'

'Past four. I'm dead. My feet feel like I just ran the Boston Marathon.'

'You would've been proud of Eddie, Barney. He did just fine.'

'Jeez, I completely forgot. Did you explain? Did it embarrass him I had to leave like that, right in the middle of Prokofiev?'

'He understood. Nobody saw from the stage; they were very busy.'

The lieutenant pulled and tugged at his clothes until they lay in a pile at his feet, then he fell back on the bed in his undershorts.

'Jesus, Syl, there's got to be an easier way to make a living.'

'Uh huh.'

'It never ends. You clean up one, there's two more in its place.'

She rose on one elbow and rubbed his temple with two fingers.

'You been saying that since the day we got married,' she said.

But Friscoe did not hear her. His breathing had already settled into a steady drone. Sylvia got up and pulled the covers over him and went into the bathroom.

A moment later the phone rang.

Before she could get back to it, Friscoe, from years of

experience, reached out and answered it without opening his eyes.

'Barney?'

'Umm.'

'Is that you, Friscoe?'

'Uh . . . yeah.'

'It's Max Grimm. You awake?'

'Almost . . . uh, you finish the autopsy?'

'Oh, on the girl? Abrams got that hours ago. I've got something else you ought to know about. Are you listening?'

'Yeah, yeah.'

'You remember, I told you Riley had a couple of John Does down here in the icehouse?'

'Right.'

'Well, I just finished the post mortem on one of them.'

'Christ, what the hell time is it?'

'Who knows? I been going so long I can't stop now. Anyway, this p.m. I just finished? They found the corpse out in the city dump yesterday afternoon. A real messy thing. Face blown off, both hands are missing.'

'Hands missing?'

'Yeah, cut off at the wrist. No clothes, no I.D., nothing.'

'Twigs, I got one too many bodies on my hands already.'

'Listen to me. Like I say, his face was blown off, nothing left, no way to identify him, okay?'

'Um hmm.'

'But that isn't what killed him. He was drilled through the right eye. A single .22 calibre long rifle-bullet, with the end dum-dummed. It flattened out and laid up against the back of the skull on the inside.'

'So?'

'So the bullet was soaked in garlic.'

And at almost the same moment that Twigs was telling Friscoe about the stiff in the icehouse with the .22 calibre garlic-soaked bullet in its head, Anderson brought the telex message to Larry Abrams, who was sitting half asleep at his table, staring at the tape he had been studying for hours.

The teletype message woke him up.

'Here's that FBI report you were lookin' for,' Anderson said. 'Looks like a dead end.'

'What do you mean?' The Nosh said.

257

'Read it.'

The bureau had made a positive I.D. on the two prints. They belonged to a fifty-nine-year-old white male from Lincoln, Nebraska named Howard Burns. But The Nosh did not read any further. His eyes jumped to the bottom line of the report and he stared in disbelief.

According to the FBI report, Howard Burns had been incinerated in an automobile accident on the outskirts of Omaha two months earlier.

Chapter Sixteen

The sleek white Grebe cabin cruiser rolled gently on a quiet sea, protected by a womb of warm fog that had drifted in from the Gulf Stream just after midnight, a fog so thick that it now obscured the crow's nest over the cabin. Hotchins slipped on a pair of faded corduroys and a yellow slicker and w at out on the afterdeck where he sat quietly massaging the calf of his imperfect leg. Occasionally, when tension and weariness weighed on him, he could almost feel the missing foot cramping up on him, the pain spreading slowly up to his knee, the artificial foot becoming a dead weight. It was a discomfort he endured alone, never mentioning it to others.

He had anchored in a cove on the inland side of the island, an unnamed hump of sand and sea grass he remembered from the early days when he worked the shallows off the Georgia and South Carolina coasts with his father. He rarely thought about those days anymore. Time had eased all that, erasing memories of the harsh work and bitter loneliness that were the realities of a shrimper's life. Now he regarded the sea with affection, a friend providing tiny islands along the coast from Brunswick to Charleston that had become his private hideaways.

He sat in the stern, rubbing the leg, drawing strength from the artificial foot, which had become a constant reminder of the humiliation of defeat, of the common weakness he saw in all people who failed, who dreamed too small, and would not pay the price for even their little dreams. His utter contempt for those who simply endured had started in Korea. There were prices to be paid and the greater the prize, the higher the price.

In the prison camp, where he lay nursing his shattered foot for almost a year before it was amputated, Hotchins had learned about survival. He needed a goal, something more than just day-by-day grovelling to stay alive. His goal, his single driving obsession to be president of the United States, was born in morphine-crazed hallucinations, but it became his goal for living. He invented methods for keeping

259

his mind alert. He tried to think like a president, act like a president, adopt the attitude of a president.

When he was released from the hospital into the prison population, he was shocked at what he found – a motley, demoralized, filthy group who reflected their senior officer, a colonel named Sacks who was a weak and disheartened shell, tormented by fear and sickness and destroyed by his own nightmares. Hotchins watched as Sacks encouraged the weak to submit to the North Koreans, to collaborate, sign confessions, to do anything to stay alive. He hated Sacks, not because he was weak, but because he had created an atmosphere that eventually would enervate Hotchins himself.

If Hotchins were to survive, he had to destroy Sacks. His became a constant and subtle voice hammering at the colonel's conscience, eroding the last vestige of Sacks's self-respect. It was an insidious and ruthless campaign, so carefully carried out that when Sacks eventually hanged himself, he did not realize he had been driven to the act by the man who assumed his position of command.

For the next two years Hotchins ruled the camp, hand-picking a small coterie of the toughest men left and establishing his own harsh rules and regulations. He restored military discipline to the prison, demanded that the men practise personal hygiene, that they exercise to keep their morale up. Twice he secretly ordered the execution of men on the verge of confessing to war crimes. He was both a frightening martinet and an inspiration to his fellow prisoners. They survived because he needed them to, and in the end he endured his humiliation with dignity and walked out of the camp a hero.

When he did, he was convinced that he would someday be president, regardless of the price. It was a passion which DeLaroza had eased to life, nurtured, encouraged and fed. And now it was happening. Nothing could stop it. In Hotchins's mind, it was destiny.

He sat in the fog, preparing himself for the tough ten months ahead, for the exhausting personal toll he knew the campaign would exact, contemplating the price he would have to pay.

He had already paid dearly by ending his affair with

Domino. DeLaroza had been right, she represented a constant danger and a foolish one. Besides, she had served her purpose. Domino had awakened new passions in Hotchins, arousing a latent need that had been smothered by ambition. She had fired his carnal desires with her incredible sensuality and given him a new vitality. Losing her was just the first of many personal sacrifices he knew he would have to make.

The decision to give her up had come quickly once he faced it. Hotchins had trained himself to make fast decisions. He simply programmed the pluses and minuses into his brain, a trick he had learned from Victor. Emotion had nothing to do with it.

It was done. Time to move on.

He started thinking about his own political machine. The nucleus was there, although he recognized that in its strength there was danger. DeLaroza, Roan, Lowenthal, each a shrewd and powerful strategist but each with his own needs to fulfil. It would not be easy, balancing their egoes, keeping the machine oiled and moving.

He did not hear her open the hatchway behind him.

'Composing your acceptance speech?' she said.

He turned, startled by her voice, ignoring the remark or perhaps not hearing it. Instead he was staring at her as she stood in the hatchway, huddled in a green jacket which she held shut with both hands, her magical features framed by tousled black hair, her blue eyes still filled with sleep, her long, perfect legs bare below the jacket.

'God you're something,' he said. 'You are really something.'

She laughed. 'Changing your mind?'

His face grew sombre again and he turned away from her, staring back into the fog when he shook his head.

'You're making it sad,' she said. 'It doesn't have to be sad. There are still a couple of very good hours left before the sun comes up.'

Without thinking he began stroking his leg. She came out and stood near him, putting her head gently on the back of his neck and moving her fingers lightly in his hair.

'Want me to do that for you?'

'No. It's nothing.'

'Did you hear what I said? It doesn't have to be sad. That's for the songwriters.'

'It got to me a little, seeing you there. A little nudge, that's all. What is it the French say? "To say goodbye is to die a little." '

She sighed. 'You're going to get emotional on me. I can tell.'

'Well, my mother always said I was emotional. "Donald," she'd say, "don't be so dramatic." '

She sat down beside him and nestled against him. He put his arm around her.

'Well, don't go getting dramatic on me. Save that for the tax-payers.'

Hotchins laughed. 'You've noticed that too, hunh?'

'Come on. When that voice begins to tremble and those eyes fire up, I just have to marvel at you.' Then, a moment later: 'You're going to win, Hotch. You're a straight-line guy and people like that.'

'What do you mean, "straight-line guy"? That sounds stuffy.'

'Not at all. It's one of your . . . charms. You get right to it, no fussing around. Now most men would have brought me out here, wined me, had a little dinner catered in a pretty picnic basket, made love to me all night, then made their little farewell speech two minutes before we docked. You gave it to me before we even got out of the harbour. And I like that about you. The only problem is, you've been acting like a little boy who did something wrong ever since.'

'Well I – '

'It's not guilt. Guilt is not one of your problems.'

'I guess I figured, when you close the door it isn't fair to climb back in the window.'

'How about me? How about the way I feel?'

He drew her closer to him, his fingers searching the jacket, feeling her nakedness under it. He remembered a time in Virginia, one of the first times she stirred feelings in him he thought he had lost forever. His hand moved around her and up until he felt the curve of her breast and she turned slightly so it rested against his palm.

Out beyond the cove a foghorn sounded, its mournful tune going sour at the end of the bleat.

'That's old Jerry Stillman's tugboat,' Hotchins said. 'That foghorn's had a frog in its throat since I was a kid.'

'You know what, Hotch? I knew you were going to be a good lay the first time I ever saw you.'

'Oh?'

The remark startled him. Her uninhibited observations always caught him off-guard. He laughed and said, 'You mean, you thought about bedding me down the first thing? Right in the middle of a cocktail party?'

She thought about that night. She had seen his picture in the newspaper, seen him on television, and had wondered about him the way any woman wonders about a man of prominence. It was Victor who had introduced them.

'Want to meet the next president?' he had asked her.

'Of what?'

'The United States.'

Now who could turn down an invitation like that? Of course she wanted to meet him. There had been a fund-raising dinner to save the historic old Fox Theatre, with a private cocktail party beforehand.

'He is a lonely man,' DeLaroza had told her casually.

'Does it show?'

'Only to those who know him. The public sees only what he wants it to see.'

'Bad marriage?'

'Typical. He married a small-town girl when he was quite young. She has not kept up. She is uncomfortable in the political arena.'

'Suicide,' she had said. 'She better get used to it.'

'Too late.'

She had been overwhelmed by his personal charm, a charisma that television never adequately captured. He was commanding, charming, friendly but formal, and she had watched him from across the room. Several times she had caught him staring back at her.

Thinking back on it, she knew now that it had been more than just Hotch. She had known commanding, charming, friendly, and formal men before, but never one who was going to run for president. It had been a challenge, no question about it. Yes, there had definitely been a challenge there.

What had Victor said? ' You are attracted by power.' No, she thought, *not really.* She had known from the beginning that the benefits of power would be denied to her. From the beginning she had been a closet mistress. Nothing would ever have changed that. And there had been affection. But love? No, that was the delusion.

And so she too was relieved that it was over.

'Hey,' he said, snapping her back to the present.

'Hey yourself.'

'I said, did you really think about bedding me down right there in the middle of that cocktail party?'

'Didn't you?'

'Didn't I what?'

'Think about laying me the first thing?'

'Uh no, but – '

'But you would now?'

'I've got prior knowledge now.'

'Hotch, if you met me in a restaurant right now, for the first time, what is the first thing that would go through your mind?'

'You win.'

'Thank you. Now you understand. I looked across the room at you and I said to myself, "He's going to be great in bed." '

'Why did you think that?'

'I saw your hunger. Not for me, not for any other woman in the room. But you were hungry. And a powerful, hungry man is a powerfully good lay.'

He turned and looked down at her. The jacket had fallen open and he could see her breasts swelling against the cloth.

'Did I disappoint you?'

'Of course not. It was fun, like waking up a sleeping tiger. Oh, you were a little shy at first, but . . .'

She smiled and let the sentence drift away in the fog, then after a few moments she said, 'You've been a very good lover.'

. More silence. She moved again, this time against him, and he could feel the heat from her body through the jacket.

'How long have we been lovers?' he said.

'Seven months this Thursday.'

'Have you been marking the calendar?'

'I never forget good things. It's a lesson I learned from my dad. If you don't expect anything from the world, everything you get is a surprise. And that makes the really good things that much better.'

'He must've been a very wise man.'

'Nope, he never kept a promise in his life. But . . . he made some beauties, so he also taught me the value of dreaming.'

'That's a very generous way of putting it. What was he like?'

'I don't want to talk about it.'

'You know, we've known each other for seven months and I don't know a damn thing about your life away from me? I don't even know your real name.'

'You don't like Domino?'

'Well it always struck me as a bit melodramatic.'

'Intriguing. I like *intriguing*. It's a much better word.'

'Okay, intriguing.'

'Good. And that's the way we'll keep it.'

'I, uh, I feel . . .'

She sensed the awkwardness in his voice and held a finger to his lips.

'Shh,' she said. And then: 'I want to make love to you. Right now. Because it's something we both enjoy and because I find you most appealing out here like this and because I'm horny as hell.'

She made a sound in her throat and moved a hand up his leg, sliding her fingers down the inside of his thigh. He turned towards her and kissed her and she reached up between their mouths with two fingers and squeezed his lips very lightly between them, and his mouth opened and their tongues touched, flirted with each other, and she moved against him, very lightly, so he could feel the fullness of her. She slid one leg up over his lap, drew her mouth away from his, and lay her head against his chest. Then she took the zipper of his jacket between her teeth and very slowly moved her head down, unzipping it almost to the waist. Then, raising her head, she kissed him again and this time both their jackets were open and as they kissed she moved her breasts lightly against him and he felt her hard nipples caressing his chest.

He was totally captivated by her, the thought of having

her was dizzying to him. He felt her hand touch him and felt himself responding. He reached up, stroked her face and throat, gradually widening the circle his hand was making until it brushed her nipple. And then he knew she was already starting the build-up and at that moment Hotchins realized fully what his obsession to become president had cost him.

Chapter Seventeen

The Majestic Grill was an obscure and unrecognized landmark that had endured on the same street corner since 1934, oblivious to the changes that had occurred around it. The shoe repair shop beside it had become a magazine store which had become a head shop which had become a natural food store which was now a pinball parlour; the theatre up the street had declined from first runs to double features to porn; and if the Majestic was a monument to early Thirties style, the hotel across the street was a six-storey monument to Early Nothing architecture. It had been boarded up for years. But the Majestic never changed. It had resisted time and transition, catering to a clientele that defied demography or caste. A bum nursing a cup of coffee received the same curt service as a college president.

Inside, bacon and sausage sizzled on ancient grills, the odours spicing the heady aroma of roasting coffee. The decor was nondescript, a well-worn combination of stainless steel, formica, pale green walls, and dark green vinyl seats. A dining room had been added to the rear of the diner years before and there Papa sat, at a corner table, mesmerized by the menu from which he was about to order a breakfast big enough to delight an entire Marine brigade. Sharky and Livingston joined him and a few minutes later Friscoe arrived, an apparition in scruffy corduroys, a peaked deepsea fishing cap, and a scarred jacket that predated antiquity.

He appraised the ragtag bunch, their eyes charcoaled from lack of sleep, their cheeks scraggly from not shaving, their bodies sagging under the weight of a sleepless night.

'Jesus,' he said, 'you all look like you just got sprung from Auschwitz.'

'And thank you, Cinderella,' Livingston said.

'So where's Abrams? He ain't gonna be one of those late guys, is he?'

'On his way,' Sharky said. 'He got hung up on a phone call.'

A gargantuan waitress with arms like a wrestler's hovered

over the table. 'Are we ready here?' she said. It was more a demand than a question.

'We'll have coffee all the way around while we're deciding,' Sharky said and she padded off towards the coffee urn on slippered feet.

Friscoe leaned back in his chair and looked at the other three detectives. 'I'll tell you what. I hope to shit you guys did better than me. I musta put in five hours trying to get a line on this Neil and what do I get out of it? Sore feet and a fuckin' goose egg, that's what.'

Papa took a tattered notebook from his pocket and licking a thumb, flicked it open. 'His name's Dantzler,' he announced. 'With a *t*.'

'What'sat?' Friscoe said.

'Dantzler with a *t*. D-a-n-t-z-l-e-r. He lives in a condo in The Courtyard, which, if you'll remember, is also where Tiffany lives. That's because she's Dantzler's girlfriend. She uses her apartment mainly for tricks. She also has another boyfriend on the sly and she occasionally shacks up at Domino's place. Dantzler's a rich kid gone sour. His game's pimping and scam. He's outa town, be back a week from tomorrow.'

Friscoe stared at Papa with a hint of indignation. 'Sounds like a pornographic soap opera,' he said. 'Where'd you come up with all that shit?'

'A snitch.'

'You got all that from one fuckin' snitch?'

'Had a little help from the security guard at The Courtyard.'

'Maybe I just should have stayed in bed,' Friscoe said, feeling suddenly inadequate.

'Sometimes you get lucky,' Papa said.

'Well, sometimes wasn't last night for me,' Friscoe said. 'Is there anything else?'

'Dantzler's sporting a new Ferrari, braggin' on the street how he took some cowboy to the cleaners. Domino is out. Didn't know about it.'

'And just how did you find that out?' Friscoe said.

'Snitch.'

'Shit, who is this fuckin' stoolie?' Friscoe said. 'Maybe we oughta put him on the goddamn payroll.'

'One more thing,' said Papa. 'Dantzler hasn't got the

guts to kill anybody or get it done. Rule him out. Ditto Tiffany.'

'Same snitch?' Sharky said.

Papa nodded.

'You sure he's reliable, Papa?' Friscoe said.

'Yes. When this guy talks, it's bankable.'

'So that retires Dantzler, Tiffany, *and* the mark in Texas as possibles,' Livingston said.

Friscoe shook his head. 'Too bad. They would have been the easiest shot we had.'

At that point The Nosh arrived, alert, ebullient, and smiling. Friscoe glared at him sourly. 'You look like you just come back from a week at the beach,' he said.

'I think I'm on to something,' The Nosh said.

'Okay, everybody gets their turn. Papa there just made himself an A-plus. Now it's Sharky's turn at bat.'

Sharky quickly described the deal on red devils made by Shoes and the layoff bets made by Arnold, the bartender at the Matador. Before he was through, the waitress returned with the coffee and demanded their orders while The Nosh complained bitterly that they might at least have selected a place that had bagels on the menu.

'This here's a diner, not a deli,' Friscoe said.

When the waitress had gone again, Sharky said, 'We didn't make Shoes. He never showed up on the street last night. But both these leads tell Arch and me that the shooter's still in town.

'Could be coincidence, Shark,' The Nosh said.

'If it was just one or the other, I'd agree' said Livingston. 'But here we got information from two completely different sources and it dovetails.'

'Yeah,' Friscoe said, 'I never been big on coincidence myself. It's like circumstantial evidence. Where there's smoke there's fire.'

'Arch and I are going to move on Shoes tonight,' Sharky said. 'But we need somebody to get on this Arnold, find out who the big better is.'

'Can you maybe get a line on this Shoes before tonight, hit him in his nest?' Friscoe asked.

'It's pushy. If we move too hard on him we could blow Ben's cover,' Sharky said.

'Okay, I'll worry about Arnold, there, see what I can

269

come up with,' Friscoe said. 'We just don't have *time*. We got nothing but maybes and probablies, and what we need, we ain't got. We ain't got a face, we ain't got a name, we ain't got a motive, we ain't got *shit*.'

'Is it my turn yet?' The Nosh asked.

'Jeez, you're like some kid in grammar school thinks he's got all the answers,' Friscoe said.

'Go ahead, Nosh,' Sharky said. 'Let's hear it.'

'Okay, I got a positive make on the prints.'

Friscoe almost swallowed his coffee cup. Sharky, Livingston, and Papa froze in mid-bite, like sculptured figures.

'You know who the killer is?' Sharky said.

The Nosh nodded. 'Howard Burns. Male Caucasian, age 59, owned a short-haul trucking outfit in Lincoln, Nebraska.'

'A *trucking* company?' Friscoe said. 'This Mafia button owns a trucking company?'

'What do you mean, owned?' Sharky said.

The Nosh smiled. 'According to the Burea, Howard Burns was killed in an automobile accident on October twentieth.'

Again silence, broken finally by Friscoe. 'That ain't possible.'

'That's right. It sure ain't,' The Nosh said. 'I checked it out again with George Barret. He says the prints are fresh, no question about it.'

'What kind of accident?' Sharky asked.

'A single-vehicle wreck on the outskirts of Omaha. Car went off the road, hit a tree, and exploded. Burns's wife made the identification using dental charts.'

'Uh oh,' Friscoe said, and a smile began spreading across his face.

'Neat,' Livingston said.

'Now that *ain't* a coincidence,' Papa said.

'And think about the date,' Livingston said.

'Yeah about two weeks before he surfaced here looking for red devils and a healthy bookmaker,' Sharky said.

'There's more,' The Nosh said.

'I shoulda stayed in bed,' said Friscoe.

'Look at this Bureau telex on Burns. Notice anything funny?' The Nosh asked.

They all looked it over, reading the lines, the background

information on the questionably deceased Howard Burns. Born in Newark, raised in Philadelphia, worked as truck driver and then in the navy yard there during World War II, returned to trucking after the war, left Philadelphia in 1960, worked at various trucking jobs until 1968 when he purchased the Interstate Van Lines in Lincoln. It was sketchy, but a resumé nevertheless.

'What do you see here that's strange?' Sharky asked The Nosh.

'Well, he's got no criminal record. So why the package?' They reread the telex.

'He's right,' Friscoe said. 'Why would they have his prints on file?'

Sharky tapped on his coffee cup with a spoon, lightly, a rhythmic tattoo that accompanied his thoughts.

'It's a cover,' said Friscoe. 'It fits. It's hand in glove. It makes sense. It's the *only* way it makes sense. This shooter has a Mafia pedigree. We figure he had to be a *capo*, right? An old-line hitman. So what's he doin' running a truck company?'

'A cover,' The Nosh said.

'Damn right,' said Friscoe. 'This shooter, whoever the fuck he is, he did a turn for the Feds and they fixed him up. He musta been in hot with the mob so the Feds give him Howard Burns and a whole biography to go with it.'

'And then something happened and he had to drop out again, only this time he did it so even the Feds thought he was gone for good,' Sharky said.

'And showed up here,' Livingston said, 'not two weeks later.'

'Okay,' Friscoe said, 'now I got a little something. What I got is dessert, buckos. Something that makes it all go down, so it ain't so hard to swallow. You remember Twigs tellin' us Riley had a coupla John Does to keep him busy down in the icehouse?'

They nodded.

'Well one of these John Does was dug outa the city dump yesterday. And it wasn't no accidental John Doe. What I mean is somebody went to a lotta trouble to make him into a John Doe, like blowing up his face with a shotgun and removing both his hands.'

'Jesus!' Papa said.

'Yeah, ain't it a pretty picture? What makes it . . . the reason, see, why we're maybe interested is that what really put this stiff on ice was a .22 bullet that was soaked in garlic.'

He leaned back, satisfied at having brought something to the party at last.

'And,' he added, 'the illustrious Mr. Grimm says this stiff got kayoed around the end of October sometime.'

More silence, then a babble, everyone talking at once. Sharky held up a hand. 'Hold on, hold on. Shit, we sound like a bad church choir here. Let's add it up, see what we got. Barney, sum it up for us.'

'Okay, we got a Mafia shooter goes underground with the help of the Feds. On October twentieth subject the same wraps a tree around his car and goes up in smoke. His wife I.D.'s him with dental plates and plants him. Ten days later this Burns or whoever pops outa the toaster in Atlanta and puts the freeze on victim number two, fixes up the stiff so it can't be identified and plants him in the city dump.'

'How come Victim Two?' Sharky said.

Friscoe shrugged. '*Somebody* burned up in the car on the outskirts of Omaha.'

Sharky whistled between his teeth. 'I missed that one.'

'Okay. So then six, seven weeks more pass by and this same Howard-Whoever-the-Fuck-He-Is-Burns comes outa the woodwork again and dumps Domino. The question is, why? Why? That may be the toughest donkey of all to pin a tail on.'

'Why don't we just take it to the Bureau? Tell them this Burns dummied up his own death, came here, and wasted two people already,' Sharky said.

Friscoe shook his head. 'I veto that one. For a lotta reasons. First place the Feds don't really give a shit about our problems unless there's something in it for them. Right now this is a local problem, so they don't stand to make any brownie points by bustin' their ass tryin' to help us. Also, if this son of a bitch *was* in the Feds' alias programme, it'll take an act of fuckin' Congress to get anything out of them. All they'll do, is come in here hot-shittin' around and the next thing you know, Riley, D'Agastino, the fucking Bat, *every*body in the goddamn world'll be in on it. We took it this far, let's take it all the way. What the hell, we got our nuts in the door jamb anyway.'

Sharky had been toying with an idea. Now he threw it out to the machine. 'This is a long shot, okay. I know that going in. But just supposing this shooter was in the service in World War Two. He's the right age for it. His prints could be in the inactive file.'

'Wouldn't the Bureau have cleaned that package, too?' Livingston asked.

'Why?' said Sharky. 'They didn't need to. The Bureau created Howard Burns. But, when I was in military intelligence there was a couple of times when we turned up an ID in the old files. The FBI doesn't have it *all*.'

'I say we try everything,' Papa said. 'You never know when something's gonna work.'

'And you got the kalibash to get in there, right Sharky?' Friscoe said.

'I've got a couple of good pals out at Fort McPherson in the intelligence unit there. What've we got to lose?'

Friscoe rubbed his hands together. His weariness was temporarily replaced by a surge of adrenalin. He had expected a few bunts, but the four of them had actually hit a couple of long balls.

'Okay,' he said, 'tuck this in the back of your minds while you're out there. This John Doe, here's what Twigs gave me on him. And remember, Riley's workin' on him, too. And Riley ain't gonna stop until he knows chapter and verse on him. Anyways, John Doe was five-ten, a hundred and fifty-five to sixty-five pounds, black hair going grey, in his late fifties. A very hard guy in good physical condition. Has two old scars down here, just under his ribs, one in front, one in back. Twigs says it's an old gunshot wound, could go back thirty years.'

Sharky said, 'Same age as the shooter.'

'Just about,' said Friscoe. 'Also he was suffering from some respiratory ailment. Bad lungs caused by inhalation of hemp.'

'Hemp?' Livingston said. 'You mean rope?'

'I mean hemp, which is what rope is made out of.'

'He worked in a hemp mill?' Sharky said.

'Yeah. And the most common place to find a jute mill is in prison. So we could be looking for an old con here.'

'We could check the county and federal probation officers. Maybe if this guy was paroled he had to register here.'

'I already got it on my list,' Friscoe said. He dunked the last of a doughnut in his coffee, swished it around, and finished it noisily. 'Well, kid,' he said to Sharky, 'it's your fuckin' machine. You call the shots.'

'Okay, Arch and I'll see what we can turn up at Fort Mac. Papa, maybe you could try to come at this Shoes from another angle, collar him without blowing the whistle on Colter. Nosh, you stick with the tapes and see what else you can dig up on this Burns. All of us keep this John Doe in mind. Maybe there's some talk out on the street about him.'

'And I'll take a shot at the local probation officers, see what that turns up,' Friscoe said. Then he smiled for the first time since entering the Majestic.

'What the hell,' he said. 'We got forty-eight hours left. It ain't forever, but it ain't Monday morning yet, either.'

Chapter Eighteen

It took them thirty minutes to drive out to Fort McPherson, a tidy but sprawling army oasis within the city limits that was headquarters for the Third Army. Sergeant Jerome Weinstock was waiting for them in front of the spotless headquarters building, a tall, florid man in starched khaki whose appearance had changed from the cherubic innocence Sharky remembered to an authoritative scowl. He had put on twenty pounds and lost a lot of hair in the eight years since Sharky had served with him in Army Intelligence.

'You like playing cops and robbers, Sharky?' Weinstock asked as he led the way into the headquarters building and down a long, stark hallway to the military intelligence offices.

'It has its moments,' Sharky said. 'What's with the scowl, Jerry? I remember you as sweet, smiling Jerry Weinstock, the pride of Jersey City.'

'I made top kick,' Weinstock growled. 'It's part of the act. Only time I smile anymore is when I'm alone in the latrine.' He looked at Sharky and winked, then said, 'So what's your problem? I don't see you for eight years and then you call me in a panic at the crack of dawn on a Saturday.'

Sharky handed him a lift of the two fingerprints. 'I need to match these prints to a face. They'd be inactive, probably dating back to World War Two.'

'You're playing a hunch, aren't you, Sharky? That's what it is. Shit, you haven't changed a damn bit. And it can't wait till Monday, hunh? Got to be right now, before the bugler's even got his sock's on.'

'By Monday I'm dead.'

'Always the same story. Eager beaver.' Weinstock looked at Livingston. 'This one'll drive you apeshit. He never stops, he's either coming or going all the time.'

'So I'm learnin',' Livingston said.

A nervous young recruit was waiting in the telex room, looking like he had dressed in his sleep. Weinstock handed him the two prints. 'Send this to DX 10, attention Sergeant

275

Skidmore. And come get us down in the coffee room when you get response.'

'Yes, sir,' the youth said. 'Should I send it urgent?'

'Willoughby, I seriously doubt that anybody in his right mind is using the twix before nine o'clock on Saturday morning. Just send it off. Skidmore's waiting at Fort Dix for it.'

'Yes, sir.'

Weinstock turned and marched out of the room followed by the two detectives.

'Skidmore? Is that old Jocko Skidmore?' Sharky said.

'The same,' Weinstock said. 'Had to get him outa bed, too. I'll tell you something, Shark. If he didn't remember you – and like you – we'd've been shit outa luck. Know what he said? He said, "That silly son of a bitch never did do anything at a civilized time of day." To which I say, amen.'

'I'll drink to that,' Livingston said. 'I haven't been to bed since I met Sharky.'

They drank coffee and made small talk about the old days, sitting in the coffee room in the basement for almost forty-five minutes before Willoughby appeared at the door.

'It's comin' in now, Sergeant,' he said.

Sharky bolted from his chair and took the steps two at a time, his heart racing in anticipation. This had to work. He needed more than just Shoes and Arnold the bartender, much more, to keep his machine rolling, to keep its adrenalin pumping. As he entered the room and saw the teletype message a shimmer of disappointment rippled through his chest. The report was short, no more than a few lines. Livingston rushed in behind him as he tore the sheet from the machine and read the peculiar print argot of the military:

POS ID, 2 PRINTS, ANGELO DOMINIC SCARDI. B SIRACUSA, SICILY, 1916. EMGRTD US, 1935. VOLTRD CVL LSN SICILY INV, JUNE, 1943. CIV ADV GELA-PACHINO-CALTAGIRONE, JULY, 43-MARCH 44. TRNSFD FIRENZE, ITALY, JNT MI/OSS OPSTITCH (TSEC), MARCH, 44-OCT 44. RET US OCT SERV TERM OCT 21, 44. SKID.

'Not too much,' Weinstock said.

But Livingston was staring at the first line, his eyes bright

276

with excitement. There it was. The name.

Angelo Dominic Scardi.

And what a name it was.

'Shit, all we need's right here on this first line,' he said. 'Angelo Scardi. Does that ring your bell, Sharky?'

'No. Should it?'

'Angel the Undertaker,' Livingston said. 'This guy was a top button for Genovese, Luciano, Costello, all the biggies. When Valachi spilled his guts to the Senate, Scardi's name popped up all over the place. Then a couple of years later who should turn up doin' the same number Valachi did for the Feds? Angelo Scardi.'

'What happened to him?' Sharky said.

'He died of cancer about six months after testifying.'

'How convenient,' Sharky said. 'And would you like to make a little bet that Howard Burns turned up in Nebraska just about that time?'

'No bet. It fits, man. It fits like a glove.' He turned his attention back to the report. 'How the hell can anybody read the rest of this shit?'

Weinstock took the sheet from him. 'Here,' he said, 'Let me translate for you. It says this Scardi was born in Siracusa, Sicily, in 1916. Came to the U.S. in 1935. In June, 1943, he volunteered as civilian liaison adviser to the Sicilian invasion forces and then worked with the Army in the Gela-Pachino-Caltagirone sector until March 1944. He was transferred to Firenze, Italy, and attached to a joint Military Intelligence–OSS operation – something called Opstitch – until he returned to the States in October '44. Service was terminated the same month.'

'What the hell was he doing over there?' Sharky said.

'Beats the hell outa me,' Weinstock said. 'That's the year I was born.'

'Arch?'

'All I remember is that he was a number one hitman for the Cosa Nostra and he blew the whistle on them.'

'But it fits, damn it, it fits!' Sharky said.

'What's so important about this guy if he's been dead for seven or eight years?' Weinstock asked.

'Jerry, when this is all over, I'll come out and we'll spend a night at the noncom club on me and I'll tell you the whole story. How about this Opstitch, what would that be?'

'That translates Operation Stitch. With the OSS involved it was probably some cloak and dagger number. TSEC means it's classified secret.'

'You mean it's still classified after thirty years?'

'Could have been a royal fuck-up of some kind. Nobody in the army wants to admit a screw-up, so they just keep the lid on. Or maybe they just never got around to declassifying it. You know the goddamn army.'

'Who cares?' Livingston said. 'We got the name, that's what's important.'

'It could relate, Arch. How could we find out about this, Jerry?'

'Forget it. You got to go through the Adjutant General in Washington and probably the CIA to bust it out. That could be a lifetime project.'

'Somebody must remember something about it,' Sharky said.

'We're pushing for time, Shark,' Livingston reminded him.

'I know, but as long as we're here, why not check it out?'

'He's havin' another hunch attack, if you ask me,' Weinstock said.

'C'mon, Jerry, this is headquarters for the whole Third Army. Think! There's probably a dozen guys on this base could help us.'

'See,' Weinstock said, 'a goddamn bulldog. He gets something by the ass and he won't let it go.'

Weinstock stroked his chin for a few moments. 'Well, your best bet, I guess, is General Bourke. Hardy W. Bourke himself. He was in Italy during the war. If he don't know, maybe he knows where you can find out.'

'Can you call him, ask if he'll see us?'

'When, right now?'

Sharky patted him on the cheek. 'Jerry, we're fighting the clock. You're a goddamn prince.'

Weinstock leered back at him. 'No, you're the goddamn prince, Sharky, 'cause this little operation here this morning is gonna cost you one gallon of Chivas Regal.'

Sharky nodded. 'Do it.'

Weinstock grinned. 'Don't have to call him. You'll find him out on the golf course.' He looked at his watch. 'I would guess he'll be somewhere around the third hole by now. And good luck. I hope he doesn't hit you with his mashie niblick.'

General Hardy W. Bourke was built like a footlocker standing on end and had the face of an angry eagle. Sharky was leaning against a tree at the edge of the third tee when he rolled up in his golf cart and stepped out, a tough little man with pure white hair cut an inch long.

Sharky walked across the trim green tee as the boxy little man leaned over and placed his ball.

'Excuse me, sir. Are you General Bourke?'

The general glared at him.

'Yes. What is it?'

Sharky showed him his buzzer. 'My name's Sharky. Atlanta PD.'

The General looked at the badge, then at Sharky's hair and snorted. 'I see,' he said. 'What's wrong? Has something happened?'

His partner, a tall, thin man whose fatigue cap covered a bald pate stepped up beside Bourke. 'Something I can handle, General?' he said.

'It's all right, Jesse. Something to do with the police.'

'The police?'

'I'm sorry to interrupt your game like this, sir, but it is important. We're investigating a murder case and – '

'Murder! Good God, sir, one of my men?'

'No, sir. No, not at all. Thing is, it relates to a military operation in Italy during the war and – '

'Ah,' Bourke said, obviously relieved. 'Well, can't this wait, young man? We should be back at the clubhouse in a few hours. We're backed up here, as you can see.' He pointed back to the number two green. A foursome was just putting out.

Bourke stepped up and planted his feet firmly in the grass, addressing the ball as if it were one of his junior officers.

'Time's pressing, sir,' Sharky said.

Bourke sighted down his club. 'If it's waited for thirty years, it can wait until I tee off,' he snapped. His club whipped back and slashed the air. The ball cracked off the

279

tee, soared out about thirty yards, and hooked drastically, plunging into the rough a hundred or so yards away. Bourke turned towards Sharky, staring at him, his face contorted with disgust.

'Did you see that?' he bellowed.

'Sorry, sir, I – '

'Goddamnit to hell!' the general screamed. He stared at his club for a full thirty seconds, his face turning the colour of a carrot. Finally he threw it down in disgust.

'All right,' he snapped. 'You've got two minutes. Get in the cart. You can help me find that goddamn ball. You can walk down there, Jesse.'

The cart purred down the fairway.

'All right,' Bourke said. 'Now, what's this all about?'

'We're interested in a military operation that occurred in December, 1944, near – '

'What kind of operation?' Bourke growled.

'OSS, sir. It was – '

'Young man, I was a command officer assigned to Omar Bradley. I don't remember some goddamn spy operation that occurred thirty years ago. What do you think I am, a military encyclopaedia?'

'No sir, but – '

'There were probably a hundred OSS operations during the time I was in Italy. Quite frankly, I was too busy trying to win the war to be bothered with those spooks.'

'Yes, sir. Perhaps if I told you – '

'Eureka! There it is. Right beside the fairway. What luck.' He pulled up and got out of the cart and looked down the fairway towards the green. 'A straight shot to the pin. Look at that. Bloody good shot after all.' He looked at Sharky and winked. 'Have to take that club over to Ordnance and have the boys take that hook out of it, eh? Heh, heh.'

'General, is there *any*body on this base who might remember the incident?'

Bourke looked at him for a few moments more, then turned to the caddy. 'Gimme that five iron, caddy,' he said. He held out his hand and waited for the caddy to put the club in it. 'Martland. Martland's your man. If anybody can help you, it'd be Martland.'

'Martland?'

'Colonel Martland. A bird colonel waiting for his star so

he can retire. He was in intelligence and he was in Italy during the war. I believe he lives on K Street.'

'Thank you, sir. Thank you very much.'

'Young fellow?'

'Yes, sir?'

'Colonel Martland has a mind like a razor, particularly about World War Two. In fact, he's a goddamn bore about it. There's one thing. He's a little whacko, if you know what I mean. His wife died about two years ago and he's been somewhat out to lunch ever since.'

'Oh.'

'He has his moments. I'm not saying he's a goddamn loony bird. He's just, uh . . . a little loose in the attic. What I'm saying, son, is it may take a little patience. So be kind to him, all right?'

'Yes, sir.'

'And don't get hit by any goddamn golf balls. I don't want to be sued by the police department.'

It was a tidy street with tidy lawns trimmed neatly to the sidewalk and tidy white frame bungalows, each one a replica of the one next to it, each one sitting exactly the same distance back from the road. The only distinction among the houses was the landscaping, an obvious attempt by the officer tenants to bring some individuality to their homes.

A white Cadillac, several years old but in mint condition, sat in the driveway. They waited for several minutes after ringing the bell before the door was opened by a wiry little man, trim and erect, with pure white hair and a white moustache which might have been elegant had it not been trimmed slightly shorter on the right side than on the left. He was dressed in a tight-fitting Army jumpsuit with a white silk scarf at his throat. He was also wearing a baseball cap, tennis shoes, and held a riding crop in one hand.

'Yes?' he said, squinting out through the screen door.

'Colonel Martland?' Sharky said.

'I am Colonel Martland.'

'Yes, sir. I'm Detective Sharky and this is Sergeant Livingston.'

Martland stared from one to the other. 'Yes?'

'From the Atlanta Police Department, sir. Sergeant

Weinstock called about us?'

'Oh, yes. Weinstock. Of course. Well, won't you come in?'

He held the door and they entered a house whose walls were barren of paintings or photographs. There was little light inside. He led them into the living room, a room so bleak, so obvious, that Sharky immediately felt burdened by its sadness. Propped against the mantelpiece was an oil painting of a woman in riding clothes with a smoking volcano in the background. That and a chintz sofa were the only furnishings in the room. No tables, no lamps, no chairs, only unopened crates shoved into the corners.

Martland pointed to the sofa and then sat down on the edge of one of the crates, his knees together, the riding crop resting on his thighs as he held it at each end.

'You must forgive the place. I don't entertain much anymore. Not since my wife, Miriam' – and he turned and looked up at the painting and smiled, 'went away' – he said. 'I really must . . . do something . . .' and then the words died as he stared around the oppressive room. He looked back at Sharky and stared at him.

Sharky said, 'Uh, Colonel, if you have a few minutes, we'd like to ask you some questions.'

He continued to stare at Sharky and frowned. 'Is it something to do with the car? Did somebody hit the car?'

'Oh, no, sir, it hasn't got anything to do with, uh, this isn't a personal matter. It, uh, we're conducting an investigation.'

Martland did not change his expression. He continued to stare at Sharky.

'What it is, sir, we uh, this relates to some things that happened in Italy during the war.'

Martland still did not speak.

'You were in Italy during the war, weren't you, sir?'

'Is that World War Two?'

'Yes, sir, World War Two.'

'Oh, yes.' And he stopped again, staring past Sharky now, frowning for perhaps a full minute before a smile spread over his face.

'North Africa, Sicily, Italy. 1942 through 1945. Then we were in West Germany for three years and then on to Schofield Barracks. That's in Honolulu, you know. We lived there for ten glorious years, my wife and I.' He looked back up at the painting and smiled again. 'I believe the years in Hawaii were the best years in our career.'

And he stopped and stared again.

'Do you remember during the time in Sicily and Italy, meeting a man named Scardi? Angelo Scardi? He was a civilian who was there in some kind of advisory capacity.'

Another frown. Another blank stare. Martland stared past Sharky into a dark corner of the room. A full minute crept painfully by, then suddenly he almost bellowed:

'The American racketeer!' And began laughing. 'Dom, that's what he preferred to be called. For Dominic, his middle name. Hah! Haven't thought about that rascal for years. Quite a fellow, you know. Very tough. And courageous, oh, yes, particularly for a civilian. Knew him well. Told some shocking stories about the underworld. He was assigned to an intelligence unit commanded by one of my junior officers. Lieutenant McReady. John Sisson McReady from Virginia. Killed at Cassino. Bloody shame. But then . . .'

He stopped in mid-sentence, as abruptly as he had started, his mind searching back in time for other memories.

'Uh, what did this Scardi do? In Sicily I mean?'

Another minute or two crawled by as Martland stared and frowned, stirring through the mass of time and dates and places. And then, once again, the words came in a rush.

'He was a native of Sicily. Let me see . . . Siracusa, a little town on the southeastern tip of the island. We made a beachhead there during the invasion. Scardi knew the place like the seat of his pants. Every road, every footpath, every stone wall. He went in a month or so before the assault, scouted the entire area, radioed information every night. Set up little pockets of resistance to badger Jerry.'

And that was it again. It was as though he were turning a switch in his brain on and off.

'What was, uh, Gela-Pachino-Calta –'

'Caltagirone. Towns in southern Sicily. A little triangle. After Sicily fell, Dom Scardi was the civilian liaison between the military government and the locals. Our objective was territory, gentlemen. Geography, not people. The sooner they returned to self-government the better. That's what Scardi did, helped them get back on their feet. And kept them out of our hair.'

He stopped again, but this time as Sharky started to ask another question he cut him off. There was a touch of anger in his voice when he spoke.

'They were going to deport him, the Justice Department, did you know that? Undesirable alien, that's what they said. Well, he acquitted himself admirably. Unless I'm mistaken he became an American citizen after the war.'

Livingston looked at the floor and muttered, 'Great!'

Sharky ignored him, pressing on. 'Later on, after Sicily, Scardi went to Italy, didn't he?'

Another long pause. More frowns, followed by the customary burst of information.

'He worked with the guerrillas, behind the German lines. They were Communists, of course, been fighting the Germans since the beginning of the war. Totally disorganized. Scardi scouted them out, got them supplies, money, medicine. He had an idea to try and bring them all together so they'd be more effective. A dangerous thing to do. He was a civilian involved in espionage. If the Germans had caught him, bang! Would've been shot, just like that, on the spot. No ceremony.' And he stopped and after a few seconds, almost reflectively he repeated the name, 'Dominic Scardi,' and it lingered in the dreary room like a mention of the plague and Sharky felt the furies building inside him, thought about Domino and a man, humiliated in death, tossed away in a garbage dump without any face or hands. *Dominic Scardi*. How could this possibly be the same man who Martland regarded as a hero?

Finally Sharky said, 'Do you remember something called Opstitch?'

Martland reacted immediately, turning and looking straight at Sharky.

'I believe that information is classified, sir,' he said.

'Colonel, that was thirty years ago.'

'Classified nevertheless.'

'Sir, this is important. We're investigating a murder case involving people Scardi knew. Anything you give us could be helpful.'

Livingston finally spoke up. 'It might prevent innocent people from getting hurt,' he said.

'Humph,' Martland said and snorted through his nose. He struggled with the question, balancing it. Then he began to nod vigorously.

'Bureaucratic folderol!'

'I beg your pardon, sir?'

'Bureaucratic folderol. Utter nonsense. No reason really for Opstitch to be classified. It was a snafu. That's all, plain and simple, a snafu. Opstitch was Operation Stitch, for "a stitch in time". A bit obvious, of course, but then nobody ever accused the army of being subtle. Stitch was Scardi's idea. Brilliant, absolutely brilliant. I'm sure you know very little about the Italian campaign. God knows, few do. The forgotten war. And a bitter one. This was in the autumn of '44. The war in Italy had gone badly. Terrible terrain. Incessant rain. Very costly. Every inch paid for dearly. So that fall the Americans and Germans were face to face in the Po Valley. A stalemate. Three months it went on like that, neither side giving up a foot.

'Scardi had gone on reconnoitre up in the northern section around Lake di Garda. There were dozens of guerrilla outfits up there. The most effective, according to Scardi, was led by a resistance fighter who called himself La Volte. The Fox. Had a price on his head. Scardi suggested that we provide him with the money and supplies to consolidate all these bands into a single strike force. Hit Jerry from behind while the American and British troops would launch a massive frontal attack at the same time. And it could have worked to break the deadlock. So . . . that was Opstitch.'

Martland stopped and smiled, as though he were proud of himself. He ran his tongue between his teeth and his upper lip, smoothed his moustache with his fingers, and looked back at the painting of Miriam Martland.

'Did Scardi pull it off?'

'Oh, no, no, no. No, sir. Scardi got sick. Intestinal malaria I believe was the diagnosis. That was in October. The mission actually was carried off in December. Two weeks before Christmas, as I recall. I was in Rome at the time. A major named Halford took over the assignment. Moody fellow. Killed in the Orient some years ago. He sent a bright young officer named Younger in several times to make arrangements with La Volte. It was Younger who actually took the mission in. But Scardi had nothing to do with it by then. Been back in the States for two or three months.'

'And what happened?'

Martland drummed on his crop with nervous fingers. His forehead wrinkled and he shook his head in short jabs several times before answering.

'A disaster. Younger and three men parachuted in. The next night the air force dropped supplies, weapons, *and* four million dollars in gold bullion. The Germans overran our position, killed Younger and two of his men. The other one was wounded and hid out in an Italian village until it was liberated. After the war Younger and his men were found buried near the lake. The gold was never recovered.'

'How about this other man, the one that got away? Do you remember his name?'

He stared out the window, almost entranced, and said, 'An Irish name . . . Lonnigan . . . Harrigan . . . ah, I've got it. Corrigon. That was it, Corrigon.'

'You wouldn't have any idea where he is today, would you, Colonel?' Livingston said.

Martland nodded slowly. 'In prison. Federal prison. Courtmartialled. Accused of murder and grand theft, tried, and convicted. I was there. Sketchy evidence really. Mostly circumstantial. Never would have held up in a civil court y'know. But in courts martial a man is guilty until he proves his innocence.'

'And the four million in gold?'

'Yes?' Martland said.

'What happened to it?'

'Oh, God only knows.'

'You mean the army just wrote it off?'

'It was wartime. Four million dollars was . . . really nothing at all. I should guess . . . hmmm . . . probably charged off to the operational budget of the OSS, although military intelligence might have had to split it. I was gone before that was all settled.'

The room was quiet. Martland seemed to be drifting away from the conversation.

'I have one more question,' Livingston said, but Martland did not answer. 'Colonel?'

'Ah, yes?'

'How were the other Americans identified after all those months?'

'Dog tags. Personal belongings. No question about it. Ah, and one other thing. A Thompson gun issued to the man Corrigon was found in the grave. It was the most damaging piece of evidence against him.'

Sharky said, 'Can you think of anything else about Scardi?'

Martland reflected a few moments and said, 'Oh, it was exciting, having an American gangster there with us. He was quite a celebrity. Quite a celebrity.' Then he fell silent again and this time his gaze became almost glassy.

Sharky stood up. 'Well, thank you, sir. You've been a great help.'

'I did well, then, eh?'

'Yes, sir. You did well.'

Martland turned to the portrait. 'Hear that, Miriam. My memory's just as good as ever. Takes a while now, but it all comes back, my dear. It all comes back.'

And he sat on the crate, his shoulders beginning to sag, his gaze fixed on another time, the memories reflecting in his faded eyes, a time of mirror-shined shoes and white gloves, of chin straps and marching orders echoing through the barracks and tattoo in the late afternoon.

They drove for ten minutes without speaking. It was Sharky who finally broke the silence.

'It was like turning on a tape recorder, listening to someone dictating his memoirs. All of a sudden it would just pour out, like rote.'

'He's probably told that story a thousand times in the last thirty years, all about the wonderful American gangster.'

'Yeah, and probably word for word.'

'I feel sorry for the old coot,' Livingston said. 'The army's all he's got left and it ignores him, letting him hang around long enough to make general, so he can get a few more bucks in a pension he'll probably never spend. Shit.'

'What about Scardi? This Opstitch thing?'

'Anybody thinks Angelo Scardi didn't have a hand in a four-million-dollar ripoff ought to be committed.'

'But why wasn't that obvious to the army?'

'You heard what the old boy said. Four million in gold

was just a piss in the ocean. All they needed was a fall guy so they could close the book on it, charge it off on some budget. Jesus!'

They drove another block in silence and Livingston said, 'Go down Spring and turn into Carnegie Way.'

'Where we headed?'

'The public library. Best place I can think of to get a photograph of Scardi.'

Sharky waited in the car while Livingston went inside. He was gone for almost half an hour and when he returned was carrying a large manila envelope. He got into the car and took out a photograph and laid it in Sharky's lap.

'There's the face to go with the name,' he said.

Sharky stared down at it. It was a copy of a newspaper photo of a man seated at a table surrounded by reporters and photographers, his hands splayed out in a gesture of innocence. But the look was there, in the vapid stiletto face, the hawk nose, the dead eyes, the humourless grin on thin, cruel lips, the slick black hair. It was a face that was easy to hate and Sharky's anger welled up anew, stirring his lust for retribution, an almost perverse passion that overwhelmed him, swelling in his groin, churning in his stomach. At that moment Sharky could easily have killed Scardi with his bare hands.

Livingston took Xerox copies of several clippings from the envelope.

'I ain't gonna bore you with a lot of details,' Livingston said, 'but I thought you might like to get a taste. This creep's got a pedigree you won't believe. When he was fourteen he had to leave Sicily because he slit a neighbour's throat in some kind of family squabble. He lived in *northern* Italy for five years before he came over here. His uncle was Lupo the Wolf, the son of a bitch who started the Black Hand movement. . . . Came here in '35, arrested the next year for extortion and kidnapping . . . Christ, here's an article says he was suspected of killing over fifty people. You know where he got the nickname The Undertaker? He supposedly invented the double-deck coffin, to get rid of hits.'

'And when did he *supposedly* die?'

Livingston checked through the sheaf of Xeroxed clippings. 'Here's his obit. February 16, 1968. Cancer.'

'And Howard Burns arrived in Lincoln in 1968. How convenient.'

'I wonder if the Feds really think they got their money's worth out of him?' .

'Anything else in there? How about that . . . heroic war record of his?'

Livingston rummaged through more articles. He stopped at one and said, 'Hey, listen to this. According to this story Scardi did his first hit for Lucky Luciano and he screwed it up and Luciano chewed his ass and told him he didn't get close enough to the mark. The next day Scardi gives Luciano a box with the guy's ears in it and says, "Here, was that close enough?" '

Sharky's grip on the wheel tightened.

'All it says about his war record,' said Livingston, 'is that he was about to be deported in 1944 as an undesirable alien, but the case was dropped after he, quote, "performed valuable and courageous services for the invasion forces of Italy". Unquote. Nothing about guerrilla operations.'

'Extortion . . . kidnapping . . . murder . . . and they made a deal with him,' Sharky said. 'That's the courageous war hero Martland thought was such a sweetheart.'

'Makes you wonder what the hell kind of deal they made with him in '68,' said Livingston. 'He musta come down on half the Mafia.'

Sharky thought to himself, *This time there won't be any deals, because this time the government isn't going to get near him, this time we're going to put that son of a bitch out of business permanently – one way or the other.*

And he said aloud, 'This time he's ours.'

'We gotta get him first,' Livingston said.

Chapter Nineteen

There were only two things in Sergeant Herb Anderson's entire life that he was proud of: a commendation he had won when, while off-duty, he had overpowered an armed robber sticking up a Seven-Eleven Market; the other was his son Tommy, an all-city football player who had already been offered three college scholarships and the season was only over a week.

The rest of his life had been a downhill slide. His other son, Harry, had been a problem since he was a child. The boy had been in and out of private schools all his life and as a result Anderson's wife, Lucy, had gradually turned into a hypertense, morose hypochondriac, a woman who complained constantly of back trouble, headaches, female problems, and lumps in her breast which the doctor somehow could never find.

Anderson himself had changed through the years from a jovial man, well liked by the other members of the force, to a depressed and involuted misfit, a man harassed by financial problems and a son he both loved and despised, who worked long hours to escape the enervating atmosphere at home. It was his reputation as a tireless workhorse that had earned him a sergeant's stripes.

He was grateful when Priest called him on Saturday morning, his day off, because it gave him an honest excuse to escape the house and enjoy a lunch at the Regency.

The man Anderson knew as Priest was actually Gerald Kershman. It was Kershman who picked the busy bars in the better hotels, which were more popular with transients than with the local trade. He usually arrived fifteen minutes ahead of Anderson, seeking out the most secluded and the darkest corner in the room. Not that anyone would recognize Kershman or particularly remember him; it was his own paranoia at work. It was one of DeLaroza's peculiar quirks, and he had many, that the corporation should always have a strong police contact in every city in which it did business. Kershman, for his own reasons, had been more than willing to oblige. He was called on to provide information from time to time, nothing particularly onerous, and yet Kershman, a man with many complexes, always became nervous when he met with Anderson. He didn't like his hangdog attitude, the inevitable spots on his ties, and mostly the fact that, while Anderson was a fair police officer, he was not too sharp. It was a struggle for Kershman to conceal his contempt and his sense of superiority when he was around Anderson.

Kershman nursed a marguerita until Anderson arrived, a few minutes late and apologizing as usual. He ordered his usual Michelob draught and sat with a forced grin on his face. Kershman avoided asking about Anderson's family, a question that usually resulted in a fifteen-minute monologue that ended like a chapter from a soap opera. Kershman had established himself as a correspondent for a European news syndicate, a perfect cover story for the kind of information he usually sought.

'I'm in a bit of a jam,' Kershman said, getting right to it.

'What's the problem?' Anderson asked and his concern annoyed Kershman.

'I heard there was a homicide in one of the fancy apartment houses out on Peachtree last night,' Kershman said. 'Thing is, there's been nothing reported so far on it. Nothing on TV, the radio, in the newspapers. My problem is I queried our news office about it before really checking it out and they're hot for the story. Now it looks like my tip may have been unreliable.'

'Did you check the police reports?'

'Yes. Nothing.'

Anderson frowned. Then shook his head as though disagreeing with his own thoughts. 'There was this John Doe turned up in the city dump yesterday. Now, that would make a good story for you. No hands. His hands were *cut off*. And he was shot in the face with a shotgun.'

Kershman listened intently to Anderson, making mental notes of everything he said. He always was prepared to tell DeLaroza more than he wanted to know rather than less.

'This was definitely a woman,' Kershman said.

'I was around until four o'clock this morning. Lot of crazy things going on, but I would have heard if there was a killing in that neighbourhood.'

'Well, if you could check around, discreetly. Perhaps, uh, there's some reason the police are keeping it under wraps. I would prefer not to create any curiosity. I just thought I might get something from the inside on it.'

'I'll go on down after we leave here, snoop around quietly. See if Twigs knows anything. He's the county coroner.'

'Remember, I don't want to make any waves. This must be done carefully just in case they are working on something they don't want the press to know about.' He paused to sip the marguerita and then asked, 'What crazy stuff was going on?'

Anderson chuckled. 'Oh, Larry Abrams was screwing around with something half the night. A tape of some kind for the Vice Squad. He's working with a new man over there named Sharky.'

'What was on the tape?'

'I don't know. Neither does he. Know what he said? He said it sounded like a Chinese orgy.'

Kershman took another sip and kept listening.

'What made me think of it is that I picked up a post mortem tape for Abrams about two A.M. from Grady Hospital. It wasn't the John Doe, because Twigs was complaining that Riley in Homicide was pushing him to do it before he went home.'

'I see. Well, if you could just kind of check around. The thing is, I'm pushed for time. If there is something I can chase down, I'd like to know by this evening.'

'I'll do my damn best,' Anderson said sincerely.

'Was there anything else?'

'Nope. Actually it wasn't a very lively night. Oh, yeah, Abrams pulled a fingerprint report for somebody, too. I took it down to him. Funny thing, he got a positive make on the prints, but the subject's been dead for a couple of months. Some truck driver from Nebraska.'

'And who is this Abrams?'

'A wiretap man, been in the OC six months or so. Nice little guy. Very talented. The Feds even borrow him every once in a while.'

'Maybe he was doing this job for the government people,' Kershman suggested.

'No, I saw the tape. It had Sharky's name on it.'

'And what about this Sharky?'

'I'm surprised you didn't do something on him. He's the narcotics cop who shot the pusher on the bus the other night.'

'Oh, yes, of course.' Kershman remembered seeing the headline, but he had not paid much attention to the story.

'He was transferred into the Vice Squad because of it,' Anderson said. 'Now keep that under your derby, okay? It hasn't been released publicly.'

'I won't say a word,' Kershman said.

Chapter Twenty

Sharky had filed a radio message through central for Friscoe to meet him and Livingston at a pizza parlour on Peachtree Street called Franco's. They had been there less than ten minutes when Friscoe arrived, puffing through the door and looking no better or worse than he had at breakfast. Friscoe plopped down in the booth with them and waved the waiter away.

'I got so much coffee in me, I couldn't eat if I wanted to,' he said. 'So, you got some news?'

Livingston was eating a submarine sandwich. Without looking up he said, 'We just wanted to say hello. We thought maybe you missed us.'

'Anything new?' Sharky said, concentrating on a piece of pizza that had everything on it but chocolate syrup.

The lieutenant smiled proudly. 'Yeah, I made a little score. I got lucky like Papa. Kenny Bautry, a Fed probation officer, has a guy who fits the description of the stiff in the city dump pretty good. Did *thirty* years plus in the joint at Leavenworth. Got out in October, reported once, and Kenny hasn't seen him since.'

Sharky took another bite of pizza. 'Name isn't Corrigon, is it?' he said.

'Well shit!' Friscoe said. 'I'm gonna get a goddamn complex.'

Livingston slid the picture of Scardi across the table in front of Friscoe. 'That's who hit Corrigon and Domino.'

Friscoe looked at the picture and reared back in surprise. 'That's Angelo Scardi!'

'That's very good, Barney,' Livingston said.

Friscoe looked back at the picture with disbelief. 'Angelo *Scardi?*' he repeated.

Sharky nodded. 'There's no question about it, Barney. We got a positive on the prints.' Then he leaned across the table and quietly told Friscoe about Scardi, Operation Stitch, and Corrigon. Friscoe listened without comment and then leaned back in the booth, letting it all sink in.

'So, what's your theory?' he asked.

'Arch and I think Scardi rigged the whole operation from the front end and somebody finished the job for him and fingered Corrigon.'

'Such as . . .'

Sharky said, 'Maybe this La Volte. Look, Scardi lived in that same area from 1930 until 1935. And Scardi was the only person who ever actually *met* La Volte face to face. Martland says Scardi only knew him by his code name, but I think that's bullshit. I think Scardi knew this guy from the old days. I think it was set up from the beginning that La Volte would hit the team when it went in. Scardi put it all together, then conveniently got sick and came back to the U.S. That took him out of action and put him three thousand miles away when it happened – with a perfect alibi. Then he and La Volte split four mil in gold.'

'That's pretty good,' Friscoe said. 'But what we can't do, we can't get too cocky yet. We got to collar Scardi. But we also got to fill in some blanks here.'

'Like what?' Livingston asked.

'Like why did Scardi come here? And why did he off Domino? And what was Corrigon doin' here? This guy gets outa Leavenworth after thirty years, gets on the first bus south, and comes straight to Atlanta. But he wasn't looking for Scardi, because Scardi was still in Nebraska at the time.'

'That's right,' Sharky said. 'Which means Corrigon was after somebody else and that somebody else pulled Scardi in to do the number on Corrigon.'

'And you think it was La Volte he was after, right?' Friscoe said.

'What the hell would this Italian guerrilla be doin' in Atlanta?' Livingston asked.

Friscoe shrugged. 'It's thirty years ago this other thing happened. Shit, in thirty years you can get born, grow up, go to college, get married, lose your cherry, have a coupla kids, and buy a house. You can do that, this fuckin ' guinea could certainly hop a plane to Atlanta.'

'Whoever it was,' Sharky said, 'Scardi can lead us to him.'

'That's right,' Friscoe said. 'But now's the time we gotta handle this here thing with kid gloves. What it comes down to, we gotta nail this Scardi with his hands full and we got to tie him to La Volte or whoever brought him in to glom Corrigon. If we don't, you know what's gonna happen. The

295

goddamn DA ends up with the case and that's like dropping a diamond in a dirty diaper. Unless we got an iron-clad case against these people, Hanson'll fuck it up. He's a legal moron, remember. I mean, shit, we could bribe the fuckin' *jury* and he could manage to lose the case.

'Look at what we got now,' Friscoe continued. 'We can put Scardi in the Jackowitz apartment, but at this point we can't get him from there to Domino's door with a shotgun in his hands. And we can't tie him to this La Volte, or whoever the hell his partner in crime is. Knowing all this is one thing, proving it is a whole 'nother ballgame.'

'So we need to tie Domino to Scardi somehow,' Sharky said.

'A big somehow,' said Livingston.

'Okay, I'm going to take on Domino's apartment,' Sharky said. 'It's been sealed up since the shooting. Maybe there's something there, an address book, letters, something that can put us closer to Scardi's accomplice.'

'Okay. Papa's still trying to run down Shoes. Your friend Abrams finally went home for a little shuteye. He'll be back in his workshop there by six. How about you, Arch?'

Livingston leaned back in the booth and grinned. 'I'm gonna do the best thing possible for this machine right now,' he said. 'I'm goin' home and grab a few hours of z's, because if I don't Sharky's gonna have a sleepwalker on his hands tonight.'

Chapter Twenty-One

DeLaroza was in a black mood and it got worse as he sat under the subdued lights in his office listening to Kershman's succinct yet detailed report on what appeared to be several unrelated events at the police station. But the more Kershman talked the more the worms nibbled at DeLaroza's insides. Bits and pieces came at him. And as Kershman continued, the pieces seemed to start fitting together. The rambling report was beginning to make an uneasy kind of sense to him. A single thread seemed now to be weaving through the information.

A sheet of paper lay on the desk in front of him, covered with doodles, with names and words. As soon as Kershman finished, DeLaroza dismissed him and then sat and stared at the sheet, at the Freudian shorthand dictated by his subconscious.

Who were these two, Sharky and Abrams, and what were they up to? The questions hammered at his brain. He began circling words and phrases on the sheet.

Sharky.
Abrams.
Truck driver.
Nebraska.
Orgy.
Chinese orgy.
Wiretap expert.
Fingerprints.

He made a new list, arranging the words in what he felt was a chronological order. Sharky and Abrams. Wiretrap expert. Orgy, Chinese orgy. Fingerprints, truck driver, Nebraska. And he added another: post mortem. And then ahead of the words 'truck driver' he added another word. 'Dead.'

Finally at the bottom of his new list he added still another word, 'Corrigon,' for that had been the first upsetting news. He had hoped that Corrigon's corpse would elude the police until after Burns was gone. It was an unfortunate stroke, but one which he did not consider serious. There was no way they could possibly connect all this to Corrigon, he thought. He scratched the name off.

The rest of it was serious. He tried to shrug off the feeling of danger that had turned the worms in his stomach to writhing snakes. The dead 'truck driver' from Nebraska had to be Burns, there was no question in his mind now that they knew it. Could Burns have made such an amateurish mistake as to leave fingerprints on the scene? And what about this wiretap of the Chinese orgy? He could not erase the memory of Domino that last night from his mind. Was it possible that this Abrams had bugged Domino's apartment before she was killed?

He threw the pencil down. No, these were not unrelated bits and pieces. These two, Abrams and Sharky, were on to something.

His panic slowly turned to rage and then to quiet deliberation. Too many dreams were about to come true for him. Hotchins. *Pachinko!* His own final release from the self-imposed prison in which he had lived for thirty years. He had outwitted governments, the army, the FBI, the CIA, some of the keenest police minds in the world, and now, at this moment, he was threatened by two simple cops. Two cops? Ridiculous!

He sat that way for perhaps half an hour, almost transfixed as he stared at the doodles. A plan was formulating in his mind. It was daring and dangerous but it would work. He considered alternatives and mentally disposed of each one. The more he considered it, the more perfect the plan became. Finally he began to smile. He reached under the desk and pressed a button. A moment later Chiang loomed in the doorway of the office, his scar accentuated by the soft overhead lights, his sightless eye gleaming like a shining coin in the shadows that masked part of his face.

'Get the car,' he said. 'We must go to the country airport and meet Hotchins.'

Chiang nodded and was gone. Ten minutes later DeLaroza climbed into the back seat of the Rolls and they pulled out of the indoor parking lot under the building. DeLaroza lowered the window between the front and back seats and spoke in Chinese to Chiang.

'There is something that must be done,' he said. 'It must be done quickly but with great caution. The doctor will help you make the arrangements. The foreign devil, Burns, who was on the junk, has become a danger to me. He is insane. He makes threats. And he also makes mistakes. Also there are two policemen who threaten me.'

Chiang listened quietly. He asked no questions as DeLaroza outlined his plan. Nothing changed in Chiang's face, not a muscle. It was as if DeLaroza were telling him the time. When he finished, Chiang nodded again.

'Remember,' DeLaroza said, 'use the shotgun. It must appear like the work of the *Gwai-lo*. When that is done, then we must deal with Burns. Do not underestimate this man. He is sixty years old, but he is still very quick. He will kill without thinking; it is his nature. He trusts nobody and he is very suspicious. That part of it must be done with great skill.'

Chiang nodded. The silent Oriental was thinking about Burns, the *Gwai-lo* who killed without honour. The barest hint of a smile touched the corners of his mouth.

DeLaroza settled back. He felt relieved. In his mind, the problem was resolved. Now he faced a bigger one. In fifteen minutes he would pick up Hotchins and tell him that Domino was dead. How he would do that already consumed his thoughts.

Chapter Twenty-Two

The JetStar sighed to a comfortable landing and taxied to the hangar where its door swung quietly open and the hydraulic stairway unfolded to the ground. DeLaroza sat in the back of the Rolls, watching as Hotchins came down the stairway and was led to the car by Chiang. He looked good, although he was limping slightly, usually a sign that he was tired or his artificial foot was acting up. But he smiled as he got into the car.

'Well, it is good you are back,' DeLaroza said as the Rolls floated onto the highway. 'There is much to be done.'

'I've accomplished quite a bit already,' Hotchins said enthusiastically.

'Ah, the trip was successful, then?'

'More than you think.'

'Excellent. And the senator, will he endorse you Monday night?'

Hotchins nodded slowly. 'He's his crusty old self, of course. Just as overbearing and patronizing as ever. I spent three hours with him this morning wandering around that damn farm until I thought my foot would fall off, but he's in. The old boy wants a cabinet post.'

'Not a great surprise to either of us. What does he want?'

'Agriculture.'

DeLaroza considered the point and nodded. 'Not an unwise choice, do you think? He is quite popular with the farmers.'

'Yeah. And the insurance companies. The food processors. The power companies and gasoline companies. God, he's sold out to every seedy lobbyist in Washington.'

'Still, he is respected.'

'He's more important to us in the Senate. We need that seniority. But I'll work that out. The important thing is that he'll be there Monday and he'll endorse me.'

'Splendid. It is going well, exceptionally well.'

'There are still a couple of other congressmen who are playing hard to get. I think we should give them a chance to get on board now or screw them.'

'You are feeling heady. I can tell.'

'I'm feeling like a winner.'

'Well, the trip was a success. Excellent.' DeLaroza took out a Havana cigar, but he did not unwrap it. He twirled it in his fingers. He had been waiting sixteen years for this moment, the moment of reckoning. Now at last was the time to test power with power. He enjoyed the moments of anticipation. Hotchins sensed his mood.

'Is something bothering you?' he asked.

'No, not really. Why do you ask?'

'Victor, I've known you intimately for sixteen years. I know when something is bothering you.'

DeLaroza smiled. 'And here I thought I was so inscrutable.'

'You may be to others. Your Chinese friends are certainly inscrutable. But I know you. What is it? Are we having a problem with Lowenthal?'

A problem with Lowenthal, DeLaroza thought. *If we were, who is more capable of handling it than I?* He was somewhat nervous anyway, although he had carefully planned the conversation. But now Hotchins was beginning to annoy him. He was being... he was being *smug*. DeLaroza smiled and said quietly, 'Not at all. I spent the evening with him and we had coffee this morning. He was nervous about starting the campaign so soon, but I believe he is convinced it is for the best.'

'Good,' Hotchins patted DeLaroza's leg. 'I'm glad you're finally getting directly involved.'

Directly involved. There it was again. The man is beginning to treat me as though he is *the president.*

'I was under the impression I was always directly involved,' DeLaroza said, trying to hide his growing anger.

'Oh, of course, of course,' Hotchins said. 'I just mean you're more open now. You were always so damn cautious about publicity and pictures. It was almost a phobia.'

'Phobia?'

'Well, you know what I mean. Anyway, of course you're involved. You've been a close confidant for years.'

Confidant. DeLaroza began to laugh out loud. *The audacity of this man.*

'What's so funny?' Hotchins said.

'You are. My God, your smugness goes beyond conceit.'

301

'Smugness. What do you mean, smugness?'

'You are smug, Donald. You think you have done this, gone this far, all by yourself? The one-man show, eh? Why do you think Lowenthal is here? Because I talked to him. Several times. Because I paid his expenses down here. Because I guaranteed that the financing is available. You think he is an amateur? And now that he is here, it is business, not charisma. Politics is business.'

'I don't believe you. The first thing we discussed was the cost of the campaign.'

'Of course. It is the key to victory. He wants reassurance, Mr. Senator. He cannot afford to ride another loser. And then, after you discussed the business, to whom did you come running? To me. Your *confidant*, Donald? I have pulled your strings for years.'

'Nobody pulls my strings,' Hotchins said. His eyes burned with fury.

'Oh? And who told you when you were ready for the senate race? You were not sure. I made the decision. And I paid for the campaign. And who decided this would be the right year for the big one. Was it you, Donald? No. I said, this is the right year, this is the year we do it.'

'Why don't you just run the race, too?'

'I wish I could. I am a naturalized citizen. It could never be.'

'Nobody owns me, Victor. And nobody's going to own me when I get into the White House.'

'Without me there will be no White House.'

'What is this?' Hotchins said. 'Why this sudden attack? What do you want?'

'Recognition. For years I have been the man in the wings, giving away the credit for everything I have achieved. You take the credit here and you take the credit there. I want recognition,' he said, and then, louder: 'I want recognition.'

Hotchins sneered at him. 'I should have known. Sixteen years and you've never asked for anything. And now, the worm turns.'

'Now the worm *can* turn,' DeLaroza said.

'What's that supposed to mean?'

DeLaroza smiled. 'It is quite a long story. I do not think now is the time to bore you with it. Besides, there is something else I must tell you. And believe me, it is not a happy task.'

'What? What's happened?'

'It concerns Domino.'

Hotchins relaxed. He waved his hand towards DeLaroza as if dismissing the discussion before it started. 'You can forget Domino. Domino is past history. That problem's solved.'

'I am not sure you understand what I am trying to tell you.'

'What the hell are you driving at?'

'Donald, Domino is dead.'

Hotchins stared at him intently. He shook his head very slightly.

'She's what?'

'A police friend of mine told me as I was leaving the office. I don't have the detail – '

Hotchins cut him off. He was wild-eyed. 'What do you mean she's dead? How did it happen?'

'She was shot.'

'Shot?'

'Yes. It happened in her apartment last night. . . .'

He stopped. Gooseflesh rose along his arm. Hotchins's reaction chilled him for a moment. He was laughing. *Laughing.*

'I knew there was a mistake,' he said. 'You better get a more reliable police friend.'

'Believe me,' DeLaroza said. 'What I am telling you is true.'

Hotchins leaned across the seat towards DeLaroza. 'It's bullshit, Vic.'

'My source is unimpeachable,' DeLaroza said sternly.

'No, my friend,' Hotchins said, 'my source is unimpeachable. My source is me. Domino was with me last night. *All* night.'

Now it was DeLaroza who looked stunned. The lines in his forehead deepened. He seemed almost angry.

'Look, she flew to Savannah yesterday and we spent the night on the boat. It was all very safe. And I told her we had to stop seeing each other. I think she was as relieved about it as I was. So relax. It was a mistake, that's all.'

A mistake, DeLaroza thought. *That maniac Burns had made a mistake. Or had he lied?*

'Was someone else staying in her apartment?' DeLaroza asked.

'I have no idea. Why?'

'Because someone was shot in her apartment last night. A terrible mistake has been made.'

'Mistake? What kind of mistake?'

'It was Domino who was supposed to die.'

'Supposed to . . .' Hotchins stopped. A frightening thought swept past his mind, but he immediately dismissed it. 'What do you mean "supposed to"?'

DeLaroza's mind was churning. He had to move fast, get to Domino before the police. But first it was time to deal with Hotchins. Now was the time of reckoning. It could wait no longer.

'Did you hear me?' Hotchins said. 'What did you mean by that?'

'Donald, maybe it is time we had that talk I referred to a few minutes ago. The one I said would bore you. You may find some of the details a bit unsettling, so prepare yourself.'

'What are you talking about?'

'I am talking about Domino. I am talking about the minute planning that went into your career. I am talking about where the money comes from to finance this gamble. And I am talking about why, suddenly, I have decided to go public, as they say. Do you want to hear the story, Donald?'

'Of course,' Hotchins said, but there was a nervousness in his tone.

'Just listen to me,' DeLaroza said. 'Please do not interrupt until I am finished.'

Hotchins was somewhat mystified by the coldness in DeLaroza's tone. He shifted in his seat so that he was facing him. 'All right, I'm listening.'

'When I introduced you to Domino, you were aware that I had known her for several months. When I first met her, she was a charming woman and of course her natural attributes were undeniable. She was like a bud and I nurtured the bud into a blossom of paradise. She was the perfect answer to my problem and my problem was you. You were teetering on the edge of disaster, my friend, consumed by loneliness. Depression hovered over you like a cloud. Domino was the perfect answer. It took several months, of course, to develop her latent treasures, but it was a task that was not without its rewards.'

'Damn it, Victor – '

'*Listen to me*,' DeLaroza snapped, his eyes afire. 'When you met her she was the ultimate seductress because of *me*. I am the one who saw the incredible potential. And you know why? Because she understands that in order to satisfy others she must satisfy herself. And she loves power as much as you or I. There was no question from the beginning. The infatuation would be total. She provided you with fire when you needed it most. And of course you took it, took it all. It was a dangerous game because it had to end. Sooner or later she would become a liability. And the liabilities must be destroyed. The danger during the campaign would have been unbearable and – after you became president – impossible. So you see, dear Donald, her death was inevitable.'

Hotchins withdrew to his corner of the seat, his expression reflecting the terrifying truth in DeLaroza's words. He could hardly speak and when he did his words came in a hoarse whisper.

'Stop talking about her in the past tense.'

'Why not? DeLaroza said, unwrapping his cigar. 'She is past tense to me. I ordered her death.'

Hotchins was hollow-eyed. 'You . . . arranged her murder?'

'Of course. It was a political necessity. It was a political necessity from the day you met her.'

'You planned it all along? You never considered an alternative?'

'I considered all alternatives. Among them the danger of blackmail, or perhaps ghost-written memoirs filled with lurid details. No, there was never was an alternative.'

'There has to be an alternative to murder.'

'Not always.'

Hotchins shuddered and looked as if he were going to be sick. He beat on the front seat and yelled at Chiang. 'Stop the car. I need some air.'

'Get hold of yourself,' DeLaroza snapped. 'And if you are considering a lecture on morality, please spare me. We are survivalists, you and I. We survive at all costs. It is one of the things that attracted me to you.'

'I won't be made part of this,' Hotchins said. 'I would never have sanctioned – '

DeLaroza waved his hand at Hotchins. 'Please. It is not just murder we are talking about. Where do you think the fortunes came from to finance your career – all the millions of dollars, all the small contributions, so carefully planned and perfectly legitimate? Everything above scrutiny. You never asked, did you? And we know why. Because you do not want to know the answer, right? Now you see the tip of an iceberg and suddenly you want to see the whole thing. Well, I say, forget it. Think about *your* alternatives.'

Hotchins could think of nothing but the horror. Like an insane newsreel, names and faces swept past his eyes. Sacks, the prison camp, the endless political campaigns, and the hollow personal life. And Domino and the energy she had brought to him. Now all the years of planning and dreaming began to crumble in his mind. Was he going to lose it all?

'The alternatives, Donald. It is really quite simple. You will either be the most powerful political figure in the world, or the most despised. Nobody likes a martyr. They are losers. If you should suddenly feel overly honest and decide to reveal all, remember that. In six months no one will care whether you revealed the truth or not. Those who believed in you will feel betrayed. Those who are against you will be delighted. And you? You will be destroyed. What is it going to be, eh?'

Hotchins leaned back and slumped into the seat. He did not answer.

'Let me tell you a quick little story. In 1945, at the height of the war in Italy, an American soldier disguised as an Italian peasant led eight mules loaded with gold bullion through the Brenner Pass in the Alps into Switzerland. The gold was stolen from the army. I spent five years in Switzerland, learning to speak like a Brazilian, manufacturing the identity of Victor DeLaroza. The millions we have spent financing your career? All of it started with stolen government money. It is not just Domino, my friend. It is your entire career. And every dollar of it is recorded, Donald.'

The bigger the prize, the higher the price, Hotchins

306

thought to himself. *And now it is time to pay. The moment of reckoning.*

'They'll find out,' Hotchins said quietly. 'Somebody always finds out.'

'No. I have been at this a very long time. I am an expert at deceit.'

DeLaroza laughed, devils dancing in his turquoise pupils. The web had been spun with such care, such patience, spreading a strand at a time across so many years that no one could comprehend the maze. It was a work of terrifying ingenuity.

'Everything is well covered, believe me,' he said. 'The last person who might have recognized me has been eliminated. There is only one danger to the entire plan right now. Domino.'

Hotchins said nothing.

'She will realize we tried to kill her. When is she due back?'

Hotchins still said nothing.

'Get hold of yourself, Donald,' DeLaroza said with annoyance in his tone. 'When is she due back?'

Hotchins looked down slowly at his watch.

'Now. She is on her way back to the apartment right now.'

'Then we have no time to lose. It must be done right this time.'

'No!'

'You prefer to be destroyed then?'

'She won't say anything.'

'Don't you understand? Somebody was killed in her apartment last night. They will put her under lights. She will break down. They will find out everything. Is that what you want?'

'I . . . don't know.'

'I have never known you to be self-destructive before.'

'I've never been involved in murder before.'

'Ah. Yes, that is true. So, you are the leader. The one-man show who does it all. Tell me, shall I forget about Domino, then?'

Silence.

'I am awaiting your answer, Mr. Senator. Now it is *your* decision.'

'I . . . can't. . . .'

'Of course you can. Think about it. The alternatives, Donald, the alternatives. What shall I do?'

Hotchins's face was drawn. The web DeLaroza had spun was indeed awesome. Had he been a mere dauphin in DeLaroza's grand scheme? The fear of deceit had lain deep in Hotchins's subconscious for years. Now the knowledge of it was like a smouldering fire that could either be fanned to life by his conscience or smothered by his avarice.

'The pluses and the minuses,' he muttered aloud.

'Ah, yes, the pluses and the minuses.'

In the end Hotchins knew he had no choice. When he stripped away the emotional considerations, as he always had, as he always would, it came down to the simple formula. The pluses and the minuses.

'Well?' DeLaroza said.

'Do . . . what you think . . . is best.'

'No. You are the one who makes the decisions. Nobody pulls your strings, is that not correct? So, tell me. Say it, Donald.'

He shook his head.

'Then we shall let nature take its course?'

'No!'

'No? Then tell me, what shall I do?'

Hotchins lowered his head like a child.

'Just take care of it.'

'*Say* it,' DeLaroza demanded.

But Hotchins just shook his head again. He tried to say it but the words crumbled in his mouth like ashes. The moment of reckoning had passed.

Chapter Twenty-Three

The lingering stench of death, the bitter smell of cordite which seemed to hang obstinately in the air, the rancid salty odour of dried blood, the oppressiveness of the closed room was overwhelming. Sharky leaned against the door, staring at the pockmarks in the wall, the brown stains streaking down to the floor. Faltering images played at the back of his mind, images he wanted to forget but needed to remember.

He was close to exhaustion. His bones ached; his lungs hurt when he breathed; his vision was fuzzy, his mouth dry and hot. He went into the kitchen, found a Coke in the refrigerator, and sat down at the kitchen table to drink it. He decided to start in the kitchen as long as he was there.

He took a legal pad and a felt-tip pen out of the small briefcase he had brought with him and wrote the word *kitchen* on the top line. Under it he would list anything that seemed incongruous with its surroundings.

The room was neat, tidy, sparkling clean. The counter-tops were bare except for an antique wine rack in one corner, some appliances, and a paper sack with two wine-glasses and a corkscrew beside it on the counter near the sink. He checked the garbage pail. It was clean enough to cook in. Next he checked the paper bag, using his pen to spread the top open. There was a bottle of wine inside and a sales slip. The wine had been purchased the previous day from Richard's Fine Wines. It cost eighteen dollars.

He started his list:

Counter: paper sack.
Bottle of Lafite-Rothschild wine, value $18.
Two wine glasses.
Corkscrew.

During the next two hours Sharky carefully analysed each room in the apartment. As the list grew his adrenalin started pumping again, warming the aches away, providing a second wind. When he was finished, he went back to the kitchen and started a new list under the heading *Significant*. When he finished the list, he sat back and smiled. His eyes had lost the dull, glassy look of fatigue. He smacked his hands together and said, '*God damn!*' aloud and reached for the phone, pacing the length of the cord while it rang half a dozen times.

'Yeah,' Livingston said hoarsely. For a moment he was completely disorganized. He could not remember what day it was or where he was.

'It's Sharky.'

Livingston opened and closed his eyes several times and cleared his throat.

'Yeah?'

'Can you get over here?'

'Where, man?'

'Domino's apartment.'

'Oh, yeah. Well, uh, what time is it?'

'Hell I don't know, it's . . . a quarter to six.'

'Shit, I've only had two hours' sleep.'

'Arch, get over here fast.'

'You got something?'

'I got enough to wake you up real good, man. Get it over here fast as you can.'

Livingston was awake now. 'On my way, baby, on my way.'

He jumped off the bed. He was wearing shorts and a tee-shirt. He pulled on a pair of corduroy Levis and slipped on a plaid shirt and strapped his hip holster to his belt. On the way out the door he grabbed a fur-lined jacket. It took him fifteen minutes to get to Domino's apartment.

'Okay,' he said as Sharky opened the door, 'what you got up your sleeve now?'

Sharky led him into the kitchen. He had made a pot of coffee and he pushed Livingston into a chair, shoved a cup of coffee in front of him, and sat down with his legal pad.

'What I did,' he said, 'I washed the place from top to bottom and I made a list of everything that was even slightly out of the ordinary. Stuff like keys on the living-room table, suitcase on the floor, bottle of wine on the kitchen cabinet, everything. Then I went back over the list and made a second list, only this time I only put down stuff that seemed to relate.'

310

'Uh huh,' Livingston said.

'Okay, here's what I got:

'Item: An eighteen-dollar bottle of wine on the kitchen counter still in the bag, two wine glasses, and a corkscrew. The wine was purchased yesterday. There are six bottles of wine in that rack over there, including a bottle of Lafite-Rothschild.

'Item: Keys on the coffee table in the living room. Six keys altogether. Two go to a General Motors car, two look like regular house keys, and one is a safe deposit box key. The other one was not on the key ring. It fits the door to this apartment.

'Item: A beat-up Samsonite one-suiter on the floor beside the bed, pushed back against the wall. The stuff in it is messed up, all pushed over to one side. It contains a tennis dress, sweat socks, underwear, no toilet articles, no make-up.

'Item: The luggage in the closet is all Gucci. Worth a fortune. Not a scratch on it.'

Livingston looked up, the coffee cup forgotten in his hand. Sharky went on.

'Item: A blue and white windbreaker hanging in the closet.

'Item: One yellow negligee on bed, spread out very neat.

'Item: One small leather case filled with make-up on the table and a Lady Schick electric razor. In the bathroom there's another electric razor. An Osterman, also for a lady.

'Item: No purse on the premises, no bank book, no address book.'

Livingston lit a small Schimmelpenninck cigar and twisted the legal pad around so he could read it. 'Well, that's a nice job, considering you musta done it in your sleep, but what're you drivin' at?'

Sharky chuckled. 'Okay, follow me on this. If Domino was going on a trip, why did she go out and spend eighteen bucks for a bottle of wine when she had one in her wine rack? And why was she getting ready to open it? You don't open a bottle of wine like that unless you plan to drink it all. So why open it if she was going to leave? Second, there's the suitcase. Look in the closet. She has three pieces of gorgeous luggage in there. Why would she carry that old beat-up job in there? Also look around here, Arch. The place is neat, neat, neat. Look in the suitcase. All the clothes are shoved to one side. But the negligee is spread out very prim and proper. Also the travelling case of make-up and the electric razor. Why two razors? And the windbreaker in the closet? It's the only jacket in there. All the rest of them are in the hall closet. Don't you see it, Arch? She wasn't packing to go anywhere, she was *un*packing. She took the make-up case and the electric razor *out* of the bag, that's why the clothes were mussed up. And she put her windbreaker in the closet. She was planning to put the negligee *on*, not pack it. The apartment key wasn't on her key ring because it wasn't hers. It was loaned to her . . . by Domino. Domino has a Mercedes, these keys are for a GM car. Don't you see it, Arch. Domino *was* out of town and the dead lady was staying in her apartment. Scardi killed the wrong person.'

Livingston looked down at the list. He was still sceptical. 'You're reaching, baby. I mean, some of this makes sense but . . .'

'No purse. No bank book. No address book. Where are they? They're not here, because Domino took hers with her and the woman Scardi killed *didn't* bring hers.'

'You're moving too fast for me.'

'I had to make sure, Arch, so I went down to the parking lot and I started checking those GM keys in every General Motors car down there. I checked fourteen before I found the one the keys fit. A seventy-five Riviera. This was under the seat. She must have forgotten it.'

He slid a woman's wallet across the table to Livingston who opened it and stared at the licence behind the plastic window.

'Je-sus Chee-rist,' Livingston said softly.

'I've never seen her before, but I'll bet you have.'

Livingston looked at the photograph on the driver's licence and nodded.

'Tiffany Paris,' he said.

'Scardi hit the wrong woman, Arch.'

'Maybe. Or maybe he was after Tiffany all the time.'

'It's possible, except for one thing. Scardi'd been snooping around here for a couple of days. It took him a while to luck into the Jackowitz set-up. So unless Tiffany made her plans several days ago to spend Friday night here, he

312

wouldn't have known she was going to be here. And if he didn't know she was going to be here, he was after Domino.'

Livingston jumped up and began pacing the room. 'Sure, it makes sense that way. Domino left here yesterday morning. Then Scardi went into the Jackowitz place and started watching the apartment. When Tiffany came in, he came across and cut down on her the minute she opened the door. She was backlit. And she and Domino are about the same height.'

'And the same colouring.'

'And if Scardi hit the wrong woman, he'll be back when he finds out. He's gonna finish it up right. I mean, his kind don't fuck up a job and walk away from it.'

'Remember the ears in the box he gave Luciano?'

'What we gotta do, we gotta find the lady and stash her someplace safe, someplace they can't find her. Then stake this apartment out and hope he comes back again.'

'Or track him down first.'

They both heard the sound at the same time, a grating of metal on metal. Someone was putting a key in the lock. Sharky vaulted out of his seat, pulling his automatic from under his arm, rushing from the kitchen towards the door. Livingston was right behind him, clawing for his .38. Sharky was six feet from the door when it swung open. He stopped, dropped into a crouch, and aimed the gun with both hands.

The door opened and he was face to face with Domino Brittain.

She looked at him, down at the gun, back at his flattened nose, and she raised an eyebrow.

'Something wrong with my elevator?' she said.

Sharky lowered his gun and sighed with relief. She did not move. She stared back and forth at the two detectives until Sharky took out his wallet and held it towards her, letting it flop open to his shield and I.D.

She looked at it, then leaned forward for a better look and stared over the top of it at him.

'A cop?' she said.

Sharky nodded.

'You're a *cop*?'

Sharky nodded again.

'A real . . . live . . . cop.'

'Detective,' he said, somewhat embarrassed.

'Detective.'

'Uh huh.'

She looked at Livingston.

'Him too?'

'That's Arch Livingston, my partner.'

'Pleased to meet you,' Livingston said, but she had already turned her gaze back to Sharky. She shook her head.

Livingston sidled up to Sharky.

'You two know each other?' he said with more than a little surprise in his tone.

'We met.'

'Oh, really?'

'We'll talk about it later.'

'You better believe we will.'

Domino stepped inside the room, but she could not see the wall, the open door blocked it. 'Would one of you gentlemen like to get my bag?' she said, pointing to the Gucci sitting in the hall, 'And then maybe we can talk about what you're doing in my apartment playing cops and robbers.'

Livingston took the bag and leaning close to Sharky, said, 'She's a cool one, buddy. But I guess you knew that already, right?'

'I said later,' Sharky muttered out of the side of his mouth.

Domino was standing very close to Sharky, and she looked at him and said, 'Now what was this about working on the elevators?'

'Sorry about that.'

'It's a pretty good act.'

He wanted to keep up the banter. He liked it and he liked her and he was grateful that she was still alive, grateful to be close to her again. He knew too that she was smart enough to sense it. But he had to change the subject and he dreaded what was coming.

'Domino,' he said seriously, 'who stayed here last night?'

'Are you grilling me? – is that what they call it?' She was still trying to keep the conversation light and Sharky was having difficulty making the transition. She looked past him, at the open door, and began to sense that something bad had happened here and then he stepped back and pushed the door shut and she saw it, the splattered blood stains, the pockmarks on the wall, and it began to register, first in her widened eyes, then her strangled cry. 'Oh, my God!'

'Was it Tiffany Paris who stayed here last night?' Livingston said.

'I-I-I-I . . .' she stammered.

'Easy,' Sharky said.

She thrust her fist against her teeth and turned away from the ghastly wall. The blood drained from her face and for a moment Sharky thought she was going to faint. He put his arm around her and as he did she began nodding very slowly.

'Arch,' Sharky said, 'there's some brandy in the dining room.'

'Right.'

'I'm sorry. I should have warned you but . . . I, uh . . . didn't know what to say. Tiffany was here last night, right?'

'Y-y-y-yes.' She looked up at him and her face began to go, first at the corners of her mouth, then the tears welling in her eyes. She started to ask a question, but the words caught in her throat and she choked. Livingston brought a pony of Courvoisier and handed it to her, but she did not take it, she kept searching Sharky's face, hoping her fears were wrong.

'I'm sorry,' Sharky said, 'she's dead.'

The tears came and she began to sag, weak-kneed, against him and he led her to the couch and sat down beside her. She covered her face with her hands, her fingers pressing against her eyelids, trying to control her feelings. Finally she broke down and began to sob.

'H-h-h-ow . . . d-d-did . . .?' she said and then stopped speaking. Sharky handed her the brandy. 'Here,' he said, 'try this.'

She took a sip and gagged.

'I h-h-hate brandy,' she said.

'Look,' Sharky said, 'I know how you must feel right now, but this is very important. When did Tiffany first know she was going to be staying here?'

Watery, bloodshot eyes peered over her trembling hands.

'I . . . decided on the spur of the moment to go to Savannah and . . . see some friends so I . . . told her she could . . . stay here for the night.'

'When was this?'

'Yesterday morning.'

'What time?'

'I had an early hair appointment at Raymond's on Piedmont Road and I called her after I was through. I guess it was about . . . ten-thirty. We met at Houlihan's for lunch and I gave her the key. Then I had to leave to catch my plane.'

'So she had no idea you were leaving town until ten-thirty yesterday morning?'

'That's right.'

'That does it,' Livingston said. 'We gotta get her outa here and fast. I'm gonna make a phone call.' He went into the bedroom.

'What's he talking about?' Domino asked.

'Are you okay now?'

'I guess. I don't know. Why . . . what happened to Tiff?'

'She was shot. About eight o'clock last night.'

Domino stared back toward the door, the full horror of what had happened working on her features. 'What *happened*? Was it a hold-up?'

'No, it wasn't a hold-up and it wasn't an accident. But . . . we think the killer made a mistake.'

The horror in her face turned to shock. 'Mistake?'

'We think . . . we're almost positive . . . that he was after you.'

'*Me!*'

'She was shot by an ex-Mafia assassin named Scardi. Angelo Scardi. Does that name mean anything to you?'

She shook her head and then said, 'Mafia?'

'How about the name Howard Burns?'

'No, no. Neither of them. I've never heard either of those names before. What do you mean, Mafia?'

'This Scardi was a Mafia killer. Someone hired him to kill you. He came here last night and got Tiffany by mistake.'

She was more controlled now, the shock and horror replaced by confusion and doubt. 'Why?'

'We were hoping you could answer that.'

'Well, I can't answer it,' she said and anger crept into her

316

tone. 'And I don't think you know . . . how do you know that?'

'This Scardi's a real pro. He's been planning it for several days. Don't you see? If Tiffany didn't know she was coming here until yesterday, it had to be you he was after. And he'll try again. He's not the kind who'll settle for a mistake. That's why we've got to get you out of here.'

She shook her head violently. 'No, I won't be forced out.'

'Forced out? We're not forcing you out; we're trying to save your life.'

Sharky understood her dilemma. Too much had happened for her to fully comprehend or accept.

'Just trust us, please. Believe me, you're in great danger as long as you stay here.'

'Trust you?' she said. 'You've already lied to me . . . that ridiculous story about the elevator. Now all this.'

'I'm sorry about that. There won't be any more lies, believe me. Now will you please throw some clean clothes in your bag so we can get out of here?'

'I want to call somebody,' she said.

'What do you mean, call somebody?'

'I mean, call somebody I know. I don't even know you. I don't know him. One minute you tell me you're one thing, the next minute you're something else. Now you want to drag me off somewhere. For all I know, you two may have killed Tiffany. Or maybe she isn't even dead. God, I don't know what to think.'

Domino's confidence was returning, the self-assurance, the impudence. Her shoulders seemed straighter, she held her chin up high, but with all the straining for composure there was still fear in her eyes. And Sharky's relief at finding her alive was beginning to turn to anger. He was tense and frustrated and his nerves tingled with lack of sleep. He recognized a volatile situation building up and he had to move to stop it. He stood up and taking her by the arm led her to the window and pointed to the other tower.

'See that apartment up there on the corner? That's where he waited. He's like a cobra. No conscience. He's killed fifty people. *Fifty* people! He killed a man and cut off his hands so we couldn't identify the victim. He found out those people were out of town and he broke into that apartment and he sat there all day, very patiently, waiting for your lights to come on and when he saw them he came over here and he rang the bell and when Tiffany opened the door he blew her head off with a double-barrelled shotgun. She was dead when she hit the floor. We couldn't even identify her. We thought it was you. Now pretty soon he's gonna find out, see, that he made a mistake and when he does he's gonna come back, because that's what he's all about. He's out there someplace, in the dark, waiting. Maybe he knows already. Maybe he's up on the roof, watching us right now. Or waiting in the back seat of your car. Or maybe just outside the door there – '

'Stop it!' she cried.

'Am I making my point?'

'He's right, you know,' Livingston said from the doorway. 'You stay here and you might just as well hang a target on your forehead and sit in the window waiting for it to come.'

'Ohhh.' She shuddered.

'We're not doing this for effect,' Sharky said. 'We want to keep you alive, Domino, and not just because it's our job. I like you. We thought . . . we thought we lost you once. We don't want it to happen again.' He turned to Livingston. 'Are we set?'

Livingston nodded. 'The place is safe and comfortable. Clean. It beats the hell out of a pine box.'

She held her hand up and stopped him. 'All right. That's enough. I don't understand any of this, but you've convinced me.'

She got up and went to the bedroom. 'May I change? I've been in these clothes all day.'

'Keep away from the windows,' Sharky said.

'Will you stop *saying* things like that!'

'I'm not trying to scare you,' Sharky said. 'I mean it. Stay away from the windows.'

'Where am I going?'

Livingston said, 'I'll tell you when we get there. The less you know now, the better.'

She went into the bedroom and closed the door. She leaned against the dresser and saw Tiffany's suitcase and the tears started to come back. She shook them off. She looked at the window and suddenly it was no longer just a pane of glass – it was an ominous threat. A sense of danger crept over her and she suddenly found it hard to breathe. She opened her own suitcase, threw the dirty clothes on the floor, and aimlessly, thoughtlessly put clean things in their place, then changed into jeans, a check shirt, and boots. And all the time the questions gnawed at her.

Why? Who?

But that only made it worse. She turned her thoughts to Sharky and she felt strangely reassured. She felt a link to him, a lifeline that tied them together. Her lifeline. Her danger was now his danger and because of that she sensed a new strength in him, something she had not felt before. *A cop*, she thought. And that was far more appealing than an elevator man.

How much did he know? About her? Tiffany? Did he know about Donald? And Victor?

She would have to tell Donald. He was certain to find out about the shooting and he might do something foolish. He was capable of such a thoughtful gesture, but he could not afford to be linked with this. The least she could do was call him, tell him she was all right, tell him to keep out of it.

She went back to the bedroom and stood beside the phone, remembering Sharky's reaction when she had threatened to call somebody.

Oh, hell, she thought, *it can't hurt to put his mind at ease. He had his own problems; he didn't need any of hers.* She picked up the receiver and quietly punched out his private number, a phone by the bedside in his suite that only he answered. It buzzed several times while she watched the door, fearful that either Sharky or Livingston might come in.

He isn't there, she thought, and was about to hang up when he answered. His voice seemed strangely cold, suspicious. 'Hello?'

'Listen to me, I haven't much time. A terrible thing happened. Somebody was killed in my apartment.'

A pause. Then: 'Where are you?'

'Don't worry about me and don't get involved in this. I'm going to be all right. A cop I know named Sharky is taking care of me.'

'Where are you going?'

'I don't know, but I'll be safe. Can't talk anymore. Goodbye.'

She put the phone down very softly.

In his suite, Hotchins stared at the buzzing telephone for a moment and then slowly replaced it.

'It was her,' he said.

'Where is she? Is she at home?' DeLaroza was standing beside him.

'Yes, but the police are into it now. Apparently they're taking Domino into protective custody.'

'Who? I need a *name*,' DeLaroza said.

'A cop named Sharky.'

DeLaroza sighed with relief and then smiled. 'Excellent. Now you can go back to the others. I'll handle this.'

Chapter Twenty-Four

At thirty-four Hazel Weems had begun to show the hard lines of a hard life. She had grown up in the South Georgia cotton country and had started to work in the fields when she was seven. Her father, a sometime preacher, sometime fieldhand, had sent her to live with an aunt in Atlanta when she was fourteen. It was her father's intention to give her a chance at a decent life, but the aunt had turned out to be an alcoholic who drank up the ten dollars a week that was sent for Hazel's upkeep and who frequently beat her in a drunken rage.

On one particularly brutal night neighbours had called the police and one of the investigating officers was Duke Weems, a kind, sympathetic ex-football coach who was twenty-five years older than Hazel. Soon after the beating Weems found her a foster home with a West End grocer and after that was a frequent visitor. After two years of courting they were married. Hazel was seventeen and Duke was forty-two. Two years later he dropped dead of a heart attack chasing a purse snatcher through Five Points.

A year after that Hazel passed the police examination and was inducted into the force as a meter maid. It took her seven more years to make the regular force and another two to become a third-class detective, one of the first women investigators on the force.

Duke's ex-partner, Arch Livingston, had talked Hazel into taking the police exam and had worked tirelessly with her to prepare her for it. It was Livingston too who had fought to get her transferred to the uniformed squad and then badgered his superiors until she was permitted to take the exam for detectives.

If Livingston had asked her to cut off her nose and send it to him for Christmas she would have done it.

She lived on the South Side of Atlanta in a predominantly black neighbourhood, her small, tidy two-bedroomed house the kind they once called a bungalow. There was an island at the end of her street that was pruned, plucked, and planted religiously by the Parton Place Garden Club. Hazel was not a member.

Hazel met them at the door and sized up Domino with the eye of a widow studying a prospective daughter-in-law. No hat, a roughouse shearling coat, blue jeans, and scruffy boots. She liked what she saw.

'These two ain't bullying you, are they, honey?' she said, steering Domino into the house.

'I'm not sure yet,' Domino said and smiled.

'If they give you any shit, you just tell Hazel. I've known this one since he was a rookie directing traffic on Five Points and this one here, I've just seen him around, but all he's good for is raisin' hell and drivin' the captain bughouse. You caught yourself quite a pair, lady. I'll put some coffee on.'

'I'll help,' Livingston said and followed her into the kitchen.

'Look here, Hazel,' Livingston told her. 'I got you fixed up with a room at a first-class hotel. Just for a couple of days. Won't cost you a dime.'

She turned on him.

'Move outa my own house! What the hell you talkin' about? You got free board. Why don't you go to the hotel?'

'Too much traffic. Too public. This lady's on somebody's hit list.'

'What did she do?'

'I don't think she knows. And that's for real. I don't think she can tell us, 'cause I don't think she's figured it out herself yet.'

'Well, anyway I ain't goin' to no Lysol-smellin' hotel. What the hell, Archie, I ain't the Avon Lady; I'm a cop just like you. If there's trouble, I'm as good as anybody else downtown. Don't come at me with that macho shit.'

'It ain't macho shit, lady. We're gonna be in the middle of the goddamndest interdepartmental ass-hittin' you ever saw. You want to get caught in the middle of that?'

'Between you and who?'

'Right now I'd say between us and Riley and Jaspers and D'Agastino.'

'God *damn*, you do things in a big way.'

'You get my point. You get out and when it hits the fan all you got to know is that I asked to use your place for a cover for a coupla days.'

322

'It ain't any of my business, Sergeant, but ain't you been in enough shit through the years? You got to stick your foot in it again?'

'Ain't my gig, this time. I come along for the ride. He's a young fella. Needs all the help he can get.'

'Good. In that case I'll just buy a ticket and jump aboard, too. Now get outa my way while I make some coffee.'

Sharky carried Domino's suitcase into the guest bedroom and put it on a chair near the door. The room, modest but comfortable, was quite a contrast to Domino's apartment.

'Is the place okay?' Sharky said.

'It's fine,' Domino said. 'What a nice lady she is but . . . why is she doing this for me?'

'She's doing it for Arch, although if she didn't like you she probably would have thrown us out. She's a detective. Her husband was one of the first black cops in the city. He died a couple of years ago.'

'How sad. She seems so young to be a widow.'

'Yeah, well, that happens.'

'Is that the way you think? "Oh, well, it happens"?'

'I can't imagine what it's like to be married to a cop,' Sharky said. 'I suppose there are realities you either accept and live with or you end it.'

'Or it gets ended for you,' she said.

'That, too.'

Domino sat down on the bed. 'I'm tired,' she said.

'There are a couple of more questions . . .'

'I thought it was going to be my turn next,' she said.

She stared at him, boring in with those green eyes, and Sharky felt the back of his neck warming up. He was moved by her vulnerability and her spirit. He would like to have said something to her but he was afraid it would come out wrong. Instead he said, 'You want to know about the elevator, hunh?'

She nodded.

'I could lie about it, you know. I'm very good at that. It's something you learn on the street.'

'Oh, I know how good you are at it. You sucked me in beautifully. But I thought we could make a fresh start – and both tell the truth this time.'

'Okay. We were bugging your apartment. I was monitoring the tapes.'

There it was, quick, to the point, and probably deadly. But her reaction surprised him. She wasn't mad or indignant or even embarrassed. She simply looked at him rather whimsically and said, 'Why?'

'Did you know Neil Dantzler and Tiffany were involved in blackmail?'

'I don't believe that.'

'Oh, you can believe it. That part we're sure of. They shook down a Texas oilman for fifty grand.'

'Tiffany?'

Sharky nodded.

'Then it was Neil. He made her do it. She wasn't like that.'

'It doesn't make any difference. They did it.'

'And you think I was part of it?'

Sharky shook his head. 'Nope, don't think that at all. But we had to find out for sure.'

'And, uh, how many of these bugs did you have in my place?'

'Enough. I could hear everything in that apartment but the plants growing.'

'How long were you, uh, up there?'

'Long enough. Since that night Confucius came to dinner.'

'Ohhh.' She sucked her bottom lip between her teeth and looked at him and then shrugged. 'What can I say?'

'You can tell me who he was. That's one of the questions. We've got to start someplace. *Somebody* wants you dead.'

Victor? she thought. *It couldn't be him. And revealing his name might eventually involve Donald, possibly destroy his career for nothing.*

'It wasn't him. He's from out of the country. Germany. He went back to Europe the next day.'

There, that was easy, she thought, *as long as he doesn't lean on it*. She changed the subject.

'Would it help my image any if I told you I'm going to retire?'

'It won't change anything,' Sharky said softly. 'Hell, I'm not here to judge you. What you do is your business.'

She cocked her head to one side and smiled. 'Do you mean that?'

'Sure. We're being honest, remember?'

'Thank you.'

'I felt like a goddamn eavesdropper anyhow.' He hesitated, then changed the subject. 'You're sure you never heard of Angelo Scardi or Howard Burns?'

'Who is this Burns?'

'It's Scardi's moniker . . . alias. Scardi was very big in the news about seven years ago.'

'Oh, hell,' she said, 'seven years ago I was seventeen and living in Mudville, Utah, and all I cared about was Warren Beatty and rock and roll.'

'Then he's just the trigger. Somebody else wants you scratched and that's the somebody I want.'

'It sounds personal.'

'Well, it got that way . . .'

'Why? Because of me, Sharky? Because you thought I was dead?'

'Uh, I . . .'

Livingston saved him.

'You gonna be okay?' he asked Domino.

'Yes. And I thank you.'

'Sure.' He turned to Sharky. 'I'm gonna check in with Friscoe but I'm not givin' him this number. I'll set up a phone drop, have him leave a number. For now I'd like to keep this place between the four of us.'

'Good idea,' Sharky said. 'What we should do, I can stay here with her. You meet the Machine someplace and fill them in. Everybody needs to know.'

'Right. Be back in a minute.' He went in the other room to make the call.

Sharky moved the suitcase off the chair and dropped into it like a sack of cement.

'You look like something out of a horror movie,' Domino said. 'When's the last time you were in bed?'

'I forget.'

'Come here.'

'If I lay down on that bed, I won't get up until Easter.'

She looked at him and mischief played at her lips. 'Wanna bet?'

325

Sharky thought about it. He wasn't too tired to think about it. Then she held out her foot. 'Would you mind helping me off with my boots?'

He went over, turned his back to her, and took the boot by the instep and heel and pulled it off. She watched him and when he had pulled the other off, she said, 'Anybody ever tell you you've got a beautiful ass?'

Sharky turned around and looked down at her. 'That's supposed to be my line,' he said.

'Oh, piffle. Haven't you heard? Times are changing.'

Livingston called to him from the other room and she sighed.

'Saved by Ma Bell,' she said ruefully as he left the room.

Livingston handed Sharky a slip of paper with a phone number on it. It was a drop, the *P* in front of the number indicating a phone booth.

'You got two urgents from The Nosh,' Livingston said. 'The first one was at six-ten, the other one about ten minutes ago. He says he'll be at this number until seven-thirty.'

A warning bell went off deep inside Sharky, but he didn't stop to analyse it. It was seven-thirty already. He grabbed the phone and dialled the number.

Chapter Twenty-Five

The apartment houses along Piedmont Road facing the sprawling inner city park were a tawdry souvenir of more elegant times. Once, near the turn of the century, the park had hosted the International Exposition and on one brilliant afternoon John Philip Sousa had introduced 'The Stars and Stripes Forever' before an assemblage that had included the President of the United States. But the grandeur of Piedmont Road was long gone. The lawns in front of the apartment buildings had eroded into red clay deserts infested with old tyres and broken bottles. Behind paneless windows covered with old blankets derelicts of every kind huddled together in the agony of poverty, cooking over cans of Sterno or, worse, drinking it to forget their lost dreams.

The Nosh sat huddled behind the wheel of his Olds watching one of the battered apartments up the street. He was getting nervous, even a little scared. He looked at his watch. Seven-thirty. Time for the meet. Why the *hell* didn't Sharky call?

He reached under the seat, got his flashlight, and climbed out of the car. And then, with blessed relief, he heard the phone in the booth ring.

He caught it on the second ring.

'Hello.'

'Nosh? It's Shark.'

'Hey, man, I was gettin' worried. I'm runnin' outa time.'

'What do you mean, runnin' outa time?'

'I got this weird phone call about six o'clock, Shark. Guy tells me he can identify the voice on the tape. "What tape?" I says and he says, "The Chinese tape." So I says to him, "I don't know what you're talkin' about" and he says, "Don't be dumb – the one from Domino's apartment" and then he tells me he can identify the guy on the tape for a hundred bucks, but I gotta come to this apartment on Twelfth and Piedmont alone before seven-thirty. So I argued a little, you know, told him I ain't goin' no place alone and then he says I can bring *you* along.'

'He said me? He said my name?'

327

'Yeah. So anyways I went by Tillie the Teller and got a hundred bucks and I'm here now, right up the street from . . .'

'Nosh, don't move. Get back in your car and wait right there. I'm on my way.'

'But he's gonna leave at seven-thirty and it's – '

'Nosh, you're not listening! Don't go near the fuckin' place. Stay there. Wait for me, okay?'

'. . . Well, okay . . .'

'Nosh?'

'Yeah.'

'You stay there, you hear me?'

'Okay.'

'Gimme fifteen minutes. I'm leaving now.'

The Nosh hung up and stepped out of the phone booth. He paced back and forth in front of the car for several minutes, watching the building.

He ambled up Twelfth Street to the front of the building. There were no lights. The street was black, the streetlamps broken or burned out.

If the canary splits, The Nosh was thinking, *I can at least nail him when he comes out.*

Paint curled from the windowsills of the three-storey building and broken windows stared bleakly out at the dark street. Here and there lights flickered dimly behind old blankets.

The pits. The absolute pits, thought The Nosh.

He stood at the doorway, waving his light around, checking it out.

A furry night scavenger dashed from the doorway into the sanctuary of the bushes. It crouched there, peering out, its amber eyes glittering in the beam of the flashlight.

The Nosh stamped his foot at it and the creature ran off up the street, its ugly hairless tail dragging behind it.

He turned the light back to the doorway and approached it. The front door was gone. Inside was a small vestibule.

The inside door was propped open by a cement block.

The vestibule was a litter of empty wine bottles in brown paper sacks, broken glass, crushed beer cans. Someone had dropped a sack of garbage down the stairwell. It lay just inside the main door, a splash of refuse, well nibbled-over.

The Nosh shuddered.

There were sounds inside the building, but he could not believe that people actually lived there.

Night creatures scurried into cracks in the wall. A twenty-five-watt bulb cast dim shadows on the stairwell, which smelled of rotten carpeting and sour cooking. The Nosh patted the tape in his inside pocket for reassurance and stood at the bottom of the stairs. High up, towards the third floor, the hallway lights were burned out. Somewhere in the building a radio blared static and country music. A child was crying behind one of the doors.

At first he hardly heard the voice. He thought it was the radio or something moving in the shadows or his imagination. He looked up into the darkness.

'Abrams . . .'

A whisper, barely audible.

He went up a couple of steps and listened.

Nothing.

He looked at his watch. Another five minutes and Sharky would be there.

'Abrams . . .'

The Nosh looked up again and pointed the finger of light into the blackness.

'Down here,' he said.

Nothing.

He went up to the first floor. The child stopped crying and started to laugh. A woman's nasal voice joined Dolly Parton on the country-music station. The Nosh felt more secure. How could there be any danger in a building where children were laughing?

He went to the second floor.

'Up here Abrams . . .'

'Who's there?'

Silence.

The stairs groaned with age as he climbed to the third floor and stood at the head of the steps in the darkness, probing the dank hallway with his light. Apartment 3-B was at the end of the hall, the number painted sloppily on the door with house paint. He walked slowly towards it and stood outside the apartment.

'Hello?'

Nothing.

He pushed the door open. It swung slowly on aged

hinges. The apartment had a long central hallway ending at the living room with bedrooms off the corridor. No lights. A tremor rippled along The Nosh's arm and across his back and he shook it off. He took a few nervous steps inside. Broken glass crunched underfoot. He was walking with his hand against the wall, following the beam of his flashlight. He passed a doorway to his right and turned towards it, swinging his light at the doorless opening.

Then he heard Sharky, out on the street, calling to him: 'Nosh!'

Thank God. He turned back towards the main doorway of the apartment. It was then he heard the movement in the room. Instinctively he dodged to his right and crouched at the same time. But it was too late.

He saw the blinding flash before he heard the dull, muffled explosion. The shotgun boomed in his face. Two barrels, shattering the quiet of the hallway with their silenced *thunk, thunk!* For an instant the corridor was lit by the ghastly yellow-red exhaust flame as the gases burst from the ugly barrels. The heat from the gas shattered The Nosh's glasses, scorched his eyes, and the pellets tore into his face and chest. He was blown across the hallway into the wall. Pain chopped through the side of his face and tore at his shoulder. His feet flopped helplessly inches above the floor and he seemed to hang there for an instant before he fell.

He saw a figure dart through a doorway. It seemed miles away. His foot was kicking the wall convulsively and he thought, *I should stop that.* But the effort was far too great. His reflexes went wildly out of control.

He pushed himself into a sitting position, his one leg bent behind him, still kicking, and fell against the wall. He was vaguely aware that his life was leaking out of him, forming a dark pool at his feet. His hand was shaking, but he managed to work his wallet out of his pocket and threw it aimlessly into the main hallway.

'P-p-p-police,' he stammered at nobody. 'P-p-p-police . . .'

And then with all the fading strength he had left, he screamed:

'HELP M-M-M-M-E-E-E-E. . . .'

330

Sharky had taken only a moment to tell Livingston he had to leave, that he was worried about The Nosh, and to tell Domino he would be back shortly.

He drove like a maniac across the city, speeding through red lights, cutting through filling stations at intersections, his hand on the horn all the way. Pedestrians fled for their lives before him. He spotted The Nosh's Olds from a block away and screeched in beside it, but he saw it was empty before he even stopped. He jumped out of the car, looked up Twelfth Street.

Darkness. The wind rattled old fences and dead tree limbs.

Which apartment? Where was he? Sharky's heart was pounding so hard he could hear it, like a pump in his ears. He cupped his hands and yelled:

'Nosh!'

And a moment later he saw in the upper-floor window across the street the hideous yellow-red flash. *Oh Jesus!* He grabbed his flashlight and ran across the street and into the apartment house, his automatic ready. Then he heard the terrible scream:

'HELP M-M-M-M-E-E-E-E. . . .'

Sharky charged up the stairs, up to the third floor, his light leading him on. When he reached the top floor he stopped, looking at the open door at the end of the long hall. He heard something thumping inside the apartment, like someone knocking on the wall. He moved cautiously down the hallway and then the light picked up the glitter of gold on the floor. A gold detective's badge.

'Nosh!'

He ran to the doorway of the apartment, saw the flashlight on the floor, its beam fixed on a foot that was jerking spastically, kicking the wall over and over again. He flashed his light on The Nosh's face. Abrams was leaning against the wall. The side of his face was blown away and his mouth was crooked and bloody. His jaw was torn loose at one side and bits of glass sparkled on his cheeks. There was a jagged, gaping hole where his shoulder had been and blood spurted from a dozen wounds in his chest.

Sharky jammed his gun in his belt and dropped on his knees beside the little man.

'Nosh. Jesus, Nosh, hold on. I'll get somebody. Can you hear me, buddy? Hay, c'mon Nosh, nod. Blink your eyes. Do *something!*'

'I . . . grahg . . . largh . . . agha . . .' The Nosh's voice was an ugly croak stifled by the blood that filled his mouth and overflowed onto his chest. He began shivering violently and Sharky pulled off his jacket and threw it over him.

'C'mon buddy, hang in there. I'm gonna find a phone, okay? Shit, man, don't fade out on me now.'

The Nosh's eyes rolled in his head. He looked up at Sharky without recognition. His eyes were turning glassy.

More blood surged up from his chest and filled his mouth.

He was limp. His head lolled against Sharky's chest.

'Nosh!'

Abrams looked up again. His face seemed to sag. The skin grew loose. He was turning grey. His eyes were no longer focusing. They began to cross. There was a clatter in his throat and then his eyes rolled crazily and turned up into his head.

'*No* . . . c'mon . . .'

Sharky's attention was riveted on his dying friend. When he heard the sound behind him, it was too late. The knife edge of a hand slashed into the back of his neck and he was thrown over The Nosh's body, the pain from the blow stunning him as he lurched into the wall. He twisted as he flew forward, swinging one leg in a wide arc in the darkness, kicking blindly, feeling it hit something soft, sinking deep into human flesh. He kept rolling, away from the wall and into the dark hall until he was stopped by two legs. He swung his knees under him, balled his fist, and shoved himself upward, driving his fist between the two legs until it slammed into a crotch. He grabbed in the dark, his hand closing around the unseen figure's genitals, and he jerked him forward. A toe found his back and buried deep just over the kidney and Sharky roared with pain and rage and twisted back in the other direction, swinging his fist in the dark. He missed, took another blind swing, and missed again, then remembered his gun and pulled it from his belt, but he was afraid to fire. He was disoriented in the dark, afraid he might hit The Nosh. He sensed movement all around him. A fist hit his shoulder and bounced away in the darkness and he rolled again, towards the main hall, away from the activity.

The beam from one of the flashlights swept the hallway, found him, and Sharky spun around, half sitting, and fired an inch above the light. The flashlight spun crazily in the dark, hit the floor, and shattered. There was a groan in front of him, the sound of a body hitting the floor.

A foot crashed down on his ankle and the pain stabbed up his leg. He swung the gun, trying to imagine his assailant there, in the dark in front of him, and raised the gun, but before he could get another shot off, a foot kicked his wrist, knocking his arm straight up. The gun flew out of his hand and clattered away in the darkness. Another foot slammed down into his stomach. Sharky gasped, grabbed the leg, and twisted hard, pulled himself up to his knees, his fury turning to blind hate. He wanted to hurt them, these unseen figures striking at him in the dark, to kill them.

And then a fist as hard as a gauntlet smashed into his temple and his brain seemed to explode. The floor tilted insanely under his knees and he floundered, trying to catch himself, to stay up. Another fist slammed into his neck and this time the pain could not be ignored. It fanned out through his body like an electrical shock. His hands went numb. His back gave out. He jackknifed and fell forward and it seemed forever before the floor came up to meet him.

The sounds around him were echoes that grew fainter and fainter. And then there was only the darkness.

Chapter Twenty-Seven

Sharky stirred and turned over on his back, but his foot was caught on something and he stopped. He tried wiggling it and felt the bite of a rope in his ankle. He was tied to something. He opened his eyes and his vision strayed crazily around the room. Nausea swept over him and he closed them again.

Pain mushroomed into his neck and temples.

He closed his eyes and lay still. He felt like he was moving, rocking back and forth.

I'm still dizzy, he thought.

Then he heard a weird scream, a sorrowful cry that seemed to echo over and over again, raising the hair on his arms.

My God, he thought, *what was that?*

It came again, a mournful shriek that died slowly and was answered a few seconds later by another echoing from farther away. He recognized the sound. It was a loon, lamenting insanely in the night, its demented love call answered by its mate.

A loon? He lay there sorting out the sounds around him. They began to make sense: ropes creaking, boards groaning, the rhythmic slap of water against wood somewhere below him. It was a boat.

He opened his eyes and blinked, trying to clear his fuzzy vision. The room was shadowed, lit only by a lantern that swung in an easy arc overhead. He lay hypnotized by it until the nausea returned. He gritted his teeth to keep from vomiting and turned his eyes away from the light.

It was a small room, a cabin, and he was lying on the lower bunk of a double-decker. One side of the room curved in and there was a porthole in it. Facing it, on the other side of the cabin, was a hand-carved lattice-work partition which separated the room from the hall. The door was heavy and made of some kind of dark wood, rosewood or mahogany. The far side of the room, opposite the bunk, was dark. The lantern shed a small pool of light over a table and chair which sat in the centre of the cabin. He smelled pork cooking in garlic.

In the darkness opposite him, a cigarette glowed briefly. He concentrated, trying to make out a shape, a form of some kind in the shadows but he could see nothing.

Then he remembered The Nosh.

God damn them. God DAMN them!

He fought back tears, but they came anyway, dribbling down the side of his face, and he reached up and wiped them away.

'Well, welcome back to the land of the living, Mr. Sharky,' a voice said from the shadows.

He squinted into the darkness.

'Oh, don't try to see me,' the voice said. 'It's much too dark. It will only strain your eyes.'

It was a big boat, too big for the river. Then the loon cried again and Sharky thought, *I'm on the lake. Seventy miles from Atlanta.*

A voice he did not recognize, hoarse and trembling with fatigue, said:

'Where's my partner?'

My God, he thought, *was that my voice?*

'Unfortunate,' the voice from the darkness said, 'but the sacrifice was necessary.' It was a weak, whining, nasal voice and Sharky hated it.

The rage built inside Sharky, like a tornado in his gut. But he held his tongue. Nothing more would be accomplished with dialogue. Escape was the only thing he could think about now. *Concentrate on it*, he thought. There will be a way. *There will be a way.* He looked down at his foot. It was lashed tightly to the foot of the bunk. His jacket was stained with The Nosh's blood. The fire roared inside him again.

Let me take one of them out. Let me watch his eyes when he goes, the way I watched Larry's eyes.

'Hai, Liung,' the voice in the shadows called out and the door opened. Three men entered. They were Orientals, short and lean, their faces wide and hard, their noses broad, their eyes beads under hooded lids. They wore white tee-shirts, the cotton moulded around hard muscles and taut, flat stomachs. One of the three had a scorched hole in the shoulder of his shirt and a bloodstain down one side. Sharky could see the bulge of a bandage under the shirt.

Sorry it wasn't a couple of inches lower and an inch to the left, you sorry son of a bitch.

Another one had a splint on his forearm.

Sorry, Nosh, sorry I didn't do better.

The one with the splint on his arm stood near the door, his arms at his sides as the other two approached the bunk, untying his foot and dragging him to his feet. His knees buckled and they pulled him upright. His vision wobbled. The room went in and out of focus.

From the shadows, smoke curled like a snake, twisting into the heat from the lantern. Sharky concentrated on the corner, letting his eyes grow accustomed to the darkness.

'If you're trying to build a mental image of me, forget it,' the voice said. 'It's much too dark. And there's no need to say anything to my three friends. They don't speak English. In fact they rarely speak at all.'

Sharky said nothing. He continued to stare into the dark corner of the room.

'You can save yourself a lot of time and pain if you will simply answer one question for me,' the voice said. 'That's all we're here for. A simple sentence will do it, Mr. Sharky. Where is the girl?'

Sharky said nothing.

'Where is she? Where is Domino?'

Sharky continued to stare at the glowing tip of the cigarette.

'All I want is the address.'

Sharky moved slightly towards one of the Orientals and then quickly twisted the other way, snapping his arms down towards his sides. As he did, the two Chinese exerted the slightest pressure on the nerves just above each of his elbows. Pain fired down Sharky's arms to his fingertips and both arms were almost immediately paralysed.

'Don't be foolish,' the voice said. 'They can paralyse you with one finger – and they will. That was a simple exercise. The feeling will return to your arms in a minute or so. The next time they will be more persuasive.'

Sharky felt the numbness begin to subside. His arms felt as though they had fallen asleep. They tingled as the feeling returned. He shook his hands from the wrists and flexed his fingers.

'You see what I mean? Now can we make it simple, Mr.

Sharky? Or will you require more complicated tricks?'

Sharky still did not talk. He peered hard into the shadows. Was it Scardi? The tobacco was brash and smelled rancid. Sharky concentrated on that for a few minutes. *English cigarettes*, he thought. *But his accent is American.* Sweat beads rolled down his face and collected on his chin, stubbornly refusing to drop off.

Gerald Kershman, the man in the shadows, was becoming annoyed.

'Stop staring over here,' he said. 'I find it irritating.'

Sharky stared stubbornly at the corner.

Kershman said something in Chinese and one of the men holding Sharky reached up with a forefinger and pressed a nerve beside Sharky's right eye. The pain was literally blinding. The vision in the eye vanished. Kershman chuckled. He felt a surge in his testicles, a sensual thrill. He was growing hard watching Sharky's ordeal. Secretly he hoped Sharky would prove difficult, that the torture would get more intense, and he began to tremble with excitement at the thought. He dropped his Players cigarette on the floor and, turning his back on Sharky, lit another. Then he said:

'Time is of the essence. You will give up the information. It's really just a matter of time.' Then, sharply: *'Pa t'a k'un tao chuo tze.'*

The two Orientals jerked Sharky to the chair and forced him down into it. There were two straps attached to each arm and two others mounted on the table. They strapped his arms to the chair, leaving his wrists and hands free, and shoved the chair against the table and fastened the straps on the table over the back of each hand, tightening them until he could hardly curl his fingers.

'Before we proceed any further, perhaps I should explain a little about the three Chins. They are members of one of the oldest Triads in Hong Kong, Chi Sou Han. Since the twelfth century the oldest male of each of the three families of Chi Sou Han has been taken from his mother at birth and trained to be the ultimate warrior. Their discipline is beyond the western mind. I have seen one of these men stand in a *crouch* for ten hours without a falter. They endure the most excruciating pain in silence.

'They are experts in *tai chi ch'uan*, karate, and judo.

337

They communicate through the use of body movements and they use only two weapons – their hands and the *yinza*. Are you familiar with the *yinza*, Mr. Sharky? *Da yu'an p'an!'*

The man near the door with the splint on his arm moved with fluid grace, twisting to his right from the waist up while his right hand swept past his belt and swung up shoulder high. Immediately, without breaking the continuity of the move he shifted his body in the opposite direction, flicking his wrist sharply as he did. There was a flash at his finger-tips, a glint in the air, and a steel disc the size of a silver dollar ripped into the table so close to Sharky's hand that he could feel the cold metal. It had twelve steel barbs an inch long around its perimeter.

'An ancient weapon, Mr. Sharky, and far more accurate than a bullet. Chi Sou Han are also famous throughout China for what we would call in English *The Perfect And*. The art of torture. The most effective example of The Perfect And is the Ordeal of the Fifth Finger. It is used to persuade the most obstinate subjects only. Very simply, a joint is cut off a finger every eight hours beginning with the little finger. Five fingers, five days. The Chi Sou Han claim that no man has ever resisted them beyond the thumb of one hand.'

Terror seized Sharky. He was drenched in his own sweat. He lowered his head, staring down between his hands. He tried to curl his fingers but his hands were strapped too tightly to the table.

Kershman said, 'For the last time, where is Domino?'

Silence.

Kershman's pulse thundered and he said, '*Nung hao la.*'

The Chin with the splint on his arm stepped from the room for a few moments and returned carrying a small hibachi only slightly larger than his hand. It was filled with glowing coals. He placed it on the corner of the table. In his other hand he held a sharpening steel and a dirk, its tapered blade about six inches long. He stood close to Sharky and slashed the knife blade down the steel several times, the blade ringing as it clashed, steel against steel.

Sharky clamped his teeth together.

They're so proud of silence. I'll give them silence.

Sweat ran into his mouth and he spat it out.

The man with the knife put the sharpening steel on the table and turned towards the shadows.

'Hai. Tuo ch'ung la,' Kershman said. He stepped forward a bit, his eyes shining with anticipation as the Chin stuck the point of the knife into the table beside the first joint of Sharky's little finger. With one swift downward chop he sliced off the end of the finger.

Sharky stifled the scream in his throat. It swelled there, hurting his tongue. He was shaking hard, but he held it in.

The Chin placed the blade over the coals until it was red hot and then held the edge of it against the stump of Sharky's finger. It sizzled. The room filled with the smell of burning flesh. Sharky stifled another scream, only this time it did not die. It was a squeal trapped behind his lips as pain triggered the nerves to his brain.

He stared at the bizarre sight of his fingertip lying on the table.

My God they did it, he thought. *The bastards cut off my finger.*

And he fainted.

He awoke with his pulse throbbing in his ruined finger. Every movement of the boat, every sound, seemed like a knife jabbing into it. He used the pain, thought about it, let it clear his head.

He lay motionless, listening. Above him, on what he assumed was the deck, there was movement. At least one of them was up there, maybe all four. He tried to separate the movements, but that was impossible.

There was another sound from somewhere down below, to the right of his prison cabin. He tuned in on it. The nasal voice. The whiner. Talking. Hesitating. Talking. He was on the phone, reporting to someone.

Sharky thought about escape.

How? Where would I go? Where am I? What the hell kind of boat is this?

Immaterial, stupid. Get out first, then worry about where you are.

He focused his thoughts on escape. He thought about weapons. The knife was still on the table and he was tied by only one leg. The bastards were confident enough. But when he checked the knot he knew there was no way to untie it with only one good hand.

Anything else?

Jacket? No. *Shoes?* Hardly. *Nothing in my pockets. My belt?* The BELT!

It was a wide leather belt with a large, heavy, square brass buckle he had bought at the flea market. It would hardly make a dent in the skulls of Winkin, Blinkin and Nod, but Whiny Voice, now there was a possibility. He had to get him in close.

He had to make the miserable bastard show his face. But then what? He thought about the three Chinese with their little steel discs. *Careful, Sharky.*

The thinking had tired him and he closed his eyes and rested. He heard someone in the passageway. He turned his head towards the door, lying with his eyes half-closed, watching the door as it swung open.

The man standing there was short and fat, wearing a rumpled grey suit with the jacket open. His belly sagged over his belt. Thick, obnoxious lips, jowls, frog eyes. So that was the body that went with the voice. Sharky felt better.

Then he saw the 9mm Mauser jammed down in Fat Boy's belt.

Kershman stared down at Sharky with contempt. DeLaroza had just chewed Kershman out. 'Five days, hell. I want the answer before morning.'

Kershman had felt humiliated.

He called out to Liung and the Chin with the splinted arm came down from the deck above. A moment later the other two followed.

All three of them are outside. Good.

Kershman handed Liung a tube of smelling salts and nodded towards Sharky. Sharky closed his eyes, feigning unconsciousness. He felt his foot being untied. Then the sharp odour of amyl nitrite burned his nose and he involuntarily jerked his head to one side.

'Wake up,' Fat Boy said, back in the shadows now. 'Time for round two.'

They pulled Sharky to his feet, shoved him into the chair and strapped him down. He felt like a rag doll in their hands.

'Look at you,' Fat Boy said. 'How much longer do you really think you can hold out? You're a wreck.'

Sharky did not answer.

'I ask you again, where is the woman?' Kershman was almost screaming.

Sharky kept his teeth clamped shut.

'Where is she?' Kershman said and there was an almost feline quality to his panicked tone.

Somebody's putting the heat on him.

'You're a fool,' Fat Boy screeched. *'Jaw sao.'*

Liung picked up the sharpening steel and the blade rang across the rough metal. It grated Sharky's nerves, turning them raw. His finger began throbbing from anticipation. Fear was a lump in his throat.

The Chin stuck the knife point into the table next to his finger and waited.

'Kan ni ti ch'ua pa,' Kershman said.

This time Sharky was more aware of what was happening. He heard the knife slice through bone and gristle a second before the pain stabbed up his arm to his shoulder. The cabin whirled around him and he groaned into his clenched teeth, stifling his agony. The finger was already numb when Liung cauterized it.

Sharky slumped forward, let his body go limp, felt them unstrap him, drag him back to the cot, and drop him on it. They tied his leg.

He was going to pass out again, he could feel himself slipping into that dark pit. He thought about The Nosh and the anger sustained him for a few minutes. He began to slip. He thought about Fat Boy, about his Mauser stuck there in his belt. That was good, that helped, but then he began to drop off again.

He thought about Domino and that was fine. Was she worth all this? The answer came back instantly. Yes. And how about the tape with the Chinese orgy? It was clear now. The man trying to kill her was with her the night he had been monitoring her. Why was she protecting him?

The worst of it passed and Sharky's mind began to clear again. His hand was a pulsating lump at the end of his arm. He tried to ignore it, to concentrate on Fat Boy.

There has to be a way to get the little asshole in here.
There is, stupid. The slant-eyed bastards are the answer.
They don't speak English. Fat Boy speaks English. He has

341

to hear you, right?

Right.

He rolled over with his back to the door, and reaching down with his good hand, he undid the belt buckle and then slowly, inch by inch, he slipped it through the loops. The belt fell loose and he relaxed for a minute.

He was lying on his left side. The only way to get any leverage and keep his back to the door was to swing the belt with his crippled hand.

Jesus!

He pressed the end of the belt into his palm and, gritting his teeth from the pain, held it in place with his thumb. With his left hand he slowly wrapped the belt around his fist until about six inches were left. The heavy brass buckle hung on the end of the belt like a ball on the end of a mace.

One shot, kiddo, that's all you get. And don't forget Winkin, Blinkin, and Nod. They ain't gonna be hanging around sipping tea.

One thing at a time.

He had one shot and he had to make it good. If they got the belt, he was dead.

There was movement on the deck above him again. Winkin, Blinkin, and Nod were probably up there, doing their homework. Fat Boy was on the phone again. His voice was up a notch. More panic.

There were nine shots left in the Mauser, counting out the one he had used in the dark.

Two each for Winkin, Blinkin, and Nod.

One for Fat Boy.

One for the rope.

One for luck.

Go for it, kiddo. Go for the bomb. Time's running out.

He heard Fat Boy hang up the phone. He was coming down the passageway. Sharky rolled over almost on his face. He slid one knee up under his leg.

Fat Boy was at the door. He was coming in.

Sharky moaned.

Fat Boy edged a little closer.

He groaned again, a little lower.

Fat Boy moved in.

'Help me,' Sharky said, almost in a whisper.

From behind him he heard Fat Boy's voice, close to his

342

ear, 'The address, Sharky. Where is Domino? Tell me and I'll help you.'

A little closer, Sharky thought. *A foot or two.*

'Domino?'

'Damn you!' Fat Boy said, leaning closer, his lips wet with saliva, his frog eyes bulging with anger.

Sharky hunched his shoulders and with a massive effort, he rolled over, straightening his arm. The buckle snapped at the end of the belt. The belt whipped in a full arc and whooshed into the side of Kershman's nose. It burst like a raw egg. The bone shattered. Blood gushed out like water from a pump. The fat man screamed in pain, his eyes bulging with horror as he saw Sharky reach out and grab at his belt.

Sharky's fingers felt the butt of the gun, but the fat man was reeling backwards. He clutched at it frantically, pulling it loose, but it fell from his hand. Sharky lunged off the bunk to the floor and grabbed the automatic as Kershman grappled with the chair to keep his balance.

Sharky could hear the Chins coming on the run. He grabbed the gun, held it at arm's length straight up at Kershman, saw the fear in his bleeding face.

'Please!' Kershman screamed as Sharky fired. The bullet tore straight up through his chin, his mouth, and into his brain. He went down on his back, his face frozen in terror.

Sharky whirled, still holding the gun at arm's length, held it an inch from the knot around his ankle, and fired again. The heat from the blast scorched his ankle. The rope disintegrated.

Liung swept through the door with the grace of a ballet dancer, his arm whipping up from his belt, the glint of steel in his fist. Sharky fired, saw the disc sparkle towards him, felt it rip through the top of his shoulder and thud into the wall behind him. The bullet tore into Liung's chest, jolted him, but did not stop him. He kept coming, his hand swept to his belt again. Sharky felt the Mauser jump and roar in his fist. He shot Liung in the stomach. The Chin made no sound. Blood spurted from both wounds. And he still came.

Jesus, it's like shooting an elephant!

His kneecap, idiot, his kneecap.

Sharky lowered the pistol and shattered Liung's kneecap with the next shot. He wobbled and fell straight forward, reaching out and grabbing Sharky's ankle. Sharky thrust the Mauser an inch from Liung's temple and fired. The Chinese died without a sound.

Six shots.

Three left.

He was on his feet when the second Chin charged the door. Sharky stepped over Kershman's body and tilted the table on end, dropping behind it as the Chin flung out his hand and sent three steel discs into the tabletop. Sharky raised on his knees and squeezed off a shot straight into the Chin's face, but he was moving too fast. It hit the corner of his jaw and tore half his ear off.

Two left.

The Chin leaped at him, kicked the table, split it in two as Sharky rolled over and slammed his back into the side of the bunk. The Chin rose over him, his hand raised, the fingers rigid, and started to chop down on him. The gun roared in Sharky's fist and the Chin's left eye exploded. He plunged over Sharky's head and died face down on the cot.

Sharky spun towards the door. The third one was there, his hooded eyes gleaming through the latticework, not six feet away.

One shot left.

Sharky swung the gun out, holding it with both hands, the belt still dangling from his ruined hand.

The Chin whirled and was gone. Sharky was on his feet. He jumped to the doorway and swung into the passage in time to see his adversary leap through the hatchway to the deck. Sharky ran to the bottom of the hatch ladder and stopped. He listened.

Nothing.

The Chin too was motionless. He had jumped up on the cabin roof and was poised there, over the hatch, every muscle tensed, his fingers curved in a classic karate pose. Waiting.

Sharky peered through the hatch and checked out the afterdeck. The Chin was not there. There was no place to hide. Against one railing there was a large emergency box. Two fuel tanks on the stern. Nothing else.

He looked overhead, wondering whether the Chin was up there. He had one shot left and the Chin had God knows how many of those whatchamacallit discs.

Sharky could take a chance, run out on the deck cowboy-style, and try to drop him with a John Wayne shot.

Suicide.

He had to get in close, put him away with one shot.

The Chin crept towards the bow of the boat, moving as soundlessly as a puff of smoke.

Sharky reasoned that the longer he waited, the slimmer the odds were. The Chin was trained to be patient. He could outwait Sharky until they were both too weak to walk. Sharky's patience was already running thin. If he missed with his last shot, the Chin could kill him with his big toe. He looked at the emergency box. Perhaps there was something in there he could use as a weapon. An axe, anything.

His finger began to throb. His nerves were screaming.

Go for the box. If it's empty, take your best shot and go overboard. Maybe the son of a bitch can't swim.

Sharky climbed to the top of the hatch ladder, hesitated for a moment, and then ran towards the emergency box. He looked back over his shoulder. The Chin was walking on the roof in the other direction, maybe sixty feet away. Sharky slid up to the box and flipped open the lid.

The Chin came after him like an antelope.

Sharky did a two-second inventory. Blankets, life preservers, flare gun, water bottles, radio . . . flare gun! He grabbed it and snapped it open. It was loaded.

The Chin leaped off the roof and landed running.

Sharky had to slow him down. He swung the pistol over the edge of the box and aimed at the biggest target he saw, the Chin's chest. The Mauser roared and Sharky heard the bullet thud home. The Chin was knocked sideways. He fell, sliding past Sharky into the stern railing.

Sharky's hand was shaking, his eyes were fogged with pain. He saw the Chin jump to his feet and he pointed the bulky flare pistol at him and fired. The flare spiralled out of the short barrel with a *chunk*. The Chin twisted as he fired and the blazing flare streaked across his chest, scorching his shirt, and ripped into the valve of one of the gas tanks. The nozzle blew off, releasing a flood of gasoline. The gas hit the blazing flare and burst into flames. The Chin, distracted by the sudden fire, turned for an instant and as he did Sharky fired again. The second flare hit the Chin in the chest, shattered his ribs and lodged there, knocking him backwards to the railing. He floundered there with the phosphorous flare shell sizzling in his chest and then plunged backwards into the lake. Sharky looked down into the dark water at the flare, still burning fiercely, its bubbles boiling to the surface, bursting into puffs of acrid smoke, as the Chin sank deeper into the lake, the glowing shell growing smaller and smaller.

A moment later the tank went.

The explosion knocked Sharky halfway across the deck. A ball of fire roared out of the ruptured tank and swept up into the mast and furled sails of the junk. The sails burst into flames.

Sharky ran from one side of the junk to the other, looking over the side. The motor launch was lashed to a floating pier.

The keys. Fat Boy had to have them. He raced to the cabin and leaped down the stairs. Kershman was still lying on his back, his crazed eyes staring at the ceiling. Sharky ran the fingers of his good hand through the pockets and found not one but two sets of keys.

The other gas tank blew up. Fire spewed out along the deck and poured through the hatchway. Sharky ran down through the main cabin and up the bow hatchway. He went over the side and dropped down to the pier.

The junk was burning like a piece of scrap paper. Bits of flaming sailcloth drifted out over Sharky's head and hissed into the lake. He tried the keys and finally found one that fitted and cranked up the launch, jamming the throttle forward and twisting the wheel away from the blazing junk. The launch roared out into the lake, tearing the pier to pieces as it went.

Sharky did not look back. He flipped on the night lights and headed off into the darkness.

Chapter Twenty-Eight

The high energy from the fight and the cold wind biting at him kept him alert. He found the main body of the lake and drove maniacally down its winding byways, keeping in the centre of the lake to avoid debris along the shoreline. It was almost an hour before he saw the green light blinking on the end of the marina dock.

He pulled alongside and got out, tying the front of the launch down. It was easy to find Fat Boy's car, at that time of the year there were only half a dozen cars in the lot. He cranked it up and sat huddled in the front seat. A wave of dizziness shook him. *Hell*, he thought, *I've come this far, don't let me pass out now*. It passed and he flipped on the heater switch, slammed the gas pedal to the floor. The car screamed out of the lot.

He drove the seventy miles back to Atlanta in less than an hour.

All the lights in the house seemed to be on. Livingston had the front door open and was standing just inside it, his gun out, before Sharky got out of the car.

'Hold it right there,' he yelled.

'It's me – Sharky.'

'Sharky! Goddammit to hell, where you been? Where's The Nosh? What – '

Sharky reeled into the light from the doorway and Livingston swallowed the rest of the sentence.

'Jesus Christ, what happened to you?'

'You're not gonna believe me when I tell you. Is she all right?'

'Sure she's all r – '

Sharky stormed past him and into the house. Domino was coming out of the bedroom, her eyes puffy from lack of sleep.

'Oh, thank God,' she said and then her face registered the shock as she saw his burned-out eyes blazing with pain and fury, his cheeks mottled with a two-day growth of beard, his shoulder ravaged and bleeding, the torn edge of a bloody rag hanging from his fist.

347

He stood in front of her, his body shaking from hypertension, fatigue, and anger.

Livingston kicked the door shut and put away his gun.

'What the hell happened, Shark?' he asked.

'The Nosh is dead,' Sharky said. 'They got him the same way they got Tiffany. Sawed-off shotgun . . .'

'I gotta call Friscoe right now. They been lookin' for you two all night.'

'Don't call anybody yet.'

'Where have you been?' Domino said. Tears were building up in her eyes.

'Where have I been? I'll tell you where I've been, lady. My best friend was ambushed. I been beat up, kidnapped, hauled out to a goddamn Chinese junk in the middle of the lake, had my finger chopped off by three wildass Chinamen. I've killed four people, blown up a boat, stolen a car. Shit, I've had a *great* night! And you know why? Because they want *you*, that's why.'

His eyes danced crazily in his head.

'We've got to get you to a hospital,' she said.

'A hospital. Shit, I don't need a hospital. I need answers. Who do you know has a Chinese junk? Who do you know has Oriental assassins doing his dirty work? Who do you know digs *Chinese orgies*? Your pal, Confucius, that's who. You lied to me. Told me the bastard went to Europe. Why? Don't you see it? He's the one behind it all, the one who's trying to kill you!'

He ripped the bloody bandage off his hand and held it out in front of her, the burned stump of his finger a foot from her eyes.

'Look at it. That's what they did to me.'

She moaned and turned her face to the wall. He grabbed her by the shoulder and whirled her around. 'Look at it. Don't turn your face away from me. That's what your life cost. That and a little guy who never hurt anybody in his life ended up on a stinking tenement floor with his face blown off. And Tiffany, what about her?'

'Please stop,' she cried.

'*Me* stop? These are the bastards you're protecting.'

'Slow down, Shark,' Livingston said, moving closer to him.

He turned to his partner and said, 'The crazy thing is, we

348

had it figured right, Arch. We were right on it. Scardi, the rip-off in Italy, Scardi's connection here. We had it by the ass.' Then he turned back to Domino. 'And we would've tied it up if you hadn't lied to me.'

'No.'

'Bull*shit*. You told me that creep went to Europe, that he couldn't have had anything to do with it. If you had given me his name, levelled with me, The Nosh would be alive now. We could have taken the son of a bitch last night. But I trusted you. You told me . . . I believed you. Should have known better. Should have . . . Goddammit, are you so much in love with him that you're willing to – '

His fury exploded and he lashed out at her with the back of his good hand, slashing her across the face with such force that it knocked her back against the wall. Livingston grabbed his arm.

'C'mon, pal, you're acting like a jealous lover, for Christ's sake.'

Sharky leaned against him. His hand was throbbing and he had a splitting headache. *Was that it, was he jealous?* He shook his head violently.

'No, nothing like that, nothing like that. Too many lies. Nobody's what they seem. All lies!'

'Shark, I gotta get you down. You need – '

'I need Scardi. And the motherless son of a bitch that brought Scardi in. I want them and if we can't take them legally, I'm gonna rip that cocksucker's heart out with my bare hands. *I need to get even!*'

He had turned back to Domino, glaring at her. Here was a Sharky she had never seen before. Gone was the roguish smile, the rough charm. In its place was a raw power that frightened her. Stripped of any elegance, finesse, cleverness, or caution.

He leaned against the wall, his knees shaking, turning to mud, his body wracked with chills, his mind teetering on the edge of insanity and bent on destruction, his strength coming from an almost carnal need for vengeance. The room began to swim around him.

He looked back at Domino.

'Who did you tell?'

'W-w-what?'

'Who did you *tell*? You told somebody about me. That's

how they knew. They were after me, goddammit. Don't you get it? They suckered me by setting up my best friend. They told him it was all right if *I* came with him. Not Arch, not Papa, or Friscoe. *Me.*'

He jabbed his wounded hand at her. 'You blew the whistle on me. You gave somebody my name.'

He was shaking almost uncontrollably and he began to sweat again.

'They were gonna cut them off. Those crazy goddamn monkeys were gonna cut all my fingers off, one at a time, until I told them where you were. Can you believe that, hunh? Cut off all my fingers. Now *what's his name?*'

'Please,' she said. She was crying hard. 'Please, let us help you.'

'Only one way to help me. Gimme the name. Just say it.'

His fingers pressed into her arm.

'DeLaroza,' she whispered. 'Victor DeLaroza.' It was all happening too fast. *Could Donald also be part of it? Of course – he had to be.* It was Donald she had given Sharky's name to, not DeLaroza. And yet, could there be an explanation? She needed time, time to reason it out.

Sharky began to sag, like a drunk losing control. It was almost an anticlimax, hearing it. 'Shit,' he said inanely. 'Wouldn't you know it? I never even heard of the motherfucker.' He looked at Livingston. 'You gotta promise me, Arch, *promise* me you won't go after them without me. Tell Friscoe, tell him nobody's stealin' *my* melons this time.'

'Sure, Shark, just take it easy.'

'Promise me, damn it.'

'I promise.'

'Don't let him flush it at roll call. Make him hold off, okay?'

'Right.'

'All I need . . . see, I need . . . couple hours' sleep . . .'.

He took a step towards Livingston and his legs went. He sagged into the black man's arms.

'Shit, where's everybody going?' he said and passed out.

When Sharky awoke the first time, Twigs was sitting by the bed with his black bag open, taking his blood pressure. Sharky looked around the room and it was filled with fog. Vaguely, faces appeared and disappeared through the mist.

'What the hell you doin' here, Twigs?' Sharky said. 'Am I dead?'

'Not quite. But I can't remember anybody recently who tried any harder.'

'I'm okay. Just, uh . . . just . . .'

'Tired?'

'Yeah, that's it.'

'Sure, just a little tired. In a state of shock. Blood pressure reads like a basketball score. Nothing at all.'

He took a hypodermic needle out of the bag.

'Whatcha gonna do?' Sharky said fuzzily.

'Antibiotics. Also got to get a little snooze juice in you.'

'Doandothat . . . gottastay . . . wake . . .'

'You got someplace to go at five in the morning?'

'Nawbdystealm'melons . . .'

'Sure.'

'Arsh . . .'

'Right here, buddy.'

'Doand . . . nuthin . . . outme. . . .'

'Right.'

'Is he going to be all right?' Domino said.

'He's got the constitution of a horse. Didn't lose as much blood as I thought. Just keep him warm so he doesn't go into shock. If he makes it until noon he'll live forever.'

'I'll keep him warm,' she said.

He felt the needle enter his arm, felt the warmth from its fluid flooding his body. The room did a little dance for him and he faded out again.

He was dreaming. A crazy dream without form. Faces floated in and out of focus. The Nosh. The fat man on the junk. And Domino, like a face looking at him through smoke. He was on fire. And then suddenly he felt cold and began to shiver.

'It's all right, it's all right,' she said, and he opened his eyes. There was only one light in the room, a lamp in the corner. He had a hard time separating light and shadow. Another chill passed over him.

'Easy,' she said. She was talking softly and he felt her hands moving over his body.

'Cold,' he said.

'It's alcohol,' she said. 'I'm trying to break your fever.'

351

His lips felt scorched and his throat was like dust. He could hardly swallow.

She put her hand under his head and lifted him halfway up and held a glass of cold water against his lips. He gulped at it.

'Not too much,' she said. She reached over to the night table, to a bowl of ice cubes, and wrapped one in a washcloth, holding it against his lips.

'Just suck on it,' she said, and lowered his head back to the pillow.

She poured more alcohol in her hands and spread it on his chest, moving her hands easily and lightly over his hot skin.

He closed his eyes. The fire was going out. He could feel it leaving his body.

'Hey,' he said, without opening his eyes.

'Hey,' she said back.

'Sorry.'

'For what? Saving my life?'

'Slapping you. Dumb move.'

'Please, it's all right.'

'No. I think. . . .'

The words drifted off, as though he had fallen asleep.

She touched his cheek, then his forehead. He seemed cooler. She started to move away but his fingers closed on her wrist.

'I thought you were asleep again,' she said.

'No. What I think. I think maybe it was jealousy.'

'Sharky, you don't – '

'You gotta understand about The Nosh. He shouldn't have even been – '

She put her fingertips to his lips.

'Don't, please. Arch told me about him. I'm sorry. I'm so very, very sorry.'

Tears flooded her eyes and she turned her face away from him. Her throat started to close up and she knew it would be difficult to say any more.

'Point is, gotta stop them, okay?'

'Oh, yes.' She leaned back towards him and the tears dribbled down her cheeks and fell on his chest. He opened his eyes and looked up at her. Then he reached up and brushed them away with his thumb.

'Don't.'

'I want to tell you about it. You have a right to know. It was like' – she swallowed and wanted to stop crying but the tears kept coming – 'it was like . . .'

He pulled her gently down until her cheek lay against his chest. The tears poured down over him.

'He was very good to me. For a long time. And I felt . . . I couldn't believe he could . . . could . . .'

'All I wanted was the name. What happened . . . what was between you . . . none of my business.'

'But I want it to be.'

'Baby, I don't care.'

'Oh, God,' she said. 'I just want it to be over. I want it to be over with them. I don't want to see Neil again. I – '

He rubbed her neck with a weak hand.

'Soon.'

And he fell asleep again.

The room was dark. She had turned out the light. He reached over and felt her beside him and sighed.

'Do you need anything?' she said.

'Feeling better,' he said. 'Just pooped. What time is it?'

He felt her hand cross his chest and she moved close to him. For the first time he realized they were both naked. He put his hand on top of hers.

'Don't worry about the time.'

'You feel good. Soft. And warm.'

He felt her cold hand on his forehead.

'You've still got a little fever,' she said. 'But it's going down.'

'Yeah.'

She moved her hand on top of his and closed her fingers around it, squeezing it. Her head moved closer to him. He could feel her hair against the side of his face and he moved it closer to her.

'Thanks for taking care of me,' he said.

'Ummm.'

'I, uh . . .'

'Shhh.'

'No.'

'Go back to sleep.'

'I want to tell you. I, uh . . . before I flake out again.

353

About The Nosh. It's okay. Everything just got screwed up.'

'Please. Go to sleep.'

'Yeah. That time in the market, when I first talked to you, I, uh . . .'

He moved his head closer to her, and lying there in the dark, he began to drift again and a moment before he fell asleep he said, 'I love you.'

A light awakened him the next time. It was a thin shaft coming from the bathroom. He held up his wrist, but his watch was gone. Water was running. He stirred, reached out for Domino, but she was gone. Then he saw her, standing naked in the doorway of the bathroom, a washcloth in her hand.

'Your fever broke,' she said. 'I'm just drying you off.'

She came to him, sat beside him, put the cold cloth on his forehead. She leaned over him, her breasts crushed against him. She kissed his throat, then his dry lips. Then she slipped into the bed beside him.

The shot was wearing off. Sharky forgot the pain in his hand, the fever, how tired he was. He put his arm around her and kissed her and she reached around and stroked his back and slid her hand down over his buttocks and drew him against her.

She smiled. 'I think you're recovering,' she said.

'If I'm not, this is as good a way to go as any.'

'Better,' she said.

She slid her leg up over his hip, moved her hand around her back and down between her legs and touched him, stroked him, held him against her, and began moving slowly back and forth.

This time Sharky didn't fall asleep.

'What time is it?'

'Four-thirty.'

'How long have I been laid out?'

'That's a terrible way of putting it.'

'Yeah, right. How long have I been knocked out?'

'Almost twelve hours. How do you feel?'

'I think I may be able to get up.'

'You did okay a few minutes ago.'

'I mean on my feet.'

'Okay, want me to help?'

'I need a shower.'

'I gave you an alcohol bath for the fever. You smell like a baby.'

'Need a shave.'

'I shaved you.'

'Need some decent clothes.'

'Arch went by your place and brought some over.'

'I sure rate, don't I?'

'Um hm.'

'How about Friscoe? Papa?'

'They're waiting out there for you, in the living room.'

'Are we still in the ballgame?'

'Do you think Arch would break a promise to a sick friend?'

'Tell them I'll be out in a minute.'

They assembled in Hazel's living room. All of them looked better. They had cleaned themselves up, had a little sleep, and recovered from the initial shock of The Nosh's death.

Sharky was wearing his only suit, a tweed, with a fawn-coloured shirt and a dark brown tie.

'How come you brought my Sunday suit?' he asked Livingston.

'You're going to a party.'

'A party?'

'We got a plan,' Friscoe said.

'A plan?'

'You got a little catchin' up to do there, Sharky,' Friscoe said. 'First off, this DeLaroza ain't your everyday garden variety squirrel, know what I mean? I mean, this guy's big potatoes. He's powerful. He's got half the world by the ass. He's untouchable. And he's Siamese twins with Donald Hotchins.'

'The senator?'

'Who's about to announce that he's running for president,' Domino said.

'Jesus! What did we get into?'

'Well,' Friscoe said, 'that depends. On the one hand, we may come out with the roses. On the other hand, we may come out with our foot in a bucket of shit, pardon the

355

French, ladies.'

'Somebody catch me up,' Sharky said. He was still feeling weak, like someone who has slept too long.

'Okay, I'll do the honours,' Friscoe said. 'First, see, we know we can pin Scardi to the Tiffany killing if we can collar him. Also The Nosh. Although we ain't found him yet, I think we can peg that one on him too because of the m.o. By the way, I scored a few baskets myself last night. That movie actor was makin' the bets at the Matador Club? Nailed *his* ass, too. Had him under the lights all fuckin' night, pardon the French, ladies, and about nine this morning he starts singin' like Frank Sinatra. What it was, see, he was puttin' down bets for this guy Kershman who works for DeLaroza. A big shot. So we get our hands on this Kershman, we may be able to tie the can to DeLaroza's tail. Incidentally, there's another tie-in. The car you pinched to come back here with is registered to this Kershman.'

'You got a description?' Sharky said. 'What's he look like?'

Friscoe took out his notebook and flipped through several pages. 'Here we go. Five-seven, two-ten, getting bald, slobby-lookin' guy, according to this actor. The actor, Donegan, he does the gay joints, picks up fresh meat, and delivers it to this Kershman's door, for which he gets paid more than you and me together. How do you like them apples?'

'I think we may have a little trouble as far as this Kershman's concerned,' Sharky said. 'If it's who I think it is, he's at the bottom of the lake with a hole in his head.'

'He was one of them?' Livingston asked.

'A guy who fits that description was running the show. A real pig.'

'Neat,' Friscoe said. 'See, the problem is, right now we ain't god diddly shit to tie this DeLaroza to *any*body. Everything we got, okay? is circumstantial. We know he knew this guy and that guy and he was here and he was there and he owned this and that and the other thing. But nothing we can hang our hat on. Unless we grab Scardi, see, and he sings, DeLaroza's walkin' free from where I'm sittin'. He's like, once removed from everything that came down.'

'Who owns the junk?'

'DeLaroza's corporation. But he can always lay the

whole thing off on Kershman. We need corroboration somewhere in here.'

'Who did you tell about me?' Sharky asked Domino.

For a long moment they stared at each other. Domino felt his eyes burning into her soul.

'Donald Hotchins.'

Sharky whistled. 'So he's in it, too. And he's running for president?'

'Yeah,' Friscoe cut in, 'but also, shit, pardon the French, ladies, see, that's another thing, it's like a goddamn Chinese wastepaper basket. Domino was with Hotchins the night Tiffany got snuffed. Obviously he didn't know what was comin' down at that point. He must've got into it, see, after he got back.'

'You were Hotchins's mistress?' Sharky said to Domino.

'Kind of.'

'Neat company you keep.'

'The pits,' she said.

'Has anybody figured out why they were after you?' Sharky asked her.

Livingston said, 'We got a couple of ideas. The way we put it together to here, Corrigon must've got on to De-Laroza some way. How, we don't know. Domino thinks the hit may have happened in front of DeLaroza's building and she saw Scardi putting Corrigon's stiff in a car. It was Halloween night, so the time jibes.'

'I think it was more than that,' Domino said. 'I think they were afraid of me because of my association with both of them.'

'So, where do we stand?' Sharky said.

'Where we stand, we ain't got nothin' on DeLaroza. We can put Scardi under if we can collar him. Hotchins? So far all he did was blow the whistle on you and fuck around a little. Sorry about that, little lady, but you know what I mean there. Anyways, we can't get to DeLaroza right now and if we turn this case over to that retard Hanson, he'll shit purple apples. The case'll flush and DeLaroza and Hotchins'll walk. We got to tie these three bastards together and make it stick.'

'We got a plan,' Livingston said. 'Actually it was Domino who came up with it. DeLaroza has this amusement place inside his building. From what we hear it must be some-

357

thing. It's been on the TV news all day today. Tonight's the grand opening, a costume thing, see, with the big shots goin' formal. Now, supposing Domino shows up there. She has an invitation, so getting in is no problem. And maybe when they see her, they'll make a move against her.'

'This was your idea?' Sharky said.

Domino nodded.

'It's too risky.'

'That's what we all said.'

'Thing is,' Friscoe said, 'if Kershman is out of it like you say – that leaves us in the shit pile with no flyswatter. And if they get smart and get rid of Scardi, we can't stick them for even runnin' a stop sign. The best we can do, we go to Jaspers, lay it all out for him, give it to the Feds, and hope to hell they can make something out of it.'

'No way!' Sharky snapped.

'So, her idea's the best thing we got goin' there, Shark,' Friscoe said. 'After tonight our string's run out. We're on borrowed time right now. Anybody tumbles to that junk, Abrams's body turns up, school's out.'

'So what are we gonna do,' Sharky said, 'just stand around and hope they make a move?'

'We freak them,' Livingston said.

'How?'

'I'll let them see me, then duck back in the crowd,' Domino said. 'If I do it often enough, they'll have to do something. I'll be in costume and you'll be in your Sunday suit with a little mask on. It'll be kind of fun.'

'Fun! These people don't play for fun.'

'Right,' Friscoe said. 'And judging from some of their moves the last few days, they ain't afraid to take big chances. Sharky, you stick to her like Elmer's glue. We'll have you wired, and Arch and I will be in the lobby if anything breaks loose. Papa's gonna try crashing the gate so he can back you up. Anything happens, we'll be in there like the fuckin' Marines.'

'I don't know . . .' Sharky said.

'Well, let's make up our minds, troops, because we got about two hours to show time. After that, it's give it to Jaspers and collect unemployment.'

Chapter Twenty-Nine

Enormous arc spotlights swept back and forth in front of Mirror Towers, their beams reaching up into a clear, star-filled sky. Live TV cameras rested on tripods beside a red carpet that stretched from the kerb in front of the building to the blazing entrance to *Pachinko!*

Celebrities had started arriving at six for a private cocktail party in DeLaroza's penthouse. The regular guests had begun arriving even earlier and now they began filing into the four elevators for the trip to the magic gates of the amusement atrium.

Newsmen crowded around Donald Hotchins as he got out of the black limousine. His wife, Elena, remained in the back seat as usual, waiting for the furore to die down. She hated the public spectacle, hated the press, hated everything about politics.

Hotchins seemed the perfect politico, his longish blond hair flopping casually over his forehead, his broad smile radiating sincerity. He seemed even taller and more handsome than usual in the elegance of a tuxedo.

As he got out of the car into a volley of popping flashbulbs and a phalanx of microphones, all thrust in his face, DeLaroza moved through the crowd of reporters to shake his hand.

'Is it true, Senator, that you're going to make an announcement later this evening?' one of them asked.

'Well, why don't we wait for a little while and see?' Hotchins said, still grinning. 'By the way this is Victor DeLaroza. You ought to get to know him. You'll be seeing a lot of him in the future.'

'So you are going to be making a statement then?' someone else asked.

'Wait another hour or so,' Hotchins said good-naturedly. 'I've never missed a deadline yet.'

The press contingent laughed and moved back as the senator helped his wife from the sedan. She smiled coolly at DeLaroza, who nodded back, and then led the Hotchinses along the red carpet towards *Pachinko!*

She appeared older than Hotchins, a stunning woman, tall and straight, although somewhat stern-looking and formal. She had silver-grey hair and the kind of features the magazines sometimes call handsome. She was wearing a glittering white gown and a full-length lynx coat.

As they approached the entrance Hotchins saw through the crowd a woman standing near the doorway, her face inscrutable behind a waxen full-face mask with high, bright-red cheekbones and a thin slash of mouth. She was wearing a gold full-length mandarin dress with a blazing red sun in the midsection and her eyes seemed to follow him through the slanted cutouts in the mask. He looked back as he entered the building. There was something disquieting about her.

'So that's the pair,' Sharky said, as the Hotchins party boarded one of the bullet-shaped elevators to be whisked up to DeLarōza's penthouse.

'He looked back at me,' Domino said, her voice muffled by the mask. 'I was afraid for a minute he might have recognized me.'

'Maybe the gown attracted him,' Sharky said. 'It's gorgeous.'

'It came from Hong Kong,' she said.

'Now, why doesn't that surprise me?' They entered the lobby and mingled with the crowd waiting for the elevators to *Pachinko!* They were a strange couple, Sharky in his tweed suit and black eye mask, Domino in the shimmering gold gown, with the eerie waxen disguise covering her entire face.

'You sure you want to go through with this?' Sharky asked.

'Too late to stop now,' she said. 'Besides, I have a little getting even to do myself.'

The elevator opened at the top of Ladder Street and Sharky and Domino stepped out into a carnival of sight and sound.

Several hundred visitors had already arrived and the enormous atrium was crowded. Jugglers roved the steps of Ladder Street, tossing fire sticks back and forth. Music seemed to swell from every doorway. Travelling hucksters offered postcards and trinkets. The smell of barbecuing

360

chicken and ribs drifted up from the food stalls.

'Look for Papa. He should be close to the top of the steps,' Sharky said.

The place made him nervous. Too big. Too many people. It was more dangerous than he had imagined.

Papa was standing in front of the first food stall, nibbling a rib. He was not wearing a mask.

'Have any trouble getting in?' Sharky asked him.

'Naw. I could crash a kindergarten party and get away with it.'

'Where's your mask?'

'There's some things even I won't do for the department.'

'The place is bigger than I thought,' Sharky said.

'Worry you?'

'A little.'

'Not me. Easier to keep an eye on her. Harder for them to spot you.'

'Maybe you're right.'

'You feeling okay?' Papa asked.

'I'm fine.' Only Domino knew that they had stopped at Grady Hospital on the way to the opening, where Twigs had given Sharky a shot of speed. 'You gonna become a junkie now that you're off the Narcs?' Twigs asked him. 'I just want to stay awake tonight,' Sharky had answered. The stuff was good. He felt strong and alert and his maimed finger was just a dull ache at the end of his arm.

'You got everything down pat?' he asked Domino.

'Sure,' she said.

'Remember, if I tell you to do anything, do it. Don't ask questions, I may not have time to explain.'

'Yes, sir,' she said and threw a mock salute.

'And knock that shit off too, pardon my French, ladies.'

'I think Friscoe's cute,' she said.

'He's as peaceful as a split lip,' Papa said.

'We'll go to the bottom of Ladder Street, check out the radio mikes. Could be a lot of interference in here. Put your hearing aid in your ear.'

'It's uncomfortable,' Papa said.

'Put it in anyway. Let's be ready when they get down here.'

Friscoe and Arch were outside, standing apart from the

crowd in a doorway to keep out of the wind gusting from the plaza. Sharky's voice came over the walkie-talkie loud and clear.

'This is Vulture One to Vulture Two. You read?'

'This is Vulture Two,' Papa answered. 'Loud and clear.'

'Vulture One to Nest. We coming in okay?'

'You're coming in clear,' Friscoe answered. 'What's it look like up there?'

'Bigger than the Astrodome,' Sharky answered. 'The place is unbelievable.'

'Well, enjoy. It's colder than . . . uh, it's very cold down here.'

'Okay, let's stay loose. They ought to be here any minute.'

In the crowded penthouse Hotchins eased DeLaroza out on the balcony.

'What about Domino?' he asked.

'Nothing. I have not heard from Kershman all day. But then, it has been quite a day, eh? Besides, this Sharky was proving more stubborn than we planned.'

'I'm worried. If she's in police custody they probably know everything by now.'

DeLaroza smiled confidently. 'Do not fall apart now. What does she know? Nothing. Relax. Enjoy yourself. Within an hour we will have disposed of another problem – and given the police their killer at the same time.'

'I hope there are no more mistakes,' Hotchins said.

'I don't make mistakes,' DeLaroza said vehemently. 'I correct them.'

'I hope you do,' Hotchins said, and went back to the party.

DeLaroza walked along the balcony to his bedroom and took the private elevator down to his office. Chiang was waiting for him.

'You know how to accomplish this?'

Chiang nodded.

'Remember. He is fast and deadly. Forget his age. He hears like a rabbit and strikes like an asp. When you move, do it quickly. You will not have a second chance.'

Chiang nodded again.

'Do not move the body until everyone has left. It would be dangerous with all these people about.'

'Hai.'
'Joy shan.'
'Dor jeh.'

He moved silently out of the room. DeLaroza returned to the party and began herding the guests towards the door. 'All right,' he said. 'It is time for *Pachinko!*'

In the guest suite Scardi was painstakingly painting a clown face over his own features. He had been cooped up too long, first on the junk, then in this fancy prison cell. He had to get out, hear people, feel like part of the human race again. This would be perfect. He was wearing an outrageous clown suit, red-and-white striped with large red wool buttons. With his face painted no one could possibly recognize him and so he felt safe going to the opening.

He had finished applying the white chalk base and the blue mouth and was painting large, round eyes when the door chimed.

It startled him. He slid open the top dresser drawer and eased out the .22 Woodsman. He held it down at his side as he went to the front door and peered through the viewer.

That damned Chink.

The Chinese was holding a silver tray with a bottle of red wine, a glass, a corkscrew, and a note. He opened the door. The note was addressed to Howard and he took it to the bedroom to read it, keeping an eye on Chiang in the dresser mirror as he did.

The note said:

> Have a pleasant evening. The wine is on me.
> Victor.

Damned white of him. He returned to his task, leaning over the dresser, close to the mirror, as he completed his makeup. He kept watching the Chinese.

Chiang was twisting the corkscrew into the bottle of wine and as he popped the cork out, the bottle slipped from his grasp. He snatched it up quickly, but several ounces gurgled from the neck, splashing down over the carpet.

'Shit! You clumsy fuckin' slant-eye!' Scardi snapped. Chiang entered the bedroom, bowing in apology and pointing towards the bathroom.

'Keep away from me,' Scardi snarled. He stood near the

dresser, his hand beside the .22, as Chiang pointed towards the bathroom and rubbed his hands together.

'You wanna towel, you ignorant gook? Go ahead. I ain't cleaning up your mess for you.'

Chiang went into the bathroom, took a towel, and held it under the cold water and then began to wring it out. As he squeezed out the water he reached up into his sleeve with two fingers and drew out a thin steel tube about five inches long. It was no thicker than a pencil. He pressed a button in its base and a pointed shaft that looked like a short icepick shot from the handle. He held it under the towel and started back.

Scardi was still leaning over the dresser when he heard the faint click from the bathroom. He almost let it pass, but then it ran back through his mind, an instant replay of the sound, and the memory of it rushed back at him from the past.

A switchblade. The fuckin' Chink had a switchblade!

He grabbed for the Woodsman as Chiang came out of the bathroom, let the wet towel fall to the floor as he entered the bedroom, and took a single swift step towards Scardi. His arm arced from the waist, swept up towards Scardi's chest, the steel sliver gleaming in his fist. Scardi moved quickly, made a feinting move to the left, and then reversed himself and fell sideways, swinging the .22 up as he did.

The icepick was already committed. It missed its mark by six inches, plunging into Scardi's side low, just under the ribs, and piercing up deep inside him. The point stopped an inch from Scardi's heart.

Scardi screamed and jammed the pistol into Chiang's neck. He fired and the bullet shattered Chiang's Adam's apple, ripped through his jugular vein and came out the back of his neck. A geyser of blood burst from the wound.

Chiang staggered backwards, but Scardi pressed after him, twisting the pistol slightly, jamming it back in the wound, and firing again. The second bullet tore up through the back of Chiang's head and shattered his brain.

Scardi shoved the Chinese servant over backward on the bed, where he fell with his hands stretched out at his sides. Scardi shot him three more times, twice in the face and once in the heart.

The pain was like a hot needle deep inside Scardi's chest.

He gasped for breath, reached down, felt the handle of the dirk sticking in his side, and pulled it out. He dropped the weapon on the floor and leaned forward, clutching his side, pressing in, trying to squeeze the pain away. He could feel it, feel the burning puncture sapping his strength.

He sat on the edge of the dresser, steadying himself with both hands. He examined the clown suit. He could hardly tell where the instrument had pierced the cloth. He went into the bathroom and unzipped the costume and examined the wound itself, a small, round hole beginning to swell at the edges. A pearl of blood appeared and winked obscenely at him. He carefully folded a washcloth and held it against the hole like a bandage and wrapped a towel around his waist to keep it in place.

He went back to the dresser. Pain came at him in waves, burning inside him. Sweat had begun to erode his makeup. Red tears etched their way down his chalky cheeks into the corners of his mouth.

The bastard, that filthy bastard, to try this after all these years . . .

The fury raged inside him again, welling up, giving him new strength. His hate was a passion. For thirty years he had listened to DeLaroza bragging, flaunting their combined wealth, taking credit. For what? *For what?* The whole scheme had been his idea, not DeLaroza's. Scardi had invented La Volte. Scardi had gone in, done the legwork, taken the chances in the beginning. Scardi had set up the dummy hit at the lake, put the fix on Corrigon, arranged to transport the gold across the Alps into Switzerland.

It wasn't for me, he'd be nothin'. A fuckin' bank clerk in Ohio someplace. Shit, he didn't even know he was a fuckin' thief until I saw it in him. A baby blue goddamn captain with no future.

He slipped the clip out of the .22 and replaced it with a fresh one. There were two more in the drawer and he put them in the pocket of the clown suit.

Got to stay up, he said to himself. *Got to stay on my feet long enough to find that fat bastard. Try to put the cross on me. Shit. Shit! I made him. Me, Scardi.*

'I made you, you fat gutless sonofabitch . . .' he screamed aloud.

He opened the small box on the dresser. Three red devils left. He popped two in his mouth and swallowed them without water.

An instant later they jolted him, setting all his nerves on edge, intensifying the pain in his chest beyond bearing. He put the back of his hand over his mouth and screamed again.

Then it was gone, replaced by the soaring rush of the speed. It cleared his vision, replaced the pain with a pure and driving hate. He snapped the silencer on the ugly snout of the Woodsman and slipped it inside the clown suit. Then he took his invitation and headed for *Pachinko!*

Chapter Thirty

Scardi picked his spot carefully, with the same instincts, the same planning, that had kept him alive for forty-five of his sixty years in a business where death was as common as winter flu.

Several factors dictated his choice of position. First, accessibility to the victim. He wanted a clean head shot.

The .22 Woodsman had a specially designed eight-inch barrel with a Colt-Elliason rear sight and a ten-shot clip. The weapon was deadly up to seventy or eighty yards. With the silencer Scardi knew he could probably get off two, possibly three shots undetected. One would be sufficient, two ideal.

Second, he checked the pedestrian traffic patterns, looking for a place he could get in a clean shot without a lot of people around.

Finally, he looked for an escape route. It would be tough, escaping from *Pachinko!*, since it was accessible by elevator only. But there had to be a fire escape, a stairwell somewhere.

His *modus operandi* did not include trapping himself.

He stood on the balcony overlooking *Pachinko!*, orientating himself, studying every inch of the place through pain-clouded eyes.

He was standing with his back to the western wall of the building, looking down into the atrium. To his left was Ladder Street, winding down six storeys to the park's main floor, where it became the main thoroughfare of *Pachinko!*, ending at the gardens. To his right were the shallow pond and the Tai Tak Restaurant. In the far corner to his left was the entrance to the pinball ride and in the far corner to his right Tiger Balm Gardens. Below him was the entrance to the underground Arcurion tour of historic Hong Kong.

There were three side streets in *Pachinko!* One was Prince Avenue, which ran perpendicular to the main street, starting at the foot of Ladder Street, and terminated at the giant figure of Man Chu, the robot who operated the ride. A second street, Queen Street, paralleled Prince Avenue near the gardens. A narrow alley connected them, the stores on its eastern side built up to the far wall of the atrium.

The alley was virtually empty. Few of the guests who jammed the spectacular complex had discovered it yet. Only two stores on the alley had been completed. One was a petshop about halfway between Prince and Queen. The other was on the western corner of the alley and Prince Street, a trinket shop with a stall in front.

Perfect.

Scardi guessed Hotchins and DeLaroza would come down Ladder Street, turn into Prince, and go to the pinball ride. They would pass within fifteen feet of the alley. From the corner, hidden by the trinket stalls, Scardi could get off a couple of good head shots and escape down the alley.

And then what?

He continued to study the far side of the atrium floor. Then he saw the fire door. It was located on Queen Street between the alley and the wall.

The fire door provided his escape route. Scardi also reasoned that there would probably be an access door from the playing field of the ride to the fire stairs. If necessary he could enter the main floor of the ride and escape through the tunnels that led to the first floor. A risky trip, particularly for a wounded man, but an out nevertheless in case the stairway itself was blocked by police or security guards.

The wound burned deeply, but Scardi went over the plan two more times in his head before he was satisfied.

Scardi smiled. He *was* satisfied. It was a daring plan, but he had pulled off worse. And even if he didn't, he was certain now that he could put a bullet in DeLaroza's brain before he died himself.

Hotchins had been introduced with glowing platitudes by the state's senior senator, Osgood Thurston. Hotchins's speech was short and to the point, a straightforward declaration that he was running for president and running to win, for the guests had come to play, not to listen to political speeches. The press would have its chance at him later at the press conference.

Five minutes, that's all it would take.

He was halfway through the announcement when he saw her the first time. A face in the sea of masks, staring up at

368

him, smiling cryptically.

He floundered, lost his place as panic seized him. He smiled at the crowd, regained his composure, and when he looked back she was gone.

A moment later he saw her again, this time staring enigmatically from between the posters in a display in front of one of the booths.

Again, a few moments later, from farther down in the crowd.

He went on, losing track of what he was saying, flashing that smile, inventing lines, frantic to get it over with. For sixteen years he had savoured the anticipation of this moment. Now it was here and he was seized with terror.

Domino was out there, in that crowd of masked revellers, taunting him.

He finished with relief, backing away from the podium, his bandwagon supporters crowding around him, raising his arms over his head. Lowenthal, Thurston, three governors, the mayor, five congressmen, a dozen state legislators, several bankers, and two of the nation's most powerful labour leaders.

The crowd was cheering wildly as the band struck up a furious version of 'Georgia On My Mind'. Flashbulbs and strobes blinded the dignitaries, and movie and television cameras swept the crowd, capturing its lusty reaction to their favourite son's entry into the campaign.

Only DeLaroza read the fear in Hotchins's eyes.

He pulled him aside after the furore had died away.

'What is the matter with you?' DeLaroza demanded.

'She's down there,' Hotchins said. He was trembling.

'What are you talking about?'

'She's in that crowd. She's *leering* at me!'

'Who?'

'Domino. She's here. In this place.'

'You are going to pieces. She would never take such a chance.'

'I'm telling you, Domino is out there. She's trying to rattle me and she did it.'

'Listen to me,' DeLaroza said, 'we have only to walk down that stairway and over to the entrance of the ride and get in that steel ball and then you will be finished here. I assure you, she will not be at the press conference.'

'I'm not going down there.'

'You are most certainly going down there. The cameras, the reporters, the public, they are all waiting for us. Everyone who sees you on television riding in an amusement park will identify with you. It is something everyone can relate to. You are not backing out now.'

He grabbed Hotchins's arm and led him down into the crowd, bodyguards and security men forming a wedge through the mob, leading them down through the noisy bazaar.

They had gone a few steps when Hotchins saw the sketch. He pulled free of DeLaroza and rushed to the artist.

'Who is that?' he demanded, pointing to the easel. 'When did you do this sketch?'

'Just before the speeches,' the young artist stammered.

'Where did she go. Which way?'

The artist waved his arm towards the crowd.

'Out there somewhere, sir. She said she'd come back later and pick it up.'

'What was she wearing?' DeLaroza demanded.

'Wearing?'

'What kind of *clothes* was she wearing?'

'Uh . . . I was concentrating on her face, y'know. Uh, gold gown. That was it, a gold gown. Big splash of red right here in the middle.'

Hotchins remembered the woman at the entrance, the eyes following him from behind the impenetrable mask.

'It was her downstairs. I knew it. I knew there was something . . .'

DeLaroza was urging him along the stairs.

'Smile. Wave at the crowd. We are surrounded by guards. You have nothing to worry about.'

'I have *her* to worry about!'

Like Scardi, Sharky too had devised a daring scheme, one designed to unnerve Hotchins, and it was succeeding. He and Domino had moved to the rear of the crowd. Now, as the spectators turned from the speaker's platform to walk down Ladder Street, they were leading the way into Prince Avenue. At the end of the street, the glowering figure of Man Chu waited ominously to send Hotchins and

DeLaroza on the first official spin through the pinball machine. Photographers were jockeying for position and TV cameramen were eagerly setting up their tripods.

It had worked like a charm. Domino had put the mask on the back of her head and faced Sharky. Every time Hotchins looked in her direction, Sharky had turned her around facing him and then, the instant his eyes were averted, had turned her quickly back around, so that when Hotchins looked up again he saw only the expressionless mask.

They had moved through the crowd, trying the trick a dozen times or so, and Sharky was sure Hotchins had seen her at least three or four times.

Now for the cherry on the sundae. Hotchins and DeLaroza moved towards the robot. When the two were safely inside the steel car, with the guard rail snapped shut and the door secured, Domino would step out of the crowd and call each of them by name. The last thing they would see before plunging down into the dazzling interior of the ride would be Domino.

Sharky hoped they would try something desperate.

As they started up Prince Avenue, Sharky lowered his head slightly and spoke into the microphone pinned on the back of his lapel.

'How you doin', Vulture?'

Papa's answer crackled in his hearing aid.

'Right behind them. Hotchins's flipping. May not work, but he ain't gonna sleep tonight.'

'Stay close.'

'Gotcha.'

On the street below Friscoe and Livingston stamped their feet and tried to control their excitement, waiting for something to break loose. They anticipated the unexpected and it was about to happen.

Scardi was in position. Waiting.

So far, so good. The alley was almost empty. Twenty, thirty people milling about.

The crowd was moving up Prince Avenue, choking the street from storefront to storefront. He could see DeLaroza's bald head and flaming red beard through the mass of people, moving towards him.

371

He checked the alley again. The people were beginning to move towards him, attracted by the noise of the approaching crowd.

At the far end of the alley a mime on stilts, dressed like Uncle Sam, stalked around the corner and started awkwardly towards him.

The wound was numb now. His chest no longer pained him. His life was ebbing away, trickling down his leg. He looked down at the clown suit, at the crimson stain, widening, seeping down over his hip towards his thigh.

He leaned closer to the wall, peering around the corner and over the stall of souvenirs. He slipped the last red devil in his mouth, waiting for its surge, suddenly feeling himself growing taller, more confident.

Come on, you bastard, just a little closer. He zipped down the clown suit and reached inside, felt the comforting grip of the Woodsman, drew it out, and folded his arms across his chest with the gun concealed, the snout pressed up into his armpit.

You pipsqueak little nothin'. A fuckin' GI that I turned into a millionaire. What a fool, to think you could kill the old pro.

The speed surged through his blood, cleared his vision. He checked out the people in the front of the crowd, looking for tell-tale signs. Cops. Bodyguards. Security guards. He could always tell them by their eyes, by the way they checked everywhere.

His gaze fell on the woman in the gold gown. She was walking straight towards him. He stared into her face. There was something familiar there. Did he know her? Was it someone who could identify him? He panicked for a moment, then remembered the clown face. Nobody could see through that clown face.

And yet . . .

He concentrated on the face again. She was twenty feet away, bearing down on him. He dipped into his memory and then it began coming to him. Slowly. A photograph. That was it, a photograph. A photograph he had studied for hours.

And then it hit him.

Domino!

Domino?

No. It couldn't be. She was dead. He had seen her face explode in front of his shotgun, seen her brains hit the wall. Domino was dead.

'You're dead,' he muttered. He started backing away from her. 'You're dead,' he repeated.

Domino saw him before Sharky did, a terrifying sight. His face had dissolved, paint melting into a surrealistic glob of red and blue and chalky white. The ridiculous clown suit was stained blood red. His eyes were mad with fever. He was backing away from her. Saying something.

'Sharky?'

'I see him,' Sharky said and stepped in front of her.

'He's saying something.'

The crowd pressed them towards him.

'He's saying . . . Jesus, he's saying "You're dead" over and over,' Sharky said.

He looked hard into the crazed face, at the hawk nose, the pointed chin, the pig eyes. Then he saw the gun in his hand, the Woodsman.

'Jesus,' he yelled, 'it's Scardi!'

The clown turned and ran.

Sharky shoved Domino into the doorway of the store on the corner.

'Stay here. Put on the mask, don't let Hotchins and DeLaroza see you.'

'But – '

'It's Scardi, don't you understand? He's all we need.'

He yelled into the mike:

'Papa, the store on the corner of the alley. Cover Domino!'

'On my way.'

'I've spotted Scardi!'

On the street the name shocked Friscoe and Livingston into action.

'Shit,' Friscoe cried out.

'Let's roll,' Livingston said.

Scardi ran down the alley, shoving people aside, plunging between the stilted legs of Uncle Sam. The mime teetered and plunged forward into an awning over the petshop, crashed through it, and fell on top of several cages. They split open and the alley was suddenly alive with yapping

373

Maltese and Pekingese dogs.

Sharky charged through the madhouse, stepping over the wreckage of the awning. Uncle Sam was struggling to his knees, his six-foot trouser legs straggling out behind him.

'You okay?' Sharky yelled at him.

'I would be if I could get these damn pants off.'

Sharky went on, racing to the end of the alley. He stepped cautiously into Queen Street and looked both ways. The street came to a dead end at the wall on his left. To his right it was clogged with merrymakers. No sign of Scardi. He walked past the first few shops, looking in through the windows.

Nothing.

The bleeding clown had vanished.

Scardi stood inside the fire door for a few moments gasping for breath. He had caught a glimpse of a big guy in a tweed suit running after him. A cop? Some irate guest? He didn't care. He saw the door on the landing below, the door that led out onto the giant pinball playing field. His escape route.

He leaned against the wall and staggered down to the landing, pulled the door open, and stepped over the spring-loaded guard rail that surrounded the tilted board.

It was like walking into his own nightmare. All around him, reflected on the mirrored walls, the Mylar ceiling, were grinning Orientals. They towered over him, mocking him, strobe lights flashing from their slanted eyes, colours kaleidoscoping from their rubber bodies, electricity humming through the springs that wound around their bases. He was hypnotized by the fantasy garden, by the flashing lights, and he lurched crazily out among them like a somnambulist.

The upper part of the board was adjacent to the bottom of Ladder Street, separated from it by a wall of mirrors and plywood. Near the top over a narrow chute with bumpers on both sides, was the control booth for the ingenious ride. The operator, who controlled the speed of the ball, was too busy to notice the madman strolling through the maze of bumpers and chutes and tunnels. He had checked out all the controls. Everything was ready.

He picked up an intercom phone. 'Okay,' he said, 'let 'er roll.'

From the safety of the trinket shop Domino and Papa watched DeLaroza and Hotchins climb into the six-foot steel sphere. An attendant pulled the guard bar up and locked it across their laps.

The press was having a field day, shooting pictures, ordering the candidate and the owner of the spectacle to wave, smile, shake hands with the mob that crowded around.

From deep inside the infernal machine, the operator pressed the start button.

The steel ball began its descent.

The crowd was cheering, lining up to be next.

The ball plunged down into the tunnel.

Sharky had walked up Queen Street almost to the main thoroughfare and then turned and started back. Scardi was close by, he could feel it, sense the evil of the man. But where?

He walked back towards the end of the street. Then he saw the fire door, discreetly marked, camouflaged by shrubbery.

He ran down the street to the door, waited a moment, listening, drew his Mauser, and then, shoving the door open, jumped inside and cased the stairwell.

Empty.

Bloody footprints led down the stairs to the other door. He followed them, waited for a second, and pulled the door open.

A moment after the operator had ordered the ride to begin he looked up and saw Scardi, wandering like a lost child among the field of flashing bumpers.

'Hey, you!' he screamed. 'Get outa here, you crazy fool!'

The bleeding apparition kept coming towards him.

'Oh, my God,' he cried, 'get outa there. The goddamn ball's coming!'

He snatched up the emergency phone.

Scardi shot him in the head.

The operator fell to the floor. Scardi could hear the

rumble as the ball began its descent. It boomed out of the tunnel at the upper end of the game, spiralled around the giant playing surface, and rolled out onto the board, struck the first bumper, bounced away from it in a blaze of lights and clanging bells. It sped up towards the top of the field, ricocheting off the guard rail into another bumper.

From inside the ball, DeLaroza saw the grinning face of Shou-Lsing, god of long life, grinning down at him as the steel car struck the springs around its base and bounced away, spinning around on its ball bearings, rolling towards another. It was picking up speed as it hit another bumper and another, jerking him and Hotchins from one side of the seat to the other. The ball sped past the control booth and he looked up.

There was no one in it!

'My God!' he cried out.

'What's the matter?'

'There's no one at the controls, no one to brake us.'

The ball struck another bumper and reeled away from it, spinning on its axis, and rolled into one of the narrow funnel-like bunkers, slowing as it went through the tight passageway.

At the other end Scardi was standing in a duelling position, his side facing the ball, his hand held straight out, aiming his pistol at DeLaroza.

DeLaroza's eyes bulged as he saw the assassin standing there, waiting to kill him.

He released the catch on the side of the guard bar and jumped out of the ball. Hotchins, confused and dizzy, tried to follow.

Something hit him in the chest, knocking him back into the car. The guard bar snapped back, trapping him inside. Hotchins looked down at his shirt front, saw the tiny hole there, reached up very slowly, and touched it.

Blood spurted from the hole and cascaded down his dress shirt.

The ball rolled out of the bunker, struck another bumper, and bounded away amid clanging bells. Hotchins sighed and fell over sideways in the seat.

DeLaroza dragged himself to his feet. His ankle was twisted, the knees torn out of his tuxedo. He ran, limping, and ducked behind one of the bumpers.

Scardi was oblivious to the ball careening from bumper to bumper around him. It whisked past him, almost knocked him down. He had one purpose now. Nothing else mattered.

'Howard, for God's sake, listen to me!' DeLaroza screamed. He was backing up, trying to keep the bumper between himself and Scardi.

'Don't call me that!' Scardi cried out. 'I ain't Howard. I ain't Burns. I'm Scardi. I made you. You hear me, Younger? You was nothin' but a dumb goddamn dogface. I gave you all this.'

He stepped from behind the bumper and fired at DeLaroza. The bullet hit the wall and one of the mirrors burst into dozens of reflecting shards.

DeLaroza turned and ran, aimlessly, dodging amid the grinning statues and flashing lights.

The pinball, totally out of control and roaring across the playing field, struck its last bumper, lurched over the floor, leaped the guard rail, and crashed through the wall.

The mirror exploded into millions of splinters. The wall shattered as the steel ball burst through it and rolled out at the foot of Ladder Street, struck one man and sent him reeling back up the steps, rolled over another, crashed into a shop at the bottom of the street and ripped through it, bursting out onto the main thoroughfare amid a shower of dolls, bracelets, and postcards.

The crowd scattered, falling over each other, as the antic pinball smashed through it, tossing people into the air like tenpins, ripping the marquee off the puppet theatre before it tore through the wall at the edge of the man-made lake and soared out over the water. It plunged down onto one of the sampans, split it in half, and hit the lake, sending a geyser twenty feet in the air, before it finally rolled to a stop.

DeLaroza limped towards the gaping hole in the wall. Scardi aimed and shot him in the thigh. He fell forward, hit the springs at the base of a bumper, and was thrown like a rag doll almost to Scardi's feet.

The killer looked down at the battered DeLaroza. He calmly snapped a fresh clip into the pistol.

DeLaroza crawled to his knees. Across the floor he saw a man standing in the emergency doorway, watching the mad scene.

'Help me,' he yelled. 'Please, help me.'

The man in the doorway yelled back to him.

'My name's Sharky. Hear that, DeLaroza? *Sharky!*'

DeLaroza moaned. He looked back at Scardi. The assassin was standing over him, grinning, aiming the pistol down at him. The gun thunked once, twice, three times, and the bullets tore into DeLaroza's chest. He screamed once and slumped forward, his head resting on its forehead in front of his knees, like a man in prayer.

Grinning maniacally, Scardi leaned forward and shot him again in the back of the head.

'Okay, Scardi, that's enough,' Sharky said.

The man clown turned towards him. Sharky stepped over the railing and started for him.

'Drop the gun, Scardi,' Sharky called to him. 'Police.'

The word seemed to trigger Scardi's dying energy. He scrambled through the ragged hole in the wall, crawling through broken glass and splinters of plywood, out into the main floor of *Pachinko!*

He got up and, half-running, half-staggering, made for the opposite end of the atrium. The crowd scattered as he waved his gun madly at them, clearing a path for him. Ahead of him he saw the gates of Tiger Balm Gardens. He struggled towards them.

Sharky stepped through the hole and went after him, slowly, deliberately. There was no rush now. There was no place for Scardi to go.

On the stairs above him, Friscoe and Livingston saw Sharky stalking the frenzied killer.

Sharky saw them too and held his hand up at them.

'He's mine,' he said coldly.

'Scardi?' Friscoe asked.

'It's Scardi,' Sharky said, still following after him.

'You gotta take him alive,' Friscoe yelled. 'We need him.'

'Not anymore,' Sharky said.

Scardi stumbled into the gardens, rushing blindly away from his pursuer. He slashed through the shrubs and flowers, scrambling up into the protection of the rocks and crevices. He fell against the side of the cliff at the far end of the gardens, looking back towards the street.

The tall guy in the tweed suit kept coming. And coming.

378

He was taking his time. Scardi fired a shot at him, half-heartedly, and it thunked harmlessly into one of the gates.

He turned and crawled frantically on his hands and knees, up, up, deeper into the crevices of the Tiger Balm. Every move now was agony. His sight was going. Every breath screeched through his tortured lungs. There was hardly enough blood left to sustain his frenetic flight.

Sharky walked into Tiger Balm Gardens, stepped over the fence, and followed resolutely after the mobster.

The silenced pistol spewed and dust kicked up in front of Sharky. He did not duck, did not dodge to one side or the other. He kept going, straight ahead, closing in.

Scardi dragged himself to his feet, backed away from him. His sight was almost gone. A vague shadow was moving towards him. He backed around a ridge in the cliffs and slumped against the rocks.

The unearthly shriek behind him was like no cry he had ever heard in his life.

He turned, looked up. A dragon loomed over him. Its mouth began to open.

Scardi screamed in pure terror.

The dragon's mouth opened wide and a river of flame poured from it, and enveloped him.

Scardi was a human torch, his clothes and body an inferno, his screams of pain as unearthly as the creature that had just incinerated him. He rolled back around the ridge, feet and hands thrashing madly.

Sharky shuddered and turned his back to him.

One shot, he thought. *One shot would put him out of his misery.*

Well, it was one shot Scardi would not get from him.

He started back down towards the gates. Scardi's screams followed him almost all the way down. Finally, they died away.

Domino and Papa came down the battered street towards him. She stopped a few feet in front of him.

'Are you all right?' she asked.

'Never better,' he said and smiled down at her. Then he took her by the arm and walked to the edge of the lake. The stainless-steel pinball lay upside down in three feet of water. Hotchins was hanging from the guard bar, his head and shoulders under water, his once handsome face distorted like a reflection in a funhouse mirror.

'So much for the next president of the United States,' he said. 'And that was the shortest political campaign in history.'

The elevator stopped and they walked rapidly through the lobby and outside into bedlam. A dozen police cars had pulled up into the plaza, their blue lights whirling. A TV newsman was interviewing a woman who seemed on the verge of shock. An ambulance screamed around the corner and pulled in with its siren dying down to a growl. They walked past a crowd of spectators, some holding drinks from Kerry's Kalibash, staring up at the building.

Livingston and Friscoe were standing away from the crowd, talking intently with Jaspers who was jabbing the air between them with an icepick finger.

Sharky kept walking, holding Domino tightly against him. He had passed Arch Livingston and Barney Friscoe and Papa before The Bat saw him.

'Sharky!' he bellowed.

Sharky kept walking.

'*Sharky!*'

He was almost to the car.

'Sharky, godammit, stop!'

He stopped, still holding her close to him, and looked over his shoulder at The Bat.

'What the hell's going on here? What the hell . . . I want some answers. Just who do you think you are, all of you? You're, you're . . .' He stopped.

Livingston came over to them. 'You okay?' he said.

'I'm okay. I'm taking her outa here.'

'Whatever,' Livingston said and smacked him on the shoulder. 'You run a hell of a machine, brother. Any time.'

'Thanks.'

The Bat snapped. 'Now let me tell you something – '

Sharky cut him off. 'No, you're not telling me a goddamn thing.'

He started back towards the car.

'Godammit!' The Bat screamed. 'You're through, Sharky! You hear me?'

But if Sharky heard, he made no response. He kept walking, past the police cars, past the crowd, away from the building, away from The Bat, away from the nightmare. The wind shifted and a cold breeze blew past them, carrying the carrion odour away from Sharky, blowing it back towards Mirror Towers and with it the hurt, the anger, the hate.

They got in the car and drove away.